CHASING FIREFLIES

Lori Berhon

"Everything was going to be wonderful.
Everything was going to be absolutely positively wonderful:
Rainbow bubbles and fireworks.
Everything was going to be wonderful.
Everything was going to be utterly magnificent and wonderful:
Sparkling diamonds and chandeliers;
And a choir of heavenly voices.
You gotta believe me.
Belief is everything."

— "Everything" from the musical *Flamingo*, Marshall Berenson

"There's a Broken Heart for Every Light on Broadway."

— Howard Johnson

Not all dreams come true. But that doesn't stop us from dreaming.
This story is dedicated to anyone who ever waited
on the wrong side of a stage door;
and, begging your understanding that, as Charles Lamb once wrote,
"your then is not my then,"
with love to those who shared my own journey.
To K & J, and R & C, and B, and T & D & A & L & L & W, and V & R & J
and most especially to O;
to everyone who ever shivered at the sound of an overture
or held their breath as the curtain went up;
and finally to the artists, too many to name, who create the magic
that we all want to capture and hold forever.
This book is my jar.

.

CONTENTS

OVERTURE

While Martha Cecchi was home in Patchogue, praying over her cancer with her Practitioner, her husband Mickey brought their kid into the city, to Cooghan's on 54th Street, where he'd sit for hours, knocking back a few with his old service buddies and Judy Garland.

This was Mickey's idea of babysitting. Well, there were always a couple of women hanging around Cooghan's who'd keep an eye on a kid and smile extra at the poor guy whose kid it was. "Broads," Mickey called them: well-upholstered gals with hair like cones of cotton candy, their eyes plastered purple and black to make them look like Liz Taylor. Frankie would spin around on a bar stool until she made herself almost sick, when one of the broads would get her a warm Coke and some pretzels to settle her stomach. They played knock-hockey with swizzle sticks and bottle caps, and gave her their eyebrow pencils to draw on the bar mats. There were also a couple of other women who felt at home popping by Cooghan's to have a few with the guys. Mickey called them "Broads," too, but with a sort of respect that made Frankie hear it with a capital B. Mary Catharine Shea—Mary Cat, as everyone used to call her—had a column in the papers. Her friend Dottie Kelly, who hardly ever laughed herself, wrote for Jack Parr or Sid Caesar...someone funny like that. Deep-voiced Annie Fallon, who kidded Mickey like a big sister, was on Broadway a lot of the time, and sometimes Frankie saw her on TV. And, for a while that most of them never forgot, there was Judy.

The first time Judy came, it was Annie Fallon who brought her. Annie walked in fast, like always, but with her eyes probing corners of the place that hadn't been looked into for maybe years. Then she nodded a kind of okay to herself and gave a high sign over her shoulder. A bunch of people walked in behind her, checking out the room with faces that were half "aha" and half "uh-oh." Anyone could see right away that they were show business types. They were mostly men. If they hadn't been with Annie Fallon, a couple of them would have been in trouble with the guys at Cooghan's. They must have known it, too, seeing how they never came back after that one time. They all of them wore dark skinny suits and, except for one, dark skinny ties. Some were wearing pretty sharp hats. Two had dark glasses that they kept on, even though at four in the afternoon in Cooghan's you could hardly see the fingers of your own hand in front of you. They piled into the big corner booth, the one farthest away from the bar, which soon became veiled with their smoke.

The regulars tried to not gawk, to ignore them, but it was impossible. In the middle of them all was a tiny woman, with a fluff of dark hair, sparkling in one of those brocade dinner suits like a diamond in a heap of charcoal briquettes. Whoever this woman was, she was the most alive person Frankie had ever seen. Her face and body seemed to vibrate, even when all she was doing was listening to someone else. A slide show of reactions flashing across her face, she made sitting and listening seem like important things to do. When she spoke, her hands flinging out in the air, she set off sparks. And the people at her table kept their faces turned toward hers, opening like flowers to the sun.

It was Annie Fallon who, picking up their drinks at the bar, told the dazzled child, "That's Judy Garland. You know, Dorothy, from Oz." And it was Annie who laughed to see the little girl scoot down to stare at Judy's shoes. They were disappointingly brocade, pointy like the ones the broads wore, just a little glittery but not red at all.

It was Annie, too, who whispered low to the regulars at the bar about how Judy got bored with fancy places and phony people. They'd been talking, the group of them, about where to go, and Annie'd said she preferred her own watering hole, Cooghan's, to all the phony El Moroccos and Rainbow Rooms in the city. That got the regulars embarrassed and proud. For years, whenever one of them was lower than usual, they repeated what Annie had said and reminded themselves that Judy had come—and come back again.

Once they realized the strangers weren't leaving and weren't asking for any trouble either, the regulars settled into their usual ways, almost. Cooghan's nephew Ronnie stopped arranging glasses in pyramids and went back to his racing sheets. Mickey's buddy Phil put a few dimes in the jukebox like he always did, only this time he didn't put his arm around Rusty's waist and sing into her ear like Frank Sinatra. Occasionally, there were peals of laughter from the corner, but no one paid them any mind.

Judy must have slid out to go to the ladies' room, which at Cooghan's was only just the one of the toilets that had a latch. Walking back, she stopped at the bar. The guys were shooting craps to figure out who was buying the next round.

"I always love a crap shoot," she said, snapping open a silvery case. "Who's winning?" She smiled and wiggled a cigarette, the way women did back then.

"More useful to know who's losing," Mickey said, flicking out his lighter. "Mickey Cecchi," he said.

"I always liked the name Mickey," she said, quirking up the corner of her mouth. And when he lost the round and pulled out his wallet with a good-natured grimace, she laughed like anything.

For a while after that, Judy was something of a regular. She usually came in with Annie Fallon, or sometimes with the anxious looking young man who'd worn the blue tie, the one that made his shirt look like someone had painted a stripe down it with the one of Frankie's oil pastels that was called "cerulean." He'd always go sit at the dark end of the bar, on the extra chair where the fluff poked through a slash in the red vinyl seat, and he'd disappear like he was sleeping until Judy looked like she wanted to leave.

When Judy came in, Frankie wasn't allowed to play Hide Out under the tables, or make xylophones out of half-filled glasses. Mickey would scoop her up onto his knee and hold onto her as if she were something precious that he didn't want to lose. She'd snuggle back against his starchy shirt and he'd rest his chin on her head and listen to Judy, or sometimes lean across her to light Judy's cigarette. And always he'd hold her close, so close that for all the next day her hair would smell of cigarettes and beer and Old Spice.

Everything was different when Judy was there, more like a nightclub in a movie than a dark, musty bar. The guys perked up, holding themselves straighter and laughing like they meant it, lighting the cigarettes of the broads, who'd lose some of that scared look from behind their eyes. Everyone laughed, and not that ugly laughter she often heard and shrugged away. They were magic, those times. When Judy was at Cooghan's, there wasn't another place in the world Frankie would have wanted to be.

Judy made everyone feel special, just by being in the same room. Frankie wanted to be exactly like her when she grew up. Once, she worked up the courage to blurt this out. Judy chuckled, that throaty chuckle. Then Mickey, feeling kind of proud, put her down and tried to get her to do a little song she'd learned from watching Darla Hood on *The Little Rascals*. She'd been too scared and hid behind his knees. Judy got down on her own knees then, smiling at Frankie with her big sad eyes. "Don't let them try and make you," she said. "When you want to do it, then you'll sing. Only then. A song has to come from your heart." That was the last time Frankie and Judy were both at Cooghan's at the same time. It just turned out that way.

On a cold April night twelve years later, Judy Garland was several years dead and so was Martha Cecchi. Mickey hardly came into Manhattan anymore, preferring to do his drinking at home, or at the bar across the street from his butcher shop, where a twice-divorced definitely-lowercase-broad named Eunice regularly warmed the bar stool next to his. And Frankie Cecchi was on 45th Street, flattening herself against the cinderblock wall of the alley.

1 – TWO YEARS

POLINA [spoken: Everything you're
looking at is history, shadows of
things that already happened,
people who walked around this
very lake two years ago. Nothing
exists as you see it now, except in
our memories...]

Two short years have fled, are done;
Just twenty-four months of sand
have run—
It trickles like lead when you're
having fun.
Two long years have gone, have fled,
And some have parted and some
have wed,
And some have done other things
instead.

[spoken: But an unconscionable
number of people have done
absolutely nothing at all. Indolent
as barnacles. And twice as thick.]

Time leaves a mark, and hardly a
trace;
It goes so fast, but looking back, so
much has taken place,
It must have been longer ago and
farther away than it seems:
Two years in the flick of an eyelash;
Two years in the space of a dream.

Two short years have ambled by.
I used to look forward, my hopes
were high;
But now I look backward and wonder
why.
Two long years have had their day.
I woke one morning, my hair was
grey—
It's hard to recall it the other way.

[spoken: It was the most glorious
auburn once. The colors of
autumn leaves at sunset. Or so
they told me.]

Time leaves a mark, and hardly a
trace;
It goes so fast, but looking back, so
much has taken place,
It must have been longer ago and
farther away than it seems:
Two years in the flick of an eyelash;
Two years in the space of a dream

[spoken: More of a nightmare, really.
When you think about it. Which I
don't. Well, not too often, that is.]

There used to be a wood here,
where bungalows now stand;
They used to call me fetching, and
now they call me "Gran;"
I used to have a lover, where now I
have a chum.
It isn't a question of better or worse;
We must learn to adapt to the
changes that come.

Two long years are fled, are gone.
No future remains to be dreamed
upon.
I wonder how long I can carry on.
Two short years are gone, are fled.
Some take to travel, and some to bed.
And some are since born, and some
are since dead...

[spoken: But most of us are still here,
just as you see us before you,
walking around this lake:]

music starts for "Lake Song"

"Red velvet curtain disease," someone's mother called it. That's what my notes say. Someone. I can't read the name. Somebody famous, no doubt, or I wouldn't have written it down. Not in 1973.

Evocative, isn't it, "red velvet curtain disease?" Of the effect of a theatre on the audience: the mingled smells of perfume and sweat, with whiffs of old liquor and tobacco, all lightly overlaid with dust; the sumptuous swags of velvet, heavy with tassels and cord, just beyond reach but somehow able to be felt; the final lemon splinters thrown by the dimming chandeliers; the rustling of other people, unseen in the darkness, settling down to the left and the right, in front and behind, the wriggle of anticipation dancing up even the most jaded spine. Evocative of the magic that grips you in that seat for those two or three hours, and lingers ever after in your memory with the seduction of an opiate, pulling you back again and again for more.

Sometimes there's true magic. That's the lure of live performance, the reason human beings can't let the theatre die. Sometimes, if you're still in the dark...very still; if your breathing is cautious enough; if you can become transparent...in the musical silence and velvety blackness, you might find yourself courted, then captured; enchanted by glimmering creatures who appear before you, skimming through the perfumed air. And then...maybe, perhaps...your body might disappear into the balding velvet seat, and you—the real you—would float free in another world.

The balcony of the Regale theatre, above the Second Mezzanine, had only the three rows, each rising two feet above the one before. Looking down from that height was dizzying: leaning on the railings, chin pillowed on your arms, peering down at the stage over the lighting equipment. That night, a bit of the apron was visible when the curtain was down. We stared hungrily at the sliver of green, waiting for something to happen. We were always waiting for something to happen; we were almost 18. The house lights dimmed and the music swelled, and we already trembled with the almost mystical energy of that room. We held our breaths as the curtains parted, revealing the shores of a lake, summer trees of a winter country against a twilight sky. To one side was a small platform with a velvet curtain strung across a clothesline: a stage within a stage. And then Lilith Brassloe entered, with her famous hoarse chuckle and knowing wink, to tell us that what we were about to see had happened, had already happened in the past.

"Red velvet curtain disease." No wonder I wrote that down. Even though the curtains at the Regale were gold.

I saw it today, in the "Arts & Leisure" section of the Sunday *New York Times*: a quarter-page ad for the first Broadway revival of *Lake Song*.

It's hard to believe that this will be the first Broadway revival. You don't have to be a red velvet curtain baby to know the name Marshall Berenson. He's an official national treasure. Remember when they gave him one of those Kennedy Honors awards and Bette Midler sang "Fireflies"? It gave me shivers. And the Harlem Boys Choir did an angelic version of "Ghosts in the Room," which is the song everyone remembers from *The Summer Lands,* Berenson's last really big musical. Since then, there have only been a couple of tentative work-shopped chamber pieces, but Berenson's glory has never dimmed. He's our major theatrical export with productions of his shows, the minor efforts as well as the legendary work, in cities all over the world. Hardly a season goes by when you can't catch one of his musicals in any American town that has some kind of theatre. For *Lake Song* alone, there have been dozens, if not perhaps an even hundred major productions over the years. So how could Broadway, which lately lives and breathes revivals, take 40 years to put together this one?

By 1973, when musical theatre was taking the first transitional steps to rock, pop and jukebox, Berenson was already a cult figure. Having segued from musical wunderkind to enfant terrible, vexing more than a little of the establishment along the way, he was ironically spoken of as the last hope for the grand old Broadway tradition. The burden on Berenson's new show was especially heavy because of the fate of his last one. *The Boy Jones* had opened in September 1971 and, despite critical acclaim and a considerable following, closed seven months later, the producers claiming that the large cast and the demands of the historically accurate Victorian costumes and revolving set made it too expensive to run. Too expensive for those days: a very lavish production of *The Boy Jones* has been running in London for more than two years now with no end in sight. My friend Tony, who is not easily pleased, says it's delightful. Times do change.

When *The Boy Jones* posted its closing notice, many theatre aficionados thought Broadway's inability to support the run might actually be "the first stroke in the death knell of the Fabulous Invalid" (theatre critics used to write like that, back in the day). You can imagine the combination of joy and trepidation with which a new Berenson musical was awaited.

Reviews of *Lake Song* were mixed. Some adored it from the first. Others grumbled that, no matter how clever it might be, a musical wasn't any good if you didn't walk out humming the tunes. A few critics wondered if, in the fiscally blighted wake of *The Boy Jones,* it was quite prudent for the same artistic team to mount another period piece. The one thing everyone agreed was that it was an odd show. What Berenson and book-writer Ian Kraft had created was as much drama as "musical comedy." That this mix doesn't seem radical to you is precisely due to the ground that was broken by *Lake Song*. The demands on casting were extreme; the show couldn't be done without performers who were fine dramatic actors and either equally fine singers or could at least act their way credibly through a song. Bronwen Davies was not then and never had been a singer, but her solos were written to her flaws, and contrary to what some critics wrote, "As I Am" has never been so poignantly delivered as in her broken voice.

As well as the unlikely emotional tone of the work, Berenson and Kraft took a big risk tinkering with material as beloved as *The Seagull*. Chekhov's following is large, loyal and vocal, and almost everyone who's been exposed to this particular play identifies with one or another of the characters at different times of his or her life. While the middle-aged ruefulness in the text seems especially compelling to me now, I know that the story exerts a particular and considerable thrall on young people of any vulnerability—which clearly includes every young person who thinks it a good idea to spend money going to live theatre. During the original Broadway run, the cheapest seats in the Regale were packed with likely "Ninas" and "Mashas" and "Kostias" and "Medviedenkos," many of whom returned time and time again. Of these, more than a handful spent hours hanging around the stage door, dropping off gifts, writing little notes, frequenting the company's usual restaurants.

The show could easily have been an heroic flop, referred to in jokes and warnings for decades to come. Instead, Berenson and his team took the fabric of *The Seagull*, augmented it in some arcane way that made the story shimmer, and created the stuff of legends.

I knew a revival was in the works before I saw the ad in the *Times*; I just didn't know the when of it. It had been months since Ahuva had told me to expect it. Unlike me, she's never lost touch with the theatre world. Even before the announcement, she knew that the production would star Meryl Streep for at least the first few months of the run. And here it is in print: Meryl Streep, and Kevin Spacey, and a pop star my niece is crazy about (presumably as Kostia). It can't have been so long ago that a cast like that would have demanded a full-page ad, even if they were appearing in the auditorium of the Bronx High School of Science, singing "The Farmer in the Dell" to raise money for the Eat Local Challenge. With printed periodicals disappearing like dewdrops at high noon, I suppose it's almost a bigger surprise that there's still an "Arts & Leisure" section and a Sunday *New York Times* at all, than that the producers went for only a quarter-page.

Ahuva said that she and Youri would of course come in from Prague to see it. Youri grew up in Ukraine. How he learned about Marshall Berenson is either a mystery or a miracle, depending on your point of view, but he became a big enough fan that he took out a subscription to *The Berenson Bulletin*. That's how Ahuva found him. When she was preparing to emigrate, she took the precaution of calling the *Bulletin* offices to ask if they had any subscribers in the Czech Republic, and then, with her singular blend of enthusiasm, sincerity and determination, persuaded them to forward her email address to all five. So Ahuva and Youri (and maybe their friend Milos, who is obsessed enough to have gone with them to London last Christmas for *The Boy Jones*) will fly in from Europe for the weekend, to see a show.

Accept that this last sentence is reasonable and you're exactly where I need you to be.

I have been waiting for the right time to write this book. It seems that the universe has just confirmed that the time is now; that's if you put any credence in signs. Time passes and you drift apart from people who were once a daily part of your life. I never lost touch with Ahuva, no matter where she moved. Ric and I always kept a line open and, since he moved back from Vegas, we've met up a couple of times. More recently, after so very long, Facebook brought Leonard and Ellen back into my life in a small way, and Ahuva made contact with Frankie. Consider all of that and a Broadway revival seems inevitable. It's as though the tectonic plates have been shifting into place, settling the landscape in which I could write this book.

We are "still here, just as you see us before you, walking around this lake."

♫

We used to sit in luncheonettes. In those days, that's where you went to hang around. Even in the boroughs, the city was running out of footprints for the classic diners that still dusted the rest of America, those free-standing neon-decked silver tubes or artificial-brick-faced triple-wides. Luncheonettes set the same basic concept into a regular storefront, with smaller menus and shorter hours. You could perch on a vinyl-topped stool around a long Formica counter and stare, across a skyline of red and yellow squeeze bottles and silver-topped glass shakers, at bell-jarred pyramids of shellacked danish and an always nearly empty coffee carafe. Or you could cram into a vinyl booth around a legless Formica table, read the "fun facts" off the backs of sugar packets, and contemplate feeding dimes into a wall-mounted jukebox that played last year's top twenty and songs your parents liked. You could get breakfast any time—just so long as your idea of breakfast was some kind of eggs or pancakes with cured pork. Salad was iceberg lettuce with creamy orange dressing. Vegetables came out of cans. Cakes and even pies were piled high with aerosol whipped cream, and corn muffins were the size of cereal bowls. Everything was served on thick ceramic dinnerware with worn, stained rims, and one of the forks was always bent and/or had something crusty sticking to it.

There was this one luncheonette we sometimes went to that had aspirations of being a café. Apart from one brick wall, it gave the overall impression of being fashionably beige. Around the tall mushroom tables, we sat on what looked like bar stools, only the cushions were linen instead of leather. Overhead, plants drooped from macramé holders. Our coffee or tea came in tall mugs that had pedestals. The food had aspirations, too: chocolate mousse instead of chocolate pudding, though the frill of whipped cream still came out of a can. We would sit there for hours, a couple of miniature loaves of banana bread or a plate or two of fries between us, and they would talk, and I would listen. I can see them sitting there, Ellen and Frankie and Ahuva, three girls with little in common except that they were all in love. And every now and then, they'd stop and turn to me and say, "you should be taking notes." And I would say, "I'll remember." It was always understood, you see, that I'd write this someday. I think they needed a recording angel, an observer to give shape and resonance to their actions. I know they played to it.

So yes, I promised them I'd tell their story someday. I've been waiting, partly for the wisdom of distance and the ripening of memory by age, but just as much for the moment when such a story, told by me, would be heard. We all had dreams back then. I was dreaming, it turns out, of an audience. Now time is at issue. I feel I can no longer wait to begin. And if my only audience is myself, at least I should have fulfilled my promise.

I believe promise should be fulfilled.

Not all dreams come true, but that doesn't stop us from dreaming. We hold our dreams in outstretched arms, shining them like lanterns against the dark and random terrors of this life. They may not lead us down the paths we'd thought to choose, but they take us somewhere—they keep us moving when it would be so much more comfortable to burrow down into a safe hole and sleep. And in moving us forward, backward, somewhere, anywhere, our dreams become our lives, for with no movement there is no life.

I used to believe that so much was possible. We all used to. I think that's the only thing I miss about my youth: the idea of possibility. Hope. No one is born disappointed. On the contrary. We had such joy and excitement. We were bursting with potential, all of us.

Anyway, it wasn't my story I was setting out to tell (though I can't help but come into it sometimes), but the story of some others I knew in those years when everything was possible.

♫

Once upon a time there were three girls who fell in love with a Broadway show. And me, because you can't have a show without an audience.

2 – LAKE SONG

SORIN

Life may be hard and life may be long,
Days may be cloudy or blacker than
    night.
People are weak, and people are
    strong,
All of them go to the lake.

COMPANY

We go to the lake; and walk by the
    shore
And wait. And walk some more.
For the shore of a lake is an endless
    thing,
Perfect and round as a wedding ring.
There to reflect, and there to
    redeem:

And you look at the stars—and the
    sky is so vast;
And you look at the lake—and the
    water's like glass;

SORIN

And you live for today, for there isn't
    a past,
There is no tomorrow, you live in the
    moment—
A moment as long as a life.

By the lake, where time stands still;
By the lake, forever and ever the same
As it was on the day that the world
    first began
In a moment as long as a life.

SHAMRAYEV

And here the world is not so big as it
    was when you were small.

DORN

And here the world is not so cramped
    as it felt when you grew tall.

POLINA

And here the world is just a place,
    the space in which we live.

COMPANY

Except for those who choose to
    embrace the alternative.

MASHA

Sometimes I feel that I struggle alone,
Nobody cares if I live or I die.
Thinking of filling my pockets with
    stone,
Wandering down to the lake.
I'd go to the lake; and walk by the
    shore
And wait. And walk some more

MEDVIEDENKO

For the shore of a lake is an endless
    thing,
Perfect and round and as wedding
    ring.
There to reflect, and there to
    redeem:

NINA

And you look at the sky—and the
    moon is so cold;

ARKADINA

And you look in the lake—and your
    face is so old;

TRIGORIN

And you reach for your soul and
    remember it's sold;

ARKADINA & TRIGORIN

You fight off tomorrow, and grab at
    the moment—
The moment that's left of your life.

COMPANY
By the lake, where time stands still;
By the lake, forever and ever
    unchanged:
In the blink of an eye passes all of a
    year,
And a moment holds all of a life.

KOSTIA

And the grey summer sky is a
    blanket of peace;
And it's calm by the lake, and the
    anguish may cease;

MASHA

So you scatter the stones and you
    feel the release.
The circles spread outward, a ripple
    a moment,
A moment that blesses your life.

COMPANY

By the lake, where time stands still;
By the lake, forever and ever
    unchanged:
In the blink of an eye passes all of a
    year,
And a moment holds all of a life.

Cocooned in her sheets in the darkness, Ahuva Geffner assured herself that she was someone in particular. She probed the wellspring of what she knew would be character, if only she could tap into it and give it form. She hated seeming anonymous when she knew she was…well…Someone. Maybe she couldn't describe exactly who she was, but not everything of value can be easily defined.

When Ahuva looked in the mirror, she never saw a whole. She saw parts. A face that was nice to look at. Healthy, shiny hair; she used a cream rinse because that seemed to be a big thing. A naturally slender body, with all the requisite limbs and appendages; a body that was easy to cover with appropriate clothes that were hemmed evenly, fastened neatly and fitted in at the waist. Somehow none of this added up to anything specific.

"How do people know *how*?" she often wondered. Jeans are jeans; brown shoes are brown shoes. What makes the difference? Why did some people look, well, special to themselves?

Like Byron, for example. Byron always wore a white shirt. He wore it over his jeans for every day. He tucked it in, with a dark suit jacket over it, for concerts and shows. It was a plain white buttoned shirt, the kind her father wore when her parents went out with friends, but it looked so different on Byron. Byron Weeks was the most incredible musician Ahuva had ever met. Even when he wasn't at the piano, he pulled you in from across an entire auditorium. There was the way he held his head, high but just a little ducked-under. And his way of looking at you: not directly; just enough to make you draw closer, so that he'd have to move his eyes that little bit where they'd have to look straight into yours. The most thrilling thing was to sit next to him on the bench while he was playing. You couldn't see his eyes then; but Ahuva knew if you could, they'd be blindly focused on a distant inner spot no one else could see, where he'd once confided he could watch the music dance like colored lights. The few times she'd sat beside him while he played, just the two of them in the auditorium before or after a chorus rehearsal, she'd been unable to breathe from the heat of the music pulsing through his body only inches away from hers. Those had been the most phenomenal minutes of her life. She still couldn't stop thinking about them, even though it had been so long ago.

Byron, a year ahead of her, had graduated in June, and spent the summer with his father, in New Orleans. In July, he sent her a postcard of the French Quarter, which she pasted into the scrapbook that she'd started for mementoes of people she knew would become famous someday. She'd been hoping Byron wouldn't forget her from the grandeur of Julliard, planning to watch out for every concert he might play in and show up with flowers. She never expected a card. It was breathtaking that he'd thought of her.

Before she turned around, it was September and Byron called out of the blue, asking if he might take her out for coffee. Of course she said yes. Then she coolly informed her parents that an almost adult Afro-American musician they'd never met was coming by the apartment to pick her up and take her to Greenwich Village, a place almost as exotic to them as he was. Abba said he was glad the young man knew to come to the house and meet her parents, and had then given her money for a taxi and told her not be slow to use it. Her mother, of course, had ignored everything except that it was—finally—a date and then started driving her crazy about what she should wear.

She wore her jeans with the peasant blouse that used to be Holly's, because Holly sometimes sang in coffee houses in the Village so it should be right, and a pair of Yemenite earrings that she usually considered too fussy to wear. Byron arrived on time, wearing his jacket though it was still summer outside. Her mother, who would always manage to do the most embarrassing thing, stared at him all the time he was there. He was shy, which he always was except when he was playing, and very respectful, answering all of her father's questions in a low voice but with a frank and confident manner. Abba was favorably impressed, but still made Byron promise to get her home by eleven o'clock.

They took the subway, almost an hour of sitting shoulder to shoulder with Byron as the car rattled and shook along the track from Queens to the Village. Byron would never raise his voice loud enough to be heard above the screeching of the train, so they were companionably mute until they reached West 4th Street. At the top of the stairs, Byron shyly reached for her hand. Until that moment, she'd kept telling herself it wasn't a "date" at all, no matter what her mother thought. She thought she would explode with happiness. He led her to a cave of a coffeehouse with sooty brick walls and scarred wooden tables. The posters on the wall were of musicians she'd never heard of, and everything on the chalkboard menu had Italian names. Jazz saxophone played on the sound system, an old and grainy recording; it was probably very famous; she was too embarrassed by her own ignorance to ask. Byron ordered her a cappuccino, which turned out to be coffee topped with milky foam. She wasn't used to drinking coffee. It was unpleasantly bitter until he poured a packet of sugar right down the middle of the foam, drilling a tiny hole that closed up as the sugar sank. She giggled, which made him smile. He didn't smile enough. Byron had a beautiful smile.

They talked about their summers—her usual visit to the family in Jaffa, his much more interesting months in New Orleans with his father. As a rule, Ahuva believed in getting to the point and didn't hesitate to ask questions that other people seemed to find surprising. With Byron, however, this never felt right. He trusted her, but she sensed that if she asked something he didn't want to answer, he'd clam up altogether. It was too great a risk, so she listened carefully and tried to ask only what she judged to be safe. This was how her parents spoke with their friends, the history around them thick with the shadows of dead relatives and unspoken horrors. Over time she'd learned enough about Byron to understand that, except for having lots of locked rooms to avoid, his family was nothing like any family she knew. It hurt to imagine the things he'd hinted at: a mother who'd died when he was small; an undependable absent father; the grandmother who'd raised him for a while until she'd died; and the step-uncle who'd agreed to keep him until he finished school, then threw him out when he turned 18. Ahuva knew that for most of his senior year Byron had lived in Mr. Gruen's basement. Ahuva once had a tiny crush on the junior high band teacher; he was everyone's favorite; he'd coached Byron for his Julliard audition, too.

Byron's father was a musician; he could have been a great one Byron said, but he messed up somehow and now he seemed to make his living doing shady things down in New Orleans. Ahuva thought maybe Mr. Weeks had smoked a lot of dope, which Mr. Gruen said musicians were doing long before the hippies discovered it, and that a lot of them, like Charlie Parker and Billie Holliday, had ruined their lives, which was a lesson everyone should learn. Mr. Gruen was probably their only teacher who knew anything about jazz.

Looking over her cappuccino at Byron, Ahuva wondered if he'd ever tried dope. If not before, then he probably had this summer, visiting his father. If she caught his sideways glance, would she see a difference? Could she? How would she know what to look for? Suddenly, Ahuva felt much younger than her 17 years and embarrassed by her lack of sophistication. It was hard to believe she was living in New York City in 1972.

A light snapped on inside her head, the realization that it was time to grow up and get a life. It so excited her that, before she could wonder how he'd react and stop herself, she leaned across the table and kissed Byron on the cheek. Her heart stopped. Had she gone too far? Would he jump up and run away? It was a good thing Abba had given her that money. At first Byron didn't move, but then he gently turned his head those two inches so that his mouth was lined up with hers and he kissed her lightly on the lips. In that

15

small world that was the two of them and the table, everything seemed enormous with importance. She could hear his breathing and the beat of his heart, and she had no doubt that his musician's ears were hearing hers, too. It was too much power to sustain. They both pulled back just enough to break the circuit. That had been when she'd noticed how sad his eyes were, even sadder than usual. He told her then. They'd all believed so strongly that the wait-list meant he'd be at Julliard, but not enough people had opted out; there wasn't a place for him.

She was ready to cheer him on, to tell him Julliard would be sorry they blew it, to show him she'd help him find something bigger and better. Instead, she heard that he thought he already had: he was taking all the money he'd saved for college and was leaving for Paris. That was why he'd wanted to see her, to say goodbye. The lights had winked out as instantly as they'd turned on.

That almost perfect night.

Byron was in Paris right now, playing in piano bars or jazz clubs or whatever smoke-filled night spots they had in that glamorous, mysterious city. Except for sometimes making her heart ache, this was good. Her father would die to hear her say so, because to him going to college was practically *halachic*, but Byron didn't really need school. He needed to be out in the world, having experiences that would help him make art. Byron was a genius. He was the only genius she'd met so far, but she knew she was right. When he sat down to play, it was liquid and beautiful and carried you away. He had only to listen to music once to be able to play it, entirely, by ear—classical, jazz, rock and roll, anything. He could play harmonies right off the cuff. And he could write it all down. Every lead sheet for the chorus, the band and every school play had been written by Byron Weeks. What Ahuva found even more exciting was how he could take music apart and put it back together again in ways that no one except a genius could ever have conceived. Ahuva was musical enough to laugh at the jokes he sometimes snuck in. That was how their friendship had begun—she could follow enough of what he was doing to be dazzled. When Byron played, he engaged more than her heart; he engaged her mind. Listening to him had the same excitement as hunting down the solution to the best kind of puzzle.

For as long as she could remember being a person, Ahuva had nearly worshipped puzzles, especially any with numbers and the patterns that connected them. She loved unraveling a problem to its bare components and fitting them neatly to a formula. Resolution was so satisfying it made her toes curl. If countries could resolve their issues mathematically, the world would live in serene harmony. Patterns in language fascinated her too, so much so that no one hearing her fluent unaccented English would guess that she'd never spoken a word of it until the age of 10. Unlike numbers, however, words were surprisingly slippery creatures; you could seek out a word that meant exactly what you wanted to say, but something in the rest of the sentence…or your voice or face while you were speaking…or maybe just the fact that no one understood that particular word, would subvert or eclipse or befuddle your entire meaning.

If being a Marshall Berenson fan were a clinically monitored syndrome, Ahuva might have been said to have manifested all the early markers.

Ahuva had only been American for two years when her parents took her to a summer theatre production of *The Buddy System*. It was an odd choice of show for a child, but she'd been too old for a sitter and too young to be left on her own; and anyway, musicals were for the whole family, weren't they? While most of the things her father was laughing at were opaque to her, the score was as clear as her own damp footprints by the pool. Ahuva sat spellbound. At the first opportunity, she'd bought the album, where the original Broadway cast had made it more exciting still. The following spring in junior high, *Rosebud* was announced as the school play. Unlike girls her age who'd been born in the States, she'd never seen the popular film version, no less heard of the actress on whose childhood memoirs it had been based. When someone pointed out the real "Rosebud" on a television Western where she played the recurring role of a frontier saloonkeeper, Ahuva was stunned by disbelief. It was because she was enraptured by Berenson that she couldn't wait to be part of the show. When she'd failed to get into the chorus, she joined the props crew and hung around rehearsals. Mr. Gruen, delighted by her enthusiastic quizzing, loaned her his records, including his prized copy of the rare cast album of *Riding a Bicycle*.

Asked by her parents what she wanted for her fifteenth birthday, Ahuva didn't have to stop to think: "Tickets to *The Boy Jones*." It was her first Broadway show, and the first time she experienced a Marshall Berenson musical in its original production. She didn't stop talking about it for months and, for her sixteenth birthday, only wanted to see it again. Her parents couldn't understand why she'd want to see a show she'd already seen. Moreover, they understood that in America the traditional sixteenth birthday present was a nice party, and they liked Ahuva to have what other girls had. By the time she'd saved enough babysitting money to buy a matinee ticket, the closing notice had been posted and tickets were impossible to get.

When word of a new Marshall Berenson musical first leaked out, Ahuva was determined to get a ticket the minute they went on sale. She'd been saving her money for something special; surely there couldn't be anything more special than this. She had two friends who agreed: Heidi, who was mad for musicals in general; and me, who....well, what can I say? These days I prefer *The Cherry Orchard*, but in the autumn of 1972 I lived and died by *The Seagull*. In an ambience defined by aged jeans and batiks, I stalked moodily across campus in a black maxi skirt and sweater, smoking gold-tipped Black Sobranies and trying like crazy to lure someone into challenging me so that I could say "I'm in mourning for my life." I was a freshman drama major, and I was very young.

We speculated endlessly about the show, and started to campaign for permission to see it. It seems sweetly innocent now, but at 17 we'd none of us ever been to the theatre without an adult. Times Square and the theatre district, teeming with junkies, drunks, pickpockets and runaways, were dubious neighborhoods for sheltered middle-class girls to visit at night. A matinee seemed too juvenile for such an event; against all evidence, we thought of ourselves as adults; Heidi and I after all, having skipped a year, were already in college. Finally Ahuva's mother, who didn't care at all for Chekhov and probably not much more for Berenson but who was relieved to do something that would please her inscrutable child, volunteered to chaperone us and even get the tickets. Ahuva wrote me at school, triumphant. Mrs. Geffner had stood on the box office line for over two cold hours; the deed was done.

Tickets for "the first Friday night you can get," as Ahuva had specified in view of my two hour train ride, ended up meaning the balcony. In the Regale, this was a breathless trek up three long stairways. When we finally reached the seats, everyone sighed. Once she'd settled in her aisle seat and stopped panting, Mrs. Geffner began to read her *Playbill* from cover to cover. Heidi felt a flake of mascara in one eye and had to remove a lens and suck it clean. Knowing *The Seagull*, I stuck a tissue up my sleeve before jamming my shoulder bag under my seat.

Ahuva was the last of us to actually sit down. She set her *Playbill* and overpriced color souvenir program on the center of her seat, then slipped her bag from her shoulder and placed it on the papers. Her long fingers deliberately unknotted the belt, undid the buttons of her coat one by one. After stepping out of the coat, she folded it in half the long way, and then in half the other way. Picking up her bag and programs with her free hand, she sat carefully, feet neatly squared. She began to drape the coat over the guardrail, but was stopped by a vision of it slipping off and floating down, an enormous woolen leaf, onto the heads of the people in the orchestra below. She folded it in half once more and placed it on her lap. Only then did she unwind the long crocheted scarf from her neck, fold that, and set it atop the coat. She smiled broadly at everyone and looked around.

Even when safely seated, the view from the top of the theatre was vertiginous. Beneath the latticed ceiling, a frieze of gilded nymphs capered in subdued mid-Victorian ecstasy. Lower down, to each side of the stage, plaster maidens and plaster lutes were twined with vines of plaster roses, all picked out in gold. Faceted crystal balls dangled from the massive chandeliers, which in turn were suspended from rods or chains that were bound in velvet wrapped with gold cord.

Everything that didn't sparkle, curved and spiraled so that your eyes had no tether; you were forced to look down to where the orchestra and a bit of mezzanine appeared as rows and rows of heads. In the Friday night audience, predominant bald domes and shellacked platinum helmets merged with fuzzy brown pompoms and the occasional blob of red-orange into an image that might have been painted by Lichtenstein or Seurat.

If you could bring yourself to stare all the way down to the stage, a bit of grass-like green edged from beneath the heavy curtain toward the orchestra pit. The curtain rippled. Was that the toe of a black boot peeping out?

Lightheadedness, coupled with our already heightened expectations, created an atmosphere of unreality even before the lights went down.

In one of the lower boxes, a balding man in a grey sweater took a chair, pulling it back so that the fleur-de-lis patterned side curtains concealed him from eyes at angles less elevated than ours.

Heidi giggled. "Can you believe this? I think I see Carol Channing." She pointed to one of the platinum helmets in the orchestra, surrounded by a pouf of white fur.

I pointed to the box. "That man must be somebody, the way he's hiding."

Ahuva jumped, her coat slipping dangerously. "That's James Lord!" She rifled through her souvenir program and stabbed her finger at a page. "See!" The picture showed a balding man in a turtleneck and sport jacket. Everyone leaned as far forward as she dared and stared, awestruck, at the man in the box. James Lord. The Director. Oblivious of the glory in her vicinity, Malke Geffner continued reading her *Playbill*.

Then the lights slowly dimmed. The new silence of the darkened theatre was underlined by a cough, a sneeze and the rustle of a candy wrapper. We reached our hands to each other, across our folded coats, and gripped them with excitement. The overture swelled, masking every sound but the heartbeats pounding in our ears.

And the curtains parted at last. And for two hours and thirty-seven minutes, even during intermission, no one seemed to breathe.

When it had ended, and multiple curtain calls had been demanded and taken, everyone followed Mrs. Geffner down the three long flights of stairs and out of the theatre. Emptying the theatre, like emptying a sack of flour through a funnel, seemed to take forever. Forever wasn't nearly long enough.

Eyes sparkling with tears and pleasure, Ahuva paused at the threshold of the city, her gloved hand caressing the brass doorplate. It was a clear night outside, dark blue with bright stars. We floated through the streets, towards the subway, magic clinging to us.

"It was a good play," Mrs. Geffner said, breaking the spell. "But the ending I didn't like. Eh. Russians. What should you expect?"

Ahuva was humming quietly to herself. As she gained confidence in the melody, she hummed more loudly and the strain became recognizable. It was that song from the play, the one Nina sang. Heidi picked up the tune and Ahuva began to play with harmony. I joined in with patches of lyrics. "*If ever you need my life, take it, it's yours…*" all along the platform, then onto the subway car.

"Girls!" Mrs. Geffner tried to hush us, then threw up her hands and found a seat, pretending not to know us. Giggling and nudging shoulders, we grabbed onto poles.

"And they say you don't walk out of a Marshall Berenson show singing the score!" Ahuva Geffner exclaimed, triumphant.

♫

Frankie Cecchi was not a virgin. She'd made sure of that. And in her first term at the Academy, she'd done a scene from *Cat on a Hot Tin Roof* wearing only a slip. She knew these were important milestones. When Frankie insisted at age ten that she wanted to be an actress, her dying mother said that if she still wanted to be an actress by the time she was 15, she should read *Marjorie Morningstar*. It was one of the last pieces of advice Martha gave her. On her 15th birthday, Frankie pulled the book from its hiding place in the back of her closet and read it from cover to cover. It was pathetic, especially the ending, but she felt a kernel of truth; she'd already met some girls she'd be willing to bet would end up being Marjorie Morningstars. There was also some useful information. Finding the world to be one big question, Frankie prospected for answers wherever she could find them. That meant reading not only *Respect for Acting* but all the actors' memoirs and biographies she could find. Her fellow students at the Academy made fun of her reading material, another reason she didn't have a lot of friends there. They seemed to think they were too good to read even *My Life* by Sarah Bernhardt or Ellen Terry's autobiography. Ellen Terry had been the best English actress of all time; not only that, but she was John Gielgud's great-aunt or something. John Gielgud! Frankie could only begin to imagine what the snobs would say if they knew that right now she was reading *Weep No More My Lady*, a memoir by Judy Garland's last husband, Mickey Deans. Frankie kept a special place in her heart for Judy, who'd been so kind to her at Cooghan's. It was too sad to read the book straight through, so she was reading in bits, breaking it up with *Four Plays* by Henrik Ibsen.

Frankie never forgot what Judy had said, that time she didn't want to sing. It was her only childhood memory that didn't involve recriminations. Rubbing her damp nose, Frankie found herself thinking a lot about the past. There wasn't much to do in the alley but think, because it was dark and she had to stay inconspicuous. To anyone walking by, there was nothing to notice except the red feather in her brown hat and the insect glitter of her oversized eyeglasses—"Volkswagen headlights," she called them. With all the lights of Broadway, this little glint was hardly noteworthy; therefore, to the casual passerby, Frankie Cecchi wasn't even there.

A professional actor wouldn't ordinarily count it desirable to blend in with the scenery; nonetheless Frankie Cecchi, a few months past 19, was a professional. She'd had her Equity card since August, thanks to the famous director who'd been at her Academy audition and had needed a compliant and genuinely young Kattrin to play against his soon-to-be-former mistress's *Mother Courage* up in Provincetown. It was interesting about show business, how you never knew which of your qualities would come in handy. Naïveté had opened an important door for her, and looking ordinary was about to open another.

In five minutes, the doors to the Regale would open and a crowd of people would spill out for their intermission smokes. Once they did, Frankie would dart around the corner and disappear into their midst, just another member of the audience. A few minutes later, she would file in with the others, looking for her seat. That there would be one, she had no doubt. Since Donny, the Musical Theatre teaching assistant and her only real friend at the Academy, had taught her how, she'd done this six or seven times at different theatres.

There always was a seat, somewhere off to the side in the back, or in one of the boxes; people didn't buy box seats much anymore. Even in a sold out house, there was usually a seat someone didn't show up by curtain time to claim. And even for the best play on Broadway, some people didn't return from intermission; there was no accounting for taste, as the broads at Cooghan's always used to say. If worse came to worst and there were no seats at all, *Lake Song* was SRO and by intermission the ushers would pay no attention to the number of people standing. "Second-acting," Donny called this; a way for the poorest theatre lovers—mostly actors—to see at least half of a Broadway show.

Two weeks ago, Frankie had seen *Lake Song* as an official member of the audience, from a seat in the front mezzanine. Looking down, you could take in the entire stage without getting a sore neck from ducking back and forth to look over the shoulder of the person in front of you on the left and then over the shoulder of the person on the right. The ticket had been her birthday present to herself, well worth a month of eating apples instead of lunch. By the time the day came, she'd already snuck in to the second half of the show twice and was almost desperate to see Act I. It had been everything she'd hoped. Frankie was a big fan of Marshall Berenson musicals. *Playing the Palace* had been the first Broadway show she'd ever seen, her best audition song was from *Rosebud*, and her beloved acting teacher Annie Fallon, the same Annie Fallon who used to kid around with Pop at Cooghan's and was almost her aunt, had played Baroness Lehzen in *The Boy Jones*. Frankie had seen *The Boy Jones* seven times, paying full price each time. She wished she'd known Donny back then; it would have been nice to see Annie sing her big number every night. Annie wasn't working at all this season. She'd left *Helen* the month before it folded, and when the students returned from Christmas break, there'd been a replacement covering her classes at NYADA. Rumor had it she was really sick this time, that she was back in the hospital, but there was no way to find out; Frankie wasn't permitted to call her anymore. Frankie tried hard to put that out of her mind. Right now she had to focus on getting into the Regale to see Act II again. And Bronwen Davies.

Frankie couldn't remember how it all fit together, but somehow she associated a babysitter taking her to see *Goin' Goin' Go Go* with understanding that her mother was so sick that she was going to die. As Martha became frail and distant, Frankie began to fantasize that she was Hayley Mills' sister and their mother was Bronwen Davies, and that they would all laugh and sing together in front of European fountains in matching outfits and short white boots with little gold zippers. Frankie went through the movie magazines, clipping out every photo and every interview she could find. She learned everything there was to know about Bronwen Davies. When James Lyttleton died, also from cancer, Frankie sent a card with angels in care of the studio. The studio sent back a signed photo, which she kept on her nightstand for months, next to a framed snapshot of Martha. That Christmas, *Photoplay* published pictures of Davies with her children and Frankie imagined a story where Mickey, who was a good looking man, would meet Bronwen Davies at a nightclub and they would fall in love and move in together, and Richard and Cressida would become her brother and sister. There had been weeks when dreaming over her scrapbook was the only thing keeping Frankie going.

Now it was Annie Fallon who was terribly ill, Annie, who was almost her aunt. Annie had pretended not to know Frankie when she'd shown up in Intro to Musical Theatre Performance in September; she had to keep her distance and not show favoritism. This was understandable, but it made things harder for Frankie than they already were. Instead of teaching at the Academy as planned, Thierry had moved to Canada to start a new Molière festival; and from the first day, the instructors at NYADA seemed to hold it against her that she'd been in *Mother Courage* before taking any of their classes. Most of the students picked up on that attitude and shut Frankie out. This wasn't how she'd dreamed acting school would be. And now Annie was probably dying; Frankie could feel it in the pit of her stomach.

When Frankie heard Bronwen Davies was going to play Arkadina, it felt like a sign, like Fate was watching out for her and things were going to be okay after all. It was comforting to second-act and see her on stage, even though Arkadina wasn't at all a comforting character. Then Frankie saw *Lake Song* all the way through. All of Arkadina's good songs were in Act I: "Moscow," "As I Am" and "Kiss, Kiss." By intermission, Frankie was shaking with excitement. It was hard to sit still for Act II, but it would have been idiotic to leave. She applauded until her hands were red and sore. She was one of the last people to leave the theatre. She didn't even remember the train ride home. The next thing she could remember was being on her knees in the closet, digging out her old scrapbook. Friday after class, she went to the big Hallmark store and bought a new scrapbook. She took some of her old, precious clippings, added a *Playbill* and other things connected with *Lake Song*, and made a new book. It took every free minute for a week. She wrapped it up in the flowered paper she'd bought for her cousin's bridal shower present and, before she could lose her nerve, dropped it off at the stage door.

The doorman, Wally, was really nice. If she stepped away from her exact spot in the alley, she could see him standing by the stage door blowing smoke rings. She stayed flat, waiting for the crowd. This close to Saturday he might remember her. She didn't want anything to stop her tonight. Act II wasn't the same as seeing the whole show, but until she could save up enough money for another ticket, it was better than nothing.

♫

Ellen Janow plucked a cigarette from the red cardboard box and stroked it. It was slim and unfiltered. Her similarly slender fingers tamped the cigarette against the top of the box, releasing a fleeting maple whiff of tobacco. Her pointed tongue darted out to wet the brown paper where it would meet her lips. To complete the ceremony, she flicked her new Dunhill lighter, a present from Mr. Black, and inhaled, deeply and appreciatively. The lighter rested with satisfying weight in her hand, the ribbed case catching the marquee lights and refracting tiny rainbows. Mr. Black; Barney. Surely she should be calling him Barney now, but Mr. Black was more, well, titillating. She arched her back against the postered wall and smiled her long ironic smile.

Ellen was advancing toward 18. She smoked with assurance and was learning to appreciate Guinness, Drambuie and gin. Her hair was finally growing out in turbulent curls, and she'd stopped shaving under her arms. She strutted braless in her vertically ribbed, horizontally striped, zipper-fronted sweaters, presenting her magnificent young breasts—arguably her best feature—to the world. It was all about attitude. It had to be, because Ellen was not a pretty girl. Her features were too long and sharp. She was small in stature, but without the proportion or grace to be considered dainty. Her voice was nasal and loud. But her skin was lovely, poreless and white, and she was learning to use her hands with exquisite fluency; her hands...and her tongue and her thighs and other less visible muscles. She walked like a sailor just making landfall, and sat with her weight tilted clumsily forward, but on her back she was lithe and confident as a cat. Ellen knew she would never be a beautiful woman, but she was determined to become more than most beautiful women ever became. Ellen Janow wanted to be a powerful woman, and she already well understood that there was tremendous power in sex.

The summer Ellen was 15, her divorced mother dragged her away to a Catskills resort for a weekend. While Sydelle sat elegant and alone in the Lounge, bored by the litany of some woeful comic, Ellen slipped out of their room on a hunting expedition of her own. The elastic neck of her gauze granny dress pulled low off her shoulders, she wandered barefoot along the perimeter of the golf course, pausing beneath the occasional lamps where the stark light would silhouette her legs and illuminate her already compelling bosom. Eventually, as she'd felt in her bones, she was approached by a man. He was the hotel's masseur, a long-limbed sometimes-drunk, with dandruff and a pockmarked face. One of life's losers, but for Ellen, Deus ex Machina; God-in-a-machine, the machine being a can opener.

"I like the way you move," he said as he approached her. It was a ridiculous thing for someone to say to her of all people, but she managed not to laugh. "I'm an artist," he said a few minutes later, "and the human body is my instrument."

She let him lead her to his room where, with his mouth and hands, he proved his claim long before he entered her and brought her to her triumphant maiden climax. Later in her bath, she basked in an afterglow mixed with smugness; Ellen had known she would excel in this sphere. Thrumming with satisfaction, she curled beneath the sheets, her back feigning sleep to her mother's entrance. She didn't want to tarnish her joy with the sight of her mother: the beautiful mother who kept her hair cropped short and her sprouting breasts plastered down in oxford-cloth shirts; the rigid mother who prohibited after-school gossips on the phone; the scorned mother who hated her ex-husband and, as much as possible, kept him apart from his only child. Freed by her body, Ellen could despise Sydelle's fears and contemplate perhaps even pitying her.

Two-and-a-half years and a string of lovers later, Ellen had ripened secretly, a spiny fruit that only a connoisseur would know to taste. She and Leonard, her best friend since playpen days, her dear and confused friend who had never been her lover, bloomed in the shadows of the city. The minute they found a place they could afford, having inveigled her father into agreeing he would sign a lease, they would move into Manhattan, into the center of the real world. They would turn 18 and Life would begin. Meanwhile, they continued to fill their time with their own sort of education: every person they met was a teacher, every street a lesson. They browsed through bookshops for biographies of people whose lives might be used as patterns. They sipped, sniffed, chewed, eavesdropped, spied, gawked and groped their way into the selves they wanted to become.

Anything was more stimulating than sitting in an airless classroom listening to some shabby husk drone on about nothing. Ellen's parents had never encouraged her to think of herself as a scholar. On the contrary, apparently affronted by her lack of gifts in the French and mathematics in which they had once excelled, they often called her "stupid" to her face, one of their few ever points of agreement. Knowing she'd never do well enough to please them, Ellen chose not to work particularly hard at all. Her report cards had often used the phrase "not living up to her potential," but no one had ever made an attempt to show her what that potential might be. Somehow she managed to pass the junior high acceleration test. After that, she stayed firmly at C level throughout high school. Instead of homework, she spent her time leafing through her parents' copies of *The New Yorker* and *Esquire*, reading reviews of whatever was new, then moving on to read the books and plays for herself. She often daydreamed of what life might have been, if only some glamorous celebrity couple had been her parents.

However irrationally (based on their assessment of her limits) and in concert for once, Sydelle and Harry had fully expected Ellen would go to college. After years of academic lassitude, the only place that would accept her was a glorified finishing school that was no measure to her true aptitude, difficult as that was to describe. Ellen liked to think of herself as "cunning," a delightfully animal description of the way she imagined her mind worked: quickly, venally, instinctively. She was constantly bored with school, but had little choice but to stay enrolled until she came of age or, more realistically, until she could afford to tell Sydelle and Harry where to stick it. Fortunately, Ellen's college had never expected much from its students beyond manners and, in this heyday of student freedom, even those were indulgently overlooked. Ellen could do pretty much as she pleased. As long as the school didn't register an objection, there wouldn't be a peep out of Sydelle and Harry. She attended classes occasionally, and only if they served her private purpose. She showed up for that slice of the Art History survey course that was devoted to 20th century art, because the lecturer with the bizarre maquillage claimed to have been a mistress of Picasso's. When the required freshman "Classics in Translation" course reached a unit on Sappho and Catullus, Ellen not only attended, but read aloud so brilliantly that the hollow-eyed Jesuit who taught it had his tongue halfway down her throat before they were safely in the darkest corner of the locked language lab.

Just as the boredom was beginning to outweigh the glamor of freedom, Ellen spotted the index card on the Internship bulletin board. Felix Ayre was trying to resurrect his Lazarus Repertory Company. That was how he put it. Ellen was quick to adopt the expression and use it whenever someone asked if she was a college student. "I'm interning with Felix Ayre," she would say. "You know—the director." Half the time they'd know, half the time they wouldn't. "He's trying to resurrect his Lazarus Repertory Company." It was interesting to see if the eyes were blank behind the knowing nod, or if she'd met a true theatre aficionado. If the eyes brightened at the name and the line got a laugh, this was an acquaintance to cultivate, either for her own use or to help Felix—which would also work out to her benefit.

Ellen and Felix clicked from the first; they understood each other. Walking unprepared into his offices, any other girl would have screamed and run. The first thing that met your eye was the "coffee table" in the reception area—a glass coffin containing the flower-decked body of a young woman. After dedicating years to learning to appear blasé about everything, Ellen hadn't even lifted an eyebrow but took a seat on the sagging couch to wait for the interview. Shifting the copy of *Backstage* that covered the maiden's face, she realized with a thrill that it was Penelope Rice. When the Royal Shakespeare Company had visited New York three years ago, Harry had taken her, against Sydelle's wishes of course, to see their notorious ultra-modern production of *Agamemnon*. Penelope Rice had been Clytemnestra. Mind-blowing. Ellen hadn't known theatre could be so intense and alive.

Felix made his grand entrance from an inner office, only slightly hampered by the cast on his left foot. He wore the black jeans, black cashmere turtleneck and burgundy Noel Coward dressing gown that turned out to be his working uniform, and leaned on an ebony-topped cane; Ellen later learned the cane was unrelated to his injury and concealed a sword. Assuming the gilded chair across from her, Felix held forth, darting from unfounded assumptions about who she was and why she'd applied for the internship, to catty criticism of nearly every show currently playing in New York, all revolving around his plans to bring repertory theatre back to Broadway. After what seemed like either seconds or years, he pulled out a silk handkerchief and blew his nose loudly. Tucking it away, he looked down his elegant nose and stared into her eyes, Barrymore playing Svengali. "Do you have any questions?" he asked, making the "you" into something sinister.

Ellen decided she had nothing to lose. "Just one," she said, trying not to be seen taking a deep breath. Felix prepared to pounce. "What's with the wax figure of Penelope Rice?" Lightly but firmly, she tapped twice on the coffin's lid.

From an incipient sneer, Felix's mouth broke into a shockingly wide grin. "Ah, Penelope!" he cooed, "The light of my life! Well played, Helen! And how do you know Penelope?"

"Ellen," she corrected, and went on to talk about *Agamemnon*. It turned into a genuine conversation about modernizing the classics and about what Felix called "authentic performances," eventually interrupted by Penelope Rice in person. Felix's ex-wife and always-muse had come to fetch him to a meeting with an investor. It was while helping Felix hobble down three flights of stairs that Ellen was finally told about their production of *Hamlet*, years before "and years ahead of its time," for which the coffee table had been a prop. *Hamlet* had been the final production of the original Lazarus company, and both Felix and Penelope had a superstition about keeping the coffin in the office for luck.

As he dragged his leg into the limo, Felix held out his hand to hers and told her he'd see her first thing Tuesday morning. Penelope smiled her beautiful smile. "That means noon, dear." Ellen smiled back foolishly and stood there waving as the limo pulled away.

The internship was almost over now. Ellen knew she'd done well. She had free tickets to *Lake Song* to prove it. They were house seats, which meant they were from the block of what were considered the best seats in the theatre, reserved for the members of the production who wanted to get tickets for family and friends; Bronwen Davies' brother Ivor lived with Penelope's brother Lionel. Penelope was on her way to London now to play Blanche DuBois, and before she'd left she'd given the tickets to Ellen "as my little way of saying thank you for all you've done."

It was a thoughtful gift. Ellen found it encouraging. She hoped it meant she'd proved herself enough to maybe wangle a paying job with the Lazarus; a real job in The Theatre. Then she could stop doing Barney Black under his desk at the import company office, where she typed and filed two mornings a week. Unless she thought Barney's connections (ahem) might turn out to be useful to her. Connections of all sorts were important when your goal was to one day be a producer. She often wondered what would it be like, to be respected enough that people would want to invest money in your dream, and to have famous people care so much that they came to your door to make sure you got to the meetings to make it happen. She imagined herself being driven around town in a limo.

"Come on!" Leonard was tugging her arm, breaking into her reverie. "Intermission's over. We've got to get back inside." A girl hurried past them in the lobby, her eyeglasses nervously winking from side to side. The feather in her hat brushed against Leonard's face. "I wonder," he said, rubbing his cheek; "how are they going to handle the 'I am a seagull' speech?"

"We'll know in about an hour," Ellen said, linking arms with him and butting her head against his woolen shoulder. She laughed with pure unguarded happiness. "God, I love this life!"

3 - BLACK

MASHA

[spoken: "I'm in mourning for my life"]

I'm in mourning for my life:
Never started, never ending—
Like those fever dreams you have.
Just a blank slate, like a black board.
Everything is black...

    MEDVIEDENKO

    *[spoken: I didn't mean, it's not
      that I don't like it]*

    It's a very nice dress,
      Only just a little gloomy—
      Maybe.
It's a statement, not a fashion!
Can't you see, I'm all in black?
Well now, when you look at that
Don't you think it has a meaning?
I am wailing; I am keening.
I'm in black.
    Masha, darling,
      Maybe if you wore
Yes, I know it's attrac-
Tive. Black's my color,
Makes me pale and interesting;
    The ribbon mother gave you or
    A flower in your hair...
But not interesting
To everyone, not to him!

    Yes, a very nice dress
    And your hair is very pretty.
    Very.
This is useless. Foolish passion.
Won't he notice, I'm in black?
That I'm always wearing black?
It's enormously emphatic:
I'm defenseless; I'm dramatic.

I would think
    Masha, darling
    When you let it down,
That at least it's distinc-
Tive. Pink's insipid
White and blue, too usual
    The way it curls about your brow
    Makes such a pleasant sight...
Maybe plaid would be
A better choice. What a joke!

    It's a very clear night
    And the stars are nearly
      showing.
I am weary of inaction,
    Nearly.
Longing for obliteration,
    If I weren't such a poor man
    Would you hear my words of
      love?

And I'm tired of wearing black
    Would you love me if it weren't
      for
    My mother or my sisters?
I would think it's conspicuous;
    Do you despise the way I speak?
Even you, it made you look.
    Or the way I earn my bread?
My whole life is ridiculous
    Is it my nature you find weak,
If he doesn't even look.
    Or the angle of my head?

MASHA & MEDVIEDENKO
(together)

Why do I go on fooling myself?
What will it take to prove to me
That s/he clearly doesn't notice me?
No s/he doesn't hear me screaming,
And s/he doesn't feel me quiver,
And s/he doesn't see me bleeding.
And though I would wait forever,
Nothing may come of waiting;
Nothing may ever
Change.

MEDVIEDENKO

All these people around...
Oh, I think the play is starting
Shortly...

MASHA

More's the pity, I'm a virgin.
Maybe it would be more apt
To wear white instead of black;
White's a banner of denial,
White's a shroud. No, white is bridal!

I'm in black!
        Masha, darling...
I'm in mourning for my life.
See I waited and I waited,
And I plotted and I planned,
But it never took off
And there's nowhere for it to go.
I'm in mourning for my life,
I'm in mourning for my love.
Everything is black.
        I think the play is starting
Black.

[spoken: "Would you like a pinch of
        snuff?"]

Harry Janow was appalled. It wasn't a "nice" part of the Upper West Side, not like Riverside Drive or Central Park West; or even Broadway, which was lined with weathered but still grand old buildings that had been built for the millionaires and divas of a past generation. Harry had recently dated a flautist with the Philharmonic who lived in a studio in the Ansonia which, despite its state of disrepair, had the cachet and louche glamor of a certified artists' enclave. This place the kids were dragging him to was on a burned out side street among other burned out streets. Amsterdam and Columbus avenues were wastelands, empty storefronts alternating with dirty vegetable stands. There were a lot of bent wire fences signaling vacant, but not necessarily unused, lots. Getting out of the cab, Harry tripped over a beer bottle and nearly snapped his ankle. He limped gingerly across sodden clumps of paper and some tacky substance that he couldn't wait to scrape off the thin leather soles of his Italian loafers.

The address was a shabby brownstone with ill-fitted window sashing and a treacherous front stoop. The building had good bones but had been converted in an ad hoc fashion over the years, the owners chopping off another bit each time money was needed and a potential tenant appeared at the door. The bit Ellen and Leonard coveted was on the third floor and had once been a large high-ceilinged bedroom with an adjoining state-of-the-art Edwardian bath. The room was two now, divided by a flimsy partition built to one side of a large plaster ceiling medallion that had, no doubt, once been the setting for a suitably elegant chandelier but from which now depended a nasty black wire, woven through a chain, ending in a single bare bulb. The original bath, with its majestic cast iron claw-foot tub, had also been partitioned, carving out a kitchenette so narrow that the oven door could only be opened to a 60 degree angle before hitting the wall. Fortunately, neither Ellen nor Leonard had much interest in cooking. Neither had the previous tenant, a jilted poetess who'd learned the hard way that the angle was also inadequate for suicide. The poetess had survived to be fetched back to Iowa by her family, but the grout by the tub still showed some bloodstains from her backup plan. In her stead, a large dead roach rested belly up on the floor next to the half-sized refrigerator. Returning to the larger room, Harry looked through the smeared windows at a gap across the street that was filled with grey-brown rubble. A bent, rusted bicycle leaned against a street sign. It reminded him of London at the end of The War.

"What about the Village?" he wondered. "Isn't that where all the young people are?"

"A few years ago maybe," Ellen replied. "Whatever's left down there, we can't afford it. Unless maybe Alphabet City." Harry shuddered. She held up a hand to forestall other suggestions. "We've looked everywhere, Daddy. We were lucky to find this place. It's big enough, it's in better shape than a lot of places we've seen and it's near the subway. If it was a few blocks further north, some Columbia students probably would have snatched it up."

"The man who lives next door is doing his Ph.D. research at the Museum of Natural History," Leonard said craftily, knowing Harry's weakness for the intelligentsia.

"And there's a cartoonist who has the basement apartment. He's been in *The New Yorker*." Ellen didn't know if that last part was true, but it could be. There were so many cartoons printed in *The New Yorker* and this guy was definitely a professional.

Harry was weakening. With Ellen turning 18, he didn't legally have to do anything, but she was still his baby girl. He couldn't help wanting to protect her a little for as long as he could. The price was a lot less than he'd been paying for child support these last seven years. He could come out ahead and still, as far as his daughter was concerned, smelling like a rose. "It's only two rooms," he said.

"Like a dorm," Leonard nodded, trying not to fiddle nervously with the zipper of his windbreaker. He and Ellen had prepared for this. "I went up to Buffalo to visit Jeff Kaplan. He's in a suite smaller than this, with three guys sharing."

"Who gets which room?"

"We'll flip for it," Ellen said quickly. There was no need to tell Harry they'd already decided to sleep in the small room and use the larger one as a living room. Why freak him out? He'd never come back here once he signed the lease.

Harry sighed. "You're sure this is what you want?" If it didn't work out, he'd worry about it then. Meanwhile, his helping her to move out would make it two in the eye for Sydelle.

Ellen flashed a huge smile and threw her arms around him. She hardly ever hugged him. He hugged her back hard, blinking away some surprising tears.

"Let's go find the landlord," he mumbled into her hair. "Then we'll go to the Oak Room and have a civilized lunch."

They picked up the keys on May first. Ellen was all for moving right in, but Leonard insisted on cleaning and spackling and caulking and painting, and then cleaning everything again. Fortunately, he had some idea of how to do all this, because Ellen surely hadn't and they didn't want to spend whatever it would cost to hire someone. Ellen turned her energies to gathering what they needed to make it a home. They would make a comfortable nest, but as cheaply as possible. "Cheap" was going to be Ellen's new motto in life. Every penny she could save was a guarantee of continued independence.

Barney produced one of those new Mr. Coffees and a television that "fell off a truck." Felix, who she continued to cultivate by dropping by with the occasional coffee and muffin, told her about the better thrift stores, where rich people got rid of the things they didn't want to give their maids. It was, he confided, his secret weapon for keeping up appearances. Most of the "thrift" was too socialite-stuffy for the apartment, but she did pick up a genuine Jaeger cashmere sweater, not a thing wrong with it, for only seven dollars. "Quality" was going to be her other watchword. She stumbled onto her best find the first time she made the walk across town from school. Just past one of the ritzy buildings on Central Park West, she noticed some wooden chairs that had been left out on the curb for the trash pickup. One had a giant hole in the seat, as if someone had punched through the woven mat; the other three were perfectly fine. She flipped one of the good ones upside down over another, balanced a chair leg on the toe of her boot and, walking backwards and dragging her foot by slow inches, made her way to the apartment. Every muscle ached for a couple of days after, but the two free chairs were worth it.

They both had classes to attend. With her share of the rent at stake, Ellen was making an effort to get acceptable grades, as well as putting in her regular schedule at the import company. Leonard's part-time job was with his family's business, so he was able to take some time off. Working odd hours every day and all of every weekend, it took a few weeks to make the apartment livable. Finally the morning came when Leonard's older brother Seth loaded their things in the old van the business kept for errands around town.

Sydelle stayed in the kitchen, drinking coffee and having her usual grapefruit and Raisin Bran, while the boys took the elevator up and down with Ellen's mattress, boxes of books, and an Army surplus duffel bag packed with the clothes she'd decided were mature enough to keep. Last of all, they dragged out the beanbag chair she'd gotten for her 16th birthday; it had been the one time she'd gotten the present she'd asked for. She was leaving the bedroom set, the walnut veneer nightstand and chest of drawers and the combination desk and bookshelf that had always made her think of a motel.

Standing in the doorway, Ellen paused to look back: even with all that furniture, the room seemed hollow; everything that was "her" was gone. She wondered what Sydelle would do with the place; it wasn't like she sewed or painted or anything. One thing Ellen knew for certain: she would never be coming back here to live. She picked up the plaid suitcase they'd bought her to use for weekend visits with Harry. Her old teddy bear was tucked under her other arm. It was a childish thing to hold onto, but she wouldn't leave it here and it made her feel peculiar to think of Booboo sitting in a dump in Staten Island.

Feeling calm and curiously detached, she went to the kitchen to say goodbye to her mother. Sydelle put down her mug and crossed her arms over her aqua velour robe. "I'll see you for dinner Friday," she said. Leaning forward, she gave Ellen a dry kiss on the cheek.

"The boys are waiting," Ellen said, giving her a quick reciprocal peck. "I'd better get going."

Sydelle nodded. Her stare was opaque. As ever, whatever was in her mind was a total mystery.

Reaching the van, Ellen threw her suitcase in the back and squeezed in the front with her bear and the boys. "Home, James!" she said grandly, and they pulled away and toward the city.

Hours later, beds were made up, books were on brick-and-board shelves, and clothes were neatly folded into the stack of plastic cubes from Broadway Bazaar.

They walked over to a bodega they'd noticed at 74th and Broadway for some groceries. On the way home ("home," Ellen kept repeating to Leonard, each time with a wilder grin), they stopped at a pizza place to pick up a pie for dinner. "With anchovies," Ellen insisted, "and olives." Leonard wasn't sure about that, but agreed he could always scrape off what he didn't like. Waiting for the pizza, Ellen examined herself in the wall of gold-veined mirrored tiles. Her hair was looking good. The chambray work shirt she'd thought practical for moving day wasn't interesting but it was what people were wearing. The couple at the table in the corner were both wearing them. The guy, who had a sexy European air about him, was also wearing sunglasses. Indoors. Ellen stuck her hand into her shoulder bag. Her eyes were pale and sensitive to glare. She always carried sunglasses, often slipping them on when it was hardly sunny at all, but it had never crossed her mind to wear them indoors. She put them on now and twisted her head to see herself from various angles. "Better," she decided; she was shaping up. She was the type of woman who ate olives and anchovies, and she was starting to look the part.

The pie was still warm when Leonard set it on their own table. The table was a piece of wood bolted to an old cast-iron sewing machine stand, covered with what Ellen thought might be a genuine Irish linen cloth from the Opera Guild thrift shop. Above it, they'd hung a slightly stained Toulouse Lautrec poster she'd found at the Salvation Army. Their plates, angular and grey like something the Jetsons might have eaten off of, had been a dime each from an odds-and-ends box in the same store. Leonard insisted they use plates even for pizza; it was, after all, their first meal in their new home. They sat on the wooden chairs, facing each other across the pizza box.

Ellen handed him a beer from the six-pack Seth had left as a housewarming gift. "To a new life," she said, quoting *Lake Song*, which they'd seen again last week. It had been the one night they hadn't worked on the apartment. Not knowing that she'd already seen it, Barney had thought to surprise her with tickets to the hottest show on Broadway. In the end, he'd been too worried about what might happen if they ran into one of his father-in-law's business buddies on the street, so he'd chickened out and told her to take a friend. She and Leonard had been just as impressed the second time.

"A new life," Leonard echoed. They clinked bottles solemnly and drank. Suddenly the room seemed very quiet. "Should we put on some music?" Leonard asked, "Or do you want the TV?"

"Put on the cast album," Ellen said. If she was hearing the song in her head, and she wasn't the most musical person in the world, he must be too. "*There's a new life / beckoning to me,*" she tried to sing, "*telling me to leave the nest / break my jesses / fly away free…*"

"Ouch! My ears!" Finding the record in the stack that was their pooled collection, Leonard put it on the turntable and gently placed the needle in the first groove. The overture started. Taking more and more confident swigs from his bottle, he paced the room, trying to decide if he'd put the speakers in the best possible positions. "So what are jesses anyway?"

"Those leashes they put on falcons. You know, around their legs. So they have to fly back to the falconer. I looked it up." Ellen hated not knowing things.

"Falcons?" It struck him as funny and he started to snigger. "I thought Nina was a seagull."

"I'd rather be a falcon. I think I'd be a fabulous bird of prey." She could see it. She would be a sleek bird with an elegantly curved beak as sharp as a scythe and talons like razor blades. She imagined soaring through the sky, picking out her victim with her sniper's eye, then swooping down and snatching it. "It could be my symbol. A falcon. And I could get a leather cord and wear it around my ankle." She quirked her eyebrows suggestively. "I think that would be very sexy."

"I'm an actress!" Leonard moaned in falsetto. "No, I'm a falcon!"

They both burst into helpless giggles and then couldn't stop. Leonard snorted beer out his nose, which hurt but made him laugh even more until he got a stitch in his side, collapsed in a heap, and starting rolling on the floor, still gasping giggles. Ellen slid down off her chair to join him. Every time they thought it was over, one of them would poke the other and start it up again. When finally they were gasping and exhausted, they lay quite still on their backs, weak and as light as air. On the stereo, Christopher Pruitt was singing *"I can create a world out of nothing / but a moment's inspiration / and the impulse to achieve it."*

"We need a rug," Ellen said, drawing a deep slow breath. "That should be the next thing we get. You know we always end up sitting on the floor." She stretched to grab a slice of room temperature pizza. Anchovies were good. Olives might be an acquired taste. Leonard, she noticed, had quietly picked his out and put them back in the box. Martinis had olives. She took a determined bite.

"Hey!" Leonard exclaimed, abruptly sitting up. "You want to walk over and stand at the stage door?" She stared at him and he started to feel foolish. "Well, not tonight; it's Sunday. But Tuesday. We can take a study break and go down to the theatre and stand outside and watch them come out. If we feel like it," he finished, lamely, since she was still staring. He shrugged. "We can do whatever we like."

"We can!" she said. In a flash, it had all become real. "We live in the city. We have our own apartment. We can do whatever we like!"

It became a routine. Almost every night at a little before 10, they'd drop their work on the floor and walk the mile down Broadway to Times Square. From there, they'd wander until they picked a theatre, where they'd wait outside with people who'd seen the show that night and also, as they quickly learned, with others like themselves who just liked to hang around stage doors. It turned out that there was a small village of such citizens, some more or less permanently haunting a single show, others like Ellen and Leonard moving from station to station along a buffet of stars.

They could stand, shyly star-struck, outside the 46th Street Theatre where Morton DaCosta had stuffed his production of *The Women* with legends like Myrna Loy, Kim Hunter, Rhonda Fleming, and Alexis Smith, who exited the theatre as grandly as at a Hollywood premier, their arms full of flowers, and graciously paused to sign programs as they made their way to waiting cars. The street practically shimmered with their glory. At the Uptown Circle in the Square, previews of *Uncle Vanya* had just begun, with the infamously hot-tempered Nicol Williamson and George C. Scott going head to head for the love of Julie Christie, who was as incredibly gorgeous face–to-face as she was up on the screen. At the Majestic, the show was *Sugar*, a musical based on *Some Like it Hot*. Most in the alley were waiting for Robert Morse and Tony Roberts, but Ellen and Leonard were more excited to spot gentle Cyril Ritchard, who would always and forever be their Captain Hook. At the Eugene O'Neill, Peter Falk and Lee Grant were in *Prisoner of 2nd Avenue*, Barbara Bel Geddes and Robert Lansing were in *Finishing Touches* at the Plymouth, and the Lunt-Fontanne had *6 Rms Riv Vu* with Jane Alexander and Jerry Orbach, to whom Leonard could boldly say "hi" because Orbach played basketball at the Y with his dad.

There were lots of attractive men to fantasize about. The very sexy Raul Julia and Clifton Davis were *Two Gentlemen of Verona* at the St. James. Even better, *The Changing Room* had a whole stage full of hot men, totally naked, to ogle. The plan was to celebrate Ellen's June birthday doing exactly that; but for now they enjoyed standing outside the Morosco, listening to the whispers of the exiting audience. Eavesdropping was always fascinating. You never knew what you'd learn. Once, outside the Imperial, someone pointed out one of the *Pippin* dancers who was rumored to be having an affair with Bob Fosse. Ellen looked hard, envisioning a possible path to the future.

Seesaw was at the new Uris theatre, which was said to have such horrible acoustics that the actors performed with radio mikes. The stars, Michelle Lee and Ken Howard, seemed to get a big kick out of talking to their fans. Ellen and Leonard also loved to catch Tommy Tune ducking under the doorframe with a grin and unfolding himself onto the street. The dancer, as long and thin as an Uncle Sam stilt-walker, reminded Leonard of Scarecrow in *The Wizard of Oz*. Actually, everything about Broadway at night was Emerald-Cityish. They'd walk along the streets, neon and marquee bulbs lighting up the sky, the city of New York rising darkly out of sight; then they'd stand in huddles, waiting for men to open blank silver doors for creatures whose simple presence had the power to hush and part the crowd, and whose smiles and "thank yous" would make people happy for days.

At least once a week, they would make their way to the Regale and wait for *Lake Song* to let out. Leonard had a thing about Lilith Brassloe, because she'd played Mona in *Riding a Bicycle*, which was probably his all-time favorite musical. Ellen, sharing Pirandello's fascination with the boundary between theatre and life, wondered where an actor playing an actor drew the line; she thought if she could watch Bronwen Davies closely, she might be able to spot the crack. That wasn't all that drew them there. They had an old hobby of picking apart pretty much anything that might be debated on the basis of taste. A show, a movie, a book...one or the other of them would inevitably find a way it could have been more effective, more thrilling...more *something*. With *Lake Song*, which they'd seen twice, neither could think of a single thing they would have wanted to be other than what it was. From the overture to the sets, in every casting and directorial decision, it was achingly lovely and they shared an unspoken superstition that if they could get close enough to that perfection, some of it might rub off on them. The stage door of the Regale began to feel like home.

Leonard had just typed the last sentence of his final paper for Philosophy 101. Ellen's classes had ended the week before. This meant that they were both now officially on summer break. It was a drizzly night, but they wanted to celebrate. They decided to do some star watching, then treat themselves to fancy cocktails at the new, aggressively black-and-silver restaurant below the Uris that was trying to position itself as a theatrical hangout.

It was too wet for a random stroll, so they headed straight to the Regale; but even the tiniest bit of rain is enough to mess up the city bus schedule. They arrived too late. The stage door was closed and whatever faithful few had waited were already dispersed. It was disappointing, but "that's showbiz," as they were wont to say when consoling themselves for setbacks large and small. Opening the big doorman's umbrella that Ellen had liberated from Felix's office, they started walking the few blocks to the restaurant.

Leonard, holding the umbrella, stopped abruptly.

The rain had picked up. Water dripped down the back of Ellen's neck. "What the fuck...?!"

"Bronwen Davies," he stammered, pointing. "Isn't it?"

Like an old French photo, a streetlamp picked out a fair-haired woman in a pale raincoat. Her head turned slowly from side to side, but though the "walk" sign was flashing, her feet didn't move. She turned in their direction; it was definitely Bronwen Davies.

Ellen and Leonard picked up their pace, afraid that if they ran she might think they were attacking her. People were being mugged left and right in the theatre district, all the time. Bad weather might keep career criminals in bed, but it was all the same to the junkies.

"Miss Davies?" Ellen said softly, as they reached her. The woman seemed so vague and lost. "Can we help you?"

Leonard, shaking and white, extended the umbrella to cover her.

"Oh, thank you so much, dear," she murmured. "My car was late and I told dear Wally I would be fine and he locked up and went home, but then it never showed." Her eyes, ringed with rain-smudged makeup, widened like a doll's. "How does one find a taxi in this city?"

With a nod to Leonard, Ellen took off down the street. All those wandering nights had come in handy; she knew which theatre let out later than the Regale. Any cabs that might be empty on a rainy night were bound to be headed that way for a sure fare. Ellen was soaked by the time she found a cab that would take her. Breathless, she got in and directed the driver back to the corner to pick up "the woman in the white coat" who, she explained, was a very tired, very famous actress who needed to get home and would give him her address. Opening the door, Ellen stuffed a five into the driver's hand and said "Miss Davies, I found you a taxi."

Leonard hadn't moved a muscle.

Bronwen Davies flashed a brilliant smile. "Thank you, my dear," she said, getting in.

Ellen closed the door behind her and waved as the cab pulled off. "Wow!" she panted, ducking under the umbrella and stripping the rain from her curls. "That was incredible! So what did you talk about?"

Leonard unwound his silk aviator scarf, and gave it to her to mop her face. "I couldn't say anything," he marveled. "I mean, I said 'Don't worry, Ellen will take care of it,' but that was it; nothing else. I wanted to. But I couldn't think. And she didn't say a word."

"You said my name. She knows my name is Ellen."

"Yeah, I guess."

"That's pretty fucking incredible!" Playfully, Ellen punched him in the arm. "Let's go get that drink! You may have to spot me; I gave five bucks to that cab driver."

"Are you crazy?"

"I don't know. It seemed like what people do. God I'm a wreck. I hope they let us into the restaurant."

"On a night like this?" Leonard rolled his eyes. "We're not the only wet people showing up. Hey! I just thought of something." He made his "I'm about to be clever" face.

She was going to have to start to train him out of that; it made him look like a dopey seven year old. "What?"

"*Famous people keep their feet dry in the rain,*" he quoted. Giggling hysterically, they bumped against each other all the way to Pub Theatrical; where they found themselves at a table next to that of a famous acting couple, who were having a post-performance bite with friends who, by a coincidence that seemed prophetic at the time, were called Leonard and Ellen.

♫

My freshman year of college ended just before Memorial Day, an event I greeted with mixed emotions. I'd arrived in a new land alone and without a map but wrapped in shiny expectations. College was going to appreciate all the qualities that high school had disdained. After all, unlike the local school district, this was a selective society; I had chosen and been chosen; the goose-girl would be revealed as the princess she had been all along. Instead, it had been a long year homesteading my first rough claim in the adult world. I slogged along and, while college was often no better than high school, it was never any worse and it held the keys to the future—which would definitely be better, right? I'd made some strides during the year. Coming home was a step backward, through the looking glass. Until three months back home were looming before me, I hadn't realized how free I'd felt on campus. I'd become used to running around at all hours: to parties; to willfully age-blind off-campus bars; to people's dorm rooms, where we'd sit and talk the night away until someone had to leave for a morning class. It was hard coming home to my childish bedroom and my parents wanting to know where I was going and with whom, every time I left the house. Even my summer job was under the eye of a family friend in the garment industry, who'd generously pretended his secretary needed an assistant to handle a season's backlog of filing. The company produced men's underwear which, possibly inspired by the counter appeal of the L'eggs pantyhose packaging, they sold in plastic tubes shaped like (ahem) bullets.

Ellen and Leonard's invitation for a sleepover was a lifesaver. Their dangerous neighborhood and the authentic bohemian air of their make-do aesthetic impressed me. I tried to impress them back with my housewarming gift of a harvest gold fondue pot. Fully expecting we'd be staying up around the clock, I also brought the ingredients for dessert. Chocolate fondue had been the midnight snack of choice for my dorm friends that spring. We stocked Baker's chocolate and those miniature airplane bottles of liqueur in our rooms; then when the mood struck, we would cadge fruit, stale cake and pats of butter from the dining hall. This was considered *très raffiné* in the dorm; I hoped it would be enough to help me hold my own with my newly-sophisticated friends.

They did seem terribly sophisticated to me, my first contemporaries to have their own apartment—and in Manhattan, no less. When I saw the narrow bedroom, like any rumpled dorm room with posters stuck to the walls and mattresses taking up most of the floor, I looked past the window shade and tried to imagine what it must be like to wake in the morning and know that when you went out your door you'd already be in the city. This odd almost-garret was as glamorous to me as any Park Avenue flat I could remotely imagine. These two, who had once been my ordinary schoolmates, had made a dream come true. By comparison, my successful passage through the alien world of college seemed a juvenile accomplishment.

As though reading my mind, Ellen opened her box of Nat Shermans with a raised eyebrow that dared me to take one. I wrapped myself in the dignity of my own embryonic taste and produced my Sobranies. Leonard proudly served a pot of chili he'd made from a magazine recipe attributed to Chassen's restaurant in Hollywood; it was supposed to be Elizabeth Taylor's favorite meal. We established that we'd all learned the "right" way to down shots of tequila, with a wedge of lemon and a lick of salt. We exchanged stories about the oddest people we'd met over the course of the year and took swipes at books we'd read. We laughed, had some more tequila, and found one another very witty. They told me about their adventure in the rain, and started to go into detail about their stage door pilgrimages. Then Leonard looked at his watch and said, "If we leave now, we could maybe just make it."

We flew down the stairs and over to Broadway. The bus doors were about to close, but Ellen put her fingers in her mouth and gave a piercing whistle, and the driver let us climb aboard, breathless and laughing. Despite that, by the time we got down to the 40s, the theatres were already dark. "Sorry," Leonard shrugged. "Next time."

"We could look around," I said, loving the idea of being on the city streets at night.

"Sure," Leonard said, linking his arm in mine. "Maybe there's still…"

"Nope," Ellen said, snapping her lighter and taking a quick draw. "Billy doesn't start sorting until everyone's gone." She pointed at a round little man crouching at the mouth of the alley, the faint street light bouncing off his bald head. He was pulling bits and pieces of paper out of the very sagging pockets of his raincoat and sorting them into piles on the ground.

"She's right," Leonard said. "He never does that until he's done for the night. He collects autographs."

"So do you," I said. They'd shown me their collection.

Ellen shook her head. "Billy collects them to sell. Goes to all the theatres and puts out pieces of scrap paper to get them signed. Then he stands around before the shows and tries to get the tourists to buy them. Everyone knows about him. The doormen leave him alone as long as he doesn't get too pushy. I think he might be retarded."

"Nicol Williamson punched him once," Leonard said with a nervous laugh.

"Yeah, well Nicol punches everybody." It was an old habit of Ellen's, to refer to famous people by their first names as if she knew them. "I know," she said, linking through my free arm, "let's go by the Regale anyway, so you can see."

I was a little affronted. "I'm not from out of town. I've been to the Regale; I've even seen *Lake Song*." But we were linked together and I soon found myself under the portico, looking at the large black-and-white photos that had been staged to look like specific moments of the play. I knew this because I'd been a villager in *House of Bernarda Alba* that term, and we'd had a special photo call. Posed pictures meant not having to hope the shutter would be quick enough to prevent blur; also, you could make sure that there was balance in the shape of the stage as it appeared in the frame, and that nothing important was obscured.

We stood by a photo of Lilith Brassloe with uplifted arms, the scrim behind her melted to show the cast standing around the lake. It had been a thrilling moment on stage. "*Just as we see them now*," I murmured.

"Yes!" Leonard smiled broadly.

"There's Joe," Ellen pointed. "And Tyler—such a love—and Fredi…" as if they were all her best friends.

"It's posed," I said, anxious to display my own small expertise. "Not an action shot," I added, in case they hadn't understood. "You can tell because Masha didn't enter until after Lilith Brassloe was mixed in with the ensemble, and in the picture she's over here."

"Your memory!" Ellen said, mocking awe, but with that raise of eyebrows and slantwise glance that was her look of respect. "She remembers everything."

"Not everything." It always made me uncomfortable when people said that. Some things stuck, others went right out the window. But if I closed my eyes…"Masha's the only one who doesn't come out in the beginning. She enters singing. Because she's singing about being alone."

"I like this one," Leonard said. It was "Kiss, Kiss," with Bronwen Davies wrapped tightly around Max Bulloch, her head flung back in wicked glee.

"Look where she's got her hand; right on his cock. I wonder what Becky thinks about that," Ellen mused.

"It's his, um…" It was a word that made me blush. "Why should anyone else care?"

She shook her head. "Well, would you want your luhh-vurrr" (she drawled the word) "to have his exe's hand on his cock?"

It reminded me of my first semester boyfriend, who'd dumped me over spring break. I'd found out by catching sight of him on line at the dining hall with his new squeeze, their hands cupping one another's asses. Whether my face was showing hurt or rage, it wasn't the reaction Ellen was gunning for.

"Max has affairs with all his leading ladies, you know. Sheldon says—Sheldon's the ASM, the Assistant Stage Manager…"

"I know what an ASM is."

"Sheldon says Bron didn't want him in the first place, but that he was determined to have her. Then she won the Tony and he broke it off. And before the body was cold he was seducing poor little Becky. Not that I blame either one of them. I mean, was there ever a man so well named?"

"Max?" I was confused.

"Bullock! Look at the size of him! You can see it right here," she jabbed a finger at another photo, where pale summer pants draped in an interesting manner that seemed to fascinate Rebecca Lewis, thereby solving the mystery of who "Becky" was. "Would I love to get hold of that!" she sighed, with a vivid shifting of her hips.

"It's good to have a goal in life," I said.

She stuck her tongue out as far as it would go.

"Ew, put that away!" Leonard squealed. He jerked my arm to pull me close, and whispered theatrically, "You don't want to know where it's been!"

"Fuck you!" Ellen flounced off—as much as someone could flounce in jeans and work boots, which was more of a fussy stride. Suddenly, she broke into a run. Leonard and I instinctively ran after her. We didn't realize her intent until the bus pulled up a foot ahead of her and she jumped on. We were still half a block behind and didn't make it. As the bus pulled away, a window shot open and she gave us the finger. We stood there, falling over each other, trying to catch our breath and wondering what the finger meant. It was always hard to tell when Ellen was acting out and when she was really hurt. So much bounced off her skin, but the oddest things got under it; sometimes it was just the timing.

"We should start walking," Leonard panted. "It'll be a while before the next bus." He was right. We ended up walking all the way. By the time we reached the apartment, Ellen was curled up in the beanbag chair in her pajamas, apparently reading a book. She'd washed up the dinner plates, and my offering was on the table.

"Took you long enough," she said, without looking up. "Are we ready for some chocolate?"

Leonard put *Lake Song* on the stereo and we made fondue.

When Ahuva called, so excited after her second viewing of *Lake Song*, I impulsively asked if I could bring Ellen and Leonard to her graduation party that weekend. It turned out Leonard couldn't come: Jeff Kaplan was home from Buffalo and they were making extra money helping Seth set up the booths for some event at the Coliseum. But Ellen thought she would combine the party with a duty visit to her mother. It would be a good excuse to get away for a few hours after dinner, and then she'd sleep over; regardless of whether Sydelle would be happy, the obligation would have been satisfied.

Ellen and I met on the corner, a receding echo of childhood walks to school. Each of us had carefully orchestrated party clothes for that season. For me it was my long patchwork skirt, a rainbow of block-printed Indian cotton gauze, which I wore, as I wore everything then, with black ballet shoes; I ran through a pair every other month, and I wasn't even a dancer. The flat shoes made my skirt so long that I pretty much walked on it from the inside, creating a natural fraying that saved me hours of hemming. I wore this with a muslin peasant blouse and a rope of fat amber beads. I hadn't yet heard of Frida Kahlo, but if anyone else had, that's what they would have thought I was aiming for. Ellen had a short-sleeved denim jumpsuit with a wide hip-slung belt, fashionable enough that her mother couldn't criticize but with the top unzipped low enough to drive Sydelle crazy; there was an elegance in how Ellen would manage that balance. She had knotted a genuine Pucci scarf around her neck, a gift from Barney Black she said when I admired it, and, even though the sun was low in the sky, she wore her dark glasses.

Since Sydelle dined at the "civilized" hour she'd adopted during her fabled semester in Paris, I knew we were late. I usually hated being late, but it was better than arriving alone. That morning, I'd found I was of two minds about going to the party at all. I wanted to celebrate with Ahuva, but I knew very few of her friends and I was shy.

The door was unlocked. I knew Mr. Geffner would be watching from the kitchen table so I poked my head in and waved. He smiled and went back to his cards. Mrs. Geffner was swooping through the living room, refilling chip bowls and clearing away abandoned plastic cups. Ahuva was nowhere to be seen, but the party was well underway.

There were a couple of dozen kids crammed into the room, "kids" being the operative word. They were uniformly decked out in candy colored stripes and checks and too-clean jeans and, in the case of the girls, those ubiquitous caramel Kork-ease sandals. To please the parental cameras, hair had been freshly cut for graduation and was therefore just a little too short. There was a lot of fruity lip gloss, and boys who didn't need to shave had slapped on spicy cologne. The fact of graduation, that "the golden gates of their childhood had forever closed behind them," hadn't yet sunk in. These were Ahuva's friends from the Yearbook and Student Government and Pre-Calculus: the smart kids, nurtured by parents and teachers to be the redeeming generation; the bright ones, confident that brains and ideals and hard work would lead them smoothly through life. They were going to college to become doctors and district attorneys and teachers and crusading journalists, and they planned to meet their perfect mates and build a perfect community in which to raise their own perfect children.

Everyone in that room seemed so young and artless, bright-eyed baby animals with no concept of the innocence they had to lose. Having been through the fire of freshman year in a college that encouraged friendship across classes, I'd watched and listened, and had already shed a few of my own illusions. I suddenly felt old and jaded, as if a single year had been five. For Ellen, living a fully adult life in the city, high school must have felt a generation away; I instantly regretted inviting her and wondered how quickly we could leave. Maybe we could go to the Wine Gallery. Neither of us were ever carded. When the drinking age was 18, any girl with a big bust was assumed to be legal. I would make it up to Ahuva; we'd do a special graduation thing, just the two of us, another time.

I exchanged stiff greetings with a couple of people I vaguely knew. The sound of a few chords turned me towards the only exception in the room. Hope leaned on the arm of the sofa, hunched over her guitar, her long hair flirting with the strings. We knew each other well, having sung together shoulder-to-shoulder through a number of high school productions. As always, Howie stuck to her like a conjoined twin. He was older and they'd already been engaged-to-be-engaged for almost three years. At first they'd said they were waiting for Hope to turn 18, but just before they'd hit that milestone, Howie's folks had asked him to wait until after he finished dental school. He'd first be starting in September, but since the parents were footing the bill, Howie and Hope didn't have much choice. With his free arm, Howie was dangling an inch of ash over a plastic cup of Fresca.

I pulled Ellen in their direction and nearly ran into Ahuva, who'd just finagled an ashtray for Howie.

"Hi!" she squealed, throwing her arms around me in a giant hug.

"Happy graduation!" I said, hugging back. "You remember Ellen."

"Of course."

"Hi," Ellen said. We found places for ourselves on the floor, Ellen putting herself within reach of Howie's ashtray. She pulled out her red box and started on her cigarette ritual. Everyone around her watched, mesmerized; only Hope, working on the last part of "Both Sides Now" and too busy reaching for the high notes, was oblivious. Lighting up, Ellen took a long draw and finished by shooting a trio of smoke rings, like fireworks, in Ahuva's direction. "Happy graduation by the way."

"Thanks," Ahuva said. I could see her wondering how it was done. We were all quiet for a bit. Hope finished her song and started noodling around with some fingering.

"Happy graduation to you, too," I told Howie, just to fill the void. "Looking forward to dental school?"

"Sure," he said with his farm boy smile; I'd always wondered where he'd picked that up in Queens. "Thanks." Howie had never been much of a talker.

"Is there something wrong with your eyes?" Ahuva asked bluntly.

"Why?" Ellen purred.

"Well, we're indoors and you're wearing sunglasses."

"It's nothing," Ellen said, in a tone implying quite the opposite. "Just some sort of minor tumor on the back of my left eye. It's not critical; the doctor says the operation can wait until he's back from his summer on the Cape. I'd rather not talk about it." She sighed and took another deep drag of her cigarette.

Ahuva was aghast. "Oh my god! I feel terrible…" You could see that she did.

I, on the other hand, was fascinated. This was the first I'd heard of any tumor.

Fortunately, Ahuva's friend Alan had walked over. "Sorry for breaking in, but my aunt wants to take me to a Broadway show as my graduation present and I didn't want to forget to ask. What was that show you said was so good?"

"*Lake Song*?" Ahuva said, brightening. "Oh, yes, Alan, you have to see it! It's amazing!"

Hope looked up from her chords. "She keeps telling me I have to see it, too. She doesn't stop talking about it."

"Because it's extraordinary," she said, with the tiniest bit of huff. "Isn't it?" she appealed to me.

"It was pretty amazing," I told him. "I think this is the first time I've ever wanted to see a show twice. Ahuva already has. Ellen, too."

Ahuva's face lit up. "That's right! You said she had." She shifted closer to Ellen. "I want to see it again when I get back from Israel," she confided, "before I leave for school. If I can save up enough."

"It's a life altering experience," Ellen stretched back her neck and took a long, deep breath through her nose. "Life altering."

"Marshall Berenson is a Genius!" Ahuva closed her eyes ecstatically.

"It's a really good show," I told Alan, trying to regain some proportion. "Tell your aunt to get tickets. Have you read *The Seagull*?" It turned out that he had. He was heading for Princeton in the fall to study math, but he was hoping to minor in philosophy. We started talking about Chekhov, and then I wanted a Coke and he walked me over to the dining room to get one, so we missed much of the conversation.

Hope, having moved across the room, was leading a group in "Bridge Over Troubled Water," as a graduation tribute to arguably the most famous alumni our alma mater had managed to produce. A couple of kids I recognized from the inter-class *Sing!* competitions had shifted nearer to Ahuva and Ellen, who were still going on about *Lake Song*.

As we got close enough to hear them over the singing, Ellen was saying "Did I mention I saw Bron a couple of weeks ago?" Ahuva must have not registered a satisfactory response, because she repeated, "You know, Bron. Bron*wen*. As in Davies?"

"Oh! You did?!" Ahuva looked like someone had given her a present. "What's she like? Is she anything like Arkadina? She seems so elegant and witty."

"She's an incredible woman," Ellen said with a sweeping gesture that nearly set my skirt on fire. "Such magnetism!"

"I'd love to meet her." Ahuva wore the earnest determined look that usually meant she would soon start working on a Plan.

Ellen glanced at her watch. "We could go now. If we don't have to wait for a train, we should get there just when it ends."

"Sounds like fun to me," I said. As far as I knew, the only time Ellen had "met" Bronwen Davies was to hail a cab for her on a rainy night. I wanted to see how far she'd take this.

"Oh, but I couldn't pull Ahuva away from her own party." Ellen's voice dripped with reproach. I almost felt guilty. "Another time. When you get back from Italy."

"Israel."

"Yes."

"You have such an exciting life!" one of the other kids said admiringly. "I wish I could move into the city and go to shows all the time. My parents would have a cow. I can't wait 'til I graduate college; then they'll have to let me."

"That'll be great," Ellen nodded, with a condescending smile that stretched into one of enormous satisfaction. "It's pretty intense. I've done so many things this year, met so many people. I feel as though I've opened myself up to the world."

"Wow!" the same kid sighed.

Ellen turned to me, to share an "in" tidbit. "Felix called yesterday. Felix Ayre." The elaboration was for the peanut gallery. "He's invited me to come to a party at Lionel Rice's house."

Lionel Rice, an eminent art historian, taught at Vassar two days a week. My friend Craig had tried every which way to sign up for his seminar "Human Scale: Residential Architecture of the 20th Century" for next year, but it was so popular that sophomores never got in. Ellen and I thought it was a funny coincidence that Lionel was Penelope Rice's brother.

"I'd tell you to put in a good word for Craig," I shrugged, "only you don't know him."

"Maybe I'll still put in a good word for him. Penelope is very fond of me." She wasn't getting much of a reaction from the group. Felix Ayre and Penelope Rice weren't household names to most of our generation; I may have been the only one of Ellen's friends who'd known enough to be impressed when she'd landed her internship. "Did you know that Lionel lives with Ivor Davies, Bron's brother? They're lovers."

Ahuva gasped. One of the other kids gasped as well. Looking at his face, I think it might have been a defining moment in his life, to hear someone matter-of-factly announce that two men were lovers. "Maybe Bron will actually be there!" Ahuva exclaimed. I noticed that in the last few minutes, she'd picked up the first name thing. "Will you write to me in Israel and tell me all about it?"

"If you like," Ellen was practically strutting sitting still. "And I'll make sure to let you know what's happening with *Lake Song*. If Max breaks up with Becky or something like that."

"Thank you!" Ahuva practically bounced with pleasure. "I'm so glad you came tonight!"

Ellen smiled, a genuine smile. "Me too."

4 - NOTHING

KOSTIA *[spoken: There's a theatre for you! No artificial scenery. Only the purity of Nature. We'll raise the curtain at nine, when the moon comes up.]*

Oysters produce their pearls out of
    nothing
But a minor irritation and compulsion
    to relieve it.
I can create a world out of nothing
But a moment's inspiration and the
    impulse to achieve it.
Why these Great Artists
Need their plaster and their limelight
    and their velvet and their paint,
When I need nothing but a blanket
    on a line across two trees,
A simple summer night, some grass,
    a lake, a lovely girl
To set my vision free.
How can that be?
How can I see what they don't see?
We need new words, new forms—
If they aren't available we might as
    well have nothing,
We'd be better off with nothing at all.

Am I the only one who knows art can
    only be as pure as artists?
Am I the only one who cares? Have I
    the only eyes to see what art is?
Nothing less than miracle;
Nothing more than total abnegation
    by the artist
In the service of a greater thing than
    we could ever be.
Art is all, and we...

Isn't it ironic,
How they're really looking backward
When they think they're facing
    forward
In their rooms with three walls?

Artificial light, when they could have
    the moon.
God, I'd have to kill myself if that
    were all I knew.
But me, I stretch my sights to gaze
    far beyond the safe and well-
    accepted.
And me, I reach my hand to touch;
    knowing well that I may be rejected.
Still I strive for miracles,
Living ev'ry day with degradation; I'm
    an artist
In the service of a greater thing than
    we could ever be.
Art is all, and we...

Don't you think it's comic
When they act like they can't see
    me,
When they ought to want to be me?
If they knew what I know,
They'd have to admit that they've
    been blind and deaf.
If I should become like that, I'd bore
    myself to death.
But I'm the kind who has to bare
    every fiber of his deepest being.
Yes, I'm the kind who'll always dare,
    I'd rather lose than miss the
    chance of seizing
A sliver of a miracle.
Risking even full obliteration, I'm an
    artist
In the service of a greater thing than
    I could ever be.
Art is all, and I am nothing.

[spoken: I have a vision!]

Annie Fallon was dead.

It started as a rumor, on the day they took her Musical Theatre class to see *Lake Song,* during intermission. Frankie knew it wasn't true, because Nancy Pardoe had been on stage for Act I and if something had happened she wouldn't have been, because Nancy Pardoe and Annie were, well, you know.

Frankie had been so excited about this outing: her third time seeing the whole show from beginning to end, and this time for free. She'd hoped that in class the next day, people would see how much she knew about it and maybe be impressed and start to like her. It was awful, the mocking way they looked at her and whispered, those rich suburban kids with their soap opera looks and Fred Braun shoes. She still didn't understand how it all began. She'd never said Annie was her aunt. She was sure that what she'd said that first week in the Autobiography exercise was that Annie Fallon *felt like* her aunt, because of how she'd been friends with Frankie's father and been around when she was a kid. Somehow the class had gotten the wrong end of the stick, as Annie herself used to say, and before Frankie knew it all of NYADA was buzzing with the story that she'd claimed Annie was her aunt, leading to the general conclusion that she was (a) a liar and (b) maybe a little crazy, too. There was nothing she could say that would make them understand that it wasn't like that at all. It hadn't helped that she'd hung around after classes, trying to speak to Annie, but she wasn't the only one that did that with the teachers; everybody was looking for someone to give them advice or a helping hand. Of course, the gossip had gotten worse when Annie had stopped teaching and everyone could see how much it upset Frankie, but why shouldn't she have been upset? She'd known Annie since she was small. Anyone would care if someone they'd known forever had gotten that sick, especially if their mother had gone the same way.

"Oh, didn't you hear?" some girl told her, with a gooey pity that she probably thought sounded sincere but which, if it was the best acting she could do, was stamping her for a future of starring roles in some Podunk Little Theatre; "Annie Fallon is dead. Or at least she's dying. Depending on who you ask."

Why would Frankie believe any of them? So she didn't; she ignored it and went back inside to enjoy Act II. But it must have gotten under her skin because she made a special effort to check the ensemble, to satisfy herself that the skinny blonde in the blue dress really was Nancy Pardoe and not the "swing" in a wig. It was, and Frankie could comfortably return her focus to the principals. She'd particularly wanted to watch Kaye Victor because it had occurred to her that, if *Lake Song* would have a long enough run, maybe after graduation she'd be able to get an audition and someday take over playing Masha.

Still, what if the whispers had been right? Frankie knew Annie truly was failing. It was all she could think about, all the way home on the train. There was nothing in the paper; then again, Mickey took *The Daily News* and only a Broadway star as big as Merman would ever make the *News*. On the way in the next day, she'd thought of looking for a *New York Times* but before she could get one, she'd run into Donny picking up coffee and he'd assured her the rumor was a crock.

A week and a half later, the morning session was interrupted with a special assembly and Miss Nelson made the announcement that Annie had died. Frankie thought she'd puke up the fried egg sandwich she'd grabbed on Ninth Avenue an hour before. She didn't, but she hid out in a stall until everyone was back in class, then picked up her things from the girls' changing room and ran from the building.

She didn't know where to go. She only knew she had to go somewhere. She started walking, because her legs had to. Then she knew where she wanted to be: she wanted to be at Cooghan's. Only she didn't remember exactly where Cooghan's was; she'd been too young to pay attention to things like street numbers. So she made her way down to Radio City and figured out the right direction from there by using landmarks. She must have walked up and down four avenues worth of West 54th Street almost three full times before she finally realized that Cooghan's wasn't there anymore. Where it used to be, there was now a Beefsteak Charlie's. She was crying by now: from grief, from fatigue, from the blister that was forming because she'd forgotten to take off her jazz tights and the half-toe was rubbing against the loose insole of her sandal. Even so, she couldn't seem to stop moving. She limped down Broadway. In the back of her head she thought if she could make it to Penn Station she'd take the train home, but she didn't want to be home. She wanted to be somewhere.

The Howard Johnson's on Broadway and 46th Street rose up like a lighthouse on a suddenly nearby shore. Choking back a sob, Frankie pushed open the door. It was an off hour, so there were lots of empty seats. She fell into a saggy vinyl two-person booth, shoving her dance bag on the empty seat across from her. Her right eye was burning from runny mascara. She didn't have to look in her compact mirror to know she was a mess. The waitress brought a glass of water and the menu. Frankie ordered a cup of coffee and a portion of fries, then stuck the corner of a napkin into the water and started to carefully wipe away the black. There always seemed to be so much more mascara running down your face than you ever thought you'd put on in the morning. Her coffee arrived at the table. She put her hand around it. There was something so comforting about the heavy cup with its familiar man and little boy. Simple Simon met a pie man. She'd never figured out what that had to do with Howard Johnson's, but there it was. She ran a finger along the rim, which had been rubbed dull by thousands of sippers. Something to hold on to. Cooghan's might be gone, and someday Beefsteak Charlie's would be too, she bet, but there would always be Howard Johnson's. With a deep sigh, she tore the corner off a sugar packet and let the granules trickle into the steaming black pool.

"Is everything alright, dearie? Bad audition?" The hostess of the Broadway Howard Johnson's towered over her, a well-corseted Rubenesque woman with coral ringlets and the posture of an empress. Watching her sweep along the aisles in her toast-colored suits, it was easy to imagine a younger slimmer version parading her feathers down the staircase in the Ziegfeld Follies, which was how she'd spent her youth. This was common knowledge. Everybody knew Miss Tiffany, but it was a shock to find out that maybe she also knew you. "Is there anything I can do to help?" She reminded Frankie of the brusque but kindly teacher she'd had the year her mother died.

Frankie gulped. She hoped she didn't look too much like a startled raccoon. A waitress zoomed by and slid a plate of french fries neatly past Miss Tiffany and onto the table. It was all too much, and Frankie dissolved in tears. "Annie Fallon's dead."

"Yes, I know. She was such a talent, wasn't she? A lovely woman."

"Uh huh," Frankie nodded, wiping her nose with a napkin.

Miss Tiffany was quiet for a moment. She leaned over carefully and patted Frankie's hand. "Take all the time you need," she said. "No one will bother you here."

Annie Fallon was dead. Allowing the door to slam behind her, Frankie dragged her dance bag into the house like a load of damp laundry. She hobbled to the bathroom and lifted her leg, resting her ankle on the edge of the sink as though it were a ballet barre. Gingerly, she unbuckled the straps and eased the sandal from her foot. It looked ugly; a blood blister; the worst kind, she thought with a shudder. As gently as she could, she washed it with soap and lukewarm water. Hopping a little closer to the sink so that her arm could reach into the medicine cabinet, she rummaged for the old baby aspirin bottle where she kept a needle soaking in rubbing alcohol. She pulled at the loop of dental floss to draw the needle out, then held it poised at the edge of the black-red swell. There was always that moment of hesitation, when it was impossible to imagine she could willfully hurt herself.

When she was little, she'd sit on the edge of the toilet, her eyes squeezed tight while her mother cleaned out the cut, pulled out the splinter or whatever. Martha would always try to get her to watch.

"When you're grown up, you're going to have to do these things for yourself. I need you to watch so you can learn how."

Martha had been wrong. Frankie had needed to start doing things for herself way before she'd grown up.

She ran the needle's tip against the grain of the skin. In her head, she tried to pull back from herself and view the scene from outside her body. When she achieved that distance, she'd be able to plunge it in. The blister was a full inch around. She would have to puncture the skin more than once and then press down to squeeze out the blood. It was going to hurt. Annie Fallon was dead.

"It's easy to take on a small hurt to get rid of a big one," Martha would say, picking up the tweezers or the razor blade. "You do what you have to do." Frankie plunged in the needle.

Frankie limped down the stairs on her bandaged foot. All these years after they put her mother in the ground, her father still went down to the finished part of the basement when he wanted a quiet glass and a smoke. When she told him, Mickey Cecchi put down his racing form with a look that said "Why do I need to know this?"

"Annie Fallon," she said, pleading for it to mean something to him, the way that it did to her. "The actress. You remember Annie, Pop. From Cooghan's. She was my teacher."

He drummed his fingers on the arm of his chair to show he was thinking.

"You used to joke around. She was the one who brought Judy Garland."

The creases melted smooth in his forehead. "The funny broad with the voice." He nodded, satisfied. Frankie's ears picked up a lower-case 'b'; it made her unreasonably angry. "Used to come in with Dottie sometimes."

"And Judy," Frankie insisted, "she brought Judy."

He waved his hand dismissively. "We used to get all kinds there, time to time. The location. Funny how you remember that; you were such a kid. Anyways," he grew suddenly defense. "I only brought you once or twice. Not like you grew up in a bar, right? I was a good father. With Martha so sick and all."

"Only a few times, Pop." It was good to agree. "I liked it there. People were nice…" she wanted to say "to me," but Mickey was looking out into memories and kept talking right past her.

"We had all kinds. DiMaggio came in a coupla times. Joltin' Joe." He breathed the name like a rye-flavored prayer. "Your generation, you see him on the television selling that coffee machine, you act like he's some big joke. You know nothing, nothing at all."

"So DiMaggio came in," she said, wheedling for a story, for comfort. She wanted to lead him back to her memories. "Who else, Pop?"

"Well that was the big one," he said, grudgingly. "No one bigger'n Joltin' Joe. But we had others. Graziano, Rocky Graziano. Came in regular for a while. And some of the newspaper guys'd come with Mary Cat, but only she came in regular. She used to bring a lot of 'em by, all kinds. Her and Dottie and that Annie."

"Annie Fallon." Frankie was exhausted, as though she'd been walking up a steep hill in cement shoes.

"Used to say the funniest damn things. Wish I could remember some of them," Mickey shook his head as if to clear it. "But DiMaggio, that was the best. Damn, I haven't been to Cooghan's in years. Wonder if any of the old gang is still around."

"It's not there anymore," Frankie said, starting up the stairs. "It's a Beefsteak Charlie's." She couldn't tell if he'd heard her. She hoped so.

There was a private service for family and close friends that Frankie read about afterwards, in the trades. She read about the public one at the Actor's Chapel in time to go. St. Malachy's was full of people, "SRO for our Annie" as the priest said. There weren't any big stars; it was filled with real theatre people, like Annie herself. Two kind men squeezed over to make room for Frankie. Some of the NYADA students came together and huddled on the other side of the sanctuary. Very sad and dignified, Nancy Pardoe gave a speech. So did Peggy Cass, who had replaced Annie in *Helen*; it had been a regular thing, the two of them replacing one another. Peggy made a joke that with Annie gone, she'd probably never get asked to work again. It wasn't that funny, but people laughed because they really needed to. Jack Gilford said Annie was the best comedienne he'd ever worked with, and then he read a poem she'd liked. It wasn't until everyone sang "Smile" together that Frankie recognized the men next to her from *Lake Song*, Joseph Bigelow, who was Sorin, and the short man who had those bunchy cheeks like the *Wizard of Oz*.

Blinking in the sunlight outside, glad her glasses kept people from seeing too much of her eyes, Frankie felt hollow. It would have been nice to have someone to sit down and talk with. She'd hoped to see Donny but he was probably worried about bumping into his ex, who was in the *Lake Song* chorus. The group from NYADA had walked right past her in a tight protective cluster. Even if they'd looked at her—which they hadn't—she would have felt shut out. There would be no comfort going home to Patchogue; this was the night Eunice cooked Mickey dinner before they went over to the VFW. Frankie decided to kill a few hours listening to old records at Lincoln Center; talk was discouraged in the library, so it always felt alright to be there alone. Later, she'd come back down and get a standing room ticket for *Lake Song*. Bronwen Davies was always a comfort. If there wasn't a ticket, Frankie would take her time over a slice at Sbarro and then she'd second-act. She wondered if Nancy Pardoe would go on tonight. Probably. No one would blame her if she didn't, but it was a memorial, not the actual funeral and the show must go on. Maybe Frankie would wait at the stage door and talk to her. It would be like a condolence visit. Unless Nancy remembered her from that time at Colony, when Annie got so angry. It was probably better not to wait. She'd go to the library, then go to the show. Annie would have liked that plan. It was how an actor should mourn.

It was a scene out of Frankie's worst nightmare. She came back to the changing room after Movement class to find an envelope stuck to her locker. Miss Nelson wanted to see her in the office. She knew immediately that it couldn't be good. Miss Nelson didn't call you in to give you a pat on the back. Frankie pulled on her clothes. Her fingers didn't want to work properly. She fixed her lipstick, then decided she had on so much that she looked like Lucille Ball, so she wiped it off hard and smeared Chapstick over what was left. Now she looked exactly like she felt—sick and terrified. She tried again, and put some spray in her hair to make it look more styled. Regina Nelson had high standards.

Fifteen minutes after that, it no longer mattered. They'd thrown her out of school. No, what Miss Nelson had said, exactly, was "We have decided not to ask you back." She wasn't the only one. Fully a third of each first year class wouldn't make the cut. This was expected, Miss Nelson told her coolly; it was planned for, a fact that was news to Frankie and, she was willing to bet, to the others who were being dumped.

Trying hard not to faint, Frankie gripped her wooden seat with both hands while Miss Nelson made an entire speech. NYADA was meant to be a training ground, not a nursery. There was no purpose in coddling young actors. Being accepted to NYADA was an opportunity to prove that your talents were competitive in the professional world. If by the end of the first year you hadn't proven this to the satisfaction of the faculty, it was a kindness to let you go.

"But I'm already...I've already worked professionally, Miss Nelson," Frankie felt so much righteous indignation that the words jumped out of her mouth. "Thierry Dupontel..."

Miss Nelson winced as though someone with a stiletto heel had stomped on her foot. "My dear Francesca, it is unfortunate that Thierry put you in a false position. This is a selfish business, child. You served a purpose for him, if I may be blunt."

That was blunt, alright, Frankie thought. "If I wasn't good enough he wouldn't have cast me. Thierry is a perfectionist. Everything about that production had to be perfect."

"You are young and inexperienced. You looked the way he envisioned the character, and I'm sure you copied every direction he gave you; I understand you have a knack for mimicry. In these ways, no doubt, you were perfect. You gave him exactly what he required, but that does not make you an actress."

"That's your opinion," Frankie retorted. If she was getting thrown out, she had nothing to lose. "They called Katharine Hepburn 'box office poison'."

"You're hardly Katharine Hepburn, Francesca. This is not to say that you might not find a place for yourself. Our faculty, while highly experienced, is not infallible." Her thin smile made it clear that she didn't believe this. "Art is subjective and there is no accounting for taste. However," she held up a hand like a stop sign, "we feel a tremendous responsibility to our young people. It is because we care, Francesca, that we cannot allow you to continue." Miss Nelson rubbed her forefingers carefully along her eye sockets, so as not to disturb her makeup, and gave her temples a rueful massage. There was silence for maybe as long a minute. Miss Nelson opened her eyes; she seemed surprised that Frankie was still sitting frozen in her chair.

"I am an actress, Miss Nelson," Frankie squeaked bravely, struggling for dignity. "It's all I've wanted since I was little. It's what I am. And I'm going to do it with or without this school."

Miss Nelson let go an implausibly deep sigh and shook her head. "Theatre is a hard business. It will be hard enough for those who are talented enough to complete this program. For those who are not, it would be cruel to encourage them to pursue this path." She stood up and walked to the other side of the desk, leaving no doubt that she wanted Frankie to leave her. "You can be extremely charming. I'm sure children love you. You might make a wonderful kindergarten teacher. Don't cry, please. I am accustomed to dealing with people who can cry on cue; it won't move me and you will only distress yourself."

From the other side of the door, Frankie heard a definitive click. She flicked her eyes up and down the hall to make certain she was alone, then walked carefully to the ladies' room by the auditorium entrance, which was always empty during the day, to pull herself together. As long as she was in this building, she vowed, she was not going to show she was upset. They were making a mistake. She was probably the most talented actress in her class. They couldn't handle it, that was the problem. If the instructors were so great, they'd be out there working instead of teaching. What was that saying? Those who can't do, teach? They wanted nobodies that they could turn into copies of themselves. They were jealous of what she could do. She was going to be bigger than any of them.

She would pretend that she was Bette Davis in *Dark Victory*. Judith Traherne. No one would know she was dying because, on the outside, she would act as though everything was just fine. Holding herself as tall as she could, she made her way back to the changing room. She only passed a couple of students. They pretended to ignore her, but maybe that didn't mean anything; they always had. It didn't take long to clear out her locker, because she wasn't neat about it. She scooped out her belongings and crammed them into her dance bag and a shopping bag that was on the floor: dance clothes, sides for scene class, makeup…There was a piece of sheet music that Donny had loaned her. It had his name stamped on it. She had no idea where to find him right now. She didn't want to take it home. She didn't have Donny's address to send it back to him. She'd have to leave it with the school secretary. She hated doing that, but she was determined to leave no loose ends. Once she walked out of that front door, she would never even think about NYADA again.

She borrowed a pencil from a clipboard used for filling out enrollment forms. On the inside front, she wrote "Donny, I won't be coming back to school. You're the only person I'll miss. Thank you. Frankie," and her phone number. As casually as she could, she gave the sheet to the secretary and asked for it to be given back to Donny. She picked up her bags and walked firmly out of the building. Somehow, she made it back to Patchogue. She stuck her head in the butcher shop to tell Mickey she was coming down with a bad cold; then crept into bed, where she stayed for two days.

She didn't say a word to Mickey. Friday would have been the end of term in any case. All he cared about was that she had some kind of work lined up for the summer, which she did. Last month, she'd finally talked a local day camp into giving her a spot as a drama counselor. At the time, it had seemed like a way to have a summer at least partly connected to acting. Now it felt ominously close to Miss Nelson's recommendation. She was glad she didn't have to start until after the Fourth of July.

She could have been acting, she thought, resentfully. In March, the trades had been full of notices for summer theatre. NYADA students, however, were limited to a selected pool of theatres "whose quality was considered to be consistent with the standards of our teaching" and who sent representatives to an open call that was held in the school. Only six first year students had been selected by any of these.

"No big deal," Donny had reassured her. "They'll be cleaning toilets and painting flats. The only acting most of them will be doing is faking it under the visiting stars."

If she'd known she was going to be thrown out of school, she thought bitterly now, she would have gone to all the real auditions and now she'd be getting ready to go to the Cape or someplace. Or maybe she would have called Thierry and he would have invited her to work in his theatre in Canada.

Donny would be up in the Adirondacks. She hoped he'd gotten her message before he'd left. There was an Equity house a couple of towns away from where he'd grown up. By the time he'd graduated high school, between summers and the annual production of *A Christmas Carol*, he'd put in enough hours there to get his union card. His first year at NYADA, he'd told Miss Nelson with all due respect that she couldn't tell him the place that had given him his start didn't meet the Academy's standards. The way Donny told it, she hadn't been able to say a word. Frankie enjoyed imagining Miss Nelson standing there with her mouth hanging open like a fish.

This summer they were doing *Babes in Arms* and *The Pajama Game*. Not only would Donny be in the shows, but he'd be assistant to the musical director. Donny had hopes of being a musical director himself someday. If he could make himself indispensable this summer, it would be a big boost to his career. Maybe someday Donny would direct her on Broadway, and they'd sit at their table in Sardi's and laugh about NYADA.

Someday seemed further off than ever before. Frankie hung around the neighborhood and biked to the water. She'd stretch out on her towel and stare at the ocean for hours. Whenever she found herself thinking, she'd pick up Martha's old copy of *Gone With the Wind* and read until she'd driven her mind firmly back to Tara. When her eyes got tired and she rubbed them and saw purple sunspots, she'd go back to watching the waves.

It took the thought of another dinner with Eunice to get her back on the train to the city. One had been more than enough: Eunice tying on that ridiculous organdy apron with the red satin apple pocket, flouncing around her mother's kitchen and making a big deal out of tossing a can of green beans with a can of cream of mushroom soup and pouring it over a pan full of tuna and cornflakes. With all that fuss, not to mention all the pots and dishes, you'd have thought she was making Thanksgiving dinner. And the way she leaned over Pop when she served him, so his nose was practically caught between her boobs. The Jungle Gardenia fumes should have knocked him out cold, but instead he had this glazed happy look like someone having gas at the dentist. It all made Frankie sick to her stomach—the tuna casserole, literally.

When Mickey started tidying up the living room and told her to "try and look nice tonight," she suddenly "remembered" that she was supposed to meet a friend from school in the city that night, to see a show. She pulled on the first clean thing in the closet and fled. She made it to the station just as the train was pulling in.

Frankie had no idea what she was going to do in the city. She couldn't afford a theatre ticket, not even standing room. Maybe she would go to a movie. She wondered how long she could sit in a hotel lobby and what hotel would be safe; she didn't want anyone to think she was a hooker.

First she needed food. It was a funny time, too late for lunch and a little too early for dinner, but she was starving. There was that restaurant where Thierry had taken them the day of the table reading. The walls were covered with framed posters for recent shows, and all the people who worked there seemed to be connected to the theatre. If she went there, she could feel like an actress. There would have to be something cheap she could eat.

Walking down the steps into Alfie's, Frankie knew she'd made the right decision. The restaurant was cool, dark and still nearly empty, and the posters hung on the exposed brick just as she'd remembered. A guy with a black JFK haircut slid off a barstool to greet her. She thought maybe he was Alfie himself. He walked her to a table and pulled out her chair. "Menu's on the wall," he said, with a little wink. "I'll give you a coupla minutes."

To see the chalkboard, she had to swivel around in her seat and crane her neck over her shoulder. Burgers, fried chicken, chili, onion soup. That was all there was on the cheap side. The rest of the menu was scampi and duck à l'orange, that sort of thing. Finally, she noticed the cramped words squeezed at the bottom. She strained through her glasses to make out exactly what it was. Alfie or whoever he was came back.

She took a deep breath and gave it a try. "I'll have the salad nickoyze."

"Sorry, babe," he said, tapping his ear to show he hadn't heard. "What was that?"

"The salad," she repeated, a little more loudly. "The salad nickoyze? What kind of dressing is that?" Her voice sounded loud and squeaky in her own ears. The man still seemed puzzled.

"The young lady will have the salad niçoise."

Knee-swahz; that was how you said it. Feeling herself turn pink with embarrassment, Frankie wanted to hide under the table, but that rich baritone voice was somehow familiar and she had to whip her head around to see who it was. Joseph Bigelow was a couple of tables behind her, sitting with the *Wizard of Oz* man and eating spaghetti. He waved kindly.

"Very good choice, young lady, for weather like this. Tuna and olives, and some fresh green beans, isn't that so, Alfie?"

"Ah!" Alfie cocked his finger in salute. "Salad niçoise it is."

The man seated with Bigelow broke into a broad, twinkly grin. "Joe, it's the little girl from Annie's memorial service! Isn't it? Hello, my dear!"

"So it is!"

"Are you alone, my dear?"

Frankie nodded. You weren't supposed to admit to strangers that you were alone, but they weren't blind; they could see she was. Besides, they weren't really strangers; she knew who they were.

"Oh, don't be! Come here; sit with us." He stood up and moved a chair out.

She stood uncertainly. With a friendly nod, he patted the chair. Feeling as if she were crossing a stage with an entire audience watching, she walked the few yards. She was glad she'd put on her makeup in the train. In future, she decided, she would always say she learned three things at NYADA: how to accept that criticism is subjective; how to second-act; and how to do her makeup in a moving vehicle.

"Tyler Moss," said the twinkly man, taking her hand and maneuvering her into the chair. "And this is Joe Bigelow." Bigelow reached across the table.

"Frankie Cecchi," she managed to say.

"Is that your real voice?" Bigelow asked abruptly.

Her voice, she knew, had a touch of the cartoon about it. Since it made things sound funnier than they usually were, it had earned her a reputation for being a "character" and had made things a little easier for her growing up. People had always laughed with her, not at her—until the Academy, that is. There, the faculty seemed affronted by her voice, not that they'd given her any help in trying to change it, and they'd encouraged the other students to treat it as an affliction. "Yes," she said. What else was there to say?

"Great!" he said from somewhere deep inside his belly, which made it sound like he meant it. "You can make a fortune with that voice! That is assuming you're an actor."

She nodded and smiled. He pushed the basket towards her and she picked out a soft roll. The butter came in a little white ceramic dish, not in foil-wrapped pats.

"Why else would she have been at Annie's service?" Tyler Moss had to reach across to another table to grab a place setting for her. "Were you in a show together? Or are you one of her students?"

"I took Musical Comedy with her at NYADA last term," was the honest, if less than complete, explanation. "It's summer now," she hurried to add, trying to cut short that line of discussion.

"Right, right," Joseph...Joe Bigelow said, shrugging it off. "So how come you're still in town?"

"They don't allow us to do stock."

"That's right." Tyler Moss made a sour-tasting expression. "You remember, Joe. Linda told us. A young lady in our company who recently graduated," he explained. Frankie nodded politely; she knew plenty about Linda, Donny's ex. "Strange rule for an acting school, if you ask me."

"They have a lot of them," Frankie said dryly, knowing they both would laugh. They did.

"But why haven't you gone home then?" Bigelow pursued. "No fun sticking around this city all summer. Expensive, and no way to keep your hand in. Unless you plan to take dance classes or whatnot in some hot studio?"

"Oh!" she finally got his point. "But I'm from here. I live in Patchogue. On Long Island."

They laughed again. She guessed Patchogue sounded like a joke name, until Moss said, "I grew up in Bayshore myself."

Frankie was impressed. Tyler Moss didn't look or sound like the Island. She'd assumed he was from the South, some place where men wore pale-colored three-piece suits and used walking sticks. He had that air about him. Or maybe that was what he wore in the show. Sometimes it was hard to sort out her impressions.

Her salad arrived. The salad knee-swahz. They smiled encouragingly and she picked up her fork and looked. She'd expected a little salad, but this was a lot of food. There were chunks of tuna, not with mayonnaise but just straight out of the can, sitting on the bed of lettuce. And little olives and green beans, just like they'd said. Also wedges of tomato, slices of hard-boiled egg and what looked like pieces of boiled potato. Moss winked at her and she realized he'd been eating the same thing. She stuck her fork through a piece of lettuce and some tuna and brought it to her mouth. There was some lemony dressing on it. It was good.

They were so nice to her, it was like having dinner with old friends. She told them about her summer job at camp, and they didn't think it was terrible at all. Bigelow even congratulated her on finding something slightly related to acting. They both told funny stories about jobs they'd had, not only when they were starting out in the business but over the years. Only major stars and a few unusually lucky character actors could make their entire living by acting. Frankie had been told that over and over again, but only now, coming from two working actors who were treating her like an equal, was it sinking in that this was the truth and not something people said to discourage her from trying. Moss noted he kept a "day job" to this very day; he was co-owner of a store down in Chelsea, where he sold theatrical memorabilia and other collector's items.

"Break a Leg," Frankie nodded intelligently. "It's in your Who's Who."

He seemed pleased that someone had read his paragraph in the program. "Ivor's a set designer and he's as happy as I am to have a little extra income and a place to go between shows if we feel like it," he said. "It's so cheap down there that we can cover the rent without having to be open all the time. Except between Thanksgiving and Christmas, when people have a lot of presents to buy, we only open up once or twice a week. Or as a special command performance—you know, if some VIP wants to pick up a few opening night gifties." This last comment was made in a fake British accent, with a glance down his nose as if he were trying to decide if something was genuine.

It was so gratifying to be spoken to like this, as though she were one of them. It was like spending a holiday living the life she was supposed to have.

"So have you seen *Lake Song*?" Bigelow asked in that abrupt way she could tell he had.

She nodded so vigorously that her glasses slipped down her nose a bit and she had to push them back. "Three times," she said, thinking she probably shouldn't mention the second-acting. "I think it's wonderful."

"Wonderful," Bigelow repeated, flexing his eyebrows.

"Wonderful. Those characters are so…Well, you know, you can really feel…" She gestured haphazardly, trying to marshal her words which refused to flow the way she wanted. "And the music, and all of you…you're all so…It makes me happy, even the sad parts. Because it's so beautiful." Thinking of "Bandaging the Wound," envisioning Bronwen Davies all distraught, trying to enfold Kostia in her arms, Frankie exhaled a deep sigh. She didn't hear how mournful it sounded. She couldn't see how pathetic she looked, her too-large blouse, her crumpled hair, her eyes behind their lenses as liquid as an abandoned puppy's. "I'm going again tonight, if I can get standing room."

Tyler Moss tapped his knife on the edge of his water glass so that it made a little ping. "Fear not, my dear," he said in a silly voice, "you shall go to the ball!" There was a box, he explained, that was kept empty on weeknights in case it was needed by Marshall Berenson or James Lord. Berenson was up at Willamstown, where he was being honored with a special cabaret, and Lord wasn't due for one of his surprise visits for at least another week. If she came with them straight from the restaurant, they'd slip her in.

They wouldn't even let her pay for her salad. She walked to the Regale with Joe Bigelow on one side and Tyler Moss on the other. It was hard not to keep looking back and forth between the two of them and their photos on the sides of the theatre. She felt as if she'd swallowed bubbles.

At the stage door, the actors had to sign in. "My niece," Moss said grandly.

"She has to leave before half hour," the doorman said, giving her a fishy look. She wondered if he remembered her from the scrapbook.

"*His* niece, Wally, not mine," Bigelow chortled, thumping the man on the back.

Wally snickered. "Nothing to worry about there!" When his back was turned, Moss grabbed Frankie's wrist and pulled her through a door. For one magic second, they were on the stage, but then he hustled her through another door, which led to the far side of the auditorium. With a finger held to his lips, he moved quietly up the stairs. Before the mezzanine level, he stopped and pushed aside a layer of gold brocade drapery and hooked out a chair. Tucking the fabric around it, he made the chair invisible from both the house and the landing.

"All you have to do is sit quietly and stay out of sight until the house opens," he whispered. "Once it starts filling up, you can move the chair back into the box. I'll talk to the usher who works this section and tell her you're with the show and to leave you alone. Okay?"

Her eyes were shining so brightly that her glasses looked like lanterns. "Okay," she whispered back. "Thank you. Thank you so much—for everything!"

"Actor to actor," Tyler Moss whispered back. "One kid from Suffolk to another. Someday you'll pass it on."

"I will," she promised.

"Have a good time." He winked at her. "And have fun with your summer camp. May it be the worst day job you ever have."

She had to put her hand over her mouth to stop her laugh from spilling out. She could see that made him happy. He bowed like one of the Three Musketeers and disappeared. Other than her breathing and the beating of her heart, she didn't make a sound for the next hour, until the audience started to file in. It was the happiest hour she could remember in her life.

5 - SOMETHING

SORIN *[spoken: You know, when I was young there were exactly two things I
   wanted passionately: to get married and to be a novelist. I never managed to pull
   off either one.]*

I always had a dream,
And through the darkest hours—
Oh yes, a man like me,
We too have darkest hours—
I'd cut the shadows with a dream of making love or art;
But dreams just seem to fall apart,
And now I haven't got the heart to even wish for something.

From my soul I kept on giving
'Til there's nothing left, believing
If my life was worth the living
There'd be something I'd be leaving when I'd go.
Little could I ever hope to know:

I'd never have a wife,
I'd never write a story;
A small and lonely life,
Without a shred of glory.
I must have asked too much! And as I stand here looking back
Confronted by the things I lack,
I'd be a cuckold or a hack
If only I could feel I had been something.

*[spoken: Yes, when all's said and done, to be even a minor writer must be rather
   nice.]*

Ahuva loved the Dead Sea, which is why the family had chosen to make the schlep there for her last weekend. Her tribe of cousins, aged two to fifty-plus, were mostly hanging by the shore, plastering themselves with mud. The older ones used it as a beauty aid, or to ease psoriasis and eczema. The little ones loved that they could throw all the mud they wanted and the adults wouldn't care. Ahuva loved the mud, too, but right now she floated blissfully on the water. On her back. She'd been warned her entire life against flipping over and trying to swim—people drowned that way, when they couldn't right themselves and their noses and mouths became stuck in the sea. Floating was better anyway. You could float effortlessly on the buoyant salt water, which meant your mind could go anywhere and not worry about your body. Unless of course you floated too far. You certainly didn't want to end up in Jordan. Her eyes flew open at the thought; that she'd never heard of that actually happening made it no less terrifying to contemplate. Even in the 33° Centigrade heat, she felt herself shiver. Squinting at the sun, she tried not to think about it.

And the sky is so vast / And you look at the lake and the water's like glass / And you live for today, for there isn't a past

The words came, unbidden, to mind. She could hear the *Lake Song* score almost perfectly in her head, which was lucky as the cassette she'd made of the cast album hadn't shown up when she unpacked. It must have fallen out when they went through her luggage at security.

She wished something else had fallen out. *Watership Down* maybe. She'd used Byron's postcard as a bookmark, making it impossible for her to stop obsessing over what he'd said or, more accurately, what he hadn't.

"Hi," it began, not "Dear." not even her name.

"I think you would like this place." But she'd already been to Amsterdam, to visit Malke's cousins. She knew she'd told him.

"Mirielle set me up with a friend who has a club. She thinks my problem with Paris was I don't have experience in Europe so she sent me here to get some." Who is this Mirielle? What problem; and how does she know so much about fixing it? She sounds bossy. And old; she must be old if she has friends with clubs all over Europe.

"Byron." Not "Sincerely, Byron" or even "Regards." Of course not "Love." She would never sign a letter to him "Love, Ahuva," even if sometimes she felt it surely had to be…No, she would never dare. So why would he, even if he…?

Oh! She should be thrilled he'd written to her at all, not looking to find fault! What did she expect? It was a postcard; anyone might pick it up to read, and in any case there wasn't much room for pouring your heart out.

Every time she read it, she tried to imagine Byron in Amsterdam. She couldn't. Paris was easier, because she'd only seen it in movies. Amsterdam had a solid reality and she couldn't make Byron fit. When she tried to imagine a jazz club there, all she could visualize was the narrow hallway in the Anne Frank house closing in on her, or the rows of canal houses with all their windows reflected in the water. She couldn't imagine Byron, in his white shirt and dark jacket, riding a bicycle over the cobblestones, strolling through gardens, brushed by the soft sunlight.

It didn't matter. She couldn't let it matter. She had to let go of the past and look to the future. This vacation was supposed to be about relaxing and enjoying herself with her family. When she got back home, all her attention would be focused on getting ready to head upstate to college. To a new life.

She couldn't imagine herself upstate any more than she could imagine Byron in Amsterdam. Forget college, which was way too big to think about; she didn't even have a real concept of what it was like that far upstate. Mountains, she expected. A lot of trees. But what would it sound like, what would it smell like? It was going to be very different, that much was certain. She was going to miss the city. She would especially miss knowing that the theatre was a subway ride away, just when she'd begun taking advantage of it. She wondered if she'd ever see *Lake Song* again. She was lucky she'd gotten to see it twice. Such a wonderful show; magic.

"Earth to Ahuva!" It was an expression Gali had picked up during her last visit to New York. Soon Gali would officially be in the Army, unable to leave the country for a few years, which was why she'd been traveling so much: to Ahuva in New York, to Greece and Italy, and then to their family in Amsterdam. As soon as she was allowed to travel again, when her tour of active duty was up, she and Ahuva were going to Disneyland and Las Vegas together; they'd sworn, and they always came through on a swear.

Ahuva lifted a languid arm and waved. Gali, running across the salt shingle in her flowered bikini, black hair whipping behind her, waved a bag of Bamba out of reach of the little ones. In about two weeks, that hair would be pinned up under a cap. Gali would be in the Army, wearing a uniform and carrying a gun. Ahuva would be back in the States getting ready for college. Equally inconceivable.

When they were little together in Jaffa, they used to pretend that they were twins. Now Ahuva felt as if she'd been caught in some Einsteinian time puzzle where she'd been left at age 11 and Gali had kept on growing. Even before their training began, Gali and her friends were men and women, harder and cooler than any of Ahuva's friends back home. When Ahuva expressed this, Gali laughed and said they were all the same; it was because she didn't really know them that she thought they were different.

They *were* different, no matter what Gali said. When she'd lived in Israel, Ahuva had been too young to sense anything other than the security of home and a large, loving family. Her parents had emigrated the year before the Six-Day War. In America, she'd never had that cold dark feeling that everything could disappear in an instant, or the certainty that it was up to her to make sure this never happened. That's what was different for Gali and her friends.

Israel made Ahuva feel small. She often felt that she didn't belong in America, but when she was back in Israel, she felt she didn't belong anywhere at all.

"*Heaven bless and heaven keep,*" she found herself singing dreamily, afloat on the Dead Sea. "*Heaven grant a quiet corner now and then in which to sleep.*"

When she got over her jet lag, Ahuva called me to catch up. We talked for nearly two hours. What she wanted most was news about *Lake Song*. I gave her whatever fragments I could dredge up from some rambling conversations with Ellen, then gave her Ellen's number so she could find out herself—if she could ever catch Ellen at home. I was a little baffled by their obsession. It was a wonderful, memorable show but, to my mind, still only a show.

Of more immediate concern to me were Heidi's last weeks in town. Her parents, both Holocaust survivors, had decided they could no longer wait to retire to Israel; her father was becoming too frail to keep driving his cab. Heidi couldn't bear to live half a world away from her father, so she was moving too. She had to be in Jerusalem soon for the pre-term intensive language program at Hebrew University, more or less swapping places with Ahuva.

Heidi's friends put together a full slate of events to fill those last weeks: final trips to Bloomingdales and B. Altman's, a concert at Jones Beach, a "kitchen sink" sundae at Jahn's. It might be a very long time before she would see another Broadway show, so some of us decided to see her off in the most extravagant, most New York way we could imagine: an entire Saturday on Broadway, seeing both a matinee and an evening performance. We would of course need to eat between the two. With what we thought was tremendous sophistication, we made reservations at Sardi's.

Seesaw, our choice for matinee, was as much a romance with the city as between the two main characters. It might have been too poignant a goodbye for Heidi. It took waiting outside the Uris stage door, collecting a few autographs, to restore her spirits.

Brimming with the insuppressible excitement that used to precede and follow every theatre outing, we were all humming "My City" as we crossed the street to the legendary restaurant and fluttered in. Hundreds of eyes stared down at us. We immediately fell silent. The famous caricatures paved the walls, from just above the chair rails all the way up to the ceilings. Even the doorways were crowned with a row of framed cartoons, each a face we felt we ought to know. We were led, single file, to our table. It seemed to be a mile away. We tried to act blasé, as if we ate at Sardi's all the time, while at the same time darting our eyes around the room in hopes of spotting a famous face in the flesh. Servers in maroon livery brought our menus, poured our water, took our orders. It was a hot day in a memorably hot summer. We were drawn to the cooler items on the menu.

"Did I mention that I went to see *Lake Song* on Wednesday?" Ahuva asked, knowing that she hadn't.

I shouldn't have been surprised. In the two short years I'd known her, I'd learned that Ahuva did nothing half-heartedly. Her passion could move mountains, turning a pair of high school musicals into impressive fundraisers for a school for mentally disabled children. At other times, she chose something as her own—an inspiring teacher, the pizza from one particular local parlor, *The New York Times* crossword puzzle…Marshall Berenson and Byron Weeks, of course—and gave herself to it entirely. Watching her with Ellen at the party, knowing she'd already seen the show twice, it should have seemed inevitable to me that every conversation would now include the words "Lake Song." I shrugged this off as a devotion that would have to level out fairly quickly, considering she'd soon be five hours upstate of Broadway.

Ahuva had a story. She'd gone around to the stage door after the matinee. Most of those waiting seemed to be with theatre parties from ladies' clubs, brandishing flowers at Davies and Brassloe and practically mobbing Max Bulloch, all three of whom had come out fairly quickly, to smile and sign *Playbills.* Once they went back inside, the club ladies dispersed. By the time the rest of the cast came out on their way to dinner, only Ahuva and a couple of others remained. When Maria Dearborne came out, Ahuva suddenly recalled that Mr. Gruen had gone to college with her and had talked about going backstage to see her in *Gal from Kalamazoo.*

She couldn't explain why she hadn't remembered before. Excited, she actually tapped Maria Dearborne on the arm and said, "Albert Gruen was my teacher. He used to tell us about you, all the time. Maria…It's pronounced Muh-RI-yuh, you know, as in 'they call the wind Maria'," Ahuva informed us, loftily. "Maria was thrilled. She had the nicest things to say about Mr. Gruen." With Maria being so receptive, Ahuva had gone on to tell her about that watershed school production of *Rosebud*, to which the actress responded with her own experiences playing Joan in the revival. When Ahuva'd said that this was her third time seeing *Lake Song*, Maria's response had been gratifying.

"She was so real!" Ahuva enthused, waving her fork. "While we were talking, Oliver Blanchard stopped by to ask Maria if she was going with their group for dinner."

"Oliver Blanchard is a little old," Heidi said, "but he's handsome."

"He's not really that old," Ahuva said. "They have to make him look old enough for Lilith Brassloe. It's the hair and makeup. And those suits they have him in. He looked a lot younger in jeans. He smiled at me." She lit up as she recalled it. "His eyes are blue. Very blue."

Then Ahuva froze, fork in midair, her face a dead ringer for Joan Crawford's in that scene from *Whatever Happened to Baby Jane* when Bette Davis serves her the rat. "There's a fly in my chicken salad!" she hissed loudly.

"Quiet," Janet couldn't resist quipping, "or everyone will want one." Heidi and I groaned and rolled our eyes at a joke that was probably old when our grandparents heard it.

Ahuva was furious. "There is," she said through clenched teeth, "a Fly. In my Plate. Look!" She shoved the plate to the center of the table. Sure enough, a large housefly was perched on a cube of white meat, nicely embalmed in mayo; it clearly hadn't just flown by the table to check out what was on offer.

The rest of us looked guiltily at one another, ashamed we'd laughed.

"In a restaurant like this!" Ahuva stood and, with a gesture that would have done Lilith Brassloe proud, summoned a waiter. He was an older man, with a toothbrush mustache, and seemed predisposed to find our table of girls amusing. Ahuva turned her glare his way and pointed a long arm at the offending insect. "My chicken salad has a fly in it," she trumpeted; "take it away!"

I don't know if everyone in the restaurant actually turned to look; I only know we felt they must and, ostrich like, quickly cast our eyes down to the fascinating weave of the tablecloth.

"My sincere apologies, Miss," the waiter said solemnly. "I'll bring a replacement."

"Don't bother," she sniffed. "This has completely destroyed my appetite!" The plate was removed. Still nursing her huff, Ahuva resumed her seat. "I am absolutely astounded. To serve food like that. A place like Sardi's!"

She was absolutely correct, of course, but we were young and easily embarrassed. All we could see was the overstated gesture, and the ringing voice that we felt could be heard across Broadway, and we cringed.

"Should we order coffee?" I said in the silence that followed, considering the meal to be over. Ahuva wasn't going to eat anything more, and the rest of us were uncomfortable enjoying another swallow.

Everyone shrugged and nobody moved. The waiter reappeared with a large plate of Italian cookies. "The management hopes you'll accept this as our apology," he said. "May I bring you all some coffee or tea?"

We all looked at Ahuva. "Iced tea," she said, grudgingly, "with lemon."

By the time we'd finished our cookies and drinks, we were talking comfortably about our big plans for the coming school year. We'd almost forgotten about the fly, but when the check came, Ahuva scrutinized it like a trig problem until she confirmed that the chicken salad did not appear. With a satisfied sigh, she made the reckoning, adding a respectable tip for the waiter who had handled the situation appropriately.

Conscious that this was not the sort of place where you paid at the register, we left the bills on the table, folded in the logo-stamped burgundy folder, and made our way to the front door.

I was the last. Still a bit embarrassed, I kept a few steps behind everyone else, pretending I wasn't with them. There was a bottleneck at the door. I found myself stuck beside a table where a man was seated alone. I felt him looking at me and was drawn to meet his eyes. Still staring directly at me, he lifted a spoon to his mouth and, with deliberation, swallowed some soup. His eyebrows twitched engagingly behind his glasses and he almost smiled. I realized I knew that face. I felt my own cheeks flash with heat. It was Woody Allen. The bottleneck broke and I practically ran out of Sardi's.

Ahuva diligently put together a list of everything she needed for college, including some rain and snow gear suggested by the school and a few recommendations from friends who freely offered expert opinions from their own experience as to what you'd actually end up wearing—as opposed to what your mother thought you ought to pack.

Ahuva's mother would have loved to go shopping with her. Malke's ideal daughter would have wanted to kick off the day by having her hair done, followed by perching on a Lucite and pink vinyl stool to have her face painted by some woman in a pastel smock who only wanted to sell her a bag full of expensive makeup that she'd never use again. After that, the two of them would presumably trip giddily from department to department, admiring all the ridiculous displays, pulling a dress here, a shirt there until their arms would be full of hangers. Then, and this would be the most excruciating part of the whole fantastic expedition, Ahuva would be expected to try these costumes on and twirl around in front of a glaring three-way mirror while Malke, staring up from the low chair that was always in the corner of a dressing room, would tell her how pretty she looked in clothes that felt as if they were walking around all by themselves with Ahuva inside them as an afterthought. It was the kind of day that, merely in proposition, made Ahuva want to scream. When such outings came to fruition, she usually ended up saying something sharp to her mother, which started them off on one of those squabbles that looped over and over itself like the infinity symbol. Determined to avoid the issue, Ahuva set aside one Saturday for a trip to MACY*S and asked Jakub for his credit card, claiming that she was meeting a bunch of girlfriends. Malke was disappointed, but approving. It was what young women should do, go shopping together. Yes, she'd been looking forward to going; so now she'd look forward instead to a fashion show when Ahuva got home with all her beautiful new things.

Ahuva was too relieved to feel guilty. She remained relieved until, having pushed through a block-long maze of cosmetics and accessories counters thronged with back-to-school shoppers, she stood on the wooden escalator, clutching the handrail like it was a black rubber lifeline, wondering where to get off. Maybe skipping out on her mother had been cutting off her nose to spite her face. She could have used a guide. How did anyone ever find anything in MACY*S? It was crazy! It took half an hour just to find the bra she always wore. How do you make sense out of an entire department, bigger than their apartment, that had nothing but jeans? Two denim legs, a zipper and a couple of pockets: how many variations could there be? A thousand, apparently. She found herself sucked into a whirlpool of blues: dark blues and lighter blues, marching seams of red and yellow and white, fringes like centipede legs, not to mention rivets and studs and patches and…racks of pants pressing down on her from every side. Her chest began to tighten. Before she lost the impetus to act, she grabbed at the first plain-looking pair that had the right size ring on the hanger and ran into the dressing room. Thank goodness it was one of those little stalls that had its own panel mirror.

Parading down the aisle to a three-way was a torture she wasn't ready to face. If they zipped and she could comfortably squat into a sitting position, she didn't need a view of her tush to buy a pair of jeans.

They fit. Big sigh of relief. Leaving the dressing room, she spotted a saleswoman disappearing into a thicket of woolen blazers. "Miss!" she called loudly.

The woman froze, the weary fear of the hunted. Ahuva closed in on her, thrusting the jeans under her woman's nose.

"I like these," she said. "I want them...something like them, in black corduroy."

"We have some adorable corduroys," the woman enthused listlessly. "All the new fall colors—russet, forest green..."

"I don't want adorable," Ahuva said flatly. "I want these. And black."

With a resigned shrug, the saleswoman tried to take the hanger. Ahuva panicked; if she let it go she might never see her jeans again. After some discreet tug-of-war, the woman looped her glasses up from their chain and peered at the label.

"You're in luck," she observed. "This manufacturer does do corduroy." She lifted an arm and pointed. "I'm not certain whether it's the exact same style or what colors..."

"Where?" Ahuva craned her neck anxiously. "Is it a big department?" She had jeans; maybe she should quit while she was ahead.

The saleswoman must have sensed her panic. Pity overtook her exhaustion. She slipped her glasses down her nose and smiled kindly. "Why don't you wait here and I'll see what I can find." She checked the label again. "I won't be a minute."

She was five, which was remarkably fast, considering that she entirely disappeared from view. Wherever she'd gone, she returned with her arms full of hangers, all with corduroy pants that, despite coming from a variety of manufacturers, were as similar as possible to the jeans. In addition to black, there were some in a color that she called "amber," which she assured Ahuva was "a wonderful neutral for fall and would go with everything."

It would have been impossible to find these on her own. Ahuva hadn't thought about it before, but people who work in department stores need to have incredible memories. While the credit card was going through, she thanked the woman from the bottom of her heart and was pleased to receive a wink in return. "You just go have a good school year," she said, folding the pants in tissue paper. "These really are the best years of your life."

Ahuva knew she'd be expected to bring home some shirts as well, although the ones she already had were perfectly nice. Fortunately, you could buy shirts without having to try them on. She made a single circuit around the perimeter of the racks and pulled out three that seemed appropriate. Three would be plenty. She was especially pleased with the plaid that had her favorite blue crossed with some of that "amber;" it was flannel, which would be warm for upstate. Heading for the register, she passed a counter heaped with those round-necked woolen sweaters that everyone wore. With the worst of her shopping behind her, she could appreciate the autumn leaf colors. The amber would match the shirt and her new cords. Ahuva liked when things matched. Her mother would be impressed she was being so fashionable. She took it. Her list included something for parties, but she had no idea what would be appropriate. Maybe she really would ask some friends to come with her another day, to help her make sense of it all. As for a new coat, Malke could buy her one; coats were a mother thing. She also needed a new pair of shoes, and boots for the snow, but not now. Now she had a headache. she was tired and she wanted to get out of the store. She'd grab a handful of socks and call it a day. MACY*S had nice socks, argyles and stripes. It was mysterious, how socks could always make her cheerful.

That was enough shopping for one day. It was hard to believe it was only 1:30.

Utterly drained, Ahuva stood at the top of the steps to the 34th Street subway station and contemplated her haul: two big bags that would keep her mother quiet and stop her father from worrying, the way he sometimes did when he thought she was missing out on something he ought to be able to give her.

She had absolutely no desire to go home but it was too hot to wander around the city, especially with shopping bags. It would be nice to get on an air-conditioned train. Even if she didn't, at least at this time of day there'd be seats. If she could sit and the car had a working fan, it would be a pleasant half-hour. Sometimes Ahuva wondered what it would be like to just stay on the subway, ride the E train from end to end. How long would that take? Did they clear the cars at the end, or would you be able to stay on and go back the other way? People thought it was strange, but she enjoyed the subway. Once you blanked out all the noise, which happened automatically the minute you concentrated on a crossword puzzle or a book, you didn't have to think about anything. *It's the only place I have where life is calm...* she realized with surprise. Medviedenko's solo. Until that very second, she'd considered "Four Miles" to be a minor song in The Show (as Ahuva had begun to think of *Lake*

Song). It wasn't minor at all. It was profound, it was moving, and she wanted to hear it right now. There was a matinee at 2:00. The theatre was one subway stop away. She had money in her pocket. She could go.

She hadn't planned to do it. She ran. She nearly flew. She got the cheapest matinee ticket, for a "partially obscured" seat behind a pillar, which didn't matter since she had already seen The Show three times, and settled into it just as the house lights were dimming. At the overture's first bar, the tension of the day drained from her body.

When Polina sidled out to deliver her opening number, Ahuva was shocked to realize it wasn't Lilith Brassloe but Maria Dearborne in the role. A good shock; this was exciting! Lilith Brassloe was a brilliant actress and absolutely perfect as Polina, but Maria was someone Ahuva almost knew personally. It was Fate that she'd suddenly decided to come to the theatre for this performance! She hoped that whatever was "obscured" from her seat wouldn't include any of the important Polina moments.

Grabbing a Coke from a knish cart outside during intermission, she checked her *Playbill*. There it was, the insert: "At this performance, the part of Polina will be played by…" She was going to have to keep that slip of paper. Maria was doing a terrific job, too. There was a different quality to the relationship between Dorn and her Polina. "Everything" had seemed, well, sadder and sweeter somehow. Bittersweet, that was it; less ironic. Maybe it was the age thing; Maria and Oliver Blanchard were more like a real couple than Blanchard and Lilith Brassloe.

It would be nice to leave a present at the stage door. If there was a florist or a Hallmark really nearby, she couldn't see from the corner and she was too worried about getting back to her seat in time for Act II to go any farther. Never mind. Even without something to give her, she was definitely going to wait around and congratulate Maria in person.

Her tears took her by surprise. She cried so much more this time when Nina left her childhood behind, and again when she came back to see Kostia but couldn't stay. It broke Ahuva's heart to watch. Leaving her seat, reaching for the bag of corduroy at her feet, she made the stunning connection: a college woman, setting off for parts unknown, she too was leaving the nest.

Time and change. So much loss. Marshall Berenson was a genius! Ahuva had to see this play again. When she came home at Thanksgiving. If not, she promised herself, then definitely Christmas break. Something to look forward to.

After checking in her purse mirror that the evidence of tears was gone, Ahuva walked around to the stage door. The crowd was taking longer than usual to disperse, which was okay; she wanted to take her time. Many of the people waiting seemed to be tourists. The group with the "Hello, My Name Is" labels on their shirts were practically begging to get their purses snatched. Others weren't so obvious and she couldn't say exactly what it was that made her sense they were from out of town. She heard fragments of conversation in several languages, but this didn't mean they weren't going home to Brooklyn or Queens. It must be the nervous excitement in their voices, or the way they took up space on the sidewalk. She wished she could understand it well enough to describe to someone else. She supposed this was why she wasn't an artist.

A young woman with a long braid plowed through the densest parts of the crowd with a basket of roses. Each time she passed a man, she pushed a flower under his nose, urging him to buy one "for your lady." There were a lot of these girls around the city lately, boys too sometimes, always selling flowers for their religion. The airport had been full of them. They reminded Ahuva of the Hare Krishna, except they didn't wear yellow robes or smell of incense, and they didn't sing or dance. They wore soft white blouses over jeans or long skirts and identically blank faces, smiling like dolls with lips together and eyes wide open. Jakub, who generally avoided sweeping statements, had expressly instructed his daughter that any group "that supports itself by turning children into street peddlers is a cult" and must be shunned. However, right now Ahuva really needed a rose and it was only a dollar. How far could a cult go on one dollar? She stuck out a bill and took the flower that was pressed into her hand, carefully avoiding eye contact and trying not to hear the girl's lilting "thank you for supporting our Church."

Ahuva kept a little to one side of the door, letting all the tourists press forward with their cameras and their *Playbills* as the actors trickled out. This must be a big deal for them, seeing Broadway stars this close up. When sisters with accents straight out of a fried chicken commercial couldn't figure out which of them should take a picture of the other two with Max Bulloch, Ahuva politely volunteered to snap one of all of them together. It was satisfying to think that, every time they looked at that photo, they would have to remember that New Yorkers were much friendlier than their neighbors had warned them to expect.

When Maria exited with Kaye Victor, tourists who'd come expecting Lilith Brassloe offered loud assurance that they had hardly been disappointed at all. Maria laughed and graciously signed her name.

She recognized Ahuva at once and gave her a giant hug. Her reaction to the rose was perfect. "How wonderful to have someone who's really here for me and not Lil!" she exclaimed. "How did you know? Did Bert call you?"

Who was Bert? Ahuva tried to hug back but she was nervous and loaded with MACY*S bags. "I umm...I didn't...I just decided to come. It's like Fate." She attempted a light-hearted laugh; it sounded embarrassingly like a hiccup.

Maria was too excited to notice. "He's here too you know. That certainly sounds like Karma," she giggled. "You ask Kaye. She's very into all that. No accidents in Kaye's universe! Not that Bert is an accident. When I learned this morning that Lil had no voice—I mean absolutely nothing, poor thing—I made a bunch of quick phone calls. You want to have some friendly faces in the audience, right? And my agent, of course." She was sparkling and couldn't seem to stop herself from talking.

Ahuva imagined that anyone else who might be watching them must think they were very good friends. She adjusted her posture and smiled back at Maria in the friendliest way she knew how.

"I'm meeting a few people at Alfie's right now. I can't eat much between performances, so it'll just be a light bite and I probably won't stay long, but Bert'll be there. Why don't you join us?"

Maria was already on the move. Ahuva trotted behind in a happy haze. There was sure to be a pay phone in the restaurant. She'd call her parents and say she and her girlfriends had finished shopping and were going out for a burger together. That would be okay. She hoped Alfie's wasn't an expensive restaurant. She still had money in her pocket, but not a lot. She wasn't going to worry. Fate was clearly working on her side today. Everything would be fine, she assured herself, as long as nobody noticed that this Bert didn't have the faintest idea of who she was.

Hoping for the best, she trailed Maria through the dark restaurant to a large round table at the very back. Among the four or five people already seated there was the glint of a pair of John Lennon glasses above a familiar sandy mustache. Glasses and mustache reached across the table to give Maria a resounding smack on the cheek and said "Brava!" in a definitely familiar voice, and Ahuva nearly fainted with relief. Bert. Of course—Albert Gruen. She'd always privately thought of him as Al.

"Ahuva?" he said, spotting her over Maria's shoulder. "Is that really Ahuva Geffner?! Look at you!! You're a young lady!" Now grinning from ear to ear, Ahuva was the recipient of her own big kiss and after, some minor seat shuffling, squeezed in between Mr. Gruen and Maria.

Maria only stayed for an hour, just long enough for a glass of wine and a salad, but it was a perfect hour. Like Mr. Gruen...Bert...the others were friends from college days, all musicians of one kind or another. They talked about the show and the music, and of course about how well Maria had done that day. At Maria's urging, Ahuva proudly made a meticulous comparison of her and Lilith's different interpretations of the role. When she voiced her observation about the scenes with Dorn, Maria laughed loudly and called out "Ollie! Come here a sec!"

Ahuva's heart started beating presto. She hadn't noticed anything in the restaurant beyond their table. Now Oliver Blanchard was striding over, looking more elegant in jeans and a T-shirt than anyone had a right to. He bent down and kissed Maria's head, and Ahuva blushed. Were they dating?

"Hello, Gorgeous!" he said. "Everyone." His grin shot around the table and, hooking a chair from behind him, he threw himself beautifully down. "Was she perfect or was she perfect?"

"Ahuva thinks we make a more convincing pair of lovers than you and Lil," Maria said mischievously. There was no need for Maria to point her out; the blush, now doubled, had done the trick.

"Does she?" Blanchard rolled his eyes to the ceiling then snapped them down to look directly at Ahuva. "You mean the *Harold and Maude* thing doesn't work for you?" He winked and her breath stopped. "I was hoping my acting was up to the challenge."

"Oh, you're phenomenal! I mean…"

"He's teasing," Maria said. "We all kid him about the age thing."

"My agent sent me in for Medviedenko," Blanchard said. Everyone laughed. He seemed offended. "Uta thinks it's a great part for me," he insisted, "and so do I. I'm a character actor. But the directors always want me to be dashing." He said it mournfully, as if to be dashing were a disability.

"Poor you," Maria said, sliding her salad near to him. "You eating?"

He shook his head. "Too late. Picking up something to go."

"If you weren't such a good actor, I wouldn't have liked it so much the other times," Ahuva observed. "You're phenomenal with Lilith Brassloe. And I think she's phenomenal, too."

"Oh, she's incredible," Blanchard hastened to say. "I adore working with her. It's a privilege. But I think—and I'm saying this as the guy who got the job—that the show would be even better if she were playing against a contemporary. You saw it yourself," he was addressing Ahuva directly now, those blue, blue eyes drilling into hers, "what a difference it makes, if they make sense together."

The waiter arrived with a brown paper bag and handed it to Blanchard, receiving in exchange a rolled-up bill.

"Very nice meeting you," he said, reaching across to shake first Ahuva's hand and then everyone else's.

Maria rose to join him. "Sorry to run," she said, brushing kisses over all the faces at the table. "It doesn't make sense, I know, but I need extra time for this, for covering this part." There were assurances of understanding, and promises to call, and thanks on both sides—for calling and for showing up. The actors departed, and some of the ozone seeped out along with them.

"Ed's going to be so pissed he missed this," one of the other men said to Bert.

"Who's Ed?" Ahuva wondered.

"Maria's husband," Bert explained. "He's a photographer. In Portugal on a shoot. Of all weeks, right? So tell me what you've been doing? You must be what, in college already?"

"Right after Labor Day," she told him.

Coffees came for the table, and the two of them caught up on her plans, what they each knew of Byron's whereabouts (Bert hadn't heard about Amsterdam), and Bert's plan to direct *Anything Goes* as next year's junior high musical. Someone overheard and made a joke Ahuva didn't get, about Reno Sweeney. Everyone else laughed, a laugh with an edge to it. She didn't like that they might be making fun of Mr. Gruen, so she began talking very loudly about his wonderful production of *Rosebud* and, even more, about how it had meant so much to her, the first musical she'd gotten close to. *Rosebud*, a Marshall Berenson musical, that Maria had once acted in and that Bert Gruen had directed for her school, and today she came to watch a Berenson musical and there was Maria going on for one of the leads and here was Ahuva having coffee with Bert Gruen.

Absolutely Fate, she thought, as she was telling the story. For all these pieces to come together, there absolutely must be a pattern to the universe.

After calling Ellen what had to be at least a dozen times, on different days and all different times of day, Ahuva finally got through.

"I know," Ellen said. "I need to look into getting a service. I'm never in." As a matter of fact, she was that minute on her way out the door to a temp job. The best time to catch her, she suggested, was one of the afternoons that she gave to Felix Ayre. She suggested that Ahuva meet her at the office on Tuesday and they could have a good long talk while she worked.

The run-down cement-grey building, snuck in between an Irish bar and a grimy looking pizza place, wasn't what Ahuva expected from the office of a professional producer-director. She found "Ayre/Lazarus" on the tarnished brass tenant list and pressed the button. Someone buzzed the door open without asking who was there.

The lobby was the size of a bathroom, a comparison that extended to every detail—the shabby black and white linoleum that would have looked like tile if it weren't curling up along the edges; the stained green walls; the acid fug of pee. She made her way carefully up the steep, scuffed flights of stairs, hating to hold the banister but too afraid of slipping not to.

On the third floor landing, she knocked on a door that had "Lazarus Rep." stenciled on it in gold.

"Come in!" Ellen called.

Ahuva turned the fat brass knob and entered. And almost immediately screamed, because there was a body in a glass box in the middle of the room. It was a good icebreaker for two people who did and didn't know each other. Once Ellen had stopped laughing and Ahuva, still hot with embarrassment, had been told the story of the coffin, they both relaxed.

Felix was in Massachusetts, directing *You Can't Take it With You* ("give the people what they want") for the Berkshire Theatre Festival, so Ellen was trying to get through all the filing that she could never do when he was around. "The second he sees me open a file cabinet, he pulls me away to tell me a story or he comes up with an errand that has to be run right that minute," Ellen sighed with her entire body. "I think it's psychological. If there are files, it must be a business and Felix can't stand thinking of himself as a businessman. Now when I'm producing plays, you can damn well bet I'm going to think like a businesswoman! It's called Show *Business*, for fuck's sake! But try telling Felix," she sighed again.

There was a lot to file. Things went faster with Ahuva helping as they exchanged the promised gossip about The Show, so much faster that the top of Felix's desk was quickly cleared and they were able to tackle some shopping bags full of papers that were sitting out front.

"Holy shit!" Ellen said, slamming the last drawer closed for the final time. "Thank you! This is amazing! Can you stick around a little longer?" Ahuva nodded happily. It had been fascinating to hear about Lionel Rice's party and Ellen's new friendship with Joseph Beckwith. Ellen had enjoyed her story, too; she must have, to invite her to hang around. Ahuva wondered what else Ellen would tell her. Maybe they'd talk about Oliver Blanchard.

Ellen grinned and leaped to her feet. "Great! I'll go buy us a couple of beers—we've earned it." Before Ahuva could say she didn't drink, Ellen was out the door. She popped her head back in before she closed it. "If the phone rings, just pick it up and say 'Lazarus Rep' and take a message. There's a pad on the front desk."

Ahuva sat herself behind the desk, hoping desperately that the phone wouldn't ring or that, if it did, the caller would be happy to leave a message and not ask any questions she couldn't possibly answer. She slid the pad over, and put a pen next to it, at the ready. She stuck her fingers between the spirals and teased out the perforated edges of paper that were left from torn out pages. Why was it always so creepy to be alone in a room that wasn't your own? She felt the emptiness pressing down on her, invisible eyes staring at her from every angle. She centered the pad precisely on the desk and moved the pen, slanting it at a different angle and setting it on the page.

She cleared her throat. The only other sound was the ticking whir of the giant fan in the corner. This was ridiculous! Why was she sitting behind a desk when she should be walking around, exploring? Here she was, in the office of a real theatre company. It wasn't what she'd expected, but it was real. Ellen had pointed out the framed poster from the same production of *Hamlet* as the coffin. Hanging next to it was what looked like a print from an old book, which, like something in a museum, was professionally labeled "Ellen Terry and Henry Irving in *Hamlet*." It was obvious that the poster was meant to copy the print. Both showed two actors in the same pose: a fair woman in a pale gown, clutching desperately at the black velvet chest of a sharp-nosed, hollow-eyed man who stared over her head into the distance. Other walls held a few old publicity shots, also labeled, and a number of photos signed "To Felix" with various kinds of affection from a lot of actors she didn't know. So much history! She was abashed at how little she knew about theatre that wasn't musical.

Maybe this was how it was supposed to be, all the clutter and battered furniture. She didn't know what she'd imagined, but maybe this was better. This was authentic. She turned her head slowly to take in the entire room, inch by inch. Now she knew: this was how art got made, in smelly office buildings and basement clubs in Amsterdam, places that were run down enough that artists could afford to rent them.

There was no need for such places to be dirty though, as Felix Ayre seemed to agree. Ahuva ran an approving finger over the bookshelf. It was old looking and had too much carving to be attractive, but there was no dust. Overall, the office was messy, but clean. She wondered if it would be presumptuous to try and shelve the books scattered all over the, um coffee table. Probably. She could at least close them; she hated when people left books open face down, breaking the spines. She picked up the first one. It had a blue jacket with photos of actors; *Theatre World 1966-1967*. She saw where it had come from on the shelves, a rainbow of similar books almost like school yearbooks. Interesting. Flipping through this one, she saw actors' portraits, scenes from plays, and photos from parties and from what turned out to be ceremonies for a Theatre World Award. 1967 was when *The Buddy System* opened on Broadway. She started looking carefully; if there were awards, surely it must have won one! She found some pictures of the show, most of which she'd seen reproduced on the cover of the cast album, but no awards. It was disconcerting, until she turned to the front of the book and read that these awards were specifically for actors making their debuts. Maria Dearborne had made her Broadway debut in *The Buddy System*, Ahuva recalled from the *Playbill*, but as an understudy. She wondered when Oliver Blanchard had made his debut. He wasn't really very old. Maybe she'd be able to find a picture.

She was peering at the chorus of *Riding a Bicycle*, laughing at the ears sticking out on a very young Peter Beckwith, when Ellen returned.

Ellen joined her on the sofa, uncapped a couple of beers and handed her one. "Cheers!" she said, pointing her bottle in Ahuva's direction before taking a swig.

"Cheers," Ahuva replied, following suit. Her nose wrinkled against the sour smell and she swallowed fast. She had nothing against alcohol, but she didn't like the taste very much, not the sour taste of beer and not the stale taste of her father's preferred whisky. The sweet, musty taste of holiday wine was easier to take, but she couldn't say she found it enjoyable. She supposed she was going to have to learn. They said people drank a lot of beer in college. Thinking it might block out the taste, she tried not to breathe through her nose when she took her next swallow.

Watching her, Ellen laughed loudly. "You'll learn," she said, not unkindly, and passed her a box of Bugles.

Grateful, Ahuva dug out a handful and popped a few in her mouth. The salty, crunchy corn flavor overwhelmed the beer. She relaxed and tried another sip. As long as she alternated the beer with the chips, it wasn't so bad at all. "This is super, that you're working here," she told Ellen.

"It's an education," Ellen said, nodding. "I'm hoping he gets so used to having me around that when the company finally has a payroll mine'll be the first name on it." She pulled out her red box. "Like one?" she said, offering it to Ahuva. "Nat Shermans. No filter."

Both of Ahuva's parents smoked but she never had. She looked at her beer and shrugged. Why not? She took one and stuck it in her mouth. Ellen leaned forward and flicked her elegant lighter. Ahuva knew you had to suck in air to get the cigarette lit and did so as nonchalantly as possible. She was proud that she didn't cough. She could sense Ellen was waiting for a reaction. "They're different," she said, shrugging again. "I'm more used to filters."

"Most people are," Ellen said. She took a long drag, with a flourish that called attention to the heavy silver ring that took up the entire lower section of her forefinger. The stone was a rich deep blue, carved with what looked like a hieroglyphic.

"I like your ring," Ahuva said. "It is new?"

Ellen held out her hand, contemplating it with great satisfaction. "A birthday present from Harry."

"It's stunning! What kind of stone is that?"

"Lapis, I think. It had better be, for that price. It's from the gift shop at the Metropolitan. He wanted to buy me one of those chain bracelets, the ones with the birthstones. I told him it wasn't my thing; too ubiquitous."

Ahuva tucked the hand with the beer so that her wrist was less obvious. Heshy and Raisel had given her the chain of tiny aquamarine beads for her Sweet Sixteen; she thought it was pretty.

"It's a *wedjat*, of course. You know, the eye of Horus, the falcon god. *Leave the nest, break my jesses, fly away free.*" She didn't try to sing. "I'm making falcons my symbol."

Ahuva nodded, trying to pretend she'd ever considered having a personal symbol. What would hers be, if she had one?

Ellen cricked her neck to one side and yawned. "Sorry," she said, sounding more proud than sorry. "I'm hardly sleeping these days. Just no time. This will probably knock me out, but I've had so much coffee already today, I'm practically peeing brown."

"It sounds exciting," Ahuva said, because it did. The end of the cigarette felt squashy in her mouth. She had to take another sip of beer to wash away some bits of tobacco that stuck to her tongue.

"It's exhausting," Ellen said, "but it's great. I feel so alive. I wish I didn't have to go back to fucking school next month."

Ahuva shrugged. "Well, we have to."

Ellen shook her head. "You sound like Harry and Sydelle. It's a total waste of my time. Nothing they teach has any relevance. I suppose college might be fine for people who don't know what they want to do in life, but I know what I want to do. This! I learn so much more that's useful here. Even temping is better than school. But as long as I need the parents to pay the rent, I'm stuck."

That certainty reminded Ahuva of Byron, playing his piano all over Europe. She had no idea yet what she wanted to do with her life. What did that kind of certainty feel like? Was college going to help her find out, is that what Ellen meant? Should that make her happy or sad?

"Another beer?" Ellen asked. Ahuva looked at her bottle in surprise; it was empty.

"I'd better not," she said. She felt a little drifty, as if she were floating on the Dead Sea. Anyway, she'd have to leave soon. Her parents were expecting her to be home in time for dinner. Her mother had started making all her favorite meals.

Ellen opened another bottle for herself. "I may as well get comfortable. No point in going home and then having to turn around and come back down. I need to stop by the theatre before half hour. Joe likes a little, uh, pick me up, before half hour." She slid the bottle suggestively in and out of her mouth.

"Oh." Ahuva didn't know what else to say to that. The thoughts clicked together in her head. "Are you going to see The Show?"

"Not tonight. I think I'll make an early night of it and try and get some sleep. You know," she said with a sly smile. "Wednesday matinees aren't selling out. I can try and comp you—get you in for free. If you don't mind a nosebleed, that is."

"Seriously?"

"Mmmm. I could probably get you in tomorrow. Should I ask?"

"Tomorrow? That would be stellar! Sure!"

"I'll call you tonight, after I see Joe, and let you know. Give me your number again."

Ahuva couldn't believe it when the phone rang at 8:30. She still didn't quite believe it at 1:30 the next afternoon, when she spoke her name into the grill at the box office and the man with the bow tie handed her a narrow white envelope with her name, misspelled, in pencil.

As Ellen had predicted, her seat was all the way at the top of the theatre, the final row in the balcony, even higher than where she'd sat the first time. That was fine with her. She wanted to hug herself with excitement. Here she was again, seeing *Lake Song* for an unbelievable fifth time! Even more unbelievable was that it had been free. She'd never been "comped" into a theatre before. It was like being elected into an exclusive club. A couple seated a few rows below twisted their heads to look up at the ceiling and accidentally looked straight at her. She beamed back, wondering if she looked different somehow, if they could see that she had a connection with The Show.

She was so happy, almost giddy with it, even at the end when Nina goes running off into the night and Kostia kills himself. It was proof of the excellence of the show. Only art of the highest caliber could affect her so differently each time she saw it.

With all the extra stairs, it took her a while to get to the stage door. She could tell by the people comparing signed *Playbills* that some of the cast had already left. That happened with matinees, since many actors ran out with their makeup still on to grab a bite between shows. After a few minutes, when Maria hadn't shown up, Ahuva thought she must have missed her. It was disappointing, but not enough to ruin such a gift of a day. She'd write a note, she decided, and leave it with the doorman.

Kaye Victor finished signing someone's album cover and noticed Ahuva leaning against the wall to write. "Hello!" Kaye said. "You're Maria's friend, aren't you?"

Ahuva was flabbergasted. Kaye Victor had recognized her. Tony Award winning actress Kaye Victor! Not only that—Kaye Victor thought she was Maria's friend. Ahuva nodded and smiled. "I missed her," she said.

"Poor thing," Kaye said. "The lie down will do her good. That bug is killing us all. At least she still has her voice. We're going to get her some chicken soup. Odd on such a hot day, I know, but it works."

"Oh, yes," Ahuva agreed vehemently. "In my family, we think it's as good as penicillin."

"Were you leaving her a note? How sweet! I can give it to her if you like."

"Um, yes," Ahuva said. "Thank you. I was just finishing." She quickly added "I'm sorry that you're not feeling well. I hope you're better soon," and handed the note to Kaye. "Thank you so much, Miss Victor."

"Kaye," she replied, tucking the note into her pocket. "Ollie, there you are." Oliver Blanchard, looking more handsome than ever, had appeared behind her.

He nodded to Ahuva with the kind of smile you give someone who looks vaguely familiar. "Hello," he said.

"Hello," she blurted out, her voice catching a little in her throat.

"Oh, you know Maria's friend, uh…"

"Ahuva. Ahuva Geffner."

"Ahuva," Kaye repeated.

"Of course," Blanchard said, his forehead clearing. "Maria's friend. We're off to get her some soup. Are you going our way?"

Ahuva hadn't been, but she was now. She walked between them, listening to them talk the way regular people do who spend much of their time together. Once or twice she was brave enough to venture a word. At the door to Carnegie Deli, they said gave her warm smiles with their goodbyes.

Ahuva floated over to 53rd Street for the subway. "Famous People" kept spinning in her head; the nice parts that is, Nina's lines:

How can life be small or bland, when the moon is in your hand...Famous people are surrounded by a glow / Famous people; knowing all there is to know...

6 - EVERYTHING

POLINA *[spoken: Oh, for heaven's sake, go back and put on your galoshes... You shouldn't need me to tell you the damp air is bad for you. You're a doctor. Irina Nikolayevna has you so dazzled, you forget to take care of yourself.]*

DORN *[spoken: I'm 46. Too old to make a fool of myself.]*

POLINA *[spoken: A man's not old at that age. You're still very attractive to women.]*

Laughing, flirting—thought it was an endless lark.
Everything I based my life on—whistling in the dark.
Longing, hurting didn't seem to play a part.
Never dreamed I'd end at lonely gamb'ling on tomorrow,
Playing with my heart.

But everything works out for the best,
Or so they would ask us to believe.
Well, life has its mysteries I can't pretend to read.
Maybe I've everything—I just can't see.

Forward motion. Secret to a happy life;
Keeping busy every moment: busy mother, wife.
Fancy footwork, all the little things I do,
Everything I've had to juggle ever so discreetly
Making time for you.

But everything works out for the best,
Or so they would ask us to believe.
Well, life has its mysteries I can't pretend to read.
Maybe I've everything—I just can't see.

No regretting: that would be a waste of time.
Everything I did or thought of, want to claim as mine.
Sense the end now, heading for the final years.
Wish that you would see what I see: you and I together;
Everything is here.

POLINA *[spoken: Admit it, she fascinates you. You're all the same. You meet an actress and you treat her like the Queen of Sheba.]*

DORN *[spoken: Artists are rare creatures. It's natural to treat them differently. It's a kind of idealism.]*

"Tell them about your wounded bird." Joe Bigelow tipped the tonic into his third gin. The choice was either that or Scotch. Based on the empties, most of the guests seem to agree the day was too hot for whisky. Most of them needed a refill, too. With a bottle in each hand, Joe graciously made the rounds to top them off. "We spotted her in Alfie's the other day, sitting in a corner looking like one of the Orphans of the Storm. Ty recognized her from Annie Fallen's memorial and called her over. Skinny girl, a little offbeat. I want to say quaint."

"You just did," Felix Ayre observed, sucking on another slice of lime.

"Alright then, quaint," Joe confirmed. "Actually more of an owl than a bird, with those enormous round glasses."

Tyler Moss shook his head. "Don't make her a joke," he said with a smile as gentle as his voice. "She reminds me of myself at that age, trying to find a place for myself. You have no idea how hard it is to be different out in Suffolk. It's New York State out there, Joe, not New York City." Not pretending to conceal it, Tyler's lover, Andy, squeezed his hand.

"Providence isn't exactly Paris," Joe remarked. "Not when you're the lad whose big number for the local radio Amateur Hour is a rousing rendition of 'Puttin' on the Ritz'—tap included."

"Joe, you didn't! Not really!" Penelope Rice's laugh was a silver spoon bouncing off the rim of a champagne glass.

It wasn't the first time Ellen had made that observation. She came by the metaphor first hand: Sydelle was fiercely proud of her wedding silver and the Waterford.

"Honestly, Joe." Nearly camouflaged by her sand linen dress, Bronwen Davies was sitting at the same end of the long beige sofa as she'd been when Ellen arrived. Ellen had smiled nervously and, being ignored, had kept a careful distance. It was thrilling to be in the same room, even if Davies barely moved other than to sip from a glass that seemed to magically refill. She sipped again now. Her voice was the tiniest bit slurred. "Are you certain you're not queer?"

"If he is, he sure fooled me," said the blonde woman who played the bitchy socialite on that soap opera. "Not to mention a few dozen other girls I could name."

Everyone laughed.

"Joe is the type of boy I used to meet in bars in New Haven." Penelope's brother Lionel had hooded eyes that always appeared half-closed, adding a lingering flavor to his observations. Ellen made a mental note to try and copy this. "Hetero down to their toenails, but so intrigued. There was always a dark alley outside where I could satisfy their...curiosity."

Everyone laughed again, this time uncomfortably.

"I've never been that curious, Lionel. Nothing personal," Joe said smoothly. "I like exploring the half of the population that smells like flowers. Speaking of flowers..." Joe's circuit of the room had brought him to Ellen. He loomed overhead, talking directly to her breasts. She was glad she'd worn the Pucci halter top Harry's most recent girlfriend, the fashion editor, had given her for her birthday, the top you couldn't wear with a bra. "Has anyone shown you the garden?"

It was impossible to miss the garden through that wall of windows. She hadn't realized you could walk there; pretty stupid of her. Lionel Rice and Ivor Davies lived in one of those half-basement apartments where the door was huddled under the brownstone's front steps and protected by a Lilliputian iron gate. Of course the garden was theirs.

An hour or so ago, tucking a gift-wrapped bottle under her arm and lifting the gate latch, Ellen had felt she was on the brink of something momentous. "Today might change my life!" she'd thought. Then she'd turned beet red. Thank God she hadn't said that aloud! And thank God she hadn't yet rung the bell; she could wait until the blush subsided. She hated that nerves turned her into such an ingénue. She'd been so nervous today. The invitation, from Felix and Penelope, had been as surprising as it was flattering. She'd also worried that Bronwen might recognize her from the taxi incident, which was embarrassing in retrospect. She needn't have thought twice; if Bronwen had any recollection of the taxi, you'd never know it. As for the rest, it turned out that this was a "bring a person" party. Ellen was one of eight or nine young protégées, all either decorative or precociously witty. Dialogue flew as if people were hurling Noel Coward scripts at one another. The setting was, appropriately, equally precious. It was the most decorated...scratch that; the most *curated* apartment she'd ever seen. She was sitting on—more accurately, in—her father's favorite black leather Breuer sling, except that here it fit the setting. Even the glass she drank from seemed clearer and more cylindrical than any she'd drunk from before. There were several pieces of what Sydelle would refer to as "original art" and, though she couldn't make out the signature, she sensed that the gigantic double portrait on that one red wall must have been painted by someone important. As a whole, there was a combined reek of success and Art that she aspired to. When she was a producer, she was going to have parties like this in an apartment like this. With a Tony or two, like the one on the slab of black stone above what the prickle in her nose said was a functional fireplace.

Yes, she belonged in this world. If only she could get started. It was wonderful to have been taken under Penelope and Felix's wing, but she needed to be paying her dues and getting her hands dirty. She needed to be working in the theatre. Any connection would help. She took Joe Bigelow's beefy hand, letting him pull her out of the chair so that she "accidentally" pitched forward and her breasts crushed against his chest. He put an arm around her and opened the French doors.

"One of the city's unsung jewels," Joe said grandly. "Ivor says he's basing his set for Felix's *Chalk Garden* on this. But you know that. You work for Felix, right?"

She used to, she thought ruefully. She still would if she could. Why couldn't she? Why stop just because the internship was over? She'd be temping as much as possible over the summer, but she planned to continue with Barney two mornings a week: a bird in the hand, so to speak. Why not give those afternoons to Felix? She could kick herself for not thinking of it sooner! She'd learned so much from Felix already. She'd learn even more and meanwhile, he'd get so used to having her around that he'd have to give her a real job when the money came through.

Ellen gave a satisfied wriggle that Joe seemed to think was due to him. He put his arm around behind her and gave her ass a swift squeeze.

"Well now, here we go," she thought. She tilted her face to catch his. "Have I mentioned," she said, "that my birthday was three days ago? I just turned 18."

"Happy birthday," Joe said with a wink. "Is it too late for me to give you a present?"

She lowered her eyelids as much like Lionel as she could manage without having mirror practice and prayed she wouldn't blush. "I was hoping you might have a package for me," she said.

Ellen enjoyed being with Joe. Even though he was legally separated or, as he put it, "between marriages," she wouldn't call it "dating." Neither of them was looking for a relationship. There wasn't a word for what they were to one another. He called them "buddies," saying he could be honest with her the way he was to one of the guys, that she was "refreshingly unsentimental." They found each other amusing. The sex was surprisingly athletic, the couple of times they had it, though mostly there was only time to suck him off. He was barrel-chested, and his curly hairs were iron grey, but all those years as a song and dance man had given him a lot of stamina. She liked his cock: he liked that she liked it. She liked him. And talking to him was an education.

Joe had stories about everyone who was anyone in theatre: if he hadn't worked with them, he knew them and, unlike Felix, he wasn't a walking museum. One night she met him at Joe Allen's after the show and when she got home, it took her half an hour to write down the names of all the people who'd waved or stopped by to say hello. It was one hell of a list. Some of the names made Leonard's eyes pop. Ellen had recorded them in the leather book Barney bought her in Mark Cross. Ellen had a theory that all the people you knew plus all the people they knew made up a pool of influence you could dip into and pull out connections to almost anything; the trick was to keep track of who you knew and create a presence for yourself. Ellen wanted to be able to walk into a room full of theatre people and seem familiar to them, to have them assume she belonged there. Then someday, when she needed help getting something done, she'd only have to ask the right person. She wasn't about to waste any important favors, not yet, but it was a kick to take a few trial runs and feel the power. Getting Ahuva Geffner into that matinee, for example, and seeing the awe on her face—that was a rush Ellen could get used to. Ahuva was a good barometer of how far she'd come. Ahuva's fascination with *Lake Song*, her thrill at being noticed by the supporting players, was cute. Ellen could almost feel nostalgia for when she'd felt that everyone who walked across a stage was a magical creature. Certainly anyone who could earn a living acting deserved her respect, but adulation was reserved for those higher up the food chain.

Max Bulloch wasn't idol material, but he was the biggest name she'd fucked to date. Not long after his split from "Becca" (not Becky after all) Lewis, he'd spotted her with Joe and walked over to be introduced. She'd noticed Joe's smirk; she and Joe understood one another. Max claimed to have a form of stage fright, that he wasn't any good without a woman to "set him right," thus accounting for his habit of pairing off with his leading ladies and, in a successful run, ultimately working his way through much of the female cast. No doubt theirs was a highly temporary relationship, lasting only until he decided where next to fix his attention, but for now Max needed regular servicing. And because she genuinely liked him, Ellen still kept some time for Joe.

Her schedule was getting harder to juggle. There was never enough time for sleep; there were so many more interesting things to do, even if it was just talking through the day with Leonard and seeing her impressions verified or blown away by his reaction. Barney Black had gotten her some speed, but she hadn't liked the way it made her heart pound against her ribs. She preferred being exhausted, and she had no intention of missing a thing.

She'd thought about giving up Barney but, as she explained to Leonard, that would be killing the golden goose. Leonard had pointed out that it wasn't the goose that was golden but her eggs. Typical Leonard, to be so nitpicky about the irrelevant. If anything was gold, it was Barney, who might be useless as a theatre connection but was extremely useful in other ways. She'd cut down his office work to once a week, which was fine for him. He didn't much care about the filing. What he cared about was doing her against the file cabinet and watching her walk down the hall after, with that hitch in her ass from walking in pants that were heavy with his cum. Barney paid well for that little pleasure.

Felix still wasn't paying at all, but she had every reason to believe that he'd put her on the payroll once the first season's subscriptions went on sale. It almost didn't matter—the experience was priceless. If only Harry and Sydelle weren't so intent on her getting a degree. What college could teach her half of what she could learn helping start a New York theatre company? But that was the logical way of looking at it, and logic had never been part of her parents' attitude towards her. Before she'd been out of diapers, they'd been entirely invested in their picture of the world and her role in it. If Ellen had been remotely like what they'd planned, it would have been harder to break away; but they'd been so wrong it wasn't even funny. The trick was to play along just enough to keep the rent paid and a door open in case of emergency. Pity she had to waste even the little time she did in classes. It was no small feat to register the way she had for fall semester: exactly enough credits to satisfy matriculation, with as much of the week left as possible for her real education.

Ellen hadn't known you could see a professional show from the wings. Joe said technically it wasn't allowed, but he could make it happen. She thought it was his way of making sure Max wasn't elbowing him out. He needn't worry.

Joe handed her over to a stagehand who leered and squeezed her ass while helping her up an iron ladder to some scaffolding overlooking the stage. She could sit at the edge, feet dangling down, with a bar pressed securely across her midriff. She breathed deeply, relishing the backstage compound of glue, sweat, old dust and greasy makeup floating in the electrical miasma of the lighting instruments.

A muffled clatter made her turn around. A huge pair of eyeglasses crested the platform. "Hi," croaked the girl who, Ellen instinctively knew, was Tyler's baby owl. "I'm Frankie Cecchi."

"Catchy," Ellen said. She stuck out her hand to help the other girl onto the platform. "And memorable. Ellen Janow. Not so catchy. I'll just have to make people remember." It was a good line; she'd have to file it away in case she could use it again someday.

Sliding down next to Ellen, Frankie started to fold her legs under the bar. She stopped, her knees jutting at an ungainly angle from her head. "I don't want them falling off and hitting someone on the head," she explained, snaking her arms under her legs to remove her wooden clogs and set them neatly behind her. She was wearing rainbow socks with little toes, like gloves for feet.

"Have you seen the show before?" Ellen asked. When you're sharing a four-by-six foot platform with someone, you feel compelled to make conversation.

Frankie nodded happily. "A lot. But not from up here. I have this job," she confided, "with Lilith Brassloe. She said I needed a treat tonight and told Sheldon to find a spot for me."

Absorbing this information, Ellen chose to let it go without comment. "Joe Bigelow brought me. I've always wanted to see a show from the wings."

"Are you an actress, too?"

Ellen shook her head emphatically and rolled her eyes. "I'm going to produce. I work with Felix Ayre at Lazarus Rep."

"Felix Ayre? I read his memoirs last year, *To Ayre is Divine,* from the library. He's pretty smart."

Ellen felt oddly flattered that someone who knew Lilith Brassloe would be so impressed. "He is. And incredibly witty. It's going to be an amazing season."

"I read about it in *Backstage.*" Frankie's voice dripped eagerness. "*The Chalk Garden,* and something by J.M. Barrie."

"*Dear Brutus,*" Ellen supplied. "Two plays with gardens, so they can get double use out of the set. Budget, you know. And Felix and Penelope are going to do *The Chairs,* which doesn't need any set all. Just chairs," she added drily.

"They're going to need someone young to play Laurel. I already know what monologue I'm doing if there's an open call," Frankie confided.

"There's a girl in *Dear Brutus,* too," Ellen thought aloud. "But I think they'll be going with someone really young. Felix has been looking at this girl from one of the soaps."

"I'm only 19," Frankie said.

That didn't matter. To play both his imaginary daughter in *Dear Brutus* and the dark, manipulative Laurel, Felix was looking for a classic ingénue, a budding Penelope Rice. Ellen was about to abruptly change the subject when Frankie added, "I was Thierry Dupontel's Kattrin, in *Mother Courage*."

Ellen couldn't deny her interest. "I heard about his production of *Tartuffe* up in Montreal, with the mannequins. Thierry Dupontel sounds crazy!"

"He's a great director!"

"Completely original," Ellen agreed. "But a little out in left field." She didn't have any details, but she knew she'd heard his name associated with behavior even stranger than that of most directors.

"He was very nice to me." Frankie seemed about to wrap herself in a huff when the stagehand poked his head over the platform edge to shush them. It was five minutes; from this point until intermission they were sworn to total silence.

Ellen was relieved at the interruption. It was too small and public a place for an argument. She shrugged apologetically, smiled and gestured zipping her lips. Frankie politely smiled back and turned her attention to the stage

Leaning forward, Ellen crossed her arms on the bar and pillowed her chin. The position of the platform meant that the curtains masking the wings were also obscuring her view of stage right. She rummaged through her memory, trying to predict which scenes would be completely invisible. Kostia shooting the seagull, she thought; no big loss. Bits of all the ensemble numbers, but there'd still be plenty to see. A big part of "Bandaging the Wound;" now that was a shame. The curtains, she noticed, were really more like stiff velour than velvet and incredibly dusty, enough to raise a quick concern about possibly sneezing. She was high enough to see the row of tarnished gold bullion tassels across the proscenium, too. The crazy mosaic of tape on the scuffed black-washed floor showed where furniture and flats belonged when they were wheeled on. How did the crew keep track of which marks were meant for which scenes? There was only white and yellow tape, so it couldn't be the colors. She would have to ask Joe.

The actors assembled in the wings. Near her scaffold, the women of the ensemble fluffed out their skirts; from overhead it looked like a dance. The overture began, louder but less enveloping than it felt from orchestra seats. Just as Christopher Pruitt sped across from stage left, running on his toes, Lilith Brassloe took her place center stage. She smirked at him, wagged her finger and broadly pantomimed wiping lipstick from her cheek. Ellen could see him flame under his pale foundation. He rubbed his unmarked face before he slunk out of her sightline. The curtain went up.

It was nothing like watching the show from the audience. Only the music was the same. Instead of a smooth quadrille, scene melting into scene, she saw splinters of action flash by, broken by grunting stagehands pushing trolleys or people in servant costume setting a shawl over a chair or laying a table. Actors slapped on their expressions as they crossed into view, or ran for a nearly-missed cue with a mumbled "fuck" under their breath. The scaffold Ellen was sitting on turned out to be a canvas-sided booth that was used for quick costume changes. She could hear the rustling inside and was thrilled once to see Bronwen Davies sail out with her dresser still doing up the back of her gown. It was fascinating how a woman who had seemed so lost waiting for a cab and who'd practically disappeared into her brother's sofa, became so magnificently commanding on stage.

Before Ellen knew it, the horses were waiting at the gate and intermission had arrived. She was exhilarated by every wrinkle and crack she'd seen. It made the show better, more exciting. Like a student of magic, she could admire the trick even more after knowing how it was done.

Looking over, she saw some of her own excitement mirrored on Frankie's face. It seemed ridiculous not to smooth over the awkwardness. It was close quarters up here. Additionally, she didn't want to alienate the first working actor she'd met who was her own age, a person who had already worked with someone as big as Thierry Dupontel. They were both starting their careers; maybe someday they'd be famous and working together. Another thing they had in common was that they'd both made friends on *Lake Song*. She had Joe and Max, and Frankie had somehow become a much bigger fish than when she was Tyler's orphan.

"So," Ellen ventured, "you work for Lilith Brassloe?"

Frankie smiled. She wanted to talk, too. "Uh huh. I'm helping her with her scrapbooks. She's got a lot of old ones that need fixing, and she hasn't kept anything up to date since...well, for years. She's got boxes and boxes of pictures and clippings and things."

"How did she find you?"

"It's funny coincidence. Months ago I made a scrapbook for Bronwen Davies. I'm a big fan, ever since I was little. After I saw the show the first time, I wanted to make her a present. I like making things. So I made this album. Tyler Moss—he's kind of a friend of mine—he saw it in her dressing room and read my name in the front. He knew Lilith needed help and I was looking for a part-time job that I could fit in around auditions, so he brought me to meet her. And that was it."

"Are you majoring in theatre?" Frankie's glasses flashed question marks. "In school," Ellen clarified.

"I graduated last June," Frankie said. "We don't have majors out on the Island. Where did you grow up?"

Ellen laughed. "Queens. I meant in college."

"Oh, I'm not going to college. I've always known I want to be an actress. You don't need to get a college degree to do that."

Ellen fervently agreed. People who were going to college to act or paint or whatever were only going because they had parents like hers and had to. "So where are you studying? HB? Stella Adler? Neighborhood Playhouse?" These were the only ones she knew by name, just enough to keep her from sounding like...what did they say in *The Hollywood Reporter*? A "civilian."

Frankie was momentarily flustered. "I have a voice coach," she responded. "And I've been looking into dance teachers. I need to get my singing and dancing stronger before I start auditioning for musicals."

"You're not in an acting class?" That was surprising. Ellen had heard plenty of employed actors, even members of the *Lake Song* cast, talk about keeping up with their workshops.

"I was at NYADA," Frankie explained. "But it didn't make sense. They don't teach you, they just try to fit you into their mold. The only reason people stay is because of the LORT audition when you graduate. I've already got my Equity card, so I decided what was I waiting for?"

Ellen was impressed. This girl had managed what she hadn't, namely dropping out of school. "What's your schedule like? We should meet and hang out."

Like a handshake, they exchanged answering service numbers. Ellen had to tear a scrap of paper out of her calendar for Frankie, who'd left her bag in Lilith's dressing room.

Climbing down the ladder after the show, they made a tentative date for coffee the next week. As Frankie disappeared to pick up her things, Ellen could hear her greeted with familiarity and affection.

Joe had said to wait for him outside. She did her spy thing, standing within view of the stage door but away from the crowd, seeing what information she could pick up. Becca Lewis came out with Chris Pruitt. They weren't touching, but Ellen saw how adoringly he looked at her. When someone gave Becca flowers, he relieved her of a dance bag so she could carry them. Aha, so that's what Lilith's little pantomime was about. They didn't seem to be "together," but it was easy to see he wanted to be. She wondered what Max thought of that. As if his name had summoned him, like Mephistopheles in *Dr. Faustus* (which she and Leonard had caught by skipping their classes one day), Ellen could hear Max's distinctive rumbling chuckle. She pulled back into the shadows to avoid being seen; it wasn't his night and she was in no mood to deal with him. She needn't have worried. He was immediately surrounded by a group of overdressed theatre patrons, who he seemed to expect. He was so busy playing to his claque that he wouldn't notice Ellen if she was standing right in front of him. Well, maybe if she was standing there naked...

Everything went black and she jumped a foot.

"Was it fun?"

She'd been so diverted that Joe had taken her completely unaware. Laughing, he removed his hands from her eyes. She punched his arm and he laughed some more.

"Yes it was fun. And I met Tyler's owl girl."

"Wounded bird," Joe corrected. "And she's Lil's now."

"And me?"

"You're still mine. Max is..." his voice trailed off and he looked guilty. "Well, you know about Max. He's a dog."

"He's a pig," she said coolly, knowing it would please him. In fact, Max was a pig. Hung like a horse, as she'd suspected, but he was the only one who got the benefit of it. Plus, his personal hygiene was nil. Like family dinners, his appeal was greater at a distance. As much as she enjoyed getting down and dirty, Ellen had learned that grime repulsed her. Max's feet were particularly gross, thick yellow callouses and nails like slabs of dirty horn; fortunately she hardly ever had to see them. But he was Max Bulloch. On stage he was sex on the hoof and, to those who didn't know better, he was a notch in her belt. "He's useful," she told Joe. "And it won't be for long."

Joe gave her the look she loved getting most, from any source: a mixture of affection, admiration and a little trepidation.

"I need a drink," she reminded him.

7 - ANYTHING

DORN

Anything I said, well they already knew it.
Anything I did, well anyone could do it.
Never did I ever think I was unique or that
It would be hard to fill my place,
Or I did more than take up space.
But this does not disturb the comfort of my days.

Yes, I'm lacking that odd passion
Other people have for life.
Or maybe that strange longing
That makes others sure they are alive.
But no specific concrete thing,
No dream I could devise
Is/was strong enough to make me feel . . .
Not anything.

Anything I got, too easily I'd surfeit.
Anything I lost, too comfortably was forfeit.
Never was there anything I felt was so important
That I'd work that hard to get it
Or I'd miss it if I lacked it
Or I'd think about with more than mild regret.

Except maybe that odd passion
Other people have for life.
Or maybe that strange longing
That makes others sure they are alive.
But no specific concrete thing,
No dream I could devise
Is/was strong enough to make me feel . . .
Not anything.

Summer passed more quickly than Frankie had expected and wasn't nearly as bad as she'd feared. Every few Saturdays, she took the train into the city and tried to second act some matinee. She always ended up at the stage door of the Regale, where Joe Bigelow and Tyler Moss gave her a big enough hello to buoy her spirits for days. Once Tyler got her into a preview of a musical revue some friend of his was doing downtown. They were "papering" the house, he explained. Early on in a run, there's a risk that people who buy tickets will find it disturbing to see empty seats around them. No matter how good the show is, this psychologically smells like failure. One way to ensure that the show feels like a success is to give away free tickets to people whose enthusiasm can be counted on. Frankie had genuinely enjoyed that show. She would probably have liked it even if she'd had to pay. She said as much afterwards to Tyler's friend Andy, making him laugh a lot.

Camp filled the weekdays nicely. It was even kind of fun, teaching the kids songs and helping them improvise little skits. She put together a talent show in July. It was enough of a success that she wrote a short musical for August, stealing the story from a Madeleine book and using songs the kids already knew. Everyone had a lot of fun. The parents were so pleased that, to her surprise, they tipped her. A few said that if she had an after-school class this fall, they'd be happy to sign their children up. She told them she was considering it.

She did consider it. She had to. One night, when Mickey was in his best mood after a date with Eunice, she summoned up the courage to tell him she wasn't going back to NYADA. If she told him the complete truth, he'd have plenty to say about how maybe now she'd give up on her stupid dreams and do something sensible, like go to secretarial school. She wasn't about to do that, so she told him she was dropping out of the program because it was a waste of money. Reminding him about *Mother Courage* and her Equity card, she explained that NYADA was for raw beginners, that she was well past what they had to offer. As if it were the preferred professional route, she laid out a plan to take singing and dancing lessons in the city while getting out and auditioning for real work. She'd picked her time, and her battle, wisely.

Mickey, half asleep already, heard her out without exploding. "Just don't expect me to be paying for anything," he grunted. "Until that acting starts to pay off, you're gonna hafta find some way to pay your own way. You always got a roof over your head with me. You're my only kid, after all. But for all that other crap, that's up to you."

She gave him a kiss on the cheek and watched him haul himself beerily up the stairs. Then she sank into the old rocking chair that had been her mother's and felt the worst of the worries lift from her shoulders. Pop knew she wasn't going back to school and the world hadn't come to an end. She'd find a job. She'd find as many jobs as she had to. It wouldn't be for long, after all. She'd gotten her first acting job without even trying. Now that she was a professional and giving it her full attention, she'd be back on stage before she knew it!

Next day she went around to the Curl Up and Dye. The owner, a friend of Martha's, had trimmed Frankie's hair since her first baby bangs. Rhoda always needed extra help, especially from people who didn't want to be hairdressers. She was glad to have Frankie on Saturdays, which were busiest, and Tuesday mornings, when her daughter taught at the mortuary science school. With that settled, Frankie started asking around the churches to see how much it would cost to rent a room for a couple of hours after school once a week. If she could charge five bucks a class per student, six kids would be enough to cover the rent and leave her with more than she'd make from babysitting for the same two hours. If she got eight or even ten kids to sign up, she'd be doing great.

As proud as she was of her many arrangements, Frankie was even prouder that she was explaining them to Donny Hopkins. It had taken almost as much nerve for her to call him as it had to tell Mickey she was leaving school.

She'd been so disappointed not to hear a peep out of him all summer. She understood how busy he must be, up in the Adirondacks, but she missed him. He was her first real theatre friend, so talented and, yeah, cute. With months to think about it, she also could admit that she had a little crush on him. And he liked her enough to tell her things, not only the theatre things that everyone talked about but personal things about his ex-girlfriend Linda. Still, he knew so many people that he probably didn't have room in his life for Frankie Cecchi.

She waited until the week before NYADA would be starting up again, thinking the message through carefully so that she wouldn't sound pathetic. "Just making sure the people in the office gave you your sheet music," is what she dictated to the operator at his service, along with her number. "Sorry I wasn't able to give it to you in person. Let's keep in touch. Frankie."

He called her back that same night. Yes, he'd gotten the envelope; but things had been so crazy, what with leaving for Long Lake and everything. He felt terrible that he hadn't called before now. What assholes they were at NYADA! It wasn't the first time those morons showed they wouldn't know talent if they stepped on it. She shouldn't take it to heart. He'd been wanting to tell her that all summer; he would have written her except he never had her address. She felt warm all over.

They arranged to meet at Howard Johnson's. Over a malt and a shared plate of fries, she poured it all out: everything about camp, Tyler and Joe, her job at the salon, teaching kids, and the lessons she was planning to take. It was so good to talk to someone who understood!

Donny agreed that with her sense of humor and funny speaking voice, musical comedy was a promising target. "You could be the next Carol Burnett," he speculated. If his schedule weren't so full, he'd coach her himself. A private club on the East side had hired him to be musical director for their fall production, a Jerome Kern review. It was bound to be pretty awful and the salary was only an honorarium, but the committee chairman had reeled off an impressive list of names who'd launched their careers by working there; the club's members were known to invest in shows. Donny expected to get some valuable contacts out of the experience.

As soon as the show was over, he promised, he'd start working with Frankie on her voice. She shouldn't worry about the cost; he'd keep it low, as a friend. He could also recommend a few dance studios. Since most shows now hired only one chorus to do everything, dancing was as important as singing. Donny didn't mean to be discouraging, but he didn't think Frankie would be able to compete with people who'd been dancing from the time they learned to walk. Tap, on the other hand, was almost a lost art. *No, No Nanette,* during a more successful run than anyone had expected, had used up every tapper in town and there were never enough for all the summer theatre productions of *Anything Goes* and *Dames at Sea.* If Frankie started now, by the next time tap got hot on Broadway she'd be as good as anyone else.

Frankie felt her world settling into a proper shape again. She listened, wrote things in her notebook, and glowed. She didn't know how to thank him.

"Just work hard and make me proud." He winked, making her blush. "And once you start taking singing lessons from me, you're going to have to cut out the malteds. Chocolate and dairy coat your vocal chords. First lesson free!" he joked.

In the years since her mother's death, Frankie had forgotten nearly all she'd learned about Christian Science, but she still believed in the power of positive thinking. Maybe it couldn't cure cancer, but it there was no doubt it made a difference in other things. Look at how her life had started coming together once she stopped moping about NYADA. She had eleven students for her after-school acting class—eleven! Between that and the beauty salon, she had enough money to take the train into the city three days every week to knock on agents' doors and go to whatever open calls were posted on the Equity bulletin board. To her delight, Equity sometimes had free tickets to distribute: "papering," she observed, with the wisdom of experience. She continued her education as she always had, seeking out books and reading plays. With more time to poke around the Lincoln Center library, she discovered the Spoken Word section: Shakespeare recorded for radio, Dylan Thomas reading *Under Milkwood*, famous actors reading famous books; she was astonished to find an old recording of Bronwen Davies reading *Alice in Wonderland*.

Frankie tried to stay away from the Regale. She'd come in soon after camp was over, planning to treat herself to a standing room ticket, and had run into Tyler and Joe at Alfie's. They offered to slip her into the box again. Tyler had to stop by the drug store for the prescription that helped his end of season allergies, so it was only Joe who walked her through the stage door. Wally the doorman, who'd been so nice before, smirked and mumbled something she didn't hear. Joe laughed it off, but she could tell he didn't like it. It made her feel dirty.

It was silly though, wasn't it, to let a nasty smirk keep her from saying hello to her friends? After a couple of weeks, she gave in and stopped by on a Wednesday, as the matinee was letting out.

Tyler saw her at once and gave her a big wave. "Stay there!" he called.

The matinee ladies, craning impatiently for a glimpse of one of the big stars or Oliver Blanchard, had overlooked him until then. A bunch turned sharply to stare at Frankie, then turned back to Tyler with fresh interest, suddenly holding out their *Playbills* for his autograph. By the time he made his way over to her, Frankie's self-consciousness had subsided.

"Just the girl I was looking for!" he twinkled, putting his arm through hers and leading her down the street. "I'm picking up my salad. Walk with me?"

She already was. She could tell they were on their way to Alfie's.

"So my dear, are all your day jobs working out for you? How are you fixed for spending money?"

"Fine," she said. He already knew the details.

Tyler squeezed her arm and continued what he wanted to say. "Well, an actor can always use a few dollars more, yes? I have a proposition for you. You make scrapbooks, don't you?"

Frankie stopped short, her heart making a painful thud against her ribs. How did he know?

"No, I'm not psychic. Eyes back in head, my dear." He pushed her glasses gently with the tip of his finger. "It happens I noticed a sample of your work in our Bron's dressing room. Coincidentally—and quite a lucky coincidence I think—Lil's been griping for ages about getting her papers in order. It's in her will, you see, ever since the Hasty Pudding, to hand them over to Harvard. And life being what it is, she's decided she'd rather hand them over when she's alive, preferably at a grand champagne reception. I told Lil I might know the perfect little elf to help her. It would only be a few hours a week. That's about the limit of Lil's attention span. Interested?"

Frankie didn't need a mirror to know her eyes were shining. How exciting, to work for Lilith Brassloe!

Tyler laughed. "I take it that's a yes? Lil can be a little, uh, careful about money. I thought I'd better suggest a price to her. Would $5.00 an hour suit?"

Frankie nodded. Two hours work would earn her a balcony seat in any theatre on Broadway. In her heart, she knew she'd probably have done it for free. She trotted happily at Tyler's side, hardly noticing the steps even though she was wearing her platform sandals. She followed him back to the theatre, right past the snooty Wally, to Lilith Brassloe's dressing room.

The room was smaller than Frankie expected. She would later learn it was one of the two largest in the theatre. This had put Max Bulloch's nose out of joint, but there was nothing his agent could do. Bronwen Davies was the star of the show and, though Max was the leading man, people all over the world knew Lilith Brassloe's distinctive gravelly voice. Her name on the marquee sold tickets, therefore Dressing Room 2, with the private toilet and an alcove large enough to fit a brocade-draped daybed, belonged to Lil.

Lilith Brassloe lounged on that daybed, looking like every actress ever portrayed on stage or screen. She was wrapped in what appeared to be a Japanese silk kimono, a purple turban covering her wig cap. Propped up by fat velvet cushions, an equally fat marmalade cat curled in her lap, she sipped broth from a china bowl.

While Tyler did the talking, Frankie had plenty of time to look around. Other than the size, the room was perfect. The old trellis-print wallpaper, reminiscent of the department store powder rooms that Frankie often used in the course of a long, peripatetic day, was nicely obscured by framed theatre cards for *Riding a Bicycle, Last Gas Before Highway*, and other of the actress's successes. Shoeboxes, covered over with bright Con-Tact paper, sat atop a genuine steamer trunk. A few large vases were crammed with such a mix of flowers that they must have been brought to the stage door by her fans.

Scattered all around were mascots and snow globes and, probably in honor of Polina's penchant for gambling, decks of cards; a clutter of treasure everywhere except the counter that served as dressing table. That was neat as a pin, with the pots and sticks and brushes set out on a cloth as clean and white as an operating room on TV. Rather than the familiar Steins, the makeup labels were Max Factor or the very British Leichner. Standing sentinel were the two wigs from the play: Act I's overly-youthful flirty ringlets and the more sober, grey-streaked Act II. Someone had drawn a clever caricature on one of the wig stands. The frame around the mirror bristled with telegrams, cards and photos.

Frankie was so fascinated, she lost track of why she was there until Tyler called her name. His voice was a little sharp. It must not have been the first time he'd said it. She blushed. "I'm sorry, Miss Brassloe. I'm just so excited to be here. This is a big honor."

The actress smiled. "Tyler tells me you've agreed to be my little elf."

Frankie got chills down her spine. That voice! Any time she heard it, even from the stage, a lifetime of movies and television shows spooled through Frankie's head. To think it was speaking directly to her! Her own throat was too dry to speak. She could only nod.

"Wonderful! I dare say you'll have your work cut out for you. I'm rather a packrat."

"I don't mind," she managed to croak. "It'll be so interesting."

Lilith Brassloe laughed. It was a wonderful laugh to hear in a tiny room. "Thank you, dear heart. I hope you feel the same once we're underway. Do you think perhaps that might be as soon as tomorrow? I find I'm suddenly chomping at the bit. Tyler's finding you must be a sign. Noon would suit me admirably."

Frankie nodded, trying not to burst with excitement. Positive thinking had done it again! She was actually going to be working for Lilith Brassloe. Even Pop would be impressed: not only was she famous, she was an absolutely capital-B Broad.

The actress scrawled an address on a piece of paper and pressed it into Frankie's hand with a lovely smile. "Until tomorrow then."

Understanding she'd been dismissed, Frankie ducked her head and backed out of the room. As she passed Tyler Moss, she whispered her thanks.

"Don't thank me yet," he whispered back. "You don't know what I've gotten you into!"

As Tyler had said, it was only a few hours a week. They decided on Thursdays. Lil, as Frankie was asked to call her, liked a couple of extra hours of sleep after the two Wednesday shows. Frankie showed up at noon, in time for Lil's breakfast, which was her lunch. They'd work until three, then have tea before Lil took the little nap that she said she needed at her age to rest up for the evening performance. Frankie could stay and finish up the pages she was working on, as long as she closed the door very quietly when she left.

Lil's apartment in the Apthorp was a lot like her dressing room: small and crammed with things and memories. Lil had moved into the historic building during her first New York engagement after the War and had hung onto the place ever since. She also had the flat in London that she'd taken after her husband died, not far from her son Martin's. When she worked in Los Angeles, she stayed in hotels or, in recent years, with her dear old friend Coral Browne. "I would never want to live there myself," she confided. "Still, it seems to suit Coral down to the ground and I do enjoy the sunshine and luxury when I'm there."

Coral Browne had played Vera Charles in the movie of *Auntie Mame*. Frankie loved these casual references to people and places she only knew from magazines. She also loved knowing things before seeing them in print. Like the Actor's Fund concert that Lil was participating in. It was a one-night-only Tribute to Marshall Berenson, with dozens of Broadway stars slated to be on stage: not only Lil and Bronwen Davies and a lot of the rest of the *Lake Song* cast, but people like Bea Arthur and Hal Linden and Jerry Orbach and Barbara Cooke. Listening to Lil tell about the rehearsal was almost as good as being there. Which she never could be: it was one night only, with tickets going for as much as $150!

The only surface large enough for them to spread out papers was the kitchen table. Because it was the kitchen, Lil kept trying to feed her. There were eggs for breakfast, with bacon and toast and sometimes, if Lil was feeling especially British, a fried tomato. Frankie always felt as if she were watching it on a screen: Lilith Brassloe scrambling eggs and the two of them eating together from the chipped Spode plates with the birds. Tea, only a few hours later, came with cookies—biscuits, Frankie learned to call them—and bread-and-butter-and-cucumber sandwiches. It was strange to bite down on a sandwich and crunch a piece of cucumber, but once she got used to it, she thought it was pretty good.

As well as feeding her, Lil occasionally gave her presents. They were gifts someone else had given her that she didn't want, but it was still incredibly nice. Frankie especially liked a genuine Vera scarf, a big silk square with red and orange swirls. It was probably very expensive, but Lil insisted she would never wear it herself.

The work was fascinating, a gift in and of itself. There were papers so old and yellow that Frankie was almost afraid to touch them: stage bills and newspaper clippings from when Lil was still a child, performing on the musical hall stage with her parents; notes from people like Noel Coward and Winston Churchill. A letter from Leslie Howard—the actual Leslie Howard, Ashley Wilkes himself—upset Lil so much that she had to stop for the day. Tyler was a little wrong about one thing: the only reason Lil didn't want to work too long was because she got so emotional going over the past.

One night, after they'd finished a particularly fat scrapbook of 1950 through 1954 (the year, as it happened, that Frankie was born), Lil decided Frankie deserved a little celebration and arranged for her to see *Lake Song* from the wings. Lil didn't walk her past Wally: she stopped and told him coolly that Frankie was her guest and that Sheldon, the ASM, would be taking care of her. Like everyone else, Sheldon did whatever Lil asked. Of course he would take good care of Frankie.

He led Frankie to a small scaffold that turned a bit of stage right into an onstage dressing room. She could sit up there, he explained. All she had to do was keep completely quiet during show time, so the overhead mikes didn't pick her up. He'd come and get her when the show was over.

Glad she'd left her coat in Lil's dressing room, Frankie tried not to trip on the hem of her skirt as she made her way up the ladder. If she'd known in advance, she would have worn pants. Definitely sneakers. Clomping up the ladder, her wooden clogs sounded like bowling pins.

Suddenly, there was a face looking down at her. A clever face with a sharp nose. If Frankie hadn't been holding on so tight to the rails, she would have fallen. She managed to blurt out a hello and her name. The other girl leaned over and stuck out a hand to help her.

"Ellen Janow," she said, with a flourish of her curly head.

8 - MOSCOW

ARKADINA

Everything is green here—not like
   Moscow,
And the air is clean here —not like
   Moscow.
But my lungs are only free
When they breathe the air my eyes
   can see,
And never do they breathe as easily
As when they breathe the air of
   Moscow.

I can hear the birds call as they glide
   low;
Most of them are seagulls, and they
   croak so.
I am fond of wildlife
After it has met the butcher's knife.
When I said I'd "play *The Country
   Wife*"
I meant on stage, in Moscow.

When it comes to exercise,
I like to hobble on the cobbles of the
   city streets.
How I miss the civilized
Routine of window shopping,
   stopping somewhere for my tea—
Somewhere where clover doesn't
   grow.

I should be so thankful, let my cares
   go.
Here it is so tranquil; days are so
   slow
Every hour feels like five
Lingering about the countryside.
You'll wonder at the years you stay
   alive
In one brief holiday from Moscow.

When we're playing cards in the
   gazebo
I look out on a garden and a
   meadow,
But the flowers don't amaze—
Not until they're plucked and well
   arranged,
Or thrown down as a curtain call
   bouquet
By the swooning fans in Moscow.

Turning to the amorous,
I find it disconcerting flirting in
   Arcadia;
Surely not as glamorous,
But quite exotic and hypnotic as
   Arabia
And twice as foreign to my soul.

Days are sweet and balmy—not like
   Moscow;
Starlit nights disarm me. Still I don't
   know:
What the good's a moonlit lake
When I'm too damned bored to stay
   awake?
I rise at dawn and yawn and long to
   take
The first train back to Moscow!

There were only ten days left before her parents would be driving Ahuva up to school and the nearer they got to seeing her off the closer they seemed to want to hold her. Next Saturday was part of Labor Day weekend and the Geffners were talking about going to the beach as a family. That made this the last free Saturday. So many lasts. Ahuva had already had last get-togethers with friends whose schools started earlier, and the traditional last sundae at Jahn's. With all the haircuts and doctors and packing and plans by her parents, today was probably the last day she would be able to use any way she wanted. And the minute she got out of bed in the morning, she knew what she wanted to do: she had to see The Show one last time—one really last time.

With an air of ceremony, Ahuva ate a single egg and two triangles of toast. She showered and carefully blew her hair dry, then stepped into the blue and white cotton dress she'd worn under her gown at graduation. She held herself in an almost tangible bubble of silence, even in the subway. Walking up the steps to the street, she proceeded to the Regale with the deliberate pace of a bride. The box office had one seat left, in the front row, and she had enough money to buy it.

She only had to sit a little taller in her seat to be able to watch the orchestra tune up. When the overture began, the swell of sound seemed to come up through her bones. Sitting so close, she could see things she'd never noticed before: tape marks on the stage, where the changing sets came to rest; a flurry in the wings just before an actor's entrance; the texture of the scrim in the opening number as it was cut with light. Yet with this closeness she felt an enormous distance, as if she were watching from the other side of a telescope, giving the performance the alien elegance of a clockwork toy. Somewhere in the back of her brain, she could feel every instant being recorded.

It was over too quickly. She let the auditorium empty before she stood, slowly and deliberately, and made her way to the doors. The sunlight was an intrusion. She headed automatically for the stage door.

Something broke through the shell she'd wrapped around the day: Oliver Blanchard, the sun raising a halo above his hair, was posing for a picture. She didn't think she could bear to watch. It was better to remember the play as a play, not to come too close. She didn't want to think that she'd soon be hours away, that by the time she might return here they would have forgotten her.

A giggling old lady grabbed Ollie's arm to get his attention and he turned. As he did, his eyes met Ahuva's and he waved. She smiled and waved back. Then she averted her eyes and, as briskly as she could in her good sandals, she walked away.

In the spots where there were trees, upstate was pretty. Everywhere else, it was just like Valley Stream: bald, ugly strip malls; borning signs on cinderblock walls sitting on smack on the highway, without even a tree-lined sidewalk. The buildings looked almost identical; it was a wonder that people didn't constantly turn into the card store on the way to the dry cleaners. Ahuva wanted to sing with relief when they drove through a small town with actual streets and buildings older than she was. Maybe she was a little artistic after all.

That would be a nice discovery for this adventure. She was on her way to college, to find out who she was and see new sights. *To soar to the ends of the earth.* That's what college was all about, right? The thought cheered her in the face of her mother's regular sniffs and her father's fake high spirits. She knew they were fake; every time she caught sight of him in the rear view mirror, his smile was frozen tight.

Ahuva was Jakub's only child. She was his only family, period. She'd been named Ahuva—"beloved"—in memory of the family who'd died in Theresienstadt. The individual names of everyone the Nazis had stolen from him would have been a list as long as the Megillah, and Jakub understood prudence. Prudence was how he'd stayed in the Czech Army until almost the last possible moment, holding his tongue and pretending everything was fine until the day he "got lost" during a training exercise in the forest and bolted. It was how he'd stayed alive—prudence, a gift for languages and considerable charm—making his miraculous way through the Italian Alps to Switzerland, and from there, all the way across the English Channel to safety. Not that anywhere on that side of the Atlantic was truly safe during the War. The safe haven was America. Which is why, years after, having built a good life in Israel with a wife, a business and warm circle of friends, when his child was finally born he told Malke that he wanted to emigrate. It took nine years to cajole her, to convince her to leave her own siblings, alive and safely resettled, and move to a new country with a language that felt uncomfortable in her mouth.

Their friends Heshy and Raisel had moved to New York to be closer to Raisel's only surviving sister, miraculously located in 1962 through a registry at Yad Vashem. Heshy wrote to say there was a store near his shoe repair, a place where local people stopped to get their newspapers and cigarettes and sweets. It was a good business, just the thing for someone as sociable as Jakub. The Irishman who owned it was old and tired, and none of his boys wanted to take it over. Jakub and Malke would like Queens. There were a lot of *lantzmen* to play cards and schmooze with, and with him and Raisel nearby, it would be like home almost at once. And there were good schools; Heshy knew how Jakub felt about education.

Jakub wore Malke out with arguing until she agreed that he could spend the money to go over and take a look. She hoped he'd change his mind. She should have known better. Jakub never saw the dirty streets or the dark rooms, so different from the bright, modern life they had in Jaffa he saw what he wanted to see. He charmed the old Irishman—Heshy joked they were two of a kind. Leaving his friends to find them a place to live, Jakub returned home, laden with presents from MACY*S, a store Malke had only ever seen in the movies, and told her to start packing. Ten months after their tearful departure from Jaffa, the UAR mobilized forces along the border in the Sinai Peninsula, setting off the events that would become known as the Six-Day War. Secure in their stuffy apartment, the Bank Leumi calendar dangling reproachfully over the kitchen table, the Geffners felt like traitors. Tucking Ahuva into her safe, quiet bed, Jakub felt a knob of guilty peace warming the deepest part of his heart; he couldn't afford any more losses in this lifetime.

Ahuva knew it was tearing him apart to send her away. He'd hoped she would go to City College. This time it had been Malke doing the convincing. Malke hadn't been much older than Ahuva when she'd left Erdély to be a *kibbutsnik*. Only now did she understand how hard it must have been for her parents to let her go; but it had to be done; a girl had to leave home to find herself and become a woman. Ahuva was shocked to find herself in agreement with her mother on anything, especially with her father on the opposite side. Nervous as she was at the prospect, going away made college seem more real; City College would be like high school all over again. In the end, his eyes fixed carefully on the brimming ashtray, his fingers blindly adjusting the flowered corners of the plastic tablecloth, Jakub had to concede defeat. As much as he needed to have his child with him, his greatest purpose was to give her everything she needed to succeed in life and he had been persuaded that leaving the nest was part of this.

Today in the car, they tried to pretend the family was on vacation; that Ahuva wasn't sandwiched between the pile of linens from her bed, her portable stereo and her precious box of LPs; that the trunk wasn't crammed with her suitcases, and cartons of other things she couldn't bear to leave behind; that Malke and Jakub wouldn't be on the road again in just a few more hours, speeding down I-95 back towards Queens, alone.

Campus was bigger than any of them had expected, a small city teaming with frantic activity. They were waved down with a red felt flag and someone handed them a map through the window. Jakub had the boy show him

Ahuva's dorm on the map, repeating the instructions carefully while Ahuva, mysteriously mortified, slumped in the back seat.

It took some doing to find a parking spot. The lot was packed with cars, spewing luggage and boxes and stick lamps and sporting equipment…and people. Dozens, maybe hundreds, of people; an ant-like stream, shifting burdens from the cars to the red brick tower.

Wanting to make a good first impression, Ahuva had chosen to wear her new corduroy pants and the plaid shirt in her lucky color. She'd expected September to be colder this far north. When she was finally able to climb out of the car, she did her best to ignore that everything was sticking uncomfortably to her skin. At least it wasn't sticking where it showed; and the style was sufficiently like what other people were wearing. There were certainly enough people available for comparison.

A young man in a Rolling Stones T-shirt, the one with the tongue, approached them. His name, he said, with a firm handshake for Jakub, was Mike. He was an RA in the dorm, a Residence Assistant, which meant he was there to answer questions and give advice. Ahuva saw Jakub write the name on a matchbook and tuck it into his shirt pocket. She wanted to duck behind her pillows all over again. It didn't fluster Mike; maybe lots of freshman parents did that. He found Ahuva's name on his clipboard and gave her a friendly grin. Her roommate hadn't arrived yet, he said. She should hurry on upstairs and snag the better bed.

"How do you know which one is better?" She blurted it out before she could think twice.

Mike grinned again. "Whichever one you want is the better one. Right? Here, let me get some of the guys to help with your stuff." He put his fingers in his mouth and gave a loud whistle. Two more boys came bounding across the parking lot, wearing similar healthy smiles and rock-n-roll T-shirts. Should she worry that she didn't have any band T-shirts or was it only a guy thing? If anyone asked her, what bands should she say she liked? She was glad for the headphones that Hope and Howie had given her for graduation. If the music she liked wasn't cool enough to fit in, no one had to know.

Before she had time to say "Hi," the strange boys had fished her bundles out of the back seat and were heading towards the dorm. She thanked Mike again and started running to catch up. Friends had warned her, but it was still a surprise to see that a room about the size of her own room at home was meant to be shared by two girls. It had bare cream walls, and wooden tiles in an up-and-down V pattern across the floor. Probably the nicest feature was that the window looked out on grass and trees, not the parking lot. There was a bed on either side of it; honestly she didn't see much to choose between them.

The blonder guy let her pile of linens plop heavily onto the mattress to her left. "You want this one." He jerked a thumb over his shoulder.

Swiveling her head to follow, she immediately saw what he meant. The other bed was the one you saw the minute you opened the door. The one he'd picked for her had a little more privacy, at least from the hallway.

"Thank you," she said, but he was already out the door. She sat on the edge of the bed—her bed now, she supposed—not sure what she was should do next.

"Hi! Should I put this here?" The second boy was about to set her stereo atop the low chest of drawers that stood at the foot of her bed. "That's what most people do."

"Okay," she said, quickly adding "Thanks. Thanks a lot!"

"De nada," he smiled. "That's what a welcoming committee is for.'

"I didn't know there would be a welcoming committee."

"Not officially. It's just what some of us do. Help out the incoming freshmen, the way people were here to help us. It's mostly the football team, since we have to be here a week early anyway."

She stared in awe. A football player! She certainly felt like she was in college now. Her high school had only managed to field a team for basketball; the yard wasn't big enough for anything else. "What, um, position do you play?" She hoped that was enough of a question to ask. She didn't know the first thing about football. It wasn't a game that Jakub and his friends followed.

"Oh, I don't play. I'm the assistant business manager. It's my campus job. I was lucky to get it. I'm a business major, you see."

"I'm going to study math, I think. Are there a lot of campus jobs?" Ahuva was glad the subject had come up. State university tuition was modest, but she was conscious that room and board made it a lot more expensive than staying home. She didn't want to have to keep asking her parents for spending money.

"There should be some information in your orientation packet." Until he pointed it out, she hadn't noticed the two fat white envelopes in the basket stuck to the door. One had her name on it. "Or else, you can ask Mike later. That's the kind of thing he's supposed to tell you guys. Listen, I'm going back down to help your folks. You just stay here and try and wrap your head around it, okay? It's a lot, the first day."

She'd only had time to realize that she'd have to share a closet, before her mother arrived. Clutching the old-fashioned train case that she'd given Ahuva to use for toiletries, Malke took a tentative step over the threshold. Her eyes darted into every corner of the bare little room. She took a deep sniff of Pinesol and ran a finger along the side of the chest of drawers.

"It's clean," she said, with grudging approval. "We should make your bed, so it shouldn't look so strange."

Ahuva jumped at the suggestion. Anything to make it seem like someone could maybe live here. She moved the pile to the other bed and pulled out her bottom sheet. "Where's Abba?"

"By the car, having a smoke. I told him not to schlep, to let those nice boys help like they want. We'll show him later, when we have everything. I don't like he should be straining himself up and down the stairs." Her face darkened for the briefest moment. They thought it was bad luck to talk about Jakub's heart. "Also, he's making friends with that Mike, so he should be nice to you." Malke laughed and shook out the top sheet. "You know how he is, that father of yours."

They both knew, so they made an effort not to argue with each other for the whole remainder of the day. The bed was made, the suitcases unpacked and stowed carefully under the bed, her books and things arranged on the shelves that were attached to the student desk. As a family, they went to the campus shop and bought a sweatshirt Jakub could wear in the store on a cold day, a decal for the back window of the car and a T-shirt for Ahuva. She would come back tomorrow to get the books she'd need for classes.

Strolling through the Student Union, they looked with interest at the bulletin boards that advertised an almost endless array of interests, events and services. Jakub was pleased to see that there was a Hillel; he'd been concerned that there might not be many Jews this far from the city and, in his experience, where there were too few Jews there was danger. They had a Coke together, sitting on achingly bright pastel chairs, staring covertly at other families who were doing the same thing.

On the way back to the dorm, Jakub stopped at the car and produced a surprise: Ahuva's favorite chocolate-covered jelly rings; an entire display box of them, like the one he always kept by the register. It was hard work not to cry, but she didn't want to make him sad, and she was also afraid that if she started she might never stop. As a family, they walked slowly up the stairs to her room. Ahuva had to jiggle her key a couple of times before it caught.

There were some boxes and a big canvas duffle bag on the floor by the other bed, signs that her unknown roommate must have arrived while they were out. Her own side of the room looked exactly as she and her mother had left it. Without her rug or her furniture as reference, her linens looked oddly unfamiliar on this bed. The walls seemed so bare. She wondered if you were allowed to hang up posters or something. There was a half-scared, half-excited lump in her throat. "Doesn't it look nice, Abba?" is what she said.

He must have had a lump, too. He nodded his head and forced a smile.

"Very nice," Malke said stoutly. "Look, Jakub, how she can see the trees. A very nice room. And such nice people. You'll make so many new friends. You'll see. This is good."

"It's going to be great," Ahuva insisted. "And wait until my classes start. Freshman English is required. Ech! But I've got Calculus, Music History and French." Confirmation of her class schedule had been in her orientation folder. She was a little disappointed that she'd been closed out of History of Theatre, but Music History, her second choice, should be just as interesting. "You're going to be so proud of me, Abba."

He crushed her to his chest with surprising strength. "You always make me proud, my Ahuva." He kissed the top of her head and whispered a blessing in Hebrew. He released her with some reluctance and walked out the door.

Malke gave her daughter a more moderate hug and a kiss on the cheek. "You be good. And you should need anything, you ask that Mike. Yes?"

Ahuva started to follow her to the hallway, but Malke shook her head. "If he sees you standing there, he won't be able to drive away. And you...So you wait here, Mamele and soon you meet your roommate and start making friends." Malke cleared her throat and left before either of them could say another word.

The room instantly seemed unbearably quiet and impersonal. Ahuva sat on the bed, thinking that the more she did this, the more it would seem like hers. Instead, all she could think was that she was now five hours further away from London, where a new production of *Always Forever Never Again* was about to open. She hoped Ellen Janow would remember her promise to Xerox the review when it came out; Abba didn't have any customers who bought *The Financial Times*, so he'd stopped stocking it.

The mattress crunched under her tush. She was sticky, too. If she were home, she'd take a shower. The bathroom here was down the hall and shared by everyone, even the boys. She wasn't feeling brave enough yet. Maybe after she met her roommate and there would be another girl to go with. She could at least change her clothes. She jumped up and locked the door; it would be terrifically embarrassing if her roommate's parents walked in while she was changing. She swapped her cords for regular jeans and, in a sudden burst of inspiration, traded her plaid flannel for the T-shirt from the last Willowbrook benefit; it wasn't a rock band but it was close, and maybe someone would ask her about it. In thinner clothes, and with the door and window both open to make a draft, she felt cooler but just as ill at ease. The packet said there was hall orientation at 4:00. What should she do until then? Venture downstairs, wander around campus? What if she got lost? Did she really want to be alone in that crowd?

In the end, there was only one thing she could do. She flipped up the latch on the orange paisley record box. Orange wasn't a color she liked much, but the box had been her Sweet 16 present from Holly. Now all that mattered was that the box was hers in this disturbingly anonymous room. She pulled out her *Lake Song* cast album and gently placed it on the turntable. The new headphones were heavy and made her feel like she was under water. The opening bars of the overture were painfully loud. She had to fiddle back and forth with the volume knob to find a comfortable level that still gave her the full swell of sound that she craved. Finally, it settled into place. She kicked off her shoes and, eyes closed, sprawled face down on her bed to disappear into a place that felt more like home.

Ahuva had never expected to meet someone named Ginger. Her roommate's name was really Virginia but even her parents called her Ginger, so there you are. Anyway, she'd probably never expected to meet someone named Ahuva. Ginger was unlike anyone Ahuva had ever known. She insisted her house wasn't a farm, but they had chickens and grew their own vegetables. She went to church every Sunday and worked one morning a week at the health food co-op, bringing back supplies of dusty granola and raw honey, which tasted no different than regular honey. She was nice, once they got used to each other. A bigger thing to get used to was feeling like an ant. New York City high schools were big; New York State universities were enormous; and in high school, with all her activities and honors classes, Ahuva had enjoyed a certain status. People had warned her that freshman year was a giant step backwards, but she hadn't believed it; she'd been sure it would be different for her.

Not since her first year in America had Ahuva felt so consistently foreign. She couldn't figure out why. At base the people here weren't so different from the people she'd been perfectly comfortable with in Queens. The difference was the air they had of being free and careless. It wasn't that they didn't work.

Classes were long and intense. In the library and the language lab, the carrels were so full that you often had to hang around for an hour or more, waiting for one to free up. People stayed up around the clock hammering out long papers, which then had to be neatly typed. There was a joke going around about a dealer who sold grass, speed and Liquid Paper; Ahuva had memorized it to tell her old friends over the Thanksgiving break.

Yes, everyone worked hard; but everyone also played so hard. Not only on the weekends; people went out drinking and dancing any night at all. The smell of grass and dope was so persistent in the halls that at first she'd thought it was the cleaning fluid the maintenance staff was using. Ahuva had tried grass once. "Had a toke," was what you said. She wanted to be able to tell Byron—if she ever saw him again. Honestly, she hadn't seen what all the fuss was about. And there was so much sex here! Ahuva had thought herself pretty broad-minded about sex, thanks in good part to her mother's European attitude. Malke had discussed birth control matter-of-factly, and offered embarrassingly frank advice about the benefit of being introduced to sex by "someone a little older, a man with experience." Except for Byron, Ahuva hadn't met anyone who attracted her in that way, but she hadn't felt odd about it until she saw what was going on here. It wasn't only people in a serious relationship, like Hope and Howie. People didn't think twice before jumping into bed with someone they hardly knew. Bed or even other places, she thought, twitching at the memory of the time she'd heard strange grunting in the shower stall next to hers. She constantly overheard conversations that began "what the fuck was I thinking last night!" Once, she'd gone back to the room after class to find Ginger in bed with the blond guy who'd helped her move in that first day. They were only snuggled up under the covers, but Ahuva wasn't stupid; he didn't have a shirt on and they had that look on their faces, that private, smug look. Ahuva knew for a fact that Ginger had a serious boyfriend at West Point; he'd sent her this official jacket that she always wore. Ginger was hoping to transfer to New Paltz next year, to be closer to him. So how could she be "doing it" with some other guy? Flustered, Ahuva had dropped her books on her desk and run back out again. They never talked about it, but after that time Ginger was careful to know Ahuva's schedule and Ahuva was careful to stick to it.

The brightest spot so far was the student production of *Pirates of Penzance*. Ahuva heard about it too late to audition for the chorus, but they needed lots of volunteers to paint sets and run the box office, things that she was more than happy to do if she could be part of a show.

"Ride the roller coaster and hang tight," Mike had advised them at floor orientation. "You'll find your groove."

That was good advice for most things; she was willing to accept that it was good advice for college. Anyway, the point of college was education and her classes, though more challenging than she'd expected, were as interesting as she hoped.

Before she turned around, it was October 6 and Yom Kippur. Ahuva had decided to fast, but wasn't so sure she wanted to go to services at the Hillel. It was a Saturday; she'd rather sleep in a little late and be by herself. When the hallway phone started ringing, she put her pillow over her ears and hoped she might fall back asleep for a little while. Before she could, someone was banging on her door. "Geffner! Phone!"

♫

In my own dorm room in Poughkeepsie, I woke up to my clock radio. I'd been trying to break myself of the inconvenient habit of sleeping eight hours a night; there simply wasn't enough time. Between rehearsals and papers, I was up until four or five most mornings. If I didn't set the alarm for 10:30, I could easily sleep the day away, so it went off even on the weekends. I kept it on my desk, forcing me to get out of bed and cross the room to turn it off. Following the logic that it was too easy to doze through music, I kept the radio turned to a news station. The news I heard that morning, the holiest day of the Jewish calendar, was that Egypt and Syria had attacked Israel. I had to hang onto the desk to keep from falling over. Heidi could be injured. She could be dead! What about her parents? And Ahuva's cousin Gali...I'd met Gali when she visited to New York; she was in the Army! Israel felt extremely close now that I knew people living there.

Hysterical, I grabbed the phone on my desk and called my parents. My mother, bless her, told me to calm down and call Heidi. Such an ordinary thing to say now; it's hard to describe how breathtaking that was when a phone call from one of the contiguous United States to another was considered Long Distance, so costly—and static-y, over fluky cables—that it was to be undertaken only with forethought and a firm budget. A five minute call to Israel would cost more than $20, half the spending money my parents were able to send me for an entire month. To pay for that call, my mother would be giving up something else. I didn't know what to say. My mother said to hang up and call Heidi, and call her back after.

It took forever to dial the number on the rotary phone. Several times, I lost track and hung up before I might accidentally connect with Tahiti. Finally, the call went through. I held my breath until someone picked up.

"Hullo?" There, at the other end, were Heidi's stereotypical New York City tones.

"It's me," I said. "Oh my god, are you okay?!"

For the next five minutes, I kept saying how worried I was and she assured me, over and over, that she was fine. We didn't know what else to say. That was another thing about Long Distance: you were so conscious of the cost that you were afraid to say anything, and inevitably ended up wasting the time on banalities. Still, I felt better for having heard her voice and, she wrote in her next Aerogram, she felt better too. Still dazed, I hung up and went down the hall to brush my teeth. Back in my room, I called home. In all the excitement, I'd temporary forgotten about Ahuva. If I'd felt so awful, how would she be feeling? Her whole family was over there! I quickly dialed the number she'd given me for the phone in her hall.

The girl who answered made an exasperated sound and shouted "Geffner! It's another one for you!" before dropping the receiver so that it banged against the wall.

"Ima?" Ahuva was a little breathless.

I guessed she must have been running. "No, it's me. Sorry. I didn't mean to scare you."

"Thank goodness. My parents have called twice already. They were trying to make me feel better, but it's only making me feel worse."

"Did they speak to Israel?"

"Uh huh."

"Is everyone okay? Gali and everyone?"

Ahuva's emphatic sigh was unnerving under ordinary circumstances. This time the drama was warranted. "They say so. But they always say so. I remember what it was like in '67."

We were silent for a moment while she remembered and I wondered if anything I could say would help.

"I called Heidi," I said lamely, embarrassed at feeling self-important. "She sounded okay."

"That's good," Ahuva said vaguely. She sighed again. "It's horrible. All we can do is wait."

119

"Fuck!" I said, feeling a little like Ellen. "Listen, if you need to talk, you can call me any time. Find a pay phone and reverse the charges, okay?"

Once I felt Heidi was safe, I was able to relax. It was my sophomore year. Freshman fears and detachment were dimming memories: I enjoyed my school friends and a crush who didn't know I was alive; I knew my place in the Drama Department; I was writing a history paper on WT Stead's "The Maiden Tribute of Modern Babylon." The war in Israel receded into background noise, uncomfortable when I thought about it, but ignorable for long stretches of the day. For Ahuva, only first settling into freshman year and with so many people to worry about, the month of October was one long nail-biter.

Everyone we cared about made it through the war intact, but Ahuva lost her place. By Thanksgiving break, she should have been sailing along, a well-adjusted member of the class of 1977. Instead, every day continued to be new and disconcerting.

♫

Midterms bled right into the two-week run of *Pirates*, which ran right up to Thanksgiving.

Ahuva had been smart to choose Props. All the talented artists flocked to scenery, costumes and makeup, and there were lots of people wanting to play with impressive equipment who volunteered for lighting or sound. Since hardly anyone wanted to do props, your hard work was appreciated. And it suited Ahuva, who thrived on organization. Like Einstein said, "God is in the details." Ahuva'd stuck a sign over the table saying "Props are in the details." It made Janet, the Property Master, laugh. That was the night Janet convinced her to join the others in the beer hall, even though she had an 8:30 French lab the next morning. Everyone was nice enough, but she still felt awkward around them. They were mostly upperclassmen, with their friendships all worked out; there wasn't room for someone new. And she was exhausted all the next day. Ahuva needed a solid eight hours sleep every night, but she didn't want to sound weird by saying so; college students didn't seem to sleep very much.

Yes, *Pirates* was the best part of college, but it only made her long to see *Lake Song* again. She found herself counting the days to Thanksgiving. Officially it was only a long weekend; there would be classes Monday and Tuesday. The professor for Music History, Ahuva's only Tuesday class, had said it would be okay to cut, that nothing new would be covered. He'd said it flat out like that; Dr. Nadich was stellar. She could have skipped her Monday classes, too—professors cut you a lot more slack than high school teachers had, as long as you kept up with the work—and headed home the Friday before, except that *Pirates* was ending that weekend. She couldn't let them down; she'd made a commitment. Plus, they'd strike the set Sunday and there would be a cast party. She'd loved the cast parties in high school.

Pirates was phenomenal. The girl who was Mabel reminded her so much of Hope; which was funny, because Hope had actually played Mabel at Bard last spring. Ahuva had taken the train to see it. Hope's voice was stronger and more confident than Jennifer's, and the costumes at Bard were more professional looking. Nonetheless, Ahuva thought her own school's production was superior. The senior who played the Pirate King reminded her so much of Oliver Blanchard, she thought she would die every time she had to buckle on his sword! She almost told him so at the cast party—not the dying part of course—but the girl who played Edith was hanging all over him and he seemed to like it, so Ahuva just said "great show" and moved on to compliment the Musical Director, who mentioned he was in the choir and suggested she come for tryouts in January.

Anyway, she'd soon see Oliver Blanchard himself. That's what she was going to do on Tuesday night. She was in college now—she didn't have to stick to matinees or wait for someone to take her. She was going to the Tuesday night performance, even if she had to go Standing Room.

Ahuva did have to go Standing Room. Of course. Thanksgiving week, New York City overflows with visitors who want to see a Broadway show. If she'd eaten dinner at home, which Malke had wanted, she probably wouldn't have gotten in at all. With a radiant smile for the box office clerk, she pocketed the last ticket and carefully rewound her new school muffler before heading out to the street. It was already night at five o'clock: dark and cold, that hard city cold that bounces off pavements and skyscrapers and goes right through your bones. She should probably have worn her snow boots; not that it was snowing, but because the rubber soles were better insulation. It didn't matter. Feet chilly, fingers stiff inside her gloves, the tip of her nose turning red as a cherry tomato, Ahuva felt better than she had in weeks. She was Home. "*And never do they breathe as easily as when they breathe the air of Moscow,*" she hummed, stepping nimbly over discarded newspapers and empty bottles and dog poo, giggling at tourists who'd stopped dead in the middle of the street to stare up and marvel at Her Town. She respectfully avoided the ragged bums who were talking aloud to themselves. Peering into shop windows, she wondered if Ginger or maybe Janet would appreciate a souvenir. Most importantly, she went past every theatre, checking out the posters to see what was coming soon and admiring the cast photos of the shows she hadn't seen. The mid-year break was only a few weeks away. She'd have nearly two months to do whatever she wanted. Naturally, she planned to see a lot of shows. Hungry, she rounded the corner, past the burned out bulbs of the giant *Burlesque!* sign, and pushed open the door to Howard Johnson's. It was hot and noisy, so packed that there wasn't even a seat at the counter. She had to go to Sbarro instead and eat a piece of greasy pizza, which she'd probably pay for later on; Ahuva's stomach had a tendency to do horrible things. She drank a prophylactic Coke and stopped at a newsstand for a roll of Tums, just in case. She needn't have worried; she soon forgot she even had a stomach.

Finding her spot at the rear of the auditorium, she unbuttoned her coat and took a deep breath. Slowly, methodically, she turned her head to greet every plaster nymph and grape, every gilded leaf of the Regale Theatre. She gave an affectionate pat to the partition separating her from the last row of orchestra seats, then scrunched up her coat so that when she got tired and leaned, it would be a cushion. Across the aisle was a girl leaning against the partition on that side. They were almost bookends, except she must have found some other place to put her coat. When the big round eyeglasses turned in her direction, Ahuva smiled.

The girl smiled back. "Great show!" she said, in a funny, croaky voice.

"I know," Ahuva replied. "My favorite."

The overture began, interrupting them and whisking Ahuva off to the lake, to a world she knew so well but never tired of visiting.

The other girl must have gone to the ladies' room during intermission, returning just before the lights went down again.

During curtain calls, Ahuva applauded until her hands were stinging. She even cheered, the way people did at the opera. She couldn't help herself. The man on her left winked at her and cheered even louder than she had, which made her giggle. She looked across the aisle, but the girl with the glasses was already gone.

She hated to leave the theatre, waiting until nearly everyone was gone, until staying was too conspicuous. Only then did she shrug into her coat and wind her scarf around her throat. Putting one foot slowly in front of the other, she walked out through the lobby. Trying to make the moment last, she drew on her gloves one finger at a time.

With all her dawdling, she still reached the stage door before anyone had come out. It was so cold that only a few of the more passionate tourists were waiting. Some of the ensemble trickled out; a couple seemed to notice and almost recognize her.

Now that it was too late to do anything about it, Ahuva realized she desperately needed to pee. She should have gone before leaving the building, but the thought hadn't crossed her mind. Only now, in the sharp contrast between the warm theatre and the cold street, did it go from not-even-a-vague-thought to a pressing emergency. She was briefly grateful that that she *only* had to pee, that her stomach hadn't let her down after all; but now that it was in her head she needed to pee more fiercely than she needed to do anything, even breathe. There was a hotel around the corner, if only she could get there.

She was looking in that direction when Maria Dearborne spotted her and greeted her with a hug. "I wondered what happened to you!"

"I'm going to college upstate," Ahuva said, momentarily distracted. It was exciting that Maria recognized her, so exciting that she could be forgiven for forgetting that Ahuva had said goodbye almost three months ago. "I'm on Thanksgiving break now. I couldn't wait to see the show again."

Maria dimpled with pleasure. "I hope you weren't disappointed. Some of us were a little chesty tonight. There's a cold going around."

"It was wonderful!" Ahuva protested. "Maybe I just forgot after so long, but there were parts…" she fished in her recollection for specifics. "Kostia and Nina's scene at the end!" she said triumphantly. "Definitely better. It's always sad, but there's something more. I think Rebecca is becoming a better actor. I mean, she's always been an amazing singer, but…" Now she'd put her foot in her mouth. She had a bad habit of voicing opinions that maybe people didn't want to hear.

Maria laughed. "Yes, well, Chris and Becca have discovered a few things."

With a treacherous lurch to her kidneys, Ahuva's body reclaimed her attention. She crossed her legs tight at the knee and discreetly shifted her weight from leg to leg; sometimes movement helped.

She must have moved too much. Maria reached for her shoulder, as if to steady her. "Are you okay? You look like you're about to faint. I shouldn't keep you standing in the cold."

"I'm fine," she said hastily.

"You're too sweet! I'll let you go. I should be going, too. My in-laws are in town for the holiday. They saw the show tonight. I'm supposed to be meeting them for a bite to eat."

"How nice! Are you meeting them at Alfie's?" Ahuva hoped so. Alfie's was even closer than the hotel. If Maria walked her in, she could use the rest room and leave without buying anything and no one would care, if they even noticed.

Maria flashed the special smile she'd used when she'd played Polina, the one where her eyebrows made quotation marks. "The Lambs? They're not the Alfie's kind. No. I'm meeting them up at the Russian Tea Room. I should really get going. I'll never find a cab, and it's a walk. Are you going that way? Oh, of course. You said Alfie's. Well, that's on the way. We can start out together."

Maria's concern and her friendliness were too much. There was no way around it. "I have to pee!" Ahuva blurted. "I thought maybe I could use the rest room at Alfie's, if you…" She wanted to die.

Maria was too kind to laugh. "You poor thing! Come with me." She whisked Ahuva through the stage door, right past the doorman. "Wally, this is my friend Ahuva. She'll just going to freshen up. She'll be gone in a trice."

Maria led her up the stairs and around a couple of corners. All the doors looked alike. She rapped firmly on one of them. Satisfied that it was unoccupied, she twisted the knob and pushed. The knob dangled perilously. "Don't worry; it won't come off. Now I'm going to run. And don't worry about Wally. Take your time. Just turn off the light when you leave. And have a very happy Thanksgiving, okay? Come see me when you're back in town!" She gave Ahuva a peck on the cheek and flew off.

Ahuva decided that Maria Dearborne must be the nicest actress on Broadway. She fervently hoped there was a Tony or, better still, constant employment, in Maria's future.

A few minutes later, she switched off the light as Maria had instructed and began to slowly make her way in what she hoped was the right direction. Backstage at a real theatre! She was surprised how sad it looked: grubby tight quarters and a worse institutional green than the high school basement where the gyms were. Whatever was metal was painted dismal locker room grey. She stepped carefully down the chipped grey stairs, wondering how the actors managed it so that there wasn't clanging all over the theatre. Reaching the bottom, the dingy little foyer pressing in on her, she was overwhelmed with the urge to make it less depressing for the cast. How? Hang some of those tinselly Christmas garlands from the pipes? No, that was probably a fire hazard. She could at least, she thought, looking at the old, pitted cork bulletin by the stage door, send them a cheerful card. Something really big. Hallmark didn't make one big enough for what she had in mind, but she could make one. A Christmas card out of oak tag, she thought, remembering classroom projects from her one year of American elementary school. She'd get red oaktag—that was cheerful—and paste things on it. There was a stellar picture of the entire cast in the centerfold of the souvenir program. She'd tear it out; she could always buy a new program next time she came to see the show. She would put some glitter on it. Maybe a tree. What else did you put on a Christmas card? She remembered the one Holly's son Jason had made her: cotton ball snowmen would be perfect!

"Can I help you, Maria's friend?"

Ahuva jumped and whirled around.

The doorman laughed. "I didn't mean to scare you." But she could tell he had.

"I was getting ready for the cold," she said, with as much dignity as she could muster. She made a show of adjusting her scarf just under her nose, then pulled her gloves from her pockets.

"Goodnight, Lil!"

Ahuva turned towards the somehow familiar nasal croak. The girl from Standing Room emerged from one of the identical doors. Now she had a floppy hat pulled almost down to the top of those glasses, a tired looking feather drooping almost to her shoulder. Her coat had big round buttons. All those circles had Ahuva thinking of snowmen again.

"Goodnight, Frankie," said the doorman. "We gonna be seeing you around here again?"

"Maybe. Lil says she'll want to get started again after New Year's, so probably. Oh, hi!" she'd spotted Ahuva behind the doorman and gave a friendly little wave. "It's you, isn't it?"

"Hi," Ahuva replied, a little shyly.

"You know Maria's friend? Sheesh. Figures all you kids know each other."

"I'm Frankie, by the way," the girl with the glasses said, once the door had closed behind them.

"Ahuva." She put out her hand and they shook gloves.

"Don't let Wally get to you. He's only sometimes a jerk. So you're a friend of Maria's. Are you an actress? I am."

125

Ahuva was impressed. This girl couldn't be any older than she was. "No. I don't have any talent. I'll probably end up being a math teacher. But I love the theatre."

"Me too. You have to do movies or television for the money, but I'd rather do theatre. Are you heading for the subway?"

Ahuva nodded.

"I'm walking to Penn."

Ahuva could take the subway from 34th as easily as 42nd Street. She decided to walk the extra blocks with her intriguing new acquaintance. Not only was she an actress, but Frankie actually worked for Lilith Brassloe; that was the story behind the little exchange with the doorman, Wally. It was one of several jobs—"day jobs," Frankie called them—that she had while she auditioned for parts. She was also working at FAO Schwartz, dressed like Raggedy Anne, demonstrating those See-&-Say toys.

"Little kids like my voice," she said. "I keep trying to get in to see the casting agent at Children's Television Workshop. You know, the people who do *Sesame Street*."

"Oh! I hope you do!"

Frankie was obviously very talented. Maybe she'd be the next Maria Dearborne. And Ahuva would be able to say that she'd met her when she was first starting out. When they parted at 34th Street, she wished the young actress good luck, from the bottom of her heart.

9 – FOR THOUSANDS OF YEARS

NINA *[spoken: Ladies and gentlemen, the performance is about to begin. Your attention, if you please. I'm going to start.]*
[knocks with a stick]

(recitative: You honored ancient shades that hover above the lake in the hours of night, make our eyes grow heavy, and let us dream of what will be in two hundred thousand years from now!)

Men and lions, partridges and larks,
Ev'ry worm that wriggles, ev'ry dog that barks;
Ant'lered stags and hawks and bees and others;
Th'unforthcoming fish that dwelt beneath the waters:
All are gone, gone, gone.
Life is done, done, done.
On the empty Earth
Is a fearful dearth.
In the wake of death
All is cold, cold, cold, cold, cold.

ARKADINA *[spoken: have you seen my wrap? I feel a chill...]*

POLINA *[chuckles]*

SORIN *[spoken: Hush! Listen to the child.]*

NINA *[spoken: Thousands of centuries have passed since any living creature walked the earth. Their bodies have fallen into dust and turned into stones, into water, into clouds. Their souls have merged into one universal soul, and this is Me. In Me are the souls of Alexander the Great, of*

Shakespeare, of Napoleon and of the very least of leeches. All, all, all do I remember, and every life I live again in my own self.]*

I am quite alo-o-one
And I walk the earth from pole to pole,
Withered all to bo-o-one,
Holding up my lamp to mock Old Sol.
Who has long guttered out.

Oh, the light I shine is weak
As if the very flames are cold with fear.
When I part my lips to speak,
There is no one here … to hear!

TRIGORIN *[spoken: Here to hear?]*

SORIN *[spoken: Shhh!]*

NINA

In the watches of the night I observe you born from rotting swamp:
Formless lifeless forms of life witnessed by the flicker of my lamp.

POLINA *[spoken: I was wondering how he'd get out of that one.]*

NINA *(getting angry at the "audience")*

In a constant state of flux!

Somehow all this sludge and mire will evolve, developing until,
With a soul that I inspire, you achieve a Universal Will!

*[spoken: The Father of Eternal
   Matter, He who is the Devil,
   influences you, as he does stones
   and water, shaping you by a
   constant replacement of the
   atoms. He challenges me to fight
   for your freedom!]*

All I am allowed to know is that
   victory will be my fate.
That can only come about after eons
   of a vigilant wait!

ARKADINA *[spoken: Seems like
   eons already.]*

NINA

Let matter and spirit merge in
   wondrous Harmony!

*[spoken, threateningly: Here comes
   my mighty adversary, the Devil,
   now. I see his fearful crimson
   eyes...He pines for human
   company!]*

Frankie's new answering service passed her a message from Ellen Janow, the girl from the scaffold, suggesting they meet for coffee. That was a surprise. Frankie called back and suggested Howard Johnson's.

The other girl ordered a soft-boiled egg with whole wheat toast and took her coffee black; she produced a gold lighter and, with some ceremony, lit a slim brown cigarette. Despite the comfort of the familiar vinyl booth, Frankie was intimidated.

But then they began to talk. Ellen asked flattering questions about Thierry and *Mother Courage* and Lil Brassloe, and told some fascinating stories about working with Felix Ayre. Despite her worldly sophistication, she was gratifyingly impressed by everything Frankie had to say about acting and pounding the pavement.

Ellen was the only person Frankie had told about Connie dePaul's offer to sponsor her to the dressers' union "if the acting thing doesn't work out, dearie." Frankie might have been insulted last year, when she was trying so hard to fit in at NYADA, but she'd spent enough time backstage since then to understand how generous an offer it was. Bronwen Davies' dresser had no way of knowing how talented Frankie was; she only saw how much Frankie loved the theatre and was offering her a way to be part of it. Ellen said Frankie's attitude showed a lot of maturity and that when Frankie was in a show, which would certainly be soon, she'd personally ensure that Connie came to see her.

Ellen was a lot more likable here than on the scaffold. They had things in common. Or people, at least. They both knew Joe Bigelow. Ellen had met Tyler, too, at a wonderful party given by Bronwen Davies' brother Ivor. She also had a funny story about finding Miss Davies wandering the street in the rain; the kind of funny story where Frankie could have laughed at Ellen as easily as with her. She understood that Ellen trusted her, an invitation that Frankie couldn't resist.

Except for Darlene, who was with the Coast Guard now, and Donny Hopkins, there wasn't anyone Frankie could call a friend. It went back to when her mother died. The other kids in school hadn't known how to behave. Conversations were stilted. They stopped inviting her to parties, either because someone made them think it was inappropriate for her to have fun or because they were afraid that death might be catching. The little bit of distance got bigger and bigger until, after a year or two, they'd become strangers. It wasn't deliberately mean; they just glided over her, like a bump in the road. She got used to being alone. There were books to read and movies to watch. It was okay. She'd expected that once she became an actress, things would be different; that she'd meet other people like herself, a new family. Then the crowd at NYADA shut her out even more firmly than the crowd at Patchogue-Medford High.

Ellen was inviting her in.

Fortifying herself with a deep pull on her malted, Frankie told Ellen about *Goin' Goin' Go Go* and what it meant to her. Ellen listened closely. Leaning on her elbows, her pointed chin resting on the knuckles of her right hand, her cigarette burning unnoticed in her left, she radiated acceptance. When Frankie admitted, with an embarrassed giggle, that she'd fantasized that Bronwen Davies was her mother, Ellen nodded in recognition.

"I used to imagine that Martin Landau and Barbara Bain were my parents," she said. She wasn't laughing. "Sydelle actually looks a little like Barbara, except for the nose job. Sydelle was born with a perfect nose. I have Harry's." She tapped if ruefully. "What can I say? I have other assets. *It's not the cards you're dealt, it's how you play them*, right?"

Frankie nodded appreciatively. She admired the deep knowledge of *Lake Song* this quote implied. "Bezique" wasn't a popular number. She also admired Ellen's businesslike air and her bold certainty. Ellen ought to be a very successful producer someday.

They left Howard Johnson's, firm friends, promising to meet on a regular basis. "A week from Thursday?" Ellen suggested. "Felix is supposed to be in London that week. After Lil lets you go, we could hang out at the office."

Frankie opened her date book to write it down. Flipping pages, another note caught her eye. "Oh! You should know this! Miss Davies is going to be on *Mike Douglas* that Monday. I know because Connie's going with her to Philadelphia to help with her wig."

Ellen's grin spoke volumes. She felt exactly the same way Frankie did: they were part of this world; they were insiders.

While waiting for Donny's schedule to open up, Frankie turned her sights on dance. It hadn't taken more than a few samples to appreciate Donny's point: even the dancers in Beginner Jazz looked ready to jump up on a Broadway stage. She refused to let it get her down. If Donny was right about that, he was probably right about other things. Tap, for example, so Frankie made her way to a studio in Carnegie Hall.

Sixty if she was a day, fiercely plain Irene Lemon taught class in a button-down oxford shirt and the kind of work pants mailmen wore. Even her taps were screwed onto the most ordinary brown lace-up shoes imaginable. But she could dance like nothing Frankie had ever seen outside the movies. It was dazzling. Her body seemed to hover, weightless, allowing her feet to move freely and with the speed of a magician's hands. If it hadn't been for the percussive flurry, Frankie wouldn't have believed they'd moved at all.

Irene's beginner class was an assorted pack. There were a few obvious actors, but the other eight or nine could have been anything. There was even a kid, a girl of maybe ten or eleven, in a pair of fluttery polka-dot shorts straight off Ruby Keeler. Her hair was tied up in a scarf and there were big ribbon bows on her patent leather shoes, but her face was as serious as any of the others. That was what really grabbed Frankie, how focused everyone was. They watched Irene without blinking, didn't flinch when she barked out the most scathing criticism. There wasn't a real dancer in the bunch, but they followed Irene's instructions gamely, and by the end of an hour, someone watching would think it was a dance number.

Frankie was hooked. No Marjorie Morningstars here; everyone was as committed to learning as she was. She told Irene Lemon she wanted to join her class and asked where she could buy the right kind of shoes.

Just when life was going so smoothly, Lil Brassloe said she was putting the scrapbooks on hold for a while. There simply wasn't enough time in the day; she was always invited onto television shows at this time of year, and there was her annual cabaret engagement at the Cafe Carlyle. They'd start up again in January.

Frankie had put her after school class on hiatus; families had so much to do over the holiday season. She'd thought that, between the money she'd saved and what she expected to make working for Lil, she would be fine until New Year's. With Lil drying up, she'd be in trouble.

One of the guys in Irene's class said he'd got a gift-wrapping job at MACY*S for the holiday season. Frankie went over the next day, but they'd already hired as many people as they needed. The nice woman in Personnel suggested she try FAO Schwartz. "They like young people there," she said, with an encouraging smile.

Wasting no time, Frankie walked uptown as fast as she could. It wasn't cold, but the air had that raw dampness that clung to every part of you that wasn't covered. Her glasses kept fogging up. She had to wipe them on her long crocheted scarf. By the time she got to 59th Street, she was sure she was a mess, but it was almost five o'clock; she couldn't stop to tidy up. She squared her shoulders and marched into the building.

"Hi," she said to the Steadfast Tin Soldier at the front door. "Where do I go to apply for a job? I'm great at wrapping gifts. And I'm good with kids, too. I teach acting."

He looked her up and down, from her rainbow socks to the drooping feather of her damp felt hat and her big round glasses. He grinned. "You're in luck," he said. "I think they're looking for a new Raggedy Ann."

Frankie had felt guilty about quitting the hair salon after Ruby had been so nice about giving her the work when she needed it, but Saturday was the big day at FAO Schwartz and a mandatory part of the schedule. Frankie was making enough money over Christmas season to pay for classes and carfare all the way through March, April if she was careful.

Her expenses now included singing lessons. As good as his word, Donny called her the minute his show was over. His only open time was in the evening; he was coaching at NYADA most days. Frankie was exhausted— even a full day running after kids at camp was nothing compared a day on the floor at FAO Schwartz—but she was afraid that if she didn't start at once that his schedule might get full or, worse, he might think she wasn't interested.

Donny taught in his apartment on West 102nd Street. For her first lesson, Frankie dragged herself there after work, walking across town to Columbus Circle station so that the cold would wake her up, then standing all the way uptown so she couldn't doze off on the train.

Donny met her at the door with a giant hug and a glass of wine. He'd been thinking back to her musical theatre classes at NYADA, he explained. He'd decided her biggest obstacle was that she was self-conscious about her voice. The wine would help her relax.

"As long as I don't relax so much I fall asleep!" she cracked.

"I won't let you," he promised. "We have work to do. So did I tell you my bitch ex-girlfriend is screwing Max Bulloch?"

Frankie almost choked on her gulp of wine. "How do you know?" she asked, once she recovered. She wouldn't contradict him. She knew it was true. Ellen Janow had mentioned Bulloch was seeing the girl who understudied Nina; she'd just forgotten that girl was Linda.

"She told me!" Donny jutted his chin forward and opened his eyes ultra-wide, a classic "would you believe it?" take. "I still coach her, you know."

Frankie hadn't. Donny was crazy about Linda; the breakup had hit him hard. She didn't understand how he could bear to keep coaching her. For that matter, she didn't get how Linda had the nerve to let him. "That's a lot of kutzpah," she declared, feeling righteous on his behalf.

Donny laughed, a big belly laugh. "That's not how you say it, but it is. A lot of *chutzpah*. Except they say it with a gargling sound that is really hard on the vocal chords. That's why Jews are belters and Italians sing opera."

Frankie had never thought about it before, but it almost made sense. She nodded gravely, looking more than ever like a baby owl.

"Anyway, it's a compliment. Even with a Broadway credit under her belt, fucking Linda, pardon my French, still thinks I'm one of the best coaches in town. And if she walks around saying that, she can do me some good, so what the hell."

Frankie nodded again. Maybe that's how it had to be if you dated another person in the business. Theatre was a small world. You were bound to have to work together sometime. She guessed it was the mature thing to do, to separate work from your relationships. She still couldn't imagine doing it. Then again, she couldn't imagine anyone wanting to break up with Donny.

"I hope Bulloch makes her eat shit," Donny continued pleasantly. "Okay, enough of that. Let's get started with some scales."

It was raining hard, the kind of freezing rain that messed up city traffic. Little Daphne's mother usually caught the last ten minutes of class before taking her home. She was probably finding it hard to get a cab. Irene Lemon had to close up; she was coaching the chorus of *Lady Be Good* and had to be downtown by 6:30. Frankie told her not to worry. This being one of her two days off this month, she was enjoying the luxury of calling her time her own. She'd wait with Daphne in the little lobby until Mrs. Rodney showed up.

They sat side by side on the bottom step. Daphne nudged her. "Are you an actress? You don't dance very well."

Kids, Frankie knew all too well, never minced words. "I'm only just learning now. Actresses have to do a lot of different things. I'm taking singing lessons too."

"Your voice is funny," Daphne said. "Like someone in a cartoon, or maybe a commercial."

"I hear that a lot," Frankie replied.

"Mamma wants me to be in commercials. I go on auditions sometimes, but I never get the job."

Frankie got the impression she didn't much care.

"Do you want to be an actress?"

The child shrugged. "If I book a commercial, Mamma says she'll get me a dog. I love dogs. Mamma says it's not right to keep them in an apartment, but our apartment is big enough. At least for a small dog. You know which ones I like? Yorkies. Yorkshire terriers. They're so cute! And they're really little. I bet the terrace would feel like a whole backyard to a Yorkie." She brightened, warming to her subject. It was the first time Frankie'd seen her looking like a kid.

"Then I hope you get a commercial. Soon."

"Thank you," she said gravely.

The glass door flew open with a dangerous groan. Margaret Rodney burst through. "There you are!" she said wildly. "Oh, Baby! There wasn't a taxi in the city! I thought I would never get here! I keep telling your uncle we need a driver. Are you alright?" She bent down, as if Daphne were a much younger child who could be scooped up in her arms.

"I'm fine," Daphne said, struggling not to lose hold of her dance bag. "Irene had to go, but Frankie said she'd wait with me. This is Frankie."

"Nice to meet you, Mrs. Rodney," Frankie said politely.

The woman whirled to face her. "Thank you so much for taking care of my little girl!" Staring fervently into Frankie's eyes, she took both her hands and squeezed them. It hurt a little; she was wearing a lot of rings.

"It's nothing." Frankie tried to extract her hands. "We've only been waiting a few minutes."

"But here, in this deserted place! Who knows what might have happened if you weren't here!"

The lobby to the Carnegie Hall studios was small and dusty, just a square of tiles where you could wait for the elevator or start up the stairs, but it had a big glass door that looked right out onto 7th Avenue. Compared to most of the places Frankie went on her rounds, it was pretty nice and definitely safe.

"Really, Mrs. Rodney, I was happy to help out. Daphne's a good kid. And she's a great little dancer."

A change came over Margaret Rodney's face. Frankie almost expected to hear a choir of angels in the background. "Do you think so? I do, but I'm her mother. It's so nice to hear it from someone with unprejudiced eyes."

"I'm only a beginner myself, but when I get confused...you know, it's always confusing when Irene shows you the step from the front and you have to switch the sides around...I know if I watch Daphne I'll get it right."

There was another painful hand squeeze. "Thank you. Thank you so much!"

"Hey, that's okay. Um, now that you're here, I'm going to go. I've got a train to catch."

"My taxi is waiting outside. You must let us drive you," Mrs. Rodney insisted.

Frankie was shocked someone could leave a taxi parked outside all this time. "That's okay," she said quickly. "The subway is right on the corner."

"Mamma, I'm hungry!" Daphne said.

Mrs. Rodney shook away a jangle of bracelets to check her watch. "Oh, dear! We have to meet some friends at Rumplemayer's. If we were on our own, I'd invite you to join us. You'll have to have dinner with us after class next week." She stared up as if there were a calendar on the ceiling. "Damn. No, next week we have Daphne's orthodontist. The week after then, Frances. Without fail."

"Frankie," she corrected. "Francesca, actually, but everyone calls me Frankie. Really, it's not necessary Mrs. Rodney."

"Margaret. And I insist!" She gave Frankie a European peck on each cheek and whisked out the door, yanking Daphne behind her. Daphne looked over her shoulder and, with her free hand, gave a little wave.

Before their next class, Daphne handed her a thick blue envelope with a monogram on the flap. Frankie was surprised; she hadn't expected Mrs. Rodney to remember the invitation. The sprawling handwriting was difficult to make out. Fortunately, Daphne already knew what it said.

"Mamma's really sorry we can't take you to dinner next week after all, but my uncle's going to be in town and she says we have to dance attendance." Daphne giggled. "I always tell her I don't know the steps to that dance. It drives her crazy. But we really do have to be with Uncle Ned before he goes to Paris. And then it's Christmas, and after that we go visit Grandmamma in Arizona. So Mamma was hoping you'd come to our house for dinner when we get back, after New Year's. That Friday, so I don't have to do homework? Please say yes. Mamma put the address and everything right here."

This close to Christmas, FAO Schwartz was a nightmare. If it wasn't screaming kids, it was hysterical parents trying to do all their holiday shopping in an hour. It was hard to say which group threw bigger tantrums. Frankie was glad she could hide behind Raggedy Anne's painted smile; she didn't know how the regular clerks managed it.

She'd thought about canceling tonight, but he was taking the next two weeks off to be with his parents upstate and that would mean three weeks with no Donny. With no *lesson*, she corrected herself. She hated to skip when she was just starting to make progress. It would be unprofessional. Also, she had a present for Donny. It was a silly thing, a piano-shaped music box they were selling downstairs. It happened to play the Christmas song from *Rosebud*, which she knew was Donny's favorite musical. So even though she was ready to collapse, she washed off the greasepaint, put on fresh makeup and dragged herself uptown.

She hadn't had lunch. Something happened to the girl who ran the Barbie counter and she got roped into filling in, and then one thing led to another. She'd had nothing after breakfast, except some orange juice and maybe an oatmeal cookie. She forgot how little she'd eaten today until she'd drunk most of her glass of wine.

She swayed a little when she stood to do her warm-up. Reaching out a hand to steady herself, she almost knocked the little music box from where Donny had set it on the piano.

"Oops!" she giggled. "Sorry, I had a hard day."

He came up behind her as he sometimes did and gave her shoulders a rub. Her head flopped back and forth under the pressure of his hands. "You feel nice and relaxed now," he noted.

"I'm Raggedy Anne," she reminded him.

"Let's see what Raggedy Anne sounds like." He sat down at the keys and gave her a chord.

Frankie took a deep breath and, with her eyes fixed on a point above his head so she wouldn't be distracted, she began her scales. She felt something miraculous in her chest and throat. It was just like Donny always said: when you relax completely your throat opens; the sound isn't forced, it just releases. Frankie thought her voice had never sounded so full and surely she'd never sung with such ease.

By the time they finished the sequence, she was beaming. She turned her eyes to smile at Donny. He wasn't smiling back. He was thoughtful, a small furrow in his forehead.

"Interesting," he said. That was all.

"But it felt great!" she protested. "And I could hear the difference…"

"Oh, absolutely," he agreed. He stood so that they were eye to eye. "A huge difference in tone. Your throat was completely open. But there was no support. I don't understand what…Here, try ma-me-mi." He stretched his left hand and plinked a key.

Frankie took a breath and began. "Mah…"

He held up his hand to stop her and shook his head. "No good. I need to see how you're breathing." He matter-of-factly undid the first three buttons of her blouse. "Now take a deep breath." Blushing furiously, she did. "Exactly what I thought. You're breathing from the chest. You need to breathe from your belly." He sounded almost like a doctor. "Breathe in through your nose, and imagine it ending up here," he instructed, kneeling down and putting one hand on her stomach. "On a count of five. One, two…" She looked across the top of his head to a spot on the opposite wall where the paint had chipped off, and tried to imagine exactly as he'd said. "Good! Now breathe out through your mouth, on a nice open 'Ah,' as long as you can and make sure it's all coming from here," he jiggled his hand on her stomach for emphasis.

"Aaaahhhh" she warbled, while Donny counted to eight.

"Not too bad for a first try," he said. "The count was really good. But I'm still hearing a little chest. If you could get rid of that, I bet you'd hold that note for a count of ten, easy. Maybe even twelve. Try again."

She tried six more times, feeling more and more light-headed. Something about this deep breathing was very dizzying. She looked down into his face. He was frowning. Not in an angry way, but like he was thinking hard.

"I know!" he exclaimed, jumping up and moving behind her. Standing so close that when he spoke it felt as if he was nibbling on her ear, he put a hand on her stomach and said, "Okay now close your eyes and when I start to count, try to imagine your stomach is like a balloon and your throat is an air hose for filling it. Your chest shouldn't move at all. Okay, one, two…"

She could see the balloon, she could feel the air hissing down. When it was time to exhale, she tried not to have that little heave in her chest. "Ahhh."

Donny began to count. As he reached three, she suddenly felt his hand inside her blouse, pressing firmly down on her chest. She jumped and started to cough.

"Sorry," he apologized, "I didn't mean to startle you. Can we try again like this?"

She felt stupid being so flustered. He was a voice coach. He was trying to help her. "Okay," she said, glad he was still behind her and couldn't see her face. She took a deep breath and could feel it all went to her chest. "Oh!" she cried, "damn!"

"That's okay." Donny was so sweet. "Relax. I know I'm pushing you hard, but it's because I believe in you. I know you can do this." His hands hadn't moved. The warmth was comforting. She could feel her shoulders loosen. She took a very deep break and her stomach swelled like a beach ball. "Yes!

Exactly like that!" This time she almost held her "Ahhhhh" for a count of ten, and she knew her chest hadn't moved at all. "Wow!" Donny said and kissed the crown of her head. "Now that's the way to do it! Think you can do it again?" She nodded happily.

They did it over and over again. Each time it became easier. Her "Ahhhh!" floated out like a raft on a river and her head grew lighter and lighter. When his hand slid downwards, she didn't notice at first. It was when he pinched her nipple in his fingers and her "Ahhhh!' turned into a moan that she realized what he was doing. By then it was too late. He'd heard the sound she'd made and felt her melt backwards into him. He slipped his other hand up to unfasten her bra, then cupped both breasts.

"Don't be nervous," he murmured, nuzzling the nape of her neck with his lips.

"I'm not a virgin," she gasped, a little frantically.

"Good," he said, slipping one hand under her skirt and down the waistband of her panties.

10 – FAMOUS PEOPLE

NINA [spoken: It's all so strange. To
see a famous actress crying her
eyes out, over nothing really. And
a famous writer, whose name is in
the papers all the time, spends the
whole day fishing and is thrilled to
catch a few gudgeon!]

Famous people are a mystery to me.
To be famous, what a magic thing to
be!
How can life be small or bland
When the moon is in your hand,
And you're looking down on clouds
and trees?
Your world has no more boundaries.
You're loved by everyone you
meet—Oh, my!

Famous people are surrounded by a
glow,
Famous people; knowing all there is
to know

KOSTIA

But they cry and sulk and bleed
Just the same as you and me.
And they stuff their maws like hungry
hogs,
They fornicate like rutting dogs,
They're commoner than dirt
because—don't sigh!

Just believe me when I tell you we
are made of finer stuff.
You and I, we rise above them.
Fame disguises worthless fluff.
Would you rather be a rhinestone or
a diamond in the rough?

NINA

Kostia, all I hear is jealousy—
Enough!

Famous people drown in orchids and
champagne.
Famous people keep their feet dry in
the rain

KOSTIA

Lay yourself down at those feet,
Make your sacrifice—how sweet!
But I know that clay is friable,
Those idols unreliable.
The glamour's undeniable, but I...

I resist that trifling power by refusing
to play ball;
I won't disappear or cower when
they need me to be small.
Famous people, see them crumble,
see them stumble, see them fall
Famous people are just people, after
all.

Ellen didn't ordinarily watch daytime talk shows. Their overly smooth, implacably chipper old Hollywood hosts were so repulsive. In any case, she was never anywhere near a TV set when they aired. Barney had acquired a little space-helmet portable last month, for watching the Series. Ellen did a fair amount of finagling to make sure she was in front of it at the right time on Monday. It was probably crazy, but she absolutely needed to see which Bronwen Davies would walk out in front of the cameras: the lost poodle, the tipsy shadow, or the vibrant Arkadina.

The woman on the sofa was none of these. She was all warmth and crinkled smiles. She told an adorably self-effacing story about visiting her daughter, who was reading History at Cambridge. Ellen took note: "reading" not studying. The story involved a pair of "gum boots" and a road "lay-by"…was that a shoulder or a rest stop? This was really very educational. Mike Douglas found the story charming and so did his audience. So did Ellen. They were all even more charmed when Bronwen, recalling her girlhood stage debut as Alice, went on to recite "Jabberwocky" from memory. Douglas and the studio audience hated to have her leave.

Ellen was enthralled. She tried to explain this to Leonard that night. "She lit up the screen. You know how it is when she walks on as Arkadina. It was like that, but completely different. I'm totally fascinated. Who was this woman? I've never seen anyone be as many different people."

"She's an actress, El. That's her job."

"This is different. Not acting—being. I want to know how she does it. It can't be conscious. She's a dumb blonde. Not like Lilith Brassloe. Even on stage, you can see Lil's brain clicking away, but not Bron's. Maybe it switches on and off by itself; a multiple personality thing, like the woman in that book your mother gave us."

"*Sybil?*" Leonard sighed. After reading *Sybil*, Ellen had spent days agonizing over whether any traumatic incidents in her childhood might have caused her own personality to secretly fracture. "I thought we agreed we were simply neurotic."

"We are. And it was a metaphor. I don't actually think Bron's got a split personality. Damn, wouldn't it be fascinating, to meet someone like that in real life?"

"I don't think we'd know if we did. Wouldn't we only ever meet one of them?" Leonard was tired of the subject. Anyway, Ellen wasn't listening. She had a puzzle and was thinking out loud. It might take her days, even weeks, to work it through.

Leonard was absorbed in his own infatuation. He'd been besotted with Bernadette Peters, ever since Aunt Lorraine had taken him to see *George M!* for his Bar Mitzvah. He'd seen her in every show since. Now that he lived in the city, he could catch her cabaret dates. The last time Bernie was at Brothers and Sisters, he'd gone every night and left flowers at the door. The final night, he worked up the nerve to hand them over to her in person. She made a big thing about asking his name, then repeated it in that funny little girl voice of hers, her expression changing to an especially glad-looking one.

"So those are yours, those beautiful flowers Nick's been giving me every night. You are such a sweetheart!" She pecked him on the cheek. A pack of friends came to claim her. She gave a little wave before moving off with them. Watching her retreating back, a grin plastered across his face, Leonard felt as if he'd been knighted. Even her mop of russet curls was vaguely Arthurian.

She was wonderful. Flowers weren't enough; there had to be something more special he could give her. He couldn't think of a thing until Jeff Kaplan sent him the *Harper's Bazaar* clipping about this woman in Nebraska who made fancy dolls for collectors. They were like fashion dolls, except she made them look like famous people. There was a picture of a Sally Bowles doll that looked exactly like Liza Minnelli. Remarkable! Leonard tracked down a mailing address through the magazine and wrote to ask what sort of photos or information she'd need to make a doll, and how much it would cost. The amount made him gulp a little, but he'd decided it would be worth it. He commissioned the woman to make a Bernadette Peters doll, based on a photo from *Dames at Sea*.

The box had arrived today, not long before Ellen came home. He'd been staring at it, working up the nerve to open it. The tension was unbearable. Leonard's hands were shaking so hard that he interrupted Ellen's *Sybil* monologue to make her open it for him. She carefully unwound the tissue paper and posed the delicate figure on the table. They gawked; it was a beautiful little thing, Bernadette Peters to the life.

"You almost expect her to start singing," Leonard breathed in awe. "I'm going to give it to her for Christmas. She'll be back at Brothers and Sisters around then."

Ellen's face lit up in that crafty grin he knew so well. "Eureka!" she said. "A Bron doll! In the blue dress." In a stunning bit of stagecraft, just at the moment that "As I Am" turned into an anthem, Arkadina's faded dressing gown slipped away to reveal a startling bold blue gown.

Leonard shook his head. "It's $125!" he said. "Are you crazy?"

"Are you?" she countered, pointing to the figurine on the table.

He made a face. He was uncomfortable discussing money with Ellen. In addition to his tuition and living expenses, his family gave him a generous allowance, a lot more than the ten bucks a week that Harry gave Ellen for groceries. Leonard had offered, right off the bat, to pay a bigger share of the rent, but Ellen wouldn't let him. He did what he could to sneak in treats, but it wasn't easy; she was very proud. So he didn't give the obvious answer, that he could afford it. Instead he asked, "How can you compare this? I've been a fan of Bernie's for years. She even knows me, kind of. She remembered my face right away, even if she didn't put it together with my name. But I bet she will next time."

"I'm doing this, Leonard. Maybe I can't explain it, but I need to do this. I need to give her something as unique as she is. I'll find the money somewhere."

By paying a little extra (which she would never admit to Leonard), Ellen was able to have the doll in her hands in time for Christmas. It was everything she'd hoped, a jewel of a miniature, perfect down to the distinctive arch of the painted eyebrows.

"Okay, it's beautiful." Leonard tried not to sound begrudging.

Ellen sighed with satisfaction. "It is, isn't it? Now all I have to do is figure out how to give it to her. I wouldn't trust the post office."

Leonard forbore to remind her that the box had travelled all the way from Nebraska in perfect safety. She wanted to deliver it in person for the same reason that he would deliver his to Bernie; you want them to know it's from you.

She continued to fuss. "I sure as hell don't want Max to see me. He'd never let me hear the end of it."

"I'm sure you know his schedule well enough to avoid him."

"Yeah. Why am I so nervous about this?" Her shoulders gave a little shiver. "Hey, would you go with me?"

"Huh?!" He hadn't seen that one coming.

"Sure! Come with me." Her smile returned. "Then I won't look like a lunatic. We'll just be some fans being seasonally appropriate. I'll give her the doll. And you can give her that book that has *The Country Wife*."

It was an old volume of Wycherley from the second-hand section of the Drama Book Shop. Leonard had bought it for his *Gone With the Wind* collection (it had belonged to Laura Hope Crews), but he'd remarked more than once that it would be fun to give it to Bronwen Davies because of the reference in "Moscow."

"Sure," he agreed. "Why not? So when do you want to do this?"

She sighed again. "I have to think about it."

Jeff Kaplan came to stay for the weekend, telling his parents that his Christmas break started later than it did. He brought a couple of joints from Buffalo; his suite-mate was a dealer—nothing serious, just enough for book money.

Happily buzzed on grass and wine, they meandered down to the theatre district. It was snowing: a mild dusting, enough to feel festive. Jeff started singing that Mel Tormé song about the chestnuts. Ellen had never realized what a nice voice he had. She said so.

Jeff clutched his heart and staggered forward. "I'm dying! Ellen Janow gave me a compliment!"

"You are such an asshole, Jeff!"

"Well, you don't really give a lot of compliments," Leonard observed. "Not unless you want something."

"So what do you want? My body maybe?"

"Don't flatter yourself," Ellen sniffed.

"Just as well," Jeff said. "I think I might be...you know."

"I think we're all a little stoned," Leonard said anxiously.

"Of course we are," Jeff agreed. "That's why I can say it. Wow! I did say it, didn't I?"

"You really did." Ellen felt genuine admiration.

Jeff heard it and smiled. "I did. You know what else? I want to go to a gay bar. Just to see what it's like."

"You should!" Ellen gave him a quick hug. "I think that's a great idea. Leonard, why don't you go with him?"

Leonard twitched uncomfortably. There were some things he didn't think about, no less say. "I don't know. I'd feel weird."

"Don't be ridiculous! If I were a guy, I'd go with him. Maybe I should go to a dyke bar some time, just to see. They have dyke bars, don't they? I wonder where you find them."

Leonard writhed. "Would you please just shut up!"

They did. They'd reached the Regale, where Max Bulloch stood under the lemony light, surrounded by his usual gaggle of female admirers.

"I hope he doesn't see me," Ellen fussed importantly. "He'll wonder why I wasn't here to blow him during intermission."

Leonard gave her a look. He enjoyed Ellen's stories, but sometimes he wondered if all of them were true. He was about to make a clever comment, when his attentions were distracted. "Look!" he hissed, poking Ellen in the stomach with his elbow.

"You're lucky this is a thick coat," she groused. "I can't afford to be black and blue for weeks."

"Shut up and look!" He put his hands on her shoulders and turned her around. Rebecca Lewis and Christopher Pruitt were making their way, shoulder to shoulder, down the alley. As they passed under a streetlight, a keen eye could spot that they were holding hands.

"Ahh!" Ellen sighed with satisfaction. "Confirmation."

"I wonder how your friend Max feels about this," Leonard teased. He explained to Jeff, "Max and Becca used to date."

Ellen's eyes glittered with reflected bits of light from the marquee. "Date? They used to fuck. But that's been over for ages."

"The things you know," Jeff said respectfully.

"I'm starving," Leonard said. "Why am I starving? We ate like pigs."

"It's the joint," Jeff informed him. "You know what I could really get into now? One of those Entenmann's cakes with the fudge frosting."

"I wish you hadn't said that. Now I want one!"

"Let's go home," Ellen said. "We can pass that 24 hour place on 78th Street. Maybe they'll have one. Damn! I can't wait to tell Ahuva! Thank god we're doing that thing with her."

♫

Between Thanksgiving and Christmas, Ahuva's idea had blossomed from a card into an entire party. SUNY let out for break a few days before my school; by the time I'd arrived home she'd already convinced the doorman, bribing him with a bottle of the liquor that customers were always giving Jakub for

144

the holidays, to let her hand out cookies and punch. She was going to bake the cookies herself, so they'd be special. Ahuva's enthusiasm was contagious and, with the constant stream of gossip from her and Ellen, it was impossible for me not to feel involved in the backstage life of *Lake Song*. The phenomenally thoughtful Maria; handsome Ollie and friendly Kaye; Max and Joe and the legendary Bron and Lil…I wondered briefly if Ellen's new friend from her scaffolding adventure could be the same girl Ahuva had met in the bathroom, but it seemed too much like a coincidence from a cheesy movie. Without consciously making the decision, I volunteered to help with the party. Somewhere along the line, so did Ellen.

The plan was for Ahuva and me to do the baking on Saturday. On Sunday, we'd bring the cookies, some candy canes her father had supplied, and the giant card that had been the seed for the whole idea. Ellen and Leonard, who had some kind of gift they wanted to give Bronwen Davies, were bringing the beverages. And Leonard had decided it would be odd to do this without seeing the show, so he'd bought us all tickets as a present. It had turned into a marvelous adventure.

We dressed for Sunday with great care. I don't need to remember what I wore, because I have a picture: my one genuine silk blouse (black, of course) with a long plaid skirt I'd bought in the Salvation Army (vintage, but with a label from Saks), my good black pumps and the (adored) moldering raccoon coat my dad had found for me at one of the thrift shops where he sniffed out antiques for our family store. I confess to a total blank as to what my friends wore, except to recall that we all looked very smart and festive, and all our eyes were bright with excitement.

Ahuva and Ellen had carefully calculated the best time for our arrival. Everyone had to clock in at latest half an hour before the show, so we showed up an hour before that. The doorman, Wally, waved us in with a grin that turned into a smirk when he caught Ellen's eye. When she cheerfully flipped him off, he laughed.

Under the flickering light of a bare fluorescent tube, we trooped behind him down a narrow corridor that was as undistinguished as the backstage area of my college theatre and probably (a thought that only occurred to me as I ran a surreptitious finger along the lumpy walls) of similar vintage. Wally stopped at the first grey door on the left. A small metal frame, nailed at eye level, held a hand-lettered piece of card that said "Bronwen Davies." He knocked. A dumpy moon-faced woman opened the door.

"Hi, Con. These are the kids I told you about, with the Christmas present for Miss Davies."

"Of course, Wally. Thanks." The woman had an extremely pleasant smile. "Miss Davies is expecting you."

"Oh God!" Ellen whispered in my ear.

"Shut up!" I whispered back. "You know how your voice carries!"

Ahuva, who seemed very much at home backstage, led the way with Leonard close on her heels. I trailed a little behind. It was their day, after all. I was only along for the ride.

"Hello. Welcome to my little room."

The voice was immediately identifiable, lilting, with the sandy quality of an old soft-shoe dance. After we'd all filed in and found a place to stand, I saw the person who went with it. Ellen had rhapsodized so often over "the many faces of Bron" that I was surprised to see the actress looking exactly the way she always did. She was a little smaller than she seemed on stage, and her head was proportionately a little large, but I'd often noticed that in movie stars and Bronwen Davies was primarily a film actress.

"How magnificent!" Ahuva was saying.

It was a pretty room, more decorated than I would have expected, the cheerful yellow floral of the divan slipcover repeated in the wallpaper and curtains. The makeup table, framed and flower-decked, was positively dainty. I wouldn't have called it "magnificent," but certainly a world away from the cinderblocks, stained boards and bare light bulbs that I was accustomed to at school. So this was Broadway.

"Thank you, my dear. I've just finished papering." Miss Davies, as pleased as if Ahuva had compared the before and after, felt compelled to point out other fine points of the room. "In here is my little loo and that sort... 'john,' I think you call it. And here is my little refrigerator..."

"Oh, good! Can we offer you a cup of cider and some cookies? We made them ourselves. The cookies I mean, not the cider..."

Ellen, insisting punch was too juvenile without booze (which Ahuva felt uncomfortable about adding), had suggested cider, which at least had the virtue of being seasonal. Leonard started fishing in his heavy shopping bag.

"Oh, no, my dear. I never indulge before a show."

The dresser, Connie, interrupted. "But if you'd be kind enough to leave some for us to have later, we'd be delighted. They made the cookies themselves, Bronwen."

Miss Davies flashed us a megawatt smile. "Oh yes, of course. How lovely of you all!"

Ahuva turned gratefully to Connie and handed her a small packet of cookies that she'd wrapped separately for this purpose.

Ellen and Leonard still hadn't said a word. Ahuva cleared her throat and gave them a freighted stare.

Leonard blushed and produced a square gold box. "Uh, we have some Christmas presents for you, Miss Davies."

Undoing the ribbon, then delicately removing a layer of tissue paper, Davies pulled out a small frosted-glass seagull that Leonard had been unable to resist in the museum shop at the Met.

"How lovely!"

Leonard's blush deepened.

"I'll put him there, so he won't be lonely." She pointed at the steam pipe that ran across the ceiling. A small flock of seagulls dangled there: plush, wood, plastic and one other glass. "This one shall be the baby." She smiled fondly at them, then gestured at an armchair in the corner that was overflowing with stuffed animals. "The reason I keep so many toy animals about is that I can't have that many live ones."

"I also have something else," said Leonard. "It's a book," he added unnecessarily. No matter how beautifully wrapped, a book like a record album, was unmistakable.

She removed the wrappings, oblivious to Connie's catching them as they left her hand. The old volume was bound in well-rubbed green leather, embossed with a pattern of lilies. Peering near-sightedly at the title, Miss Davies seemed confused. She rallied with a resourceful smile. "Thank you so much. It's quite lovely."

"I thought it would be significant," he continued bravely. "It's the complete Wycherley. Well, pretty complete. It has *The Plain Dealer*." When she didn't react, he added quickly, "and *The Country Wife*, of course."

"Ah!" The penny had dropped. "And all these others, too? How lovely! I don't have a copy of Wycherley here."

"And now you do!" Ellen had finally found her voice.

I understood that Ellen didn't expect to be recognized. After all, the infamous cocktail party had been half a year ago; a famous actress would have met hundreds of people since then. What surprised me was how she stood, blending into the wallpaper. Now that Ellen had embraced her wild side, I'd almost forgotten that this other girl existed, the one I'd sat next to in sixth grade, the one who'd hardly raised her hand in tenth grade History.

"Yes, well thank you all so very much. It was lovely of you all." Miss Davies kissed Leonard, who was nearest, on the cheek and moved to kiss us all.

Ellen looked as if she might burst. "Wait! Miss Davies, there's one more thing." She stepped forward and stuck out her box. Wrapped in foiled paper and thick with green velvet ribbons, it was almost too beautiful to open.

Miss Davies nonchalantly slipped off the ribbons and pulled of the paper, letting everything fall to the floor. The cover came off the box, followed by several sheets of tissue. Connie, who'd been busy finding a place for the book, stooped to retrieve it all.

"Oh my!" Bronwen Davies had been terribly polite before, but the doll clearly affected her. She lifted it high, showing it to Connie, turning it to see every side. The pile of pale golden curls, the sparkle of the blue beaded gown; it was her Arkadina to the life. "Oh my dear!" She looked directly at Ellen, who was, I think, holding her breath. "This is so…so…" She seemed to search her mental thesaurus for an exclamation that would express her feelings.

"I hope you like it," Ellen said shyly.

Davies beamed at her. "So extraordinarily lovely! Thank you, my dear!" She bestowed a kiss on Ellen's cheek.

"Merry Christmas," Ellen murmured, turning the same shade of dark pink as Leonard.

"Merry Christmas," Ahuva said. Connie, catching her eye, had signaled that it was time for us to leave.

"Merry Christmas," I whispered, because it seemed less conspicuous than being the only one keeping silent.

Leonard backed towards the door. I just about heard him mumble "…Christmas." We waved goodbye to Connie, who closed the door softly behind us. Somewhat dazed, we found Wally.

Ahuva had warned me how unimpressive it was backstage at the Regale. The corridors had certainly confirmed this. Still, I was surprised that the greenroom was less than half the size of the one I was used to and the badly painted cracked walls, the miscellaneous furnishings and the row of ancient framed black and white production photos were identical to those in Avery Hall.

Ahuva had bought a paper tablecloth printed with goofy snowmen and ice skating elves. We spread it over a card table and started setting out the cookies on paper plates. As soon as Wally disappeared, we began a frantic rehash of the events of the last ten minutes.

"Did you see?" Ellen said, completely unnecessarily. "Did you? Wasn't she…? Perfect! Her room was so cozy!"

I agreed. "It looked like someone's home."

"That woman could have been a designer," Ahuva declared. "She ought to win an award for taste, if there is such a thing. That robe she was wearing was stunning."

"I thought I'd die when she said 'welcome to my little room.'" Ellen's eyes rolled back in her head—ecstasy.

"When she said 'my little refrigerator,' I thought she was going to ask us to have a drink," Leonard confessed.

"And I almost thought she was going to ask us if we wanted something to eat!" Ahuva laughed with him.

Ellen paused in mid-pour. "You know she thought this was hard cider, right? When she said she wouldn't 'indulge.' It was obvious."

"To you, maybe," I countered.

Ahuva weighed in. "I thought she meant she doesn't like to eat before a show."

On a dime, Ellen turned direful. "Did you see the empty J&B bottles?"

"What is it with you?" I objected automatically. Dark forebodings were typical Ellen drama. "Maybe she had a bunch of friends stop by after last night's show."

With a little lift of her shoulders, as if to say she knew better, she changed the subject. "Did everyone see the Tony?"

I hadn't been able to take my eyes off it. It was the first Tony award—the first award statuette of any kind—that I'd ever seen in person, and it had shot an arrow through my ambitious little heart. "It was hard to miss. What about that that antique sheet music?"

"What music?" Ahuva demanded.

"Some old sheet music for a dance called 'Betrayal Tango,'" Ellen informed her. "Don't you wonder who gave her that?"

Ahuva sniffed. She hated missing out on anything. "How do you two notice everything? I didn't see that!"

"It was on the shelf near the armchair," I explained. "Right near the cast picture in the silver frame."

"How…lovely!" Leonard called, from the bench where he was standing, trying to drape Ahuva's card (signed by all of us) over the nearest production stills.

We broke into hysterical giggles.

"I couldn't believe it," he marveled. "She really couldn't think of another adjective!"

"I told you," Ellen said triumphantly. "She's a dumb blonde!"

Suddenly Ahuva's eyes flew open. She pulled something out of the shopping bag and ran out the door. We were still blinking our confusion when she returned, breathless, but smiling with relief. "I almost forgot the invitation!" It had been a last minute thought, a piece of construction paper with "Xmas Cookie Thanks From Your Fans!" in my best fake calligraphy. "I borrowed a pen from Wally and added 'in greenroom.' Should I have put 'now'?"

Ellen shook her head. "They'll figure it out. Or else, when we hear people walking around, one of us will go out and get the ball rolling."

There was no need to worry. Blindfolded and hogtied in the vacuum of outer space, an actor will always find the way to free food. The first to arrive were Joe Bigelow and Tyler Moss.

"It's your young friend," Moss said delicately, with a warm smile for us all.

"Indeed it is!" Bigelow made much of his living with the rich embrace of his voice. He'd recently completed a commercial for canned soup that would go on to win every advertising award and put all three of his children through college. Joe's been gone for years now, but they still run the commercial at those times of year when nostalgia runs high; it'll probably outlive us all. Harry Janow was the agency's account executive for Campbell at the time. I wonder if Harry ever knew that Bigelow was shtupping his daughter.

Bigelow grabbed Ellen and gave her a smack on her bottom. "What a delightful surprise!" Still basking in the glow of her success with the doll, Ellen leaned comfortably against Bigelow's beefy side. Seeing them side by side reminded me how tiny Ellen was; her personality was so outsized that I often forgot. "It was actually Ahuva's idea," she said graciously.

"Well then, thank you Ahuva!" he boomed, reaching his free arm to pull Ahuva into a brief embrace.

"It's nothing," she mumbled, flustered.

"It's a lovely idea," Moss twinkled, reaching a hand to shake hers and thereby rescuing her.

Leonard stifled a giggle at the adjective.

Fortunately, Ahuva didn't notice. "I just wanted to thank you all for such a stellar show," she told Moss earnestly. "You've all given me so much pleasure…"

From my corner, I could see Bigelow about to open his mouth and Ellen put her small hand up to stop him. She was assisted by a commotion at the door.

Five or six actors burst in at once. At their head was Oliver Blanchard, handsome even through the age makeup that was far less convincing this close up. He grinned at Ahuva in recognition. "I know you!"

Pink roses bloomed across her cheeks, and I saw the dictionary definition of "starry eyed." I wondered if Blanchard really was gay, in the homosexual sense of the word, like Ellen said. Then again, as I'd reassured Ahuva, Ellen thought everyone was gay or at least bi until she had indisputable evidence to the contrary.

Before Ahuva could faint, Maria Dearborne surfaced from the pack and gave her a hug. "Are you back in town! I'm so glad! And what a delightful idea! Did you bake these?"

"Yes. I…all of us…" Perfectly at ease now that Maria was here, Ahuva gestured to include me and Leonard in the shadows, where we clung discreetly to a pillar, sharing the unspoken view that this wasn't our scene but that we were thrilled to watch from the wings.

Maria flashed a smile in our direction. "Wonderful! Thank you!' Ahuva took her aside to give her the silver kitten pin that she'd bought her as a Christmas present.

All the actors were so charming that even Leonard and I found ourselves engaging in small talk. Fortunately, Max Bulloch was otherwise engaged and didn't show to spoil Ellen's radiance.

Connie came down for a few minutes to say "thank you" again. She offered to take some cookies to Lilith Brassloe who, like Davies, ate sparingly before a show but would be "most appreciative." Ahuva made up a very pretty plate, and thought to tell Connie to take as many more cookies as she liked and give them to the other dressers. We'd made dozens and dozens of the things, dropping lumps of Toll House dough, cutting sugar cookies in the shape of stars, and slicing little squares from batches of brownies we made from a magazine recipe that claimed to have originated from Katharine Hepburn.

The half-hour call came and we had to leave. While Ellen and Ahuva brought the remaining cookies to Wally, to distribute to the stagehands and anyone else backstage, Leonard and I tidied everything else away, leaving only the giant card to show that we'd been there. Hearing we'd be watching the show, Wally said to leave the paper goods and boxes with him and pick them up after.

We were so keyed up that it was difficult to settle into our seats. Ahuva and Ellen especially kept whispering about what this person or that person had said. Leonard, hands clasped peacefully in his lap, was quietly content.

I was thrilled by the adventure of it all, and by the wonderful story it was going to make for people at school, especially those unfortunate enough not to have Broadway as their local theatre. I was also a little anxious about seeing the show a second time. Back in May, I'd thought *Lake Song* was wonderful. I knew both Ahuva and Ellen still thought so after multiple viewings, and I still loved listening to the soundtrack; but I was worried that, with everything about it now so familiar, the magic wouldn't be there.

It wasn't; and that was okay. This second time, familiar with the material and with another semester's worth of Drama Major slogging under my belt, I passed beyond wonder. I spotted the gears and braces beneath the effects, and it was a revelation: rather than being disillusioned, I was overwhelmed by respect for the excellence of the work that went into the production. When the curtain fell, I jumped to my feet—not to applaud for Arkadina or Trigorin, nor in empathy with Masha or Nina, but to salute the actors, and the musicians, and the wigmakers, and the people pulling the levers on the light board. It was the first time I'd sat in an audience and felt like a fellow actor.

We applauded ourselves sore; then staggered to the stage door where we waited, wondering when we could go in and get our things. The first actors who came out were members of the ensemble. They greeted us with big waves and "thank yous." It struck us as hilarious that all the autograph seekers turned to stare, wondering if we were Someone. Wally appeared in the door, holding it for Oliver Blanchard, who had a lot of packages. Blanchard called out to us, which spurred Wally to throw a thumb over his shoulder and yell, "Come on already." Ahuva and Ellen looked at each other and bolted for the door, with me and Leonard close behind.

Wally was incredibly friendly. Ahuva's bottleh must have been the good stuff. "Hey," he said, when we were safe inside. "You wanna stand on the stage?"

We were all, even Ellen, as wide-eyed as little kids at Santa World. Wally winked and led us through a door.

Following close behind Leonard, I took a few tentative steps forward. The stage was larger than any stage I'd ever stood on. Yawing on the other side of the apron was the auditorium of the Regale theatre. I looked up, all the way up, to the balcony where we'd sat in May. It was so far away, my neck hurt.

Everything was far away. I walked over to the work light and tried to imagine playing a scene in this vastness. I didn't feel like an actor anymore; I felt like a mouse.

"Stand over there!" Ahuva called. She was pointing to the large tree stage right. It was the tree in the illustration on the posters. At the start of Act I, it held one end of the rope for Kostia's outdoor stage. While other parts of the set came and went throughout the play, that tree remained: sheltering Kostia when he killed the seagull; supporting the tired Medviedenko; hiding Nina before her final entrance. First checking to see that Wally wasn't looking my way, I put my hand on the bark. It was real bark, glued over a foundation of some kind. I smiled and a bright light blinded me. Ahuva, thinking of everything, had brought a camera. We look turns taking pictures by the tree.

Wally just laughed. "Come on. I'll show you some more. Only no pictures when we get back there." He walked us through the wings to where the rolling sets waited: Nina's garden bench; Arkadina's dressing table; Kostia's study; the card table from the final scene. Wally took a proprietary pride in it, saluting the stagehands who were tying it all down, pointing out the half-sleigh that was used in the Act I Finale. It was a bunch of old junk that we could have found in any thrift store in the city, but we were as awed as if it were Versailles.

We ended up where we'd begun. Wally produced our shopping bags from the open cubbies by the front door. He laughed off our effusive thanks, saying "The pleasure was all mine."

We stepped out into the cold, clear darkness of a December night. A little drunk with it all, we stood for a minute by the door, smiling hard.

"What do we do now?" I asked. I couldn't bear the thought of going home.

"Alfie's!" Ahuva and Ellen said together.

"You still haven't been, have you?" Ellen asked.

I shook my head. I'd only heard about the place from both of them.

"Well then we absolutely have to go," Ahuva decreed, looping her arm through mine.

11 – NOTHING (REPRISE)

KOSTIA

Am I the only one who knows art can only be as pure as artists?
Am I the only one who cares? Have I the only eyes to see what art is?
Nothing less than miracle,
Nothing more than total abnegation by the artist
In the service of a greater thing than we could ever be.
Art is all and I...
Am nothing.

Sometimes you get lucky. Of course, there are two kinds of luck.

Like when you come home Christmas Eve on the last train, footsore and completely frazzled from crazy last-minute shoppers, and your Pop greets you in a cloud of rye fumes that almost knock you out when he hugs you, and he tells you in this thick choky voice how wonderful it's going to be, because Eunice has agreed to marry him and she'll be moving in sometime after New Year's. That's luck, alright; only not the good kind, even though Frankie had to pretend that it was. From the first time they'd met, Eunice had made it obvious that she wanted to have Mickey all to herself; his daughter was a piece of gum stuck to the sole of her shoe.

Then there were her acting classes. Frankie tried to start them up again, but she couldn't enroll enough children to make it worth her while. "Kids are fickle," one of the parents explained. "They lose interest. Try again in the fall, when camp is fresh in their minds and they're used to seeing you." So that was more bad luck. Not entirely, since it would mean another full day for making the rounds, but definitely bad financially.

Frankie needed a lift. When not having money is one of the reasons you needed consolation, it's especially crappy that most consoling things cost money. She resolved not to worry too much about it. Lil would soon be ready to get back to work. Bob, the clown who'd demonstrated the juggling balls at FAO Schwartz, was confident he'd be getting lots of kids' parties from all the cards he'd given out and had promised to give her a call when he needed an assistant. Something else would turn up. You had to have faith.

Frankie decided to treat herself to a hamburger at Alfie's. She took a table by the brick arches that divided the bar from the main restaurant. You could see most of the dining room from there and, if you took the chair facing the door, you also got to see who came and went. It was quiet. On non-matinee days, most people who came in for lunch were regulars who liked to hang out when they were in rehearsal or not working. She'd seen some of them before. A few waved as they passed. She was pretty sure they were actors, at least the one with the mustache was. She waved back. It gave her a warm feeling, to think they knew her.

The waiter who brought her burger also brought a Coke she hadn't ordered. "On the house," he'd winked. That was so nice!

Alfie's felt more like home than home did, now that Eunice's personal touches were creeping in. The worst part was finding some of Martha's special things in the trash. Frankie had only just managed to retrieve the kitchen canisters with the roosters and the sampler she thought was maybe her grandmother's, the one that had "Smile Upon Our Home and Bless Those Who Dwell Within It" worked in cross-stitch. The sampler was hanging on her closet door now, and the canisters tucked under her bed. She'd touch them sometimes, to reassure herself they were safe.

She wondered if she'd ever stop aching for her mother's old rocking chair. It had gone to the junkyard almost as soon as Eunice had moved in. Frankie had been in the city that day. She didn't notice until the next morning, when she came down for breakfast. In place of the rocker, which had stood there for her entire life, she saw a ruffle covered armchair. She'd thought she was hallucinating.

Mickey and Eunice were in the kitchen, having coffee. Trying to be calm, keeping her voice as low and steady as a professional actress could, Frankie asked what had happened to the chair.

"It was old and crappy," Mickey said. "Should have gotten rid of it long ago. Anyway, we need room for all of Eunice's stuff."

"Only the nicer things!" Eunice said, with a fake laugh that any first term NYADA student would have sneered at. "Frankie, dear, you have to agree that my chair makes the whole place seem brighter."

"You could have asked me, Pop. I would have put the rocker in my room."

"We have too much junk in this house," Mickey said. "Let it go, Frankie." His voice was gruff and defensive. He knew he'd done something wrong.

Eunice just sat there, with that smug smile on her fat face. Okay, she wasn't fat. She was…what did Pop's buddies always say…? Well-upholstered. Exactly. Just like her chair.

For all the years since Martha's death, Frankie had sat on that chair for comfort. Losing it was like losing a piece of her mother all over again. Frankie didn't say another word. Saturday, while Eunice was out getting her hair done, she snuck the family photo albums out of the breakfront in the living room. She made sure to check the trash cans every day. What else could she do? Pop thought he loved this woman. He wanted to marry her. Valentine's Day, they were going down to City Hall. Once a thought got stuck in Mickey's mind, nothing could change it. Frankie had to find a way to live with it, or find a way to make enough money to move out fast.

Frankie sighed, so lost in thought that she'd forgotten the straw in her mouth until she heard the bubbles. Jerked back to the present, she was completely embarrassed. No one else seemed to have heard; there weren't too many people in the room and most were far away. As her eye travelled the room, it caught Alfie's. Relieved no one had noticed the bubbles, she smiled automatically before remembering she found him a little scary; he looked, she thought, like a gangster. She'd once confided that to Tyler Moss who'd smiled as if her observation amused him but didn't contradict her.

And now Alfie was walking towards her table. She hoped the waiter wasn't in trouble over the Coke. She'd offer to pay for it.

"Hi, there," he said. "I'm Alfie. I've seen you here with Tyler, haven't I? Tyler Moss? And I think you sometimes pick up Lil's order."

"Yes. Hi. Nice to meet you."

"Nice to meet you, too. I bet you're an actress. You look like one." He didn't sneer it, like Eunice did; he said it as a compliment.

She smiled with pleasure. "I am, yes. I'm Frankie," she added, remembering her manners. "Frankie Cecchi."

"Frankie Cecchi." He tapped his forehead with his finger, showing he would remember. "Paesana! So, Frankie. I've got a little problem and it occurs to me a nice Italian actress like yourself might be able to help. One of my coat check girls has the flu. At least that's what she says, but I don't know. I mean, she's an actress too." He made an extremely funny face.

She laughed again. Actually, when he smiled he looked a little like Robert DeNiro.

"She's a good kid, so I'll give her the benefit of the doubt. But it means I'm stuck without a coat check girl for a coupla nights. Donna usually covers Tuesdays, Wednesdays and Thursdays. From 4:30 to 11:30. I thought maybe, seeing as you're an actress, you might need to make a few extra bucks. Or else you might know someone who does. The pay is ten bucks a night, but the main thing is tips. Tuesdays aren't so great, but you'd be surprised how much you can make on a cold, wet Wednesday. And you get dinner, of course."

"I'd love to," she said promptly. She didn't need to stop and think. Even someone as broke as she was always left a quarter if she checked her coat. Plenty of people gave more. A coat check girl working all night would make at least twenty bucks in tips. Plus dinner. This, finally, was *good* luck. "When would you need me?"

"I could use you tonight," he said. "If you're available. Donna only just called. So tonight and tomorrow. Probably next Tuesday, if it's really the flu."

"Okay." She'd have to miss Irene's class tomorrow, but that was alright. She could go to the Advanced Beginners on Monday. It was harder, but it would be practice and Irene wouldn't mind.

"Fantastic!" He held out his hand for a shake. She had to wipe some ketchup off hers, which made him laugh. "And that hamburger is on the house," he said. "Now that you're on the payroll. You've got plenty of time, but as soon as you're done, you tidy up and I'll show you the ropes. What's the matter?"

He read the dismay on her face before she said anything.

"I'm not dressed right." Frankie pointed to her red plaid shirt and stood up enough for Alfie to see she was wearing it with jeans. "I just came in to go to the library."

"Don't worry. I'm sure we've got a spare white shirt somewhere. That's all you need, a white shirt. Usually with a black skirt or pants, but jeans will be fine for tonight. You give your hair a little comb and put on some lipstick and you'll be a-okay." He gave her a wink and sauntered back to his usual spot at the end of the bar.

If she got a lot of tips, maybe she'd splurge and buy that new Berenson album, the live recording of the Actor's Fund concert. It was a double-album, so it was a little expensive. She'd hinted hard to Pop, but he'd turned over the Christmas shopping to Eunice and she'd ended up with a horrible yellow angora sweater that made look like she had mono and, to boot, made her sneeze.

Alfie was really very nice, once you got to know him. This was *very* good luck.

♫

Someone at Equity told Frankie about the casting agents who supplied actors for advertising promotions. Standing on your feet all day in the street, no matter what the weather, was pretty crappy work and the pay wasn't much; but if you did it, the agents owed you a favor and they were the same ones who often cast movie extras, the people in the background. If you did promotions, they almost always thanked you with extra work. With enough film work, she'd be able to join the Screen Actors' Guild. As a matter of fact, if she got more than a couple of jobs she'd *have* to join; but that was okay. Union membership would get her more extra work; it would pay for itself. Besides, people were always telling Frankie how great she'd be on a sitcom. Maybe if she belonged to SAG, she'd get some auditions.

She took a bunch of headshots around to those particular agencies and expressed her willingness to do promotions. The very next week she was hired for a three-day job, giving out samples of a new style of Virginia Slims.

Frankie didn't smoke, but she had nothing against cigarettes; her mother had died from a different kind of cancer.

They said to wear a dark skirt, panty hose and dark pumps. Because it was freezing, the girls would be allowed to wear their coats but only plain cloth coats, not those padded ones that looked like sleeping bags. A dark hat was okay, and dark gloves. Frankie's coat was gray wool and she had an old navy beret, but her only gloves were the red ones that matched her favorite hat. She had to buy a cheap pair of black ones at Bolton's. It was an investment. Maybe she'd need dark gloves someday to be in a film.

At the meeting place, a building lobby on East 56th Street, the agency representative gave her a Virginia Slims scarf to wear. She thought that was nice of them, until they told her she'd have to return it at the end or else the cost would come out of her pay. There was a cardboard tray to hang from a strap around her neck. It was filled with tiny boxes, each holding four cigarettes. She found this out during the lunch break, when one of the other girls popped one open and lit up. Virginia Slims were feminine and elegant: long and white, with a floral pattern below the filter. The same pattern, in pale green and blue and lavender, covered the boxes they were handing out. They were so pretty that you felt like you were giving people a present, not forcing them to try a product they didn't want. Frankie said as much to Kim, the girl who'd lit up.

"Are you kidding?" Kim laughed. "Even guys'll take them. Who doesn't want free cigarettes?"

For three days, Frankie stood on her assigned corner from 11 AM until 6 PM with only two five-minute bathroom breaks. They took lunch at 2:30, when the streets were a little quiet: fifteen minutes to eat a cheese sandwich and thaw out your feet. Standing on Park Avenue with a box around your neck, toes numb and nose running, is a strange way to spend the day. It was hard to think of it as having anything to do with acting.

You were supposed to need to refill your tray at least every half hour—the agency was monitoring. Frankie had worried she'd need to walk up to strange people and wave the packs in front of them, but Kim was right. All she had to do was stand there. As soon as people noticed what was in her tray, they came over and grabbed boxes. The only thing she had to say was "yes" when someone asked if it was okay to take more than one. Day One went by fast. Day Two went on forever, one of those raw, grey days when people stayed inside and had lunch at their desks. It was impossible to empty a tray every half hour, no matter what the agency people said; you couldn't approach people who weren't there. Some of the girls dumped their trays in the lobby, telling the agency it just wasn't worth it. Frankie was tempted to do the same. They were only getting paid $25 a day and a cheese sandwich. She'd made more teaching acting to kids, and the church basement had been so nice and warm. But an actress had to make sacrifices. If she got film work, the cold and the boredom would have been well worth it.

On Day Three, an obnoxious man started an argument over why Frankie was giving out "girly cigarettes" and then complained that there were only three in his box and he'd been cheated. Frankie tried desperately to reason with him. People were staring, and not in a good way. What if the cops came? Was it really okay to be giving things out on a street corner? She was about to break down and cry, right there on the sidewalk, when the agency man, alerted by the girl on the opposite corner, came to save her. He talked tougher than the obnoxious guy, poking his chest with a finger, until he went away. And that was only the morning. The afternoon wasn't as bad, but it wasn't easy either.

At the end of the day, Frankie gratefully unwound the green and blue and lavender scarf from her neck and handed it over, along with her tray. The agency man handed over her check with a businesslike smile. "Nice work, Cecchi," he said. "Cool under pressure. We'd be happy to use you again."

"Thanks," she said. She devoutly hoped he didn't mean more days giving away stuff on street corners. She squatted beside her dance bag to swap her pumps for sneakers. Her knitted leg-warmers felt so good, she stayed where she was for a minute, just to enjoy the warmth.

"Hey, Cecchi!" the agency man called out. "Feel free to take as many as you like." His assistant was emptying all the trays into a carton.

It seemed stupid not to. She didn't want them herself, but other people might. Ellen only smoked those fancy brown cigarettes from the store by the library, and Margaret Rodney smoked Benson & Hedges, but she bet Casilda would be happy to have them. So would Connie dePaul and Lil's dresser, Beryl. Frankie plunged her hands into the carton and grabbed as many of the little boxes as would fit in her dance bag.

ARKADINA

Something crept into my room...
Must have been while I was
  sleeping.
Something stole away the bloom
  from my cheeks
And the twinkle from my eyes
And a thousand other things
That made me what I am. Was.
Now everything is upside-down
  because
When I look in the mirror, a strange
  woman looks at me.
I can't imagine who she is, or who
  I'm now supposed to be.
All the things you've had in life
  everything you were
Stolen in the dead of night, leaving
  you with...her.

As I am. When the applause
  disappears,
I feel the silence start to paralyze.
  Why must I face my fears?
I've been happy with illusion—or at
  least I've been content;
And if every day I have to fight
I've always felt so full of life,
The life I'm leading as I am.

Must I stand upon the brink of old age
With my book already over? I don't
  want to turn the page.
There's no fairy tale conclusion in
  the chapter dead ahead.
Like Scheherazade, I must delay
And fight to live another day,
The life I'm leading as I am.

Life is suddenly so fragile. A simple
  breath could crumble it to dust;

And every day a burden too heavy to
  be shouldered, yet I must.
Time to face the music, time to beat
  the band,
Time to make a reckoning as I am.

I refuse to be alone and afraid!
When all the monsters are familiar
  and there's always a parade
Of the people who adore me and the
  people who I pay:
Just a big unhappy family
That suits me satisfactorily;
The life I'm leading as I am.

I could fall into a ravening rage!
But there is gold anesthetizing me,
  and precious masquerade
And as long as there are lovers,
  there are always games to play
Though it may not be a paradise
It's fine compared to other lives,
The life I'm leading as I am.

Living in the moment—no memory of
  the past, memories pain.
Heedless of the future—tomorrow
  might not come, hope is vain.
Smash apart the hourglass, grab
  each grain of sand.
Time! There still is time to be as I am.

As I am! I am unique and I'm brave!
I made my life myself: I cut the cloth,
  from cradle to the grave;
For there never was a pattern that
  resembled what I dreamed.
So I took the chance, I paid the price.
I seize the most I can from life—
The life I'm leading as I am!

Leonard's family had tickets to opening night of the new Julie Harris play, so when Felix gave Ellen passes to the final preview she decided to invite Frankie Cecchi. Frankie was turning out to be kind of a character. She had a way of making everything sound like an adventure; even her childhood, which made Ellen's look almost tolerable by comparison. She also had this spunky waif thing that made people want to help her. And Thierry Dupontel seemed to think she was talented. She could end up famous someday.

Ellen suggested Frankie sleep over after the show, so she wouldn't have to take the train back to the ass end of Long Island. Leonard had invited Jeff Kaplan to stay over the same night. By the time the girls got home from the show, the boys were pretty spaced: they'd found the nerve to go down to the Stonewall for a couple of drinks. Jeff was enraptured; he'd actually been asked to dance, and it had been wonderful.

Leonard seemed happy, too, but he was very quiet. Ellen didn't want to question him in front of the others, but she meant to have a long talk with him at the earliest opportunity.

The next day, Leonard left for the traditional Kirschner family pre-theatre dinner at Joe Allen's before Ellen got home. She was alone in the apartment, a pretty rare thing. It was rarer still to have absolutely nothing that she needed to do. Opting for hedonism, she had a long hot bath, then slathered herself with her favorite cucumber lotion. There was a spot on her forehead. She pulled the pin out of the vitamin E capsule and squeezed out a drop.

Wrapped in a beach towel, she padded over to their small but interesting collection of bottles. The rolling aluminum cart had been rescued from the trash in Barney's building. Once Leonard sprayed it with silver Krylon and they put that piece of mirror on the top shelf, it looked almost Art Deco. They'd christened it "the drinks trolley," which they thought sounded very Burton and Taylor. Ellen thought that Richard Burton and Elizabeth Taylor were the sexiest couple on the planet. Any time you saw the two of them together, you knew they were panting to run into the next room and tear off their clothes. Those eyes—both of theirs, not just her famous violet ones...and his voice! His voice had a caress as palpable as fingers; just listening to him made her wet.

Though he said he was too old to get up to such adventures anymore, Joe liked to describe threesomes to her. It was food for fantasy. Ellen's favorite was to imagine a threesome with Burton and Taylor. Preferably on a pillow-strewn divan beside a perfumed pool in Morocco. Ellen wondered what they drank in Morocco. Whatever the Moroccans might drink, Burton and Taylor probably drank champagne. There wasn't any on the drinks trolley; anyway, it wasn't fun to drink champagne alone. She poured herself a Drambuie. Sprawling on the rug, she closed her eyes and tried to imagine herself at that pool. Perfume might help. Her eyes flicked open. She'd been waiting for an excuse to light that expensive Rigaud candle.

She jumped up to get her lighter from the other room. As she passed the table, she spotted a book of matches that would do just as well. Leonard had taken them from the Stonewall. Nice. Almost historic. Maybe they should start a matchbook collection; they did go to some interesting places.

The wick was a little short; she had to use two matches before it caught. Once it did, and that little pop of sulfur dissipated, she inhaled appreciatively. The scent was divine, worth every dollar Penelope had paid for it. Ellen was about to put down the matchbook when she noticed the writing on the inner flap. A phone number. Aha! Maybe that explained Leonard's secret little smile.

"His name is Preston," Leonard said, when she confronted him over breakfast. "I was going to tell you. I felt funny talking in front of Frankie."

"Jeff knows?"

"He was there," Leonard reminded her. "He went to dance with that guy and left me alone at the bar. I didn't know where to look. I thought everyone was staring at me. I almost left. A man came over to order a drink. It was pretty busy. He was having a hard time catching the bartender's eye and he started doing silly things to get his attention. Like he quacked. You know, like a duck. With his fingers in his armpits. It was funny. I laughed. He heard me, so he looked at me and rolled his eyes and winked. I...I don't know. I winked back. And then the bartender finally came over and he ordered a drink, and he asked if he could buy me one too. And then we started talking. His name is Preston."

"You said."

"Preston Harrold."

"Shouldn't it be the other way around?"

Leonard ignored her. "He's an architect," he said happily. "He's very smart. And funny. He's 34. I know that sounds old..."

"Not to me," she said dryly. Most of the men in her life were grey.

"You know who he looks a little like? Robert Culp. Well, I think he does. And he wants to take me on a date."

His smile was so shy that she often forgot how beautiful it was.

"Wow. Leonard, that's... So I guess you're gay then." She wanted to bite her tongue as soon as she said it.

She might as well have slapped him. He crumpled into the beanbag, the smile reversed into a Charlie Brown wiggle. "I...I don't know!" It came from his heart. "How am I supposed to know?"

"But you liked him. *Liked* him liked him."

He nodded mutely. "But I like girls. I used to like Lisa, remember? And I think Bernie is beautiful."

"So, okay." She sat on the floor and put her head against his legs. "Maybe you're bi-sexual. A lot of famous people are bi. Julius Caesar. Danny Kaye."

"Danny Kaye?" He sounded both shocked and hopeful.

"Uh-huh. Joe said. I think maybe Tyler Moss...Maybe. I definitely think Felix might be."

"Felix? You think so?"

"Oh yeah. He and Penelope are inseparable, so why else would they have gotten divorced? She's dating this banker now. She tells Felix stories about him and they laugh..."

"What about Felix? Is he, um, seeing anybody?"

"I don't know. It's funny. Felix is so out there that you don't notice how little you actually know about him. Other than his career: he'll talk your ear off about that."

Lost in their own thoughts, they sat quietly.

Ellen reached a hand up and squeezed his knee. "I'm really happy for you," she told him. "I think it's great that you're going on a date."

Ellen was surprised to find herself at loose ends.

Since the Day of the Doll (as she thought of it), she'd hardly seen Joe. He spent a lot of time with his family at this time of year. At least he'd had the decency to warn her in advance.

Unlike Max. Ellen had shown up for one of their usual appointments, only to have Wally to tell her Max was out. It was annoying. She'd gone out of her way to leave Felix's office early, to get there on time. Wally was still showing residual friendliness (she would definitely have to wangle the occasional bottle of scotch out of Barney), so he let her go upstairs and use the loo before she left. Which was when she heard the giggling and, popping the door a crack, spotted Mr. Bulloch doing one of the ensemble in the stairwell. The one who understudied Nina of course. Linda, Ellen thought her name was. Disgusting. Not that he was doing this Linda, but that he was too much of a pig to tell Ellen that her services were no longer needed. Well fuck him. More accurately, don't fuck him! Let Linda enjoy his dubious attentions. He was a lousy fuck for all he was hung like a horse. He thought himself such a treasure that he never gave any gifts, and he'd proven worthless as a contact. Ellen could do a lot better with her time and her skills. It was only that her feelings were a little hurt. No one likes to feel they're so easily replaced.

She tried to talk this through with her female friends, but they were all such virgins. Maybe not technically, but the way they acted, so insistent on coupling sex with romance, they might as well have been. Leonard was the same way, but at least he let her talk about it without making her feel she was wearing a scarlet letter.

It sucked that she hardly saw Leonard anymore. He was spending all his free time with his beloved Preston. Who she'd finally met. They didn't get on. At all. He was a snotty bastard, intellectually pretentious. Whatever she said, Preston found a way to turn it around. She assumed he saw her as a threat.

The house felt too quiet. Ellen's hours were far too regular for her taste: going from school to her various jobs; coming home; having sensible salads or picking up a pizza. Though it wasn't really her thing, she got in the habit of turning the television on for noise. Almost despite herself, she found herself getting into that British show, the one about the rich people and their servants.

The only slightly interesting thing in her life was that Felix had finally put together the financing and pre-production was finally underway for the brief, three-play season.

She was wide open for a new experience, any kind of experience.

Felix sent her to pick up some *Dear Brutus* sketches from Ruth Mann, the award-winning costume designer who'd committed to design his season: a standard messenger run but, as the designer of Bronwen Davies' fabulous blue beaded gown, Mann was not without some interest.

The elevator's out-of-order notice was old enough that the tape was flaking off the corners. Ellen walked up three flights to a dusty hallway. The doors held the kind of pebbled glass that usually had Humphrey Bogart or Robert Mitchum on the other side. She pushed at the one stenciled "R. Mann." It wasn't locked, which was more than a little unusual in a city where people locked the door behind them to throw out the trash.

Her eyes were assaulted by a jumble of color and pattern, blazing from racks of garments and from the heaps of fabric that covered tables and every available surface. A few dress forms were draped with bits of cloth that, when looked at quickly, became the rough shape of a gown or something a dancer might wear. There were sketches everywhere: on the walls, piled on chairs, hanging off clotheslines that stretched across the ceiling.

She didn't know what she'd expected. A room full of old Eastern European women bent over rows of sewing machines? She later learned that this was Ruth's studio; the costume shop was somewhere in Long Island City, a surprisingly industrial choice that reminded her "that's why they call it show *business*."

"Hello?" she called.

"Yes?" A skinny man in a sweater vest bobbed out from behind one of the racks. A tassel snagged his glasses. Lunging to grab them back, he almost fell.

"I'm from Felix Ayre's office? I'm supposed to pick up some sketches from Miss Mann."

"Ruth! What do you have for Felix Ayre? The messenger is here."

"I'm not a messenger. I'm Felix's assistant."

He wasn't listening. He was rummaging through a heap of papers on an extremely messy desk. "I don't see anything here. What did you put them in?"

"You don't see them because I'm still working on them."

Ellen hadn't even seen the woman. She was at the farthest end of the room, camouflaged by swatches. Her hair, an impossible red, almost matched her lipstick. The rest of her was covered by what would have looked like a lab coat, if it hadn't been painted with a dizzying collection of Day-Glo shapes and black brushstrokes that might have been a Japanese poem.

The man glared in a fussy way. "Well, the messenger is standing right here…"

"I'm not a messenger," Ellen repeated.

"Then get her a chair, Robert. I won't be a minute." She examined the paper before her and wrinkled her nose in distaste. "Make that fifteen. Give the girl a drink, why don't you?"

With a little huff, he whisked a stack of file folders and a bolt of orange stuff from a chair and dumped them on the floor. "Bourbon or gin?" he asked.

She was expecting a Coke or maybe a cup of tea. "Um…gin?"

He nodded curtly and fetched a bottle and glass from somewhere. "We don't run to ice," he said, pouring out a healthy slug. "But there's a bathroom down the hall if you want water." He disappeared behind the rack again. The woman, Ruth Mann, Ellen assumed, was completely absorbed in her sketch.

Always take advantage of a bathroom when you see one, because later on there may not be one around. Leaving her coat on the chair, she wandered back out to the hall. Assuming that the glass-paneled doors belonged to other people, she tried the knob of the only one that was all wood. The bathroom was much cleaner than she would have expected from the state of the building. After she washed her hands, she let the water run until it was as cold as it would get, which wasn't cold but was drinkable.

She returned quietly. Mann was exactly where she'd left her. Ellen sat and sipped her gin, looking around. Some of the sketches looked familiar. They were costumes from shows she'd seen. She tiptoed around the room for a closer look.

"Oh!" she exclaimed, louder than she'd intended. Everyone was always on her about how her voice carried.

"Pardon?" Mann looked up. Her tone was polite; her expression wasn't.

"I'm sorry. I didn't mean…it's the blue gown. Arkadina's blue gown."

Mann didn't exactly drum her fingers on the table but she gave every impression of wanting to hear a better reason for having had her concentration interrupted.

Ellen swallowed. "I love how perfect it is…when she stands up and the robe drops and there it is…revealed. It's….it's as if you crystalized the character in that one dress." Now she was babbling. She felt herself turning red. Damn! She hated how easily she blushed.

The corners of Mann's lips briefly turned up. "Precisely what was intended. You've seen *Lake Song*, I take it."

"More than once. It hit me the same way every time. As a matter of fact, I gave Miss Davies a doll of herself in that dress." The gin was going straight to her tongue.

"Ah."

Ellen didn't know what to make of that syllable, or of the way Ruth Mann was looking at her now. Mann was standing now.

"I've seen that doll. Quite well made. So, you're the…ah…donor. Interesting. And you work for Felix?"

"I'm his assistant. Ellen Janow."

"How do you do, Ellen Janow." Mann approached, hand outstretched.

Ellen took it to shake. Like the gin, it was surprisingly strong. And warm. The heat seemed to travel up Ellen's arm. She startled and shot a quick look at the designer. The way that Ruth Mann was looking at her was very familiar. A lot of people had looked at Ellen that way, only all of them until now had been men.

Leonard's romance with Preston was worlds different from Ellen's various affairs. They met at Preston's apartment, on the top floor of a brownstone on Charles Street. Preston cooked elaborate dinners, with candles and flowers on the table. Then they climbed a ladder, through the ceiling of the bathroom, to the roof where he kept a telescope. They sat up there for hours with a bottle of wine, looking at the stars.

Ellen watched her friend carefully, looking for some change in his face or the way he held his body that would tell her that he and Preston had consummated the relationship. There was only the bandanna that he'd recently started to wear in his back pocket; hardly proof. The night he didn't come home at all, she thought she'd caught him; but it turned out that Preston had smashed his finger hammering cutlets for veal marsala and they'd spent the night in the Emergency Room of St. Vincent's.

The day he told her that he and Preston had finally had sex, she didn't see it coming at all. It was a Monday, the night they'd agreed to always stay home and have dinner together. They'd ordered a pizza, with anchovies, olives and Leonard's new favorite, artichoke hearts.

Leonard was picking the olives off his slice; he still didn't like them. Ellen had her mouth full of cheese when he nonchalantly said, "So we did it last night."

Ellen swallowed hard, burning the roof of her mouth and half her throat. She gulped half a glass of water, then had to blow her nose on her napkin because some of the water went the wrong way.

Leonard waited, chewing placidly, until she'd regained her composure. Then he raised one eyebrow, a talent Ellen wished desperately that she had, and grinned. "Uh-huh."

"You fucking asshole!" It was halfway between a holler and a cheer. She sprang over to his side of the table and wrapped her arms around his neck in a strangling hug. She let go just as quickly and turned his head to face hers.

"What are you doing?"

"I want to see if you look different."

"Do I?" He seemed tickled by the idea.

She examined him carefully. "No. No you don't. Well, that's another lie Sydelle told me. So?"

He giggled. "So what?"

"So tell me all about it. Was it wonderful? What do two men actually do? I mean when it's real men and not a porn film."

Leonard blushed violently and giggled again. "I can't say it! I'm not you. I can't! But yes, it was wonderful. I think I love him."

"Wow." Ellen was taken aback. "Love? I know you like him a lot, and I'm glad you finally popped your cherry, but don't you think 'love' is a little extreme?"

Leonard was offended. "Just because you've never been in love doesn't mean that I'm not."

"How do you know I've never been in love?"

"Because you would have said. You tell me everything. You tell everybody everything."

It was Ellen's turn to be offended. "I do not! I just don't happen to believe in hypocrisy."

"Oh quit being dramatic. So what if I love Preston. I love you, too."

"Do you?" She knew he did. Leonard was the most entirely honest person she knew. Whatever scramble of emotions had possessed her a minute ago was replaced with a warm liquid feeling in her stomach. She took his hands and pulled until he stood up. Walking backwards, she started moving him away from the table.

"Whaaat?" He smiled nervously, his eyes flicking from side to side.

She stopped suddenly and reached for the flies of his Levis.

"What are you doing!" he squeaked.

"You're a Lit major. Guess?"

He had no idea what she was talking about. His hands, fluttering, tried to push hers away from his buttons.

Her eyes gleamed wickedly. "Compare and contrast. You had sex with Preston. Now you need to have sex with a woman. Otherwise, how will you ever know?" She made it sound entirely reasonable. "And what better woman? Who could you trust more, than your best friend in the world?"

They were already in the bedroom. She pushed him, still protesting, onto his mattress and yanked off his jeans.

"This is ridiculous!" he sputtered.

She'd straddled his hips and leaned down, her nose touching his. "Ridiculous? You call these ridiculous?!" She whipped off her t-shirt. Her breasts were bouncing inches from his eyes. She picked up his hands. Fixing him with her eyes, she placed one hand over each breast. He was mesmerized. "Now lie back and think of Greece," she ordered.

"*Grease?*" he squeaked. "Are you supposed to be Rizzo? Who am I supposed to...?"

"Greece. Alexander the Great. Socrates. All the lovely little boys, presenting their shiny pink cheeks..."

♫

"Do you still have that wig?" Ellen asked.

I was too groggy to wonder why she'd called Poughkeepsie to ask me this. I squinted across the room at the clock. 9 AM. I'd only finished my last term paper three hours before. I should have had another hour's sleep before having to wake up, deliver it and catch my ride down to the city. Ellen sounded disgustingly wide awake.

"Fuck you," I grumbled.

"Not now, I'm busy," she replied. "Do you?"

I had several by then, part of my Drama Major equipment, but I knew the one she meant: the cheap mop of brown Dynel curls I'd worn the first Hallowe'en we'd trick-or-treated together. It was the year I pierced my ears and decided to be a gypsy so that I could wear my grandmother's hoop earrings.

"Yeah," I said. "Why, what about it?"

"What about a skirt with an elastic waist? Something you could wear this time of year?"

I propped myself halfway upright against the pillows, curiosity clearing my head. "I have one of those print challis things," I said warily. "Sort of a French print, you know what I mean? Brown and black."

"Brown and black? That's excellent! Bring them. The skirt and the wig, both of them. We've got a little project. I've got to go. Barney's calling me. See you at *Moon*."

I'd returned to campus after New Year's to finish off the semester. Now I had a week's Intersession before the spring term would begin. Ahuva's school calendar was different than mine, with fall semester ending at Christmas, followed by SUNY's six week winter break, enough time to cram in an accelerated version of a required course, or make some money, or, if you were a freshman, pull yourself together.

I was home in time to help Ahuva enjoy her last slice of genuine city pizza and hang out while she finished packing. Playing in the background was the Actor's Fund Tribute concert recording. We were all playing it constantly these days; my own copy had been a combination birthday-Christmas present from Ahuva. The album was more or less Berenson's Greatest Hits, plus some unknown songs that had been cut from shows before they'd opened. A particular favorite of our little circle, sung by Bronwen Davies, had been cut from *Lake Song*. We declared it to be the ultimate song about Theatre. It wasn't only us. "Fireflies" has had a long afterlife with numerous recordings by everyone from Bette Midler and David Bowie to Willie Nelson and, most recently, Lady Gaga, and it's often played behind the Necrology slideshow on televised awards shows. Rumor has it that it's going to be restored to *Lake Song* in the upcoming revival; another reason for me and Ahuva to cry.

Ahuva had a lot to tell me. She'd seen an extravagant total of eight shows during her time off. *Moon*, she declared, was absolutely stellar.

She'd also Seen *Lake Song* yet again. "I see something different every time," she informed me. "This time, I was totally fascinated by Sorin. You know, Joe Bigelow is a very talented actor. When you see him off stage, he's so, I don't know…healthy. But as Sorin, you really feel as if he's wasting away."

"That's why they call it acting," I said, rather snippily. Already experiencing the theatrical frustrations that would fill the next fifteen years, I often felt compelled to remind my friends of my vocational expertise.

Ahuva was too sunk in her own musings to take offense. "I can't believe I have to go back tomorrow."

I could empathize. The transition between home and school was always a little bumpy. "You're just out of the habit. You'll be fine in a few days," I assured her. "As soon as classes start back up, you get back in the swing of things."

"I guess. I got into Theatre History II this semester." She brightened at the thought. "It's 19th Century through Modern, so I bet we'll do Chekov."

"You'd pretty much have to," I agreed. "Chekov, Ibsen, Strindberg…all of that. And O'Neill, you know."

"Maybe I can write a paper about *Lake Song*."

You can only catch red velvet curtain disease when you're flooded with the unique intensity and vulnerability of youth. Everything that touches you then is enormous. Everything is mind-blowing, or earth-shaking…or stellar. "Stellar" was never my particular superlative, but it's apt here. To say that *A Moon for the Misbegotten* was humbling to my tender aspirations was like saying it was humbling to stand out in an open field during a meteor shower. What was I, compared to that? What were any of us? *Lake Song* had awed and enchanted me, but I'd already known that a musical could do that. I'd never known that a play could shake me so. It wasn't the play. It was the performances: Jason Robards, so broken and beautiful; Colleen Dewhurst, a force of nature. It was Biblical; it was Greek. It was unlike anything I'd ever seen on a stage.

I was glad to be staying with Ellen and Leonard. I could never have survived a subway ride in that condition. As it was, there was no way we were going to sleep, not for hours. Shaken to the bone, we wandered away from the Morosco, somehow silently agreeing that what we were looking for was an Irish bar. We passed quite a few, but some were too raucous and some were too sad.

A soft gentle snow began to fall. Snow had nothing whatsoever to do with the play, but it suited our mood. We embraced it, never altering our meandering pace. When my overnight bag got too heavy, the others took turns carrying it. Bits of snow settled on our hair, on the sleeves of our jackets. Squinting up through a spinning curtain of flakes, we laughed at the three-quarter moon.

Blurred by the snow on our lashes, soft red neon spelled out an Irish name. Ellen, closest to the door, pushed it open. We stepped into a quiet place, a neighborhood spot for a polite neighborhood, with a long J-shaped bar and a row of button-backed leather booths. Set into a bit of side window was a narrow counter with three stools. We ordered Irish coffees that arrived in glass mugs: a slick of Irish Mist, poured over strong coffee and topped with a thick dollop of fresh, unsweetened whipped cream. With each sip, the coffee cut a channel through the layers, hot and bitter riding piggyback on sweet, grabbing a garnish of creamy chill before hitting my mouth. Outside, the snow continued to tumble past the moon.

It wasn't until breakfast the next morning that they explained the wig and the skirt. Leonard had a boyfriend. I wasn't at all surprised that he wanted one; I was impressed and also a little envious that he'd found one. I was having lousy luck in the boyfriend department. Surely, with all that secrecy, it should have been even more challenging for homosexuals; yet here was Leonard, happy as a clam, with someone who sounded utterly perfect.

Preston was handsome, clever, and so sophisticated. A brilliant (of course) architect, he knew all about art, wine and astronomy. Not only did he speak fluent French, but he'd lived for a time in Paris; also Switzerland and, more exotically, Morocco. He even knew how to pilot a plane. He was straight out of a romance novel. Leonard had to pinch himself—often—to believe that this hero wanted to be with a quiet, gawky kid from Queens.

Preston's birthday was in early March and Leonard was driving himself sleepless trying to come up with present worthy of his love. It was Jeff Kaplan who'd said, with some level of exasperation, "Chill out already. The man's clearly happy with what you've got. Just put a bow on it." Somehow this clicked with one of Preston's Moroccan stories, a tantalizing encounter with a transvestite hooker. Leonard decided he would make reservations somewhere romantic in the Village and surprise his lover by showing up in drag.

He had no idea where to begin. He could hardly ask his mother, and Ellen, the other important woman in his life, wasn't a girly girl. Leonard wanted my help.

After a quick run to the nearest drugstore for supplies, we got to work, Ellen taking careful notes so that Leonard would be able to duplicate my efforts. Though he hardly needed to, I made him shave before I covered his face with the creamy beige Cover Girl foundation. I did his eyes in a soft palette of Love's oyster, fawn and bark shadows. My stint in the makeup room for *Mrs. Warren's Profession* had given me loads of practice applying mascara to virgin male lashes. I advised him to practice this task carefully or he'd be likely to poke his eye out on The Day. His cheekbones were touched with coral blush and his lips with peach-scented gloss. We'd even found a pearly nail polish to match.

Thanks to the elastic waist, my flouncy skirt fit; and with a sweater belted over—the look favored by girls who wanted a Bohemian touch without going all over Hippie—there would be the illusion of curves. Rummaging through the closet, we found a peach colored Izod sweater that Leonard had worn on a family vacation on Cape Cod, a sweater anyone could wear, male or female. Ellen and I had a riotous time making boobs out of rolled-up tube socks and pinning them to his T-shirt while Leonard, ticklish, squirmed. The look demanded boots, but the only ones he had were galoshes; I agreed he could wear his loafers if he bought a pair of black dance tights from Capezio.

While I was fixing my wig into place, Ellen produced a small shoulder bag and, as a final touch, a long scarf of heavy black silk with a repeating pattern of beige and rust.

"This is gorgeous," I said, playing with different ways of arranging it around Leonard's neck. It looked and felt very expensive.

Ellen smirked. "Souvenir from Ruth. She likes to tie me up with them."

She caught me off guard. She'd hinted before about an affair with Ruth Mann. I was ready to believe her. Half the people I knew in college were claiming to be bisexual, so why shouldn't Ellen? She always liked to try whatever was out there. But tying her up? What kind of person does that? The shock flashed across my face before I could stop it. Ellen smirked again.

"She has this four-poster bed," she continued, letting her eyes roll back slightly in her head, as if remembering ecstasy. "And this basket of long silk scarves. Like this one. She ties me up, so I can't move...well, I can move some things, or it wouldn't be fun...and then she has a peacock feather..."

"Well, at least she has good taste in accessories," I said tartly. I was angry at myself. Ellen loved shocking people, which was why I tried so hard never to seem shocked. I gave the curls a final tug and turned Leonard around to face himself in the mirror.

I didn't know the first thing about drag. If I had, I would have plastered on a ton of glamor makeup, including the blood red lipstick I bought for myself, at quarter a tube, from a vending machine in the nasty Grand Central Station restroom; and I would have taken him to the Salvation Army for an over-the-top cocktail dress, turning him into a parody of Jayne Mansfield. But this was years before my meta period. As we were then, I had tried to make him look like a real girl.

Which he did. Curls and pastel makeup didn't make Leonard pretty, but he looked enough like a plain, studious girl to take the bus down to the Village unmolested, and certainly enough to fool Preston for a few minutes in a dark restaurant. And he had a radiant smile.

That spring, the result of making a generous donation to the American Theatre Wing, Leonard's name was entered in a lottery for tickets to the Tony Awards and he won. He invited me to use one of them, so I guess it went okay.

13 – A SUBJECT FOR A SHORT STORY

TRIGORIN

When you're a writer there's no way of shirking
That hearing and seeing and being is working,
And if you're not working, you don't make a living.
Your life is a luxury if it's not giving you work.
A writer's a clerk:
I'm always filing away what I've done or seen or heard;
Life is merely whiling away, 'til you put it down in words.

A subject for a short story: an image;
Something to trap on a page, imprison with words,
Frozen forever; time suspended in ink,
Shackled by grammar—less than you think.
A fragment of a novella, a glimmer
Of an exciting new world. Everyone craves
Somebody else's life, protected by prose,
Thrills at a distance—safer to know.

A subject for a short story:
That one shining thread something drops at your feet;
But the wind starts to toss it the moment you see;
And you run, like the wind, 'cause you have to grab it now
Or it's blown away forever on the air.
And you need to have that thread so you can weave it into cloth.
But then it looks a little bare,
So you must pad it out and fill it in with silk imagination.
And you fringe the edge and wrap it up, an artful little package.

And you hope that no one notices, when all is done and read—
That there's really nothing there beyond that single honest thread
That somehow flashed before your eyes;
Or, like an insect hair, it rubbed behind your ears to make you hear:
A filament that planted in your brain and became
A subject for a short story.

Going to the Rodney apartment on East End Avenue was like going to the White House. After calling upstairs on the house phone, the doorman showed Frankie to an elevator and even pushed the button. The door closed before she could ask the apartment number. It didn't matter. When it opened again, she was already in the apartment; like that audition on Greene Street, where the elevator opened onto what used to be a factory floor and looked as if the machines had only just moved out...in that same elevator, which was big enough for a grand piano and which, in the seconds it took to get to the fourth floor, had penetrated her wool coat with a stink so strong it took a whole can of Lysol to get it out. On East End Avenue, the elevator smelled like lemon polish. There was gleaming wood paneling and shiny brass. The little red leather seat was probably left over from when there used to be elevator operators, which wasn't so long ago, after all. When Frankie was little, her mother would sometimes go to visit friends in her old office, taking Frankie along to show her off. There were two things Frankie always remembered from those trips: the man with the gold-braided cap and white gloves who took them up to the office; and going out for ice cream afterwards, to Schrafft's.

A Spanish-looking woman, wearing a light blue nylon dress that was certainly a uniform, greeted her in the tiled entry. The woman had a nice smile but worried-looking eyes, a combination Frankie knew all too well.

"Hi," she said, holding out her hand for a shake. "I'm Frankie. Frankie Cecchi."

"I am Casilda." Casilda didn't seem sure of what to do about the hand. She hid her own hands under her apron.

Frankie wasn't offended. There were probably rules she didn't know. "It's really nice to meet you," she told Casilda. "I hope I'm not too early."

Casilda smiled again and gestured that she wanted to help Frankie with her coat. Frankie nodded. She handed over the flowers so that she could unbutton. A paper cone of Gerber daisies and eucalyptus from a deli was probably the wrong thing to bring to such a fancy home, but it would have been more wrong to bring nothing.

Casilda draped the coat over her arm and returned the flowers. "Mrs. Rodney is in the parlor. Follow me."

The entryway held a mirror, a small crystal chandelier and a bench you would probably sit on while you took off your bad-weather boots; all pretty normal. It was only after she'd followed Casilda for several twists and turns that things started to feel odd.

The apartment was enormous; probably as big as the entire Cecchi house in Patchogue, if you didn't count the attic or the basement. Maybe you could count in Mickey's den; it was honestly that huge. Frankie couldn't stop wondering why the poor kid couldn't get a Yorkie; a tiny dog would have been ecstatic running through these halls. The whole place, every corridor and room after room, was paved with beige carpeting. That was nearly all there was. The white walls were unbroken by a single painting or poster. Peeking out the sides of her eyes, she saw not a stick of furniture.

Even the room where Casilda stopped was almost bare. There was an old rug in the middle of the floor, spread right over the carpeting. At right angles to an empty fireplace, with an equally empty mantel, were a mustard brown sofa and one of those big square Formica coffee tables. That was it. The table held an overflowing ashtray, copies of *Backstage*, *Show Business* and *Variety*, and a large scrapbook with a tooled leather cover stamped in what was probably real gold.

Margaret Rodney sat on the sofa, staring into space.

Casilda's murmured "Mrs. Rodney" didn't make her turn.

"Hi," Frankie said, a little loudly.

Mrs. Rodney blinked and shook herself back into the room. "Frankie! How nice to see you!"

"Thank you for inviting me, Mrs. Rodney." She extended the flowers.

"Margaret, please. You must call me Margaret." She made pleased noises and handed the bundle to Casilda. "Come, sit with me." She patted the seat beside her and drifted back into her trance.

The sofa was the squashy kind, where if you sat back too far you could sink down, which would be so embarrassing later when you couldn't get up. Frankie perched at the edge. From that angle, her eye went straight to the ashtray.

Casilda's eyes did, as well. The housekeeper snatched up the glass bowl and disappeared. She returned a couple of minutes later with a fresh ashtray and the flowers, now standing in a tube-like vase. Margaret hadn't moved. Casilda placed the vase on the mantel and, with a tiny nod at Frankie, disappeared again.

Frankie didn't know what she was supposed to do. She cleared her throat. "You have a lovely home, Mrs.... Margaret."

Margaret blinked again. She seemed surprised to see Frankie sitting there. "Do you think so? I suppose it's well enough. For what it is. I can have Casilda show you around if you like…"

Frankie was relieved to hear a nearby peal of laughter.

Margaret's eyes brightened at the sound; she seemed fully awake for the first time. "Or Daphne can. Daphne! Darling!"

Daphne bounded through the door into her mother's arms. After a quick embrace, she rebounded at Frankie. Frankie, caught off guard, took a beat to react and hug back. Daphne didn't seem to notice. She wriggled to make a space for herself between them on the sofa, turning her head from one to the other, beaming. Frankie felt a tug at her heart. She didn't think anyone had ever been that happy to see her.

Daphne butted Frankie's arm with her head, the action of a much younger child. "Want to see my room?" she asked. "Mamma, is that okay?"

"I'm sorry, Baby. What?" Margaret had lapsed again. What could someone find to distract them in a practically empty room?

"Can I take Frankie to see my room," Daphne repeated patiently.

"Oh, I suppose so." Her eyes shifted back into focus. She smiled. "Yes, of course. What a good idea. Don't be too long. Dinner will be ready soon."

Daphne jumped up and took Frankie by the hand. "Don't worry," she whispered. "Casilda will call when dinner's ready."

"Casilda seems very nice."

"Oh yes. Much nicer than anyone we had before. I hope she stays. Good help is hard to find." Daphne said it so gravely, Frankie couldn't stop herself from laughing.

"I'm sorry," she said. "You sounded so serious."

Daphne tilted her head and frowned. "It's a very serious thing. If Uncle Ned doesn't approve, we're not allowed to keep them. He hardly ever approves of anyone, and never anyone we liked until Casilda."

"I see," Frankie said, though she didn't.

"Tah-daaaah!" Reaching her room, Daphne flung open the door and ushered Frankie in with a grand gesture.

It was a pleasant shock. After the rest of the house, Frankie had expected a mattress on the floor. Instead she saw the gauze-draped canopy bed and dressing table of every little girl's fantasies. Anything fabric was a soft rose, masses of fluffy pink that contrasted oddly with the framed signed photos of Ann Miller and Eleanor Powell. The floor was bare wood, but that made sense once you spotted the mirrored wall with the ballet barre; this was Daphne's studio as well as her bedroom.

The room was neat, everything appearing to have a place. Daphne flitted from treasure to treasure, making certain that Frankie saw and appreciated them all: a stuffed Snoopy as large as toddler; a chorus line of dolls of all nations; a Lucite box that held a faithfully copied pair of the Ruby Slippers. Daphne was especially proud of her "wall of inspiration," a bulletin board collage of moments from famous and not so famous musicals, cut from magazines. She giggled delightedly when Frankie pointed out some of her own favorites there.

"Did you make this yourself?" Frankie was fascinated. Some of these musicals were pretty obscure. "Oh my God!" She clapped a hand over her mouth. She tried not to swear in front of kids, but Daphne had a picture from *Goin' Goin' Go Go*! "I love that movie! You didn't actually see it did you?"

"Uh-huh! It was on the Disney Sunday night movie once. It was so funny! I wish I had boots like that."

"I did, when I was your age. We all did. It was the style."

"Did you do that funny thing with your hair?"

"I tried. My mom used to set my hair with Dippity-do..."

Daphne shrieked with glee. "Dippity-do!"

"It was like jelly that you smooshed in your hair," Frankie started to act it out, "before you rolled it up on the curlers. So sticky! When it dried and you unrolled your hair, you had a curl. Only it felt all stiff and crunchy."

"Crunchy?"

"Uh-huh. If you pressed down on it, it made a crunch sound, like when you ball up a candy wrapper. That sound. You know how, when you have a scab, you can't stop picking at it? That's what those curls were like to me. I couldn't stop crunching. After a while, I crunched out so much of the gel that the curls fell down."

"You have curls now."

"I use a curling iron. The heat makes them hold."

"I have hot rollers."

"So do I, at home. But I can carry the curling iron in my bag, so I can fix my hair before an audition."

"Smart. Frankie, do you think you could make my hair do that? With my hot rollers?" She stabbed her finger at Bronwen Davies' flip.

"I could try. I'd have to tease it. We'd have to get a rat tail comb at the drug store."

"Rat tail? Ew!"

"That's what they called them. The combs with the long skinny handles."

"You know the most interesting things."

Frankie couldn't resist. "You know what else I know? I know her." She tapped a finger against the picture. "Bronwen Davies."

"She's pretty."

"She is. And she's a very good actress. Right now she's on Broadway, in *Lake Song*."

"I've heard of it. Mamma says it's too old for me. Also she says there's no dancing."

"There isn't much," Frankie agreed.

From somewhere far away came the tinkling of a bell.

"Dinner!" Daphne yodeled joyfully, tugging Frankie by the arm. "It's my favorite! Pancakes and bacon! I'm usually not allowed to have them because, well you know, a dancer can't be fat. But Mamma said we could have them in your honor."

Frankie hadn't expected dinner at a fancy Upper East Side apartment to be pancakes. For Daphne's sake, she made sure to act like she was delighted. She was starting to feel protective of the kid.

Nothing here was really what she'd expected. Okay, maybe the dining room table, which was straight out of *Citizen Kane*. It had a shine like patent leather, except for the tiny black scars by Margaret Rodney's place. Cigarette burns, Frankie assumed. Even while they were eating, Margaret lit one after the other with the marble lighter squatting near her elbow and, from the look of the table runner under the ashtray, she either had crappy eyesight or crappy aim.

If they hadn't all been clumped together at one end of the table, they'd have been yelling like Teamsters. Whatever had caused her earlier inertia, Margaret was back to herself at dinner. That's to say, she was the woman Frankie had met at Carnegie Hall: effusive, maybe a little dizzy. Definitely chatty. Her hunger to talk was so sudden that it came on like an attack.

Of course they talked about dance. Frankie had a few questions for Daphne about the routine in the Advanced Beginners class. There was one step in particular where Irene's legs seemed to move at a different pace from her feet. Daphne happily talked her through it. Margaret maintained a fierce attention to her daughter's words, as if even "okay" and "um" were precious.

When Daphne drew shapes in the maple syrup to clarify, her mother didn't bat an eye; in fact, when they'd finished, she jumped up to give her a big hug, sticky fingers and all.

Both Margaret and Daphne had a lot to say about the dancing in the Radio City Christmas Show, which they'd seen three times this year. Frankie had only gone twice in her entire life and said so.

Daphne was plainly astonished. "Twice ever? At all?"

"It's expensive for a movie," Frankie explained, "so it's a big treat. My parents took me when I was seven. The line wrapped around the block. We had to wait almost an hour to get in. My Christmas dress that year was green velvet. I remember my mom did my hair with a barrette that was shaped like a star, and Pop said I looked just like the Christmas tree." It was one of Frankie's nicest memories of her childhood: *Babes in Toyland* and the Rockettes, sandwiched between her parents, everyone looking so special in their best clothes. Afterwards, they'd walked around Rockefeller Center, and watched the ice skaters from a little table where the hot cocoa came in gold-rimmed cups and had whipped cream on top. It must have been one of Mickey's happiest memories too, because he'd tried so hard to recreate it. "The year my mom died, Pop took me again. I kind of wish he hadn't. We both tried hard to enjoy it, but it wasn't the same. It made me not really want to go back."

"You can never go home again." Margaret blinked back a tear. "How sad! We must see what we can do to change that. We'll make a new memory for you! Next year you must come with us."

"Oh yes!" Daphne bounced in her chair. "Please say you will!"

Frankie felt a little teary herself. They were so kind! "Thank you. I'd love to. If you're sure you'll even be going after seeing it so much this year."

"Oh, we will." Margaret sounded unusually definite. "Daphne needs to observe different dancers perform the same routine. Before selecting dates, I consult with a friend in the Organization to make certain we see a rotation."

Frankie nodded, impressed. Margaret was certainly a supportive mother. "Did you sit through the movie over and over, or sneak out?"

Daphne laughed. "*Robin Hood*? It's for little kids, but it was fun. Mamma put on her sleep mask after the first time."

Margaret rolled her eyes while quirking one corner of her mouth. It was an expression Frankie had often seen on Daphne's face in class. "Believe me, I had to. I brought earplugs, too. I ask you, Frankie—Roger Miller, Andy

Devine and Pat Buttram? One began to wonder whether it was Sherwood Forest or the Great Dismal Swamp."

Casilda brought around a plate with more pancakes, hot off the griddle. Margaret groaned and waved her away. "Please, no more for me. I'm absolutely stuffed. I won't be able to eat for days after this." Margaret had barely touched her food except to cut it up and move the pieces around on her plate. No wonder she was rail thin. She wagged a finger at her daughter. "And you, my darling, this is the very last one. Poached chicken and spinach salad tomorrow."

Frankie didn't want another pancake either, but she accepted one in solidarity with Daphne.

Reaching for the syrup pitcher, Daphne caught her eye across the table and grinned. As if to divert her mother's attention from the stream of syrup, she piped up: "Mamma, Frankie knows a Broadway star."

"Does she, Baby?" The tactic worked; Margaret's eyes turned immediately on Frankie

"Uh-huh. The one from that movie, with the white boots."

It was the boots that had made the impression, Frankie realized. "*Goin', Goin', Go Go*," she explained. "Bronwen Davies. There's a picture of her on Daphne's wall. She's starring in *Lake Song* now."

"And you know her? How fascinating!"

"I have some friends in the cast. And I work for Lilith Brassloe, helping her with her scrapbooks. She has mind-blowing stuff, boxes and boxes of it. Winston Churchill sent her flowers. I found the card. Lil was sure she'd lost it, but there it was, stuck to the back of a postcard from Shepard's Hotel in Egypt."

"Lilith Brassloe." Margaret threw up her hands in a dramatic gesture that probably added a burn mark to the table. She swiveled back to face Daphne. "Now that, Baby, is a career to emulate. Lilith Brassloe was a child star, and here she is, old enough to be your grandmother and still a star."

"She's very nice, too," Frankie noted. "Gracious. She makes me scrambled eggs."

"My goodness!" Margaret looked at Frankie with new respect. "You must tell us everything!"

Donny had apologized after the first time. They'd gotten carried away; they'd both had too much wine on empty stomachs, not to mention how light-headed you could get from really deep breathing. Plus, people did crazy things around the holidays. It wasn't that Donny didn't like and respect her. Frankie was a great girl. It was him. He had too much baggage. He sincerely hoped he hadn't ruined their friendship. He thought the world of her.

If that was supposed to make her feel better, it hadn't. It made things worse. Sure she'd gotten carried away; she'd never have had the nerve otherwise, but deep in her heart she'd wanted to. She liked Donny. *Liked*-liked. It had been wonderful to think that he felt the same. But he made it pretty clear that he didn't. The next couple of times he coached her, he kept things very cool and professional. He didn't even offer her a glass of wine.

After her first day back with Lil, she'd brought her own. Not wine. Cointreau. Lil had given it to her as a welcome back present. It was orangey, Lil said; "Too sweet for me, but I think you'll enjoy it." She must have gotten it from someone else for Christmas. Still, it was probably expensive; she could have easily given it to someone more important.

"I was hoping you'd hold on to it for me," Frankie told Donny, as breezily as she could manage. "If I take it home and Eunice sees it, it'll be gone before I get to enjoy it."

"You could hide it," he pointed out.

"I could," she agreed. "I thought about that. But then I'd feel like I was...you know. *Days of Wine and Roses*. Like I had a drinking problem."

"Yeah, I get you." He did get her. He gave her this serious look that went right through her.

"We could have a glass before we start," she suggested. "No strings attached!" She made sure to laugh, like it was a joke they both shared.

She did it well enough that Donny relaxed a little and they did have a glass. Lil was right on both counts: it was sweet and she did like it. She and Donny joked around more than they had since That Day, and her lesson went exceptionally well. He even gave her a kiss on the cheek before she left.

He had two glasses of Cointreau waiting on the coffee table for her next lesson. He was moody that day and not a hundred percent in the room. Out of sorts, that was what her mother used to say, and Frankie would ask what "sorts" were and how you could run out. What Donny had run out of was any amount of tolerance for Linda-the-bitch. That was how Donny always referred to her. Frankie had repeated it to Ellen and it became a joke between them to the point that Frankie now thought of it as the girl's actual name. She was a little nervous she might accidentally use it in front of Lil or Tyler.

Now Linda had asked Donny to squeeze her in for an extra session, because they were casting the National Tour of *Lake Song*. Though Jim Lord was favoring the actress he'd originally wanted for Broadway (but who'd been unavailable at the time), Bulloch had talked him into giving Linda serious consideration. As an actor, Frankie was intrigued that Becca Lewis, who seemed so perfect as Nina, hadn't been the director's first choice; she made a mental note to tell Ellen. What was significant to Donny, however, was the part about Max Bulloch.

"I guess he's trying to get rid of her," Frankie said smartly. She took a glass and held it up like a toast.

Puzzlement, amusement and finally satisfaction washed rapidly over Donny's face. He lifted the other glass and touched it to Frankie's. "Couldn't happen to a nicer girl," he said.

"I don't know. It sounds like she's getting exactly what she wanted. You can almost admire her. She probably planned it that way all along." Frankie was proud of that: it sounded like something Ellen would say. "I mean I couldn't have done it. Max Bulloch is disgusting. But maybe she just thinks of it as a day job." Frankie hadn't meant to make Linda sound like a hooker. Or had she, maybe very deep down? People made the mistake of thinking Frankie Cecchi was too nice to have a catty side, but she did; and if there was anyone she felt completely justified in being catty about, it was Linda Schiller. She smiled sweetly at Donny. "And when she gets back from the tour, she'll be free to come back to you. So I guess I should say congratulations."

Frankie hadn't dated much, but she'd grown up on bar stools. There was only one response she would expect a man to make to that comment. Donny made it automatically. "Who says I'll want her back?" he snapped.

"I thought you did, that you were hoping..." Frankie deliberately hesitated. She was discovering she had a femme fatale side. Or maybe the longer she pounded the pavement the more she realized you had to be a little ruthless to get what you wanted. "Your baggage, I mean. I thought that you were holding back because you were waiting for Linda to come back."

Donny looked at her as if she were a different person from the one who'd walked through the door. She turned her head. She wasn't pretending; she really did have tears in her eyes.

"Hey," he whispered. He reached a hand to her chin and gently turned her face to his. "Frankie..."

It was different from the first time, and not only because her head was clear. Donny was different too. Not as passionate; which was good, because she was more nervous. Instead, he was slow and considerate. It was personal.

They'd done it twice since then. Each time they were more comfortable together after. Frankie wondered if maybe now she could start thinking of Donny as her boyfriend. He hadn't used that word, but they were definitely more than friends.

14 – MOSCOW (REPRISE)

COMPANY

Days are blue and blazing with the sun's glow.
If it should be raining, there's a rainbow.
But she has a sharper gaze
When she sees the world in shades of grey.

ARKADINA

Colors only cause my eyes to glaze.
I miss the soothing haze of Moscow.

Nestled in my cozy flat,
I know the city's humming, thrumming with activity.
How I love the feel of that!
I only need to lace my boots to chase le dernier cri…

DORN

And now your nerves are shot to hell!

COMPANY

Here the eggs are fresher, and the milk flows,
And the simple pleasures make your skin glow.

DORN

I prescribe a country scene
As part of any worthy health regime
For actresses who want to look eighteen
When they return to Moscow

Harry, being the one who paid the bills, was the one who got the official letter, but he immediately called Sydelle to confer. Not that Ellen didn't already know. The rumor mill had been grinding away since almost the first week of classes; even someone who hung around as little as she did couldn't miss it.

The former finishing school had been hemorrhaging money for years. It hadn't made a bit of difference that they'd scraped together the accreditation to give out a bachelor's degree. Girls who were looking for actual bachelors (the population on which Fetherston relied) sensed they'd lost too much ground to their mop-headed, silver-ringed sisters and migrated to institutions that provided more immediate access to potential husbands. Either that or they succumbed to the 60s, decamping to Laurel Canyon with their trust funds or backpacking luxuriously through Europe or finding God in the pretzeled limbs of a Himalayan yogi. With attendance down and property taxes ever rising, it merely took one inept, albeit well-connected, portfolio manager to plunge the school into a fiscal abyss. The trustees, mostly old and all preferring pretty causes to lost ones, quasi-reluctantly voted to throw in the towel. The building was sold to New York University at a price that would cover the most egregious debts. As a deal sweetener, NYU graciously offered to allow any students who remained after May to matriculate and complete their studies.

Harry and Sydelle were ecstatic: they could stop pretending to be pleased about Fetherston; their daughter would have a respectable NYU degree.

"Read the fine print," Ellen advised. She hadn't, but the rumor mill was thick with details. "It's a joint diploma."

Harry dismissed the quibble. "Who'll notice?"

"What if I don't want to go?"

He was too busy being pleased to hear her. He was so pleased that he wasn't even uncomfortable in Sydelle's living room, which remained exactly as it had been on the day he'd packed his bags. "This is great. It'll probably be a few bucks more, but I'll find a way to swing it."

"Could you, Harry?" Sydelle cooed to her ex. "Maybe we could get her one of those student loans."

Ellen's mind took a moment off to boggle. So her parents were cooperating. Well, they'd soon be bonding even closer. The enemy of my enemy is my friend, right? She hadn't learned *that* at Fetherston; Felix had said it once, to John Houseman; she still wondered who they'd been talking about. Twisting her ring around her finger for courage, she cleared her throat, interrupting their planning. "Father. Mother. This is very good of both of you, but I'm not going."

Sydelle's lips turned white. Before she could open them, Harry laughed.

"Don't be stupid," he said harshly. "Of course you are. Do you not get how fucking lucky you are? What do you want? You want to go to Queens? Or can you even get in there? I sure as hell know you can't get into City."

"I don't want any of it. It's a waste of my time and, frankly speaking, your money. I haven't learned a damned thing in college."

"Language!" It was an automatic response. Sydelle narrowed her eyes. "NYU is quite a few rungs up from Fetherston. Uneven, yes, but considerably better. I expect you'll find it more challenging than you think. Or perhaps that's the issue. You don't want to put in the effort."

Ah, the "put in the effort" speech. How many fucking times in her life had Ellen been told to put in the fucking effort?! She exploded "I work my ass off! I have a job and I go to school. You think that's not effort? And I put in so much time at Felix's office he says I'm starting to look like the wallpaper."

"And what's he paying you for all that work?" Harry demanded. "That internship was over a year ago. You still haven't made a dime, have you? And you never will. Why buy the cow if you're getting the milk for free?"

"I don't think that metaphor applies to volunteer work, Daddy. How's Sandy these days? Or is it Shelley? Or is there one you haven't mentioned?" Harry's face turned the dark brick color that scared her. She didn't like contemplating his mortality. He could be a bastard but, in some corner of her being, she loved her father. The problem was they were too much alike; that and all the walls Sydelle had put between them. Ellen hastily dropped her little barb and tried to argue reasonably. "Felix pays me when he can. When his grant comes through...And there are other compensations. I learn more in one week typing contracts for Felix than I learned all semester in Rudiments of Law and even you said the connections I'm making are invaluable. I didn't want to go to college in the first place, remember? I only went to Fetherston because you said you'd cut me off."

Harry's blood had dropped to a low simmer, but he wasn't much calmer. "And who's to say I won't now. I swear, Ellen, if you drop out..."

Whenever Ellen argued, her throat tightened, turning her naturally loud voice strident. She could feel it starting. Leonard had told her over and over again that it made her sound crazy and sabotaged her. He'd been helping her develop a way to rope it in. She was supposed to think about Penelope Rice, the most charming person Ellen had ever met. Penelope had people eating out of her hand. Okay, how would Penelope answer Harry?

Ellen took a deep breath and smiled. "I'm sorry you feel that way, Daddy." She made herself sound contrite. She could see that Harry was confused. Sydelle was more skeptical. Even Penelope Rice would have her work cut out with Sydelle. Didn't matter; it was Harry who held the purse strings. "I understand where you're coming from. College is great for a lot of people. Leonard, for instance, who needs a chance to sample different things. Or someone like Ron who's been heading for medical school since Aunt Marlene bought him that plastic stethoscope when we were what, three? What I don't understand is the point of going to college just for the sake of saying you did. I know you see it differently. You think it's a great opportunity. But I've got a once-in-a-lifetime opportunity, working with Felix Ayre! I'm getting hands-on experience with someone who's doing exactly what I want to do. That's like Ron getting a chance to hang out in the operating room with Christiaan Barnard."

"Ronald would never be allowed anywhere near an operating room until he finished college," Sydelle observed tartly.

"It was just an example." Ellen forced herself not to holler. "So maybe not the most effective example, but do you see my point? I can always go to college. In a few years, if I think it's holding me back, I can go at night. But right now, I want to be out there in the world, working in theatre. I appreciate how generous you've always been." The little observer who lived in her head gave her a big thumbs up for not sounding sarcastic. Fixing on her parents' grim faces, she took another deep breath for the tricky part, the ballsy part. She knew she had to be prepared to go through with it. "Please…let me finish. I've felt a little guilty about how much you had to pay for school, especially this year, since I'm only more and more certain about my plans. I know how expensive it is. You could have stopped back in June when I turned eighteen, but you didn't. Because you've always wanted me to have a good start in life. But now I'm legally an adult and you have no obligation to support me. I mean, financially. Because I hope you'll always support me the other way, as my parents. I'd like to finish out this year, because it seems like the sensible thing to do."

Sydelle made the rudest noise of which her refined nostrils were capable. "So you're suddenly being sensible?"

Ellen ignored it and plowed ahead. "That will give me the equivalent of an Associate's, so if I ever do decide to go back, I'll be on firm ground. When the term is up and the school closes, if Felix can't pay me, I'll make it up with temp work. I've got solid work experience and both Felix and Mr. Black will give me excellent recommendations. I'm not expecting it to be easy, but I'm confident I'll be able to make enough to cover my share of the rent and all my other expenses. At least I know I can get free theatre tickets." She thought it good to end with a little joke.

Sydelle did the equivalent of throwing up her arms. She rose in a single motion and strode to the breakfront. Her mules clicked emphatically on the parquet. "I give up," she said, lighting a cigarette with a decisive drag.

Harry was still frowning, but the thunder and apoplexy had passed. He shook his head. "I don't get you, Ellie. I love you, and I wish you well, but I don't get you. I need to think."

Her inner observer gave a little cheer. This was the best result she could have hoped for. She'd meant it, every word. She'd be hitting up Felix and Barney next week, writing her own recommendations for them to sign. Once Felix saw she was serious, she was willing to bet he'd find some money, with or without the grant. And Barney could probably get her a day with one of his connections who would agree that her other services were exclusive to Barney. She could make this work; and because she could, she knew that Harry would decide to cover the rent for at least the two more years she would have been in school. Considering the thousands he'd be saving in tuition, it would seem like nothing; plus it would annoy the crap out of Sydelle, who was still adjusting to the child support payments having dried up back in July.

"I made reservations at Dante's." Sydelle threw out the name of the priciest local restaurant like a challenge. "Not that anyone's in the mood, but we do have to eat."

♫

The second half of Freshman English was as ignorable as the first. French was okay. Calc was…definitely more challenging than first semester, which had been much harder than she'd expected. Ahuva had made an oblique reference to this when her father noted the B- on her first semester transcript. Jakub gave her that mild look of disappointment he reserved for her occasional transgressions and suggested working harder. "Perhaps," he considered, "that opera of yours was too distracting."

She'd fumed silently, her anger nearly canceling out the wash of guilt inspired by that look of his. "That opera" had positively saved her life. Without it, this new semester was a yawning chasm she could more easily imagine tumbling into than crossing. Maybe it would be different if she'd made the choir, but she caught the most horrific cold just before tryouts; what voice she'd had was smothered in phlegm and, most damning, sounded flat. She'd tried to explain that it was the cold, that in fact she had excellent pitch, that she could call out the pitch in a squeaky door hinge. Pleasant, but steely on this point, the committee suggested she try out again in September.

Theatre History should have been a life raft, except the professor was snooty about musicals. She'd made the mistake, after an early reference to *The Seagull*, of raising her hand to ask if he thought *Lake Song* correctly captured the essence of the play's themes. It set off a sarcastic ten minute rant that had the rest of the class struggling to control their laughter. After class, some people came over to commiserate. Maybe she could have made new friends, but she was too upset to properly respond. She took the rant personally—how could she not? And how could she not take it personally when he kept throwing little zingers her way, referring to her as "our own Ethel Merman?" Which had nothing whatsoever to do with *Lake Song*. She didn't even like Ethel Merman whose voice, she thought, lacked nuance.

So Ahuva was thoroughly miserable.

Immediately after break, the West Point almost-fiancé apparently history, Ginger moved in with the blonde junior. It made life easier, not having to deal with Ginger's love life, but the loss of her friendly, upbeat presence made the days lonelier. Class, library, as little time as possible in a corner of the dining hall with her face in a book. Then back to an empty room, where she'd listen to *Lake Song* and the Tribute concert album a million times. Or *The Buddy System* or *The Boy Jones;* or maybe sometimes *The Rothschilds* or *Pippin*, which everyone had sung a lot in high school. On very bad days, there was the copy of *Riding a Bicycle* that she'd found in Colony Records over Christmas. It was rare, so she was afraid to play it too often, but there was one song, "No Reflection on Me," that was becoming her personal anthem. Even singing that over and over in her head didn't help fill the hole that was the rest of her—a black hole, sucking everything down into it.

Ahuva physically ached from the emptiness. Sometimes she had to take a hot shower at 2 AM, the stream of water beating her shoulders until they gave up and released enough tension for her to fall asleep. Other nights she'd sleep through her alarm and wake up having missed half the day. She was tired all the time. It looked as if she'd smeared pudding under her eyes. She lost weight, never a good thing for a skinny girl. And her grades were falling, even French, because it was so hard to concentrate.

She decided to go home for the Washington's Birthday holiday. Her parents couldn't hide their dismay at what a few weeks had done to their child.

"Maybe you have that mono they all have." Malke always grabbed at practical explanations.

Ahuva went, uncomplaining, to the family doctor who thoroughly checked her over, with special attention to the size of her pupils. He said she was a little anemic, but otherwise sound, and prescribed red meat and fun. "I know you, Ahuva Geffner," he scolded in his phony jolly way. "You drive yourself too hard. Cut yourself a little slack; let yourself be young."

She didn't feel young. She felt ancient. Ancient and heavy as a statue. With her parents so busy fussing over her for the entire three days, she wasn't even able to get to the theatre.

She took the bus back upstate, almost grateful to be alone again, and slept most of the way. The next day, her first class was Theatre History. She sat listlessly, marking time, her mind wandering until he gave out the assignment.

"...and his opinion of women. So for next class, I'm asking you to read *Mrs. Warren's Profession* and *Pygmalion*. And I mean *Pygmalion*, Ethel." He was looking right at her, every head in the room turning along with his. "Not *My Fair Lady!*" His mirthless chortle was the final straw. Ahuva burst into uncontrollable tears. She was consumed with weeping. She wasn't even embarrassed; there wasn't room for anything except her overwhelming grief.

In the silence that followed, one of her more compassionate fellow students approached Ahuva's chair and squatted to be at eye level. "It's okay," the girl said kindly. "It happens to all of us. Come on, let me walk you to the infirmary."

Gulping, and wiping her nose with the tissue the other girl produced from her jeans, Ahuva allowed herself to be led across campus and deposited at the door of the red brick building. A calm nurse took her pulse, led her to a room with four beds and allowed her to climb between the covers in her own T-shirt. Ahuva pulled the sheets over her head and stared blankly into the grey cave. When the young doctor came, he asked her a few questions. It's hard to answer when you don't really care. He seemed to understand this. He said he was going to give her a little shot, to help her relax and get some sleep. She tried to protest, but she wasn't quick enough. She slept for hours. She slept through dinner, waking up around eight o'clock with a dry mouth. The curtains had been drawn around her bed for privacy. There was a glass of water by the bed, with a straw. She took a few swallows, turned over, and went to back to sleep. Her body woke her up at 6 AM. She threw her legs over the side of the bed, wanting to spring up and find a place to pee. Her head didn't want to cooperate. Her kidneys didn't care, so Ahuva forced herself to stand. Putting one wobbly foot in front of another, she made her way to the curtains and fumbled to part them. Two of the other beds also had their curtains drawn. She wondered if the occupants also had stress. It made her angry, thinking of all of that stress, thinking of all of them being incapacitated with it. What if her father had allowed himself to be swallowed up by stress? What about her mother's sisters and brothers, every last one of whom had survived the Camps? How could she be so weak when her entire family was so strong? She wanted to curl up in a ball and sleep forever, and she hated herself for that weakness.

With more determination than she'd felt in weeks, she shuffled to the bathroom door. She peed. She splashed water on her face and swished some over her furry teeth. She opened the door carefully. Nothing had changed. She crept back to her curtains, found her clothes in the bedside cabinet and got dressed. Holding her books tight to her chest, she slipped out of the room. She could hear sounds in the distance, but the hallway was empty. It gave her time to manufacture an air of nonchalance, to become the girl who'd been braver backstage at the Regale than big-talking Ellen Janow. She pulled herself as tall as she could and headed to the stairwell.

There wasn't a soul to stop her until she reached the lobby. The nurse on duty was the same one who'd checked her in. "Miss Geffner? Ahuva? Where are you going?"

Ahuva made sure to smile. "I'm fine now. Really. The doctor was right. I only needed a good night's sleep."

The nurse must have heard this before; she looked skeptical. "You should wait. The doctor is expecting to see you at eleven. Go back upstairs and I'll see that you get some breakfast."

This time Ahuva gave a little laugh. "No, really, I feel great. I just want to take a shower and change my clothes, then I'll head out to the dining hall. If it makes you feel better, I promise to stop by later and check in."

"I do wish you'd stay. But we can't keep you against your will." She consulted a large book. "I'm making an appointment for you with Doctor Miller at four o'clock, okay?"

"Four. Absolutely." She couldn't wait to get out of that place. Halfway through the door, something struck her and her manners kicked in. It wasn't the nurse's fault. She paused to look back. "Thank you so much for all your help. You've been super kind."

"You students, always in such a rush." The nurse had a rueful smile. "No wonder we see so many stress cases on campus. Take care of yourself, Miss Geffner."

Ahuva nodded brightly and darted past the glass door. It was a pretty day. The sky was so blue that it made her light-headed. *A vertiginous blue sky.* From "No Reflection on Me." Such a stellar word, vertiginous. She'd had to look it up in the dictionary, but she didn't mind. Some people said Berenson was pretentious for using words you had to look up. She disagreed. The man was a genius. He used these words naturally. It probably never occurred to him that everyone didn't know what they meant.

Everything was so intense. The unmelted patches of the most recent snow were sparkling hard in the morning sun. The evergreens gave off that Christmas tree smell. *Everything is green here,* she thought, *not like Moscow.* As soon as she was safely behind the trees, she leaned against one and bent her head down to her knees to catch her breath. The last hour had drained her of every last bit of energy. She needed to get back to the dorm. She would take that shower. She'd try to eat some of the Cheerios she kept in her room. She needed to recharge her batteries, so that she could call her parents and tell them she was coming home to stay.

15 – IF EVER YOU NEED MY LIFE

NINA

If ever you need my life take it—it's
  yours.
I never had a life to give until you
  came along and made me live,
And if you wanted, I would die for
  you; I could.

If ever you need a love, here is my
  heart.
I never had a heart to lose or break,
  and now if you should only choose
To take it, that would make it real. I
  feel it would.

And if you needed a haven from the
  world, I'd gather you in my arms.
Comforting you with understanding,
  soothing you, keeping you calm.
How I would adore you!
And you would be free.
I'd be there forever—if ever you
  need.

TRIGORIN

If ever I needed hope, this is the day.
When someone offers you a candle
  do you curse the feeble glow or fan
The flame to see the visions
  candlelight provides?

If ever I needed change, this is a
  chance.
If what I need is innocence, she's clear
  as mountain water, pure as rain-
Drops, near as yesterday, as rare as
  truth or bliss.

And if I needed a mem'ry of the time
  when all that I felt was new,
Taking her hand would take me back,
  would let me recapture my youth,
What she would surrender
I use to breathe.
She waits to be wanted, if ever I need.

NINA/TRIGORIN

If ever I dreamed of love, what did I
  know?

NINA

I thought that love was teasing
  glances. Now I know it's boldly
  seizing chances

TRIGORIN

So we seize the day together If we
  dare.

If ever I'd stop to think, it should be
  now.
You offer me your dearest treasure;
  not to mention many hours of pleasure. Am I cruel enough to take it?
  Do I care?

NINA

And if you needed a rocket to the
  moon, I'd carry you on my wings

TRIGORIN

Together we'd soar beyond the
  stars. I'd show you some
  wondrous things.
For only an hour,
And then I would leave.

NINA

An hour is a lifetime; if ever you need

Margaret Rodney was late again and Irene had to run. Frankie told her not to worry; she'd be happy to wait with Daphne.

"Are you sure?"

Frankie didn't see what the big deal was; it was only standing in the lobby for a few minutes.

Irene put on her stern face. "I don't want you making a habit out of this. Margaret Rodney is the type to take advantage. She wouldn't dare try anything with me—I'm too important to her plans for Daphne's career, poor kid. But if she sees you're willing to wait, she'll start being late constantly. You'll see."

That was Irene for you: she might dress like a gym teacher, but she had as much artistic temperament as Lil Brassloe. Like the time she yelled at Vern for ruining the routine when all he'd done was mix up his arms in the Maxie Ford. She inflated everything. This was way more *agita* than the situation deserved. Frankie was happy to wait a few minutes.

Daphne was a good kid. Maybe too good. In addition to Irene's classes, she took jazz twice a week, with a former Fosse prodigy who'd left dancing because of a sprung hip, and her singing coach was important—and expensive—enough to impress Donny. It was a lot to expect from a kid; especially as, the more time they spent together, the more Frankie felt Daphne didn't want it, that she was playing along because it mattered so much to her mother. She practiced everything rigorously, had all the steps down pat, even the tricky ones. Like pull-backs: Frankie could never figure out what you were supposed to do with your weight to make even one possible, but Daphne could do a faultless double. While they waited for Margaret, Daphne tried to show her how. The kid danced with the precision of a machine. But something was missing. Something that "switched on the lights," as Annie Fallon used to say. Joy maybe? Frankie's tap sucked by comparison, but she sure loved doing it.

"Oh my God!" Margaret Rodney burst through the glass door in her usual cloud of frenzy. "I must seem like the most irresponsible mother in the world! What you must think of me! Whatever it might look like Frankie, I assure you…everything that I do, everything, is for Daphne."

"It's no problem Margaret." Though the name felt odd in Frankie's mouth, she sensed the woman would be offended if she didn't use it.

"At least you must let us take you to dinner. I won't take no for an answer."

Why not? It was a school night. How long could it take? She'd probably still be able to make the 8:37.

Standing in the phone booth in the Equity Lounge, a painfully wide smile stretching the corners of her mouth, Frankie made the guy at her service read the message again, slowly, so she could write down the important parts. The agency from the cigarette promotion wanted her for a movie crowd scene that was shooting Friday, on location in Brooklyn. She should call as soon as she got the message, to let them know.

The call to her service had taken her last dime. Her purse held a couple of dollars and her train ticket home, but no more change. She looked around for someone who could break a dollar. There was no one around except the old people who seemed to almost live here. She'd once asked the door monitor who they were.

He'd shrugged. "Fred used to understudy Alfred Lunt back in the day. Maisie was in all the comedies after the War, and George was in the original production of *Lost in the Stars*. They used to work all the time. Theatre's not what it used to be."

They all had wrinkled skin like Chinese dogs, and sparse fluffs of grey hair; the men always needed a shave. Their clothes were frayed and they toted canvas bags of old newspapers and oranges; yet they sat with the confidence of kings and their voices, often ringing out over the hum in the room, were hearty and true. They fascinated her, but she'd never had the courage to introduce herself. Today she had to. "Hi," she said. She said it too quietly. They had their heads together over a crossword puzzle book and didn't hear her. Also, they were probably a little deaf. "Hi!" she said again, pitching her voice louder. "I'm sorry to bother you, but would anyone have change for a dollar?"

The Afro-American man smiled at her. "Sorry, darling. I don't have any change."

One of the women rummaged in her change purse, and frowned. "I do. But not a dollar's worth. Sorry, dear."

Frankie's face fell. "I need to make a phone call," she sighed. "My service had a message. A movie. I have to call the agency to accept."

The old woman with the change purse produced a dime and pressed it into her hand. "Then you go call them. Right now."

"I couldn't…" It was obvious these people were pretty broke. They were old and not working, and some of them had hardly any teeth.

"You'll pay me back when you get that movie."

Frankie nodded and took the dime. "It's just for extra work," she said hastily; it had occurred to her that they might think she was up for a real part, and it made her feel guilty.

The Afro-American man must be the one who was in *Lost in the Stars*. His laugh sounded like singing. "No small parts, darling! Many a fine career started with carrying a spear."

She laughed at that.

"Good girl! Now go make that phone call!"

The movie starred Al Pacino. She never did see him, but she heard him in the distance couple of times, from across the street. That's where she was, on a street corner again—in Brooklyn, this time.

It was pitch black out when she left the house. At 7 AM sharp, still a little groggy, she checked in at a Winnebago with a "Holding Area" sign taped to the door. It wasn't the real holding area; it was just where someone checked your name off a list and handed you a bunch of papers to fill in and give back before lunch. The assistant in charge was a guy her own age, bristling with self-importance. All the time he was talking to her, he kept one wary ear trained on a walkie-talkie that buzzed static from the table that served him as a desk. Frankie was not to talk to the principals, he warned, unless they addressed her first. Nor to the director. She was very lucky that the director would be running today's shoot. Frankie tried not to show her confusion: who else would be doing it?

The assistant sent her to a trailer marked "Makeup," to get checked out. She'd hoped to see some of the stars there, but later found out that they kept to their own trailers. Makeup said she was fine, that if she felt a little shiny, she should come by during a break and they'd powder her. Frankie had specifically worn her Vera scarf because the casting agent had said "business attire," but Wardrobe asked her to take it off. A bright red scarf would call too much attention to her. Extras were background, a useful reminder for Frankie to tuck away along with the scarf.

Cleared for filming, she was told she could pick up coffee and breakfast from Craft Services, but to remember that there was no eating on the set. Frankie followed the signs to the bank's parking lot, where the other extras were already waiting. She asked a guy with a Styrofoam cup about coffee. He pointed out a long table against the side of the building, with urns of coffee, plates of danish, and baskets of fruit. The danish were diner style, big and glossy. She took an apple for later, just in case there was no place to get lunch. She also took note of where the porta-potties were located. There were no chairs in the official holding area, and all the good spots for leaning were already taken. Some people sat on the pavement, with their morning newspapers under them. Frankie didn't have a paper; anyway it was too cold for that. A lot of the extras seemed to know each other; she could tell by how they were talking about their kids or a mutual friend. But the great thing about actors is that even strangers are part of the same tribe. When she found an impersonal conversation, all she had to do was look friendly and listen.

"We're in luck today," the tall girl said, as if Frankie was already one of them. "We have the director.'

"Who else would it be?" Frankie couldn't help herself. She had to know.

"An AD," replied the girl, who introduced herself as Gwen. "If the scene's only for texture."

"Or an establishing shot," added the guy, DJ. "You must be new."

If she admitted it, she could ask all the questions she wanted. On the other hand, they might start asking her some questions and find out she wasn't in the union. It was perfectly okay for her to be working here, but she was leery of people's attitudes. If they knew she was non-union, they might decide she wasn't professional enough. Frankie tried for a non-committal shrug.

DJ decided she needed clarification. "The director being here means the scene's a critical part of the action. We might get some decent face time."

As they kept talking, mostly about themselves, she learned that Gwen and DJ did a lot of extra work. DJ, who thought of himself as a young Michael J. Pollard, said it was a way to keep his hand in while he was growing into his type. Plus, you never know. Last year, a director spotted him on a shoot and flew him out to LA to play a junkie runaway on *Streets of San Francisco*. DJ had seriously considered staying out in LA, but all the agents had too many junkie or runaway types on their books already, and without an agent out there, you were just spinning your wheels. If he had to wait out a few years until he got some "gravitas," he might as well do it cheap, in his parents' basement in Sunnyside. Also, the separate background performers' union in LA meant there was some stigma for a serious actor in taking background jobs. In New York, where extra work came under SAG, he could do as much as he wanted without screwing up his future. DJ was pretty philosophical.

Tall, beautiful Gwen was a person people noticed. She said she'd been upgraded on the set four times, by four different directors. Frankie acknowledged this with the open-eyed nod that showed people you were impressed, even though she hadn't the faintest idea what Gwen was talking about. They hadn't even started shooting and she was already learning so much! Gwen was studying with Stella Adler (this time Frankie was honestly impressed), who didn't think she was ready to audition for real parts. Gwen seemed to accept this, which Frankie wouldn't have been able to do. Stella didn't think extra work counted, so Gwen took as many jobs as she could get, learning her way around a shoot, and ensuring that her face would be familiar when her time came. For the same reason, she worked in the office at Circle Rep. Compared to DJ and Gwen, the NYADA crowd were embarrassingly naive.

Frankie spent hours crossing the same street, back and forth, with a pack of other people in business attire. They were told to act like they were in a hurry to get wherever it was that they were going. She pretended to herself that she had to get to an important meeting—and that she was old enough for that to be plausible.

When the assistant director, the AD, blew a whistle, they were supposed to react as if they'd heard gunfire.

"Scream if you want..." the AD started to say, then cut himself off. "No, not everyone. We don't want a screen full of open mouths. It's not *The Poseidon Adventure*. Let's see. Just you, you and you." He pointed at Gwen, a loud guy who'd been calling all the crew by their first names, and a fat woman with grey hair. "And the little girl, if she feels like it."

Frankie had been surprised to see the woman with the stroller, but she realized, with respect, that it would probably make the crowd look a lot more realistic.

The adult actress nodded professionally. "She probably will, when the whistle goes off. Especially if she hears other people doing it. Daisy's a good screamer."

"Great. So you three...and Daisy...you should scream. Everyone else, figure out another way to react. But no four-letter words! I know, I know; it's all going to be re-voiced in the loop, but there's always some lip reader out there who spots a Fuck or a Shit and calls the studio to complain."

For the entire day, they crossed that street. There were breaks to reset the cameras, and breaks to reset the lights. There were union-mandated toilet breaks, and breaks for lunch and an afternoon snack. Otherwise, they assembled on that corner, waited for their cue, crossed, reacted to the whistle, and ran. And waited to see if the director wanted them to do it again. It was fascinating to be on a shoot—for the first few hours. By noon it was as engaging as being stuck in a revolving door.

16 – BANDAGING THE WOUND

KOSTIA

Place the bandage on me gently, softly—
Careful not to hurt too much.
Kiss the wound and make it better quicker.
Mother has a healing touch.

With your arms around my shoulder
How the room is getting colder,
When it should be getting warmer;
When I should be feeling closer
Than I've felt since the days in the womb,
As you sit by my side, with your hands on my temples
Bandaging the wound.

Mother's hands, cool and light wrap the gauze about me now
Where her lips in the night used to brush against my brow,
Placing a kiss I scarcely could feel,
Leaving a scar nothing will heal.

Curtains have been drawn against the daylight
Making us a secret place.
Lavender and lemon in the water
Dabbed across my fevered face.

If I'd only known you'd choose me
When it looked as if you'd lose me,
I'd have never tried to win you—
All those sad attempts to please you!
Now you cling when I'm flirting with doom
And you sit by my side, with your hands on my temples,
Bandaging the wound.

Mother's hands, cool and light wrap the gauze about me now
Where her lips in the night used to brush against my brow,
Placing a kiss I scarcely could feel,
Leaving a scar nothing will heal.

I sought to hear angels singing me to rest,
But all I hear is the beating of my heart
And the whisper of her breath
And there's not another sounc
As the bandage is unwound
In the silence of the room
As we're bandaging the wound.

The very next day after she called, Jakub was there, holding the back of his hand to Ahuva's forehead to check for a fever that wasn't there. It was a knife in his heart to see her like this.

"You should come home for a week, get some rest. Let your mother feed you up. Then you'll be fine and you can come back, yes? I'll talk to someone here and explain."

Ahuva was adamant: she wasn't sick; she didn't want to come back here; she only wanted to come home. She hugged him as if it were possible to crawl into his ribcage and hide there.

He gave some boy ten dollars to help her load the car. They didn't say much on the long drive back, but every now and then he would turn his head and see the pain draining away.

Ahuva unpacked, putting all her belongings exactly where they'd been in August. Her parents tried to understand what had happened. What was it about the school she didn't like? Was it too far away, or too hard? Were the people not friendly to her?

"Was it a boy?" Malke prodded.

"What are you going to do now?" Jakub asked. "Another school? Don't you need an application form?"

She didn't have answers to any of it. When she opened her eyes every morning, she checked to see that everything was where it should be. Satisfied that it was, she showered and returned to her room and got dressed. And waited. She couldn't say what she was waiting for. It was pleasant, somehow, to wait.

♫

Knowing that school would end entirely in a few more months made it almost enjoyable for Ellen. She attended more classes in that final semester than in the preceding three combined. She belatedly discovered that, by writing theatre reviews for the school paper, she'd get free tickets with no strings attached, while simultaneously building a portfolio that might come in handy someday. She could have kicked herself for not realizing that sooner.

Once he understood that he might lose her altogether, Felix managed to cough up a token salary. He also introduced her to a ticket broker who had a decade's worth of filing mounting up and was willing to pay to have it done. Papers were the only thing Mr. Nudler needed handled, which made working for him almost a vacation. Yellowed and smelling faintly of ash, like his papers, Mr. Nudler was a sweet old thing, especially if she unzipped her top an extra inch or two and jiggled where he could watch. She got a lot of free tickets that way, too.

As well as a small legitimate paycheck for her office work, Barney continued to provide numerous little extras that made life comfortable. She was currently nudging him toward a portable electric typewriter. She wrote down everything she picked up from Felix and her handwriting always atrocious, became almost illegible when she wrote quickly. She needed to transcribe her notes while she could still recall enough to read them. She had access to typewriters at Felix's and Barney's, but not time enough to use them for own purposes; juggling so many jobs, she could barely get through the work she was being paid to do. Life was so crowded!

Not crowded; it was crammed full and she relished every bit, even the hard parts; sometimes the hard parts most of all. That's why she'd stopped second-acting *Lake Song*. Chekhov's ending annoyed her. Kostia killing himself? He's a published writer, with fans. So what if he'll never have his fantasy girl? Every time she saw that scene, him staring into the empty garden, she wanted to scream, "For fuck's sake, grow a pair!" And the girl...Ellen could never decide which disgusted her more: that Nina turned martyr over her affair with Trigorin, or that she thought being fucked and dumped validated her lousy acting. "Stupid bimbo! You're young and free. Find another man! Get another job! Emigrate to America!" Which, come to think of it, was pretty much what Ellen's grandmother had done at just about that point in history. Maybe she was genetically predisposed to despise the Ninas of this world.

In Ellen's book, you didn't back down from challenges, you faced them and wrestled them down. That's what made life exciting—conquering where you were supposed to run, turning failure into triumph. Every day she dared life to fuck with her; and she adored it, because she knew that, one way or another, she would win. She firmly refused to cave in to the very tiny whisper in the back of her head, the one that told her life wouldn't go on this way forever. It only made her more determined to experience as much as she could while she was still young and the world was hers for the taking. Lovers, for example. Everyone wanted you when you were young. Why the hell not enjoy it? There was nothing and no one Ellen didn't want to sample while she could: whatshisname, the philosophy instructor; Max Bulloch; Leonard...It was exquisite how different they all were: their scent; the touch of their skin; the way they moved inside whatever parts of her; the way their eyes closed or opened when they came. Barney made a whimpering sound that she found oddly touching. Someday she'd have to drop Barney, but not yet. He'd been her training wheels. It seemed rude to dump him as soon as she'd found her balance. She was certainly in no hurry to get rid of Joe. Joe was great in the sack, and the longer she knew him the more she liked him. She especially liked how they understood one another: no strings, no guilt, only good sex and fun.

Ruth Mann was in a class all by herself. Ruth had an intensity that gave a dangerous edge to their encounters. Was it because she was a woman? Ellen wouldn't know until she'd been with other women: "compare and contrast," as she loved to needle Leonard. Maybe it had to do with the nature of Ruth's art. She was a creator—as opposed to an interpreter, like the other artists Ellen knew, who adorned themselves with eccentricities, deliberately selected and worn with charm: Felix's 1920s wardrobe and grand mannerisms; Penelope's scatterbrained lightness; the pretended casualness that caused most people to never give Joe credit for what a very good actor he was. Ruth, in sharp contrast, said she didn't have the time or the energy "to play tea party." People either had to take her as she was or leave her, and she made it pretty clear that she didn't care either way. It was too honest to be arrogance. Lots of people, including Ellen, said they didn't care, but Ruth meant it. Her self-sufficiency was stunning. It was also tremendously enticing.

Ellen wished she could speak with Harry about Ruth, but she wasn't brave enough, certainly not while he was still paying the rent. Too bad, because she knew on some level he would understand. He'd introduced his new lady at brunch last week. The Chinatown dive had been less of a shock than the unkempt, blunt-spoken Maureen; Harry liked his women decorative and mannerly. Ellen was utterly confused by the haze of lust in his eyes until someone mentioned that Maureen was a painter. Then she got it. Like Ellen, her father was dancing with danger.

Right now, Ruth was designing costumes for a new film set in the court of Louis XVI and a Wild West production of *Titus Andronicus* for the NY Shakespeare Festival. She was a raving lunatic, halfway between a wicked witch and a woman pushing out a ten-month pregnancy. When Ellen wasn't scared shitless by the spectacle, she was awed; in either condition, she was completely turned on. Sure, it was crazy, but Ellen wouldn't change a thing about her life. Life was full; so deliciously, deliriously full.

♫

The family doctor told the Geffners not to worry. College could be challenging. It wasn't unusual for the stress to prove too much, especially for girls. "Let her be," he said. "Give her time. She'll find her way. Have you considered other options? Secretarial school maybe? There's an excellent school in Rego Park that trains dental hygienists."

Malke thanked him quickly and hustled Jakub out the door before he'd say something he'd regret. The man was a good doctor and he knew Jakub's history; she didn't want to lose him.

"What kind of dental hygienist?" Jakub demanded at least once for every block of the walk home. "My daughter could be a doctor if she wanted, a better doctor than he is."

"He means well," Malke reminded him. "So he's wrong about the school. Maybe he's right the other way. We should let her be for a while. Give her time."

Jakub disagreed. "Time is something you lose, not something you give. I don't want her sitting in a dark house all day listening to records. The world moves on before you know it. I don't want it to move on without her.'

Malke knew that it was his own moving on that Jakub feared. The future wasn't certain for anyone—their own lives had proven that. He didn't want to leave his daughter unprotected, and to Jakub, education was protection.

After a few weeks, at a loss for what to do, they took the uncharacteristic step of confiding in their friends.

"After all," Malke observed, "nothing to hide. They see she's come home." Their friends variously suggested a psychologist, a rabbi and going back to Israel to join the Reserves. Jakub had objections to all of these. It was their neighbor, Holly, who provided a viable solution.

Holly, the mother of a young son whose father no one in the building had ever seen, worked for the local pediatrician and was putting herself through college at night. "Queens has a mini-term that just started. Maybe Ahuva would like to take a class."

With the term already underway, Ahuva would audit until her paperwork came through. That was fine with her; for now, the less official the better. She'd decided to take Theatre Appreciation. The catalogue mentioned that students would attend an Off-Broadway production, something she could enjoy.

Jakub offered to drive her, but she insisted on taking the bus. It was bad enough to know he'd be waiting all night to hear how it went. She felt horrible about how she'd let her father down. That she'd rather live with his disappointment than stay upstate said everything about how miserable she'd been there. Whatever happened in class tonight, she would have to stop by the store after, have a Coke at the counter and tell him something that would make him happy.

The campus was bigger than it had seemed when Holly brought her to register. The building she needed looked exactly like another one nearer the bus stop. She got confused. Despite leaving the house early, she didn't reach the correct door until ten minutes after class had started. If she'd ever been able to lie to her father, she would have walked away and found some way to kill the next couple of hours. Instead she gritted her teeth and yanked open the door before she could change her mind.

Naturally everyone in the room turned to stare. There were only about a dozen people, but when they're all staring directly at you that can feel like the whole world. A slim woman with almost-a-crewcut sat cross-legged on top of the desk, her ripped jeans and suede boots adding to the overall impression that she was Peter Pan.

"Welcome! I'm Deb. you must be Ava."

"Ahuva."

"Ahuva. Sorry." She didn't seem at all annoyed, already a big improvement from that horrible Theatre History professor. Her grin beckoned Ahuva to join the rough semi-circle of chairs around the desk.

♫

It was cold in the little theatre on 7th Avenue. Frankie was glad to have a sweatshirt to put on over the new leotard that she'd splurged on for this audition. She already had two perfectly good ones that she'd had to buy for NYADA, but this one, the girl at Freed's said, was a serious dancer's leotard. It was grape colored (not green grapes, but jelly grapes), sleeveless, with a pucker at the neck that almost turned it into a V, and it was cut higher in the hips than she was used to, to make her legs look longer. She felt a little self-conscious in it, another reason to keep the sweatshirt on as long as possible. She'd looked really nice in her bedroom mirror, but this was her first time wearing it in public.

First times were always nerve-wracking. This was also officially her first professional chorus call. It was for the National Tour of a popular Off-Broadway show. Donny agreed the audition would be a good experience. "You're not where we want you yet, but that's okay," is what he'd said. "We're trying to expand your range and beef up your endurance, not change your sound. Anyway, if you get work, it'll be from someone who likes you the way you are." Donny was working like crazy these days. As well as NYADA, he had more than a dozen private students. Plus he was putting in tons of hours working with a team he'd met at an ASCAP workshop, who were doing a backers' audition for their new musical. Imagine if they got the money!

She was so proud of Donny. It was selfish to wish he'd had a little time to help her prepare for this audition. She wanted so much to get the job. She'd just have to take heart from remembering what he'd said: she wasn't going to worry about her voice. She wasn't going to worry about the dancing either. She'd seen the show in previews, with Equity paper. It was more singing than dancing, and the choreography was old-style hoofing. She should be able to pull that off; her months with Irene had given her a lot more confidence. When Ellen told her about this audition, she hadn't panicked at all; she felt ready. All she'd had to do was run out and buy a leotard that would keep her from looking like an amateur.

It wasn't the usual open call with all the girls in Equity fighting to get in. The audition was by agent submission only. It was a mystery to Frankie how Ellen had gotten her in here. She'd said something about knowing one of the producers. Ellen seemed to know a lot of people. It was incredibly nice of her to make this happen. Frankie would make one of her famous clove oranges to say thank you. She'd given some to Lil and Bronwen for Christmas. She tied them up with fancy ribbon and hand beaded her own tassels to hang from the bottom. Lil kept hers on the dressing room hook with her kimonos, which proved how much she liked it. Frankie would absolutely have to make one for Ellen.

At the sign-in, they told Frankie that she was in Group 5. To make sure later groups wouldn't get an unfair advantage by watching the earlier ones do the routine, everyone had to wait in the greenroom. Frankie looked around to see what other people were wearing. They were either in leotards and leg warmers, or else they were quickly climbing into them, right in the middle of the open room.

Frankie only had to step out of her skirt. She'd layered herself for warmth. The heating in the Patchogue station shelter was always broken; she'd frozen her butt off waiting for the train this morning. It would have been warmer to carry the skirt and wear pants but, what with makeup and tap shoes and books and the white shirt and black pants for her shift at Alfie's, her dance bag was heavy enough to lug around all day. She always travelled in her audition clothes and Frankie never auditioned in pants unless it was obvious from the cast breakdown that the character would wear jeans—like if it said "Hippie College Student." She thought a dress or skirt made a better impression. Only now did it occur to her that this didn't apply to chorus calls, where you were taking off your clothes anyway.

Frankie folded her skirt and blouse and tucked them away. She sat on her dance bag to buckle on her character shoes. The few chairs were taken. Girls were even sitting on the table. More of them were spread across the scuffed brown linoleum, stretching their hamstrings and doing breathing exercises like the ones she did for Donny. Since it was an agent submission, there were maybe 60 girls here, 80 at most, every one of whom would be seriously considered for one of the 10 jobs. Those were amazingly good odds. Everything would hinge on being one of the types they were looking for. There was certainly an assortment for the casting people to choose from: tall, medium, short; blonde, brunette, redhead; girls like pipe cleaners and girls with Angie Dickinson curves. There were even a handful of girls with brown skin and one who was Chinese; Frankie was surprised their agents had submitted them, considering that everyone in the Off-Broadway production was white.

Every single girl was so poised and sophisticated. Frankie felt very young and awkward all of a sudden, even though the others couldn't have been much older than she was, if at all. She tried to do her own breathing exercises, but she was too nervous. She knew there was no point in taking out her book; she could never focus on reading when she was waiting for an audition. A couple of girls were knitting; she should start crocheting again; she thought she remembered how to make a granny square. For now, all she could do was go over her song in her head. She hoped she'd made a good choice. Donny said it showed off the best of what she was currently capable of singing. He wasn't being mean; he was treating her like a fellow professional.

She could do this. She only had to believe in herself. Musical comedy was where she belonged. It was where her heart was, where she was meant to be.

When they called for Group 4, Frankie found herself too nervous to stay seated. She stood up and started shaking out her legs. As long as she moved in slow motion so that her foot didn't come down too loud, she thought she could practice some of her tap steps as a warm up.

One of the other girls caught her eye and winked. "Hoping for a tap revival?" she said.

Frankie nodded. "Also, I really like it."

"Me too. So far out it's in! I did *Dames at Sea* at Paper Mill last year. Who do you take with?"

"Irene Lemon."

The other girl nodded respectfully. "Lemon's classic. She'll give you a good foundation. But," she asserted, "if you want to get up to speed for the season, you may want to take some classes with Lou Manzini. He's flashy, all hands and teeth, but sometimes that's what you need to get the job. And getting the job is what it's about, isn't it?"

Frankie nodded. "Lou Manzini," she repeated, to show she was listening. The girl returned to her own stretches. Frankie felt a little twinge in the pit of her stomach. It had been friendly advice, offered as one actor to another, but it made her realize what she was up against. She had *Mother Courage* to prove her worth in drama, but musicals were different. This girl, who spoke with so much authority, had already done a show at the Paper Mill Playhouse. Frankie was probably the only girl here who didn't have at least one similar credit on her resume.

By the time they called Group 5, there wasn't a breathing exercise ever invented that could have helped Frankie calm her nerves. She was halfway out of the room before she remembered to pull off her sweatshirt. There wasn't time to go back to her bag. She slung it over a hook by the door and hoped it would be there when she came back.

They trooped up a small flight of stairs. Frankie had enough presence of mind to lick her lips and smile before walking out onto the dusty stage, pretending she was used to all this. The work lights were very bright; even with her glasses on, everything beyond the apron was fuzz. She wondered who was out there. Her other senses told her it wasn't a lot of people. The casting director must be there, of course, but was the show's director? The musical director? The choreographer? It shouldn't really matter. You gave it your all, even when it was only a casting assistant.

A short muscular woman greeted each of them as they emerged. Her hair was scraped into a utilitarian ponytail. She wore dance trunks over snagged black tights, an old T-shirt tied up to her midriff; it was the polar opposite of the fashionable rainbow sported by the auditioning dancers. "Thanks for coming out today," the woman said, briskly pushing them into two rows. "I'm Kate. I'm the dance captain for the show. I'll be showing you all a short routine. We'll rehearse it a few times. Then you'll do it twice. In between, you'll switch so that the back row is in front. Okay? Then you'll wait while they decide who'll stay to sing."

Frankie's heart sank. If they let her sing first, they'd see how well she could put over a song and how funny she was. If it was all based on dancing, there was no way she'd get far enough to show them anything. Well, she couldn't walk out; she'd just have to do her best.

Luck put her in the back row; no one would be looking at her the first time through; she'd have an extra chance to practice. Kate showed them the routine from beginning to end, so they could see what it was supposed to look like. Then, with her back to them, she broke it down into smaller segments. She slowed it down, but it was still too fast for Frankie to follow. Sometimes Kate would call out the names of steps that you were obviously supposed to know. Maybe Frankie should be taking a jazz dance class after all. Once or twice the step reminded her of something she'd seen in a movie. She could fake these: the running step that you did with your arms windmilling, like in that vaudeville number in *Rosebud*; and the hoppy thing that reminded her of Debbie Reynolds and Donald O'Connor in *I Love Melvin*.

Far sooner than Frankie wanted, Kate gave them the signal for the first run-through. The music came of nowhere, probably a tape. No one else even twitched; Frankie jumped, grateful again that her inexperience was hidden in the back row. Kate yelled out "5, 6, 7, 8!" and they were off. Weirdly, the music seemed to help. With music, Frankie could pretend she was in a show, acting the part of a chorus dancer. The audience wouldn't know if she made a mistake, not if she stayed in character and really sold it. The key was to keep moving, look straight ahead and smile a really big smile. Frankie went all out. She tripped over her own feet a couple of times, but at least she didn't bang into anyone else. As they reached the end, she was actually feeling good about it. Then Kate swapped the rows. Frankie's heart thumped painfully in her chest. She stared out into the bright glow of the auditorium and focused on her imaginary chorus girl character. Before she could sneak in a deep breath, the music started up again. "5, 6, 7, 8!" Frankie went all out, all over again. She wasn't use to kicking at this speed or all the extensions that made her legs feel wobbly. She stumbled once or twice, but pushed on. When they got to the *Rosebud* step, she could have cried with relief, it felt so good to be doing something familiar. Through it all, she sold that routine like mad; Ann Miller couldn't have given it more heart and sparkle than Frankie Cecchi. When they finished, she felt triumphant. She'd done it; she'd made it through a professional chorus call and hadn't embarrassed herself. She could feel the pride shining off her as Group 5 waited to hear who would be asked to sing.

A male voice penetrated the glare. "Thanks everyone. We'd like to hear Jamie, Carol, Monica and the girl in the blue leotard. Everyone else, we enjoyed meeting you, but you can go." Frankie didn't move. Maybe under the stage lights her leotard looked blue. Then she heard a happy little squeal behind her and turned to see a tall blonde in an unequivocally royal blue camisole-strap leotard.

She gulped hard and forced herself off the stage and back to the greenroom.

"I knew they'd play favorites," griped the redhead in brown. "Only people they've worked with before, except for that one girl with the legs."

"She just came in from Vegas," supplied the girl with the very short black curls. "Hard to beat that experience. I was talking to her before. She's been training to try for the Rockettes, but she missed the open call and has to wait until August."

"Of course. It would be someone who doesn't even want the job."

"I'm sure she wants the job as much as any of us. Don't be a bitch about it, Beth."

Privately Frankie found herself agreeing with the redhead. If they were mostly considering people they'd worked with before, why did they bother having auditions? She was completely demoralized. A Rockette...even an aspiring Rockette...was this what she was going to be up against every time? Even for a singing role? There was no way she could compete. She dressed as quickly as she could and ducked out of the building. She was halfway up the block before she realized she'd left her sweatshirt behind. It took every bit of strength she had to turn back. If she could have afforded to lose it, she would have kept going; but money didn't grow on trees—especially not her money.

She turned around, forcing herself to act cool and lah-di-dah, as if she had so many auditions that this one didn't matter much in the scheme of things. The door handle wouldn't budge. Of course it would be locked from the inside; the building was only open for the audition. She waited by the door; other girls would have to leave eventually. She hoped she didn't freeze first. That would be so pathetic: Frankie Cecchi as the "Little Match Girl," frozen to death, staring longingly at the theatre she couldn't get into. It was a good thing she had a sense of humor. She was still laughing when door flew open, almost banging her in the face.

It was the tall girl in the blue leotard, the would-be Rockette, jamming her fingers into her gloves, a pissed off expression on her face. Not such a great singer then, a thought that made Frankie giggle more. The other girl glared. "Yeah?" she spat.

"I was here before. Such a space cadet! I left some of my stuff."

The other girl tilted her head to one side and held the door. "Knock yourself out," she said, stalking off.

Frankie stood in the doorway for a moment, watching. When push came to shove, she hadn't done much worse than a girl who had professional dance experience and was good enough to try out for the most famous chorus line in the world. It was all in how you looked at it. Frankie Cecchi had done okay today. And next time, she'd do even better. She was working hard at her training and making good progress. She had friends now, people who believed in her: Ellen, and Lilith Brassloe, and the Rodneys, and even Alfie, who had given her a regular shift. And she had a wonderful boyfriend! There was so much to be thankful for already and it was only February. Yes, 1974 was going to be her year.

♫

Ahuva helped out in the store, taking over in the middle of the morning so that her mother could force her father to take a nap. And she helped out in the house, giving Malke some extra time to go shopping with Raisel or play canasta or whatever they liked to do. And one night she went to school, which gave a shape to the week and made everybody happy.

She liked her class. After Professor Patronizing, it was an absolute pleasure to be treated like a responsible, thinking adult. She wondered if it was just Deb, or if it was always like that in night school, because of who the students were. Ahuva was Deb's youngest student. Mr. Klein, who nobody called by his first name, was the oldest. He reminded her of some of her parents' friends. It was brave of him to be going to college at his age. The three women who pushed their chairs close to one another and whispered together in Spanish were younger than him, but certainly older than anyone Ahuva had ever been in school with.

There were two guys who'd didn't say very much: one was pretty nervous; the other seemed to be with him for moral support. Mr. Klein told her they were back from Vietnam. Ahuva treated them with great respect. She hardly ever met any young person in America who'd served with the Armed Forces. It was probably because she'd mostly been in Honors classes in high school, where all the boys claimed to be pre-med or pre-law and everyone was strongly anti-war. She didn't think anyone would ever actively want to go to war, but her Israeli family and friends considered it a sacred duty.

"Vietnam is different," her American classmates said. "It's not our war, not like Israel, fighting to protect your own country. And it's not a righteous war, like World War II." They'd all had elaborate plans for avoiding the draft. Fortunately, the draft had ended before they had to put those plans into effect.

Ahuva thought Ric, the guy with the glasses, had been in the Service, too. The Army, probably, because he almost always wore fatigues. So did a lot of people her age, but Ric was almost thirty, and he wore his casually, not as if wearing them made a statement. It was this, together with his hair being so short and a passing mention of Yokohama, that made her think he was probably a Veteran. Cathy, who always sat next to Ric, was only 21, but she'd been married for almost a year, which made her seem much older. So did the fact that she was expecting a baby. Cathy always wore a poncho, so Ahuva didn't realize this at first. When she caught on, she decided it explained why Cathy was so mature. Cathy worked a register at Alexanders during the day, while her husband studied accounting at City College. Their parents had begged them not to start a family yet, so they were trying to be as independent as possible.

Ahuva found it bracing to be among these people. They lived in an entirely different world from the people she'd met upstate. All those sheltered teenagers, pretending to be sophisticated, seemed childish in comparison to her new night school classmates. The adult world was so much more substantial. Ahuva didn't belong here either, but it didn't reject her and it seemed more possible for her to float alongside these people and find her way.

She felt a similar ease when she was with Ellen Janow. Of all her contemporaries, Ellen was the only one who wasn't appalled to hear she'd left school. On the contrary: Ellen passed her into a matinee of *Find Your Way Home* and offered to buy her a celebratory cocktail at the bar at Alfie's after. The drink reminded her of something she'd tasted at the dentist, but they split a delicious portion of fries and she managed to get down a little more cocktail than she'd planned. Ahuva was pleasantly light-headed when Ellen paused at the coat-check. Maybe that was why she called out "Hi! I know you!" in such a loud voice. But she did know the coat-check girl with the big round eyeglasses. They'd met the night she'd used the bathroom at the Regale. Frankie. Frankie said "Hi" back, and then Ellen asked how they knew each other, and Ahuva, who was certainly a little tipsy, babbled the whole story, even starting with how badly she'd needed to pee, which should have been too embarrassing to mention. When the coat check got too busy to hang around, Ellen said they should all have coffee together at Howard Johnson's next Thursday afternoon, because that was always a good time for Frankie, who had two jobs on Thursdays and a few hours to kill in between.

In the end, it was Ellen who couldn't show up on Thursday. Ahuva got to the restaurant early and grabbed a booth. Ten minutes later, Frankie arrived. They waited ten more minutes before they ordered. Then Frankie went to the pay phone to call her service and found the message from Ellen saying she had to cancel because of something she had to do for Felix. It felt odd, staring at a stranger across the table, but they'd already ordered and it would have been weirder to leave. *Lake Song* was the obvious icebreaker. Ahuva was fascinated by Frankie's job with Lilith Brassloe, and that she'd known Bronwen Davies when she was growing up. Which led to some stories about Frankie's aunt, Annie Fallon, who Ahuva remembered from the original cast album of *Rosebud* that Bert Gruen had loaned her in the year she discovered Marshall Berenson. They talked a lot about Marshall Berenson musicals, and James Lord. Frankie told some stories about auditions and working at FAO Schwartz. Ahuva thought the stories were hilarious and told Frankie she could be a comedian, like Joan Rivers. When Frankie explained about her musical theatre studies, Ahuva opened up about leaving college...which had now turned into a decision, rather than a reaction...and about her class in night school. Frankie was even more supportive than Ellen. Ellen said Ahuva was making a rebellious statement, which wasn't true. Frankie, on the other hand, didn't think everyone was supposed to go to college; leaving it meant nothing special to her. Her attitude warmed Ahuva through and through. To have someone accept you like that, especially someone clearly wonderfully talented and, to boot, connected with *Lake Song*...it was absolutely *beshert* that they'd met and were becoming friends.

17 – KISS, KISS

ARKADINA

Kiss, kiss, my love.
Ah, such a cozy little tryst, my love.
Now you're recalling what you've
    missed, my love—
Such bliss, my love.
Admit it, the passion isn't dead.

Hold tight, my love,
The way you used to do at night, my
    love.
I know a sure way to excite my love...

TRIGORIN

Don't bite, my love.
A migraine is pounding in my head.

ARKADINA

No, that's your heart accelerating;
I feel it beating next to mine.
And as your pulse begins to rise
I see a swooning in your eyes.

TRIGORIN

I think...another glass of wine.

ARKADINA

Restraint is so intoxicating;
Release is twice as much divine.

TRIGORIN

You've caught my thigh between
    your thighs,
And now I'm breathing in your sighs,
It would be pointless to decline.

ARKADINA

Kiss, kiss, my love.
The room around us seems to list,
    my love...

TRIGORIN

I think we're getting rather pissed my
    love.

ARKADINA

My fist, my love.
God damn it—you're ruining the
    mood!

Just cling, my love,
And I'll forget that little fling, my love.
Oops no! I didn't say a thing my love.

TRIGORIN

No slings, my love.
It isn't attractive to be rude.

Besides, you lead me to remember
The reasons why I left your bed:
The nights of petulance and pouts;
The tears that forced me to a route;
The poisons better left unsaid.

When April's flower meets
    November's
The sweeter blossom shrinks in
    dread.

ARKADINA

To think you're wasting all that wit
To court a moony little chit.

TRIGORIN

Have you heard anything I've said?

ARKADINA

Kiss, kiss, my kiss, my love.
Or, as the French would say 'bis bis',
    my love.

TRIGORIN

Don't get your knickers in a twist, my
    love.

ARKADINA

No risk, my love:
No knickers, no corset and no
    shame!

TRIGORIN

Low hit, my love!

ARKADINA

I see you've finally got the drift, my
    love.

TRIGORIN

You're too enticing to resist, my love.
I lift, my love!
Upstairs my love?

ARKADINA

You dare to love?

TRIGORIN

But wait, my love!

ARKADINA

Too late my love.
Kiss this!
Kiss off, my love!

Having kicked off her career with a paying job, Frankie was shocked at how many professional actors, members of Equity, were willing to work for free. She once said so to a guy behind her on line at an open call. She later heard him tell someone else that she was "stuck up and self-impressed." That hurt. She decided he was jealous that she'd worked for Thierry Dupontel and didn't have to act for free. After six months of pavement pounding, she began to question that assumption.

Frankie had tried every agency in the little blue booklet they sold at the Drama Book Shop, mailing her pictures or, manila envelopes and postage costing almost as much as the prints themselves, saving money by dropping off her 8x10s in person whenever possible. The agents she managed to see face to face, usually by planting herself in a waiting room all day, never wanted to hear her monologues or give her anything to read. When she finally got called into the room, she'd shake hands and smile hard—"Sparkle Plenty," people called it, like the character in Dick Tracy—and say hello. They'd perk up for a second at the unusual sound of her voice and flip over her photo to see her resume. She'd peeped at enough of other people's by now to know that her own, even padded with high school plays, looked pretty thin by comparison. She stretched it out with a bunch of specialty skills: singing, tap, children's theatre and, after some consideration, foreign and regional accents. She was confident that, if she got a job, she could learn whatever she needed to know; she'd already picked up an English accent from watching movies, and she did an absolutely perfect impersonation of the girl from the Shake & Bake commercial. Not that anyone asked her to prove any of this. They'd either do nothing, or hand her a card and say "Send me a flyer for your next showcase." Frankie didn't want to work for free—less than free, really, when you added up the coat check tips she'd lose out on—but apparently they wouldn't give you work unless they saw you working. Which turned out to be why everyone did showcases. To her chagrin, they weren't all that easy to get into. She'd submitted herself for more than 30 without anyone showing the faintest interest until Wardell O'Hare responded to her mailing.

The address was in a part of town that Frankie had only been in once, for an audition in the old machine loft that had nervously reminded her of the Triangle Shirtwaist fire. Everything here looked like old factory buildings, connected by actual cobblestone streets so empty that you could easily imagine horse carriages just out of sight. The entire walk from the subway, she never saw a living soul on the street. The building walls were sprayed with cryptic slogans and plastered with posters of bands she'd never heard of. She'd never heard much about the neighborhood either, until that boy went missing and it was suddenly all over the news: Etan, a name as odd as the neighborhood. Supposedly a lot of artists lived here, some illegally setting up studios in buildings that had been abandoned because of taxes or something. She'd never heard of there being a theatre.

The building looked like all the others, but the sign on the metal door said "Soho Art Theatre." She pushed a button, said her name into the speaker and someone buzzed her in.

Though it wore the daylight air of sadness shared by all theatre lobbies, it looked more like someone's rec room. Maybe it was the fake wood paneling and the faint whiff of damp. There was one single hard plastic bucket chair with wire legs and a mismatched pair of shabby piano benches. The box office was behind a thin laminate partition. The table next to it, spread with a wrinkled cloth that could have used a good wash, held some rumpled programs and a packet of Sweet 'N' Low. The space ended in a half-wall, hung with thick velour curtains to mask whatever was beyond.

"In here!" a confident tenor called from the other side of the drapes.

Frankie shrugged off her coat and gave a quick tweak to her skirt, making sure it hadn't rucked up over her tights. She hoped her lip gloss was okay; there wasn't time to fix it. She cleared her throat, and walked through the gap to what, makeshift though it was, was unmistakably a theatre. Lighting instruments hung from overhead pipes and the exposed brick walls. Rows of elderly seats, bald patches obvious even in this dim light, were separated into two blocks by an aisle. They faced a large rectangular patch of floor that wasn't raised at all but was most definitely a stage, set for rehearsal with an old kitchen table and two chairs, and a blue Victorian sofa with a large duct-taped hole on the seat.

The man was dressed, like the Irish fisherman on the soap commercial, in a flat cap and a butter-colored sweater that was knit of braids and bumps. He had a small beard. It was hard to tell how old he was.

"Wardell O'Hare," he said. Without rising, he held out a hand.

"Frankie Cecchi," she replied, taking it.

"Let me tell you about our company," he said, using the handshake to pull her closer. Considering how the sweater hung on his wiry frame, his grip was stronger than she expected. The beard only partially covered a gaunt, pitted face. His eyes were such a light brown they were almost yellow. His free hand patted the sofa beside him.

She perched gingerly, not trusting to the safety of either the duct-tape patch or Wardell O'Hare. She remained sitting stiffly for a good quarter hour, while O'Hare's tenor voice—thin and reedy when he didn't have to raise it—droned on about his Mission: to stage all of Chekhov.

O'Hare could have done anything he wanted with his life, at least anything money could buy. There was a lot of money. His mother was one of the bread company Wardells (the label was one of the first things Frankie could remember learning to read). His father's family had manufactured plumbing supplies in this very building for sixty years, until the factory moved out to Trenton. The building was his now. Having converted the street level into this theatre, he lived on the top floor and rented the rest to artists.

O'Hare had met his vocation at Columbia, when Chekhov was suggested as supplemental reading for the Dostoyevsky unit of his freshman Humanities class. He'd devoured everything he could get his hands on, including the grim-sounding *Island of Sakhalin*. He'd even tried to learn Russian.

"But turns out I don't have a knack for languages. If only we'd had a Polish nanny! Really, translations are for shit." When he'd embarked on his Mission—every time he used that word, his face lit up like a painting of the Virgin Mary—he'd had the brilliant idea of commissioning literal translations from a pair of translators. "Word for word. The raw text only; no interpretation. Though Shlomo, the old Jew I met at Ratner's, he can't resist pushing in a few of his own touches. 'Shlomo,' I tell him, 'if it says red just give me red. I don't need you trying to figure out whether Chekhov meant blood or cherry.' See, that's why I like having two translations. Once I have both sets—there's always some student at Columbia or NYU who can use the extra bread—I bring in my people. We talk it through, scene by scene, and build our own script. I think we get to the meat of it that way. It's how Stanislavsky would have done it."

Frankie had only ever read *An Actor Prepares*, which hadn't impressed her. She was turned off by "affective memory," the idea that if your character is sad, you remember your dead mother. Frankie didn't believe acting should be painful: you act to be someone else, someone who's not yourself. She'd stopped reading after that. Apparently, though, there was more about Stanislavsky that you're supposed to know. She was ashamed at her ignorance.

"I have my core company," O'Hare explained. "All committed actors. No theatrical dilettantes. Nobody marking time until it's time to fly west for pilot season." Frankie could tell from his cold laugh that this had happened to him once. He ticked them off on his fingers: "Leading lady, leading man, a pair of good juveniles. A fantastic older man. Bob Carpenter?"

She didn't know the name.

He waved away her embarrassment. "You'll know him when you see him. He had an arc on *Dark Shadows*."

Dark Shadows had been really popular when Frankie was in high school. She'd tried watching, in an attempt to make friends. The show was supposed to be a soap opera, but there were vampires and ghosts and werewolves. Unless you knew someone who'd been watching a while and would fill in the blanks, it was impossible to get started. Frankie'd thrown in the towel, though not before seeing enough episodes to be surprised that someone as intellectual as Wardell O'Hare would be impressed by an actor who'd been on it.

"And I found a wonderful older woman to play all those faithful old retainers. Cathleen Penney. Been in the business forever. She was once married to Fred Crane: you know, the other Tarleton twin. She was with the Group for a little while. And with Quintero at Circle in the Square. Living breathing theatre history, Cathleen; an absolute treasure. And such passionate commitment to what we're doing here. All of them. You'll see when you meet them."

She would? She hadn't even auditioned yet. All she'd done was mail her headshot to the address in the *Backstage* ad: "Chekhov repertory company seeking actress for upcoming season. Young woman, 18-25, for small roles in two act short story adaptation, *Gooseberries*. Equity Showcase contract." The only gooseberry story she could find in the library didn't seem too promising, but she had a rule of trying for at least two jobs every week no matter what and, because of *Lake Song*, she made a particular point of trying for productions of Chekhov. Getting a call had been a pleasant surprise.

O'Hare was staring intently into her eyes. "Do you like Chekhov?"

She couldn't help a tiny jump of embarrassment. "Oh, yes! That's why I'm so excited to audition for you. I..."

He held up his hand to stop her. "What's important here is your enthusiasm for the work. And how well you fit in with the rest of the company, of course. Our goal is to stage all of Chekhov. The narrative fiction, too, even if we have to adapt for theatre ourselves. I think Chekov subconsciously meant even his prose to be staged. Reaction is the essence of his writing." O'Hare paused, letting the phrase hang in the air.

He clearly relished the sound; she wondered if he'd come up with it himself. Frankie would have to remember it.

He continued. "We do three productions each year: one of the major plays, an evening of one-acts, and an adaptation we create on our own. We've built the upcoming play on a trilogy of short stories. "Gooseberries" is just one of them. Great title, don't you think?"

She nodded. She would have nodded no matter what he'd said. Three shows a year! And Wardell O'Hare somehow made it seem like a privilege to be part of his plans. They talked for another half hour: O'Hare talked; Frankie mostly listened, becoming more and more convinced that he was someone who did important things, the kinds of things that maybe even became history. She desperately wanted to fit in with his company.

He never did ask to hear her monologue, or even to have her read a scene. He simply told her that he had a small part available: only a line or two in each act, but an excellent opportunity to work her way into the company. If all went well, there'd be larger parts in future. "I also, naturally, expect you to be my ASM," he added, once she'd pretty much accepted the offer.

Was that natural? Actors were actors, and stage managers were stage managers. Frankie had never done a showcase before; maybe things were different. "Is that…" she groped for a way to ask without sounding like an idiot. "Is that okay with Equity?"

Wardell O'Hare brushed off her concerns with a flick of his hand. "This isn't some vanity scene study evening. We're a company; we all pitch in to do what we can to help the production. This is a tremendous opportunity for you to internalize our process."

She nodded her agreement. When he said it that way, it made complete sense. He leaned his cheek closer to her face and beckoned. She realized he expected her to kiss it. She also realized this seemed like the appropriate thing to do. Before she could feel too self-conscious about the quick peck, they were interrupted by the slamming of the outside door.

O'Hare checked his watch. "The troupe assembles!" he said, with some satisfaction. "Which reminds me…" He fished a lanyard from his pocket and unhooked one of the keys. "Be careful you don't lose this," he cautioned.

"I won't. I mean, I will. Be careful." She was too flustered by his show of trust to be coherent. Digging into her bag, she found her own key ring.

She nearly dropped the key before she could thread it on. Bronwen Davies in Arkadina's blue gown didn't make a more impressive entrance than this bony young woman, sweeping down the aisle to the rhythm of the clumping work boots she wore beneath her long full rehearsal skirt and a baggy man's sweater that had seen much better years. She couldn't have been much older than Frankie.

"Dawn, my dear!" Wardell's face lit up again.

She strode right up to the sofa and bent to kiss his cheek. "Maestro!"

"Maestro," repeated the silver-haired man behind her. Frankie hadn't even noticed him enter; Dawn had taken her full attention.

"Bob."

This must be the *Dark Shadows* guy. He did look a little familiar. He also kissed O'Hare's cheek. Frankie started to feel less weird about her own impulse in that direction. So everyone called him Maestro, huh? She was learning already. Filing in, one by one, they came up to Wardell O'Hare and kissed his cheek. Two younger guys—not Bob—moved the table and chairs.

They all formed a circle in the cleared space, O'Hare shuffling to take the place reserved for him between Dawn and the woman whose heavy cornet of grey-white hair seemed familiar from Equity. Frankie remained on the sofa. He hadn't said to leave, and he didn't invite her to join them. When you felt as if whatever you do is going to be the wrong thing, Frankie thought it was better to do nothing. O'Hare mumbled some things she couldn't make out. There were murmurs of agreement, followed by a few simple stretches and a zoo of vocalizations—trills and caws and growls and ooks—that lasted for what seemed ages. Then everyone sank to the floor, sitting cross-legged, eyes turned to Wardell O'Hare.

"Before we begin our session, I remind you that this will be our last meeting before we start rehearsals. So I expect us to make the most of today. We must spend the time between now and Monday absorbing the source material and preparing our vessels for complete immersion into *Gooseberries*." O'Hare turned towards the sofa and beckoned to Frankie. She stood carefully and walked closer. He was still holding out his hand. She put hers out and he grabbed it. "A process that should flow more smoothly now that Frankie will be here."

"Frankie who?" Dawn smirked at her with those skinny lips. The mop of frizzy brown hair did nothing to soften her long nose and sunken eyes, but she acted as if she were as gorgeous as Julie Christie. "Frankie Addams?"

The circle rippled with sniveling laughter. A prickle of annoyance overrode Frankie's basic discomfort. What was the point? That she'd read *A Member of the Wedding*? Who hadn't? What was this woman's problem?

"Frankie is my new right hand," O'Hare said. Something in his eyes made Dawn shut up and everyone else twitch a shoulder or duck their head. "She joins us officially on Monday. I know she'll be grateful for your help as she learns our ways."

She stood there awkwardly and smiled. Someone started a polite round of applause. "Thank you," she said. What else could she have said?

"No, thank *you* Frankie." Wardell O'Hare nodded his head and dismissed her. "See you on Monday. Noon sharp."

Frankie devoutly agreed that there were no small parts. Every role was critical to a play's success, and there were tons of stories about actors who'd made big impressions in a bit part. Despite this, once the initial excitement had faded in the cold light of the Long Island Railroad, she began to have second thoughts. Six weeks of rehearsal and four weekends of performance. She'd be giving up paid work and a lot of auditions for only a few minutes on stage. This showcase might not be worth it. She'd have the chance to become part of the company, but did she want to be part of this company? They hadn't been exactly welcoming, especially not that Dawn and, as mesmerizing as he was face to face, Wardell felt a little creepy the further she got from the theatre.

The showcase did have one thing in its favor: it would be such a slap in the face for Eunice, who had this way of asking about auditions, all sweetness and light, and then saying "Don't be disappointed, dear; there must be so many pretty girls to choose from…" in the most patronizing way, as if Frankie were some freak of nature. Frankie didn't kid herself she was a pin-up girl (neither was Eunice), but she knew she was more than cute enough; she had Donny for corroboration. Nor could Eunice say anything that would ever dent Frankie's confidence in her talent. Frankie was only tired of blocking out the noise; it would be so satisfying to strike back. She imagined casually dropping the news, over breakfast coffee maybe: "By the way, I'm doing a play downtown. With a highly respected Chekhov company." Eunice's face! Cinderella's stepmother when the glass slipper fit; that's what it would be like, exactly. Frankie was looking forward to that moment.

Who was she kidding? That wasn't the real reason to take this showcase. It was because it was the only offer she'd had since leaving NYADA. Whatever it would or wouldn't be, she could add it to her resume and invite agents to see.

♬

Ahuva starting having coffee with Ric and Cathy after class. She still didn't like coffee, but it was what people did. She'd learned to order tea and stir in a lot of honey.

Ric Medina was even more interesting than she'd initially realized. He had indeed been in the army. He said he'd enlisted right after high school, because he was bound to be drafted and enlistees got better postings. He really had been in Japan—for a year—and in Germany for two; "The Axis Tour," he joked. He wouldn't talk about his tour in Vietnam, but she knew she'd find out some day because he was a writer. A professional writer. Ric had already written a novel. "A coming of age story," he laughed. "Like every first novel, right?" In Ric's case, coming of age was coming to live with his older sister in the Bronx when he was twelve and his father died, his mother having died a couple of years before that. What made the story "interesting enough that someone was willing to give me a few thou to publish it," was that until then he'd lived his whole life on the same mountain in Puerto Rico where he was born and where his family had lived as far back as anyone could say. Despite his last name, Ric's people were Indian, not Spanish. Maybe one or two Spanish over a couple of hundred years ("unavoidable, right?"), but at least 90% pure Taino. His father, who was old enough to be his grandfather really, saw himself as a custodian of the old ways. With the sons and daughters of two previous marriages grown and long since moved on, he concentrated on handing down his heritage to his youngest child. That's what Ric had written about, growing up on the mountain with an old man who had one foot in an ancient culture that was legend and badly remembered rituals, and the other foot firmly in the modern Independence Movement.

It was all fascinating. Once the FBI had streamed up the mountain, looking for one of his older brothers, who wasn't there. His father, Ric recalled, had been torn between pride and rage at Angel for getting himself involved.

"What happened to your brother?"

"Oh, nothing much. Papi gave him money to bribe someone with a boat. Papi thought I didn't know, but Angel made a point of seeing me before he left. He ended up in Costa Rica for a few years. The kicker was, he was up to his eyeballs in that shit, except he hadn't done the one thing they were accusing him of. Later they found the right guy and put him away. Angel ended up in Florida, not far from Boca. He sells used Chevys now. Has kids who go to swim meets and sell Girl Scout cookies."

Like Ahuva, Ric had come to New York without a word of English; yet he wrote entirely in that language, which had seduced him away from the Spanish that was his milk tongue. It was his editor who'd urged him to take a few writing and literature classes. "He says to broaden my horizons," Ric joked, "but more to make it easier for me to understand what the fuck he's talking about. The publishing people? They all go to those Ivy League schools, but they couldn't form a simple declarative sentence if their lives depended on it. It's a pisser: they tell me they love how my work is so 'raw and immediate,' but they still want to polish the shit out of me."

Ahuva made a mental note to find a copy of Ric's novel if she had to search every bookstore and library in the city of New York. Second hand stores, too; Ric claimed the book hadn't sold much. He'd gotten some good reviews, though, and people wanted to see what he came up with next. Important people. People like Marshall Berenson.

That was how special Ric was: he had actually met Marshall Berenson. Ahuva almost died when he said, so casually, "We hung out a few times." Someone had sent Berenson the novel, because they thought the subject matter would appeal to him. "The Taino stuff. You know, Berenson has a piece on the back burner that's all about Indian myths and legends. He was completely fascinated by Papi's stories, especially the ones about men who could fly."

♬

Ellen staggered out of the Winter Garden, making a beeline to Pub Theatrical. She could barely hold it together to cross Broadway. What she'd just seen! She had to have a scotch. She'd have toughed it out until she got home, except Leonard was spending the night with Preston and she'd decided to stop drinking alone, before it became a bad habit. Tonight would have to be an exception. At least if she sat at the bar, she wouldn't technically be alone.

Who would imagine you could put James Joyce on stage? Now she had to get her hands on a copy of *Ulysses*. She'd been meaning to read it anyway, though it wasn't because of Joyce that she'd taken the ticket from Mr. Nudler. She'd wanted to see Zero Mostel. There were some artists everyone should be obligated to see perform, at least once in a lifetime. Zero, high on that list, was brilliant in this role, born to play it. It was an honor to have witnessed his performance. But that woman! What was her name? Flanagan. Not Fiona...something else Irish. She would check the *Playbill* and repeat it a hundred times until she had it memorized.

The balls that woman has! Ellen chuckled reminiscently to herself. That monologue—"Yes, I said yes!" Sprawled across the bed, practically crawling the walls. It was an orgasm! On stage!

The bartender set down her glass on the chic black bar mat.

She extracted a cigarette and, having first briefly wetted it with scotch, flicked her tongue along the paper at one end.

He leaned across the bar to light the other. "You look happy."

"Saw a great play tonight. Got any nuts?" Damn, sometimes everything she said came out double entendre. She wasn't in the mood to flirt tonight;

she wanted to digest the play. Forefinger leading, she brushed her right hand across her face and rolled her eyes, a gesture she'd rehearsed to seem worldly and self-amused rather than flustered. It was the ring that made the difference. The longer she wore that damned ring, the more she loved it, the satisfying weight of it as much as the look. Every gesture she made with her right hand had such panache. "Forget I said that."

He laughed good-naturedly and produced a squat silver dish of almonds. "Let me know if you run out," he said, moving down the bar to tidy up the cut fruit. His day was winding down.

Ellen took an appreciative sip of her Chivas. She crunched an almond, relishing the contrast between the milky nutmeat and the salt.

"Yes, I said yes!" Fucking amazing, that Flanagan woman! *Lake Song, Moon* and now this…This was why she wanted to make theatre.

She hoped Felix was having half as good a night. He'd gone to the Players' Club with the couple from Brewster that Penelope had trapped at a benefit for City Ballet. The wife, who'd been a child actress, was yearning to resume contact with the business, now that her own children were grown. Felix was charming them tonight, in the hopes that they might decide to invest in Lazarus. They probably would. Charming was Felix's thing. It would be fantastic if he'd been charming enough to convince them to get their friends to invest as well. There had been so many almosts, but now they were this close to having enough money to float the season. Ellen was getting itchy; it was time to get this show on the road.

♫

Frankie rang the bell that first Monday, forgetting for the moment that Wardell O'Hare had given her a key. She fished it out of her bag. It felt weird to let herself into a place she'd only been to once. She rang again. It was windy on the street. She'd missed the morning weather report and had dressed for spring. Even with thick socks, her toes were cold in her clogs. She was exactly on time. Didn't O'Hare live right upstairs? He should be in the theatre by now. Was this a test? Steeling herself against the unimaginable, she fitted the key to the lock, turned it and pushed. The door groaned a little, as steel doors will, especially those exposed to weather. As soon as the opening was large enough, she squeezed in and closed it quickly behind her. The lobby was pitch black. It hadn't occurred to her to keep the door open until she found a light switch, probably because it hadn't occurred to her that it would be so dark.

If she smoked, she'd have a lighter. She did have a book of Alfie's matches, for emergencies, but she couldn't feel them in her bag. When she found them, she'd stick them in her makeup bag. An emergency source of light isn't really useful if you can't find it in the dark. Maybe she should get one of those tiny keychain flashlights they sold in the souvenir shops. She could hook it to one of the rings of her dance bag…In this manner, she fought off panic until the logical thought finally surfaced, that all she had to do was open the door again to let in the daylight. She groped for the knob, twisted it and pulled. Nothing happened. O'Hare had buzzed her out, she remembered, which meant it was one of those doors that locked from both sides. The key still in her hand, she brushed her fingers across the plate to find the hole.

The sudden light, grey and cloud-splintered as it was, made her squint. Turning away, she saw the same make-do lobby she'd passed through the week before. Empty and sad. Where were the actors? Shouldn't they be here for their exercises? O'Hare had said that acting exercises were critical to the fabric of the company. Even when they were between productions, they came together a few times a week just to do the exercises. That was what they'd come for the day of her audition. Remembering Dawn's smirk that day, it became imperative that no one find her standing paralyzed in the middle of the lobby. They would think she was a total idiot. She had to act efficient, as if she were used to being part of a theatre company.

Dropping her bags, she fairly flew along the perimeter, searching anxiously for a light switch. By the time everyone arrived, all the lights were on, her coat and clogs were off, and she was sitting cross-legged on the floor (avoiding the sofa after she's seen a roach crawl out), apparently engrossed in a library copy of the Oxford Russian Reader edition of *Anton Chekhov: Selected Short Stories*.

Rehearsals were interesting and dull at the same time. The Maestro, as she got used to calling him, had her doing exercises along with the rest of the company but, unlike when she did Donny's or practiced her shuffles and flaps, she couldn't feel anything happening. Maybe you had to repeat them for a long while before they started to make sense. Everyone else had this expression on their faces, as if they were being transformed. Kind of the way they looked when they kissed his cheek. She would probably feel more at ease if she could get up on her feet and act.

What she mostly did was move furniture, and go out for coffee, and make lists of costume and prop ideas that came up during rehearsal. She'd expected to learn a lot by keeping the director's book, but Wardell O'Hare's approach was very different from Thierry's. At the first read-through of *Mother Courage*,

Thierry had produced all sorts of drawings and blocking ideas, and played some music that he said held the essence of what he was trying to accomplish. It was probably easier to do that for *Mother Courage*, which was already a play. The company had only just finished the first draft of *Gooseberries* when rehearsals began. Still, she was surprised that the Maestro didn't seem to have made any artistic decisions. He watched what the actors did, and listened to them argue about motivation. Her job was to write it all down, even if one day's work contradicted the next.

Frankie wouldn't believe a play was going to come out of this muddle, except that Wardell O'Hare had been doing this for eleven years. She trusted that he knew what he was doing. It was important to believe in the director, even if you didn't understand him. She often didn't understand O'Hare; he was brilliant as well as eccentric. Frankie found his eccentricities creepy at first, especially the kissing and the touching, but she'd gotten used to them once she saw how everyone else took them in stride. He could be inspiring: every time he addressed the troupe, she was completely blown away. And when he selected people for special one-on-one coaching, which meant coming back downtown after they finished whatever work they did, they looked completely ecstatic. He must give them some kind of special insights for them to look that way. Maybe when her part came into focus she'd find out. She might be confused now, but he would probably turn out to be a great director.

She needed to let go of her expectations and go with the flow. Working with the Soho Art Theatre was a truly valuable experience. That's what she ended up telling her friends in the end.

Her announcement met with a brief moment of shock from Lil, who'd gotten so used to having an elf that she'd forgotten Frankie was an actress. It was true Frankie never mentioned her auditions, considering them too trivial to discuss with an international theatre icon, especially since nothing ever came of them. However, she'd told Lil about her day of extra work (Lil had laughed a lot) and she mentioned her lessons enough that Lil sometimes asked how they were coming along. Frankie was hurt; but then Lil kissed her on both cheeks and said "Bravo!" in that amazing voice, so heartily that she thought she must have imagined the shock. When Frankie explained that the company rehearsed in the afternoons (because they all had night jobs except Cathleen, who lived off a combination of Social Security, her Equity pension and extra work), Lil even suggested that they work on the scrapbooks on Fridays, rather than putting it on hold as Frankie had expected. It was extremely nice of Lil. Even nicer, the very next week she gave Frankie a small china dog to have as a dressing room mascot; she said Bea Lillie had given it to her, when they did *Madwoman of Chaillot* together.

Alfie wasn't quite as accommodating but he did give her the phone numbers of the other two girls so she could try and arrange a shift swap. Stacy was willing to swap her Saturday lunch for Wednesday, but Frankie had to agree to also swap tips if, after the first week, Stacy thought the Saturday matinee tippers were that much better. That took care of the rehearsal period, but no one was willing to take Thursday nights for the performance weeks. Alfie only shrugged when she told him. Why did she think he was always looking for coat check girls? They were all actresses. She'd leave when she had to, and she'd be the first person he'd call next time he had an opening. He promised to put a *Gooseberries* flyer in a prominent spot on the wall by the coat check.

Frankie was philosophical: it wasn't the best outcome, but it could have been worse. In the big picture, a coat check job wasn't much of a sacrifice. So what is she only had four lines (it was one line, really, but she would get to say it four times)? She was in a play.

♫

Jakub paid Ahuva a salary, so that she would understand that working in the store was a responsibility, not a favor to her parents. She came in from 10 AM to 2 PM. It was quiet then, mostly mothers with toddlers. The mothers wanted a break as much as a pack of cigarettes. Twenty minutes of peace at the counter was worth the price of a cup of coffee, and a cheap plastic toy. Ahuva was good with little kids. Some of the mothers offered her babysitting work. She also took care of Jason on the nights that Holly went to the Village.

Wednesdays, her day off, she went into the city to see a matinee. Sometimes she grabbed a slice after and stayed to do a double-feature. Her goal was to see every play on Broadway that season, even the ones that didn't sound at all intriguing. Thanks to the new half-price ticket booth, she could afford it.

She read all the reviews before she went, then carefully monitored her own reactions to compare them. Was she seeing what other people, knowledgeable people, saw? When she didn't, why didn't she? Plays, dramas and comedies both, often left her unsettled. When her assessment was at odds with the critics', she couldn't explain it. It often seemed that the characters she found most compelling were the ones the reviewers disparaged. Sometimes she felt that the longer she lived in America, the less she fit in. She felt on firmer footing when it came to musicals, or at least more confident: her ear wouldn't let her down.

All of this was part of the task she'd set herself, of working out where theatre fit into her life, or maybe how she might fit into theatre. Ahuva wasn't an actor or a writer or a designer. She could almost see herself learning to produce, like Ellen Janow, except that she wouldn't enjoy raising money; she'd always rather earn money than ask for it. What she enjoyed most was organizing. She'd spoken with Deb about this. Deb was only teaching for extra money. She was really a lighting designer. Deb said Ahuva would probably make an excellent stage manager and suggested she sign up to work on one of the productions at Queens, for the experience. Ahuva put the idea on the back burner; she wasn't quite ready to make a commitment.

At *Lake Song* again one Wednesday, Ahuva was surprised by a slip of paper in the program that said "At this performance, the part of Arkadina will be played by Nancy Pardoe." Nancy had a lovely singing voice, much stronger and better trained than Bronwen's, but she was too dull to be Arkadina. She gave it a good try. If anything, she tried too hard. The laugh lines were forced. Ahuva wanted to laugh, to be nice, but it felt fake. "Kiss, Kiss" was especially painful to watch, at least it was for Ahuva. The rest of the audience didn't seem to mind; they didn't know what it was supposed to be like.

As usual, Ahuva waited by the door of the Regale afterwards, to see Maria. Other cast members waved as they passed her. They were always so friendly. The best was for Ahuva to be speaking with either Maria or Kaye Victor, who was almost as friendly as Maria, when Oliver Blanchard came out. Ollie. After careful consideration, Ahuva had concluded that Ollie Blanchard was the single most handsome man she'd ever seen in real life. His name alone made her heart flip over. He was such a lovely person, too. He always, absolutely always smiled at her; and if she was with Maria or Kaye, he'd walk over and actually talk with them. It was hard to breathe when he did that, but she thought she was getting better at pretending it was normal to have a conversation with someone who looked like every Prince Charming imaginable.

Ollie didn't show up today. Kaye, who seemed to be his best friend in the show, said he was nursing a chest thing. She was going to pick up some soup for him at the Chinese place on Ninth Avenue; not won ton or egg drop, but a sour soup, which sounded terrifically unappealing. Kaye laughed at the expression on Ahuva's face and explained that it was just the thing for a chest. Chinese and Indian foods could be used like medicine, she explained. Kaye knew the most fascinating things. She'd been to India, Ahuva knew, though naturally not to China.

Ahuva wasn't in a double-feature mood today. Maybe she was coming down with a chest thing, too. She decided that she'd stop by Alfie's before heading home and treat herself to an order of fries. They made exceptionally good fries there; you could see the shape of the potato, but they were just as crispy and golden as the skinny McDonald's kind.

Frankie Cecchi, in a fresh white shirt and a black skirt, was eating a burger at the bar.

"Can I join you?" Ahuva asked.

Frankie smiled. "I've still got a few minutes before I take over. You can sit with me then, too, as long as you're not eating."

"I forgot you work here." Ahuva was a little embarrassed.

"So did she," the bartender broke in, "now that she's got a showcase." He set a Coke in front of Ahuva with a wink. "On the house," he said. "Any friend of Frankie's…"

Ahuva thanked him three times and ordered her fries, putting her purse on the bar so he'd know she wasn't trying to get them for free, too. He seemed to think she was very funny.

"You're in a showcase?" Thanks to Deb, Ahuva knew what that meant.

Frankie nodded, swallowing some burger.

"That's so exciting! When is it? I am definitely coming to see you.'

"Next month," Frankie told her. She reached over the edge of the bar for a pencil. "Write down your address. I'll send you a flyer."

There wasn't any paper. Ahuva didn't need another *Lake Song* program. She was about to write on the cover when she spotted the slip of paper poking out of the top. Pulling it out, she jotted her address down on the back. "So, is Bron okay?"

"Huh?!"

Ahuva held out the paper. "I was there today. Nancy Pardoe went on for her. Not impressive."

Frankie made a careful sweep of the room. Her glasses magnified her rolling eyes. It was hard not to laugh. Ahuva knew that Frankie had made her debut in *Mother Courage*, but it was impossible to imagine her doing anything other than comedy.

Satisfied that there was no one within eavesdropping distance, Frankie leaned close to Ahuva. Keeping her voice very low, she confided that, stopping by the Regale to leave a message for Lil, she'd run into Bronwen's dresser backstage. Clearly upset, Connie said that Bronwen had shown up at one o'clock, too ill to perform. It had taken Connie and the ASM combined to convince her to go home in a cab and let Nancy go on in her place. Ellen had always said there were rumors that Bronwen had a drinking problem, and putting that together with a little crack Lil made last week, Frankie thought "ill" meant drunk. "I hate that Ellen's right about this."

"Maybe she's not. You probably only got that feeling because Ellen put it in your head. She does that to me sometimes," Ahuva confided. "It's amazing how convincing she is! Maybe Bron has a stomach flu or something like that."

Frankie seemed to find this comforting. She was smiling by the time she left to take over the coat check. When she finished her fries, Ahuva hung out with her for a while, listening to funny stories about the Soho Art Theatre, until the dinner crowd heated up and things got too busy for Frankie to socialize.

Ahuva's phone rang early the next morning.

"So I hear Bron's on a bender," Ellen cackled over the line.

"She probably has stomach flu," Ahuva said crossly, stretching the extra-long cord so she could walk the receiver into the other room. Her mother, sitting with her coffee in the kitchen, didn't need to hear this.

"You think so? That's not what Joe tells me. Joe said she was reeking, they could smell it in the hall. Milt Foxe had Pardoe getting ready while Connie was trying to push her into a cab."

"It doesn't mean she was drunk."

"Why are you in denial?"

"Why are you getting off on this?" Ahuva countered. "Or is it just *Schadenfreude*?"

"*Shadden* what?"

"*Schadenfreude*. It's a German word. It means getting off on other people's misery."

"I like that. Say it again."

"Oh for…Why do you have to turn this into some scandal? The poor woman probably caught a bug. You should be admiring her for trying to go on. You would if she were Penelope Rice."

"Penelope is not a lush. Bron is," Ellen said with relish. "A beautiful, sexy lush, but definitely a lush. This isn't the first time she's shown up tanked. It's just the first time she couldn't make it onstage."

"You're disgusting!"

"No, I'm not. I'm realistic. That's how I'm different from the rest of you. You have such an infantile view of this business. They're not perfect. None of them is perfect. Your darling Marshall Berenson spelled it out for you: famous people are a fucking mess! If you want to love this business, you have to embrace that reality. Love them for the assholes and fuck-ups and sluts that they are. Grow up, Ahuva!"

♫

What did Shakespeare say…? Right, what *didn't* he say? But specifically, what was it he said about artists? "The poet's eye, in a fine frenzy rolling, doth glance from heaven to Earth, from Earth to heaven." For the four years I was in college, my eye darted back and forth between my own two worlds—heaven being whichever one I was not in at the time. As much as I longed to be back on campus when I was in Queens, my friends' letters, with their Brons and their Ollies and their insider gossip, made me feel seriously rusticated when I was 75 minutes from Broadway. Ellen wrote to say she'd be house-sitting her dad's Upper East Side apartment and could use some company. Taking advantage of a surprisingly rehearsal-and-paper-free weekend, I went down to join her.

As I stepped through the door, a puppy hurled himself into my arms.

"He isn't trained yet," Ellen informed me, unnecessarily. The tiny bundle of fur had left a trail of excited wee across the parquet tiles and down the leg of my jeans. "That's why I'm here."

I'd never been to Harry's place before, but tales about his second bachelorhood were part of the fabric of my adolescence: the customized German sports car, the conversation pit in his "pad" and the Joe Namath mink coat could have been ripped from the pages of *Esquire*; just as his string of educated clothes-horse girlfriends were straight out of *Cosmopolitan* (in some cases literally). Harry, a charming man with a great appetite for life, seemed born to jump from airplane to stewardess and back again, always with a cocktail in his hand.

Ellen watched me look around, enjoying my frustrated search for the legendary white leather conversation pit. What I saw instead was a large burlap sofa and a couple of those fan-backed rattan chairs that show up in tiki bars and movies set on Malaysian tea plantations. Despite the neutral furnishings and the bare wood floor, the foyer and living room blazed with color from the large, riotous canvases than hung, unframed, from nearly every wall. I stared at the one over the sofa, hoping that those pulsating shapes were merely flowers.

"So what do you think of my stepmother's work?" Ellen finally asked, then laughed uproariously at the changes in my face as I digested what she'd said.

"No shit," she assured me. She picked up a framed photo from the end table. Two people on a beach. The man was dressed beachcomber style in a gauze tunic with embroidery at the neck, his white pants rolled up to the knee. The beaming face beneath the ragged brim of the straw hat was definitely Harry's. He had his arm around the bare waist of a sturdy woman in a bathing suit top and a flowered sarong. She squinted joyfully at the camera from under a wreath of flowers. They both had ropes of flowers around their necks. Leis.

"Hawaii?"

She nodded. "Week after I met her, they went on vacation there and got married. Pretty spontaneous. I never would have thought Harry had it in him."

"Far fucking out." That was what we said when we didn't know what to say. The last thing I'd expected was to hear that Harry had remarried. Scratch that; second-to-last. The very last thing I would have expected was for him to date, no less marry, an earthy crop-haired artist who painted along the lines of a feminist Gauguin.

"Right?" She put the photo back, giving it one final appraising look. "I think he's happy. I hope so. I even like her."

"That's good," I said lamely. Even knowing her issues with Sydelle as well as I did, I thought Ellen was being incredibly mature.

"She's a hell of a lot better than any of his harem. At least she has something to say for herself." She gestured at the paintings. "And she talks to me like I'm a person, not an annoying accessory. It's even okay if we disagree. None of the others ever dared to. They thought kissing up to me was a way to lock up Harry." A reminiscent grin spread across her face.

"So what did you and...?" Ellen hadn't told me the woman's name. I peered at the nearest painting, trying to make out the signature. The first name was only an M. "What did you disagree about?"

"Mo," she supplied. "She wanted us to bond, so we went to the Museum of Modern Art, just the two of us. To the Duchamp exhibition. I thought it was funny; she didn't. We were still arguing by the time we met Harry for dinner. It was pretty cool. I tell you, I like Maureen Lannigan. Can you dig how fucking Irish? No accent though; she was born here." Ellen and I both had a thing for accents, particularly those from any part of the British Isles. She sighed, then brightened. "But her father sounds exactly like Barry Fitzgerald."

Mo, I learned, also came equipped with a 13-year-old daughter from a previous marriage. When not staying with Mo's parents outside Philadelphia, Kelly attended a boarding school. The newlyweds were now en route for Parents' Visiting Day.

An angry buzz cut through the room. I jumped and Jackson—named not for Pollack but for Jackson Hole, Wyoming, where Mo and Harry had literally stumbled onto one another in the hotel's hot tub—began to chase his tail, yipping loudly.

Ellen pushed the intercom button. "Send her up," she told the doorman. She scooped up Jackson and put him back in my arms. "Hold him while I let her in, will you? So he doesn't run down the hall."

"Who?" I asked, struggling to hold the ultra-excited puppy; today was the height of his social season.

"Frankie," she said, standing with the door open, craning her neck towards the elevator. "She's been staying with me this week. Saves her schlepping in from the Island every day."

Ahuva and Ellen had been talking about Frankie Cecchi for months. I couldn't stop myself from making an inventory of her celebrated features: the hat with the feather; the oversized round glasses; the infamous toe socks, revealed when she slipped off her clogs at the door. I knew them all before I ever saw them.

"Hi," she said. Her friendly grin matched her funny croak of a voice.

It was almost like meeting a movie star. It was also the first time I'd met someone my own age who was already what I most longed to be, a professional actor. I was tongue-tied. "Hi."

She disappeared briefly down the hall. When she returned, having swapped her white shirt and black pants for a pair of jeans and a Snoopy T-shirt, she settled cautiously into one of the rattan chairs and grinned again. "I always wanted a chair like this, ever since *The Addams Family*. They creak a lot, but Ellen says it's okay to sit on them."

I nodded. My parents had a shop that sold what they called "collectibles." In a childhood spent prowling auctions and flea markets, I'd picked up a lot of random knowledge that I tended to spout when I was self-conscious. "The rattan gets dry. That's why it creaks. It's reeds, you know. People sometimes hose them down." As usual, once I'd spouted my tidbit, I thought it sounded pompous and clammed up again.

Ellen reappeared with a bottle of wine and three glasses. "Is red okay? It's one of Harry's, so it should be drinkable. And I called out for pizza." She filled our glasses and, lifting her own in the direction of the Hawaiian photo, toasted: "To love. Not that I plan on finding out, but they say it's even better the second time around."

"Just like Mickey and Eunice," Frankie observed, her tongue very definitely in her cheek. I had no idea who they were, but Frankie's delivery made me smile.

"Tell her," Ellen urged.

Frankie launched into the story of how a neighborhood divorcee had spotted her widowed father at the VFW and stalked him until she caught him. Eunice was presented as the kind of woman who likes her man wrapped around her little finger, even while she's telling the world how he wears the pants in the family. I had no way of knowing if Frankie's impersonation was accurate, but it was hilarious, especially after drinking a glass of wine too quickly on an empty stomach.

When I laughed, Frankie glowed, a visible effect that seemed to confirm her status as an actor. I would come to see this again and again in the years to come, Frankie expanding under laughter, like a thirsty flower in the rain.

As we ate, Ellen and Frankie took turns telling stories.

Frankie's stories were hilarious. There was one about giving away cigarettes on a street corner and some man, who decided he wasn't getting enough free stuff, accusing her of cheating him. Ellen practically curled up in a ball from laughing so hard. Then there was one about an audition where you waited in the hall and could hear everyone who went ahead of you. Frankie did impersonations of the three girls in front of her as they realized, one after the other, that they'd each come prepared to sing "I Could Have Danced All Night."

"I felt so bad for the last girl," she said. So did I, but I was also in stitches the way she told it. Ellen and Ahuva were right. This girl was probably the next Lucille Ball or Judy Holliday. I was awed to be sharing a pizza with her.

Ellen was bursting to tell us about how Harry came into the studio where they were recording another soup commercial and started trading stag stories with Joe. "Harry couldn't wait to tell me what a blast he had with 'that guy who's in the play you like.' That Joe didn't lose it!" she said, shaking her head admiringly. "I may have underestimated his talent. He could be doing Shakespeare at the Old Vic."

"Falstaff!" Blurting it out in unison, Frankie and I giggled with delighted surprise.

"Oh, yes!" Ellen lowered her lids until her eyes appeared hooded.

"I auditioned for a production of *Merry Wives of Windsor* last month," Frankie noted. "I really thought I'd get a call back for Anne Page. Kurt Blount is playing Falstaff."

"June Mason is playing Anne. You remember." Ellen was looking at me. "The girl in that Czech play."

I did remember. It had been a big deal when Ellen got the passes. The play had been smuggled through the Iron Curtain and there was a lot of press about it. We were dumbfounded. The translation was so clumsy that it was hard to tell if the play behind it was really any good. The direction was highly stylized—a loud, choppy style I couldn't understand. We'd left at intermission. I'd never even been tempted to do that before. June Mason was easy to recall—there'd been only one female role.

Ellen cocked her head at Frankie. "I could have told you not to waste your time. Mason had it all sewn up. She's Blount's mistress, after all."

"But he's married to Margaret Lane!" I was appalled. Lane and Blount's mutual devotion was as famous as their immense talent. June Mason, half Lane's age, was not much older than we were.

Ellen's sigh was almost a groan. "Welcome to the real world."

"At least I've got *Gooseberries*." Frankie bit philosophically into the carbon-flecked crust.

"You're in a show?" Awed, I dripped pizza grease on my sleeve.

"A showcase," she corrected. "It's only four weekends, and you don't get paid except for carfare."

"Kind of like school." My disappointment must have shown.

"Everyone does them," she assured me. "The agents come and see you work."

"Sometimes it's a new play," Ellen elaborated. "Trying to get enough attention to have a full production. The actors are getting in on the ground floor. That's probably how I'll have to start when I find a property."

"Is that what your showcase is?" I asked hopefully.

Frankie shook her head. "Not really. I mean, it is a new play, but it's not…It's an adaptation of some Chekhov stories that have never been a play before. My part's pretty small. I'm doing it for the experience. It's a rep company, so if I work out, maybe next time I'll get something that'll show me off more and then I can get an agent."

"Do you need to have an agent?" I realized I'd struck a valuable lode of real-world experience and I meant to tap it. Frankie could tell me everything that my college professors insisted was irrelevant to a liberal arts education.

"There are open calls," she explained. "But a lot of the time it's only because the Union says they have to. The casting's already been done before you get there."

"June Mason," Ellen intoned, drawing out the syllables.

Frankie ignored her. "And no one will even see you for film or commercials unless an agent submits you."

"You'd be great at commercials." I meant it sincerely. "I'm surprised some agent hasn't already grabbed you."

She shrugged. "I keep making the rounds, but they always ask when I'm going to be in a showcase. So, knock wood, right?"

"Too bad Max isn't around," Ellen raised an eyebrow. "Talk about a nice piece of wood."

I sighed. "I thought you said Max was disgusting. And a lousy lay."

"He is," she agreed. "Linda Schiller can have him." She reached to refill Frankie's glass, but the bottle was empty. She zipped into the kitchen, calling out as she disappeared: "Did you know that Max's latest squeeze is Frankie's boyfriend's ex?"

I turned to Frankie, not disguising my interest.

"Uh-huh. She's in the chorus. She broke up with him when she got the job, which she probably wouldn't have even gotten if it weren't for him. He's also her vocal coach. Mine too. But he's really a musical director."

"That sounds pretty bitchy of Linda." I was attempting to be nonchalant, to fit in.

"Donny says she and Max Bulloch deserve each other." Frankie grinned.

"Amen," Ellen said, returning with another bottle. She topped off our glasses and raised hers in a toast. "To people who deserve what they get."

Laughing, we clinked glasses and sealed the toast with a sip.

"Speaking of deserving what you get, she didn't get the road company, Frankie. Joe told me. And with Becca and Chris renewing their contracts, she won't be taking over here any time soon. She must be pretty pissed off."

"Max too, if he was trying to get rid of her."

"Was he?"

"Donny thinks so."

"Hmmm. Interesting. The man makes alley cats look monogamous." There was a note of admiration in Ellen's voice. "And speaking of monogamous, did I tell you about Penelope's Art Historian? Lionel introduced them at Thanksgiving and he's still hanging around. Felix is skulking around like Hamlet."

Through the haze of wine and smoke, I listened as one story led to another. So this was life in the theatre. Enthralling and sometimes appalling, it was the plot of a giant soap opera, except that all the characters were real. Including, their faces alight with excitement at being part of it, the two sitting right in front of me.

♫

Kaye Victor's West 49th Street studio matched her clothes. Floaty Indian prints piled one on top of the other without any attempt at matching; big blocks of muslin in soft, bright colors: moss green and gold, brick and purple and pink, and every shade of blue Ahuva could think of. The prints were rough flowers and paisley leaves. They hung from the walls and windows, draped over the bed, and covered the heap of large pillows that were the only other furniture except for a footed brass tray that served as the table.

It went against everything anyone had ever tried to teach Ahuva. All the clashing patterns should have been horribly distracting to the eye. Instead they were fun. Free. As if Kaye didn't care what was supposed to go together, took it for granted that anything she liked belonged together. The sheer chutzpah made it work.

The room had the slightly inky smell that Ahuva associated with these kinds of fabric, with a powdery overlay of incense. One wall had a square recess; a niche, Ahuva thought you called it. She would have used it for a bookshelf, but Kaye had set up some rocks, a bead-studded clay vase filled with weeds, and a few exotic statues. Ahuva could identify the Buddha, but not the man with the elephant head or the serene Japanese woman holding out her hand.

A large brass wind chime hung from a pipe overhead. "I used to have a bunch of those." Kaye seemed a little wistful at the recollection. "But they'd start ringing in the middle of my exercises. All the different keys made it difficult to focus my practice. I had to take them all down. I donated them to

Daytop. Then, the Universe brought me this beauty." She struck it fondly. It rang out with a pure tone, in the key of C.

The pipe, stretched halfway across the ceiling, didn't seem that strong. Ahuva was surprised it could support that heavy chime without buckling. Imagine what water damage would do to all this fabric!

"It's an old gas pipe," Kaye explained. "Never seen one before? You see all kinds of things in the old buildings. Urban archaeology!" She gestured at her little shrine. "This was once a dumbwaiter. From when this was a dining room. It doesn't go anywhere now. Whoever converted the building to flats filled up the shaft. My father knew what it was, the minute he saw it. My whole family's in construction."

Ahuva nodded, soaking in every detail. Today she was here to "get a sense of the flat" and have a cup of tea. The tea, as pale as grapefruit juice, had a sharp aroma and made her tongue tingle. You weren't supposed to put anything in it, not even honey. Instead of cookies, there were flattened balls of what Kaye said were "ghee and sesame." Whatever ghee was, they were very filling, almost like eating butter. Ahuva wasn't sure her stomach would take too kindly to it. She nibbled one slowly, to be polite. She couldn't say what Kaye Victor needed an assistant to do, but she was more than happy— deliriously happy in fact—to accept the position. Assuming a Tony award (like the one sitting discreetly on a cinderblock not five feet away) to be an indication of rank, Kaye was probably the most impressive person that Ahuva had ever known. Known, as opposed to simply met. Sure, she'd *met* Bronwen Davies and once, at a benefit for the All City High School Chorus, Beverley Sills; but she *knew* Kaye Victor. Kaye Victor recognized her in the street, and invited her to tea, and practically begged for her assistance.

There were so many little things, Kaye said vaguely, that disturbed her aura. One needed to focus one's energies on art and on maintaining one's inner balance. One could not be fussing with, oh, bringing shoes to the cobbler or sorting through correspondence. It would be a blessing beyond words to have someone save her from such petty distractions. A blessing she would pay for, naturally, as she believed strongly that work should be valued. She only regretted that she could afford to pay so little. An actor's life was not a luxurious one, as Ahuva doubtless knew. She only hoped that her gratitude would help compensate for the modesty of her purse.

Ahuva nodded, her eyes large and shining.

Kaye impulsively reached across the table and squeezed her hand. "Thank you, Ahuva. I felt instinctively that I could count on you. I have a sense that we've known each other before, in a previous life."

Ahuva blinked. This was a concept she'd never considered before.

Kaye raised her eyebrows and sighed, as if confirming something she'd suspected. "Yes," she breathed thoughtfully. "You are a very old soul. You will have to meet Maharishi Narang on his next visit. Meanwhile…" She unfolded herself gracefully from the cushions and crossed to the niche. Squatting by a stack of books on the floor, she ran a finger along the spines until she found the one she wanted. The slim saffron-covered paperback between her two hands, she made a small bow. Handing it to Ahuva, she smiled.

Ahuva had never seen anyone smile like that. It wasn't about being happy, or about finding something amusing or even pleasing. It seemed to come from a great distance, maybe even from a long time ago as well as from far away. That was it: it was an old smile, and full of wisdom.

"Here," Kaye said. "You must read this. It will change your life."

♫

"We're not exclusive." Leonard said it carelessly, and Leonard was never careless. Ellen knew he wasn't happy. He squirmed a little and there was a tiny furrow above his nose, between his eyebrows.

"Makes sense," is what she said. "It's only smart to date around a little. Good for you."

"It wasn't my idea," he admitted.

She hadn't thought it was, but she was glad he was willing to say so. "Okay. Well, Preston's older. He probably knows you're too young to be exclusive."

"Preston has this friend who just got back from Italy. Someone he knew before we met. I think maybe I was…you know. A rebound." He looked miserable.

She wished he didn't take everything so much to heart. Her way was so much better. "Maybe." It would be insulting to lie to him. "But that doesn't mean he doesn't really like you."

"Like me. Great. Well I don't like him. I love him."

"Maybe you do," she said, reasonably. "But how do you know? Preston's only your first. You need to live a little, see what else is out there. You know, compare and contrast."

"I wish you wouldn't always say that." He made a face like a little kid tasting something sour.

"Yeah, but you know I'm right. Don't be in such a rush to settle down. It's a big wide world. So much to savor." She extended her tongue and rapidly flicked it back and forth.

He punched her in the arm. She pushed back and wrestled him to the ground. They tussled for a few minutes, until it turned into tickling and they dissolved into laughter.

"Okay," she panted. They lay side by side on the rug, trying to catch their breath. "So who is he?"

"Huh?"

She reached out her hand and slapped him lightly on the thigh. "Who is he? The man you're going to be not-exclusive with?"

He sat up abruptly, hugging his knees. "I'm not."

"Come on. Haven't you met anyone interesting? All those gallery openings and cocktail parties? I'll say one thing about Preston, he knows how to run a social life."

"I meet a lot of interesting people. Sure."

"But no one *really* interesting?"

He lifted his shoulders almost to his ears, then let them fall. He squirmed again. "There's this one guy. Preston introduced us a couple of times, almost like he wants us to get together."

"Hmmm. *That's* interesting. Maybe he feels guilty and is trying to set you up."

"That's what I think. It's not fair to hold it against Kevin, but…"

"Aha! Kevin!" she yodeled triumphantly.

He put his hands over his ears. "Would you please stop that?!"

"Is Kevin cute? Tall? Broad-shouldered? Blond hair or brown?"

"He is kind of cute," Leonard admitted. "Taller than me. Brown. Green eyes. There's a dimple in the middle of his chin."

"I can see you're completely uninterested."

"I didn't say I was completely…I just can't switch gears the way you can. And I don't like the feeling Preston's passing me down, like some suit that doesn't fit him anymore."

"Hey, maybe you're the one who's outgrown him. Right? Preston was there to break the ice. He served his use. But you don't need him. You're too good for him. Maybe he knows it. He's breaking up with you because otherwise, you'd be dumping him for someone who deserves you."

"We're not breaking up. We've just agreed we can see other people."

"Right. So when are you going to get that Kevin to go out with you? Show Preston how unexclusive you can be. Either he'll grab you back and apologize, or he'll smile and you'll know he really is breaking up. He's doing you a favor."

"It doesn't feel like a favor."

"I know. But someday it will."

"You don't know, El. You never felt like this. But maybe you're right. If he doesn't want me, then I don't want him."

♫

In the last of the three Chekhov stories that had been patched together into *Gooseberries*, the Countess had to call the maid and ask for a samovar. It was critical to the plot. Since she had to exist, the Maestro planned to establish the maid earlier, during scene changes, when she could also be used to represent the passage of time. This was a device he was "adapting" from a production of *Three Sisters* that he'd seen in London last year. Frankie hadn't been surprised to end up playing a maid. There were always a bunch of servants in Chekhov. A lot of the time they were funny, like the servants in Shakespeare. The Maestro was surprised when she made that observation during rehearsal. He gave her a look down his nose and asked, a bit sharply, where she'd heard this. It was insulting. Frankie didn't understand why people thought you had to go to college in order to make intelligent observations. Once she'd made it, the Maestro acted as if it was his idea to have her maid be a bit of a clown

Frankie didn't care where the idea came from. Since nearly all her stage time would be in between the bits of story, her part could be as funny as she could make it. Even Dawn, who came up with all kinds of clever reasons why people couldn't do certain business that might take the audience's attention away from her, couldn't object to what Frankie did during a scene change.

Dawn was such a bitch. Like the crack she made on the day they were discussing costumes.

"I hope you're not planning to wear *those*," she'd sneered.

Frankie hadn't known what she meant, so she'd made circles from her thumbs and fingers and held them up to her face. "The bug eyes. This is Chekhov, not Kafka."

As if Frankie were stupid.

"Of course not!" Frankie had expected to leave her glasses off, the way she had for *Mother Courage*. It was hard, being as nearsighted as she was; she wished she could afford contact lenses. At least in *Gooseberries* she only had to walk back and forth across the stage.

The Maestro never asked her to stay for a one-on-one character session, so her acting was obviously fine. Her part might not amount to much in minutes, but she could make it count for any agents in the audience. That was the only important thing, she reminded herself. She needed to remind herself often. She'd tried her best to fit in at the Soho Art Theatre. She could pull off the daily exercises unselfconsciously now, even though, like the Maestro's speeches, they still hadn't yielded any revelations. She was always friendly and made a point of showing an interest in everyone. Except for the Maestro, who seemed to confuse her with her role as the maid, and Dawn of course, the company members were nice enough, but Frankie continued to feel like an interloper there. Would she ever get any of their private jokes? They had so many of them. A lot had to do with people she'd never met who they all seemed to know. Sandalphon? Must be a nickname, like Maestro. He sounded important, whoever he was. Maybe they weren't jokes. No one laughed much, though everyone seemed to smile. She often had the sensation, for no reason, of having heard or seen something she wasn't supposed to. She was living on tiptoe.

It didn't matter. The show was going to be great. Between Lil and Alfie, she was managing to work enough hours to cover the cost of her rail pass and keep up with Irene's classes. She even fit in another job for the promotions agency, giving away cubes of cheese at a fancy food show at the Coliseum. Wearing a Dutch Girl costume, complete with one of those wigs that was wired to turn the ends of the yellow braids into a pair of Js, it was really acting. Plus she ran into Gwen from the Al Pacino film, who was demonstrating electric coffee grinders. Gwen only had time to say a quick hi, but she promised to come and see *Gooseberries*. It felt great to be part of the New York acting community.

It was exhausting, though. The week staying with Ellen had felt like a vacation. If only she could have stayed over at Donny's a couple of nights a week, even on his sofa, to get some extra sleep, things would be perfect.

♫

The restaurant wasn't easy to find in the phone book. It wasn't spelled right. O'Neal's Baloon. It turned out to be right across the street from Lincoln Center. The bell over the door jingled when Ahuva entered. The bartender looked up from his magazine.

"I'm, um, meeting someone."

He nodded and waved her across the room. "Grab any table," he said.

It would probably be packed in a couple of hours, but right now it was too late for lunch and too early for dinner so it was quiet, like Alfie's at this time of day. She couldn't imagine why Maria hadn't wanted to meet at Alfie's.

Also like Alfie's, there were bare brick walls and small tables covered with thick shellac. Only three were occupied. Ahuva picked one that seemed far enough away from the others that it wouldn't seem like she was trying to listen in. They all looked so interesting. A pair of skinny girls whispered across their coffee cups, their high, tight buns so close together that they might lock bobby pins at any moment. A man with bushy sideburns and a leather vest was having a heated argument with someone in a red dashiki who was either a woman with really short hair or a man wearing eye makeup; Ahuva honestly couldn't tell.

At the table furthest from the door, there was a trio of older men, one with very white hair, all wearing suit jackets and shirts but no ties. For some reason, they felt Russian to her, which made her think of classical music and set off a tickle in her brain. She had a physical craving to listen to classical music. Chopin's nocturnes, that's what she wanted to hear. When she got home, that's what she'd do. She'd put on her headphones and turn off the lights, so she could dissolve into the music. She should probably try some other composers as well, expand her taste. Next time she was at the bookstore by the subway, she'd take a careful look at the bins of cheap cassettes.

Wouldn't it be amazing if someone invented a tape player so small you could fit it in your purse? Even if they could, it would probably be too heavy to carry around all the time. But it would be so nice to be able to listen to music while you were waiting, like now. She wished she could distract her thoughts. Why wasn't Maria renewing her contract? Who would want to leave *Lake Song*? It was a good thing Ahuva had seen the show again on Wednesday or she wouldn't have known until it was too late. Maria said she would have called if she'd had her number, which was nice, but didn't make up for the fact that she was leaving. Maybe Maria was going to be in another show; someone so talented deserved more than being in the ensemble and standing by for Lil.

Curiosity was driving Ahuva crazy. And she felt conspicuous sitting here alone. It wouldn't be polite to order until Maria arrived. She wondered if there was a cigarette machine. Maybe by the ladies' room, wherever that was. She'd never had a desire to smoke, even though both her parents and Ric…nearly all her friends did except for Hope, but it would be something to do.

The only thing she could safely do was stare at the mural. It took up the entire back wall and showed a big group of people. They were all staring back at her. The painting style was a little smudgy but the faces were distinct. Ahuva got the feeling she was supposed to recognize them. You could tell by the way they were dressed that it was certainly a recent painting. That alone was an interesting fact. If she ever thought about murals at all, she thought of them as historic, from hundreds of years ago. She wondered who these people were. She really liked the dress the woman in the middle was wearing, the woman who had the choker.

Maria must have seen her through the windows. She burst through the door and came straight to the table. "Oh! I hope you haven't been waiting long!"

She gave Ahuva one of her warm hugs. It was wonderful, how happy she always seemed. However did she manage that? It soon became evident that she had a particularly good reason right now.

"I'm pregnant!" she said, almost as soon as they'd sat down, before the waiter had even arrived with the menus. "It's not completely a secret, but I don't need everyone at the theatre talking about it. Four months."

"Oh, how wonderful!" It wasn't the news Ahuva was expecting. It was better. She didn't have to fake her enthusiasm. "You are going to be the most wonderful mother!"

"You are such a sweetie! I can't wait! Ed and I want to have a bunch of kids. But he's freelance, you know? We decided to hold off for a while, because I wouldn't be able to work for months at least, and we need one of us to have a steady gig. Well, we thought we were holding off, but we must have been a little careless and boom!" she caroled, "here we are! But it's all working out. I was able to work through to the end of my contract. And Ed just landed a staff job at *New York* magazine. It's an excellent thing for him. Even better for me, if you want to know the truth. He enjoys traveling to the end of the world and beyond. I'd rather have him in the city, especially now. Do you read *New York*? They have some great writers working on it."

Ahuva read most every magazine, one of the few perks of working in her father's store. *New York* was one she'd probably read even if she had to pay for it, though John Simon's reviews could be a little cruel for her taste. She was honestly impressed. "This is all absolutely stellar! I'm so happy for you. But," she couldn't stop herself from saying it, "aren't you going to miss *Lake Song*?"

Maria shifted her shoulders in the lightest of shrugs. "If this hadn't happened, I probably would have renewed my contract. The box office is healthy, knock wood; the show should keep running strong. What can I say? It's always tempting to stay in a steady gig; but really, it's time. It's never good for your career to stay too long in one place. For one thing, casting people forget about you. And you get stale after a while, which isn't fair to the audiences. Sure I'll miss the show. The music is gorgeous. And you always miss things when you move on. But that's show business, right? Anyway, it's a small world. I know I'll meet up with most of these folks again. Probably even the ones I'd rather not. We're all just one very large crazy family." She laughed.

Ahuva understood. She wanted to be part of that family. "Well, I'm going to miss you...miss seeing you in *Lake Song*."

Maria laughed again. "Don't sound so sad, Ahuva! My career isn't over. I'm more of a character actor, to quote Ollie. I've got years and years of work ahead of me. You'll come see me in a whole string of shows. And you'll come see the baby when she's born. Or he. Oh! That's going to drive me crazy, wondering which one it's going to be!"

18 – THE HORSES ARE WAITING

SHAMRAYEV

The horses are waiting at the gate.
They really hate to wait.
I hear them pawing, pawing at the ground.

TRIGORIN

Waiting would be more fascinating
If they were skating.
In the winter. Just a thought.
I'm a writer…

SHAMRAYEV

On the ice. Now I see!

MASHA

But that would grate
Like nails across a slate.
My nerves would percolate!

ARKADINA

It's getting late!

COMPANY

Hurry, hurry up! The horses are waiting!
Giddy giddy yup! But she's still debating
What to be leaving and what to be taking?
Whose breast is heaving? And whose heart is breaking?
There's no mistaking—at the center of it all
Is an actress getting ready for a smashing curtain call.

NINA

There's a new life beckoning to me
Telling me to drop my dolls,
Scale the walls and run like the breezes.
Run to the ends of the earth,
Go as far as my dreams can lead
To that new life that's beckoning to me.

POLINA

The horses are waiting at the gate.
I have to celebrate!
I'm tired of fawning, fawning like a hound.

SORIN

Waiting. I find it agitating
And enervating.

DORN

You should lie down.

SORIN

When she's gone…

DORN

I'm your doctor!

KOSTIA

He'll be fine. Wait and see.
It will abate,
His pulse decelerate.
Our lives recalibrate…

ARKADINA

It's getting late!

COMPANY

Hurry, hurry up! The horses are waiting!
Giddy giddy yup! But she's still debating
What to be leaving and what to be taking?
Whose breast is heaving? And whose heart is breaking?
There's no mistaking—at the center of it all
Is an actress getting ready for a smashing curtain call.

    NINA

    There's a new life beckoning to me
    Calling me to leave the nest,
    Break my jesses, fly away free and
    Soar, with my wings spread wide,
    Just as far as my heart can see
    To that new life that's beckoning to me.

Even if Frankie hadn't said, Ahuva would have found it obvious that the show had three sources. The characters were inconsistent and some of the plot seemed to come out of nowhere. The only thread of continuity was Frankie's tiny role, which indicated the passage of time. She accomplished this by walking across the stage twice in each act, checking the tea table, and calling out "Alexei Grigorovich, the samovar is empty." Then a man would remove the urn and bring on a different one. The first time she did it, she seemed so surprised at the discovery and her voice was so funny that people laughed. A grey-haired man in burlap strode in and shouldered the urn. She fluttered her eyelashes and trotted after him. People laughed again. Next time she came out, it was to cover a scene change in Act I. There was a pillow shoved up her dress, and she kept one hand supporting her back. People laughed the minute they saw her. This time, there was a whiney touch to her voice; the man shuffled and had a little difficulty with the urn. She waddled after him and called "Alexei Grigorovich," once more.

"Your friend is funny," Ric said during intermission.

"I know. I mean, thanks."

She noticed he didn't volunteer an opinion of the play. She was relieved. She wasn't sure what she thought of it and didn't want to have to say. The production had the make-do air of a school play. That didn't necessarily mean bad; Ahuva had seen some stellar school plays. This show, however...Somehow she'd expected more from a professional production, even if everyone was working for free. Maybe they were simply miscast. The leading lady, for example, came across more like one of Holly's folk singer friends than the wealthy Countess she was supposed to be. But the bigger issue was the play itself. For example, the main story of the two mismatched couples was pretty serious while Frankie's appearances, as funny as they were, struck a discordant note. Or was Ahuva wrong? Was she missing some clever undercurrents, some subtle humor in the text?

She hoped Ric wasn't bored. She had no idea why she'd invited him. Yes she did. He was a writer; he could articulate things about books and plays, where she had only wispy thoughts. And he was so cute.

Why do you call guys cute? Babies are cute, and kittens: small creatures with faces made of circles and arcs. Guys...correction...men. Deb said if we want the respect of being called "women," then we have to offer the same respect by saying "men." Men weren't cute. Even if some, like Oliver Blanchard, were beautiful. It was incomprehensible that no one had snapped up Ollie for movies, with that beautiful face and his shoulders…the way he'd looked in his T-shirt in the summer. Beautiful. Ric, on the other hand, was handsome, with his flat high cheekbones—his Taino cheekbones, he said—and full cushiony lips. That is, they looked cushiony. Ahuva didn't know what they felt like, not yet, but she kept accidentally imagining. His nose was flattish, crooked where he'd broken it during Basic Training. His eyes were hazel, with a little fleck of gold that you could only see when he took off his glasses. His glasses had a light smoky tint. Ahuva didn't understand the fad for tinted glasses. Ellen's drove her crazy. You wore glasses in order to see. Hence sunglasses, so you could see in the sun. Otherwise, glasses should be clear, to give you the best vision possible. Though she had to admit Ric looked cool in his almost-grey wire rims. He was slim and muscular, probably from being in the army. He had this way of sitting forward when he talked to you, listening with his whole body. It gave her stomach a happy flutter. She was happy enough lately that her parents had noticed, Malke of course asking if she'd met a boy. Even by definitions narrower than Deb's, Ric was a man, so Ahuva could say "no" and still be truthful. She wanted to keep her feelings private for now. Maybe if she found out they were reciprocated…Ric spoke sharply in class and about other people, but he was always very kind to her. She noticed he'd never mentioned a girlfriend, and he never said "we" when talking about the things he did for fun. She wondered what he did for fun. She only ever saw him in class and at the diner with Cathy.

She knew it was okay now for women to ask men on dates, but she couldn't see herself forming the words. It was a different story to ask a friend to join you for something you were going to do it anyway. She'd asked both her friends, which was kind of a cop out since she knew Cathy would say no. With the baby due in June, Cathy was only just making it through the semester and that was mostly thanks to Deb being so understanding. Ahuva had told Ric and Cathy that her friend Frankie, a professional actress, was working with a repertory theatre that specialized in Chekhov, and that she was going to be in a production of a new play called *Gooseberries*.

Ric had been puzzled. "Chekhov's been dead nearly 100 years. How can there be a new play?"

"Frankie said it's an adaptation of some short stories. The director specializes in them."

Ric had grimaced, obviously stalling for time. "Hmmmmm."

"It's free," she'd added quickly. It wasn't, but she would happily cover the five dollars for his ticket if he'd come.

"Can't beat the price," he'd said. "Why not? It could be interesting."

She was worried now that it wasn't.

When they filed back to their seats, Frankie was pretending to clean the set with a feather duster. The pillow was gone, and her hair was tucked up under a big, ruffled cap, a definite contrast to the saucy little frill perched on her head during Act I. As the lights dimmed, sure enough, she called out for Alexei Grigorovich. It wasn't as funny the third time. The man shuffled in very slowly. He was all stooped over, his hair powdered pure white. It seemed to require his last bit of energy to pull the samovar from the table and drag it off the stage. Frankie rolled her eyes, then tapped briskly off after him. Nobody laughed.

Her final appearance, towards the end of Act II, was the only one at all related to the main action. The Countess said something about refreshments and rang a bell. Frankie walked out, much more slowly than before. She wore a black cap, and the bits of her hair that showed underneath had been powdered. A few shadows had been applied to her face. She set down a plate of cookies and put a cup below the samovar's spigot. As before, nothing came out, she checked the urn, and registered surprise.

"Grigor Alexievich!" she bleated. "The samovar is empty!"

A different man came out, a young man who lifted the samovar and shot the Countess a look of disdain before stalking out. Frankie bobbed a curtsey and exited too quickly to match the attempted illusion of great age. Ahuva later told Ric she thought the young man gave the best performance of the night. Ric agreed.

"I did like that gorgeous piece of beefcake who came on with her in the end, didn't you?" Ellen leaned against the front of the building, dragging on her cigarette. They were waiting for Frankie to come out, so they could take her to Fanelli's. She was sleeping at their place before the final matinee. They were glad she was taking her time getting changed. It gave them a chance to unload their worst criticism on each other before she joined them.

"Frankie was good, too," Leonard said tentatively. He seemed to realize how weak that sounded. He repeated it, more firmly. "I thought she was very funny."

"Yes," Ellen agreed. "But she always is. The show was for shit. Everything she's been telling us about this Wardell O'Hare, like he's the Second Coming of Tyrone Guthrie. What is that girl smoking?"

"You mean what's O'Hare smoking," Leonard corrected her with a smirk.

"I know what O'Hare is smoking. He's smoking 'my trust fund is so big I can do whatever the fuck I please,' that's what he's smoking. Asshole. You don't make good theatre with your own little cult. Theatre is collaborative. You need challenge, ideas that rub up against each other. What this guy is doing is artistic masturbation."

Leonard squirmed. "Does everything have to be about sex?"

Ellen laughed. "Tell me you don't think O'Hare is screwing that Dawn. We know he didn't cast her for her acting ability, so she must have talent in other areas."

"She was a little wooden," Leonard agreed.

"Maybe she's not so wooden on her back."

"Jesus! Be serious."

"I am! I think she is seriously hot! She and that hunk who came out with Frankie at the end. What a waste! I would make that boy a star. So would O'Hare if he was thinking with his head instead of his dick."

"It was cool to see Cathleen Penney. Remember that movie, where she and Gig Young were in the haunted house? That was probably her biggest picture."

"McCarthy ruined her, you know. It's sad she's sunk to this."

Leonard rubbed his earlobe thoughtfully. Since the ear piercing, it was becoming a habit. "Maybe you could talk to Felix. It's too late to bring him down here…"

"He'd never sit through this piece of crap. But you're right. I should at least let him know she's alive and kicking. He's still looking for the grandmother in *The Chalk Garden*." Ellen preened a little at the idea. Felix was hell bent on getting someone genuinely old enough to play the part. Eva Le Gallienne and Margaret Hamilton had already turned him down. Penney could be the perfect answer, and she'd probably work cheap enough for Felix's budget. It would be a real coup for Ellen. She'd only come out to this farce to support a friend. Maybe goodness was rewarded after all.

"So what do we say to Frankie when she comes out?" There was probably some etiquette that applied to the situation, but Leonard didn't know what it was. This was the first time he'd been to something like this.

"The truth, of course." Ellen looked surprised that he'd asked. "That she was funny and delightful. She only really cares what we thought of her. Then whatever she says about the show, we just nod as if we agree, and she'll be happy."

Tomorrow was the final performance and not a single one of the agents Frankie had invited had shown up; or if they had, she didn't know. It was a slap in the face. They'd said to do a showcase, so she had. She'd worked like a horse, given up weeks of auditions and lost a perfectly good job. She'd used almost the last of her savings on envelopes and stamps, and on postcard versions of her headshots to mail with the flyers. Everything been for nothing. Monday she'd have to start all over again, back where she'd been six months ago.

Sloping dejectedly over to the props table to dump the needlepoint and the Countess's "lap dog," she almost collided with a man. Frankie was still in costume, which meant without her glasses. Striding across the performance area, he seemed to come out of nowhere.

She knew his name when he said it: he was a casting agent Dawn had invited, the one Dawn said was going to get her a lot of work.

"I liked what you did out there," he said, pumping her hand energetically. "Funny. You're damned funny. Very appealing, too. You can feel the audience likes you, can't you?"

"Umm…" It felt egotistical to agree.

"Hey, no false modesty. You've got it, flaunt it. So tell me, you know what you've got, right?"

"I guess so. I can feel them out there and yeah…I know they like me."

"There you go! That wasn't hard, now was it?"

"No." She giggled.

"Great. Great. So Frankie…Is that all there is? What's that short for?"

"Francesca. But no one calls me Francesca. I've always been Frankie Cecchi."

"Frankie Cecchi. Frankie Cecchi. Cute. Keep it."

Frankie didn't expect not to. "Okay?"

"So Frankie. You got a lot of potential. You're bright and perky. Wholesome. I can see you in commercials. You could be the counter girl in the McDonald's ad. The babysitter…they use a lot of babysitters, right? I gotta be honest with you. Standing talking with you like this, up close, face to face, I see only one thing standing in your way, Frankie Cecchi. It's the teeth."

Mickey had taken her for braces when she was eleven, but she had snaggle teeth on either side of the front ones, which would have meant surgery as well. The bills from Martha's final months were still piled on the desk; even for a Christian Scientist, it cost a lot to die and get buried. Mickey thanked the orthodontist and told him maybe in a little while. A little while never came. Frankie had almost immediately stopped thinking about it. She'd seen herself as a stage actress. For stage, it didn't matter what her teeth looked like. Lately, though, enough people were telling Frankie she'd be great on television that she was starting to think about the possibility.

She listened attentively to what the agent had to say.

"You had a camera-ready smile, I'd be sending you out tomorrow," he continued. He wasn't being mean; it was all very matter-of-fact. "Straighten them out, nice and even. Get yourself braces. A couple of caps, if you need. You get a big, bright smile and some new shots to show them off, you come see me." He flashed an enormous slice of crooked, nicotine-stained teeth and pressed a card into her hand.

"I will!" she promised. Back then it had been more than two thousand dollars; it would have to be more now. She couldn't even afford contact lenses. How could she get that kind of money? Would Pop give it to her? He knew how bad her teeth were; he'd wanted to fix them when she was a kid. She would wait to get him alone. Eunice was making it very clear that she didn't think Frankie should even be living in the house. Mickey had put his foot down on that one, declaring it was Frankie's house, too, and she should stay as long as she wanted. All the same, he hardly ever slipped her a few dollars, the way he used to. She would ask him for a loan, emphasize how fast she'd pay him back with the money she'd make from commercials Unless Ellen had another idea. Ellen was good at making things happen.

♪

The 25th time Ahuva saw *Lake Song*, she blurted it out to Ric and Cathy. She hadn't planned to talk about it, it was a private thing, but the number was too momentous.

Cathy dropped her spoon and laughed. "You're shitting me. Really?"

Ric shifted the power of his focus from his burger to her. He finished chewing and swallowed. "Why?" he asked. Not in a sarcastic way, but as if he honestly cared to know.

"It's a wonderful show!"

He nodded his agreement. "It's not Berenson's best, musically, but I was certainly impressed. I never thought *The Seagull* would make a decent musical."

"It's more than decent," she declared hotly. "It's brilliant! I think it's better than *The Seagull*." Even before that dismal Theatre History class, she'd made a point of reading Chekhov's play. She read it three times. It was dry, compared to *Lake Song*, and the difference in some of the characters…Arkadina, for instance, wasn't anywhere near as exciting. In *The Seagull*, you wondered whether the others were right about Arkadina being such a major actress; in *Lake Song*, you know she's a star, no question.

"And you think that's a good thing?" Ric probed, after she'd attempted to explain. "Maybe Chekhov wants you to doubt her. He certainly does that with Trigorin. He's supposed to be a famous writer, but Kostia doesn't seem convinced."

"Kostia is jealous!"

"Okay, fine. But even if Trigorin is a good writer, he's no hero. He's cruel, he steals from people. He gets writer's block. So does Kostia. And Nina admits she's a lousy actor. You see what I'm saying? The artists in Chekhov's play, all of them, are regular working stiffs. Which is exactly what I think is so great about it." He could see she wasn't convinced. "You know, originally *Lake Song* was leaning more in that direction. Until the out of town run. People were walking out at intermission. Even the ones who stayed…you know those audience cards they pass out? They all said the same thing: 'I hate these people.' James Lord told Berenson they had to start making changes."

"Marshall Berenson is a genius! He should be able to write anything he wants to!"

"People don't show up for genius. They show up to be entertained. No asses in seats, no money for the investors. You know how much it costs to mount a musical these days? Hundreds of thousands. This show was in deep shit. So Lord decided if the audience wasn't going to be able to root for the characters, they'd damned well better envy them. 'Give them Taylor and Burton,' he told Berenson; 'give them Hemingway. Stars, like they read about in their magazines.' So they cut some songs and Berenson retooled some lyrics…Now this is where you and I agree, Ahuva. Not about the show. But that man. He is a motherfucking genius."

"That's what Berenson told you?" Cathy liked gossip, even about people she didn't know.

"Not the part about being a genius. He's too cool. But all the rest, yeah."

Ahuva nodded vigorously. "I've read all the interviews. Berenson never blows his own horn."

"Maybe not a great metaphor," Ric muttered under his breath.

"Huh?"

"Completely agree with you. He let me read some of the original lyrics. The entire slant of a song changed by shifting three or four words…" He shook his head and sighed. "Fucking genius. And he added a few songs, to make some of the characters more sympathetic. There was this one song he wrote for Arkadina. It had me thinking about Prospero's speech. You know, 'our revels now are ended'? The part about the vision melting into thin air. Berenson's was…Damn! I wish I could remember. Something like butterflies, fireflies…Really got to me."

"Did he play it for you?" Ahuva couldn't keep the envy out of her voice.

"Not that one. That's how good the lyrics were; I only had to read them. Lord decided the song was too wistful, it undercut Arkadina's strength. So Berenson wrote 'As I Am.' But you know what he did play for me? It was the chorus of the song that got replaced by 'The Man Who Wished.'"

"I hate 'The Man Who Wished.' Well, not hate. I just think it's weak compared to the rest of the score."

"This one wasn't weak. Not at all. Okay, you tell me. Here goes…" He took a deep breath. "*The mind numbs, the dark comes, the whole damn thing is through,*" Ric tried to warble. "Yeah," he added. "I think that was it. I forget the rest."

Ahuva and Cathy looked at each other and shrugged. Ric had what Bert Gruen used to call "a toy piano voice," thin and with limited range. The tune might be right enough, but there wasn't enough substance to let you feel it.

Ric could see he'd lost his audience. "It laid me out. The words. And the music. Damn! I wish I could sing." What Ric could do was tell a story. He told them what it had felt like to have Berenson talking with him as one artist to another. Heady stuff. Never, not even the first time he saw his own book in print, had Ric felt as much like a real writer as he did that day. Then to have Berenson walk over to the piano and play this song, his voice not much better than Ric's, but his hands on the keyboard providing the fire. Ric could describe all of this, but he couldn't make them feel the song.

Ahuva vibrated with frustration. "I wish I could climb into your brain and pull it out!" she exclaimed.

He gave up. "It ripped my guts out," he said simply. "Berenson's too, I think, because he suddenly stopped. Like that. Jumped off the piano bench and walked all the way across the room to his armchair. He told me he had to take the song out of the show, that Lord insisted on it. 'Jimmy thought it made suicide too compelling.' Gave me a shiver when he said that."

It gave Ahuva a shiver right now.

"Imagine the power," Ric mused. "Being able to write like that!"

Imagine hearing it, Ahuva thought. What if she'd heard it when she was feeling like she'd been feeling a few months ago? She might have done anything. She smiled weakly. "Wow," she said.

"Yeah, wow!" Ric had a devastatingly beautiful grin.

♫

Frankie hadn't landed a summer theatre job, though not for lack of trying. She'd submitted herself for every last tent and barn and outdoor theatre in the United States, at least for every one that did their casting out of New York. Despite all her vocal work with Donny, and the hours and hours spent practicing tap, she hadn't gotten a single call back. Two of the larger festivals responded to her mailings with invitations to come in and read, but when she got there it turned out they held their ingénue and juvenile slots as apprenticeships, for earning Equity points. They would provide somewhere to sleep, but no pay. No carfare. Not even food, except for breakfast; the apprentices were expected to handle their own catering. Frankie already had her union card. She didn't need Equity points. She did need to build up her resume, but not if she had to go into debt to do it.

She'd resigned herself to going back to camp when Margaret Rodney called and invited her for coffee at Rumplemayer's.

Ellen was impressed. Apparently, the café was also one of Elizabeth Taylor's favorite places. Ellen said that she used to save her high school lunch money all week to come into Manhattan for a pot of hot chocolate there on the weekend. She'd stolen a couple of cloth napkins, with the name printed in gold, and she always used the ladies' room before she left. "I tried every seat," she informed Frankie. "Which means I've peed in the same toilet as Elizabeth Taylor."

Frankie couldn't imagine Elizabeth Taylor using a restaurant toilet like a regular person. She couldn't imagine Elizabeth Taylor here at all. It was enough of a stretch to imagine Margaret Rodney, although everyone seemed to know her. She'd thought Margaret belonged in one of those French restaurants where all the women wore pearls. Rumplemayer's was a very fancy Schraffts, all white and pastels, with shelves and shelves of outrageously expensive stuffed animals. Half of Daphne's bedroom probably came from here.

It seemed a waste to order coffee and pie in a place that looked like this. Frankie ordered an ice cream sundae. She plunged her spoon through the whipped cream, digging down to the bottom so she would get all the layers in one mouthful.

"Daphne does the same thing," Margaret said.

Frankie felt self-conscious until she registered the note of approval in Margaret's voice.

"You two have so much in common," she continued. "Which is why this is utter inspiration!" Her spoon tapped a happy little rhythm on the rim of her coffee cup. She leaned forward, in a conspiratorial manner. "I have a proposal for you," she whispered.

Frankie nearly jumped. Was Margaret trying to sell her drugs or something? That would explain the far-away look she often had.

"How would you like to spend the summer at the beach with us?" At her older daughter Melina's beach place, she explained, "A large estate near Bridgehampton. We always summer there. I want Daphne to enjoy the sun and the sea, the way I did as a girl at Newport. It broke Mother's heart to sell the cottage when Father died, but Ned insisted. He said the estate had been hemorrhaging funds for years, that Father had been spending capital! Well, what could we do!? Mother, like all that generation, hadn't a clue. Ned, of course, knew everything about business. I was little more than a child. My brother is much older than I. Much. People often take us for father and daughter!"

Not for the first time, Frankie noticed the odd, artificial quality of Margaret Rodney's laugh, as if nothing ever struck her as funny and she'd taught herself out of a book.

"I want Daphne to experience everything she deserves. If Ned weren't such a miser...Never mind!" She tossed her head and smiled brightly. "Melina has married very well and has a lovely place, just over the dunes from the water. And there's a sweet little cottage that Cooper graciously insists we use."

Margaret needed to spend part of each week in town, but there saw no reason why Daphne should have to travel back and forth with her. Casilda, alas, would be in Ecuador for all of July, visiting her children.

Casilda had children?! And she left them to take care of someone else's kid? Frankie was so shocked that she almost missed Margaret's blithe dismissal of the "couple" Melina and Cooper had out at the beach, who didn't have time to also keep an eye on Daphne.

Margaret was looking for someone who would enjoy spending the summer at the beach "as part of the family. A companion, really, with maybe a few light chores around the house." In other words, an au pair. The main job would be taking care of Daphne, which Frankie didn't consider to be work at all. Room and board would be taken care of. And Margaret would pay her $100 a week.

Frankie swallowed a spoonful of sundae and promptly said yes. Donny would be in the Adirondacks again, so there was no reason to hang around the city. At the beach, she'd be out from under Eunice's thumb. Even if she had to cook and clean—and she wasn't so naive that she didn't expect to get stuck doing both—the work wouldn't be hard. With all her expenses covered, she could clear at least six hundred dollars for her bank account; maybe more, depending on how long Margaret meant by "the summer." She would try not to think about acting or auditions, and come back full of energy. Maybe a change of scenery would bring her a change of luck.

The only complication might be Lil. The library was pushing hard for the scrapbooks. Frankie didn't like abandoning her, but she would have to anyway, if not for this then for camp; it all came down to money. Maybe Ahuva would like to take over. Ahuva was smart and well-organized, she had lots of spare time, and Frankie knew how much she loved hanging around *Lake Song*. It was the perfect solution, if it was okay with Lil.

It was perfectly fine with Lil. Frankie was almost jealous at how quickly Lil and Ahuva hit it off, but she had matured a lot since being asked to leave NYADA. She was able to look at things calmly and take the long view. As interesting as it was, working for Lil was never going to help her acting career. Neither would a summer as Margaret Rodney's au pair, but at least that job would bring in enough money to get her through the fall.

♫

Leonard won six tickets in that Tony lottery. He invited Ellen of course; and Jeff Kaplan, who was so excited that he made a dire prediction that there would be a once-in-a-century May blizzard, then immediately swore that not even a disaster of that magnitude would keep him in Buffalo.

A piece of Leonard's heart wanted to invite Preston, who would have to acknowledge him as a man of substance, not some naïve boy he'd amused himself by seducing at a bar. It would be so romantic, sitting shoulder to shoulder surrounded by glittering stars. The rest of Leonard was too angry, both at Preston for not wanting him and at himself for being such a sucker. If only he could make himself cool and distant, Preston would realize his mistake and try to get him back; and when he did...if Leonard could shrug and say "Oh, Preston, I enjoyed myself tremendously, but you were right, we have to move on"...Oh! if he could count on himself to do that, he would invite Preston so fast raindrops wouldn't get him wet. But Leonard knew that the minute, the second that he saw Preston in that tuxedo, his knees would turn to jelly and Preston would be able to squash him like a bug all over again. *If ever you need my life, take it, it's yours...*

So he picked up the phone and offered a seat to his new friend Kevin. Kevin had to turn it down; he'd be on his way to New Mexico for a month-long anthropology residency. Leonard was as relieved as he was disappointed; a once in a lifetime moment should be shared with people he cared about, not someone he hardly knew. Clearly flattered by the invitation, Kevin invited Leonard to join him at the opera the next week. It was an equivalent compliment: subscriptions to the Met were hard to come by; Kevin had inherited his from a friend of his thesis adviser at Columbia. It would be *Don Giovanni* that night, with Sherrill Milnes. Frederica von Stade would be singing Zerlina. Leonard pretended he understood how great that was. It was probably a good thing that Kevin would be out of town for a while. If they were going to spend time together, Leonard would have to start learning a lot of things he currently knew nothing about.

After discussing it with Ellen, Leonard decided to bestow the other three tickets on Ahuva, Frankie and me. They called me at school, so jubilant that I had to hold the receiver at arm's length. Once I understood that we were actually going to the Tonys, I started screaming back. My next door neighbor had to bang on the wall. Unbearably excited, I spent the next three weeks obsessing over what to wear. When I wasn't driving my mother crazy, I was racking up phone bills with Ellen and Ahuva, both of whom were unusually eager to discuss wardrobe options. Ellen's primary focus was shock value. Ahuva's only worry was that she look "appropriate." Me, I secretly cherished the Cinderella dream that some director would see me there and wonder who that beautiful young actress was, that I would be Discovered at the 1974 Tony Awards.

In the end, wardrobe was a simple choice. It had to be. As a group, our pockets weren't remotely deep. Fortunately, tossing over the murky straights between the Bohemian chic of our adolescent aspirations and the Disco glamor that would rule over our 20s, fashion was clinging to a maxi moment. We girls had easy access to long party dresses—emphatically not evening gowns—that could be, and in fact were, worn to other events. These floral wonders grazed the insteps of our regulation slab sandals, which were worn with panty hose (naked toes were strictly casual). They had a Victorian air. The exception was Ellen's, which prefigured the upcoming decade with its plunging halter neckline.

Sydelle produced a white angora shawl, sparkling with beads. As we all had shawls (it was what was worn with, possibly even crocheted specifically for, such dresses), Ellen accepted it without protest. Of course, it was hard to argue with your mother when a friend was holding a loaded mascara brush to your eye. We were dressing together at Sydelle's, to which we planned to return for our post-Tonys sleepover, Ellen and Leonard's apartment being too small for six of us.

"It'll be cold, sitting in the air conditioning," Sydelle said when she emerged from her bedroom with the shawl. It was her only comment other than the "very nice," that later accompanied her twitch of approval as we filed toward the elevator.

Considering a standard limo too ordinary for such an event, Leonard had found a service that offered vintage cars. The car that met us downstairs was a yellow Rolls Royce. Below his uniform cap, the driver flaunted an exuberant pair of waxed mustaches, the mere sight of which had the effect of laughing gas. We giggled all down Queens Boulevard and along the LIE, waving through the windows any time we drew close enough to another car to catch someone's eye. In the darkness of the Midtown Tunnel, the excitement became nearly unbearable. We dissolved into meaningless babble, each skimming along a personal stream of suppositions about the moment so nearly at hand. Surfacing on the East side, we were silent for the remaining five or six minutes of crosstown stop-and-go, hyperaware of the contrast between the familiar streets and our own uncommon splendor.

The Tonys were in the Shubert theatre that year. Squeezing each other's hands, we rolled up to Shubert Alley. The streets were packed with spectators, standing behind police barricades, autograph books and cameras at the ready. Our driver came around to open the door. As we emerged, flashbulbs popped and there were screams. When you arrive at a red carpet event in a yellow Rolls, the people on the sidelines assume you must be Somebody. Hating to disappoint them, we tried to act as if we were.

Like us, the others in the lobby weren't anyone the crowds were waiting to see. The celebrities would either arrive later or were already packed into the dressing rooms preparing to perform. We were gently but firmly encouraged to make our way to our seats. They were way up in the balcony. We didn't care; we were there, in the building, about to be part of the most important night of the Broadway year. We'd be breathing the same air as Carol Channing and Joel Grey, as Jason Robards and Colleen Dewhurst, as Julie

Harris and Zero Mostel, as Mike Nichols and Neil Simon and Marshall Berenson. We would witness History.

To prove it, we had our *Playbills*. When it started feeling too much like the hour before any other curtain, we'd steal a peek at the large foil-printed Tony disk on the cover. And catch the eye of one of the others, doing the same thing. And we'd all start to giggle again.

From where we were, could see a good amount of the orchestra, and a few of rows of front mezzanine. Ahuva and Leonard had brought opera glasses, which we kept passing around, trying to spot celebrities. The crowd was so glamorous it was hard to pick them out. In simple terms of sequins and beads, it was certainly the most glittering assembly I'd ever been near.

It was strange to hear the Tony Awards with all the rustles and the coughs and other theatre noises we were used to but which the television microphones never picked up, to watch performers and stagehands prepare one portion of the stage while the camera was tight on the face of a presenter. Stranger still were those funny lulls during which the audience at home would be watching commercials.

The strangeness was nothing compared to the electricity of being on the spot. It went beyond the usual fellowship of a mass of humans sharing a live event. Sometimes the name of a winner, or even a nominee, would raise a cheer from friends in or near enough to the nosebleed section that we could crane our necks and spot the source. We didn't know them, but the immediacy made us part of them, just as thrilled as if the name shouted out had been one of our own.

When it was over, it took a while to get down the teeming stairs. By the time we reached the lobby, all the Important People were long since gone; there was no reason to linger. Clutching our *Playbills* so that the big foil Tony disk, proof of our elective status, faced anyone we might pass on the street, we floated the few blocks to Alfie's. Lucky for us, Frankie had used her influence to reserve a table. The place was packed; moreover, it was packed with faces we recognized. It was even better than being in the Shubert.

"Is that Bernadette Peters?" I asked, thinking I was being subtle by pointing with my nose.

Leonard turned red, then pale. "It can't be!" he exclaimed, twisting around to be sure. "She's out in California, rehearsing the new Jerry Herman show."

It wasn't. It was another short woman with long curly hair. But the woman at the next table was definitely Madeleine Kahn. She was only maybe a foot away from Jeff, close enough that it would have been rude of him to turn and stare but near enough that her voice was driving him crazy.

The tables along the back wall were pushed together and crammed with the cast and crew of *Candide*, three shiny new Tonys serving as centerpieces.

Ahuva came back from the ladies' room trembling, ready to explode. "James Lord is making a call from one of the phones outside the bathrooms! I stood right next to James Lord!"

"I hear Lord Jim's not planning to direct the new Berenson musical," Ellen said. Her eyes glinted with the excitement of having a scoop.

For some reason, we all looked at Frankie. She opened her eyes as wide as they would go, her glasses magnifying the effect to cartoon character proportions. "Why would I know? I didn't even know there was a new one."

Jeff and Ahuva nodded in perfect unison.

"He's still writing it. It's about Stanley and Livingston," Jeff said.

Ahuva's eyebrows shot across her forehead. "No it's not! It's Robin Hood."

They glared at each other.

"How do you people know these things?!" I said it as much out of curiosity as the need to break the sudden tension.

"Berenson told Ric," Ahuva told me.

I nodded; I'd been hearing a lot about Ric lately. Sight unseen, I liked him. He made her smile. Whatever had happened upstate, he and Kaye Victor seemed to be making it go away.

For the benefit of the others at the table, Ahuva explained: "My good friend Ric Medina...Frankie, you remember Ric. I brought him to your show. Ric's a very talented writer. Berenson was giving him advice."

"I met this guy at the Stonewall," Jeff countered. "He was in the chorus of *The Boy Jones*. Berenson called him in to sing a couple of songs for Lord and Frank Pirelli."

"I don't believe either of you," Ellen licked the tip of a Sherman, preparing to light up. "Three period pieces in a row would be box office poison. And Ahuva, I think you're becoming a fag hag. Ollie Blanchard and now this Ric?"

"What are you talking about?" Ahuva was exasperated. She had limited tolerance for Ellen at her most oblique.

Ellen waggled her eyebrows. "Berenson doesn't give advice without expecting a quid pro quo."

"Oh!" Ahuva turned to stare ostentatiously at the chalkboard menu that she already knew by heart.

It was rotten of Ellen to push someone's buttons that way. She only did it because there was an audience. Frankie and I locked eyes and willed one another not to laugh.

Since he hardly knew Ahuva, Jeff felt no such compunction. "Ha!"

"Anyone want to get tickets to *Scapino*?" Leonard asked, changing the subject just as the waiter arrived with our drinks.

By the time we'd placed our food order, equilibrium had been restored.

"So," Ellen said, after we'd raised our cocktails in a happy toast to the evening. "Wayne Alan Carney."

"Wayne Alan Carney what?" I asked.

Ellen peered inquisitively at each of the others, trying to nose out whether anyone else knew what she thought she knew. "Wayne and Bron" she whispered.

Ellen's whispers were always so loud. I immediately turned to be sure that James Lord was nowhere near us.

"The peasant, right? The big blonde guy?" Jeff sparkled with interest. "I can dig it."

"Right?" Ellen grinned wickedly.

"That's ridiculous," Ahuva sniffed. "She's old enough to be his mother."

"So? More power to her."

A wave of eye-rolling rippled around the table. No one was buying this.

"It's absolutely true," Ellen protested. "They're not exactly being discreet. Everyone on the show knows they're screwing. They practically want to give Wayne an award. She's been drinking like a fish. This is a much less destructive way to work off her tensions."

Frankie made a face.

"So what other gossip do you have?" Jeff wanted to know.

"Becca and Chris are engaged," Ahuva piped up.

Ellen shrugged. "Old news. Everyone knows they're together."

"Together isn't the same as engaged," Ahuva said, with some satisfaction. "I was dropping off Kaye's keys the other day and Becca was in the dressing room. She showed me her ring. It's stunning. A ruby, not a diamond. Kind of an antique. It's so romantic, don't you think? Kostia and Nina falling in love?"

19 – NEW LIFE

In addition to helping out Kaye, Ahuva was now working one afternoon a week for Lilith Brassloe! It was all thanks to there being a critical deadline just when Frankie would be out of town. Timing, right? Of course if Lil hadn't liked her, Frankie's recommendation wouldn't have mattered; but Ahuva and Lil clicked almost instantly. It turned out Lil's great-grandparents had come from Plzen, which is where Jakub was from. If you went back far enough, they were probably even distant cousins because...drumroll, please...Lilith Brassloe was Jewish! This completely freaked Ahuva out. She didn't know why, but she never thought about English people being Jewish.

Abba was already a Lilith Brassloe fan, but when she told him this, his face lit up as if someone had trained a godspot on his face. He dismissed her carefully couched request for more time off from the store, brushing it away like a bit of fallen ash. "Whatever days you need, my Ahuva. Go, enjoy."

"It's only half of Thursday." She felt a little guilty. The bags under his eyes had lessened since he'd begun taking a daily nap. She couldn't say so; her father hated any implication he might not be Superman. "I can still do the morning, like I do when I help out Kaye. We had a bargain, and you and Ima need the help."

"If I need help, I can get the boy to come after school sometimes. My bargain was so you wouldn't be moping in the house. I like to see you out in the world again. This makes me happy."

Even without the big tobacco-scented hug, she could see that it did, the happiest she'd seen him since that long drive down the Thruway. Yes, shining like a godspot. She could make this comparison with proud confidence now that she'd learned all about godspots. Also lekos and fresnels and snoops and gels...all kinds of things, thanks to the other stellar thing that had entered her life: the hours she was spending downtown at the Swan Theatre Collaborative.

The name was misleading. Despite the current production of *Richard III*, STC wasn't named for Shakespeare but for the residential house the founders, including Deb, had shared at Bennington. STC operated on a shoestring. Volunteers were beyond welcome; they were an utter necessity. Deb's teaching gig at Queens College enabled her to draft a steady supply of flat painters, prop assistants, ushers and other necessary drones.

Everyone in the summer Stagecraft class was required to put in some hours, which was fine with Ahuva. A theatre preparing for performance was possibly even more magical than one when the show was going on. The hammering and thuds. The sudden shouted curse cutting through the rattle of lines being run at top speed by actresses wearing muslin rehearsal skirts over their jeans and actors practicing sword fights with wooden dowels. Over it all, the heady smell of dust on old wires blended with musty fabric, sweat and the gluey reek of sizing: better than all the fresh air in all of upstate. *And nowhere do I breathe as easily*, she hummed happily, leaning dangerously far over the edge of a catwalk to hand a gel frame to Ric.

From their class, it was only she and Ric. Cathy was home with the baby, who was so cute you could eat him up! They'd gone to visit, Ahuva and Ric and Ric's friend Jay. Ric had ignored her a little that day, but she'd understood; Jay hadn't known anyone else there. Ahuva had a sneaking suspicion Jay might be, well, gay...There must be another word to mean homosexual. "Jay is gay" sounded ridiculous...though this particular Jay was hilarious, so maybe he didn't mind.

"Earth to Ahuva!" Ric wiggled his fingers, ready for the next gel. A blue one. You alternated, she'd learned: blue or green, then amber or red. Cool and hot, that was called, which was how faces on stage looked three-dimensional instead of washing out flat from the strong light. She could absorb the science of lighting, but the art remained a mystery. How did artistic people get their ideas? She'd gotten up the nerve to ask Ric. He thought she was being funny, but said he didn't know either, that it just happened. Well, not to her. She'd have to find a different way to be part of the theatre. This for example, hanging the instruments; she could never be a lighting designer, but she could do this; it was math really. Were there women stagehands? She could get into that. Or stage-managing, like Deb had once suggested.

Deb knew everything about professional theatre. Craning her neck, Ahuva could see into the wings where her instructor was working on the lighting board. It was a terrifying piece of equipment, bristling with old black knobs and switches tipped red like kitchen matches, like in that Frankenstein movie she'd accidentally tuned into one babysitting night. Deb, casually flipping screwdrivers from her tool belt, was completely unfazed, completely in charge. It must be wonderful to feel that. Yes, she would have to have another talk with Deb, ask her advice. Maybe tomorrow, after they were done with the lights.

Handing Ric the snoop to which he was pointing, she took a long wistful look at the hive of creativity all around her. This would soon be over. The mere thought brought back that awful hollow feeling. It would be worse if she hadn't already volunteered to help in the box office and usher. There had to be something she could do for the next show, so she could stick around. Maybe Deb would need an assistant. It would be stellar, working with Deb. She was a stunningly competent woman.

Almost as if the thoughts were words, Deb spun around suddenly and peered up at the catwalk. She flashed Ahuva a wide grin and a thumbs up. Ahuva felt herself blush. She'd felt Deb watching her a lot. It was exciting that Deb, who had the larger-than-life air of someone famous, maybe thought she was somehow special. Sometimes Ahuva felt daring and looked back. Then she got nervous because she didn't know what it meant. She had a strong hunch Deb, like Jay, was gay. She didn't want Deb to kiss her or anything. Or did she? Maybe subconsciously? Ahuva prided herself on being open-minded, but this was something she'd never considered. She'd only ever been attracted to men. Definitely. Like Ric. Exactly! She shouldn't let Ellen confuse her. Not everyone was necessarily bisexual. Just like not everyone in the theatre constantly screwed around or drank themselves blind. Ellen had a tendency to say things just to see you react. Kaye, for example, was practically a nun, in fact she had that same shining serenity as nuns in the movies. Ahuva respected Kaye tremendously. Deb, too. Why couldn't Ellen understand basic respect and admiration?

Ahuva hoped she was too far away for Deb to have noticed how flustered she was. She gave a small wave, then turned resolutely towards Ric, who felt her and stared back. The blushing got worse. Ric had such beautiful eyes, and they were looking directly into hers. And she could still feel Deb's eyes at her back. Ahuva felt powerful and happy, at the same time sensing that the world could easily spin out of control.

♫

Of course this would turn out to be the one summer that Donny was actually staying in town. The music director at his old theatre had moved on to the Cape Cod Melody Tent, which had a full staff, and his Long Lake replacement was bringing his boyfriend as his assistant. Donny hadn't wanted to upset Frankie by mentioning it until he was able to tell her he'd nailed down a golden opportunity to work on an exciting, no-holds-barred production of *Pericles* at the New York Shakespeare Festival. Donny kept quoting that old saying about God closing doors and opening windows.

Frankie was proud and happy for him. The New York Shakespeare Festival was a top-tier credit. She only wished she could make him just as proud of her. Like an idiot, she said that out loud. Danny laughed and pinched her nose and told her not to be silly. She was making great progress. He expected she'd have lots of time to practice out at the beach. "Sing into the waves as loud as you can," he suggested. "Great for your breathing and your confidence. You'll come back belting like the next Liza Minnelli."

Before heading out East, Frankie stayed with Donny two whole days. She made him a special dinner on their last night: Martha's famous chicken casserole and a pitcher of Yago sangria with fresh fruit. They went to the deli on the corner and splurged on a container of Häagen-Dazs coffee ice cream. They shared it by the river, with plastic spoons, trying to pick out the constellations over Jersey. It was incredibly romantic. The next morning, Frankie left while Donny was still asleep, so she wouldn't have to say goodbye.

"Sealed with a kiss," she whispered, blowing a kiss from the door before slipping quietly out. Like a scene in a movie.

♫

Her legs uncomfortably pretzeled beneath her on the hard floor, Ahuva tried to focus on what Maharishi Narang was saying. Her mind kept wandering as it did when she tried to read that book Kaye had loaned her. It was baffling how she couldn't concentrate. She wanted to, very much. Ahuva knew she would never have Kaye's talent, but if there was a chance she could acquire her confidence and serene dignity, she might not mind so much about the talent. She'd find something just as good, something meaningful. The book and the frail brown man in the biblical robes were the key.

Ahuva had devoted hours to attempting to penetrate the mysteries between the yellow paper covers with the almost-Arabic turquoise design. It was thoroughly confusing. Unfamiliar words would swim across entire paragraphs until every sentence read like nonsense. Ahuva was ordinarily attracted to new languages. Maybe the problem wasn't language as such, but the peculiar way that everything seemed to have several interchangeable names. How could you keep track of where you were? Take *Devi*, for instance, which seemed to be the name of a goddess. Ahuva had expected goddesses once Kaye had explained that her being a *Shakta* meant she honored the female aspect of *Brahman*. According to the book, Brahman is the highest of everything. Like *Hashem*, Ahuva assumed, except whereas Hashem was emphatically One, the Indians had an apparently endless population of gods and goddesses and, unlike the ancient Greeks and Romans, they were mostly parts of the same main god. Parts, as in pieces of a whole. Puzzle pieces. A puzzle Ahuva couldn't wrap her head around. She could see where Kaye's particular goddess of knowledge and culture, *Sarasvati*, was a little like Athena, but she was also—as were *Pavarti* and *Lakshmi* and *Durga* and *Kali* and all the less important goddesses whose names popped up here and there—like cells in the body of that Devī…who sometimes seemed to be called *Mahadevi* or even Durga…which meant Durga was a part of Durga…?? Who could make heads or tails of this?! Polytheism didn't only go against the grain; it was messy. Ahuva could never abide a mess. On the other hand, it was hard to deny the appeal of sanctioned goddesses. There wasn't a whole lot of female aspect in the Torah, not at that level.

This last bit was the only observation she'd dared to make aloud to Kaye, who'd laughed and said that's exactly why she wasn't a Methodist anymore. Ahuva must have looked a little nervous then, because Kaye quickly assured her that it wasn't necessary to convert in order to benefit from the teachings and invited her to come to the next of the Maharishi's prayer meetings.

And here she was. Deeply conscious of the honor of being here, Ahuva felt like a fraud. She'd hoped the guru's speech would make things more comprehensible, but it made no difference at all. Maharishi Narang had such a soft voice that his words made no more sense to her than the rustling of leaves. Darting a glance to her left or right, she caught sight of knowing smiles. Occasionally there was a murmured laugh. Maybe she missed too much while her mind was wandering; or else the other people were already familiar with the story he was telling, because they clearly understood him just fine. All she could pick up was that it had to do with a journey. This was enormously frustrating! She discreetly adjusted her lower back so that she was sitting straighter. Surely it couldn't be that complicated. She simply had to pay attention and not give up.

Her determination brought no clarity, but the sense of purpose kept her patient. When people were invited to ask questions at the end, she was encouraged that she could understand some of them—although the guru's responses continued to be a total mystery.

They all rose after the Maharishi did, one by one going before him for a greeting or a blessing. It would have been rude to leave without saying goodbye to Kaye. Ahuva waited quietly by the door, admiring a wall hanging, a large square of silk painted with an exploded star of pale blue and lavender triangles, a firm geometric oasis in this muddle. The closer she looked, the more she thought she could make out other shapes along the edges. Some kind of bird. A swan maybe; or maybe she was thinking about the STC logo.

"There she is! By the *yantra*."

Kaye's voice rang out as loud and clear as it did from the stage of the Regale. Ahuva whipped around. There was no option but to walk over

"My guru, I introduce my young friend, Ahuva Geffner. Ahuva, I'm honored to introduce you to Maharishi Jashith Amitosh Narang." Kaye performed a bow almost like a salaam, except her palms were pressed together instead of one against her head.

Ahuva felt funny bowing, and it didn't seem appropriate to shake hands. She ducked her head awkwardly. "How do you do."

"Namaste," the old man replied, echoing Kaye's bow with a smile. "We feel great joy that Shashikala brought you to us today. Welcome."

It took her a second to realize he meant Kaye. Even Kaye had two names here.

"Thank you. Um, Namaste." She thought she said it right; her ear was usually pretty good. She decided to try the little bow.

He smiled again. The man had a truly lovely smile, the kind that goes all the way up to the eyes and wraps around as far as the ears. "I hope you feel at home among us."

Ahuva knew she was a terrible liar. It was better to find a positive way to tell the truth. "I'm only just starting to learn about all this. Kaye...um ..." she couldn't remember the Indian name. "Kaye gave me a book. It's a little difficult to understand, but I'm sure it gets easier."

"Knowledge cannot be forced. You must open yourself and allow it to enter."

Ahuva couldn't stop the frown from showing on her face.

Laughing, the Maharishi gently placed a hand on her hair. "You are one who does not surrender easily. You fear the loss of self, yet it is only by losing yourself that you will find what you seek. You don't believe me, I see. You like certainty in all things, a formula to follow, yes? There is no formula that can help you on your way to happiness, but there is one small thing that I think you will like. Shashikala has told you of Sarasvati?"

Kaye caught her eye with a reassuring smile. Ahuva nodded.

"So. I will teach you the *sloka* of Sarasvati. You will chant this every day, to invite her blessing on your studies. To sharpen your memory and strengthen your mind."

"When do I chant?" she demanded promptly. "Just once a day? Does it matter what time?"

He laughed again. His eyes, dark brown, the same as hers, crinkled with amusement. "Once each day. Whenever you wish, but it should be the same always. To shape intent, it is important to keep a pattern. Say now with me: *Sarasvati Namasthubhyam...*"

"Sarasvati Namasthubhyam."

"*Varade Kamarupini...*"

"Varade Kamarupini..." Sarasvati Namasthubhyam Varade Kamarupini. Good. She could do this. It was like learning a song.

"*Vidhayarambam Karishyami...*" he continued.

That phrase was a bit trickier. Her tongue stumbled over the first word and he made her repeat it.

"*Sidhir Bavathume Sadha.*"

As soon as she repeated the last line, he went back to the beginning and gestured for her to recite along with him. They chanted together, seven or eight times, until he let his voice fade out and heard that she could manage it for herself. When she finished, he nodded his approval. "You must say the sloka 108 times." He unwound a string of pale sandalwood beads from his wrist and placed it over her head. "To count," he explained.

"Thank you," she whispered.

He bowed. She managed to pick up the cue fast enough to meet him halfway, her "Namaste," coming almost in chorus with his.

"Namaste, Maharishi." Kaye's voice rang out.

Dazed, Ahuva followed her to the door. A slim boy in an oversized tunic met them there and pressed a tiny roll of red paper into her hand. Ahuva slipped it into her pocket.

In the excitement of having tea with Kaye, she forgot all about it until much later, when she put her hand in that same pocket to get out a subway token. Waiting for the E train, she unrolled it. It was the chant the Maharishi had taught her, written out so that she could follow it. What a relief! She'd already forgotten everything except the Sarasvati part. What was it about this language that just wouldn't stick in her mind? Well, she'd have to repeat it until it did. She ran one finger lightly over the sandalwood beads. Rough guess it would take about 108 times.

♫

Ellen leaned against Joe, one bare foot propped up on the edge of the beige sofa, her right arm snaking around the back of his neck to dangle on his shoulder. It was okay to do that. Joe's wife, who wasn't as estranged as Ellen had originally thought, was never brought to these parties. Joe kept work and family in two separate compartments. "It's like being gay and being in politics," he liked to joke. Despite the closeness of the friendships here, this party was considered part of his work world. Ellen could be here with him and no one would blink an eye.

Ellen was completely at ease among these people. It was hard to believe that at this time last year they'd all been strangers, except for Felix and Penelope.

Penelope wasn't even here today. She was in Stratford-upon-Avon, doing the Scottish Play. "A revelation," Ellen heard Lionel Rice telling George S. Irving, "And you know I don't say that easily, not even about my own sister." Ellen didn't need Lionel Rice, or anyone else for that matter, to tell her—the woman was a brilliant actress, playing the role of a lifetime. Damn, Ellen wished she could see it! If only they'd been able to pull off Leonard's crazy idea for flying over. She was philosophical about missing the new production of *Always Forever Never Again* and there'd be plenty of years to see London, but missing Penelope as The Lady was harder to shrug off, especially since it was Felix's fault that her finances were so complicated.

Felix was absent today, too. He could have come. He'd be in town a few more weeks before going off to the other Stratford to earn some money and lick his wounds. "Exiled!" he declaimed, though it was no one's fault but his own that they'd lost the funding for the Lazarus season. When you finally land enough backers willing to lose their money on classical repertory, you don't screw things up with their attorneys. If Ellen had told Felix once, she'd told him a thousand times to get those documents notarized before tax time. You'd think maybe he'd skipped the party because he was embarrassed to face her, except Felix didn't embarrass that easily. It was more likely he was already mentally in Stratford, editing it into a new adventure and discarding uncomfortable details about the last shabby chapter of his life. That was Felix. You could almost admire the aplomb, if you weren't drowning in his shit. At this moment, as fond of him as she was, she wasn't in the mood to be charmed. He'd exit upstage to Canada, leaving her to clean up the mess in whatever spare time she had; which wasn't much. Since he'd had to stop paying her, she was scrambling to make enough money to cover expenses. Fly away, Felix, and fare thee well.

Her thoughts about frigging Ruth Mann were less charitable. Another winner, that one. All her talk about "theatre is my life," then yesterday, carefully choosing a moment when Ellen was in no position to argue, it's "Oh, did I mention I'm relocating to LA?" She was needed out there, she declared; she had two films in pre-production. Interesting that she felt no similar compunction about the multiple Broadway shows she had scheduled to open this season. Film, Ruth claimed, was subject to constant and last-minute changes requiring her physical presence; she couldn't possibly delegate construction and fitting to her assistants as she could for theatre. She was already bi-coastal, Ruth said airily; the only difference was that now her primary coast would be the one on the left.

Felix gone. Ruth going. Ellen gave Joe's shoulder a tiny squeeze. She was glad he was sticking around for now. Change was exciting, but it was pleasant to have an anchor. In any case, she refused to feel she'd been set adrift. She was moving forward, that's what she was doing. There would always be new jobs, new connections, new lovers, new friends. Lots of fresh starts, like being here today.

When Joe invited her, she'd assumed the party would be the same as last year's. It took a while for her to figure out the subtle difference: not that she was now an old-timer, but that everyone was; no "bring a person" theme, with its chorus of overly-animated voices and nervous hands. This was a family affair. Either Joe had done some convincing to bring her or maybe, she thought with pride, she was a familiar enough presence that it hadn't been necessary.

She could appreciate why Ivor Davies might prefer not to introduce strangers into his home: he was protecting his sister. Behind her tinted glasses, Ellen discreetly skewed her eyes to where Bronwen Davies sat. As far as possible from last year's decorous stupor, Bron was smack in the thick of things and mostly on Wayne Alan Carney's lap.

When she'd blurted it out in the roller coaster frenzy of Tony night, Ellen hadn't a hundred percent believed it. She would have said anything that night: soaring so high on the glamour, on the proximity to greatness, while at the same time feeling like a roach in the giants' castle, feeding off crumbs and in danger of being squashed, she'd needed to prove, mostly to herself, that she'd acquired some status in this world. The Bron and Wayne rumor was the first gossip that sprang to mind. She'd tossed it out, relishing everyone else's total belief in something that was only maybe possibly true. She was Harry Janow to the bone. Well, if she had to be like one of her parents, at least it was the successful one.

Now she had the evidence of her own eyes. Bron was hanging all over the guy. He looked a little desperate, trying to cope. Ellen had never given much thought to Wayne before. Maybe she should have. He had a nice ass and his khaki shorts showed off a pair of extremely good legs. Perched on the knees of those muscular legs, Bron leaned forward to the tipping point; Wayne had to grip her around the waist to keep her from falling. Tall, innocuously handsome and almost as young as Ellen was, Wayne had a walk-on in *Lake Song*, but his primary role was standing by for Chris Pruitt. Which made Bron's confirmed lover Arkadina's sometimes son, a titillating scenario. Ellen could see his lips move, whispering in Bron's ear, while his free hand massaged her shoulder. If the poor boy was trying to calm her, it wasn't working. She was rambling endlessly in a loud, not entirely clear voice, her hands gesticulating wildly, her eyes wide and glassy. There was a fascination in observing it. Not a pleasant fascination. More the *Wild Kingdom* kind, where you know the gazelle is headed for disaster, but you can't tear your eyes away from the screen. At least Ellen couldn't. Most everyone else was doing a brilliant job of ignoring the situation. She understood how the actors among them could pull that off, but how was everyone else being so cool? After all her efforts, was she still deplorably naïve?

Maybe it wasn't the situation that was getting to her, but that it was Bron. Ruth Mann had accomplished that much for her: Ellen could stop disguising it as a joke and admit she had a major thing for Bronwen Davies. Playing with the small curls at the base of Joe's neck, she watched in anxious pity as Bron spilled half a glass of gin down Wayne's bare calf. Ivor stuffed a napkin into his hand. Without changing his strained smile, Wayne wiped what he could. Ellen suddenly had the uncomfortable feeling that someone was watching her. Shifting her eyes, she met the hooded piercing glance of Lionel Rice. It was a considering glance, as if he'd stumbled on something in the street and was wondering if it might have value. She felt herself blushing, that deplorable, embarrassing tell she couldn't get rid of. She was furious at herself, which meant she only blushed more fiercely, but she refused to look away. Despite the heat in her face, she held the exchange with all the dignity she could muster. He nodded briefly, then turned to answer a question from Tyler Moss's lover, Andy.

Not long after, Bron told a rambling story. It ended with something no one else recognized as a punch line. Bron was the only one who laughed, which turned her petulant and increased Wayne's whispering. Finally she nodded, whispered back and disappeared towards the bathroom. Wayne made a quick circuit of the room, shaking hands.

Bron made a final brief appearance in the doorway. "Toodles, all!" she caroled gaily. She stumbled, her wave turning into a clutch at the wall. Wayne sped to grab her and Ivor walked them out.

"Such a nice young man," Tyler Moss sighed once they were out of sight. "We're all going to miss him."

"Miss him?" asked the redheaded woman whose name Ellen had never caught and whose face was too familiar to question. "He's leaving?"

"Road company," Joe volunteered. "They leave July 1. He's playing Kostia. Talented kid. He deserves the opportunity and good for Jim for giving it to him."

"We're all delighted," Tyler agreed. "But he'll be sorely missed."

Only a year ago, Ahuva Geffner had been floating on her back, in limbo, on the Dead Sea. It wasn't even six months ago that she'd stumbled out of a college infirmary with her heart pounding erratically against her ribs. Now, without exactly noticing when it happened, she was involved in life again. It was like when Novocain wears off after a visit to the dentist. At first you're relieved to not feel pain. You can't quit playing with the numbness, to see how far it goes. Later it gets in the way of eating and talking, and even though you can feel the pain hiding, you're ready to take a couple of aspirins and move on. Only the Novocain won't let you. It hangs on. You either have to take a nap and sleep it off, or else you force yourself to pretend it's already gone. Until it is. That amazing moment, after you forgot all about it, when Coke suddenly tastes like Coke again and you can move your lips without needing to blow your nose.

Awake. Alive! Thanks to *Lake Song*. Everything good was because of *Lake Song*. The pure magic of the show had nursed her back to life. She'd seen it 37 times and had never once been disappointed. The cast were her family. Everyone had said "hello" to her for ages, and now that she was working for Lil they called her by name, even Milt Foxe, the Stage Manager, who was in charge of everything.

Working for Lil was indescribable. Poor Frankie, having to give this up! Lil was everything a legend ought to be. On the other hand, there were things, like the famous scrambled eggs for instance, that made her almost like a favorite aunt. And her apartment! Every scrap and *chachka* had a story. Lil had forgotten more theatre history than Professor Patronizing had ever known. Ahuva was learning so much from Lil.

And from Kaye, of course. Kaye had practically adopted her, taking her to the Maharishi, literally giving her the shirt right off her back. Out of her closet, to be technical about it. It fell off a hanger while Ahuva was putting away the laundry. "What a stunning blouse!" she'd said, because it was, a watery blue print dotted with little mirrors that were rimmed in gold and purple thread.

Kaye looked up from signing the batch of fan mail replies Ahuva had typed at home that week. "It's yours," she said.

Until Kaye tucked it into her shoulder bag, Ahuva thought she was joking.

"I can't!" she protested.

"Why ever not?" Kaye laughed. "It's more you than me. I always wondered why I bought it. Now I know; it was waiting for me to meet you."

Ahuva wore the blouse on her next visit to Maria's house, where it was greatly admired.

The story made Maria laugh. "That is so Kaye! Tell me, what else is new? I need to hear the gossip." She patted the cushion next to her.

The woman was enormous. Ahuva hoped it wasn't twins; she'd already volunteered to babysit any time Maria wanted.

Pulling over a chair, so that Maria could stretch out full length on the sofa, Ahuva told how Andrew Stowe being so much shorter than Wayne meant they'd had to re-block the bit with the trunk in "The Horses Are Waiting." And how it was supposed to be a secret but the new swing guy was whispered to be George M. Cohan's grandson. And that Martin Korn's "arc" on *Ryan's Hope* (she was proud of the word) was going to get very big starting in the fall, so he was leaving the show and Tyler Moss would be bumped up to play Shamreyev. Oh, and the story Joe Bigelow had told Ellen, how James Lord stopped by the stage door on his way home from London and Wally the doorman didn't recognize him because he'd grown a beard. The weird part was that the beard was red, but the hair on Lord's head, when it was still there, had been dark brown. Oh, and poor Becca! Her mother and Chris's were fighting over whose wedding gown she should wear, to the point that she drove everyone backstage crazy until Nancy Pardoe, usually so polite, suggested she tell both ladies she planned to cut the two dresses in half and sew them together.

Maria laughed so much she kicked one of the throw pillows off the sofa.

"Don't you miss everyone?" Ahuva asked. "I did when I was away, and I hardly knew them then."

"A little. Not as much as I thought. And probably even less pretty soon." Maria was radiant, her hand resting on her stomach in the casual, powerful way of pregnant women.

That would be her someday, Ahuva thought. It didn't matter if she had no idea what she was going to do with her life. She was certain there was going to be a future and something special would happen there. Hope was a good feeling. All she had to do was stay close to the theatre. You didn't have to perform on stage or write or design to be part of this world. She was working on *Lake Song* already, wasn't she, in a way? And at STC said there would always be work for a willing volunteer. Somewhere in all of this there was a career for her. And friends. You didn't have to be creative yourself to hang around with creative people. She had proof. Lilith Brassloe wasn't really a friend, but Kaye and Maria were.

And Ric. Ric was going to be a famous writer. Marshall Berenson already admired his writing. Now Ric was working on a play. It was brilliant; he'd told her about it at coffee one night. Ahuva felt a tingle imagining it, just thinking anything about Ric. Since he'd bought that old car, the gold Dodge Dart, he'd taken to driving her home after the diner. She could hardly breathe sitting next to him, the way she used to feel around Byron. Ric reminded her a lot of Byron: brilliant, so smart and talented; and very handsome as well, which shouldn't matter but was hard not to appreciate. Only Byron, though enormously sophisticated compared to everyone else in high school, was still, despite his musical genius, a boy, traveling around the world trying to find himself. Ric had already been there and back. Ric was an adult. A man. Ric would make a stellar father. He would.

♫

"School's out forever!" Followed by a screech that fell somewhere between a wail and triumph.

Ellen wasn't big on Alice Cooper, but Leonard had included the song in the mix tape he'd made to keep her company on the weekends and she couldn't stop hitting rewind. Maybe if she played it often enough, the reality would sink in. Or maybe nothing would feel real until everyone else headed back to classes in September and she kept doing exactly what she was doing now: leading the adult life, out in the real world. She should probably be scared. Maybe subconsciously she was. Why else would the apartment feel so hollow around her? It wasn't as though she hadn't spent plenty of days and nights here on her own.

She'd better get used to it. Even while missing Leonard, she was grateful to the unknown guy who'd pulled out of the beach house at the last minute, and to Kevin for offering Leonard first dibs on the extra share. She still hadn't met this Kevin, but he sounded like a decent guy. If they weren't already sleeping together, they would be. Soon. She'd know the minute she saw Leonard's face on Sunday.

He'd probably come home from the weekend sunburned, the idiot. She should pick up some Nivea for him. Or maybe he'd come back pale as ever.

For all she knew, they'd never see the light of day. Who knew what eight gay men did in a share house? It might be orgies all weekend. Moonlight skinny dipping, now that would be worth going to the beach for. She'd never see for herself. Leonard had said they each got one weekend to invite a guest, but she assumed he'd invite Jeff.

The important thing was that Leonard would have a good old-fashioned summer fling and get Preston out of his system for once and for all. Meanwhile, she was skulking around the apartment, feeling bereft. She needed to have something to do other than filling empty corners with loud music and soaking in a lukewarm tub to keep cool. It was too hot in the house to try and read, and too hot to go outside without a damned good reason.

She would pop over to Harry's, but Ellen didn't want to break into Kelly's time with Mo. She liked her stepsister...Urgh! That word! How fucking corny! And it wasn't as though they lived together, so whatever relationship they were starting to have, there was nothing sister-ish about it. But Kelly was a good kid, innocent and sweet-natured, and Ellen had an urge to keep her that way. It was best not to hang around too much and set a bad example.

She almost felt desperate enough to trek out to Queens for some nagging. Thank God Sydelle was in the country with Aunt Marlene, so she wouldn't be tempted. She definitely wasn't in the mood to see any of her high school friends. They seemed so young these days, moaning over some boyfriend candidate or worrying about grades, as if grades meant anything.

If she'd thought about it sooner, she could have gone to a museum. An afternoon of air conditioning and art, and it would have been free; she still had a student ID, which was probably the only useful thing she'd gotten out of Fetherston. No point now. By the time she got dressed and dragged herself all over town, she'd only have an hour before they'd be throwing people out.

Felix's office was as hot as the apartment. Not that it was an option, seeing as she'd turned the key in the lock and mailed it to him at Stratford as soon she'd shoveled as much shit as she'd been willing to handle. The rest would be up to him when he got back. Whenever that would be. It could be years. It wasn't as if he had to worry about losing the office. He had it for free. The building was owned by some rich "old dear" (one of the RADA affectations Felix gloried in) who'd adored him in his pretty youth. As long as she hung on to breathing, Felix was home free. Literally home; he shacked out there "when needs must." She could hear him saying that in his deliciously stagey voice, see him winking a single eyelid with impossibly slow control and flashing a cockeyed grin.

The image made her laugh enough that the orange juice and vodka went up her nose. The glass sides of the Tropicana bottle were slick with condensation, dangerously easy to drop. She managed to set it safely on the bathmat and reach across to the roll of TP. She'd mastered the trick of setting a finger against one nostril and blowing straight out, but it still felt wrong.

There were some attributes of her bourgeois upbringing she couldn't shake. Perhaps instead of fighting, she should embrace them. Sinking back into the tub, she reached for the bottle to toast the idea. *As I am! I am unique and I'm brave.* The eccentric Ellen Janow, who lived fearlessly, never giving a flying fuck about consequences or what the world thought, would be infamously fastidious in her personal hygiene. Mother would be so proud. Ellen tried to mimic Felix's wink; as usual, she failed. How did he do it? Fucking Felix. She wondered if she'd ever see him again. Maybe, if he needed something from her. She wouldn't mind if he suddenly rang up out of nowhere, years from now. Asshole, yes, but such a lovable asshole. She understood why Penelope hated to let him go.

It was important to learn how to let things go, to let people go. Lessons like that were why Ellen couldn't stay walled up in some college. Here's to the School of Life, where all her marks were As! How cool she'd been, when Ruth called from the airport. "Ciao, bella!" Ellen had said, as casual as Marcello Mastroianni in that movie. "Don't do anything I wouldn't do." Her reminiscent throaty chuckle had been carefully pitched to torture the older woman with memories of their last night, a night of such intensity that Ellen would have been sore even without the chafing from the belly chain. Ellen had decided that if a relationship had to have a bitch, she would prefer it to be Ellen.

She ran a soapy finger between the links and the still-angry red splotch by her navel. Of course she didn't want to lose it, but had it really been necessary to solder it on? That jeweler friend of Ruth's was just a tiny bit of a sadist; not to mention a heavy letch, the way he'd leered at her body. Okay, it had been exciting. For both of them. Those few minutes were the only time she'd ever seen Ruth get hot and bothered.

Ellen raised her hips above the water, relishing the memory along with the weight of the chain. 14 karat gold. Nice. It would be pretty cool to see Joe's reaction when she saw him this week.

She could hardly wait, but she'd have to. She never saw Joe on the weekends unless they planned ahead. With two shows on Saturday, he was too pooped to be fun unless he rested in advance. Also, if anyone from the "family" side of his life—some cousin, or an old PTA friend of his first wife—was going to turn up at the theatre, it was most likely on the weekend.

The theatre. There was a thought. Ellen was constantly at the Regale, but she hadn't seen the show in weeks, maybe as long as two months. She still hadn't seen Wayne Alan Carney's replacement. She wondered if he was sexy. Would Bron try and seduce him? Ah! There was a reason to get out of the tub—she'd second act. She would take a nice air-conditioned bus downtown and hang out at the counter at HoJo's until intermission. If she didn't go around to the stage door, Joe wouldn't have to know she been. It was a good plan. She started smiling as soon it took shape in her head. Considering that the plot was honestly pretty depressing, it was amazing how *Lake Song* always raised her spirits. Something about it made her feel as if she could conquer the world, or at least the part of the world that was the theatre.

She stood carefully and stepped over the edge of the tub. Without bothering to wrap herself in a towel, she padded out to the bedroom and checked the green digital numbers on the new clock radio. She didn't need to leave for another couple of hours. There was still plenty in the screwdriver bottle. Leaving a trail of wet footprints, she padded to the kitchen and dug out an edible chunk of cheese and Leonard's box of Carr's crackers to bring back to the tub. That ought to hold her. A milkshake would make an excellent cheap dinner. *It may not be a paradise, it's fine compared to other lives. The life I'm leading as I am.*

♫

There was an old bike Frankie could use, a man's bike with a cross bar, a little higher than she was used to and rusty from beach salt, but it could get her to and from Watermill in one piece. She didn't get why Margaret's son-in-law had bought the old potato farm when there were so many pretty houses nearer to one or another of the villages. The "cottage," as Margaret insisted on calling it, was a two-room shed, across the yard from the main house where Melina and her husband lived. The bedroom was Margaret's. Frankie shared the attic loft with Daphne. The heat collected up there all day. Frankie got into the habit of hosing down at the outdoor shower before bed and climbing on top of the sheets while still wet. Sometime around two or three in the morning, which was usually when Daphne woke up from one of her dreams, it would be cool enough to sleep for the last few hours before dawn.

Frankie had been inside the main house once, the first week. She and Daphne had helped bring the baskets back from the beach after the big clambake. Melina and Cooper's kitchen was as big as the entire cottage. They also had an "outdoor kitchen," built at the edge of the patio, with a bar that had a working sink, and a big brick grill. Mickey's war buddy Vic once built a grill like that, out of bricks he'd scavenged from the haunted house on Maple. Frankie had always wondered whether it was the ghosts or Vic's limited skills that left it looking like a breeze would blow it over. The bricks on Melina's grill were so true that the most determined weed couldn't find a crack in the grout to take up residence.

Frankie had imagined there would be kids at the shore for Daphne to play with, and maybe a group of older siblings or babysitters like herself who would hang out after dark and build a driftwood fire and have a beer, like they did in beach movies. Instead, it turned out to be just her and Daphne. Margaret, when she was around, spent half her time having lunch at the Bath and Tennis in Southampton. For much of the week she disappeared to the city for her charity events or whatever else socialites did. Since meeting the Rodneys, Frankie had started flipping through *Women's Wear Daily* and *Harper's Bazaar* in the library. It was amazing how often Margaret showed up on those pages; Melina and Cooper too, once she knew to look for them. Frankie started piecing together their life stories. Only Margaret's middle child, Roland, remained a mystery. Daphne seemed fond of her brother. Whenever he sent her a postcard, she'd show it off to everyone in Irene's class. That's the only reason Frankie even knew Roland existed. Margaret never mentioned him. What had he done wrong? Maybe just be born. If Margaret hated his father as much as she hated Daphne's—Frankie had been the recipient of several unwanted confidences in that area—it would explain a lot.

Frankie's job was twofold: to babysit Daphne, as she'd expected; and also to practice with her. Every morning, they did a half hour jazz warm-up. Following that was tap: Irene's exercises and almost an hour spent perfecting one of their class routines. After lunch, Frankie set out the top-of-the-line Casio keyboard and accompanied Daphne as she practiced her singing. Only then were they free to go down to the beach or bike into the village for an ice cream.

Frankie felt too shy to vocalize in front of anyone. Now and then, Melina collected Daphne to take her to what were called "Junior Cotillion" events, mostly tea parties in the gardens of the nicer homes. On those occasions, Frankie waited until the coast was clear, then took out the keyboard. Instead of rushing though Donny's exercises (as she was ashamed to admit she usually did), she ran through them slowly and deliberately. Twice. After that, she let it rip, taking several stabs at one of the songs she was working on for auditions. It was such a relief to sing; or maybe it was a relief to have some time alone. Whatever it was, she'd move on to sing her way through all of the *Wizard of Oz* and *Guys and Dolls* before ending up at *Lake Song*.

She was pleased with her progress. She could feel the vibration exactly where Donny told her it ought to be in her chest, and mentally "placed" her high notes so that they'd release into the room instead of sticking in the bridge of her nose. She was willing to bet she sounded good, too. Maybe good enough to dare to try Donny's idea about singing into the waves.

On her way to the beach, she passed the gardener. "Did you have the radio on?" he asked. She was hugely complimented, until he added. "I don't understand the music you kids play. All that screeching and yowling."

She tried not to take it personally. Stupid man couldn't even tell rock and roll from show music. Eventually, she found the humor in it and wrote to Ahuva.

Frankie hardly felt out of touch. She wrote to everyone, once a week each, and people were so good about writing back. Except Donny, who was so busy with *Pericles* that he'd sent her just the one postcard, the very first week. She didn't mind; and of course she kept writing to him! He was her boyfriend! But he was also her vocal coach, so she decided not to tell him what the gardener said. He might be insulted, and she wouldn't know, because he didn't have time to write.

She also read a lot. She read *The Great Gatsby*, because it took place out here, and wondered whether Melina would have been important enough to be invited to parties at the Buchanans'. Melina surely thought so.

Watermill was pretty dull, but it was better than staying home and dealing with Eunice every night after camp. At least the people she was living with wanted her there. Especially Daphne. Frankie didn't think the kid had any real friends. Frankie's heart went out to her. She knew too well what it was like to be a lonely kid.

♪

Ellen got Joe to sneak her into a box on Tuesday. Saturday's second-act had felt off; she needed to see if it had been the quart of screwdrivers doing the thinking for her.

It hadn't. Bronwen Davies was several sheets to the wind, moving unsteadily and laughing loudly where she oughtn't to have been laughing at all. The woman did have talent. If it was your first time seeing the show, you might have been fooled into thinking it was part of her interpretation of Arkadina. Ellen wasn't fooled. She knew the lines well enough to see when one was dropped, and to spot the disturbed flash on the face of the actor who jumped in to cover. Bron stumbled more than once. Max looked like he wanted to kill her (more than usually) during "Kiss, Kiss" and Joe reached out to catch her, in the nick of time, when she tripped during the sweeping circuit that was her choreography for "The Horses Are Waiting."

"Wayne was keeping her straight, you know," Joe said later, when they were cuddling on the sofa-bed in the apartment of the mysterious friend who was conveniently never around. "For months, until…well, you were there."

Ellen nodded and reached up to play with her favorite little curls, the ones he said only showed up when he had to keep his hair long for a period piece. He liked when she did that. She could see all the air go out of his shoulders.

"She went on such a bender when he left. Showed up at half-hour stinking. Milt sent her home and Nancy went on. After the show, Connie went round to check on her. Good thing Connie has a key; she'd passed out without reaching the bedroom. Connie cleaned her up and called Ivor. She came back full of apologies and promises, and she hasn't missed another show, but you never know what you're going to get. If it gets any worse, the Equity rep'll have to get involved. Glad that's his problem and not mine." He shook his head slowly, as if it were heavy.

"I thought it was me on Saturday," Ellen confessed. "I was a little smashed that day myself."

"Any reason?" he asked mildly.

"I was lonely." She could say that to Joe. He would never try to analyze her, and he would never get on her case. Another reason she liked him. "And the weekend was so frigging hot. That probably didn't help. Anyway, I don't make a habit of it."

He leaned his head backwards so that he was grinning at her upside down. "Don't give up control to anything, baby. It's not your speed."

"No way!" she agreed, proud he saw her this way. "So what else did I miss the last couple of weeks?"

He tweaked her nipple. Gossip was foreplay for another round. "Max has another new one."

"Who's left? What's-her-name, who took over for Maria?"

"Dinah? Nancy's more her speed. Not that we can confirm it, they're both so fucking discreet. No, old Max officially ran out of candidates on our show and had to start casing the street. He's seeing one of the *Pippin* gypsies."

"Easier for Becca, Linda and Fredi, not to have to see him balling someone in the hallway."

"Becca…you know, I almost forgot? You'd think Chris was her first, the way they are, the lovebirds. Andy Hardy and the virgin next door. Linda's not moping any either. She's happy as a clam with her new guy. Who Tyler says is her old guy from before we started our run."

"Donny?" Ellen blurted. Cat's away? Or was Frankie getting dumped while she was out of town?

"I don't know. Don't care, either."

With Joe's hand in her crotch, Ellen didn't either for the moment, but she forced herself to file it away for when she could. Should she tell Frankie or not?

♫

Bad news shouldn't come on a postcard of the Statue of Liberty. Frankie's great-grandfather had helped to build that statue. Well, the pedestal. Mickey used to tell her the story when she was little. Somewhere inside, in a place that no one ever saw unless they worked for the Parks Department, they'd written their names in the concrete, all the workmen. His name was there, Michelangelo Cecchi. Like the painter. Mickey was named for him.

Frankie always thought of Lady Liberty as part of the family. Her picture shouldn't be on the front of the most horrible note anyone had ever written. She hated Ellen for writing it, for saying that Donny, her Donny, was seeing that bitch Linda Schiller behind her back.

He would never! Not after the way Linda'd dropped him the minute she got a Broadway show. She'd hurt him so badly, throwing him away the minute she didn't need him anymore. He'd felt like an idiot, that he'd let himself be used like that. Linda had embarrassed him in front of everyone who knew them, which was a lot of people over two years at NYADA. And now Donny was doing the same thing to her, to Frankie.

There it was. In Ellen's signature bookkeeping-green ink. "Hi. Wish you had a phone out there. No good way to say this. Wouldn't, except you haven't said, which means he's not man enough to tell you. Linda's doing Donny. Stupid prick. You can do better."

All the blood drained out of her head so fast she almost fainted. He hated Linda. And he liked *her*, Frankie; he always said so. He did. But how did he say it? "Like he meant you were a good kid," said a dry little voice in the back of her head that sounded an awful lot like Annie Fallon. Frankie wanted to hit something. She wanted to hit herself, for being so stupid, for wanting something so much that she saw things that weren't there.

She was twenty times a bigger fool than Linda had ever made Donny. The two of them probably deserved each other, she thought bitterly. Frankie *did* deserve better. Much better Why couldn't she believe that? Donny was so wonderful. Or he had been, until she'd read that postcard.

It was the most horrible postcard anyone had ever written. Frankie couldn't believe Ellen would write such a thing, no less mail it. When she stopped crying, she'd be very grateful.

♫

"Is this Ellen?"

"Yes," she said. The voice was male and soft. Familiar. She couldn't place it

"This is Tyler Moss. I hope I'm not disturbing you. Joe Bigelow gave me your number."

That was curious. "Not at all," she said politely. "What can I do for you?"

"It's rather delicate." He paused.

This was getting interesting. Tyler Moss was certainly not calling to set up an assignation. Ellen liked the word "assignation." She made encouraging sounds into the receiver for him to continue.

"I'm, ah, calling on behalf of a friend." He paused again.

Maybe she was wrong about the assignation. "Yes?"

"Ivor Davies," he said finally. "I'm calling on Ivor's behalf. Joe mentioned that you were at liberty, that you might be looking for a new job. And Penelope told Lionel you were extremely trustworthy."

"That's very kind of Penelope." She was burning with curiosity but refused to ask. She wondered what it was that Ivor Davies couldn't ask for himself.

"Would you by any chance be free tomorrow evening? To meet with Ivor and Lionel over dinner? Nothing formal, just a light bite at around seven."

"I'd be delighted," she told him.

She told me the story during our window shopping walk. This was a regular thing with us, from back when our parents first allowed us to take the subway in by ourselves. We made pilgrimages to parts of the city that thoroughly intimidated us, daring one another to enter the expensive shops and examine the goods on display. It took a lot of nerve for middle class girls from Queens to brazenly push past the doors to this other world. The impoverished widows and divorcees, often European, who staffed such places, gave no quarter; they were delighted to have someone to look down on. We taught ourselves not to shrink under their glares, equally important as what we learned about good cashmere and leather. Six years later, we could stride into any shop in the city of New York, quite as blasé as any to Park Avenue born. I doubt the salespeople confused us with genuine shoppers, but we were confident enough that we provided no sport. They left us alone. Now that we no longer needed to challenge ourselves, we only window shopped the places we imagined we'd patronize when we were rich and presumably famous: Jaeger and Missoni for Ellen; Fred Leighton for me; and both of us cherished a special fondness for the delirious ground floor bazaar of the skinny 57th Street wonderland that was Bendel's.

It's frustrating to spend a day shopping and come home empty handed, so we'd usually end up somewhere that had small items that we could potentially buy. Today we chose the Caswell Massey shop in the Waldorf. Its wood panels and marble appealed to our pretensions, looking the way we imagined London must look and stuffed with affordable luxuries: English hairbrushes; shiny Easter eggs of soap in rich cinnabar and Wedgwood blue; wooden tubs of shaving soap. Ellen developed an attachment to the cucumber lotion that was said to have been Sarah Bernhardt's favorite beauty aid. I was enthralled by Vinolia soap, the brand provided in the staterooms of the Titanic.

Poking around, sniffing bottles and bars, rubbing creams on our arms, we caught up on the news. The only remotely interesting thing I had to tell was that the bookkeeper at this year's summer job was a former Balanchine dancer who walked with a permanent limp from hyperextended hips. Ballet, we agreed, was institutionalized torture.

Ellen, a natural storyteller, brought me up to date on Leonard's Fire Island summer—he'd been at a party with Charles Nelson Reilly last weekend—before skillfully revealing her big scoop: Ivor Davies had offered her a job.

"You don't know anything about set design." That was my automatic response, before I paused to think. "Oh! You mean in his office? Cool!"

She shook her head and backtracked to the counter where we'd seen little red plastic nubbins that, when unscrewed, proved to contain domes of solid menthol. The gentleman behind the counter—and "gentleman" was the operative word for this courtly, faintly citrus-scented being—explained that you were meant to rub them on your temples when you had a headache.

"Or a hangover," Ellen pointed out, after we'd tried the sampler and experienced the icy balm. They were only a dollar apiece. A bargain when you thought of what people were paying for exotic sensations. "You know, I think I'm going to get a few of these. For my job." She turned to me and flashed her most puckish face, her thin lips pulling back into a deep v-shaped smile, her eyebrows at full waggle. "My client might need them."

"You are such a fucking tease!"

"I'm famous for it," she said, with satisfaction.

"Not as famous as you like to think," I objected.

She laughed. It was a knowing superior laugh. "Let's just say I'm getting a name for myself in a certain community."

"So what's the job?" I was getting impatient.

She raised a finger, the implication being that she didn't want the hovering salesmen to overhear. If she honestly had a secret, it was a fair concern. Ellen's whisper could hail a cab. We paid for our menthol and soaps, and her skin cream. At the last minute, I grabbed a sea sponge from a large basket on the floor. I had no idea what I'd use it for, but when I held it to my nose, it smelt wonderfully of ocean (it still does).

We left through the door that connected with the Waldorf lobby and made our way to the ladies' room. When you were out for an all-day walk, it was only smart to take advantage of any opportunity that might present. As a bonus, nothing makes you feel richer than the toilets in New York's posher hotels.

We had the place to ourselves. At the sinks, with the water running, Ellen confided her news. "I'm babysitting Bron."

"What?!" I spun around, splashing myself with soapy water.

"I told you what's been going on. Well, it's worse than I realized. Ivor's nervous. He's paying me to be her companion. We're calling me an 'assistant' so she doesn't freak out, but really it's babysitting."

"What are you supposed to do? You're not a nurse or...I don't know, an AA person?"

"If she doesn't get it together, Ivor'll have to find someone like that."

As always, Ellen was a clash of emotions: concern, warring with satisfaction, wrapped in an aura of sparkling excitement. I opted to address the concern; this sounded like a sad situation.

"Well, you always said she had a drinking problem."

Ellen seemed offended. "I never said it was a problem."

"You said she was a lush."

"I said the woman drinks. She seems to manage well enough except when she's under a lot of stress. Ivor says it was the worst when James Lyttleton died but she got it together for the kids. She didn't go on a binge for years after, and never more than a couple of days. He thinks this one is probably from menopause. No wonder she was fucking Wayne."

I was shocked to hear the word spoken aloud. No one ever said "menopause." When unavoidable, the experience was coyly referred to as "change of life."

For once, Ellen was too interested in her train of thought to react to my reaction. "I think after the show, she'll probably go someplace to dry out."

"Oh! Is the show closing?" I was disappointed. I had some friends at school who still hadn't seen *Lake Song*.

Ellen rolled her eyes at my stupidity. "You don't post a closing notice six months ahead. No, it's her contract; she was always supposed to leave. Joe thinks they'll bring in Madeleine Blair."

"Madeleine Blair, Madeleine Blair?" Like Bronwen Davies, Blair was never a huge star but had a name people recognized. She was best known for a post-war movie about blind soldier who falls in love with a crippled girl. A temporarily blind soldier. It was what my mom, who adored them, called "a three-handkerchief picture." She'd watch this one whenever it cropped up on *The Late Show*, which was why I'd heard of Madeleine Blair. I'd never heard Blair could sing, though, as I told Ellen.

Ellen shrugged. "The reviews have been good in London."

"She's been doing the show in London? So doesn't she have to stay there?"

"It's easier to put in someone new there. They expect short runs on the West End, you know."

I knew now.

"All Bron has to do is hold it together until the end of the year. Ivor thinks it's better if she's not on her own until she's adjusted to Wayne being gone. When he was around, she kept it under control enough to show up for work. Mostly. So I gave Mr. Nudler my notice and told Barney I'd be out of touch for the summer. I started the other day. I get get some food in her in the morning, then do whatever she needs: help her answer her mail, take her shopping. The point is not to leave her alone until it's time to go to the theatre, when Connie takes over. Every day except when they're dark. Ivor's covering Mondays himself, so I get some time off."

"So how are you here now?" It was Saturday.

"Matinee. That's why I said to meet at one instead of twelve. Connie's on duty until tonight."

"Uh-huh. And what about nights?"

She grinned. "Guest room. Bron thinks I got dumped by my boyfriend and need a place to stay for the rest of the summer. Part of Ivor's plan. That way she thinks she's doing someone a favor. Lionel in fact. We told her I'm one of his Vassar students. That was my idea. I know enough from you to fake it if she starts thinking clearly enough to get suspicious."

"What does Leonard think?"

"Probably happy to have some extra time to himself. Kevin has a roommate too. That's definitely a thing now."

♫

"Dear heart, I wonder if I might trouble you…"

It was one of Lil's typical openers. Either that or "If it wouldn't be too much bother…" Ahuva understood it was meant to show Lil wasn't a diva, but she often wished the woman could make a simple request. She tilted her head to indicate she was amenable to whatever it was: climbing the stepladder to pull down a box from the closet; running downtown to the British pharmacy for the headache powders Lil preferred to aspirin.

"I finally found that photo!" Lil raised herself from her favorite chaise and glided to the mantel. "I put it here for safekeeping."

Ahuva looked at her blankly.

"Oh, of course. It was the other girl, Frankie, who was looking it out for me. We must remember to tell her, she'll be so pleased!" With a flourish, Lil picked up a silver-framed photo. "Dear Noel. I still can't believe he's gone. But we all have our exits and our entrances, don't we now? Which is why I've been wanting this so. The youngest of us ought to have it."

She extended the frame. Ahuva took it and gasped. It was a much younger Lilith Brassloe, in evening dress, apparently singing with Noel Coward. At the piano was a very young Marshall Berenson.

"What a baby he was!" Lilith cooed with delight. "Hank Peet's little protegé! That was in Port Maria, of course. A marvelous party." She laughed. "Oh, I never forgave Noel for giving that song to Bea Lillie!"

Ahuva had no idea what Lil was talking about. The actress often made references to people and events she'd never heard of. She felt quite ignorant sometimes. Right now she was too fascinated by the photo for that to bother her. "What a magnificent photo! You look stunning," she hastened to add.

"Thank you, dear heart. That was sweet. I wasn't fishing, mind." Lilith reclaimed the photo and smiled at it fondly. "Yes, I was rather dishy in those days. I remember…Never mind. What I would adore, if it wouldn't be too much bother, would be for you to run this over to Marshall's. Let's see. Ah! This'll do." She pulled piece of tissue paper from a drawer in her little French desk and quickly rolled up the frame.

"You mean now?" Ahuva felt her heart stop. "To his house?"

"If it wouldn't be too much bother. You have to go that way in any case, don't you," she asked ingenuously, "To get to where you live?"

"I'd be happy to." Ahuva replied.

Lilith's understanding of New York City geography was purposefully vague. It didn't matter. Ahuva would have gladly detoured through Jersey if it meant ending up at Marshall Berenson's house. She was desperately glad she made a particular effort to look right on the days she worked for Lil. It was so hot today, it had been tempting to throw on an old sundress and scrape her hair into a ponytail. She was glad she hadn't, that she was wearing Kaye's Indian blouse and her silver jewelry.

Before she left Lil's, she combed her hair smooth with her fingers, adjusted her head scarf so that her Yemenite earrings showed to good advantage and freshened her lip gloss. Her mouth tasted of sugary strawberries. She resisted the nervous temptation to suck it off while she waited for the crosstown bus.

There were no trees by the bus stop. Ahuva stood in the blazing sun, feeling the sweat gather at the base of her neck and trickle down her back, reminding herself that she was suffering for Marshall Berenson. The bus took forever to show up and another eternity to inch down Broadway to 59th and across to Third. A steamy eternity. She walked the remainder of the way with the paper shopping bag in her arms, pressed against her chest. She was afraid that if she held the bag in the usual way, it might swing against something and the glass, wrapped in only one sheet of tissue, might break. Other peoples' belongings are such a burden.

She didn't need Lil's slip of paper. She already knew where Marshall Berenson lived. It had been in a magazine once, or at least there had been enough information to make it simple to puzzle out the rest. Whenever she had to be in the general vicinity, Ahuva found reasons to reroute her path along his side street. There was a fireplug in front of the house next door. If you used it to adjust the strap on your shoe, you could linger a good minute or more, your head down, your eyes carefully skewed to watch the door. Once there'd been a UPS man waiting on the steps and she'd performed an elaborate pantomime about a contact lens she didn't wear so when the door opened, she had her hand over her face and could peek between her fingers. Instead of a glimpse of horn rims and a sandy beard, she'd seen a white coat and patch of shiny black hair.

She hoped she wouldn't be as disappointed today. Pausing at the foot of the brown steps, she took a deep, cleansing breath to steady her nerves. She wasn't spying, she reminded herself. She was here on legitimate business, from no one less than Lilith Brassloe. Still bracing the bag with her left hand, she placed her right on the wrought iron banister and hoisted her left foot. Like most brownstones, including the shabby one where Kaye lived, the steps were tall. These were in better shape than Kaye's, with no treacherous dips and cracks, but her platform sandals meant she still needed to put a lot of knee in the climb. It was hot out. A little woozy at the top, she clutched the handrail while she took another steadying breath.

Did she have enough composure to do what she had to do next? While her mind was still weighing this, her hand jumped off the rail of its own volition and punched the doorbell. She stared at it, horrified. What was she going to say if it opened?!

It opened. The butler…no, Ric had called him a "houseman." Actually, Ric had called him a "houseboy," but Ahuva thought that sounded patronizing. He was probably as old as Ric. The houseman, then, waited patiently for her to respond to a question she hadn't heard. "Can I help you?" he repeated.

"I have a delivery for Mr. Berenson," she said, clearing her throat before and after she said it. "From Lilith Brassloe. It's personal," she was inspired to add.

He didn't ask for any proof, nor did he ask her to hand over the bag. He nodded and opened the door wider so that she could come in. Could she have barged into Marshall Berenson's house at any time, just by saying she had a package from someone he might know?

"Come this way," he said. "It must be close to 100 out there. Would you like a lemonade?"

Lemonade sounded heavenly: wet, tart and, best of all, probably full of ice cubes. How thoughtful for him to offer.

"Oh! I would love one! Thank you!"

She followed his white coat down the hall, her eyes darting everywhere, trying to take it all in. Marshall Berenson's hall. It was dim; maybe that helped keep the heat down, because it was almost cool in here. An enormous framed poster hung in the entry, obviously old and advertising some French brand of alcohol she'd never heard of. Across from that was one of those tall narrow tables, holding an arrangement of white flowers and—her nose prickled at the familiar astringent scent—eucalyptus leaves. Her heavy sandals thudded across the tiles. The white coat turned a corner, and so did she.

Looking over her shoulder as she passed an archway, she thought she could make out the shadow of a grand piano. "Thank you so much!" she repeated, hoping she was making her gratitude clear.

"Who is it Lu?"

Shocked by the familiar voice, Ahuva almost dropped the precious bag.

"It's the messenger from Miss Brassloe, sir." Even half-stunned, Ahuva was able to appreciate how the houseman managed to keep his voice low and even, but somehow make it carry into the other room. "I was about to give her a lemonade. It's terribly hot out there."

"Ah, Lil's messenger. Show her in here, Lu. And bring the pitcher. I could use a glass myself."

He was expecting her! Lil must have called to say she was coming. She started chanting frantically in her head: I will not faint, I will not faint. Maharishi Narang wouldn't think much of it as a chant, but under the circumstances it made more sense than the sloka. Clutching Lil's now quintuply precious parcel, she tiptoed behind Lu under the arch.

Marshall Berenson was rising from the piano bench. It could only have been more perfect if he'd still been playing. "Hello," he said, putting out his hand.

Hers was so hot and sticky. She wished there was some clever way to wipe it on her jeans first, but that would have been even more embarrassing. She held it out and he took it. "I'm Marshall."

"Yes, you are," she said, stupidly. "I mean…I'm Ahuva. Ahuva Geffner."

"Nice to meet you, Ahuva Geffner. Please, have a seat."

"Oh, it's such an honor to meet you, Mr. Berenson!" She made a concerted effort to sit slowly, so that her knees wouldn't collapse before her butt found the sofa.

The great man laughed, bless him; a friendly laugh. He flung himself down into the leather chair opposite. "I take it you approve of my work."

"Oh, yes! The first show I ever saw was *The Buddy System*. I was eleven at the time. I was in total awe. I hardly spoke a word of English."

"Maybe that's why you were in awe," he joked.

She shook her head. Not even Marshall Berenson could disparage Marshall Berenson to her. "No, that's the thing. Somehow, I did understand a lot of it. It made me stop being afraid of the language. I wanted to learn it. I wanted to learn it well enough to understand all your lyrics." She was on steady ground now. "And then we did *Rosebud* in my school. I listened to all your scores. It changed my life. My biggest regret is that I didn't get to see *Always Sometimes*

Never Again. But I loved *The Boy Jones*. And I absolutely adore *Lake Song*. I adore your work. All of it!"

"Wow! All of it? I wish you were John Simon." His eyes twinkled behind the famous horn rims.

"Well…" Ahuva was pathologically honest. She couldn't stop herself. "Not all equally. Some of the lyrics in the early work are a little silly, but you were so young and just starting out. And 'Emerald Hills of Home' has always bothered me. Not as a song, per se. But it doesn't fit with the rest of *Playing the Palace*."

"You're absolutely correct in that. Ahuva, right?"

Lu returned with a tray, which he placed on the table between them. Berenson poured out two glasses and handed one to Ahuva.

"What made you think that, Ahuva? It's very well spotted."

It was a verbal pat on the head and it made her glow. She hoped she wouldn't mess things up with her explanation. "The mood is different, of course. But you do that a lot in your scores, mix up the mood. This one stands out especially because it's the only one in this particular show that's not comic. But that's not what doesn't fit. It seems to me…I don't know enough about music to say exactly, but it seems to me that 'Emerald Hills' comes from a completely different musical tradition. There's something in the tonal scale…I'm sorry. I don't know how to describe it."

"No, no. You're doing fine. And yes, that's it exactly. The three jesters were exiles from other countries, if you recall. I wrote songs using the tonal scales of their homelands, to emphasize the alien nature of the men. Bernard is Irish. 'Emerald Hills' is Ionian. Fyodor was from Russia." He sprang to the piano. His hands wandering over the keys, he picked out a haunting melody in an octatonic key.

She could hardly breathe; Marshall Berenson was actually playing the piano for her.

He switched briefly to a pentatonic scale. "And what's his name, the acrobat, was Chinese." He sounded a chord, breaking the spell.

"Wong Sing," she giggled.

"Of course it was," he grinned, plopping back into the leather chair as suddenly as he'd left it. "The other two got cut out of town. Jim wanted to cut 'Emerald Hills,' but Heshy sold the hell out of that song. He said it was the only reason he'd wanted to play the part. His was the name selling tickets, so it stayed in." He handed her the plate of cookies. "It's always bothered me, but you're the only person who's ever mentioned it."

She held the cookie between her fingers, afraid if she bit it she'd choke. Marshall Berenson took her seriously. He was maybe even impressed with her! And he was so nice!!

She sat there, radiant, for nearly half an hour, listening to him talk about his work, making comments of her own that she herself found surprisingly insightful. It was perfection. Everything else that had happened this month paled next to this. *An hour is a lifetime...* That was so true.

She would have to give him a gift, to say thank you. Something as unique as he was.

♫

It was too embarrassing to admit after she'd protested so strongly—she certainly could never admit it to Leonard—but Ellen had utterly confused Bronwen Davies with the character she played in *Lake Song*. Maybe it was because she'd had nothing to compare it with. If she'd seen any of those kid movies Frankie was always going on about, they hadn't left any impression. Her every speculation, even the varied personalities she'd attributed to the woman, had begun with the assumption that Davies was, to some extent, Arkadina. The extent turned out to be pretty meager. Except for being an actress, Arkadina shared nothing with Davies. The splendid air of disregard with which Arkadina swept through her scenes? Nothing but the result of Davies' lousy eyesight; if the stagehands weren't so meticulous, the woman would be black and blue from colliding with the set. Whatever source Davies tapped for the rest of her performance was a mystery. And it was one hell of a performance. Ellen understood that better now that she'd seen behind the curtain. Onstage, the woman was a force to be reckoned with; offstage, she was a timorous shadow of whispers and blinks.

Listless, where her character was hungry for life, self-effacing where she was brazen, the actress seemed to draw neither pleasure nor catharsis from her work. It was chilling to think a person could spend two hours each day so completely divorced from herself. No wonder Davies was frightened. Scratch that: she was terrified, all the time. When she'd been on the job a few weeks, Ellen blurted that out to Ivor, thinking she was offering a fresh insight.

"Oh yes," he'd calmly agreed. "Since we were children, my dear. You know that we lost our parents in the Blitz?"

Everyone knew. It was in the *Playbill*.

"There were plans to evacuate us to Father's cousins in Glamorgan, but we were still in London. Father was home on leave. They'd sent us to sleep with neighbors that night. We resented it like hell at the time, of course, but as I got older I was glad to think they'd had a those few hours to themselves. I hardly remember them, but you can see in the photos how in love they were. We went to the tube station as usual, when the sirens went off, but our parents never showed. I think I remember the sirens that night, but I was so small and there were so many nights with sirens, I might be confusing them. The next morning…this I do remember, quite clearly: the front of our house, all open like a doll's house; my bed quilt was very red and I could see it, still on my cot. Bron says she remembers the stretchers, but she was older. Old enough to feel responsible for me and put up a strong front on the boat coming over. She didn't allow herself to cry, not until our aunt met us on the docks in New York. Aunt Marion looked so much like our mother, you see."

Ellen was glad they were on the phone and Ivor couldn't see her wiping her eyes. As fucked up as her parents were, stories about orphans always made her feel grateful to have them. "I can't imagine going through that," is all she said.

"People go through worse," he observed. "Honestly, we had a very happy childhood after that. Sunshine, oranges, playing on the back lots. Aunt Marion was a trooper. But we could never quite shake off that shadow. Bron especially. You know that to this day she refuses to take an underground train, in any city? We all have our ways, right? You avoid what you think might set you off, and it'll disappear. Bron has been fine for years and years. Nothing major since Richard's accident. Minor setbacks, yes, but when you feel it coming on you fight it. Which she does. She's been fine. Otherwise, believe me, she would never have taken the show, no matter how much Jimmy Lord begged. Sometimes she drinks a little too much. That's her way. And she finds someone safe to hold onto. Wayne was doing the trick. Once he left…Well, my dear, I can't produce a lover out of thin air. And I can't be with her all the time. So I have provided a surrogate. We only need for her to see out her contract. Then I'll take her to my villa in Greece. She finds it a comforting place to be. And I think you are doing a splendid job."

21- TWO YEARS (REPRISE)

POLINA *[spoken: See how quickly two years can pass? I'd bet it only seems like twenty minutes to all of you. Yet in that time.....]*

Two short years are gone, are fled.
Some take to travel, and some to bed,
And some are since born, and some are since dead.
Two long years have gone, have fled
And some have parted and some have wed,
And others have done other things instead.

[spoken] But an unconscionable number of people have done absolutely nothing at all. Indolent as barnacles. And twice as thick.

Time leaves a mark, and hardly a trace;
It goes so fast, but looking back, so much has taken place,
It must have been longer ago and farther away than it seems:
Two years in the flick of an eyelash;
Two years in the space of a dream.

Frankie and I had been corresponding, ever since that riotous pajama party at Harry's. I looked forward to finding her cards in the mailbox: she always had a funny story to tell, and even her clear round handwriting was somehow smiley. Of course, I wrote to her while she was out at the beach that summer. I knew Ellen and Ahuva kept her up on the gossip, but I had my own perspective to offer, mostly about how Ahuva was gradually turning into Kaye Victor and Ellen's gleeful gossip didn't match with the shadows under her eyes.

Frankie's job with the Rodneys ended a week before I was heading back to school. By picking Monday, Ellen's day off, all four of us were able to be together. For the first time ever, if you don't count Tony night. It was pretty momentous, which was probably why we splurged on the unusually nice café across the street from Bloomingdales, a place popular with the shoppers and interior decorators who made up the daytime population of the neighborhood.

The first to arrive, I secured one of the tall round tables, perching on one linen-capped stool and dumping my patchwork hobo bag onto another to claim ownership.

Frankie arrived soon after, her face alight with smiles. "I missed the city so much!" She beamed appreciatively at the setting from behind her giant glasses. "It smells like banana bread in here."

As soon as there were two of us at the table, the waitress approached. We said we'd wait for the rest of our party but would have our coffee right away. She didn't mind; an hour earlier, during lunch rush, she would have.

Ellen appeared at the same time as our coffee, bustling as always. Behind her dark glasses, she could be looking anywhere and no one would know, except that that she could never stop jerking her head as she checked out the room. Like a bad spy, I once pointed out. Plunking herself down, she waved at the waitress and pointed to our mugs, then dragged the ashtray closer to her place and began her usual routine with the cigarette. I'd tried it once, bumming a Nat Sherman off of her and licking the tip as she did. It was sweet and soggy, and a bunch of tobacco shreds stuck annoyingly to my tongue. Either she had a knack that I lacked, or she was willing to excuse the discomfort for the effect.

"God it is so good to have a day off!" she exclaimed, her voice potentially carrying to Lexington Avenue. "It's been total hell. Connie dePaul's brother died..."

"Oh, no!" Frankie was as upset as she was shocked.

Ellen had forgotten that Connie was a friend of Frankie's. "Hit by a bus," she announced concisely. She took her first drag and moved on. "So Connie had to head up to Boston to take care of everything."

"Poor Connie!" Frankie's eyes were welling tears. Magnified by her glasses, it looked like a teaspoonful of water brimming in each one.

"And it means I've had Bron to myself since Thursday. Four longest days of my life," Ellen moaned.

"The woman's brother died!" I objected. "I'm sure you can manage for a few days. Anyway, I thought you adored Bron."

"That was before I found out how stupid she is. The boredom is driving me crazy. She's gorgeous, but she is such a dumb blonde."

"I thought you said it was a wig," I countered. I could never resist challenging Ellen's outrageous claims.

"She's still a blonde. Same color as the wig. The wig is because she's allergic to hairspray or something. I don't know. Does it matter? God! She wears wigs. She also wears glasses when she's not at the theatre; blind as a bat without them."

"*Famous people are just people after all?*" Unlike my friends, I didn't regularly quote from *Lake Song*, but I couldn't resist.

Midway through blowing her nose, a thought struck Frankie. "Wait, who's doing Connie's job while she's out? You can't. It's union."

Ellen smirked. "And you should see the substitute they sent over! A shit-eating grin, and so fat she takes up half the dressing room. Bron refuses to be left alone with her. I can't even blame her, but it means I have to hang around the dressing room, too. At least when Connie's here I get a few hours off."

"Namaste," said Ahuva, inclining her head to each of us in turn. She'd wafted in, smiling serenely.

Ahuva used to wear jeans that looked as if they'd been pressed. Today's denim was soft and faded with frayed hems, and worn with a long embroidered gauze tunic. Her bag was macramé, the bottom fringe held in place by blue wooden balls. Her hair flowed off her face, held back by a folded mirror-embroidered scarf that set off the dangling silver earrings Gali had brought her from Israel, the ones that she used to say were "a bit much." She seemed happy, but so much had changed over this summer that I sometimes felt my friend had disappeared. I was relieved by the familiar deliberation with which she took her seat and lifted the menu for inspection.

"Ellen was telling us about Connie," Frankie said. "I feel terrible."

Ahuva nodded gravely. "The Maharishi says that a violent, unexpected death traumatizes the soul. I hope he can find peace."

"I hope I can," Ellen grumbled. "Maybe I should ask your Maharishi for some magic words."

Ahuva began to bristle.

"Maybe," I hastily butted in, "you should tell Bron's brother that you want to quit." I knew she wouldn't. This was only the latest in a string of complaints that had begun the minute she'd started the job. Ellen used to complain about Felix, too. She loved to complain, especially when she really cared.

She gave me the finger and turned her attention to the menu. "I hope they have some decent salads here. It's too frigging hot for anything else."

"I'm just happy to have air conditioning," Frankie said wryly. "We didn't even have a fan out at the beach."

Ahuva frowned. "That makes no sense. They're rich, aren't they?"

Frankie made a face. "Yeah, I know. I can't figure it out. It's like the furniture thing." We all knew about the lack of furniture on East End Avenue.

"Old money," I said wisely, having read a few mid-century comedic novels that dealt with the topic. "They think it's vulgar, to be too comfortable."

Ellen snorted. "Give me new money any day."

"It was still nice that you were able to get away from Eunice. All those negative vibrations."

"Tell me about it." Frankie shook her head. "She hasn't stopped glaring at me since I got home. I wish I could afford to move out. It would be great to get a LORT contract. Imagine getting paid to live in Boston or San Francisco for a year."

"What you really want is a sugar daddy," Ellen smirked. "Couldn't you find one, at any of those parties?"

Melina and Cooper threw a lot of parties, often inviting celebrities.

Frankie laughed. "Like I could have gotten anywhere near them! Did I tell anyone the Michael Bennett story?"

"Michael Bennett's gay," Ellen remarked, apropos of nothing.

"Not everyone is gay!" Ahuva and I retorted, practically in unison.

"I thought he was with Donna McKechnie," Frankie said, puzzled.

Ellen wiggled her eyebrows, back on form. "Still gay."

"Would you let it go?" I punched her arm.

Ahuva gestured to Frankie. "I would personally like to hear this story."

Frankie launched into a long anecdote about Margaret, having heard that Bennett was coming to the party, wanting Daphne to dance for the guests. Melina put her foot down. "Cooper got all red in the face and refused to talk about it. That's kind of his thing, refusing to talk." Grimacing fiercely, her mouth shut tight, Frankie sat as tall as she could and shifted her shoulders to indicate someone storming out of a room. Acting out all the parts, she was especially hilarious as Melina, lifting her chin and pushing her jaw forward. "No, Mother!" Frankie repeated, in a voice of infinitely chilly hauteur. Then she dropped character and frowned. "Margaret doesn't deserve to be talked to like that. She can be a little dippy, but she's never mean. Melina is a real rich bitch."

"A total cunt," Ellen agreed, shocking us with what was officially my first time hearing someone say that word aloud.

In the end, Frankie and Margaret snuck Daphne into the house early in the day. She hid until the caterers started bringing out dessert, then burst out of the laundry room in full costume and tap-danced out, belting "The Candy Man Can" as if she were part of the planned entertainment. Melina and Cooper were set to explode, only the guests thought she was adorable and applauded and offered her strawberry shortcake. Daphne had been a great success. Unfortunately, Michael Bennett had already gone home, having been surprised by sunburn on what had been an overcast day.

"Timing," Frankie concluded philosophically. Her face briefly darkened; we knew she was thinking about Donny's betrayal. "Good and bad. Everything is timing."

"Speaking of timing, dear hearts," Ahuva sighed dramatically. "Thursday was my last day with Lil. The scrapbooks. Are. Officially. Done!"

Conscious of the smattering of well-groomed adults at other tables, we mimed applause.

Smiling again, Frankie lifted her water glass in salute. "Wow! I kept thinking she didn't want to finish. You know. Because she didn't really want to give them up."

"I think Harvard was a little worried about that too," Ahuva confided. "Someone actually drove down to pick them up in person. He took her to lunch at The Four Seasons first."

"The Four Seasons," I breathed. It was probably my earliest dining fantasy, to eat in the Pool Room of The Four Seasons.

"Smart," Ellen said, with honest admiration. "Not only get her nicely lubricated, but show her how important she is."

"I was only relieved I didn't have to put them in the mail," Ahuva said earnestly. "What if the post office lost them? You can't exactly insure something like that. They're priceless! Completely irreplaceable!" No one could argue. "Anyway, I have some spare time now, at least until STC needs me for *Hedda*. So if anyone hears of anything…" she gestured towards Ellen and Frankie.

Ellen shrugged. "These days the only people I speak to are at *Lake Song*. I don't hear anything that you don't."

"Well, if you do, I get first dibs," said Frankie. "I want Margaret's money to last a while, but unless Alfie has room on the substitute roster, I've got nothing. I could use a new voice coach too." She forced herself to laugh.

"I'll ask Joe if he knows someone."

Frankie pulled out last week's *Backstage*, folded to a page where she'd circled several ads in orange grease pencil. She handed it to Ellen. "Ask him what he's heard about any of these."

Ellen pulled out a datebook and wrote down the names.

Voice coaches and gurus and tap classes. Show people at work. I was already starting to miss the city.

22- THE SCHOOLMASTER AND HIS WIFE

MEDVIEDENKO

Like doves in a cote, like peas in a pod,
Like oars in a boat, like coals in a hod,
Like horses and oats,

MASHA

Like Satan and God:

MEDVIEDENKO

The schoolmaster and his wife.

Like bumps on a log,

MASHA

Like rot in the walls,

MEDVIEDENKO

Like ships in a fog,

MASHA

Like drunks in a brawl,

MEDVIEDENKO

Like princes and frogs,

MASHA

Like nothing at all:
The schoolmaster and his wife.

MEDVIEDENKO

Happily…

MASHA

Un-

MEDVIEDENKO

Happily,
We rub along from day to day
Gratefully

MASHA

Disgracefully

MEDVIEDENKO

In harness together,

MASHA

We pull our own ways.

Like water and oil,

MEDVIEDENKO

Like berries and cream,

MASHA

I drink and he toils.

MEDVIEDENKO

We follow our dreams.
And nothing can spoil that wonderful
    team—
The schoolmaster and his wife!

MASHA

The schoolmaster…

MEDVIEDENKO

…and his wife.

Ellen slipped in beside Joe on the sofa bed, leaned her head against his comforting shoulder and sighed.

"Poor baby." He reached his arm to give her a good squeeze. "She's really got you beat."

"Longest six weeks of my life. I want to help, but I don't feel like I'm doing anything except watching." Watching, that was the word. Staring at herself in the bathroom mirror, she'd seen the sleepless nights in plummy shadows under her eyes. "It's a hell of a thing for a kid to deal with, but don't you ever get over it? I know people whose parents were in the camps and they have it more together."

"So Ivor gave you the Blitz story. Tugs at the heartstrings, doesn't it."

"Weeks ago…wait. You mean it's not true?"

Joe gave his hand that quick back and forth flip that he claimed he picked up from Ezio Pinza. "There are a lot of truths. I'm not denying it happened. And like you said, a hell of a thing for a kid. But it never made sense to me, that this is what it's all about. Sure, if something happens to set it off…I don't know, like watching a movie with an air raid siren? But I've known Ivor for ages, and I can tell you, it comes out of nowhere. Him and his sister. Happy as clams, then boom! Garbo time. I have this cousin. Manic depressive. They had to talk her off a ledge once, give her the shock treatment. You ask me, that's what they both have. They just don't want to say. People don't look at you the same if they think you're crazy."

How long could the woman hold it together before she ended up in the funny farm? How long could Ellen? This was not a job for a 19-year-old woman…a 19-year-old girl. Ellen hated feeling smacked in the face with her own youth, but there it was. She was in over her head. She hated feeling she was in over her head. And she was angry with Ivor Davies for putting her there. When he'd told her about Greece, she'd secretly hoped that she'd be invited to come along. Now she only wanted the woman to hang on that long, and then she'd be glad to never again see Bronwen Davies in anything more intimate than Panavision.

♫

The cliché that everyone knows is that an actor's life is all about walking; what no one ever mentions is how much waiting is involved. Frankie's days started early and ended late. She waited for the train in the morning and the train at night and, in between, she waited on long lines to get into public restrooms. She waited outside buildings and in grubby hallways, in musty stairwells where giant roaches crawled right next to you and you had to keep jumping up so that they wouldn't march into your bag and come home with you, and on hard seats in the tired old Equity lounge. If the call was uptown, she could wait a couple of hours at the library, where at least there was something to do besides listen to other actors talk about their showcases and their callbacks, their past glories and their near-misses. When she thought she could afford it, she had a bite to eat at Howard Johnson's or the nearest luncheonette; otherwise she'd grab a bag of chips to eat walking, or maybe take a break at the little place near Carnegie Hall that sold stale donuts and cheap coffee. Walking and waiting, that's what her days were like. And all the time lugging around a heavy dance bag full of headshots and resumes, paper and envelopes, copies of her monologues, sheet music, makeup, her hairbrush and curling iron, extra clothes if there were two auditions where you had to look different and, yes, all her dance gear.

Every week she read through the trades, looking for casting notices that said "Women 16–25." At first, she only considered roles she was positive she was right for: "kooky babysitter with a dark secret" or Viola in *Twelfth Night*. There weren't nearly enough of these to keep her busy. Anyway, who was she to guess what a director might be looking for? She started submitting herself for everything in the right age bracket unless it was impossible, like Afro-American or opera singer. It didn't help.

Without an agent, her best chance was to go to as many Equity open calls as possible. Everyone knew the good shows were mostly precast, only holding calls because the union required them; but sometimes smaller roles were still available, and there were always understudies. The bigger hope was that you could catch the eye of a casting director, who'd remember you for the future. It was a shot.

You had to show up at least two hours before the call was supposed to start and wait on line. Not to audition: to sign up for an audition slot. She'd learned that the hard way. She'd shown up a little before nine for her first couple of nine o'clock calls, and found the lines snaking around the block. By the time she'd reached the sign-in sheet, every last slot was taken. By taking earlier and earlier trains, she'd concluded that the two-hour window was her best bet. She still didn't make the very front of the line, but she was close enough to be sure of getting seen. They said you never wanted to be one of the last couple of auditions, either before lunch or at the end of the day, because whoever was seeing people would already be mentally halfway out the door. You also didn't want to be the first one or two after lunch, when they were probably sleepy from food. When Frankie was lucky, there'd be time available in the middle of the afternoon; since she had to leave home at 5:30 to sign up, it helped to be able to curl up on a couple of chairs in the lounge and take a nap before the actual audition.

Open calls meant killing pretty much a full day for the sake of three minutes. That didn't sound like much, but it was enough if you made the most of it. Sometimes it was only an interview but usually, unlike agency rounds, you got to show what you could do. They might give you sides to read. More often, you did a monologue. It was better to do a shorter monologue and leave them wanting more. A shorter monologue also left some time to talk. If you enjoyed talking to new people, like Frankie did, it was worth spending less time acting and more time making the person behind the table like you. They said connections got you the job and talent let you keep it. There was, Frankie had learned, as much auditioning folk wisdom as there were backstage superstitions.

A lot of the folk wisdom was around headshots. For example, a headshot had to be up to date so that, if you got called in, the director wouldn't be angry that you'd wasted his time. An agency in LA called this girl to be a stand-in for Susan Dey and found out she'd just cut off her long blond hair. Which she'd only done because the casting people kept telling her there were "too many Susan Dey/Peggy Lipton types" out there. They blackballed her, making such a stink that she decided to pack it up and come back east, at least until next pilot season when hopefully everyone would have forgotten. It was a true story. Frankie heard the girl herself telling it to friends who were looking at her new proof sheets. Headshots were very expensive, but they were probably the single most important tool an actor had. Frankie liked her own pictures a lot, which was good, since she couldn't afford new ones. A Toronto friend of one of the guys in *Mother Courage* had taken them during rehearsals. There were two poses: one with glasses, and one without. Donny said the one without made her look like that girl on *All My Children*, Season Hubely; but the one with the glasses felt more like her.

It was hard to believe, but those pictures were already two years old. Luckily, she didn't look much older and she still wore her hair the same way. Two years since *Mother Courage* and more than a year now since leaving NYADA, more than a year of open calls and mailings and knocking on doors, and what did she have to show for it? Crossing the street within earshot of Al Pacino? Playing the maid in *Gooseberries*? As Eunice loved to say, Frankie Cecchi was not exactly setting the world on fire.

She'd run into Cathleen Penney at Equity the other week. Cathleen said Wardell was doing his own version of *Uncle Vanya* this fall. You couldn't be more perfect for Sonja than she was, but he hadn't even given her a call. She knew she'd been good in *Gooseberries*. The reviewer for *Show Business* had even mentioned her by name: "brief but welcome appearances by the charming Frankie Cecchi..." And she'd been a diligent ASM, sweeping the floors, setting the props, running all their ridiculous errands. Guess she hadn't kissed ass enough. Or maybe there was something else Wardell had expected her to kiss. So much for the Soho Art Theatre.

It wasn't that she'd expected things to fall into her lap. Even at the time, she'd known that *Mother Courage* was almost miraculous. Frankie had expected rejection. What she hadn't expected was how hard it would turn out to be to get anyone to look at her long enough to reject her. She didn't mind paying her dues; she only thought that when you paid, you should get something in return. Like a callback; just for the ego boost. Was it always going to be so hard, or only while she was starting out?

"Frankie Cecchi," called the bored guy in the Todd Rundgren T-shirt. He pronounced it "Sechy" but he wasn't the first.

"Cecchi," she corrected, with a big smile, grabbing up her dance bag and patting her hair into place. She'd been waiting so long she'd forgotten what part she was submitting for. It was interview only, no monologue. As she passed the table, she threw a quick glance at the breakdown. That's right. "Carla. 18-22. Steve's girlfriend from home. Loves Steve but does not understand his new life. Understudy." Okay, so sweet and confused. Probably. Anyway, Sparkle Plenty.

♫

Maria's baby was cute, but phenomenally fussy. He screamed himself red in the face when Ahuva tickled him. It was mortifying; babies usually loved her! Maria was so cool; she laughed and said he did that all the time, that she hoped it didn't mean he was going to be a tenor. And she loved the blanket Ahuva had crocheted for him. It had been an unusually creative summer, between the blanket and her game for Marshall Berenson.

That game! Absolutely inspired! She'd had the hardest time coming up with a suitable way to say thank you for the lemonade and cookies. She'd wake up in the middle of the night, thinking about it. It was finally the *Times* interview that did it, the one where Marshall hinted that his new show had a connection with one of his hobbies. He wouldn't say which, but the reporter noted that he collected puzzles, games and boys' adventure books. Ahuva had no idea what boys' adventure books were, unless he meant comics, which seemed unlikely. Puzzles and games, however, were her hobby too. She doubted she could come up with a satisfactory puzzle for Marshall Berenson; the man was an absolute genius. Then the idea for Berensonopoly popped into her head and she immediately knew that it was perfect! She bought a real Monopoly set and carefully glued new labels on the board, naming the properties for locations in each of his shows, with "Moscow" and "The Lake" as Boardwalk and Park Place. The utilities were theatres, of course. The major challenge, but also the most fun, was coming up with clever ideas for Community Chest and Chance. She hand-wrote all the cards, using her new Rapidograph that drew a line as fine as an eyelash. Ahuva was pleased to have a legitimate reason to buy one. It was just like the one Deb used one for lighting plots. The writing took forever, but it was worth it: a labor of love and, if she did say so herself, absolutely stellar. She'd been proud to hand the box over to Jun. She still couldn't believe how boldly she'd marched up those stairs and knocked on the door. There hadn't been much choice. She wasn't about to leave her precious package on the stoop, not even in that fancy neighborhood.

"I'm sorry," Jun said. "Mr. Berenson is not at home right now."

It sounded so nice, like maybe Jun remembered her. She wasn't at all flustered. She acted so casual, saying that she was on her way to an engagement nearby and simply wanted to drop off a package. "Drop off" was an especially nice touch. Okay, "nearby" wasn't remotely true, but it made the whole thing sound better. She also liked the way she'd added, "Thank you so much, Jun" before turning to leave; and that she never looked back, but headed straight over to Maria's, to drop off her other package and have tea with Maria's sister-in-law's lemon squares. Which were stellar. Maria promised to send her the recipe.

All in all, today was a perfect day. Leaving Maria's, she decided to go to Lincoln Center. She could sit by the reflecting pool and enjoy the sunshine for a while before hitting the subway. She walked lightly, singing softly under her breath, reliving the highlights of the day. Which was probably why she didn't notice the man fall into step beside her, and why she let out a little yelp when the voice at her elbow said "Ahuva? Ahuva is that you?"

It was a familiar voice. She stopped short, her head swinging so quickly towards the sound that her earrings banged into her jaw. "Byron?!"

She was incredulous. It was Byron Weeks. In New York, in the flesh and just the way she remembered: Byron, in a white shirt and jacket; the same exact ones, if the rubbed collar and the sagging pockets were any way to judge. What used to look so smart had an air of sadness now. The same could be said of Byron's face: the droop at the corners of his eyes, the furrow across his forehead. He looked older and a little defeated.

"Oh, Byron!" She threw her arms around him, right there on the corner of Broadway and 67th Street, something she hadn't dared to do before, not even in the protective shadows of her own front door. He didn't pull away after all. "This is amazing! I can't believe it! I thought you were in…Europe." She realized she had no idea where he'd been. The postcard from Amsterdam had been followed by a Christmas card from Vienna and then silence.

"I got back in July. I guess I should have called…" He swallowed hard and fidgeted with the button on his jacket. "I've been…well…" He scratched his neck with the back of his middle finger. "You know how it is."

She didn't, not really. But he'd been the one to spot her on the street just now and call her name, so he must want to see her. The joy inside was too strong for her not to be magnanimous. "Do you have time for coffee?" she asked. "I know a good place not far." She spoke with confidence; she'd been to O'Neal's several times now.

"Okay." His smile still had a way of reaching inside her ribcage and squeezing at her heart.

She smiled back and extended her hand. He took it, standing an arm's length away, taking in every bit of her from head to toe.

"You look so different," he said. The note of admiration in his voice was thrilling.

Pleasantly self-conscious, she fingered the bead-tipped drawstring of her gauze tunic. "It's been an interesting year." She laughed, because it was such a cliché, but it was true. O'Neal's was nearly empty, except for two guys who had their heads together over a thick scatter of manuscript and an overflowing ashtray. Plunking herself down at a table, she waved a casual hand to indicate the brick walls and shellacked wooden tables and the mural of what she now knew were famous dancers. It was as bohemian as his Greenwich Village coffee house, but different, more modern.

"A lot of musicians come here. And ballet people, of course," she said, feeling worldly, and was pleased to see his look of respect.

Ahuva was still full from the lemon squares, but she ordered a portion of fries with her iced tea, to give them an excuse to linger. Byron ordered a beer and lit a cigarette. She coolly produced her own pack and held one out for him to light.

"You smoke?" Was it her imagination or did he sound disappointed?

Once they sat down, it was hard to get a word out of him. One thing that certainly hadn't changed was his reticence. He wanted her to do the talking.

So she did. She told him how dissatisfied she'd been with the education upstate and how she'd decided to come home and get some life experience. The best decision she could have made, she assured him, enabling her to immerse herself in theatre: in *Lake Song*, and her classes with Deb, and STC. She finally got to tell him about Mr. Gruen—Bert—turning out to be such a good friend of Maria's. She thought he'd like that, but it seemed to make him sad. So she rambled on enthusiastically about night school, about the English Lit class she and Ric were taking this fall and how she was also starting Spanish—so much more practical than the French she'd studied in high school. She described how the Maharishi, so phenomenally wise, had made her feel so welcome; and how stellar it had been to work for Lil.

"I'm looking for a new job now, maybe even full time. Abba said that if I want to experience real life, that includes being financially independent and not working at the store." And of course she told him about meeting Marshall Berenson.

She talked herself dry. They ordered a second iced tea, and a second beer for Byron, which finally loosened his tongue.

"Life agrees with you," he said. "I'm glad."

"I want to hear about yours," she insisted. "I was surprised you left Paris so quickly. I thought that was your dream."

"Yeah. It was. Jazz in Paris. I was going to be the next Bud Powell." He scratched his neck again, and lit a fresh cigarette. "Not the same Paris anymore. All politics. I ended up playing between shows at the Crazy Horse. It's like the Moulin Rouge, except the dancers wear even less. That's how I met Mirielle."

Ahuva must have looked shocked, because he chuckled.

"No, she's not a dancer. She's a concierge, at a hotel. She goes to all the shows to keep up with what's happening. She liked my sound. Long story short, she said I'd do better if I had a rep. Obviously, she knows a ton of people. She fixed me up with this guy in Amsterdam. Which was good for a while. But the clubs there. Too much junk around. I don't do well around junk." He grabbed his glass and took a deep swallow of beer. "I kept hearing Bert's voice in my head. So I got out. Took a gig in Vienna. And when that was done, moved up to Copenhagen. Lots of clubs there. But I couldn't seem to get started. It was wild. So I used my ticket home, before I was tempted to sell it. Gotta thank Bert for that. He's the one who bought me that ticket, you know."

She hadn't. One more amazing thing to know about Bert Gruen.

"Anyway, that's when I realized I didn't have a home. I couldn't come begging to Bert. I went down to Louisiana, to my dad. Been playing down there. I'm heading up to Alaska in a couple of weeks. I'm catching up on some sights before I take off. I'll be there two years."

"Alaska?!" she said. "Two years?"

"Yeah. The pipeline. A lot of jobs."

"Wait, you're giving up music?"

He laughed, the best laugh she'd heard out of him today. "No way! They've got a lot of bored guys up there, looking for entertainment. You can make good money. I got a contract to play with a band. Only I had to sign on for two years to get it."

She wrinkled her nose. It sounded dubious. "You're telling me the pipeline guys want to sit around listening to a jazz band?"

He shrugged. "Hey, you know me. I play anything. Mr. Versatility. That's how I got the job. We'll play whatever they want us to play. They'll probably care more about the singers anyway."

"As long as you're not giving up." She mustered as much enthusiasm as she could. "That's the important thing. You'll make some money, and it'll be a great experience. I've always wanted to see Alaska."

"Right. It's only two years, and then I can come back with a solid bankroll and give it a go here." He looked at her with sudden intensity. "I was going to call you, you know. If I hadn't run into you this way. It's really good to see you."

It didn't matter that she was wearing long earrings and sandals from West 8th street, that she'd drunk lemonade with Marshall Berenson and Lilith Brassloe had cooked her scrambled eggs, that she went to night school with adults and studied with a genuine Maharishi. When Byron looked at her like that, she blushed just as hard as she had in high school.

♫

Someone at Irene's had recommended a jazz class where the instructor was a former Dance Captain for Peter Gennaro. Kiki, a tiny Barbie in her ponytail and ballet pink leg warmers, pushed like a Marine sergeant. It was maybe the hardest class Frankie had ever taken in her life—worse than trigonometry— but she was determined to keep going. Last year she'd been too cowed to even try such a class. Gennaro leg extensions and Fosse hands and hips made no more sense to her body now, but she was tougher; she'd had some experiences.

Frankie knew things now. She knew dance was where the jobs were. Donny, when she was still talking to him, had called it "the *Chorus Line* effect," making it sound scientific. *Lake Song* had practically the only chorus on Broadway that wasn't packed with dancers-who-sing. It was smart business sense to focus on dance, her weak spot. Meanwhile, she had to hold on to what she'd accomplished with her voice. If any calls managed to crop up for actors-who-sing, Frankie was confident of doing well. She'd made big strides this year and, fuck you Donny, she wasn't about to lose them. She could forget about him, but she'd be an idiot to forget what he'd taught her; the jerk was a really good musical director. She'd do his vocal exercises to keep from slipping back. It was no easy task to find someone new to help her forward. The people with the great ads were either so intimidating that she could hardly open her mouth in front of them, or else they seemed totally crazy and Frankie was still too shaken from the Donny thing to want to deal with an out-and-out crazy. The guy Joe Bigelow recommended was amazing, but he was super expensive; definitely out of her league. She decided to save her money and keep asking around.

It was probably just as well. She couldn't afford any coaching right now. Her nest egg was dwindling fast enough as it was. Except for two last-minute fill-ins at Alfie's, Frankie hadn't earned a nickel since coming back from the beach. She was starting to worry. It helped to be able to confide in Connie dePaul. They were better friends than ever now.

Connie always got to the theatre by three o'clock on Tuesdays, to check the costumes that came back from the cleaners and any replacements the costume shop might deliver. She'd give the dressing room a thorough going over and stock up on whatever was running low. The Tuesday she'd returned from her brother's funeral in Boston, Frankie had baked some brownies and dropped them by. Connie had hugged her hard and invited her to share a brownie over a cup of tea in Bron's dressing room. Nibbling brownies on the flowered sofa, they'd talked about what it felt like to lose someone you loved, and why it hurt that people expect you to go back to normal almost instantly. It was a good talk. Frankie had always liked Connie, and Connie had always been extremely kind to her, but that talk made them solid friends. The following week, Frankie looked in after Kiki's class. They had a cup of tea while Connie worked. Connie said she needed some aspirin and thread. Happy to be helpful, Frankie ran out to Woolworth's. When Bron showed up with Ellen, Frankie said hello and waited in the hall until Ellen could leave. That was their routine for the next few weeks: Bron growing progressively paler and more vague; Connie ever more protective; and, Ellen, meeting over a grilled cheese somewhere or maybe some fries at Alfie's, getting edgier.

Then Bron had the breakdown. Frankie knew practically the moment it happened, because Ellen had called her, hysterical. She'd sat on the kitchen floor for more than an hour, listening, with Eunice stalking in every ten minutes to give her the evil eye. Next night, she stayed over in the city with Ellen and heard it all again. There wasn't a lot to tell. Bronwen Davies had honestly broken down, like a wind-up toy that completely unwound. She'd stopped. Said she couldn't do it anymore and sat in front of her makeup table, staring into space.

"Hardly blinking. Wouldn't answer if you called her name. Even Connie couldn't make her budge. A total head case. Scariest half hour of my life." Ellen said it without a trace of her usual relish, twisting that Egyptian ring of hers around and around until she rubbed her finger almost raw. "We finally told the Foxe, who got Nancy Pardoe ready. I was the one who had to call Ivor. Who called the car service. He had a list of things I should go back to the apartment and pack. He had *everything* prepared, just in case. Would have been nice to let me in on it, don't you think?" She laughed bitterly.

The next day it was in all the papers about Bronwen Davies having pneumonia: how she'd be out for a few weeks and that while she was out the part of Arkadina would be played by Madeleine Blair, who'd originated the role in London.

Frankie resolutely insisted Bron was only exhausted. That's all. Who wouldn't be, playing such a demanding role for almost two solid years without a break? "All she needs is a little peace and quiet," she assured Ellen.

"I wish I could be so positive," Ellen sighed.

Frankie had to be. In her hour of deepest need, Bron had been Frankie's lifeboat. Anything other than positive was unthinkable. She reminded herself that Ellen always exaggerated and was probably extra upset because of suddenly losing her job. She pushed all worry firmly out of mind, replacing it with a litany of select facts. How Bronwen made the first Debbie Webber movie only six months after James Lyttleton died. How she hadn't missed a single episode of *Our Bron*, not even when her son Richard was in that riding accident and had to spend a month in the hospital. It had been in all the magazines: proof, in print, that however fragile she seemed, Bronwen Davies was strong inside. And hadn't Ivor said that she would come back soon? Who knew her better than her own brother?

Bron would be fine. That was what Frankie said to Connie, who knew her longer and better than Ellen and whose care went deeper. She wrote it in a note. It seemed wrong to hang out backstage that week. Connie left a nice thank you message on her service. It ended "see you soon" so, after Kiki's the following week, Frankie picked up a package of Pepperidge Farm cookies and made her way to the Regale. Madeleine Blair had already arrived. The furniture was still the same. On the rack, Frankie spotted what looked like the familiar yellow garden dress, the Act II furs and the famous brilliant blue gown. When she took a really deep sniff, she caught a hint of Bron's Arpège. But the dressing room felt weird, sterile, as if no one lived there anymore. For one thing, there were hardly any flowers; only a single tall glass vase with five white calla lilies. Madeleine Blair had a superstition about them, Connie said, and had told her to expect a fresh bunch from the florist every Tuesday and Friday. The old bunches were to be disposed of so that Madeleine wouldn't see them wilt. Any flowers that people brought around to the stage door were to be collected and donated to St. Vincent's. In addition to the missing flowers, Bron's cards and pictures and all the little animals had been packed away. Madeleine Blair had brought only one personal touch: sitting on the shelf previously tenanted by Ellen's beautiful doll was a hat, perched on a stained old wig stand, protected by a Lucite box.

It was a little creepy. Frankie did her best Lucy grimace. "Eeewww."

"I know," Connie laughed.

Frankie was pleased. Connie probably needed a good laugh.

"Her mascot, she calls it. It belonged to someone. A strange name. I don't know. There's a label."

Curious, Frankie peered at the small brass tag and gasped. Nina Boucicault. "Oh my god! She was the first Peter Pan!" The very first Peter Pan ever, and that scrap of brown felt had once sat on her head. Now worshipful of this relic, Frankie stood on tiptoe and peered into the box. She supposed Madeleine Blair must have played the part when she was younger. It was a London actress thing. Frankie remembered the notices in Lil's scrapbooks. "Does Lil know this is here?"

Connie shrugged. "Miss Blair doesn't like to have people in the dressing room while she prepares. But they know each other, so maybe. Last night after curtain, Lil made a joke about feeling like she was back in the Haymarket."

Frankie was longing to touch the cap, but she didn't want to put Connie in a funny position by asking. Anyway, the Lucite box might not even open. "I would die to play Peter Pan," she sighed.

"I could see you in that," Connie agreed. "You'd be great."

Great nothing; she'd be perfect. It was a part she was born to play. Every time she opened the trades, she hoped to see a call for a production: for the musical, for the Barrie play, she didn't care which. No such luck. "I bet if I lived in London I'd do it someday. Maybe now. I'm a perfect age. I would probably be in rehearsal this very year, for Christmas. That's when they do it over there." She sighed. "Oh well. FAO Schwartz said last year they'd want me back. Maybe they'd let me be Peter instead of Raggedy Ann."

Connie nodded her approval. "I like how you do that, Frankie. Always find the silver lining. It's a good way to be."

"It feels better than the other way," Frankie said philosophically. "Anyway, it's the one acting job I'm almost positive I can get. There's nothing out there. None of Alfie's girls seem to be getting any shows either, which would make me feel better except if they did I'd at least get back some nights on the coat check."

"I'll keep my ears open," Connie promised. "And my offer still stands. I mean, if FAO Schwartz doesn't come through you could give it a try. I have a friend at City Ballet who always takes on a few extra hands during *Nutcracker* season. No strings attached. I might be there myself, if Blair decides to bring in her own girl when she comes back permanent."

Frankie still couldn't imagine ever wanting to be a dresser. It would be torture, hanging around backstage and helping other girls get ready to go on. But Connie's offer to help was the nicest thing in the world. Frankie threw her arms around Connie's neck and gave her a giant hug. "Madeleine Blair would be an idiot not to want to keep you. You're the best!"

Connie grinned. "Maybe you're a little prejudiced? Anyway, she's got a right. I always figured I had a 50/50 shot at getting renewed. My contract ends with Bron's." Her face, which had relaxed since Frankie's arrival, darkened again. "Damn, I'm so freaking worried about her. I tried calling, but they won't put anyone through. You'd figure Ivor would let me know what's what."

"They just want her to rest. She'll be fine," Frankie insisted stubbornly. "I know she will."

♫

Ellen had expected that Ivor would keep her on retainer while Bron was in the rest home. Either he was cheap, or famous theatrical designers don't make as much money as you might think. In any case, having unceremoniously dumped Nudler to take the job in the first place, in a season when her finances had to look particularly strong or she'd risk catching fresh hell from Harry and Sydelle about her refusal to continue college, she had nothing to fall back on except her once a week with Barney. A survey of everyone she could think to ask concluded that there were lots of fascinating opportunities if you could afford to volunteer, but nothing interesting that paid actual money. She knew she could tolerate the worst crap job if it were only for a few days. It would have to be the office temp route.

So here she was, with a resume that had taken some damned creative writing to come off sounding more like a seasoned office professional than a theatre-crazy kid. She'd slipped it into a leather folder that someone had once given Barney, keeping her hand over the liquor company emblem while she waited, so that no one would notice.

The seats here were terrifically uncomfortable, as if sitting in them was another test. If so, it was no less obnoxious than the typing test she'd already taken, or the little speed round to see how quickly she could alphabetize a list. She sat up straight, knees together and calves slanted, as Sydelle had taught her. Sydelle would probably be thrilled if she could see her daughter now. Ellen was wearing the stupid beige cotton shift Sydelle had insisted on for high school graduation. It was a personal brand of torture to squeeze into the underwire bra and suffocating pantyhose it required, but it was the only potentially secretarial garment Ellen owned, and even if she could afford to buy more she wasn't about to. She could wear the damned thing every day. She had plenty of scarves to vary the look, or she could belt a shirt over it and pretend it was a skirt. Hopefully she wouldn't have to wear it too often, not the dress and not the drugstore hairband that was holding back her hair, which she'd washed and blown almost straight. Together with the lipstick and eye shadow left over from Leonard's little venture into drag, it made her acceptably unexceptional. Catching sight of her reflection in the glass door, Ellen hated it. She wanted to tear off everything except for the impeccable Ferragamo pumps she'd found at the Opera Thrift Store. She tried to calm herself by admiring her legs in those pumps. Not bad at all; quality never let you down.

She toyed with her Cross pen and eyeballed the clock above the receptionist's head. Two hours already. How long before someone—not some flunky, but someone who had work to give out—would talk with her? Guess she wouldn't be working for pay today. It was too late to try another agency. She might as well wait it out here for another hour. She'd try somewhere else tomorrow.

She wished there were a magazine to read, or anything she could do besides stare at the walls. Bronwen Davies was lucky. At least in a sanatorium—or whatever euphemism they were using—there would be drugs.

Was that a heartless thing to say? Not really. Bron had scared the shit out of Ellen, freaking out like that and absolutely refusing to go on stage, terrifying and heartbreaking at the same time. But now the pressure was off, and Bron was in a quiet place with fresh air and people bringing her fruit. Ellen imagined a bare white room with clean linens, the windows open to a sun-washed lawn and the smell of something green. Contrasting that with this grimy waiting room and the distant sound of traffic, she could absolutely see the appeal of breaking down.

I prescribe a country scene as part of any worthy health regime... No, no need to worry about Bron in her nice, safe retreat. Ivor swore she'd be coming back, to see out her contract. She'd be the charming, flirtatious Bron again. She'd probably look younger, too. Ellen wondered if Ivor would have the balls to ask her to live in again. Fuck him!

She had to stop thinking about this; too much potential for anger, when she needed to stay calm and demure. She shifted in the hard chair. It would feel good to cross her legs, but the dress didn't cover her knees; she slanted her calves in the opposite direction.

She would think about Joe instead. He'd been very sweet to her, consoling. Tonight would be his first performance with Madeleine Blair. Was Nancy Pardoe pissed that they'd brought Blair in over her head? Ellen could understand the producers' reasoning: Blair was good box office, better than Bron, more of a movie star. The poor man's Elizabeth Taylor, Harry called her. Ellen was tempted to second act tonight, to see what Blair would do with the part. She was curious to see her, period.

"Miss?" chirped the poodle-headed receptionist.

It took Ellen a minute to realize that she was being called and haul herself out of the chair.

"Room B, Miss, right down the hall."

♬

"Keppel and Grace," Ellen repeated for the hundredth time that morning. "Franklin Li's office." She knew her voice had a tendency to blare. She struggled to keep it low and pleasant. Control was essential if she was going to stick out the two weeks, and she very much wanted to. The job paid more than decently. Not only that, the agency would owe her for saving their skin with an important client. She'd gotten lucky.

The agency had told her plainly: Ellen's experience did not qualify her as a legal secretary, however this was in the nature of an emergency. Keppel and

Grace, a venerable client, had regretfully dismissed the excellently qualified young lady they'd originally provided, due to her decided Bronx accent. It was not a voice that would do for Keppel and Grace. So said Old Mr. Keppel, when he happened to hear her answer the junior partner's phone. The old man, whose dictates of taste ordinarily remained up in Pound Ridge where they could be safely ignored, had stopped by the office on his way to lunch at the Yale Club. The timing was unfortunate. The agency's best girls—and yes, the girdle-armored virgin who'd turned up her nose at Ellen's resume called them "girls"—the cream of the crop were already booked for the week. With only the implied bottom of the barrel to scrape, the agency decided Ellen "sounded cultivated." With the message "beggars can't be choosers" stamped across her face, the agency spinster deigned to send Ellen to Keppel and Grace on approval. To Ellen's pleased surprise, the law firm approved.

Ellen was doubly pleased because Franklin Li assisted senior partner Sullivan Grace who, it turned out, loved theatre and enjoyed dabbling as a matchmaker between shows and the potential angels among his clients. Grace's clients were the sort of families that had "places" in Newport and Paris and sat on the boards of operas and museums. Families whose mothers and wives, odds were good, had been through Fetherston, which was probably the reason the firm's HR had given her a thumbs up. In the beige dress and with the odd shyness that possessed her whenever she was out of her element, Ellen seemed like the real deal, "a Fetherston girl." Which goes to show how no experience is ever a waste.

She only had to keep up the act until Li's regular secretary got back from vacation. Aside from keeping her voice down, it really didn't take much effort. Despite the agency bitch's forebodings, Ellen was perfectly competent to handle the work. Summer was quiet. Anything complicated, Li instructed, could wait for Adele's return. Ellen mostly had to handle the phones and do some light typing. There was occasionally a little steno, about the same as she used to do for Felix; much of the vocabulary was the same, too, so that was a piece of cake. And by keeping her eyes and ears open, by using the quiet hours to read through the files, she was learning things.

As soul-selling bourgeois jobs went, this one was pretty good. She wouldn't mind coming back here next time Adele went away, or covering for other secretaries. She made a point of being extra helpful with things like making coffee and keeping an ear out for the phones when someone took a toilet break, and she made certain to learn the names of all the partners so that she could greet them by name with a smile. Not her usual overtly seductive smile, but a new one she created on the spot, a smile that was utterly respectful but had an almost imperceptible sideways curve and was paired with briefly lowered eyes, implying she might be more interesting after five o'clock.

Leonard almost peed himself laughing when she demonstrated it, but he agreed that was only because he knew what a crock it was. "So, what does Franklin Li think?" he asked, putting a hmmm on the end of the phrase. He knew her so well.

Ellen wasn't about to deny it: she was definitely attracted to Franklin Li. It was natural to fantasize about that slim athletic frame, which he set off in suits that draped as elegantly as those of an Italian movie star. And he was Chinese; born and raised in San Francisco, but still exotic; she'd never had sex with someone who wasn't white. Moreover, he was already proving extremely useful. Yesterday, he'd capped off her first week by asking her to sit in on a meeting with Gloria Korn, one of the top press agents in the business. Possibly the very top. Felix hadn't been able to afford her, not even after charming her into reducing her fee. Li wanted Ellen in the meeting to take notes. That usually means to be as invisible as possible, but he'd gone out of his way to introduce her to Korn by name. When Korn called to thank him for sending over the transcription so quickly, Li had credited Ellen and mentioned that she was a temp. Korn said she might need some help soon. He asked Ellen if she would be interested in having him pass along her number.

Ellen was extremely grateful, as she told him in the most demure way possible. Monday morning, she planned to leave a breakfast treat on his desk, maybe something fancy from Zabars. She was determined to thank him more thoroughly after Adele was back. The minute she left Keppel and Grace with a spotless reputation, she was jumping Franklin Li's bones.

♫

Ahuva tried to explain it to Ric. "The main thing is intent, to form the correct intent in your mind. Which is why I asked for translations. Not because you need to understand every word. You don't. After you repeat it enough times, it sounds like nonsense anyway. The way it makes you feel is mind blowing, especially the one we chant together to start the meeting. The sound vibrates off your bones, especially your ribs and the bridge of your nose." She lifted her hand to her sternum, remembering that feeling, and smiled blissfully. "Maybe it's the way the Maharishi has us breathe. You know how singers and dancers talk about their instruments? The way they call their bodies their instruments? I always thought that was pretentious. I never felt the truth of it, not even when we had that chorus director at All-City who'd gone to Julliard. The sound resonates and then it pours out…I feel myself letting go of everything. All that pain I felt upstate…" She grimaced extravagantly. There was no need for further explanation. She'd long since told Ric the whole story of what she referred to as her "moment of truth." "I can completely let go of that now and embrace all the wonderful things that have happened since I came back to the city. Everything I have now: *Lake Song* and STC…and you…" she flicked him an adoring glance from under her eyelashes.

He noticed. "Look, Ahuva. I think we need to talk." He seemed so dark and serious.

"Okay." In her own ears, her voice sounded very small.

"Yeah." He craned his neck, looking for something. A place to pull over, as it turned out. He made a sharp left into the driveway of the church with the red door, and shifted into park. "Okay."

He left the engine idling. He wasn't expecting it to be a long talk. Whatever it was about. Ric cleared his throat. He knocked a cigarette out of the pack and lit it off the dashboard lighter.

Ahuva kept her eye on the dull red glow, not daring to break the silence.

"Shit," he said, blowing a stream of smoke through his teeth. "Look, there's no way to say this without sounding like an asshole. I get the feeling you may have gotten the wrong idea. Maybe I gave you the wrong idea, I don't know. I really like you, Ahuva. You're a good kid. I'm glad we've become friends. But I think you want something more and, well, it's not going to happen. Damn, I really suck at this."

He took another deep drag, burning enough ash that he had the excuse of turning towards the open window for a moment to flick it out. It wasn't long enough. When he turned back, she still hadn't moved. She couldn't. If she did, she might break into pieces.

The silence was uncomfortable enough that Ric couldn't stand it. He cleared his throat again. "Hey, it's not about you. It's about me. Bad timing. That's what it is." He tapped on the steering wheel for emphasis. "Bad timing. I like you. Who knows if maybe…but like I said, I'm already with someone."

Her heart began to beat again. Bad timing was an understatement. Horrible timing. Lethal timing. If only she'd met him sooner…"I feel so stupid," she mumbled fiercely. If they were closer to home, if they weren't on an unlit side street, she'd jump out of this car.

"Don't."

Did he have to look at her right now? It was his eyes that always grabbed at her insides and squeezed. They held so much sorrow, as if he'd seen more than a person ought to see in the world. "Well I do," she snapped. "And I'm sorry I make you uncomfortable."

"You don't." He put a hand on her shoulder. She wished he hadn't. It felt too good; her body didn't yet know she'd been rejected. "I'm the one who's sorry. I don't want to hurt you. I really like you…"

"Would you stop saying that?!" She couldn't hold back the words, but she could push that hand away. "Can we please get out of here? I would really like to get home."

He flicked the cigarette out the window and shifted the car into reverse. "Look, I understand if maybe you won't want to hang out much for a while. But I'm hoping we can still be friends. And no, I'm not just saying that. We *are* friends, Ahuva. You just need some time."

She tried to imagine that much time and failed. Time. If you'd asked her half an hour ago, she would have said that life, while not perfect, was certainly on the way up. Now someone had crashed the whole light board. You can't be angry that someone doesn't feel the same way you do. She looked for something that she *could* be angry about; she needed to. "You never said you had a girlfriend. You never even say 'we' all the time."

He wasn't quite near enough for her to feel it, but she could sense his shrug. "You're right. I guess it's still too new."

How new? Maybe if she'd spoken up sooner…

It was as if he'd read her mind. "It was right before I got to know you. And it happened so fast. It's been a few years since I'd been in a relationship, but the minute I met Jay…"

"Jay?!" She was incredulous. "You and Jay??! You mean you're…Oh my god, I am such an idiot!" She raced through her memories, trying to find a clue. There wasn't one. Ric was so…masculine. He'd been a soldier, he hiked. There was his story about some older woman who'd taken him on a yacht. Unless it hadn't been a woman at all. Had that been wishful thinking on her part, twisting the facts? No, she could swear he'd used the name "Rosemary." No man was ever named Rosemary. "What about Rosemary?" she blurted.

"She was something else," he laughed.

He laughed, damn it! "But you just said you're…" she couldn't make herself say the word.

"That's a label," he said calmly. "I don't believe in labels. You shouldn't either. Especially not when it comes to love. You love who you love. I wasn't looking for a man to fall in love with. I fell in love with a person, Jay, who happens to be a man. If Jay was a woman, I'd still be in love with him."

It sounded very beautiful, and someday maybe she'd be able to appreciate the sentiment, but right now it was all she could do to keep herself from bursting into tears. She didn't say another word, until the car pulled up in front of her building.

He didn't either, not until she grabbed her shoulder bag and popped open the door. He leaned across the seat as she got out, so he wouldn't have to raise his voice for her to hear him. "See you in class next week. Okay? Please, Ahuva, just tell me you're okay."

She managed to close the door without slamming it. "Fine. I'm fine. And I hope you and Jay will be very happy together." She felt proud of that

Almost as dignified as Kaye Victor's Masha, she walked stiffly up the brick paved path, opened the glass door to the lobby, and made the turn for the elevator. Finally out of sight of the street, she leaned against the mailboxes for a couple of minutes and sobbed until she thought she'd vomit. When she could catch her breath again, she rang for the elevator, hoping she could hold it together long enough to get to her bedroom and lock the door.

For days afterward, Ahuva felt as if her whole body had a charley horse. When Malke questioned her red eyes, she claimed she'd caught a cold that was going around STC. Which was a double lie because she wasn't even at STC. They said they didn't need her. *Hedda Gabler* was a small show. Deb's classes were building the set and hanging lights. They'd set it in the 1950s, so the costumes were coming from the Salvation Army. Until it was time to usher, there was nothing she could do. But since Malke and Jakub didn't know this, Ahuva pretended she still had to run down to the theatre. What she did instead was hang out at the Lincoln Center library and listen to old original cast albums. With those big, heavy headphones they had, you could brood by yourself no matter how many other people were around.

Ahuva needed some time alone for a while—utterly, inviolably alone— because disappointment came in what her father, who didn't gamble much but loved watching the horses, called a "trifecta": Ric's disclosure, hiatus from STC and...drumroll please...Marshall Berenson's thank you note. Oh, it was a perfectly lovely note, especially when you think how busy he must be. It's impressive that someone like Marshall Berenson writes thank you notes at all. A lot of famous people would have had their secretaries send her an autographed photo. It was probably a secretary who'd typed this one, but she knew it was his real signature because she'd seen his autograph on the rare

Riding a Bicycle poster they had on the wall at Colony. Even if it was a secretary, he must have dictated it, seeing as it was clearly meant for her.

"Dear Miss Geffner, What an exceedingly thoughtful gift! I'm honored that my work could have inspired the tremendous care and effort you took in devising this game. Thank you so much. With best regards, Marshall Berenson." She could tell he'd really liked it. That should make her feel good. It was only a downer because…because she'd hoped he'd remember who she was. The card she'd included had carefully mentioned Lil and the lemonade. She'd wanted him to say…oh, she didn't know! Something like "Dear Ahuva, I so enjoyed our lively, intelligent conversation. Every time I play Berensonopoply, it will remind me of you." Had she possibly, deep in the back of her head, hoped he would invite her to come over and play it with him? She couldn't have honestly imagined she was going to be friends with Marshall Berenson?! Get real! Of course not! That was total fantasy and she knew it. She'd made the game because she wanted to thank him for being so special. That was all. And yes, she wanted to think she was a little special herself. It had been a great conversation. He'd said it himself, that she'd made some excellent observations. Wouldn't he remember that? She would never forget it.

Why couldn't she be happy with that memory and a nice thank you note? Or with having Ric as a friend? Why did she always want more? It hurt to want. Maybe if she listened to the Maharishi long enough she could change that about herself and find peace inside herself, like Kaye.

It was too bad not to be able to hang out with Kaye right now, but that was gone too. Kaye had regretfully informed her that she couldn't afford to keep paying for her services. She was tightening her belt to save up for when the show closed.

"Eventually closes," she'd hastened to assure Ahuva. "Nothing on the horizon. The box office is doing great. But nothing lasts forever, and the best part of a long run is that I have a chance to put money aside so I can spend a few months at the ashram after."

The ashram was where the Maharishi lived when he was in India. It was a monastery. Or was it a school? Ahuva didn't completely understand the concept, except that people went there to meditate. Kaye had been there before, more than once. It would be selfish to resent Kaye for wanting to return to a place that made her so happy; the woman absolutely shimmered when she talked about it. Ahuva would miss being able to hang out at the apartment, but at least she'd still see Kaye at the Maharishi's.

It was the other thing that had stabbed her in the heart; that was, on top of the "trifecta," the icing on the cake. Or did she mean the final straw? It was phrases like this that could remind her she was a foreigner in this language, no matter how broad her vocabulary and how neutral her accent. Instead of springing naturally to her lips, sayings like these always stopped her in her tracks. Did icing on the cake, like whipped cream and a cherry on top, always have to mean super terrific? What about the cake from *Peter Pan*, the one Captain Hook sang about? That icing was poison. That was a clever song, not as clever as Marshall Berenson of course, but impressive the way it twisted something that could have been ugly into something funny. Hook's songs were all in dance rhythms. That was clever, too. The cake song was a tango. Maybe she should turn her life into a song and call it "The Last Straw Tango." If she could find the humor in it, maybe she could diffuse the dark cloud. So very dark, from that one final thing that she'd never thought of before but which, once Kaye said it, she couldn't get out of her head: someday *Lake Song* would close.

♫

Gloria Korn was a powerhouse. She always answered her own phones—both of them sometimes, with one receiver under her chin and the other held up to her ear so she could listen in on one conversation while putting in her two cents elsewhere. She had a bookkeeper who came in occasionally and a "girl," old enough to be her mother, who came in for twice-weekly half-days to handle correspondence and contracts; not enough to keep up with the volume of work that passed through the office. Gloria's son Pete used to help out but, as his mother couldn't help repeating almost constantly, he was up in Ithaca this fall, at Cornell Law. Gloria hadn't gone to college herself. To have a son who'd graduated City College Phi Beta Kappa and was now in one of the top law schools in the country was more than a Jewish mother could handle without bursting. Without Pete, Gloria's papers piled up faster than they could be filed, the changes to Gloria's calendar never made it into her tax diary, and they were always running out of coffee and Kleenex. What was worse was that Gloria had lost her one reliable sounding board for copy. She'd tried to fill Pete's shoes with a journalism student from Columbia, but the boy had been shit, so concerned with rules of usage that he lost the point of communication, and he'd been completely unwilling to stand on the passport line at Rockefeller Center. Gloria dumped him after a month, deciding she would to learn to live without—as soon as she cleared up this mess. Franklin Li assured her his girl learned fast and worked hard; in a few weeks, Gloria would be able to see the surface of her desk again.

On Ellen's first day, Gloria sent her to over to Rockefeller Center. Ellen asked if there was anything helpful she'd be able to do while she was waiting on line—proofreading, for example. With an approving nod, Gloria handed her an envelope of soft pieces she was preparing for a musical that was on the way down from New Haven: a couple of fake interviews with the composer and the leading man, and a few paragraphs about the show's inspiration.

Three hours later, Ellen brought them back, red-pencilled, along with a receipt from the passport office. Gloria put her hand over the receiver of the phone she was currently working and pushed back the receipt. "Thanks, hon. How about you keep this. Start looking through that pile by the window and pull out any others you find. My bookkeeper's coming on Wednesday. Why don't you take lunch first? You can pick me up some cottage cheese on your way back." She fished in her handbag for a dollar bill.

As soon as Ellen finished one task, Gloria came up with the next. Nothing thrilling, but at least the day was busy.

Gloria stayed on the phone most of the day, even while forking cottage cheese into her mouth. Around 4:30, having laughed loudly during most of this particular conversation, she slammed down the phone. She stood, slowly, making a big show of getting the kinks out of her neck and wiggling her fingers. She saw Ellen watching her and winked.

"You'll see, when you're my age. The bones get stiff from sitting all day. Time for a little break." She produced a bottle of scotch from a bottom desk drawer and poured some into the coffee mug she'd been using all day, then held out the bottle to Ellen. "You too, hon." She cast an appraising look around the room. There were still piles and piles of paper, but they seemed significantly neater. "Franklin's right. You're quick. You got a lot done today."

Ellen felt herself flush. It was such brainless work that she hadn't expected any applause. She got a paper cup from the water cooler and brought it over. Gloria poured in a generous slug and gestured for her to sit.

"Chin chin," she said, lifting the mug in salute before taking a sip.

"Chin chin," Ellen echoed. She pushed over the bookkeeper's chair and took a seat.

"So, your first day. Got any questions hon?"

Ellen cleared her throat, hoping she wouldn't sound stupid or pushy. "Was my proofreading okay?"

"Right, almost forgot." The envelope sat, untouched, exactly where Ellen had placed it. Gloria flashed a token smile and shook the paper out.

Ellen sipped cautiously at her scotch, glad she'd trained herself to drink it neat. She tried not to stare at Gloria, ripping through the pages at the speed of Evelyn Wood.

When Gloria was done, she set the papers down on her desk and gave Ellen a considering look. "Interesting. You ever done any writing yourself, hon?"

The next day, Ellen brought in the reviews she'd written for the *Fetherston Inquirer*.

Gloria gave Ellen a handful of names, celebrities with whose agents she had reciprocity deals, and asked her to come up with a few lines for each that could be planted in Earl Wilson's column, showing them being enthusiastic about one of three shows on Gloria's client list. One of those shows, ironically, was *Lake Song*, and one of the celebrities was an actor who'd famously played opposite Madeleine Blair.

That made it easy: "Seen at the Regale Theatre—everyone's favorite Detective DaVinci, the dashing Edwin Tomlinson, taking time out from filming to admire the performance of his *Bedford Square* co-star, the luminous Madeleine Blair, as Arkadina in *Lake Song*. Blair, you will recall, is playing the role as a special favor while her dear friend Bronwen Davies continues to recover from her battle with pneumonia."

"On the right track," Gloria said, knocking back her third black coffee in as many hours. "Got it all crammed in there. Gossip columns only have so many inches, right? So we make it even more compact. Tomlinson's people only care we give a boost to the next one of those damn Italian detective movies. Check. So what is it *we* want to say? 'See Madeleine Blair in *Lake Song*.' Period. The Regale goes without say. And we cut 'as Arkadina.' It's the show we represent, not the actors."

Ellen nodded, paying close attention. She would learn things here. Damn, she hoped this lasted longer than the month or two Gloria'd promised.

Gloria noted the intensity of Ellen's focus and was pleased. "Now we move things around, see how we can still say all of this while keeping down the character count." Ellen watched over her shoulder as she red-pencilled the copy: circling, crossing out, moving things around with arrows. Gloria frowned and hummed and finally blew out a grunt of satisfaction. She jotted down a fresh paragraph and slid the paper over to Ellen, who read it carefully aloud.

"Fresh from the set of his latest film, dashing Edwin 'Detective DaVinci' Thomlinson was spotted catching his *Bedford Square* love Madeleine Blair in

Lake Song, a limited engagement while Tony winner Bronwen Davies recovers from her battle with pneumonia."

Ellen read it carefully aloud. Feeling more than a little disloyal, she asked "If we don't represent the actors, then why did you leave in the part about Bronwen Davies? It makes it a lot longer."

Gloria gave another nod of approval. "That's right. If I were sending it to anyone else, I'd probably cut it. Or I'd expect them to. But this is going to Earl, and he has a thing for her. He'll probably leave it in and drum up some sympathy for the poor bitch. I like your 'battle' by the way. Nice touch, implies she's fighting for her life. It'll help with the box office when she comes back. Also why we replace 'dear friend' with 'Tony winner.' People don't buy tickets for friends, they buy for winners." She watched with pleasure as Ellen digested this dictate and accepted it.

The little alarm clock on the desk shuddered into frenzy, brassy bells tinkling like a shower of coins. Gloria jumped up and grabbed her bag. She was running up to New Haven, to see the incoming musical. "I'll look at the others on the train. We'll go over them together tomorrow morning. You're doing good, hon."

The door closed behind her. Ellen stood stock still, but inside she was jumping up and down, as giddy as if she'd had two vodka martinis on an empty stomach. As if she'd won something big. Not a lottery. Something that took skill to figure out. Poker. No, she thought hilariously: *Bezique!*

She shouted the word into the empty room, then broke down giggling. She was doing good!

Even the part about Bron, which she'd come so close to not putting in. Gloria had actually liked it. Ellen was glad. She'd had to push Bron out of her mind to focus on her own situation. Writing the *Lake Song* plug, she'd felt a pang of guilt that she could forget so easily. It was Ivor she was angry with, not Bron. It wasn't Bron's fault that she hadn't turned out to be so glamorous close up. Now that Ellen didn't have to fetch and carry and lose sleep over the woman, she could remember what a crush she'd had at first. She liked thinking she could still be helpful.

However, she sternly warned herself, she couldn't let herself get sucked in again, not to Bron's drama or to anyone else's. The Bron thing had been like Felix all over again. Love turned you into an idiot and took away your power. Ellen had always known this, but she'd made the mistake of thinking she only had to worry about the kind of love that could be confused with lust. Loving theatre was much more dangerous.

This was what made Gloria such a revelation. Gloria liked theatre. It was clear she enjoyed the hell out of it. She wallpapered her toilet with *Playbill* covers, for fucks sake! But Gloria didn't let it take over her life; she was the one in control. Like Ellen was with Barney Black. Now that was an excellent relationship, clean and satisfying on both parts, everyone getting what they wanted. What Gloria could teach her was how to make this work for theatre. No, not theatre: show business; which wasn't about love but, just like sex, about selling and bartering and coming out ahead, and Ellen had been given a golden opportunity to learn how.

She would start by going through Gloria's old tear sheets, getting a feel for how to write a press release. They were so banal, nothing but stringing together bald facts. But the more of them she read, the more she respected the craft. It took discipline to resist flowery language and squeeze all the information into the accepted formula. It was a skill she knew she could easily master.

Time to go home. Ellen made a quick circuit of the room. She put the cover over the typewriter and made sure all the file cabinet drawers were closed. She threw Gloria's half-eaten morning corn muffin into the same garbage bag as the wrapper from the bookkeeper's egg salad sandwich, to take downstairs. Gloria was clear about putting the food trash out every night; the building had mice. Didn't every building in this neighborhood? The glamor of show business. She collected two mugs and a tumbler, to pour out the dregs and wash off the lipstick stains in the little sink in the toilet. She needed this job to last. She would work her ass off, make Gloria see she simply couldn't function without Ellen Janow.

Ellen owed Franklin Li big time for this one. She was looking forward to paying him back, but had promised herself not to push too fast. Tonight, they would have a very civilized dinner at the Oak Room, one of his favorites. She would accept his offer of a taxi, and would add a little tongue and pelvis to their goodnight kiss before she got in. That would be enough for a first date. Whether it was being Chinese or because he was a posh attorney, Li was an old-fashioned kind of polite. A gentleman. She would enjoy leading him astray, and she would prolong the enjoyment by going at his pace. She returned to the sink to put on some lip gloss. It would be unsettling enough for Franklin Li that she wasn't wearing that beige linen dress. She wondered how far she should pull down the zipper on her jumpsuit.

23 – A WOMAN LOVES

POLINIA [*spoken: Give a woman a kind glance sometimes, Kostia, and she won't ask for more. I know that....My heart aches for you, Mashenka*]

I see it all, you know, my love; I
  understand.
You're not the only girl who ever built
  her castles out of sand.
I have walked this road before you,
  as did others before I.
Listen to the lessons of our
  sisterhood. Don't cry.
It isn't time that dulls the pain or
  stops the screams.
No life will ever grow if all you choose
  to nurse are broken dreams.
There's a gift in keeping busy, in
  avoiding empty time.
Listen to the wisdom of your mother,
  love. Just try.

A woman thinks;
A woman keeps her nose in books
And still she tries to keep her looks.

MASHA

A woman thinks;
And if her thoughts lead her astray
A woman tries to melt away.

POLINA/MASHA

A woman does the best she can;
It's not as though she were a man.

MASHA

Imagine the freedom, the luxury of choice!

POLINA

You must hold yourself together,
Keep a firm grip on your hopes.

POLINA/MASHA

Love must never shake your purpose.
If it sneaks in, you must

POLINA

Hide it.

MASHA

Chuck it out.

POLINA

A woman winks;
A woman putters in the yard
And plays a wicked game of cards.

MASHA

A woman drinks;
And if the vodka doesn't numb,
She can resort to laudanum.

POLINA/MASHA

A woman does the best she can;
It's not as though she were a man.

MASHA

Imagine the freedom, the luxury of choice!

POLINA

You must hold yourself together,
Keep a firm grip on your hopes.

POLINA/MASHA

Love must never shake your purpose.
If it sneaks in, you must

POLINA

Hide it.

MASHA

Chuck it out.

MASHA [*spoken: If only I didn't have him constantly in front of me. Just let them give my Semion his transfer. You'll see how quickly I forget all this nonsense.*]

Frankie got out of bed, took a shower and dressed, all before she put the kettle on for tea. It was an electric kettle. Frankie wondered why she hadn't seen one before. Such a smart idea, like an electric frying pan except to boil water. She made tea the way Lil had taught her: swilling out the pot, to warm it; throwing in a handful of leaves—Ceylon, instead of Lil's earthier Irish Breakfast blend—and pouring a careful stream of hot water to ensure they were thoroughly wetted before the rest of the pot was filled. Almost immediately, the leaves released their fragrance. She breathed it in happily. While the tea steeped, she poured milk into the little pitcher and set it on the napkin-lined tray together with the sugar bowl, the cups, saucers and spoons, and a delicate silver strainer shaped like an open flower. Nudging the bedroom door open with her foot, she carried in the tray and set it at the edge of the bed. When she drew the curtains and let in the light, Bronwen Davies would wake up.

Bron...Frankie had started out respectfully saying "Miss Davies" but it turned out she really did prefer to be called Bron...Bron liked to have company while she ate, even if it were only her morning "eye-opener," but "felt peculiar" if the other person was watching her, so after the first morning Frankie knew to bring two cups. While they drank their tea, they talked about the show or shared backstage gossip. Then Frankie made breakfast while Bron washed and dressed. Routine was important. They would spend a quiet day together, until it was time to go to the theatre and Connie.

Frankie was very grateful to Connie for recommending her for the job. She wondered if Ivor had offered it to Ellen first. Probably not. Ellen would have said. Anyway, even if Ellen weren't working for Gloria Korn she would have turned it down. It was understandable. The way Ivor had let her go was kind of disgusting. Before saying yes and missing out on FAO Schwartz, Frankie had carefully confirmed with Connie that she would be kept on for the rest of Bron's time on *Lake Song*. Connie must have had a word with Ivor, because he said how much he appreciated her "giving up other work to help out Bron" and said how much he hoped she would "join the family" for Thanksgiving and for the party that weekend after Bron's last show.

Once the terms were clear, Frankie dismissed any other concerns raised by Ellen's stories. Everyone knew how Ellen exaggerated. Bron wouldn't have left the rest home if she didn't feel up to it, right? And how wonderful not to have to deal with Eunice or the LIRR for more than a month.

Either the rest had done the trick, or maybe Frankie, who'd lived with a sick mother, was better suited to give Bron what she needed than Ellen had been. What had Ellen expected from the poor woman? Bron was lovely. As for being a dumb blonde, she read the newspaper every day—with her glasses and a large Sherlock Holmes style magnifying glass. Ellen was right about her being blind as a bat without her glasses; also about the wigs. Okay, so Ellen was right about some things, but not everything; not about what was important. What was important was that Bronwen Davies was exactly the way Frankie had always hoped she would be. Not exciting, just nice.

Frankie was enormously content to putter around the apartment, help answer fan mail, and make comforting small talk over meals. She went days at a time without ever thinking about that asshole, Donny. She had to forget about auditioning, of course, that would take too many hours; but Bron had no problem with Frankie going to her dance classes. Bron got a big kick out of Frankie taking tap, even showing her the soft shoe routine she'd had to learn for *The Fabulous Flanagans*. That was the movie Frankie's dad had taken her to see the Christmas after her mother died. It was one of those movies that was supposed to make you feel like anything was possible: a family, having lost everything they had in a horrible fire, went on to become famous in vaudeville. It was a true story. The father was Donald O'Connor, so you had to love him, even though the fire had been his fault. And Bron, naturally, was the mother. The beginning of the movie had been too sad for Frankie that year, especially the scene where Maggs, the oldest daughter, found out her pony had been killed. You didn't see it happen, but there was this long close-up of Lesley Ann Warren trying to be brave; Frankie had known exactly how she felt. The movie got better once the little brother met the juggler and the whole family turned out to be able to sing and dance, but it still wasn't a great choice for her and Mickey that year. She didn't tell Bron that, of course. She told a little fib about how much she'd enjoyed it. When Bron offered to show her the dance, however, her enthusiasm was completely honest.

She was living her childhood fantasy, almost. It was as if Bronwen Davies really was...well, not her mother, but maybe like a godmother. Or an aunt, like Annie Fallon. Frankie was sorry that it would end with Thanksgiving. She would have been happy to do this forever.

♫

Ahuva printed the name neatly on the slip of paper and clipped it to a pair of tickets that she stuck in the slot with the other reserved tickets for Thursday night. It was a familiar name; not famous, but she'd seen him act on Broadway. There were a lot of familiar names calling in for tickets. *Hedda Gabler* had been so well received that STC was talking about extending the run. That was great for STC. It wasn't so great for Ahuva. Oh, they were super grateful to have her help, but only to handle reservations at the box office. This was basically the same thing she was doing three days a week for Mr. Nudler, which was not what she'd had in mind when she'd thought of working in the Theatre. It was one thing to do it for money, but as a volunteer, she deserved to be doing something more exciting. Even ushering would have been more stimulating, but the show was so popular that every unemployed actor in New York was volunteering to usher so they could see it for free and maybe connect with a company that was suddenly on the rise.

She felt itchy from disuse. It would be better once Maharishi Narang got back from India. Her practice didn't go nearly as well when one of the more advanced *adhiyanas* led the meetings. She chanted until she was blue in the face, but it didn't make her feel the least bit serene. When she was near the Maharishi, she could embrace the flow of life. Without his benevolent presence, acceptance was unacceptable. She was counting the days. Breathing into her sternum, Ahuva tried to fix on a Peaceful Image.

After this run, STC was staging *Iphegenia*. Surely such a big production would have work that would let her feel she was part of making the show happen. Too bad Deb only taught those two classes; if there were a third one, Ahuva would have taken it. She'd deliberately hung around the other night, when Deb was giving her latest Intro to Theatre class the grand tour. Her hope was that Deb would give her some support, or maybe even tell her about another theatre where she could volunteer. Deb was friendly enough when she went to say hi, but impersonal. They talked a little, but Deb's eyes were all the while fixed on the back of the house. Ahuva followed them to where the Intro to Theatre people were waiting for their instructor. One of the girls felt them looking, grinned and waved. Deb's face it up; she laughed and mimed five minutes. The girl blew her a kiss.

Ahuva felt obscurely angry. She was so tired of being surrounded by public displays of affection. Even the constant implication. Ever since coming clean about Jay, every sentence out of Ric included "us" and "we." Their English Lit class was torture. At least Ric wasn't actually in her Spanish class, though she couldn't stop thinking about him when she was speaking Spanish. Honestly, she could hardly wait for this semester to be over.

Was everyone a couple except her? Kaye wasn't, but Kaye preferred to stay celibate to reserve her energies for Art. Ellen found this hysterical, saying all the theatre people *she* knew did just the opposite. By now Ahuva knew Ellen well enough to feel a little cynical about comments like this. Surely not everyone in theatre *fornicated like rutting dogs*. That was a Kostia line. Kostia resented theatre, but Ahuva loved it. All she needed was to find the way for it to love her back. Was that so unreasonable? Loving Byron, even though she knew he felt something in return, was loving a dream. She'd thought her love for Ric could be real, and look what happened. Ahuva was 19 already. If she couldn't have someone of her own to love, couldn't she at least have some*thing*?

♫

I left the Helen Hayes in the dazed state that I will always associate with exiting a theatre. I'd come down from Poughkeepsie for the day, to catch a matinee at a new classical repertory company that had managed to succeed where Felix Ayre had failed. It was twilight; my mind was in Restoration England, my eyes weren't focused. Heading east on autopilot, I collided with a speeding pedestrian at the corner of 46th and Broadway.

"Sorry!" we both automatically exclaimed. Street etiquette dictated we each move on, keeping our eyes studiously averted so as not to register the face of the other party, but I knew that voice.

I looked and laughed. "Frankie? Oh my god!!" Maybe I shouldn't have been so surprised. I knew she'd taken over Ellen's job as paid companion to Bronwen Davies.

"Oh my god!" she agreed, giving me a hug. "What are you doing here? Aren't you in school?"

"I subscribe to the Phoenix. I had a matinee today."

"What was it?"

"*Love for Love*. Congreve."

"Not Wycherley?"

We giggled. Poor William Wycherley was a private joke in *Lake Song* circles.

When the light changed, we automatically crossed Broadway together. "Where are you headed?" Frankie asked belatedly. "I don't have to be back for an hour. You want to have a coffee?"

We paused in front of the TKTS trailer to decide. "I was going to hit the Drama Book Shop before I head for Grand Central. They sometimes get *Plays and Players*. The British magazine?" The greatest dream of my life was to see London with my own eyes. In the meanwhile, I read British books, watched *Upstairs Downstairs* and listened to the Monty Python albums that an English girl in my dorm had brought back after the summer break.

"I'll go with you and see what's on the boards."

New York is a city of layered realities. Pressed against everyday lives is a shadow zone of gods, rarely seen but near enough that you feel them brushing against you. To walk amongst them, dreamers seek out their temples. Back in the 20th century, a lot of these sanctuaries were bookstores. In the hushed precincts of Rizzoli, art books with richly colored plates were curated and displayed like rare gems, which many of them were, printed on paper as luscious as velvet, where a single page might be printed in three languages. "Wise men fished here" in the shadowy aisles of the Gotham Book Mart, stumbling upon poetry and iconoclastic literature and wonderfully odd picture books by an artist named Gorey. At Weiser Books intrepid seekers, who probed beyond the incense-fragrant counters that served tarot and stars to Aquarian dabblers, could disappear into the dim stacks and cautiously browse within trembling distance of scholars of obscure religions and serious occult practitioners. My own particular shrine was The Drama Book Shop.

Frankie and I walked to 48th and caught the rickety elevator. It was often necessary to force the doors to slide back and forth multiple times before they completely closed. They were dented, with a single diamond of glass-sandwiched chicken wire that was so dirty it only let in shadows. The air tasted of metallic dust. Getting inside always made my stomach flop. Though it was tenuous enough that I would sometimes wait around for someone else to show up before I dared to board, it wasn't the elevator that unnerved me; it was the store. The store was the heartbeat of the community. Anyone who was remotely involved in theatre ended up there. Every time I stepped off that elevator, I was one of them—and I knew that I was not.

Merely to step through the portal of my yearning was to be simultaneously legitimized and marginalized—because I was a native. Regardless of whether you come to New York City as a big fish from a small pond or as an ugly duckling longing to find your flock, if you grew up somewhere else, you arrive in town with a desperate ambition that either cancels out or does a hell of a job of masking your inadequacy. When you grow up here however, when your local paper is *The New York Times*, your local Christmas pageant includes the Rockettes, and the kid who lives upstairs shows up on your television screen yelping about having only one cavity, you enter the race halfway to the finish line without ever having warmed up. I envied people who could walk off that damned elevator as if they owned the world, as if they had nothing to lose; people who thought they'd already won, simply by getting on that bus or train or plane and standing in Times Square. Me, though I'd found my vocation at the age of 7 and had been studying since junior high, I couldn't think of calling myself an actress until someone had paid me to act.

The Drama Book Shop was a dingy warren of shelves. What must have been thousands of play scripts, the slim performance editions by Samuel French and the Dramatists' Guild, crammed in Necco wafer layers. There were collected works in scholarly editions, the older the work the more editions. An entire towering bookcase was devoted to Shakespeare: various editions, collected and individual; modern and historic analyses; histories of the Elizabethan theatre; documentation of famous productions. Stacks of biographies, autobiographies and memoirs of actors, directors, writers and designers. A burgeoning Film section, already outgrowing its allotted corner. And the professional tools: agent addresses; tapes that taught foreign accents; audition monologues collected by age and sex.

The bulletin boards Frankie wanted to consult were plastered with flyers and postcards for everything the working actor needed: acting workshops, singing teachers, dialect coaches; apartments to share or sub-lease; photographers who specialized in headshots; rides wanted—or offered—to LA; student films looking for "mature actors to play parents;" friendly notices about shoemakers who specialized in attaching taps, and hair salons whose trainees would cut or color hair for free; and, frequently tacked up over other slips of paper, advertisements for every showcase being presented over the next few weeks. Even a glance at these boards was a harsh reminder of the sheer volume of actors struggling to work in this city. They were at once an invitation and a warning.

It was much less intimidating being here with Frankie than when I came on my own. Frankie belonged here. Frankie was an actress, a real actress.

"So was it worth seeing? *Love for Love?*" It was a serious question.

Flattered that Frankie thought my opinion counted, I thought carefully. "I always feel like I'm missing half the jokes in Restoration. I don't know. It's good to have a feel for the style. We're doing a Goldoni in the spring…But the exciting thing…You know, Mary Ure was supposed to be the lead, but she hasn't been well." Though I wasn't the Broadway insider the rest of them were, I did read the gossip columns; my mom clipped them out of the newspaper and mailed them to me. "So I wasn't completely shocked to find the substitution slip. But when the understudy walked out on stage…She can't be that much older than us! Still, you know how you always read about understudies walking on and everyone says wow that person is going to be a star? Well, this girl…I couldn't take my eyes off her, she has that much stage presence. She has a guy's name. I want to remember it. Restoration is hard, but she did it as if it was no effort. And so poised, you'd think she's been carrying plays on her back forever. Glenn. That's what it was. Amazing. I don't know about the show, but I would definitely urge people to try and see her."

Frankie nodded. What a relief. She understood what I meant.

"How is Michael Flynn?" I asked, wanting to make some reference to *Lake Song*. Flynn had taken over from Max. I wasn't a huge Max Bulloch fan, but it was hard for me to imagine someone else in that part, especially someone with Flynn's sweet smile.

"Good," Frankie said, without hesitation. "Different from Max. Like he seems honestly confused in 'Kiss, Kiss,' which makes it very funny. You like him more."

"Does that make you hate him more in the end?" It was interesting to contemplate how a change of actor could change the play itself.

"Come see for yourself," Frankie suggested. "There's standing room tonight."

I'd planned to take the 6:10 back to Poughkeepsie. I wasn't usually spontaneous, but I was in an elevated mood. I could take the last train and still make my Sunday rehearsal. "Sure! Why not?"

I'd never seen a show standing room before. The minute I committed myself, I wondered if my feet would make it. Then I decided this was something I needed to do, a rite of passage, like the practice all-nighter some upperclassmen had urged on me and Craig our freshman year. I didn't know if I'd ever strictly speaking *need* to stand through a full length play, but I might as well test the waters with a show I'd already seen; if I got tired, I could leave.

I stayed. Michael Flynn was a talented actor and a marvelous singer. I completely agreed with Frankie about "Kiss, Kiss," and you did like him more, but Bulloch's interpretation was overall more in keeping with my own sense of Trigorin. I was glad to have seen both performances. The day had been full of lessons for me.

I suppose I could have gone to the stage door and asked for Frankie, but I would have been too self-conscious. It felt inappropriate to be backstage for anything unless I'd been onstage in the first place. In any case, I suddenly realized how little time I had to get to Grand Central. I practically ran across town and fell, exhausted, into a seat on the train. I think I slept as far as Croton Harmon.

♫

Drawing a deep centering breath for her final namaste, Ahuva sank gratefully down onto the towel-sized Persian rug that she'd appropriated from the front door hallway after Prajit, the Maharishi's young attendant, had taught her how to do the salute to the sun. She wasn't very good at *Surya Namaskar* yet—she was always a little breathless at the end of her series of five—but it pleased her to keep trying. All of her practice pleased her, starting with the fact that it was called a practice. You weren't expected to be perfect immediately, maybe not ever. The whole point was to make the effort. Every morning she did her bit of yoga, said her sloka and then tried her best to meditate. She wasn't very good at meditation yet, either. It was extremely challenging to empty her mind, partly because life ran on a schedule and she was afraid of losing track of the time. It would be logical to leave meditation for night, but she conked right out when she tried it that way. It had to be morning. Ellen said Gloria Korn used one of those old-fashioned looking alarm clocks, the ones with the Mickey Mouse ear bells on top, to keep from missing appointments. It was worth a try. She could keep one on her shrine.

Ahuva was particularly proud of her shrine. She'd cleared the top shelf of her low bookcase and spread it with an antique handkerchief that had been Malke's mother's, the only tangible connection she had to her ancestors other than that same grandmother's cameo pin, which lived in the box in the bank. On top of that, she'd set a chunk of salt from the Dead Sea and a porcelain bud vase with a bit of eucalyptus sticking out. Between them was the tiny Sarasvati statue Kaye had given her. The prayer beads the Maharishi had given her that first time were too much like a Catholic rosary to comfortably leave out; Ahuva had stuck them in the back of her underwear drawer where they were mostly forgotten. Behind this pleasingly spare grouping, she'd arranged her most precious photos: her parents, young and smiling in front of their first home; Gali in her Army uniform; Byron at the piano in the high school auditorium; a *Lake Song* cast picture cut from the souvenir program; and a genuine photo of Lil and Marshall Berenson rehearsing for *Riding a Bicycle*. Mindful of the risk of fire, she kept her incense burner and the fat rainbow candle that was supposed to smell like the ocean carefully distant, at the far sides of the shelf. It was very personal and satisfactorily authentic. The rest of the room was shaping up, too. It had taken considerable negotiation for her parents to allow her to discard the box spring and keep her mattress on the floor, like Kaye's. Covered with one of those Indian print bedspreads, and with a few mirror-embroidered pillows on top, it looked pretty good. She'd found glass wind chimes small and light enough to hang from the bottom of her lighting fixture. It was too cold to keep her window open, but they'd tinkle whenever she fanned something in that direction. Every morning, she deliberately shook out her bedspread a certain way to make them sound. Malke didn't want her ruining the paint job with nails or tape, so she'd put up her posters with soft wax. The one over her bed was the same yantra as the Maharishi's silk hanging; the starburst looked nice with her bedspread. Elephant-headed Ganesha hung from the back of her door, where her parents wouldn't see it and freak out. Ahuva found the whole idea of Ganesha extremely appealing. He took care of both arts and sciences, a balance of which she strongly approved. More critically, he was the remover of obstacles, which she almost desperately needed. Everything started off so well, but then it fell apart or disappeared. There must be some invisible obstacle blocking all her efforts.

From her vantage point on the floor, Ahuva had a good view of her poster of all the chakras, which hung above the shrine. Her throat chakra, the *Vishuddha*, which had to do with creativity and communication, needed work. She tried to focus, but her attention kept being drawn to the *Anahata*, the heart chakra. The symbol for Anahata was pretty much a Magen David, which was fascinating, almost as if love were fated for her. Maharishi Narang said it wasn't meant as falling-in-love kind of love (okay, sex) but about opening yourself to love and compassion for the world. You had to start, he said, by loving your own self.

Ahuva had assumed that she *was* open to love and compassion. Who didn't want to love and be loved? Loving yourself, though…that sounded a little conceited. Couldn't she just like herself? Which she did. She was a good person, at least she thought she was. She was certainly highly intelligent. Beyond that, she had yet to unlock whatever she was, but she still believed she was special; even during those worst days upstate she'd never stopped believing in her own worth. But did she love Ahuva Geffner? Such an odd concept! She thought about the people she loved. Not people like her parents and Gali and the cousins who'd always been part of her, the people she loved back, but about the people she'd started loving before they'd had a chance to know her. About Byron and Ric; and Mr. Gruen and Maria and Kaye and even Lil. About Marshall Berenson. Love was such a mysterious thing. What was it about those people that she loved? They *could create a world out of nothing*, that's what. Ahuva Geffner couldn't. What Ahuva was, she thought, was a highly intelligent, attractive, decent human being. She could hope that was sufficient for other people to love her, but why should it be when it wasn't what made Ahuva love someone else? Could she possibly be thinking about it too much? Love was, after all, a feeling, not a logical puzzle you could work out.

Why couldn't she empty her mind and think of nothing? She uncrossed her legs and crossed them in the other direction. They were getting stiff from sitting too long. How long?! She scrambled to her feet and peered at her clock radio. She still had ten minutes before she had take over at the store. Whew! She better pick up one of those alarm clocks soon. She'd be in the city tomorrow; she could run by the Bazaar on Broadway after work.

She quickly pulled her favorite corduroys and Kaye's Indian blouse over her leotard. She wished she could put her hair up in one of those messy buns, the way Kaye did. Not right now; not enough time to play! She gave it a few swipes with a brush and stuffed her Yemenite earrings and her new Ganesha ring into her bag, along with mascara, a kohl pencil and lip gloss, and ran to grab the elevator. She could finish up downstairs. She wanted to look nice.

Bronwen Davies' last performance as Arkadina was historic. That's why Ahuva, Ellen and Leonard had bought their tickets in advance instead of risking the half-price trailer. Leonard's boyfriend, too; she'd finally get to meet him. Frankie would have joined them, except she'd volunteered to watch from the wings in case Bron needed her. Or in case Connie did. Everyone was going to be on edge today. She wondered how Frankie was holding up. Bron meant so much to her. It was a good thing Margaret Rodney needed her for a couple of weeks. Unlike her father and the horrible Eunice, the Rodneys would at least be sympathetic. Frankie would need sympathy. She'd probably spend the next few weeks feeling like someone had died. Ahuva would and she didn't have that same personal connection to Bron. For Ahuva, it was all about the show. When Maria left, even Wayne, it had an odd texture around the edges, but the fabric still held: *Lake Song* was still *Lake Song*. Max Bulloch's leaving had been harder, making everything seem off kilter. The idea of *Lake Song* without Bron, permanently without Bron, was hard to wrap her head around. She'd forced herself to go to one of the Madeleine Blair performances and had not been pleased at all. Bronwen Davies was Arkadina and Arkadina was the show.

Life was changing. Kaye and the Maharishi would try to convince her that change was exciting, that she should open herself up to it. Ahuva was already feeling that dip in her stomach that signaled overwhelming sorrow. She was glad she'd be with friends tonight. She'd probably be a wreck tomorrow. This would be an interesting test of her practice. She wondered if it would make any difference. She would work extra hard at meditating tomorrow morning. Maybe she'd have more success if she didn't face the chakra poster.

♫

The famous Uncle Ned must stay in a hotel when he came to the city. Frankie couldn't imagine he'd stay in the guest room. It was as weirdly empty as the rest of Rodney apartment: just a bed without a frame, a mirror and an antique-looking table of the kind where the sides fold down. The table had been pretty once; there were still mother-of-pearl chips in a lot of the floral border. Was it from Margaret's family or had someone found it in a dumpster? Thanks to Casilda, at least the linens were clean, and so was the little bathroom. Frankie was glad she'd made Casilda one of her clove oranges for Christmas. She was also going to give her a box of cherry chocolates and some expensive soap from the store Ellen liked so much. She'd gotten the same soap for Margaret. That was okay. Margaret would never notice.

The private bathroom was a happy surprise. Sharing out at the beach had been a little disgusting. She couldn't be angry with Daphne; the kid didn't know any better. Frankie had considered it part of her job to teach some basic manners, like rinsing the spit-out toothpaste down the drain and hanging a wet washcloth to dry so it wouldn't get all sour. Margaret, however was a grown woman. Even someone used to having maids shouldn't be such a total pig. Frankie hadn't minded keeping the kitchen tidy, especially since she did most of the cooking, but mopping up the bathroom after Margaret had been gross and shouldn't have been necessary.

Even if Margaret were staying home and they'd had to share a bathroom, Frankie would have come. She would have put up with any amount of mess to avoid Christmas with Eunice this year. The season felt flat enough as it was. How long before she'd stop feeling so peculiar? She'd be feeling better, then some memory would pop into her head and pull off whatever scab had started to form. She wouldn't have given up these last weeks for anything, but it was over and now she felt worse than if she'd never met Bronwen Davies at all. At least then she'd still be able to fantasize about meeting her, which had always been so comforting. What made this extra hard to bear was how perfect everything had been in the end. Frankie had been backstage at *Lake Song* every day that final week; Bron had wanted her there, and so had Connie. A lot of celebrities had stopped by to catch one of the last performances, and she got to hang out with them. She didn't tell Ahuva (why make her feel bad?) that Marshall Berenson had come to the Saturday night show and they'd all had champagne afterwards. Thanksgiving at Ivor's was probably the best meal Frankie had ever eaten—Lionel split the cooking with a friend who was a professional chef—but it was more than good food: they were a family there, and everyone was so warm and, well, jolly. Not a word she usually thought to use, but there you have it, that's what it was. Jolly. Like the end of a Christmas movie. The party after the final performance, also at Ivor's, was completely different but also wonderful. The whole cast came, and people from other shows, and a lot of English people. When the crowded room felt stuffy, people would go out to the garden, where Ivor had strung Christmas lights and set out heaters. Someone made a joke that only the *Lake Song* people understood, about tiny lights, and they got Bron to sing that song that she'd sung at the Tribute concert, the beautiful sad one about theatre, about how magic didn't last even though you wanted it to. Frankie wished she'd had a tape recorder. Sure she had the Tribute concert album, but it was different being in the room with Bron when she sang it. Frankie wanted to hear it that way again.

Frankie wanted everything back again. Returning to Patchogue had been waking up from the most wonderful dream to total hell. No matter what she did or said, it was wrong. Eunice snapped, Eunice sneered. Mickey just sat in his chair with his rye or a bottle of beer. He was drinking a lot more lately; or maybe it just seemed that way, the way everything is exaggerated when you haven't seen it for a while. He didn't seem happy with the situation but, since the summer, any time Frankie tried to discuss it he got angry and said she was spoiled from having all of his attention for too long. He put it all on her: she needed to make an effort to get along. If Eunice screamed at her right in front of him, all he'd do is say "now, girls…" in a tired way that no one would take seriously.

She'd be afraid except for the one time she accidentally overheard them in the kitchen, the morning after she'd gotten home so late they never heard her come in and probably thought she'd stayed in the city. She heard Eunice demanding that Mickey throw her out. Pop got furious. Frankie couldn't see him from where she'd stopped dead in the hall, but she could imagine his face, and how his shoulders and back would be tensed up like the boxer he'd been in his Army days. She wondered if Eunice had ever seen him that way before. Eunice probably thought he was going to rip her head off. He said Frankie was his only kid and as long as he had a home she had a right to live in it. So at least Frankie knew she wasn't out on the street. That didn't stop Eunice from trying everything she could think of to make her leave.

Why couldn't her acting career to take off already?! She'd give anything for a National Tour. If only the shows that were casting weren't all such heavy dance shows. She was starting to get the hang of jazz, but not enough for something like *Pippin*. She'd have to hope for a LORT company in another state; if not a whole season, at least a single show. She was working on a new audition piece: Magg's pony story from *The Fabulous Flanagans*. It had been pretty easy to cut out the other people in the scene and turn it into a monologue. All she needed was a chance to get it heard. A lot of the LORTs were mail-in submissions. She was mailing like crazy, but she wasn't getting called. She still liked her headshots, but was ready to concede that the agent who'd spoken to her at the open house may have been right: in some mysterious way, they fell short. She would get new ones, with the money Margaret was paying her for being here. This was surplus money, seeing that Ivor had paid her well and expenses had been low while she was staying with Bron. Honestly, she would have stayed with Daphne for free, but Margaret insisted on paying her—paying a lot, considering Casilda was there too.

Margaret must be feeling guilty about going away. This man she'd been seeing had invited her to stay on his yacht. Frankie had a hunch that she was trying to land a new husband, a rich one. She'd dropped a lot of hints this summer about how she hated living on Ned's stingy charity and Melina and Cooper's leftovers. And lately she kept talking about the rumor that someone was making a musical out of *Little Orphan Annie*, which didn't seem so far-fetched once you remembered that they'd once done *Li'l Abner*. Irene hadn't heard anything and neither had Ellen, but Margaret seemed pretty sure it was in the works. She couldn't stop talking about what a perfect vehicle it would be for Daphne, and that if she had the money to get in on the ground floor as a major investor, it would be a done deal.

If she was gold digging, Margaret was doing it for Daphne as much as for herself, but that didn't stop her from feeling guilty about leaving her daughter alone for Christmas. They were going to miss their annual trip to Arizona, too. That was the part that upset Daphne. Rosamund Eschenbach never came to New York; at 87 she'd gotten too frail to fly. Margaret had promised a short make-up visit over Washington's Birthday weekend, but it wouldn't be the same and February seemed years away.

Casilda would take good care of Daphne, but Margaret knew she'd be bored with nothing to do but hang around the house. Frankie would be happy to take her to the movies or Rumplemayer's or maybe a museum. They could practice tap. They might even do some things Margaret hadn't put on the list. Daphne could feel like a regular kid, Margaret was free to go after her yachtsman, and Frankie would have not only a pleasant Christmas but new headshots. Everyone gets what they need.

♫

It was my fate to always be the first at any meeting place, the result of my mother's fanatical attitude towards being on time. She never said but I've always assumed she was traumatized in her youth by one of those teachers who think children learn from embarrassment. Whatever the source, she drilled us to the point that, to this day, my sister and I always leave too much travel time and arrive early.

Alone in the booth and facing the door, I watched Ellen limp into the luncheonette using an umbrella as if it were a cane. It was too big an entrance for an audience of one.

I wasn't surprised. She'd called everyone after it happened, to tell how she and Leonard had some stupid fight and she threw his new cock ring out the window to get back at him. How he got hysterical, which made her feel terrible. How she ran down the stairs to retrieve it, pulling her sweater over her head, and tripped. It was the Irish sweater some playwright friend of Felix's had left behind in the office, thick and heavily cabled enough that it protected her arms and face. "Though if I'd smashed the ski slope, I might have considered asking the doctors to do a little tweak," she'd added. I was surprised; Ellen hated her nose, but she'd never mentioned wanting to change it, not even the year we turned sixteen and so many people came back from school breaks with tiny shiny nosebuds. As it turned out, her face wasn't even scratched. Her pajamaed legs had taken the brunt of the fall, especially her right knee. Leonard, by then doubly hysterical, had managed to help her upstairs and pack it in ice, which hadn't stopped it from swelling to the size of a grapefruit.

Since then, Ellen informed me now, the bruising had developed into what sounded like the entire spectrum of half-mourning. She volunteered to take me to the ladies' room and unwind the ace bandage so I could see.

I assured her I knew what bruises looked like.

Ellen shrugged. "You know, we never found the frigging cock ring. Leonard looked the next day, but it was nowhere. He said it was okay, but you should have seen his face."

I had no idea was a cock ring was for, but I was damned if I was going to ask. I flicked my hand in the gesture that means "oh well."

"I feel like a total shit about it. I'm going down to the Pink Pussycat later to get him a replacement. A really good one. Maybe I'll make him up a Christmas stocking. Depends what I find. Want to come with me? Help me pick out a vibrator? I keep meaning to. Ruth had one. I miss it more than I miss her. It was a revelation. You should get one, too."

"There you are!" I waved at Ahuva.

So did Ellen, briefly craning her neck to look over her shoulder.

Apple-cheeked from the cold and smiling broadly, Ahuva stopped behind Ellen. She pulled off her wooly mittens and stuffed them into her shoulder bag. Her long fingers made their habitual march down the front of her coat, undoing each button at a measured pace. She unwound her long crocheted scarf and neatly tucked it up one sleeve before hanging the coat on the hook between our booth and the next. Like nearly all of Ahuva's movements, it gave the impression of matching to a silent soundtrack.

Task complete, she headed towards the empty seat on my side of the booth, carefully dodging Ellen's leg, which was sticking out into the aisle. "Someone could trip over you," she asserted. "Namaste."

"It feels better if I don't bend it," Ellen said.

"It still hurts? Maybe you broke your kneecap. Have you been to a doctor?"

Ellen shook her head. "I can walk without passing out. I just bruised the fucking hell out of it."

Ahuva threw her hands in the air and rolled her eyes in extravagant exasperation. "It's your leg. Oh, and before I forget, Mr. Nudler says hi." She folded herself onto the red leatherette cushion beside me and fished out a mirror from her bag to check that her kohl hadn't smudged.

"I'm at Keppel and Grace for a while. Not far. I should stop by one day and give him a thrill."

"What about Gloria?" I asked.

"I'm not needed while Perfect Pete is home from Buffalo…"

"Ithaca." The correction was a reflex.

"Same thing." She flexed her eyebrows. "My own fault for being too efficient. All the backlog is taken care of. She probably won't need me until the spring openings."

Ahuva sniffed. "Outrageous. She can't expect you to wait around for months and months."

"Sure she can. Do you know how many people would give their left tit to work with Gloria Korn? Anyway, it won't be that long. She'll have to start working the campaigns by February. Meanwhile, lucky me, Keppel and Grace thinks I'm charming and intelligent and all their *girls* seem to take Christmas vacations."

"It's a good thing your voice carries. I had to find you by sound."

It was freezing out and the luncheonette was overheated. Just walking from the door to our booth, Frankie's glasses had completely fogged over. She wiped them with the tips of the jaunty red scarf bow at her neck and replaced them, grinning. "It's a miracle! I can see!"

"You'd think they would invent something to fix that," Ahuva observed.

Ellen pushed herself up.

Hooking her coat over Ahuva's, Frankie slid in past Ellen. The bill of her knitted newsboy cap knocked against the tabletop jukebox. As she adjusted it, she fluffed her bangs with her fingers.

"Cute cap!" Ahuva and I said, more or less in unison.

It was, and a happy change from her usual headgear. Her favored deep floppy brims and droopy feathers lent Frankie a quaint, wistful air. In this cap, she was fresh and perky. It was a look that could get her a lot of work, I thought.

"You should wear it for one of your new pictures," I suggested. The proposed new pictures were a current topic of discussion for the group. We were all heavily invested in Frankie's career.

"Do you think so?"

Ahuva agreed enthusiastically. "You look like someone in a commercial."

Ellen had set her new Hunting World satchel on the table, so that Frankie could get by. Now she pantomimed a fussy decision before placing it between them on the seat. The fuss was on my behalf. To Ahuva and Frankie, it was only a bag. Ahuva's attention to style was limited to the fashion influence of Kaye Victor. Frankie was interested in fine distinctions of cut and fabric, but resolutely shut her eyes to what she couldn't afford. Ellen and I were shamelessly covetous of what we judged to be the finer things in life. She knew that I knew how obscenely expensive that satchel was. With only half the leather, it easily cost twice the list price of my medium-sized Coach mailbag, which I'd only been able to buy because a friend of Heidi's mother still invited me to wholesale "parties" in her living room.

I didn't disguise my envy. "Lucky you! Christmas present from Harry and Mo?"

She flashed a smile so bright that the light seemed to refract off her tinted glasses. "Franklin said my old bag was disreputable. He couldn't stand looking at it."

It seemed Franklin Li was getting serious.

"Poor Mr. Black." My attempt at cool irony was as much for my own practice as for Ellen's benefit, an effort to acquire an air of what I thought of as British sophistication. A senior, who I had somehow previously missed meeting, had returned from his junior year abroad as the next best thing to an Englishman, and I was determined to catch his attention.

"My rainy day fund? With Franklin coming along so nicely, I think I can let soon him go." This was said with Ellen's more customary foxy smile.

I was sure that if push came to shove Harry would step up to bail her out of any emergency, but I admired how fiercely she rejected that option. I did admire Ellen, as much as she unsettled me. Everything she did seemed to be part of a master plan. Being a theatrical producer was an unlikely goal for someone our age, but Ellen made it believable. She was the Cosmo girl, a confident and savvy career woman, just as the resolutely upbeat Frankie, trudging through the city with her heavy dance bag, was every plucky girl off the bus in every backstage movie ever made, bound to become a star. Whenever I was with them, my own routine of classes and papers and Drama Department politics seemed juvenile by comparison—as did my crush on the self-impressed Simon with his European man-bag. They were center stage, while I was warming up in the wings.

If what I was doing was warming up, what was Ahuva was doing? In high school, she'd been a more committed student than I'd been, with a whole rack of honors classes. I'd been shocked by her leaving college. I'd been worried, too, until her zeal for her new life made it sound daring and glamorous. But it was almost a year now and the novelty had rubbed off. Everything she was doing seemed like busy work, as if her life were directed by a substitute teacher. She sounded happy enough and she didn't have an empty hour in the day, but none of it would get her anywhere—other than seeing *Lake Song* 100 times, which was the only specific goal she ever mentioned. She could already boast well over 80, a number that boggled the imagination. I couldn't imagine seeing *anything* that many times. And unless she was counting second-acting, the cost was unthinkable; even standing room was five bucks a pop. I knew that, thanks to knowing everyone connected with the show, she was occasionally passed in on off nights. I assumed old Mr. Nudler sometimes got her free tickets, too. There was no other reason to be answering his phones. The job didn't pay much and, the way Ellen used to describe it, it was no more connected to theatre than the people who vacuum the aisles. Between Nudler and her parents, Ahuva was basically working a couple of endless summer jobs. Night school sounded way beneath her abilities. Her theatre downtown and that Maharishi she was obsessed with? She was marking time. My life wasn't exciting, and I wouldn't have said I was happy, but at least I was headed somewhere. I was only warming up, but I was pointing straight at my dreams. And I was more than halfway to my BA; if for some unfathomable reason my dreams didn't pan out, that degree guaranteed me a job with good money and a future. What was going to happen to Ahuva?

"Don't you ever think of going back to college?" I couldn't help myself from blurting it out.

Ahuva didn't hear me. She was busy explaining to the doughy waitress that she wanted a chef's salad with cheese and hard-boiled eggs but no ham and no turkey. "I don't eat dead animals," she proclaimed loftily. "I've been purifying my body."

The rest of us guilty ordered our burgers and I let my question fade away. We got "specials," which meant a couple of slices of tomato, a leaf or two of lettuce, a pickle spear and a small heap of fries. Ahuva ordered fries on the side.

As the waitress was about to walk away, Frankie changed her coke to a coffee shake.

"This is dinner," she explained. "They're eating at Sign of the Dove after Radio City, as a treat."

It was why Frankie had been able to meet us today. It was Daphne's last day with her mother before Margaret took off to cruise around the Greek islands like some movie star.

"Wouldn't it be hilarious if Margaret ended up at a party with Bron?" Ellen leered provokingly.

"Huh?"

"Well, she and Ivor and Lionel should be in Greece by now."

Frankie shook her head. "They were going there to rest."

"You can't tell me Ivor isn't throwing a Christmas party. Or New Year's."

"Isn't Greek Christmas on a different day?" I asked.

Ahuva was after more relevant facts. "Where is Ivor's house? It's so American to think Europe is so small that two people could accidentally run into each other just because they're in the same country."

"Somewhere that ends in 'os'?" Frankie hazarded.

"Mykonos?" Ellen suggested. "That's where Onassis lives."

"Maybe." Frankie sounded dubious. "I don't know. Does it matter? It's not as if they know each other."

"I was in Athens once, with my cousins." Ahuva was the only one of us who'd ever been abroad. We all turned to her, expectantly. She shrugged. "I have no desire to go back. I don't see why people make such a big deal."

"Who said they did? People don't go to Athens," Ellen explained patiently. "The in thing is to cruise the islands. Mykonos, Santorini…"

"Crete," I sighed.

Ellen laughed. "I'm talking about where beautiful people go, not archaeologists."

"I'd rather see history," I insisted.

"Wasn't Crete where the minotaur was?" Frankie asked. "Ariadne and the ball of thread?"

I nodded. "Knossos. That's the palace. Can you imagine seeing it with your own eyes?"

"It's probably dirty and crowded, like Athens," Ahuva flung out her hand dismissively. "I'd rather see something different. Something spectacular. India, for example. I would love to go to the ashram someday."

The wide sleeve of Ahuva's gauze blouse slipped back towards her elbow, revealing a crude metal bangle.

"Is that copper?" Ellen reached across the table and touched a finger to the slim band of metal.

"Yes!" Ahuva's eyes lit with enthusiasm. "I was having so much trouble breathing through my *Anahata* and then I got this and I completely opened up. I felt strong and centered. And absolutely cleansed. Copper is associated with the heart, you know."

"Harry and Mo are wearing copper bracelets for arthritis," Ellen observed.

Ahuva frowned. "I'll have to ask the Maharishi about that."

"While you're asking people, could you ask Nudler what we'd have to do to qualify as a theatre party? I think we need 25 people, but I was hoping maybe it was less."

"For what?"

Ellen grinned. "A block of tickets for *One for the Books*. It would be cheaper that way."

Ahuva gave a little jump in her seat. "What a stellar idea!"

"It was Leonard's. He was counting and it made sense. With us and him and Kevin, that's six already. Jeff would come down from Buffalo."

"Ric and Jay would want to come. Maybe Cathy and Tim." Ahuva was genuinely excited now. "I bet we can get enough people."

"What's the show about?" I asked. "Maybe some people from school would come."

Their looks ranged from puzzled to pitying.

"It's first Marshall Berenson show without James Lord since *The Buddy System*." Ahuva made the pronouncement with the gravity of the Oracle of Delphi.

"I hear Linda Schiller is pissed off," Ellen cracked. "Joe says she still thinks Lord owes her for not giving her the road company."

"Fuck her," Frankie said pleasantly.

"Everybody does," Ellen agreed. "Apparently she went all out to get Nina."

"Then now she's lost twice. It's nice to know that sleeping around isn't as important as talent," I said primly.

"It is when you have the right equipment."

I shook my head. "Linda Schiller seems to have no trouble using her equipment. No offense, Frankie."

Frankie laughed. "Not this time. *One for the Books* is all men and boys. I saw the cast breakdown at Equity. Not even a maid!"

"That's surprising," Ahuva said. "I wonder what the impact will be...Oh, of course! The boys will supply the soprano and alto voices. But still..."

Something jogged a faint memory loose from some months back. "Wait, is this the one about Stanley and Livingston or something like that?"

"Boys' adventure books," Ahuva corrected grandly.

"You mean like *The Hardy Boys*? That would make a pretty strange musical."

Ahuva neatly avoided a direct answer. "Anything Marshall Berenson writes is sure to be brilliant."

♫

Ahuva had a late lunch at the crepe place near Keppel and Grace, listening to Ellen rehash how she'd broken up with Barney Black. If you could call it breaking up. It was more of a business relationship, and Ahuva found it pretty disgusting. How could you have something as intimate as sex with someone you didn't love? She wasn't sure Ellen even liked any of the lovers she was so proud of, except maybe Joe Bigelow. Ahuva found middle-aged, barrel-chested Joe completely unappealing but that, as Jakub liked to say, is what makes horse racing.

At least Ellen's self-centered rambling was a distraction. Ahuva felt so restless these days. Maybe it was the season. Cathy, who, now that the baby was big enough to leave for a couple of hours, was taking Psych courses at Queens, said that more people committed suicide during the holiday season than at any other time of year. Not that Ahuva was feeling suicidal: she didn't want life to end; she only wanted it to move on. All her activities seemed so pointless.

Not exactly true. Her practice had a point. When she performed her sun salutes and her new yoga poses, she gave herself completely over to them, and she'd gotten so much better at meditation. Her *sloka* for wisdom had some challenges: after the first maybe ten repetitions, no matter how she strained for focus, she tended to slip into autopilot for the rest of the *mala*. She'd done reasonably well this morning, as well as could be expected considering. Then she'd gone downtown and had transcribed the contact information and preferences for all of Mr. Nudler's clients from Draas through Gaylord, typing the information neatly onto cards for the new Rolodex that she'd finally convinced him to buy. It was expensive, but she loved how it put all the information at the tip of your fingers. Pulling order out of chaos always provided some satisfaction, but it wasn't quelling that bumpy feeling in her stomach or the flutter of the pulse in her neck.

She needed some kind of project to fill the hole inside. It was just as well Cathy had convinced her to take Intro Psych in the winter mini-term. A class would be better than nothing, plus it would keep her parents happy.

The obvious cure for today was *Lake Song*. She'd have to wait for standing room to go on sale. She needed to be frugal for a while. She'd spent more than she'd planned on holiday gifts, but it was worth it. When you see perfect presents for people, it's hard not to buy them. How could she have passed up that music box with the lullaby from *Rosebud*, when it was exactly right for Maria's baby?

Leaving the restaurant, she headed over to the Donnell to wait, thinking they might have some of the books on the Psych reading list. Then she wouldn't have to buy them. The one about dreams sounded interesting. She got as far as the library door before losing her enthusiasm for the idea. She was not at all in the mood to study today, not even to go through the motions of taking out a book.

Instead, she walked to Colony. It was a dangerous place if you were trying to save money, but she had a specific goal: she wanted to get Holly the new Joni Mitchell songbook for her birthday. Browsing the racks, she ran across a book of simplified piano arrangements for the music for *Riding a Bicycle*. It had "No Reflection on Me." Ahuva hadn't touched a keyboard since graduation—not on purpose; it simply hadn't been a priority. She should start playing again. That would be another excellent project for the winter, and this would be the perfect place to start. At the register, she noticed they didn't have a *One for the Books* poster up yet. She felt a little smug, already having tickets.

Ahuva was running out of ways to kill time. Thank goodness it wasn't snowing, but it was too cold to wander aimlessly. Her nose was starting to run. She went to Howard Johnson's and had a hot chocolate at the counter, making it last as long as she could. It was still a little early when she got to the Regale box office, but no one would mind if she stood there and waited.

The woman with the old-fashioned cat's eye glasses waved her over to the window.

"Hi, Maureen. Early Happy New Year."

"Happy New Year, Ahuva. One for tonight?"

"I'm waiting for standing room."

Maureen cocked her head. "Sorry, hon. No standing room."

"Disappointing. Must be the weather, huh? Thursday's usually such a busy night."

"Nnnope...we haven't had standing room since maybe Thanksgiving. We're done with that, I'd say. Let's see if I can find you a bargain..."

It caught Ahuva off guard. Since Bron left, she wasn't going as often as she used to, the show didn't have the same feeling anymore, but she knew she'd been here five times since Thanksgiving. Hadn't she gone standing room? Once had been her Chanukah present from Mr. Nudler, and there was that Tuesday when she'd been lucky getting at the half-price booth, but the other times? She guessed she hadn't asked.

Maureen was shuffling through the slots. "I can give you...balcony, of course. But it looks like you can be wherever you like in the second mezzanine, only a dollar or two more."

"It's a hit show!" Ahuva was horrified.

Maureen gave a weary smile. "Yeah, and doing better than some of the others on the street, just between you and me. Hey, don't look like that."

"Like what?" Ahuva replied automatically. She was too dazed to think about how she looked.

"Like your cat just died. That's the way it goes. We've been doing well here, for a Berenson musical. Better than that *Boy Jones*, though between you and me I liked that one better. And he's got that new one coming, so you gotta figure the fans are waiting for that."

Even me, Ahuva thought, with a trace of guilt.

"Tell you what!" Maureen said, in the voice people use to announce a treat they think will cheer you up. "I was just about to send over a bundle to the TDF booth. How about you run them over for me? And I'll give you row R, left side of Orchestra, for half price, the same as if you bought it there. They'll be fine with it. Saves them from having to send over a messenger."

Ahuva thanked her numbly and tucked the ticket into her bag. Maureen opened the side door to the where she sat, the steel door that was usually locked, and handed her a thick manila envelope.

"You go over to the guy who stands outside and tell him you have a drop off, okay? Enjoy tonight's show."

Ahuva couldn't imagine how she could with a death knell ringing in her ears. She walked the three blocks as quickly as possible and found the man in question. He was dressed almost like a policeman, but with a vest that said TDF over his jacket. He gave a big smile when he heard she had *Lake Song* tickets

"Those'll go like hotcakes!" he enthused. "Fantastic show! I'm guessing you've seen it?"

She nodded happily and returned to the Regale with a bounce in her step. There were people at the ticket window. Plenty of people still wanted to see *Lake Song*. What was she worried about? There were shows that ran for years and never had standing room even once. She managed to catch Maureen's eye to give her the okay sign. She waited in a corner of the lobby until half hour, when they opened the doors. She ran downstairs to pee before the ladies' room line got too long, then settled happily into row R, left side of Orchestra, to dissolve.

♫

Ellen only went to the party because she had nothing else to do and she didn't feel like spending the night alone.

Franklin Li was still in Hong Kong, and Joe was, of course, with his family. Leonard had invited her to go with him and Kevin to the drag cabaret for a champagne supper. It might have been amusing any other night, but New Year's Eve was not for playing fifth wheel to a clutch of gay male couples. She certainly wasn't joining Harry, Mo and Kelly for a jolly family gathering with Mo's friends from the art co-op; as Harry's daughter, she'd never be accepted as an adult, and she was far too old to hang out at the "kids table." No one she knew was doing anything that she found remotely entertaining.

An hour or so before the office closed, a messenger came from ASCAP with some last minute papers for Mr. Grace. While he was waiting, he mentioned this party in a squat on East 6th street. The whole building was having an open house, he said. It was a cool crowd: actors, musicians, a couple of writers. Everyone was welcome to bring a bottle and hang out. She should come; she'd have fun. She said thanks and maybe. He scrawled the address on a scrap of paper. She stuck it in her bag, not expecting to use it. By 8 o'clock, the silence in the apartment was driving her crazy and she decided what the hell.

It would be tacky to show up empty handed. Ellen eyeballed the drinks cart. She had a nice stock of bottles, most of which had fallen off of one of Barney's trucks. She wouldn't miss Barney, but she would certainly miss the perks. What to sacrifice? Not the French burgundy and certainly not the Chivas; she wanted those for herself; she wasn't giving them up unless she knew for certain it would pay off and she doubted a houseful of squatters would appreciate them. Even if they did, offering it might mark her as very bourgeois. Ditto for the gin, though it was a brand she didn't really like. She settled on a bottle of cheap vodka that she and Leonard had bought for Bloody Marys but had never gotten around to opening. That ought to strike the right note. She pulled on a pair of jeans with boots and a black sweater. She didn't need anything else except her wedjat eye ring.

Ellen took the B down to Lafayette and walked the rest of the way. Harry would be horrified; it was a pretty shitty neighborhood. With the whole city out in full force on New Year's Eve, she felt safe enough, even if her knee was making it hard to walk as fast as she preferred. Besides, she had a Swiss Army knife in her pocket, another gift from Barney, which she kept on her key ring along with a police whistle.

The address that matched the slip of paper was four stories of brown brick. It looked sufficiently inhabited. She wouldn't have said the windows were blazing, but there was obviously something more than candlelight. It was Ellen's first visit to a squat and she didn't know what to expect. Someone told her later that people either used a network of cables, thick as her wrist, to tap into a nearby Con Ed source, or else were plugged into one of the generators. The generators were up on the roof. So was the original water tank, which provided the ability to flush the toilets. For cooking water, most everyone filled buckets from fire hydrants, and they showered at the Russian bathhouse a few blocks away.

As much as Ellen liked the idea of a bunch of people reclaiming an abandoned building, pioneering wouldn't be her thing. Limited electricity was one thing, but the idea of no running water frightened her. What had Kevin said that time? There were risks that only the poor or the rich would take, because the rich had nothing to lose and the poor had everything to gain. The problem with being raised in the middle classes was that you were always afraid of falling out of them. Plumbing was more than inconvenience; the symbol was a line Ellen couldn't cross.

She pushed. The front door wasn't even locked. Inside, the doors to the two ground floor apartments stood wide open, light and laughter spilling out to meet her. There were no signs posted anywhere. Ellen poked her head in. Both rooms were packed, not an inch of wiggle room as far as she could see. Now she was curious. From the sound of things, the entire building was one big party. Someone had put a punch bowl full of floating candles on a chair by the front door, so you could see your way up the stairs. She was here already, she might as well see what she could see. If her knee started to ache, she'd stop and have a drink until it felt strong enough for her to leave.

It was the same on every landing: candles, doors either open or non-existent, a raucous clamor of conversation and laughter. The air was scented with a combination of cinnamon, balsam fir and weed. She heard a couple of guitars, bongos and some kind of horn—Ellen didn't know enough about music to say what kind. People ran in and out of doors, ambled past her on the stairs. She didn't spot the messenger. She had no idea if he was anywhere in the building, she wasn't even sure she remembered his name. It probably didn't matter. Anyone who spotted her smiled and gave a friendly wave. She could never live here, but it was pretty cool for a party. She was doing nothing but walking through and she felt almost happy. Either it felt good to be surrounded by that much life or she was getting a contact high.

When she heard the piano on the third floor, she decided it was a good stopping point. She had to see what kind of piano someone would bring to a squat.

It was an old upright, painted yellow and plastered with showcase flyers, all heavily autographed. Other than a dumpster armchair, a table and a folding screen, it was the only piece of furniture in the room. People were sprawled on the floor, a few on what looked like old sofa cushions.

The pianist was around her own age and wore a green velvet smoking jacket with a cravat around his neck. Except for the torn jeans and auburn Jewfro, it was very Noel Coward. As she entered, he started singing.

The people in the room let their conversations peter out and swiveled to listen. He wasn't the greatest singer, but Ellen liked the song. She'd never heard it before. It was clearly from a musical. She wondered which.

He finished. Everyone applauded. There were a few catcalls. Someone called out "Pam, where's Pam?!"

The guy at the piano kept playing a random melody with one hand and pointed the other towards the door. Another guy jumped up and, making a megaphone of his hands, ran into the hall shouting "PAMELA! PAMELA STONE! RITCHIE'S PLAYING YOUR SONG!!!"

There was a response, which Ellen couldn't quite hear, followed by the percussive approach of a woman running up a flight of stairs in 1950s metal stiletto heels. A disheveled blonde appeared. She wore a silver lurex slip. Arms outstretched, she braced herself against the door frame, and made great show of catching her breath, dipping her neck so that her Louise Brooks bob swung like a silk curtain. Ritchie kept playing. Pamela, for obviously that's who this woman was, pulled herself upright and tossed her head. There was a scatter of applause. Heels clicking, she sashayed across the room and posed by the piano.

"So you ready now?" Ritchie asked, mildly.

"Play it, Sam," she commanded.

Ritchie ran his hands over the keys, rippling an introduction. The room quieted down again. Ellen found a spot on the floor and gingerly slid down.

Pamela opened her mouth and sang what was musically a torch song, but with lyrics that had everyone rolling with laughter. She finished to uproarious applause.

"Thank you," she said, doing a bad Elvis. "Thank you very much."

"One more!" someone yelled.

"Okay?" Ritchie asked her. He played a few tentative bars and she nodded. This one was a snappy duet, clever repartee set to music. Again there was loud applause.

Ellen was enthralled. She hoped he'd keep playing, but after that number, Pamela laid a butterfly kiss on his cheek and, blowing kisses to the crowd, clattered out of the apartment. Ritchie stood up from the bench and made a show out of flexing his hands.

"Okay, who's up next? Jim? Your turn?" He pointed to a big bearded man who took his place at the piano and began to play jazz. Freed from his shift, Ritchie went over to the table, which was doing service as a bar and started examining the offerings.

Ellen scrambled painfully up with her bottle, to meet him at the table. "I've got…um…well the name is Russian," she said breathlessly.

He shook his head. "I'm gin tonight. Gin and It. Part of the persona." He indicated his smoking jacket and cravat.

"Ah," she said, not certain what else to say. She was used to posturing, just not to people admitting it.

Selecting the gin, he poured a healthy splat into a Flintstones jelly glass. His eyes continued to rove the table.

"I really enjoyed your playing," she said. She decided she might as well start the vodka herself.

"Thanks. Ah, here it is!" He grabbed the bottle of vermouth and poured some over the gin.

Ellen had always thought "Gin and It" meant tonic water; she was glad she hadn't handed him the Schweppes. "Those songs you did with Pamela were really great."

"Thanks." He used a knife to stir the contents of the glass before taking a sip. He gave a little shudder. "Perfect!"

"What show were they from?"

"Oh, they're not. Not yet. They're part of a show I've been writing. *A Thing or Three*. Working title, you know what I mean?"

"Yes I do. I'm a producer." It was the first time she'd ever said it aloud. It sounded good. Happy New Year to me, she thought.

He shifted slightly, new interest in his eyes "Are you? I'm Richard Edelstein. Call me Ritchie. Everyone does." He gestured around the room at his public.

"Ellen Janow," she said, sticking out her hand. They shook. "A pleasure to meet you. So tell me about this show."

Ellen spent the next hour sitting with Ritchie on his futon, behind the folding screen. Several times they had to shoo off drunken couples who were looking for a place for a quickie.

Ritchie sketched out his musical. He was writing everything himself, with Pamela's help: book, lyrics and music. It would be a cabaret, he explained, but with a plot line. For three women and two men. Pamela, of course, was meant to be the leading lady. They'd been best friends practically forever. They'd grown up in the same town in Michigan and moved to New York together last year. *A Thing or Three* was going to be their ticket, both of them knew it. He was polishing the rough edges and soon they would be starting to look for backers. In the meanwhile, she was working at Phebe's and doing the occasional Industrial, and he was selling socks at Brooks Brothers.

Ellen explained that she was still new to producing, but was well connected with a number of potential backers. She'd only been waiting for the right property. From what she'd heard tonight, *A Thing or Three* might be it. When could she hear the rest of what he had so far? He would have to work it out with Pamela, but he thought a week from Sunday would be good. If she didn't mind coming back down here. Ellen didn't mind. Ellen would be delighted.

They exchanged service numbers and solemnly toasted what they hoped would be the start of a new partnership.

"Ten!" a ragged chorus began to chant on the other side of the screen.

They grinned. Ritchie helped her up from the futon. They joined the rest, just as the number reached "six."

"Five, four, three, two, one! HAPPY NEW YEAR!!!!"

Ritchie gave Ellen a quick hug, before turning to be kissed by one of his legion of friends.

She stood there, absurdly delighted to not be kissing anyone. It was a new year. It was going to be HER year!

24 – FOUR MILES

MEDVIEDENKO

Only four miles
Between here and my own little
   home.
I don't need to see the way
Because I walk it every day.
And the walking gives me pleasure!
God has given me so much, I can't
   complain:
An honest way to earn my bread,
The girl I love to share my bed
I know I should be grateful;
I must cherish what I have, not ask
   for more.
I'm a humble schoolmaster.
I must strive to be better.
I must strive to be good.
My resolution strengthens me,
And walking through the woods.

Only four miles,
Which I travel every day;
Travel twice, but that's okay.
It's the borderland between two
   separate worlds:
From my humble family cottage
To exalted realms where I pay
   homage.
Do I rule or do I beg?
I live between the two extremes.

These four miles;
This small journey that I make,
From where I give to where I take.
Is the only place I have where life is
   calm.
At point A, my son, elated;
At point B, my wife—more complicated.
So much pressure, so much scorn!
And all I have to balance this

Are only four miles,
Through the woods, where I tramp
   on my own.
Soaked by rain, blue with sleet,

I don't need to feel my feet,
Because Masha doesn't love me!
And the others cling so close it
   drains me dry.
But mile by mile and pace by pace
I try to find a way to grace.
I know I should be grateful;
I must cherish what I have, not ask
   for more.
I'm a humble schoolmaster.
I must strive to be better.
I must strive to be good.
My resolution strengthens me
And walking through the woods.

Only four miles:
All the time I have to be,
Nothing more than merely me.
It's the only life I have that's really
   mine.
At point A, I'm someone's hero,
At point B, I'm something less than
   zero.
But within the space between
There's no one makes demands of me

For four miles.
There is sanctuary there,
My every step becomes a prayer,
As I walk this road, my burdens are
   released.
At point A, I'm suffocated;
At point B, I'm barely tolerated.
While I walk, I can forget
And find my way to harmony

Four miles!
Which I travel every day;
Travel twice, but that's okay.
I would travel so much farther if I
   dared.
What kind of man would dream of
   walking away forever?
Before I can think such a thing,
It's only four miles and I'm there.

Wiry, sandy-haired, Dinah was nothing to write home about—as Mickey Cecchi always said about skinny, flat-chested women, something that had made his skinny daughter feel inordinately relieved when her own bust finally developed. Dinah's pale eyebrows and lashes disappeared without makeup, her nose was bony and a little crooked, and she had pencil-line lips: the exact opposite of Annie Fallon's round, generous features. It was hard to imagine how Nancy Pardoe could fall in love with two such completely different people, but she had. Maybe instead of mooning over Donny look-alikes Frankie should turn her attention to curly-haired Jewish boys. It wasn't romantic tips Frankie was hoping for from Dinah. Anyone who looked so un-actressy and kept getting work must know a few things about the business.

Sometimes Frankie had a cold feeling that she'd made practically no progress at all since leaving NYADA. On those days, it was hard not to feel disheartened. She longed for some kind of guidance. It never would have occurred to her to approach Dinah who, in all the months since taking over Maria Dearborne's role, had barely even said "hello" when they met backstage. Today, however, running into her at the Equity Lounge, Dinah must have finally understood that Frankie was a professional too. She'd almost immediately pulled out the proof sheets and asked for an opinion.

The request had been flattering, but a potential minefield. It's a fact that you can never get too many opinions about headshots. No matter how certain you feel about your choices, you need other people's assurance; and if someone picks out a shot you hadn't considered, you start the whole agonizing decision process all over again. It's nerve-wracking for the critic, too, knowing how much is riding on their opinion: hundreds of dollars in session fees and 8x10 blow-ups and retouching, then $40 or $50 more for every hundred prints or postcard run; money not easily spared but necessarily invested in the single best hope an actor has of getting work. Whenever she was shown someone's proofs, Frankie wondered queasily if her opinion was good enough to state, or if it was better to give a yes to wherever the wax pencil circles already fell.

This time, Frankie needn't have worried. The proofs were outrageously good. The lighting was kind to Dinah's nose and she had a wonderful, open smile in every shot.

"He's such a sweetheart, you can't help but relax." Dinah responded to Frankie's compliments with the same smile. "I can't remember ever being so comfortable at a shoot."

Frankie asked if he was expensive. The price Dinah quoted—$225 for six rolls and three changes of wardrobe, with two 8x10s included—was over her budget, but only a little. She took out her datebook to write down the name and number.

"I'm going over now with my decision. Why don't you come with me? You can see his book and say hello, see if you get a good vibe."

Frankie had nothing else to do today except go back to Patchogue. It was bowling league night: if she hung around the city a couple more hours, Eunice and Mickey would be gone before she reached the house. And it was a golden opportunity to make a friend who might have something to teach her. She thanked Dinah and said she'd be happy to.

Instead of taking the bus, they walked down Broadway. Dinah claimed she needed the exercise. "Once you hit 30," she confided, "you have to burn a lot of calories to stay thin" and the choreography for *Lake Song* wasn't especially strenuous. The walk was fine with Frankie, who tried to save her 35 cents where she could. It didn't take long to reach the spot where Broadway crossed Fifth Avenue, a neighborhood full of sad, weathered buildings that had once been grand. Frankie hadn't been around here since she was little and Mickey's brother was working maintenance at the Toy Center. She'd almost forgotten. The toy companies used to get rid of showroom samples once a year. The people who worked in the building would bring their kids for milk and cookies. Since Uncle Joey didn't have kids of his own, he would bring Frankie. She always came home with a bag full of showroom samples—mostly dolls that never made it to market—and a cold from all the dust that got up her nose. No wonder Uncle Joey had to move to Arizona for his lungs. Looking over her shoulder, Frankie saw workmen on the ledge of the Commodore Criterion building. They were taking down the carolers, always the earliest Christmas decoration of all and the last to come down. She'd almost forgotten about them, too.

Avoiding the little park—ragged and neglected, though not as bad as the one behind the Library—Dinah crossed at the Flatiron, where Broadway opened into an unfamiliar checkerboard of retail oddities: stores that sold china and stores that sold rugs; a shop that sold absolutely nothing but light bulbs. Frankie hurried to catch up. They veered east, to a neighborhood of art supplies and the sort of camera shops that made window displays out of tripods and white umbrellas.

The air in the old brick building on East 19th Street was heavy with painting smells: oil, resin and turpentine. Following Dinah up the stairs, Frankie sneezed. Reaching the fourth floor, she sniffed a pungent odor that reminded her of Elmer's glue and she sneezed again. Modernage, where she had her prints and postcards made up, smelled like that, so she wasn't surprised that Dinah stopped and rang the bell.

They were buzzed into a very white room, walls studded with framed headshots. Frankie tried not to gawk. She didn't want Dinah to think it was her first time at a photographer's studio. No one came out to meet them. Apparently they would have to wait.

"He must be in the darkroom," Dinah said. "When I called, he said it was fine to come." She folded herself onto a white Naugahyde loveseat and got busy with a magnifying glass, making one final pass at her proofs.

Frankie settled into the loveseat opposite and looked for a magazine. The oval table held only an album, as thick as the Yellow Pages. She slid it closer, to flip through the photos. The people were improbably beautiful. Even the wrinkly white-haired man and the little girl with the missing tooth had a kind of glamour. Frankie felt homely and ungainly by comparison. She was also possessed by an absolute need to have this man take her pictures. If he could make her look like this, she'd have so many job offers that she'd have to turn some down.

Quiet as a cat, the photographer emerged from wherever he'd been and crouched down next to Dinah. Frankie was so absorbed in his work, she didn't notice until Dinah used her name.

"My friend Frankie was so impressed that she came to meet you. She's in the market for new shots."

Frankie looked up, flustered. "Hi," she croaked.

"Hi. Gio," he said, springing up, holding out a hand. He had a strong grip and intense blue eyes. "So what do you think?"

"I think you're great!" It came out automatically. She blushed and tried not to cringe. "I mean, I like your work a lot."

He dipped his head in thanks. His long James Taylor waves swung forward. He shook them back. "So what about them appeals to you?"

"Um…" She shrugged. It would to mortifying to say "you make everyone look gorgeous."

"She liked how natural my smile was, didn't you Frankie?"

Frankie found her voice. "Yes," she said, looking firmly into the blue eyes. "Especially the picture with her hair down. Dinah looks so happy that you start to smile back."

"Alright!" He slapped his hand against his knee, which was poking through a hole in his jeans. He flashed a grin at Dinah. "I like your friend. So, Frankie...it's Frankie right? Any chance you've got your old pictures with you?" He pointed to her dance bag.

She quickly pulled out the cardboard portfolio that kept them from bending and handed it over. Darting back and forth between the pictures and her face, his eyes gave her a weird feeling, as if she was a thing instead of a person.

He handed them back with a dark sigh. "Old fashioned," he said. "Worse; they're boring. No life. I can't believe you're getting any work out of these." It didn't sound cruel when he said it, just a fact, like the dentist saying you have a cavity. "We can do a lot better."

She nodded. She had complete faith in Gio. "When can I make an appointment?"

♬

Within 72 hours of Peter Korn fastening the lid on a cooler full of Katz's pastrami, pecking his mother on the cheek and peeling off towards Ithaca in his new third-hand Volkswagen Bug, Gloria was on the phone with Ellen, campaigning for her return.

Ellen had been hoping for that call. Relieved as she was to actually receive it, she made sure to sound both surprised and chagrined. "Oh, no! I'm committed to another two weeks at my current engagement. How disappointing! I really loved working for you." It was a respectable performance, if she did say so herself. Ellen might have given acting a try, if only the criticism weren't so personal; she'd had enough of that from her parents to last a lifetime.

"I'm sure you can work something out with Keppel and Grace," Gloria said breezily. "If you'd like me to make a call..."

"No, they didn't need me anymore, so I got in touch with some of my previous clients. One of them had a special project right up my alley. Lucky timing." There was no such client, but Franklin Li and her father both said to always negotiate from strength. Besides, Ellen felt like playing a little hard to get. She was fed up with people who cut you at a moment's notice, then expect you to come running back the minute they snap their fingers. "I made a commitment. It would be unprofessional to leave them in the lurch."

Gloria made an "mmmm" sound. Ellen could visualize her frowning at the chaos on her desk.

"I wouldn't do that to any client," Ellen added self-righteously, before abruptly switching to a more conciliatory tone. "I could come in a couple of nights, when the office is closed," she offered. "Do some filing for you, straighten things out?"

Gloria's "mmm" changed to a considering "hmmm."

"If that's any help," Ellen added. She knew it would be. Why had Gloria thought that Perfect Pete would want to hang around the office? He was on break from law school, for fuck's sake! "It was just a thought. I understand if you need someone right away..."

There was an obvious chain of reasoning: by the time Gloria found someone she didn't hate and broke him in, Ellen would be done with her mythical job.

"Well, until your other commitment is over..." Gloria said begrudgingly. "Why don't you come by Tuesday around six and we'll talk."

"That would be wonderful! Thank you, Gloria! See you Tuesday." There was no reason not to sound grateful: she was, and it would stroke Gloria's ego. Ellen was overjoyed. This time, there was every reason to hope it would lead to a permanent job. Now that Perfect Pete had a life that didn't include being his mother's gofer, Gloria needed Ellen to pick up after her as much as Ellen needed what she could learn from Gloria. They were perfectly symbiotic—an incredibly expressive word that was Ellen's single recollection of tenth grade biology.

Ellen poured herself a celebratory whisky. There was no point waiting for Leonard; he and Kevin were at the opera tonight. She lifted her glass in the air and toasted: "To Gloria!"

It was a bottle Franklin had given her, imported stuff that left an expensive dry aftertaste, a different class from even the best of what used to fall off Barney's trucks. She still felt an occasional small pang over Barney, almost like when she'd thrown away her Ben Cartwright doll. Another man she'd outgrown.

Her snicker sent whisky burning up her nose, a minor annoyance now that life was falling so nicely into place. Gloria wasn't merely the best press agent on Broadway (if you could call that a "merely"), but had actually helped produce a couple of small shows. Alone in the office for a few nights, Ellen would manage time for a little extracurricular research before approaching her about *A Thing or Three*.

♫

Gio said the biggest mistake most women made was thinking that their everyday makeup would be good under the lights. He insisted Frankie get hers done professionally, recommending a makeup artist who did a lot of his clients. When she explained she couldn't afford it, he suggested she go to the Makeup Center on West 55th Street, which was a lot cheaper. For Frankie, it was still a splurge.

"It's not an expense, it's an investment," Dinah advised. "You need to spend money to make money."

Dinah was right. Ellen had also once said something like that. Frankie forgot about what, but at the time she'd been impressed at how businesslike it sounded. Frankie had to remember the business part of show business. That was another thing Ellen liked to say.

One o'clock found Frankie staring at her own face in the large, light-bulb-bordered mirror, awed by what she saw. She looked like herself, except mysteriously perfected. Her eyes were larger—she could see that even before she put her glasses back on. Her cheekbones were gorgeous and her skin had a soft, even tone it hadn't had since she was eleven.

"I didn't get all the scars," confided the girl with the daunting Cleopatra eyes, referring to some acne and chicken pox scars on Frankie's cheeks. "It would have caked up. Your photographer can airbrush whatever bothers you."

Frankie bought a pot of the soft pinky-coral lip stuff and a brush she could use to apply it: an investment. Instead of the translucent power the girl urged on her, Frankie decided to stick with the powder from the Bob Kelly kit she'd bought for NYADA and had so far only used for *Gooseberries*. She was running out of money to invest. Anyway, it was probably the same stuff.

She wasn't going to ruin this artwork by walking two miles in the damp cold. On the RR from Carnegie Hall to 23rd Street, she held her head with care. She wondered if anyone thought she was famous and taking the subways incognito. Maybe not, but as she was crossing 23rd, a truck driver hung his head out the cab and called out "looking good, sexy lady!" It gave her a little strut, until some street bum lurching from a cardboard tent on 20th spoiled it by making those disgusting kissy noises. She moved faster after that, careful not to catch anyone's eye and stopping only for traffic.

In Gio's little white dressing room, she removed her shirts from the dry cleaner's bag and hung them on the pipe. She hoped they weren't too much alike. He'd said to bring things that made her feel confident, and shirt collars were what she liked. She'd also packed a scarf and the tweed newsboy cap she'd picked up after everyone had been so complimentary about her knitted one. The articles in the trades said to never use accessories in headshots, but her instinct was to express her personality. She'd let Gio decide.

She laid her new lip color down on the counter with her old powder and the brushes. By then, her curling iron was ready. Seated before the mirror, she sectioned off her hair with clips. With greater gravity than maybe even on opening night of *Mother Courage*, she wrapped the bottom of the first piece reverently around the metal rod and rolled it up to where it made her scalp uncomfortably hot. She began to hum under her breath: *Everything is green here—not like Moscow / And the air is clean here—not like Moscow / But my lungs are only free / When they breathe the air my eyes can see / And never do they breathe as easily / As when they breathe the air of Moscow.* One verse was the exact amount of time it took for a curl to set. To get her entire head done, she'd get through the song three times.

She had two more curls to go when Gio knocked on the door.

"Hey, Frankie! Are you decent?"

"Sure!" she called out, glad she'd thrown on one of Mickey's discarded work shirts instead of sitting around in her bra the way a lot of actresses did.

Gio held out a glass of wine. His smile was friendly but quick, the blue eyes immediately veering upward to the row of shirts. She put the wine down, needing both trembling hands to hold the hot curling iron. It was the moment of truth. What if all her clothes were wrong?

"The blue one," he pronounced. He was strong and positive. She could breathe again.

"The blue," she echoed, able to start on her next-to-last curl.

"The contrast will be good against your skin. The white'll wash you out too much." He turned a keen eye to her face and broke out in a wide grin of approval. "You look great! Perfect!"

She felt herself flush and grinned back. "Thank you."

"You're one of those girls who looks super cute with glasses. And it can be a good commercial look." He nodded, as if he'd been having a discussion with himself and had finally reached an agreement. "Yeah, I think we'll mix things up, shoot a couple of rolls with and a couple without. Definitely in the blue. And for a different look…" He whipped around to stare at the shirts again. He laughed.

Was there something funny about her shirts? "What?" she asked.

He whirled around again and winked. "And then I think we'll try the plaid. Usually I advise against patterns, but I think you're the plaid type. Definitely. Good choices, by the way. You know what works for your neck. Finish up and get into the blue, then come on out to the studio. Bring the wine. Oh, and no shoes. People are much more connected to their feelings when they're barefoot."

"Sure," she said, trying not to stare at herself in the mirror. What was wrong with her neck? It was a little long. Is that what he meant? Did it matter? It was a compliment, saying that she knew what worked for her. That was more important than if her neck was a little long.

The high wooden stool was planted on a white cloth in the middle of the studio. Perching on it, Frankie found herself staring into a large black box of a camera. She stopped thinking about her neck immediately. Gio switched on a turntable with a stack of what turned out to be jazz albums and began fussing with his lights and his white umbrellas, to get the light exactly how he wanted it on her face.

This was very different from having her picture taken by Larry's friend in Toronto. Frankie forced herself to look away from the camera, watching him instead, sipping her wine and listening to the music. Gio positioned himself behind the tripod and looked down into the viewfinder. He clicked a meter next to her cheek. He pulled out a Polaroid and took a few pictures. He made tiny adjustments to the lights again and again.

Finally, he was satisfied. "Okay, gorgeous," he said with a grin, taking the wine glass out of her hand. "You can have it back while I'm changing rolls." He got back in position behind the camera, and winked at her. "Welcome to the Frankie Cecchi show! Magic time!"

He'd said her name correctly. She felt a surge of warmth through her body, bursting out into an enormous smile.

"Alright!" he chortled. "Now that's what I call star power!"

The next ninety minutes flew by. Frankie understood what Dinah had meant. She felt so special, and so comfortable. Although it was impossible to ignore the tickle she felt from the gaze of those deep blue eyes, she could see Gio wasn't trying to sleep with her. And not because she wasn't attractive. On the contrary, he made her feel certain that she was beautiful. It was because his purpose in life was to help her. He was a handsome doctor: utterly professional and respectful. Even Ellen wouldn't be able to get him to look at her any other way.

Gio had her turning left and right, looking thoughtful and dreamy, pretending she'd just told a joke and that she'd just seen the person she loved most in all the world. Any time she got a little stiff, he'd make a face, or ask a ridiculous question, like "What color was George Washington's white horse?" He said she took direction really well. She could also see he thought she was really talented. Every time she said something funny, he cracked up.

"You are such a hoot!" he said, more than once. "You would be so great on TV."

She basked in his approval. So much so that, when she changed into the plaid shirt, she boldly brought the scarf and cap with her into the studio.

"I thought maybe before we finish, we could take some with these. I wear a lot of hats. It's my personality."

He rotated the newsboy cap thoughtfully in his hands, and set it on the table beside his film canisters and extra bulbs. Midway through what he said was the final roll, he paused. "If you want that cap and scarf, now's the time."

She hopped down from the stool, knotted the scarf around her neck and perched the cap at the angle she liked. Without even looking in the hand mirror, she hopped right back up.

Gio laughed. "Alright! The real you. I can dig it. And that scarf...like I said, you know what works for you. You have that great Balanchine look: small head, long neck. You're a swan! You know how many dancers would kill for that look?"

"You know how many dancers I would kill to be able to dance?" she cracked. So that was what he meant about her neck. She was a swan.

He laughed again and came over to tilt her chin slightly to the left. "Perfect. Just a few more shots. See if you can keep that pose and still smile as if you mean it."

He didn't have to tell her to smile; she couldn't have stopped if someone offered to pay her. The way he said it struck her as so funny, and she was having such a good time. She smiled with all her heart. "Damn, Frankie," he said, suddenly serious. "The camera loves you. I'm telling you, as a friend, you have to do something about those teeth. The commercial people want 'em white and even. I'll touch them up in the prints, but you'll never get past a go-see."

The lights went out. Her heart dropped and her face fell. Same as the agent last year. She still had no way to get hold of that kind of money. She needed to get work to earn the money to fix her teeth, but it seemed like she couldn't get work until she fixed them. What was the point of being here?

Gio felt the change immediately. "Hey, don't sweat it! I only meant...I want you to get the chance you deserve. And you will, babe. You'll see. Commercials and soaps aren't everything. There's plenty of other work out there, and with that energy, it's gonna roll your way. We've got some totally boss pictures in the can. The world's gonna stand up and take notice of Frankie Cecchi!"

♫

Ahuva had deliberately chosen the last preview, when the show would be set and polished but she wouldn't be influenced by the critics. By intermission she knew what the reviews would say. The score was somehow familiar, as if the composer had listened to too many musicals in his lifetime and had them stuck in his head, and the lyrics were completely simplistic. She had no tolerance for a mediocre score. Marshall Berenson had spoiled her appetite for lesser talents.

Except for a few numbers where the musical director seemed to be showing off just for the sake of proving he could, *Lost in Harrogate* was phenomenally pedestrian. And yet Maria had spoken about it such glowing terms! The only excuse was that she was playing the lead. Maria wasn't the glamorous, romantic leading lady type. She was more what they called a "character" actor. Until now, her biggest part had been Joan in *Rosebud*, the title character but, because of the way the show was written, a supporting role; plus, she'd played it in the revival. Creating the lead in a brand new show must be so exciting that it blinded you to the flaws in the material. Fortunately, Maria was giving a stellar performance or it would be impossible to go backstage later and congratulate her. Ahuva was horrible at lying, her face gave her away. That's why she was trying to get all her negative comments safely out of the way now.

"Is she always like this?" Jay asked Ric. "Intense!"

Ric laughed and said, "Chill out, Ahuva. So it's not great. It's better than a lot of what passes for musicals these days. You have to at least give them credit for the concept."

Ahuva rolled her eyes. "It's ridiculous! Exactly why I don't read mysteries." People assumed that someone who liked puzzles as much as she did would be an enormous fan of the genre, but she found it a waste of time. The plots were entirely too easy for anyone who paid attention to details. Or if they weren't, it was because the writer put in convoluted distractions, and Ahuva's taste was firmly on the side of stories that made sense.

"It's not one of her books," Ric informed her. "It's a true story. Agatha Christie's disappearance was major news when it happened. It's still famous in mystery circles. There are a few different theories. This one has never convinced me, but a lot of people buy it."

Now she felt like an idiot. She took a drag of her cigarette. Smoking could be a useful mask.

"I would have thought the same thing as Ahuva, if you hadn't told me before we came," Jay admitted. "It does come off like bad Christie."

If Jay meant to make her feel better, he wasn't succeeding. Now she could resent that Ric had told Jay and not her. Tonight wasn't working out at all the way it was supposed to. Her impulse had been to create a more intimate occasion than the *One for the Books* theatre party, something for only the three of them. This was a mature and sophisticated gesture, confirming her acceptance of Ric's relationship. She and Jay were going to become good friends. She was cool and adult. The show, starring her dear friend Maria Dearborne, would be great. She would take the men backstage after and they would see how Maria greeted her. Ric would be impressed.

"Is there even such a thing as good Christie?" she said, huffily. "I read the one about the train…"

"*Murder on the Orient Express*!" Jay's eyes sparkled with enthusiasm. "God, that movie was stunning! And that cast! We're both huge Lauren Bacall fans."

Ric whistled, which made Jay laugh.

They had so many private jokes, she thought crossly. She'd seen the movie, too. It was good, despite being impossibly elaborate. Why hadn't she remembered that it was an Agatha Christie story? "No, this one had a nosy old woman solving the puzzle. And knitting all the time. So ridiculous. Someone got killed on a train, and this woman—not the old woman, someone else—saw it because a window shade went up just at that precise moment…What a coincidence! And it only got worse."

"Okay, okay. I'm not going to pretend Christie's my favorite," Ric said it with a good-humored smile that she found patronizing. "Just don't write off the entire genre. I'm going to lend you one of my Nero Wolfes. See what you think of him."

"A major honor, Ahuva. He's crazy about Nero Wolfe." Jay patted Ric's forearm. "Every time we pass a second-hand bookstore, he has to stop and go through all the shelves. Drives me crazy."

"I want to have them all," Ric explained. "And some are out of print."

The lights in the lobby began to flash. The people who hadn't already fled back in started stubbing out cigarettes on the pavement.

"Well, I'm looking forward to Act II," Jay said, with every appearance of sincerity. "No matter what, your friend is very good, Ahuva. I'm enjoying this."

"Me, too," Ric said, putting an arm affectionately around her shoulder. "Thanks for asking us along. How about you come to dinner next Friday? Jay can try and make his father's famous pierogi."

Jay clutched dramatically at his chest. "Are you shitting me?! He's kidding, Ahuva. He knows I burn water. He will make a nice steak and I will pick up a cake from the bakery. And there will be much wine."

Ahuva forced herself to smile, her mind moving rapidly. Had Jay moved into Ric's apartment? It sounded that way. How could she be a woman of the world if every time she thought she'd learned the game, someone changed the rules? Ahuva took a deep, cleansing breath to free herself of negative thoughts and embrace love. There were the things in life you couldn't control, she reminded herself. She had to open herself to change. "Sure," she said, proud of the certainty in her voice. She mashed her cigarette against the pavement with her boot. "That sounds great. Could we make it fish? I don't eat dead animals. And I'll bring the dessert. There's a Hungarian bakery on Queens Boulevard. They close early on Friday but I can go...Oh, no! Not next Friday!" It was saying "Friday" that made the connection. The wash of relief relaxed her more than any ten cleansing breaths. "I can't! I have theatre tickets!"

"Another time then." Ric waved it off.

"Sure," she said. "Thanks for inviting me."

"So what are you seeing?"

"*Lake Song.*"

Ric laughed.

Jay blinked. "You've seen that a lot, right?"

She nodded, a huge smile crawling across her face. She felt the warmth of a small sun in her second chakra. "Friday is special. Lil got me house seats. It's my 100th time."

♫

It made absolutely no sense to Ellen that the belly chain had to come off. Her waist was a good two feet away from her knee—if not quite, then close enough—but the doctor had been adamant. Truth be told, she was glad to have a reason to be angry. A little righteous indignation did wonders to push away the fear. It was reasonable to be afraid. They were going to put her out, for fuck's sake! They'd cut open her knee and who knew what the hell they'd do in there. Would she ever walk normally again? The doctor warned she'd continue limping for months. Leonard had promised to buy her a walking stick, something with style, Byronic. She wouldn't mind limping if the pain was gone. What she did mind was that it would look like crap. Her creamy, unblemished skin was her one beauty and now it would be ruined by a big ugly scar. Harry said it was all her own fault to begin with, for running stairs blind, and then for refusing to go to a doctor until Mo practically dragged her there. He'd been red in the face, yelling how if she hadn't waited a month to get medical attention, maybe her knee would have only needed therapy. They had a huge fucking row over it, both of them screaming, to pretend they weren't scared. They were so fucking alike. Hating each other would be like hating yourself. They knew it, which was why Sydelle had failed to drive a wedge between them. They often didn't like each other but, as long as they didn't spend too much time in the same room, they loved each other fiercely. Harry was scared of losing her. Right now, she was scared of losing herself. She wished the surgeon didn't have to put her out.

The day before the procedure she went down to 47th Street to have the chain cut off. The jeweler gave her a little silk bag to keep it in and promised to solder it again the minute she got the okay. She would bring it with her to the hospital, for good luck. Not into the operating room, they'd never allow that, but to hold onto until they wheeled her in, and it would be there when she came out of the anesthesia.

Leonard had a treat waiting for her at home: lox from Zabars. Since she wasn't supposed to have anything in her mouth after six o'clock (no rude jokes please), he'd cut his afternoon class so they could have an early meal together, just the two of them. Kevin, sensitive to feelings, had chosen to stay away, sending his apologies and a promise to visit her in the hospital. He was a good guy, Kevin. The more she saw of him, the happier she was for Leonard.

Leonard said this time of day was technically tea, which is why he'd bought the thin brown German bread instead of bagels, and two mini-éclairs from the French bakery. He offered to go to a movie after, to take her mind off waiting, but she wasn't in the mood. They made do by flipping channels between a bunch of *Lucy* re-runs and a very odd movie they found on channel 11, about an astronaut marooned on Mars with a monkey.

Not for the first time, Ellen wished you could watch whatever movies you wanted, whenever you wanted. When she was rich, she was going to have a screening room in her house. The studios would of course lend her prints; after all, she would be a force to be reckoned with, a wunderkind who'd produced her first successful show at the age of 20. Maybe 21, what with the surgery slowing her down.

She was gradually winning Franklin Li over to *A Thing or Three*, enough that she thought she'd soon be able to get him to pay Ritchie and Pam for an option and make things official. The next step was to get Gloria interested. Ellen was planning on the indirect approach, dropping little hints here and there. If she could carry a tune, she'd hum some of the songs, but she couldn't. Never mind. Once she had an option, she'd have Ritchie and Pam tape a few numbers and she could "accidentally" play them at the office. Once she was back in the office. If it weren't for the surgery, she'd be starting with Gloria on Monday. Instead, she had to postpone it two weeks. Gloria had been very cool about waiting, thank god. That after-hours work had been a smart move. Thank you Felix for that lesson.

Sooner than she would have thought, it was time for *The Tonight Show*. Carson had George Carlin and Orson Bean tonight, so it was pretty funny. She still couldn't believe Dick Cavett was off the air. Tom Snyder was good for another hour after that, at which point, Leonard was exhausted, so they turned off the set and went to bed.

Eyes staring into the dark, she listened to the soft even puffs that meant Leonard was asleep. She started to count them, like counting sheep. She didn't expect it to work, but the next thing she knew, Leonard was shaking her awake and hovering to make sure she didn't accidentally drink some orange juice. She would have killed for a glass. She didn't mind fasting, as it happens, but she hated being thirsty. He practically herded her into the cab that Harry was paying for. At the Hospital for Special Surgery, he delivered her into Mo's hands to be checked in. Sydelle would have driven her insane. She'd proposed going in alone, but Mo had insisted; with her own parents handling most of Kelly's needs, she sometimes needed to do the mother thing.

It turned out to be comforting to be cherished. Then Mo left, and she had to change into that ridiculous surgical gown. And a nurse's aide came to shave her pubic hair, of all things. Ellen didn't even shave her pits; she believed in going natural. Physical therapy was going to be pain enough, she fumed. Why did she have to deal with frigging crotch stubble? Anyway, it was preposterous! She wasn't giving birth, for fuck's sake. On the other side of the curtain, she thought she heard a woman laugh.

The aide dragged in the head nurse, who definitely didn't appreciate it and stated coldly that they would be putting tubes in Ellen's thigh and "could not afford any extraneous matter that might interfere." There wasn't much Ellen could say after that. She lay like a corpse, her silk bag clutched firmly in her hand, while they shaved her and swabbed her with some blue antiseptic. They gave her a pill to make her sleepy.

There was a block of time she didn't remember. At some point, someone put a needle in her hand. Then someone called her name, from very far away. It hurt her throat to answer.

"Good girl," the voice said.

Which made her feel like Jackson, so she giggled.

"What did you say?" the voice demanded. "Can you say your name?"

"Ellen Janow," she said obediently. She didn't want to be hit on the nose with a newspaper.

"Good. How many fingers am I holding up?"

Ellen hadn't realized her eyes were open. Everything was white. "I can't see," she cried. A rush of panicked adrenaline flooded her veins. "I can't see!" She tried to sit up, but there were tubes and wires, and strong hands pushing her shoulders back down.

"Careful." Low and calm as it was, it was a command. "You don't want to sit up too fast. Lay back a minute and let me fix the lights."

She lay where the hands had placed her, her heart straining wildly inside her chest. She heard a switch snap and the brightness dimmed.

"Sorry about that. Some fool had it angled this way. You okay now? How many fingers?"

"Four," Ellen said promptly.

"You know what day it is?"

"Thursday."

"Good. Now let me help you up. Take it slow." The back of the bed, slowly tilting forward, did most of the work. It stopped well before she was upright. "That's as far as you go for now."

"My leg!" She couldn't see her leg from this angle.

The nurse...at least Ellen thought this was a nurse...seemed pleased that Ellen remembered why she was there.

"Doctor says the procedure went like clockwork. Once we know you can swallow, we'll get you in your room. Try and relax now."

Relax wasn't a word in Ellen's vocabulary at the best of times, but there was clearly nothing she could do and she was so tired. She leaned back against the mattress and tried to be patient. She'd had some strange dreams under the anesthesia. Faint wisps floated across her mind. She tried to capture them, as much out of boredom as curiosity. Something about Richard Burton wearing surgical scrubs?

They wheeled her back to her room and set her up, elevating her leg with some kind of sling. It felt bizarre and a little kinky. She said as much to the intern who strapped her up. He turned brick red and ran.

Ellen heard someone laughing. She turned her head. The room was a double. Now that the privacy curtains weren't blocking her view, she could see her roommate.

"I like your style," said the attractive blonde with the expensive haircut. "Valda Oelrich. *Guten Abend.*" She gave a little wave.

Ellen waved back. "Ellen Janow. Sorry I can't get up."

Valda laughed again. "You're funny. Excellent. The other woman was so boring."

"Have you been here long?"

"I had my procedure Tuesday. Another day or two, I go home. So we have time to be friends. Ah, yes. I think I have something that belongs to you." Valda carefully swung her legs over the side of her bed. One ankle was in some kind of black brace.

"Should you be doing that?"

"Ach! They tell me I should try to move." She hobbled towards Ellen's bed and collapsed triumphantly into the chair beside. "*Sehr gut.* So." She tossed something onto the bed. "It fell when they took you away. You were holding it. I thought perhaps it was important to you, so I picked it up. To make sure it didn't disappear, yes?"

It was the little silk bag. "Oh!" It must have still been in her hand when they knocked her out. What if it had got caught in the sheets and ended up in the laundry or the garbage?! Thank goodness this woman had found it. "Thank you so much. I don't know what I would have done if I lost it."

She opened the bag and spilled out the chain, letting it play through her fingers.

Valda's face sparkled with interest. "Such a beautiful necklace. So long. It must be Italian. I love Italy, don't you? Italians know gold. It is gold, yes?"

"Yes. But not a necklace." Ellen grinned slyly. "It's a belly chain."

Valda crinkled her eyes and shook her head. "I don't know that."

Ellen doubled the length and held it against her waist. "I wear it here."

"*Wundebar!* I never saw this. May I try?"

Ellen held it out to her. "There's no fastener. The jeweler had to cut it off for the surgery. I wear it all the time." Her lashes briefly dusted her cheeks.

"Ahh!" It was an appreciative sound. "I think my Dieter would like this on me. Did you get this in Europe? You will have to tell me where."

"Right here in New York. I'll give you the name." Ellen smiled.

"You are a very interesting person, I think." Valda tilted her head. "I am not tiring you out with all this talking?"

"Not at all. I'm too hungry to sleep anyway. They said they'd bring some food. All they would give me in recovery were a few saltines and some juice."

"Ya, well soon..." Valda flapped her hand, indicating the relativity of time. "So, we talk and keep you awake until then. Talk is what I do best. Dieter does the business and I go with him to dinner and parties and charm. You understand. I think Dieter would like to meet you, too."

Ellen nodded, bemused. She almost had the feeling this woman was chatting her up. Maybe she was still a little fuzzy from whatever they'd used to knock her out.

"Tell me, Ellen, what do you do for work?"

"I'm in theatre. I work for a press agent, but I've also optioned the rights to a new musical revue that I'm going to produce."

Valda clapped her hands together. "Wundebar! I adore revues! When we are in Paris, Dieter and I, we go to the Crazy Horse. We have such fun! And you are producing! And so young too. How clever you are! You must tell me all about it."

♫

The new photos almost instantly netted another call from the promotions agency, this time giving out toothpaste down on Wall Street. If the meeting place hadn't been around the corner from the new World Trade Center towers, Frankie would never have found it. It was so confusing down there. It was also windy and bitter freezing cold this close to the river. The worst part was that people didn't want toothpaste the way they wanted cigarettes or cheese. The cigarettes had given themselves away on a street corner. Even free, toothpaste had to be sold, and Wall Street people were in such a rush that it was hard to get them to stop and pay attention.

Just like the other times, Frankie was rewarded with a day of extra work. It was a comfortable day, spent sitting in a diner on 10th Avenue, pretending to drink the same mug of coffee over and over while talking with DJ, of all people, and an old man named Arnie. Frankie had to keep watch over Arnie's shoulder for the AD to wave his hand in a circle, her cue to signal for the waitress, an actress Frankie hadn't seen before who was playing Richard Dreyfuss's girlfriend in the movie.

She liked having something special to do, but the rest of it quickly got dull. To make their conversation look more realistic, the three of them decided to pretend that she and DJ were students and Arnie was their teacher. That let Arnie do most of the talking, which was good because the old man turned out to have a lot to say. He was a retired cop. According to him, most of the cops in movies, at least in the background, were actual cops. For a guy who was used to standing on his feet, it was an easy way to make a few bucks. And the casting people loved them: they were dependable, took direction well and came with their own costumes. Arnie was a bottomless pit of stories, mostly about famous actors being drunk or stoned or getting blowjobs in their trailers. He reminded her a little of Ellen, except Ellen saw everything as an adventure, while Arnie only had a nasty mind.

It was a good day, and she got to see Richard Dreyfuss up close (he was shorter than she'd realized). But if it weren't for DJ, she would have missed the most important thing. After they signed the timesheet, since they were going different ways, they said goodbye at the diner door. She was halfway to the corner when she heard him give a piercing whistle. Wondering if she'd left something behind, she whirled around.

"Hey, Frankie! I almost forgot!" DJ was loping towards her. She went to meet him halfway. "Congratulations!"

"Huh?"

"The union card. Well, right on!" He raised his fist in an air punch.

She blinked. She thought she had to work on a few more films in order to qualify.

"Didn't they give you a contract to sign?"

"We all got one."

"Yeah, but they should have given you…here, let me see. You know how you had to signal for the waitress? That counts as a Silent Bit."

She fished her copy of the contract out of her bag and handed it to him. DJ moved under a streetlight so that he could see better. It was still pretty dim around the smelly meatpacking warehouses at six o'clock.

"Yes!" He crowed. "There you go!" He jabbed a finger at a paragraph up at the top. "Day player! You see? You bring that up to the SAG offices and you've got your card."

Frozen in place, she tried to digest the information. Her mouth fell open, but no words came out. DJ laughed and gave her a quick hug. "See you in the movies, okay?"

She stood under the street lamp and watched him swagger away. If she had enough in the bank, she could join SAG tomorrow! There ought to be enough saved. Winter was usually slow, but Alfie had rented out the place for a couple of parties on her nights and those guys were big tippers. Like that old Italian guy she helped to find his hat, the one who'd said she reminded him of his late wife when they first were married. He made her so sad, she couldn't help crying, and he said she was a sweet girl and gave her $100. She would go up to SAG tomorrow before Jazz and find out how much it cost. She didn't care if it took every penny she had. They were all wrong: Gio, that stupid agent. Her teeth could wait. They weren't perfect, but they weren't standing in her way. So what if no one would put her in a toothpaste commercial? She'd never expected them to. She was an actress, not a model. A good enough actress that the director had picked her out for a special bit. And soon she'd be a card-carrying member of the Screen Actors Guild.

♫

Second semester of my junior year, I was rather hilariously cast as Lydia (the Bea Arthur role) in a student production of *The Buddy System*. In addition to being nearly 30 years too young, I was a light soprano. Even so, the casting committee had decided I had the best shot of all the undergraduates to wrest the bitter humor from Lydia's iconic "Never Mind Your P's and Q's." I thought it was the dawn of a glorious acting career; it would turn out to be the pinnacle. This would become a familiar trope in my life, mistaking an ending for a beginning.

My friends back home were almost as excited as I was. Student production or not, it was an iconic Marshall Berenson role. Everyone wanted to hear how rehearsals were going, and everyone promised to come up and see it. What a season! With *One for the Books* about to open, we now had three Marshall Berenson shows to talk about at once!

Happily for my rehearsal schedule, we'd booked our theatre party for Washington's Birthday weekend. I came down after my last Thursday class and spent the night with Ellen and Leonard in their garret, listening to Leonard's Original London Cast recording of *The Buddy System* and absorbing how different Patricia Routledge's fruity operatic performance was from Bea Arthur's familiar wry baritone. That night was the end of an era, my first taste of La Vie Boheme already allocated to history. A few days earlier, Leonard had broken the news to Ellen that he and Kevin were looking for a place to share.

Pleased as she was for Leonard, Ellen was anxious about her own situation. It wasn't as if she could do likewise and move in with Franklin Li, whose parents were in the process of negotiating with connections in Taiwan for a traditionally raised and no doubt properly dowered wife. Ellen would remain in his life only as long as they could pretend she wasn't. Under ordinary circumstances, she considered that a feature rather than a flaw. "Commitment is not a word in my vocabulary," she liked to say. She also thoroughly enjoyed referring to herself, albeit inaccurately, as a concubine. Li took her out to nice restaurants and gave her expensive presents, but his sponsorship was unofficial. With the senior Lis balancing the checkbook, the most she could get from Franklin was pin money that he could later disguise as petty cash.

Harry had agreed to subsidize Ellen's portion of the rent for one year beyond what would have been her expected college graduation. Would her pay from Gloria suffice to cover Leonard's share? It wasn't likely she'd find a new roommate. The only way this apartment worked for two was if they shared the bedroom, the way she and Leonard did. Should she start looking for a cheaper place? Was there such a thing? For neighborhoods Harry would accept, this place was about as cheap as it came. Maybe there was a studio in the area. One room was sufficient. It didn't even need to have a kitchen; she could live fine with a hot plate and a toaster oven, as long as there was a decent bathroom. If she could save 30 bucks a month, she could breathe easier. 20 might be enough.

The atmosphere at the apartment was a little strained, Leonard radiating guilty joy while Ellen alternated between declaring how happy she was for him and making pointed little remarks about loyalty and park benches. I was glad to have a dentist appointment to go home to the next morning.

Saturday at six, we met at Alfie's for dinner. "We" included Frankie, who was losing money by trading her full day Saturday shift with the girl who had Friday night. Calling it an early birthday celebration, Alfie comped her dinner and offered a free glass of wine to any of us who wanted. I thought this was very European. Up at school, the year of the tequila sunrise had segued into the year of 151 rum. Except for someone's abortive attempt at turning dining hall oranges and a jug of Boone's Farm into sangria, we hadn't ventured into wine. I wasn't certain I liked my Lambrusco, but it seemed an appropriate way to celebrate Frankie turning 21. Alfie wasn't the only one who'd thought to celebrate early. I'd brought her present with me, rather than mailing it to Patchogue. So had some of the others—nobody trusted Eunice. Ahuva had bought her ticket for tonight.

As advertised, *One for the Books* was inspired by boys' adventure stories. What this turned out to mean was a wholly American pastiche of Horatio Alger, Zane Grey and Mark Twain, with a soupçon of Damon Runyon. Despite the mostly 19th century sources, the story was set in an unidentified period that looked and sounded like the Great Depression: newsboys and millionaires; Robin Hood bank robbers versus The Law; brave soldiers; stalwart cowboys; and intrepid explorers. All these archetypes were lovingly collected and just as lovingly dissected. Quick-witted and shrewdly staged, it was, despite several infectious numbers, a cynical show. This wasn't the first time Berenson had been tarred with the C-word. *Riding a Bicycle* was notoriously cruel satire, and despite many endearingly funny moments and a poignant ending, *The Buddy System* was riddled with nasty zingers.

During intermission, I listened to the others, reserving my own judgment until I'd seen Act II. I was most interested in Kevin's observations, made with a keen anthropologist's eye that brought to the foreground references I'd barely begun to sense; it was that kind of show. Ahuva and Ric were strong in their praise of the score, the two of them already quoting lyrics with Jeff Kaplan not far behind. Frankie and a friend from her tap class went over some details they'd caught in the sand dance number. She also made several funny cracks about one of the younger actors, a former NYADA classmate. Not surprisingly, Ellen's comments were primarily about the difficulty in marketing such a piece.

Identifying entirely with the creative team, I wasn't comfortable with Ellen's pragmatic point of view, but I could understand she was right: in the end, it wouldn't matter how exciting the vision or how fine the execution if no one came to see the show. And they didn't. Maybe the Watergate-stunned theatre-goers were tired of seeing their illusions skewered. Maybe it was the confusing storyline. Or maybe it was the complete lack of a love story. People flocked to musicals for pretty girls and a love story. Even *Chicago*, in its louche and twisted way, satisfied that requirement. A world conjured by a Scout master around a campfire (that was how *One For The Books* opened), with the occasional wicked woman or damsel in distress played by a youth wearing a floor-mop wig, wasn't going to pull in either the matinee ladies or the tired businessmen.

I always liked to think of myself as someone who didn't need the comfort of the usual thing, who was excited by theatre that takes risks, but I wasn't certain how I felt about *One for the Books*. Even now I'm not. It was an indisputably clever show—possibly brilliant, if everything Kevin spotted was intended—but it lacked a heart. Berenson fans and the overlapping gay community did what they could by going several times each, but it wasn't enough to keep the show alive. In the end, *One for the Books* didn't last a year.

♫

Ahuva prodded a match and a button into the dustpan. Humming to herself, she tipped the pan into the trash and tied off the bag. She surveyed the room with some satisfaction. Done.

The first time Ahuva arrived early to a session, she'd found Prajit sweeping frantically. He explained that the AA group who borrowed the studio twice a week always left the trash can overflowing with paper cups, but missed a few things: the occasional tissue and gum wrapper; a couple of cigarette butts; a lot of spent matches. The wooden floor needed to be swept so that everyone could sit on it, but he had so many other errands to do that it was hard to finish in time. "Let me," she said, taking the broom out of his hand, "You have other things to do." Since then she'd deliberately shown up half an hour early to every session, to sweep and get rid of the trash.

Still humming, she dragged the bag into the hallway and bumped it carefully down the stairs. The song surprised her: *Grit, determination and a clean white collar / Grit, determination and a creed to foller / Honesty, integrity, enthusiasm, pluck!* Her sub-conscious at work? She grinned. Ahuva didn't care what the critics said, she thought *One for the Books* was brilliant. She was already planning to see it again—alone this time, so she could concentrate. She was especially fascinated by the psychological overtones. Or did she imagine those because she'd seen the show right after taking Intro Psych? The structure was fascinating. She was also increasingly curious about the source material, those boys' adventures. The Berenson interview in *The New Yorker* was practically a reading list.

It was almost *beshert* that she had so much free time now to pursue the reading. Not that Abba and Ima saw it that way. They were upset about her not taking any classes this semester. They didn't want to hear when she said it was a waste of time, that she wasn't learning anything in night school.

"Then go to day school," Ima retorted.

She knew her explanation was weak but it was the truth. "That's a waste too, unless I know what I want to study. And I don't." She didn't. If she thought she had talent of any kind, she'd go for a degree in Drama or Music. But it would feel like lying if she did. There was something out there for her.

She remained absolutely certain of it. She needed time to figure it out. The idea was still new to her parents. Once they saw that she was absolutely fine, they'd adapt to it. The important thing was to look busy and definitely not hang around the house too much.

Ahuva dumped the bag in the alley, dusted off her hands and stomped back up the stairs to the studio. She felt energized. Even a minor purpose like this refreshed her, brought her thoughts into focus.

She would give STC another try. If they didn't need her, there were plenty of other small theatres in the city. Circle Rep, American Place, La Mama...Frankie would know. Surely one of them would be happy to have her services.

She knocked on the door to the office, to ask Prajit for a fresh bag for the trash can. He didn't answer. She pushed lightly on the door. It opened, but Prajit wasn't there. Neither was the Maharishi. She'd never actually been inside the Maharishi's inner sanctum. She wondered if anyone ever had, besides Prajit. She couldn't resist stepping in to peer around.

The room was dim, the bamboo blinds half-drawn and partially masked by the ubiquitous printed cotton bedspreads. Ordinary looking file cabinets and a couple of bookshelves along the walls; a lot of cardboard boxes, and piles of books on the floor. In the middle of it all, a large desk, heaped with papers, with a chair to either side: one a weathered desk chair with comfortably dented leather padding; the other made of aluminum tubes and a vinyl seat, like the ones in her kitchen. Undercutting the haze of incense (the same one that Kaye used, no surprise) was an odd sweetness. Her nose prickled, drawing her, on tiptoe, to the shrine. A flickering lantern burned a substance she couldn't identify; not oil, it appeared waxy, but it wasn't wax. Keeping an ear trained for sounds behind her, she bent closer to the sizable shrine. There was an entire family of statues, gods she mostly couldn't identify, with tiny sprigs of flowers and herbs, and small dishes of rice and brightly colored candy-coated seeds. She felt a strange happiness, a physical lightening of her heart. She wanted to leave while she still felt it—and before anyone would catch her snooping around.

Backing up too quickly, Ahuva tripped over a box and, trying to stop herself from falling, clutched at a corner of the desk, causing a few papers to slide down to the floor. She hurried to replace them, but she couldn't tell where they belonged. Really, this desk was a mess! Papers of every shape and size, with no apparent rhyme or reason. Helter skelter, she thought, pleased at having an accurate use for that utterly senseless English colloquialism. Poking out from them, what looked like a very old, beautifully painted map. A tambourine? More of those sugared seeds.

This was so wrong. A great teacher should be surrounded with light and tranquility, a space to match his thoughts. This was a gift that Ahuva Geffner was uniquely qualified to give. She was suffused with a sense of purpose. There was no point in asking now. Maharishi Narang would be on his way to India soon. He wouldn't have time to sit with her. But when he got back, she was going to insist he let her help him get organized. A noble project, and one that would keep her occupied for months and months. She'd do it as an offering, not for money. Still, she reflected, insisting would be tricky. For all his gentle serenity, the Maharishi liked to be in charge. And, like most people her parents' age, she supposed he was a creature of habit. She would have to figure out how to make him think it was his idea.

♫

Ellen had her own desk now. Okay, she had a table, the table by the window that held the coleus and a tired geranium plant that Muriel, the part-time secretary, confided had never bloomed in all the years she'd worked for Gloria. The geranium's pot had the rubbed remains of a little kid's handprint and "I love Mom" in tilted letters, which probably explained a lot. The rest of the table, now that Ellen had shoveled off, sorted and filed several strata of tear sheets and photos, was all hers. Like everything in Gloria Korn's office, it was bare bones and functional. Invigorating.

As much as Ellen had loved her time with Felix Ayre, she had to admit the office had often left her drowsy. In late afternoon, with light filigreed through lace curtains, the aroma of lemon wax rising off Felix's precious antiques would mingle with the must of leather and books until she'd half expected to see George Bernard Shaw smoking his pipe in the armchair. Felix was good at making you believe his world had existed forever. Too bad that wasn't how business was done anymore. Now Gloria's place, with its junk store furniture and cardboard boxes, looked like it had been unloaded off a truck an hour ago and could easily be packed away in a matter of minutes. The sole nod to décor were the *Playbills* on the walls of the toilet, a gesture that might have been ironic but was probably just a matter of covering cracked plaster with an endless supply of free paper. Back in October, shifting trash and begging Gloria to adopt such innovations as in and out trays and desktop racks for file folders, Ellen had wondered whether the woman was honestly oblivious to her surroundings or just plain cheap. Now that Ellen had a property of her own in hand, she was inspired. The overall air of impermanence did more than floral-medallion rugs or rosewood furniture to underscore Gloria's relevance to modern theatre, to Show Business. The excellence of her work spoke for itself. She had no need to woo clients with atmosphere and no time to waste on such trivia as decorating.

Ellen found it daunting to imagine herself as a producer in the Felix mode but she could easily see herself with a place like this, really just one large room and a toilet. She and Franklin and Valda could find a small place in some crap building downtown, maybe as soon as next year. Meanwhile, she was thrilled to be here, learning everything Gloria could teach her. When the time was right, she'd ask Gloria to listen to Ritchie's tape. Once she heard it, Ellen was sure she'd want to help get *A Thing or Three* on its feet. Ellen was going to be more than the apprentice of Gloria's dreams, she would be the daughter Gloria didn't have. It wasn't as though she were cutting out Perfect Pete. If the boy wanted to be in the business, he'd have stuck right here instead of running halfway to Canada.

Ellen beamed at her utilitarian table. Sitting squarely between the stacked baskets and the rack of neat folders was one note of elegance: her Florentine-papered datebook. With the year a quarter done, it had cost her practically nothing at Lee's. Together with the round Harrods tin she was using for pens, and Kevin's Mexican papier mâché box for paper clips, it lent the Spartan workspace a faint whiff of international sophistication that pleased her immensely.

Months of dining out with Franklin Li was rubbing off some rough corners Ellen had arrogantly assumed she didn't have. It was one thing to hold your own in a room full of actors, or to act out in front of the easily shockable, like her mother or those girls she'd grown up with, but she could see it was better business sense to present a more subtle eccentricity to the wider world. Small touches, like her wedjat ring, were more than enough to have on display. It was more effective to keep the rest hidden and imply.

Like her belly chain. Ellen certainly hadn't been conniving that day in the hospital, she'd been zonked on anesthesia. The simple fact of that chain's existence set Valda's imagination running wild all on its own. All Ellen had to do was smile and drop her eyelids—that was hardly flirting. Valda called her from home twice a day. Once Ellen got out, they had coffee a few times, always at Valda's invitation. Again, Ellen did nothing to actively engage the attention. Initially, she was too exhausted from the combination of physical therapy and the strain of lugging her brace up and down Gloria's stairs. Later, it became a game to see how little she had to give out while Valda peppered her with questions, mostly about the theatre, and occasionally let her eyes flicker down towards Ellen's waist, as if seeing beneath her clothes to where she knew the chain would be. The day Valda's cast came off, she and Dieter gave a party at their apartment in the Sherry. Ellen brought Franklin, which seemed to fascinate the Swiss even more.

"Ass backwards," Joe Bigelow laughed, when she told him. "Most girls start out teasing and have to learn to give it away. You, sweetheart, are a fucking freak of nature."

Joe also made the occasional crack that she was getting too classy for him. Ellen didn't mind the kidding. He was the only person who noticed the changes she could feel in herself. When he wasn't ribbing her about it, he was her biggest supporter. It was sweet. He'd been frankly impressed by Gloria giving her a full-time job, and was being very encouraging about *A Thing or Three*.

And now, so was Valda. During the party, the Swiss socialite requested a "business" meeting with her and Franklin. Franklin, shifting his weight off the promising European business cards padding the back pocket of his Italian leather pants, told Valda he would book a table for lunch at the Four Seasons when she got back from Basel. Ellen had been drifting a little on the combination of hash and the painkillers she was still taking. The offer cut through the fog like a thunderclap. It wasn't that she hadn't taken herself seriously, but that she never believed that anyone else did, not until that moment. That was the biggest change.

With the last of the messages copied to Gloria's To Do list, and the coffee things washed and turned upside down on the shelf to dry, Ellen was free to leave for the day. She straightened the items on her desk, adjusting the file folders to keep them clear of dead geranium leaves, and made sure her pens were capped. She was in no rush. It was early, not even 7:00. Franklin was in Boston. With Leonard gone, the apartment was so quiet; empty. It would have been a good night to second-act *Lake Song*, but Ellen found the show a little flat without Bron. She'd have to put on some music, or maybe Channel 13. She felt that little bit of blue creeping in, the way it did, for no good reason. It would only take a phone call to arrange an evening out, free tickets being a concrete benefit of working for Gloria. She wasn't in the mood. It had been a long couple of days, and her leg ached since the painkillers had run out. Valda said she knew a guy, but Ellen didn't want to start down that road. What if she got hooked on pills? She didn't like the idea of something being able to control her. She'd have to tough it out. She'd walk home slowly. Walking was good therapy as long as it wasn't up and down stairs.

What she needed was a little jolt of energy to get her ass moving. She opened the Florentine book to the 11th. "Four Seasons Grill Room." Beautiful. She'd used her gold-nibbed fountain pen with the bottle green ink. She smiled.

She'd been dying to go to the Four Seasons. Harry, who'd drunk many a business lunch in the Grill, had promised he'd take her for her birthday when she turned 21.

"It's not a place for kids," he said. Like most fathers, he'd gone blind to any changes in his daughter once she'd started sprouting breasts.

Ellen wasn't a kid. She was a producer. Maybe she didn't have a show in production yet, but lunch in the Grill was her diploma. Companies were bought and sold there, as were politicians. They probably allowed women in pants by now, but she'd give Franklin a thrill and wear the leather skirt he'd brought her from Italy. With her Jaeger cashmere sweater and, of course, a scarf. Those silver earrings that were almost Georg Jensen would give her that subtle touch she was now craving. She'd wear them all the time if they weren't so uncomfortable. She really ought to get her ears pierced. Someday she'd get over her phobia about needles, if only for the jewelry.

Running a finger over the datebook entry, she shivered with delighted anticipation. Wouldn't it be a riot if she ran into Harry, if he was sitting at the bar when they walked in?

Feeling better now, she grabbed her bag and locked up. She limped down the stairs with her mind fixed firmly on thoughts of a hot bath and a couple of fingers of scotch. She remembered a couple of slices of pizza in the refrigerator. That was a good thing about Leonard being gone: she could get the whole pizza with olives and anchovies, exactly the way she liked it.

♫

If only her father would have asked her to come to Rocco's tonight for a plate of osso buco, just the two of them, it would have felt like a birthday. They would have shared a carafe of red wine, drinking it out of glasses as small as the ones with the painted oranges that Martha had used to serve the morning juice. The wine, thin and a little sour, was from the farm Rocco and his brother owned out on the North Fork and was served with an air of apology. They did their best, Rocco said every time, but what could you expect? Long Island ain't exactly Tuscany.

In response, Mickey always protested that it was perfect, he wouldn't dream of drinking anything else, it was 100% authentic Italian. Not that

Mickey had ever been in Italy himself. He'd been born right here. So had Rocco, but his family had land in Montalbano and he'd spent a few years after the War living with the cousins. That's why his menu had things like *ribollita* and the *pappardelle al coniglio* as well as the usual things people expected to find.

When Frankie was little, her parents would pour a splash of wine in her glass and top it off with water. When she'd turned 14 and Mickey announced he wasn't going to water it down for her anymore, it felt like an honor—until she'd tasted her first sip. She'd tried to be cool, but couldn't stop the pucker. Mickey teased her forever about that. Though she tried to be a sport, she was upset for the longest time. Being Italian was important to her. Was it the legacy of Martha's Dutch father, that she couldn't like wine? She worried right up until the first time Alfie poured her a glass. The wine at Alfie's was a very different thing from what Rocco's served. Alfie's wines were the rich red of jewels and tasted like actual grapes had been involved. Some had an undertone of strong tea. The strength had surprised her at first. Now she preferred it to most other alcoholic beverages.

Alfie got a kick out of this. It was so sweet of him to comp that bottle, the night they went to see *One for the Books*. Most of the people in their group drank beer or gin and tonic, so she got to have two glasses. She probably should see the show again, to see what she really thought of it. It had been a great night. There was the wine. Then the guys in the kitchen put a candle in her parfait and everyone sang: the front of house team, her friends and their friends who she was meeting for the first time. She'd seen a show and been given presents. So what if it was a few weeks ahead? That was her birthday. A fine one. She couldn't ask for more.

Still, it hurt that Mickey hadn't even said "Happy Birthday" once today. Not at breakfast. Not when she kissed him and said she was heading to the city.

Maybe it was better this way. If he'd done the least little thing, Eunice would have been pissed off, like she was whenever Mickey gave Frankie any attention. They all knew Eunice was embarrassed by her jealousy and tried to justify it with anger. Her eyes rolled up and focused inward. You could imagine the facts spooling across her brain, assembly line style, stopping under a magnifying glass so she could consider each one, a little muscle in her temple twitching as Eunice wondered: collect? or discard? She always managed to dredge up some minuscule thing that she decided gave her a right to be angry. Then she'd strike out and yell her head off. Frankie had learned to sit motionless until the storm died down, to not put any fuel on the fire. She'd stopped hoping her father would defend her. Mickey only slumped in his chair, trying to pretend it wasn't happening. The few times Frankie tried to fight back, she had him on her case as well. He couldn't deal with thinking he'd maybe made a mistake in picking Eunice. Mickey didn't like to make mistakes. It was better not to stir the pot. There would be 10 or 15 horrible minutes, and then she could disappear. Sometimes Mickey would slip a ten dollar bill under her door after, to try and make up. If Mickey had done anything at all for Frankie's birthday, Eunice would have figured out that Frankie was now 21 and there would have been a fresh campaign to throw her out of the house. So it was probably just as well that Mickey had ignored the day. Maybe that was why he had.

While she was turning this over in her head, Frankie's feet took her automatically from Penn Station to Times Square. She popped into 1515 to see if any new productions had posted casting contacts for SAG extras. There was no need to stop by Equity to check the boards; she'd be there tomorrow for the Oregon Shakespeare Festival call.

There were a few feature films and one television movie. All the agents listed already had her 8x10, so she pulled out a few postcards and addressed them. That's what postcards were for. She paused to admire hers, glad she'd decided to do the two-picture card. The one Gio called the "straight" shot was more versatile, but even he loved the one in the cap. She made a wish for birthday good luck and popped the cards in the mailbox on the corner. Job well done.

Next stop, the Regale, another place she couldn't call home anymore. Madeleine Blair had wisely decided to keep Connie, who was not only an incredibly nice person but could do all the quick changes in her sleep. That didn't mean Frankie could come and hang out the way she used to. It had been extremely uncomfortable on that Tuesday when Blair came in early and gave her the funniest look. But Connie had left a message on her service, specifically asking her to stop by today, if she had time. She felt almost like a stranger, knocking on the stage door. Wally gave her a big hello. He must have been told to expect her, because he gave a whistle and Connie came running out to meet her. They didn't go near the dressing room, which was just as well. Seeing it without Bron's things in it was always too sad. Instead, Connie gave her a big hug and took her down to the Green Room for tea. There was a box of delicious petit fours from a French bakery on Madison Avenue.

"She sure knows how to live," Connie cracked. It was the only thing she said about Madeline Blair, but every few minutes her eyes went to the big clock on the wall.

Connie had a present for her, too. Frankie thought it was a card, until she opened it and found the photo. It was from Ivor's party and showed Frankie on the sofa talking to Bron.

Frankie was thrilled. "I'll treasure this until the day I die! It's wonderful, Connie! I don't even remember you having a camera."

"I don't make a fuss about it. I like pictures better when people don't pose. It makes them more like real memories."

They talked about Connie's family and Frankie's problems with Eunice. Frankie told her about the *Most Happy Fella* chorus call where she got typed-out for not looking Italian. It was somehow always easy to make the worst auditions sound funny to someone else. Connie laughed like crazy.

"You should tell Lil that one," she said. "She's been asking about you, you know. Said I should tell you to stop by one Wednesday between shows and say hi."

"Sure!" Frankie felt a happy hum of belonging in her chest. Not such a bad birthday after all. It wasn't a long talk, but it was a good one, like always.

Warm from Connie's final hug and a thumbs up from Wally, Frankie headed for jazz class.

In the changing room, she wrapped her new dance skirt over her good grape leotard and the skin-colored footless tights that were like Kiki's. Daphne had given her the skirt yesterday at Irene's. It was black. She tied a purple scarf around her hair like a headband, making the ends into a puffy bow and smiled with satisfaction at her reflection. She was straight out of a Busby Berkeley musical.

Daphne wore skirts all the time now. Margaret Rodney insisted they gave a professional polish to a leotard, though not a single girl at Frankie's one and only professional dance audition had worn one. It was probably more a ballet thing. Margaret had studied ballet when she was young, until Balanchine told her that her head was too big and her neck too short; Frankie always assumed that's why she'd chosen tap for Daphne.

Right or not for Broadway, Frankie loved the way the skirts looked, but had never thought to own one. Such extravagance! Every time she saw them in Capezio or Freed, she reminded herself that she could either get a skirt or pay for six weeks of classes. What a thoughtful present for the Rodneys to have given her! And she was invited for dinner at the house next week, when Daphne was on break for Easter. Casilda wanted to make her a special cake. So what if she only did ordinary things today? She felt special! She felt more graceful, too. How could she not, with that fluttering scrap of chiffon tied over her hips?

She danced her heart out in class. Kiki said she was really putting over the routine and gave her a nice compliment about how she'd made so much progress since she'd starting coming. Flushed with exertion and pleasure, Frankie decided she'd treat herself to a late lunch at Alfie's. Or was it an early dinner? Didn't matter. She deserved a nice meal. Maybe she'd even go to Duffy Square and see if there was anything interesting on half price for tonight. If not, she'd still go home happy. Maybe she'd splurge on a bag of Pepperidge Farm cookies and have a midnight snack in her bedroom. She could snuggle up with her photo album and maybe reread *The Secret Garden*, which always cheered her up.

She ordered a hamburger at the bar with a nice glass of wine. Alfie refused to let her pay, even when she reminded him he'd already given her a birthday drink. He mussed her hair, the way he sometimes did. "So much like Yolanda," he said. He said that a lot. Yolanda was his kid sister, who'd died from a burst appendix when she was 14.

The bell over the door rang. Frankie heard loud giggles and a shriek. She twisted her neck to look. It was a couple, so tightly entwined they seemed to be sharing a single coat. They paused in the archway for the kind of kiss that looks like people drinking each other's air. The light hit the woman's upturned face. It was Linda Schiller. Frankie didn't recognize the man, but he sure as hell wasn't Donny Hopkins.

Turning her head so that she could see herself in the mirror above the bar, Frankie lifted her glass and toasted with a grin. "Happy Birthday to me," she murmured.

♫

Ten days later, James Lord, Sara Bradley and the various investors whose names no one knew posted the closing notice. In one month's time, the original Broadway run of *Lake Song* would come to an end.

KOSTIA

The man who wished,
He wished for heaven right here on earth—
Or maybe peace; why not peace?
The man who wished
Dreamed of perfection, a peaceful heart—
Or maybe love; why not love?

The man who wished,
He wished to love and be alive,
To greet each day with open arms and open eyes.
The man who wished
Wished for too little and too much—
He wished for happiness.

What am I to write at the bottom of the page
Just before I write 'finis?' What am I supposed to say
To have the last word?

Is it thought? Is it action? Or maybe conversation?
What would be the right—or should I say appropriate—sensation
To hold them, their attention;
Or release them, loose the tension?
What to give them as my very final moment?
The last word...

That's the story of my life.
That's the story of my art.

Do I think? Or do I act? Or will they talk about me?

With stops to refuel, it took more than a full day of travel to get from New Delhi to New York. Someone said they'd landed at JFK at 7 AM. Prajit kept rubbing his eyes to stay awake, yet the old man was leading the chants and telling stories as easily if he'd spent the day before dozing at the beach. Had the Maharishi actually conquered jet lag with his superior control over bodily functions, or was he merely better able to conceal the evidence? Either way, he seemed alert enough that Ahuva felt no compunction about going up to him at the end of the session to make her proposal. Strike while the iron is hot, she told herself, though she wasn't sure what she meant, other than feeling that she'd lose some momentum by not approaching him on his very first day back. She wasn't alone. Everyone seemed to need to make personal contact. She lagged behind the crowd. It wasn't easy to wait, but Ahuva preferred not to feel rushed when her moment came. Finally, there was no one else in the room except the two of them and Prajit.

Serenity wrapped Maharishi Narang in a blanket of sunbeams. When she was seated among the others on the ground, Ahuva felt it as the calm of a warm bath. Yet whenever she addressed him directly, she was strangely intimidated.

Fighting not to clear her throat, Ahuva pressed her hands together and bowed her head. "Namaste, my guru." She lifted her eyes. All her hard work went up in smoke. Her breath, diligently tempered to a languid beat, came quick and ragged, and her contrary heart skittered across her ribs.

He gazed into her face and smiled his gentle smile. "Namaste, Daughter. Still impatient, I see. But you have come far." His eyes crinkled delightfully.

It was an enormous honor, for him to know her so well. Someday maybe he'd give her a special name.

"You have a question."

She nodded. She'd thought for hours about how she was going to approach this. She didn't want to offend him. And she certainly didn't want him to think she'd been going through his office like a spy. "I want to be of service."

These were nowhere near the words she'd planned. They jumped out before she could stop them. Her face was hot, her hands were cold and she wanted to disappear.

The Maharishi waited patiently for her to continue. He tilted his head in what she decided was encouragement.

"I'm very organized," is what she finally said. "I don't mean any disrespect, but you're not. That's perfectly fine. You don't have to be. That's not what you...You have more important things to do. Phenomenally more important things. But frankly, Maharishi Narang, I don't know how you can concentrate...I mean, I know you can concentrate—*you* can—anywhere. And I get what you say, about how the outward shape doesn't necessarily reflect the inward..."

She'd once heard him say this to a woman who was upset about her weight. She could see he had no idea what she meant by repeating it now.

She hated the desperate squeeze of her throat when she couldn't find the right words. "What I mean is, wouldn't it be better...more productive ..if you didn't need to spend so much energy getting around these things?"

"It would," he agreed. Was that a twinkle? His voice was solemn. "A straight path to enlightenment is rare, but welcome."

"Exactly!" The word came out as a squeak. "Think of how much more efficient...how much more good you could do, if you didn't have to waste so much energy on clutter. If you could find things when you needed them. If supplies got ordered before you ran out of things..."

"You want to work in my office?"

"Yes!" Her reflexive sigh of relief was deeper than any hard-fought centering breath. He sounded astonished, nothing more. Of course, he had no idea that she'd intruded on his privacy. "As a volunteer," she hastened to add. "I could start by straightening things up. If you'd like. Then, if you needed someone to write letters, manage your calendar...Anything that would be useful."

He beamed at her. "Positively beamed" is how she'd describe it when she told the story.

"Such a generous offer, child. I won't pretend the offer is unwelcome. Prajit is somewhat overwhelmed. He tries his best, and with great love and devotion, but worldly matters often elude him. The poor boy was meant for study and meditation, not things of a practical nature."

"I'm very practical," Ahuva declared happily. "And I would love to help."

"Well then," he nodded. "When would you want to start?"

When she showed up the next day, Prajit had a key for her. He pressed it into her hand with a look of such profound gratitude that for years, whenever she felt superfluous to the world, the memory of it lifted her heart.

She began by familiarizing herself with where things currently were, and immediately discovered that the file cabinets were being used as a kind of attic: clothes, a box of light bulbs shaped like candle flames, a sack of lentils, a patchwork cat...she found everything there except papers. The first step had to be to systematically unload things into whatever receptacles she could muster up, which were mostly shopping bags. When the Maharishi arrived a few hours later, the cabinets were empty and ready for a good dusting, and Ahuva was more than ready for a cup of tea and a breath of fresh air.

While Prajit made the tea, the Maharishi rummaged gleefully through the bags, exclaiming over odd items he'd forgotten he ever owned.

"Here it is!" he said, for what was the eighth or ninth time that hour. "Look!"

Ahuva turned obediently to look yet again. This time the treasure was one of the nicer finds, an unusual book, the binding made of two prettily-painted wooden boards that closed with a brass hook and eye.

"Shashikala's book." A delighted smile lit his face. "The book I found for her last year, in Jaipur. Wherever did you find it?"

"In an old Pan Am bag." It paid to be thorough. The bag had felt too heavy to be empty. Inside were a pierced brass votive holder decorated with a monkey, a bag of stale airline peanuts and the book, wrapped in a half-unraveled muffler.

"Ah! I knew I had it in the airport, but then I could never find it again. And here it is! What other treasures will we uncover?! I didn't expect becoming organized would be so exciting." It was adorable how the guru's eyes sparkled, like a little boy with a shovel.

"You should go through the shopping bags carefully. Anything you don't want, leave in that box." She indicated a large supermarket box in the corner that she'd mentally labeled "trash." The torn bag and the muffler were already in there. "We'll figure out where to put everything once we see what you have. And next week, now that the file cabinets are ready, we can make a start on your desk."

Striding through the streets of Manhattan on a glorious almost-spring day (even if the sky was a little grey), the temperature warm enough to unbutton her coat, Ahuva felt more content than she had in ages. All she'd needed, all she ever needed, was to feel useful. She'd made a good start today, but at the glacial rate required to not disturb the Maharishi's work, it would probably take a couple of months to really get the office in shape. And after that, well, who knows? Look at Ellen. Her job with Gloria Korn had started in almost the identical way. Once he got used to having her around, maybe the Maharishi would want her to take on more permanent responsibilities. Imagine going to the ashram, to India!

She patted the book she'd tucked under her arm. She couldn't wait to tell Kaye. Well, she wouldn't be crazy enough to say she was hoping for India, but she would tell her she was helping Maharishi Narang.

Ahuva flashed Wally a brilliant smile. "Is Kaye here yet?"

He grunted and waved her in. Not in a chatty mood, then. You never knew with Wally.

Ahuva bounded up the stairs and rapped lightly on the dressing room door. "Knock knock!" she caroled. "I come bearing gift!"

Kaye called her to come in. She was sitting on her cushion in lotus position, preparing. Ahuva felt a little guilty interrupting, but not much. Her timing couldn't be better. Becca, who shared the dressing room, hadn't yet arrived.

"I won't stay long," she promised. "Maharishi Narang asked me to bring you this."

Kaye unfolded the typing paper that Ahuva had used to protect the precious parcel. Away from the rest of the Maharishi's stuff, the book looked even prettier and more special. Kaye opened it and closed it, turned it this way and that, exclaiming over every aspect.

"He got if for you over a year ago," Ahuva informed her. "But he...he misplaced it. It turned up today. I was over there...I'm kind of helping him out, the way I used to help you. I said I was coming over and he asked me to drop it off."

"Today!" Kaye marveled. "Today of all days. It's a reminder for me—circle of life. The Universe sends reminders, you know. The difficulty is in keeping yourself open to receive them."

It was an odd reaction, and Kaye's smile was more solemn than suited the moment.

"Circle of life?" Ahuva echoed.

Her hands still on Ahuva's shoulders, Kaye looked earnestly into her eyes. "Then you haven't heard. Oh, sweetheart, when you knocked, I thought that was why..."

A curtain of dread dropped down on Ahuva's happiness. "Heard what?"

"They've posted the notice," Kaye said simply. She brought her hands together, fingers apart, fingertips touching. "Six weeks. Circle of life."

♫

I didn't get to see *Lake Song* again before it closed. Junior year classes were demanding. As well as *The Buddy System*, I'd been cast in someone's Senior Honors project, a readers' theatre piece: perched on one of a circle of black-washed chipboard cubes, creating three major and a sprinkling of minor characters with nothing but my body and voice. It still ranks as the most fun I ever had as an actor. I was also cast in that wretched Goldoni, decidedly one of his lesser works. My role was mercifully small. Rehearsals were an utter waste of time except for mastering the lost art of maneuvering a pannier gown without sideswiping the furniture, a knack that would have come in handy if only my post-graduate career had included acting in Restoration plays or if I'd accidentally time-travelled back to the 18th century. Somewhere in all that, I went to class and wrote a substantial research paper on the prostitutes of late-Victorian London.

The only time off that I can recall was the night Willa and I went down to the city with her generous friends the Nedwins, a youngish married couple (younger than our parents but older than us) who lived in one of the nicer villages near Poughkeepsie. Teddi Nedwin was associated with the college and Willa had done a lot of typing for her over the year. As an extra thank you, they invited her out for a gala evening on the town, including tickets to *Private Lives*. The star was Maggie Smith, then and always my acting idol. Willa knew this and, since her boyfriend was up to his ears in law school in Boston, she asked me to be her "date."

I can't believe I nearly forgot about that night. I wore my Tonys dress. Willa, who didn't always, wore a little makeup. The Nedwins picked us up at the dorm and we drove down to the city, luxuriously cushioned on leather and breathing that new car smell. To me, theatre had always meant catching a glimpse of something rare and precious and private: fireflies in a garden. That night, I got my first taste of the tribal ritual meant by "dinner and a show." No HoJos or second-mezzanines for us; we dined elegantly and enjoyed the show from prime orchestra seats. Afterwards, Bruce couldn't come down from the carnival buzz. "The night is young!" he declared, too young to leave the city that never sleeps! He decided that it would be fun to go to The Blue Angel, for the drag show and some dancing. At 19, I'd never been to a nightclub and the only cross-dressers I'd seen were Jack Lemmon, Tony Curtis and our dorm diva, the glorious Jackie St. James. Willa, the Nedwins and I sat at a tiny table, drinking bubbly wine and watching gorgeously painted men lip synch as Liza and Marlene and Marilyn. Overhead, someone was swinging on a trapeze. There was a lot of glitter. After the set, colored lights bounced and swirled across the pocket-sized dance floor where we took turns doing The Bump with Bruce.

Around that same time, I began to see Simon. I can't call it "going out" as he never took me anywhere until long after our first breakup, when we met at a preppy bar on the East Side for a scotch-and-water that was probably the only thing Simon ever gave me. I was too much in thrall to his world-weary glamour to care. He wasn't great boyfriend material for any number of reasons, but the only one obvious to my star-struck eyes was that he was hardly ever around. London had spoiled him for campus life. Craftily arranging his senior year classes for Tuesday through Thursday, he spent the bulk of the week on East 88th Street, in an apartment that he shared with two friends who'd already graduated. Simon was a writer—no Joyce Maynard, but with a story already published in *The Hudson River Anthology* and a very encouraging rejection letter from *The New Yorker*. He only saw films that had subtitles. He preferred single malt scotch, almost unknown in New York at the time, to which he would add, with the absorption of Dr. Jekyll, "a soupçon of water to open it up." Over his faded, ripped jeans, he wore white dress shirts, washed until they were soft and unbuttoned to display a scarab, held by a fine leather cord, nestling in the hollow of his throat. The links in his French cuffs were his grandfather's, enameled gold, with the seal of Pembroke College. Simon's mother was English, a war bride whose upper lip had increasingly stiffened over her twenty-plus years of exile in suburban Maryland. Prone to wearing navy blue, and sporting a certain helmet of hair several years in advance of Margaret Thatcher, she sat straight-backed as a cadet, her close-pressed legs parallel vertical lines down to her sensible pumps. She had one of those silly flower names that the English sometimes give their girls…Poppy, Marigold, something like that. Why am I kidding myself? I know it was Primrose. Who could forget? His dad, a self-effacing man obligingly named George, called her "Prim," which took me aback until I realized it wasn't a tease.

Prim hated me on first sight (which is probably why there was never a second): I was too American, too poor and, despite having set foot in synagogue a grand total of four times in my entire life, too Jewish. Soon after that single strained parental luncheon, Simon and I broke up. He returned to campus the following year to see a student production of *Much Ado About Nothing*, directed by and starring a friend of his. He claimed not to have known that I was playing Beatrice. He found the character's sharp tongue irresistible. We got back together and saw each other on and off for some time, until he finally left me forever for a Presbyterian Scot, a stockbroker, named Alexander. But all this was yet to come. When *Lake Song* posted the closing notice, I was deliriously in love, and very, very busy. What I know about those weeks, and about the case of Margaret Rodney, I learned in bits and pieces of frantic phone calls and over the course of the following summer.

♫

On March 25, 1975, aspiring actress and sometimes coat-check girl Francesca "Frankie" Cecchi received a shocking morning telephone call from Casilda Meijas, housekeeper to New York City socialite Margaret Rodney. A few hours earlier, Federal investigators had arrived at the exclusive Park Avenue apartment building and arrested Rodney for conspiracy to commit murder. The victim was Rodney's half-brother, Edward "Ned" Hewett Eschenbach of Paradise Valley, Arizona. According to Mrs. Meijas, Rodney's final words before she was taken into custody had been "call Frankie."

To state only the facts, culled from the sensational reporting that flooded the media over the next few weeks:

One week prior to Margaret Rodney's arrest, Ned Eschenbach's gardener had arrived, as usual, just before the sun was fully up. He noticed a ground floor window uncharacteristically wide open. Silvio Torres went around to the kitchen door and knocked. The door was opened by Angelina Little, who cooked and cleaned for Eschenbach Mondays through Fridays. Little had been in the house only about half an hour, putting up a load of laundry. Entering through that same kitchen door, she'd noticed nothing out of the ordinary. The two assumed their employer must have forgotten to close the window the night before. Eschenbach was at an age, Little observed, where his mind sometimes wandered. She offered Torres a cup of coffee, after which they both got back to work. It wasn't until 9:00 that Little began to feel some concern. Eschenbach, a habitually early riser, hadn't appeared for his breakfast. She knocked on the bedroom door. There was no answer. Worried her employer might have fallen in the bathroom, which had happened once before, she called the gardener to assist her. They entered together and found Ned Eschenbach lying in his bed, dead of gunshot wounds.

There were no signs of a struggle and, as far as Little could judge, no evidence of burglary. During their examination of the house, investigators found a folder of papers sitting open on the desk in the library. They were begging letters from Margaret Rodney, stretching back over several years and couched in increasing levels of intensity, annotated in what was determined to be the hand of the deceased. Most passionate were those from recent months, demanding a quarter of a million dollars, which Rodney said she "needed" to invest in a Broadway show. Lawyers confirmed that Eschenbach managed the family trust; that the sister was constantly demanding money for various luxuries; and that she had recently become obsessed with this theatrical investment, a proposition that Eschenbach, a Christian man, viewed as next door to flat-out gambling. Eschenbach had turned her down in a firm letter (carbon copy filed), stating that Margaret's continued lack of judgment had led him to decide to impose tighter control on her allowance. He'd further stipulated that the portion of the fortune allotted to Daphne, which Margaret had previously been allowed to utilize as she saw fit, would henceforth be entirely administered by Ned until the child had reached her majority.

Clues led investigators to one Salvatore "Sal" Altamura, erstwhile lifeguard at the Southampton New York Bath and Tennis club. Taken into custody in Sasable, a few miles north of the border crossing, Altamura confessed to having provided access to the Eschenbach home for an anonymous gunman, believed to have been a Mexican national. The gunman was still being sought.

"Come quick," Casilda whispered shakily over Daphne's choking sobs.

Frankie threw a bunch of things into her suitcase, slung her dance bag over her shoulder, and raced to the Patchogue station. While she waited for the train, she grabbed a copy of *Newsday*. There was nothing there.

By Good Friday there would be plenty, in every paper and on the television news, much of it wild speculation. Frankie tuned it all out. The whole idea was insane. Sure Margaret Rodney was neurotic, but she wasn't crazy; she didn't have the personality to be a killer; she'd always been so kind. Sure she went to the Bath and Tennis during the summer, but only once in a while. How well could she have known this Altamura? It was a weird coincidence, that was all.

Once she'd heard and read enough to be certain the accusations were ridiculous, Frankie focused all her energies on taking care of Daphne. What the kid needed was for things to feel normal. It wouldn't be easy but she thought she and Casilda could carry it off.

It was the press that made it impossible. For the first few days, they were all too sad and confused to want to stir from the apartment, and it was Easter break so they didn't have to. Then one morning, needing milk and things, Casilda took the service elevator down and exited the basement door. Since none of them knew to look for her, she was able to walk right by four photographers skulking in the garbage alley. Long ago, on the way over from Ecuador, Casilda had learned how to keep a low profile. She was careful not to hurry and not to catch anyone's eye. She made it to the grocery store and back without incident, but along the way she spotted what she called "suspicious peoples" as far as three blocks away. The front of the building was thronged.

The following Monday, Frankie tried to take Daphne to school. The press was on them like pigeons on popcorn, so thick and fast that the poor kid screamed in terror. It took Frankie and Casilda together more than an hour to stop her shaking. Frankie called the principal, who suggested the wisest course would be to keep Daphne at home until the dust had settled, and arranged for the teachers to drop off assignments so that she could keep up with her class.

They settled into a routine. Every day, Frankie walked Daphne through her lessons. Together they did vocal exercises and a daily barre. After dinner, they'd all three watch TV. Then Frankie would read aloud a chapter of *Anne of Green Gables* before tucking Daphne into bed.

Melina never showed up, never so much as called. Frankie found this shocking. If it were her little sister, she would have been there in an instant; she had anyway. She was willing to excuse Roland. She had the impression he was a lost hippie kid, the kind that backpacks through other countries, smoking grass. The last postcard he'd sent Daphne was from Peru. What was Melina's excuse?

Casilda finally rang the Fannings' housekeeper. Melina and Cooper had left town almost immediately, distancing themselves as much as possible from the scandal, dodging the media. The decent thing would have been to take Daphne with them. That's what Frankie would have done in Melina's place, but the bitch, had taken off without a word, without even checking whether there was money for groceries. There was, enough for a month Casilda thought, by which time Margaret would surely be home.

♫

Carefully nonchalant, Ellen slid the stiff white paper rectangle across the table to her father. He flipped it over. Upside down and backwards, the stylized green 3, secretly commissioned from Mo, smiled at her. She waited to see if Harry would smile as well. It was her first business card, proof that she'd chosen the right path. The phone number was an answering service and the address was a post office box, but they were a company. Once Franklin Li finished filing the papers, in a few more weeks, they would be legally incorporated: Threesome Productions.

Harry raised his eyebrows. "It's memorable," he said drily.

She raised her own. "High praise from an ad man."

The name had been Dieter's idea. He'd suggested it with a wink, leering at Ellen's cleavage, not the first time either he or Valda had made a crack like that. Was it really a joke? It didn't matter: they were all stoned enough by then that even Franklin, uptight compared to the bawdy Swiss Germans, had found it hilarious. Upon more sober consideration, they'd agreed the name was inspired. What could possibly be more appropriate for a trio of producers (Dieter insisted he was merely silent partner to his wife), with a show called *A Thing or Three*?

Harry laughed and signaled the waiter. "Two glasses of the Pol Roger, Maurice." He turned back to Ellen. "I'll spring for a bottle of the Dom when you show me an opening night." His voice was sarcastic, but Pol Roger was nothing to sneeze at.

She sank into the chubby leather cushions, grinning from ear to ear. He was proud of her, as proud as she was of herself. She was giddy with it. By the time the champagne arrived, she was jabbering wildly about what a great team she'd put together, about Franklin's legal expertise and all of the Oelrichs' arts-loving wealthy friends. They'd already amassed over ten thousand dollars! Five of this had come from a single person, one of Franklin's clients, who'd been so impressed by Ellen's fuzzy tape that she not only wrote a check but offered up her living room for backers' auditions when the time came. The time would come pretty soon, maybe in the summer, definitely before Labor Day. Threesome had been able to pay Ritchie and Pam such a generous option they could cut down on their survival jobs and concentrate on finishing the show. Ritchie had played Ellen a new song just the other day. It was fantastic. So funny and smart. Clever, that was it; Richard Edelstein was an extremely clever man. Harry would see what she meant. She couldn't wait for him to hear it. If he was up for an adventure, she'd love to take him down to the squat some time. No, Gloria wasn't part of it, not directly, but she was being extremely supportive, promising to put in a good word to encourage the reviewers to show up when the time came, and offering to let Ellen use her letterhead for the press releases.

Once she'd started talking, it was hard to stop. Harry didn't seem to mind. He didn't cut her off, not even once. When he interrupted, it was to ask a serious question. He listened to her almost as if they were equals, as if she were another adult.

They sat together until Harry had to leave for the airport. Helping her on with her coat, he stuck a piece of paper into her pocket. He wasn't smooth enough; she felt him do it. It was a check, she just knew it! She'd impressed him so much that he wanted to invest! She fished it out gleefully.

Not a check; a hundred dollar bill. She stared at it. The brief shimmer of triumph receded, but not fast enough.

He noticed and laughed. "What? You thought I was going to blow a couple of grand on this Threesome thing? Ellie, you're a smart girl. I always knew that; I only thought you were lazy. But you're not. I hear you now, it's like listening to myself at that age. Sounds like you can do anything once you put your mind to it. What I don't get is why you're putting all that energy into this. Theatre isn't a business, it's a crap shoot. Fucking waste of time. It's not gonna work out and I've gotta be honest, I can't wait for that. Get it out of your system and let me fix you up with a real career. After you finish college, which you still can. For *that*, I'm willing to stake you."

He wasn't proud, he wasn't impressed; he was throwing her a few bucks for the same reason he over-tipped the coat check, to make himself feel big. "Thanks, Daddy. I don't want you to think I only ask to see you when I need money. My 'thing' may not be a hit yet, but I'm doing fine." Forcing a pleasant smile, she tucked it into his hand. It wasn't easy. A hundred was half the rent. "I'll save you a good seat opening night."

When Harry got embarrassed, the tips of his ears turned red. It was where she got her blush. He pushed back the bill. "Don't be stupid, Ellie. Buy yourself something nice. A reminder of what you could have if you weren't so goddamn stubborn."

She wasn't stupid. Anyway, a cab pulled up.

♫

Ahuva didn't want to think about it. She couldn't stop thinking about it. Never had six weeks gone by so quickly, each day dropping off the calendar into the growing void, the black hole. How was she going to fill it? Was it possible to fill a black hole? Maybe that wasn't the right metaphor. She didn't know much about astronomy...not anything, to be honest. Marshall Berenson would know. *One for the Books* was still running, that would be some comfort. Not enough. Brilliant as it was, it wasn't *Lake Song*, it didn't have that same piece of her heart.

She was determined to go as often as possible, to the bitter end, but some nights it hurt so much that she had to leave at intermission. How could all the cast and crew stand it? How could they be so cheerful on Death Row?

Kaye said you were grateful for the experience and simply moved on.

Lil laughed at her sad face. "It's long overdue, dear heart! Theatre is supposed to have short runs. It keeps us from getting stale. Only on Broadway do they beat the poor old horse for years and years."

She couldn't empathize, but she would have to accept that it was different for the actors. *Lake Song* wasn't a job for her, the way it was for them. It was a friend, probably her best friend in the world. It was home. It was the one piece of the world that was completely dependable. It had been. Not anymore.

Ahuva had expected Ellen would empathize. When Ahuva called to tell her the news, she'd been surprised; Gloria hadn't gotten word yet.

"Holy fucking shit!" Ellen said. An entirely satisfying reaction that she killed by adding a flippant "Well, that's Show Biz," before launching into a description of a sketch Ritchie Edelstein was writing for her show.

Ahuva had to cut her short. Maybe the sketch would be hilarious, but she was in no mood to find out. "*Lake Song* is ending, Ellen. I thought you would care."

"Of course I care. I'll miss it. The same way that I miss Bron. She'll always be an important memory. So will the show, for all of us. It was a great show. Transformative. But it's played its part, so to speak. Time to move on. This is just a formality."

It had taken every ounce of control to not slam down the receiver. So typical of Ellen, to pretend she'd outgrown it, when deep down she had to be just as upset as Ahuva. The knowledge was no consolation. Ahuva needed to talk with someone who would understand and commiserate.

It was so frustrating not to be able to talk to Frankie. Now there were only twelve days left and Frankie might not even know. No one had been able to get hold of her, not her, not Ellen, not Connie. The phone number they had from when Frankie had stayed with the Rodneys over Christmas had been disconnected. She hadn't returned any of the messages they'd left on her service. It would be awful if she hadn't gotten them, if she didn't know. Inconceivable. None of them would have even met Frankie if it weren't for the show.

Ahuva threw herself into chanting and meditation, hoping to find that elusive Balance. Maybe if she could go to India…If she had that to look forward to, if she could study there, she would find that same serenity that Kaye had achieved.

She said as much to the Maharishi. Not the part about needing something to look forward to, of course, but her desire to study.

He didn't say a word in response. He only looked at her. If she didn't speak, they could have stood there all day, staring at each other in silence. The Maharishi could outwait a mountain. "Please, my guru. I humbly ask you to consider. You know I would devote myself to my studies."

It was the solemn smile. "I understand, Daughter. Your feet want to follow your heart. Ah! Yayaati! This should be your name."

A name! A bubble of excitement tickled her ribs. And almost instantly fell flat. He'd held up his hand, the universal sign for "Stop."

"But now is not the time. You are not ready. Not yet." He touched her lightly on the head. "You will be. Someday Yayaati. Not now."

The Maharishi had named her. She should be floating on air. But he'd said no.

♫

You'd think that after a couple of weeks the press would get bored and frustrated and go away, but they hadn't. Every time Frankie called down to the lobby for a status report, they said the same thing: there were reporters and photographers lurking everywhere. Some of the photographers were waving twenties. Frankie was grateful that Daphne was such a lovable kid that the doormen and the elevator operators wanted to protect her. Even so, she dipped into Casilda's housekeeping money to add something tangible to her heartfelt thanks. It was a war zone down there.

She and Daphne were going stir crazy. They were trapped inside the apartment which, big as it was, had begun to feel like a closet. They couldn't even keep the shades up, no less use the balcony. A photographer with a camera lens as long as a baby's arm had camped out, in an actual tent, on the roof of the old brownstone across the street, just about eye level with the Rodney windows. Frankie had no desire to venture into the fray, but they were suffocating. They had to get some air. Irene's class, she concluded, was their best hope. They'd be surrounded by friendly faces and the dancing would do them both a lot of good. It was a safe haven—if only they could get to Carnegie Hall.

Frankie decided they wouldn't carry dance bags. The press was churning out headlines about "the Stage Mom Murderer" and she refused to add any fuel to that fire. They would wear their tights under their street clothes, and Frankie would conceal their shoes in an ordinary Bloomingdales bag. She also decided they would go out the front; it was too easy to get trapped in the narrow garbage alley. When they got downstairs, she'd have Sean hail them a cab. She knew you could call a car service and arrange a pickup, but she'd read Sherlock Holmes and knew that car services could be bribed. Holmes said you shouldn't take the first cab, either, because it might be a plant; but she didn't think the press could pay a New York cabbie enough for him to waste a day waiting around the corner on the off chance of their emerging from the building.

Preparations for the expedition brought them both near to hysteria. They couldn't eat a bite of lunch. Daphne's lips were white with nerves. Frankie kept humming the *Mission Impossible* theme song to break the tension. They left the apartment an hour earlier than they should have needed to.

The elevator stopped on four, letting on a nanny with a trio of adolescent boys who were dressed for the park, carrying mitts and a bat. Daphne was wearing jeans with an old baseball jacket of Roland's that seemed to give her some comfort. The only thing that kept her from blending right in was her hair. In a single moment's inspiration, Frankie grasped a lesson most actresses would only learn after years of seeing their faces in magazines: you didn't have to be a master of disguise to get past the press, you only had to look different from what they expected. She yanked the newsboy cap off her own head and, before they reached the lobby, had pushed it onto Daphne's with the long ponytail stuffed inside. She gave the girl a little push, making sure they kept close enough to the others that they looked like a single group of noisy kids heading off to play. Frankie and Daphne stuck with the boys all the way to Fifth Avenue. None of the press followed.

By the time they reached Carnegie Hall, they were quivering with suppressed tension. It was too much for Daphne, who tore down the beautifully deserted hallway, flung open the door and burst into the studio with an explosive whoop.

Irene dropped the cane she'd been rehearsing with and spun around. Frankie couldn't tell if she was going yell or have a heart attack. She did neither. She grabbed up Daphne into a fierce hug.

Frankie had never seen Irene hug anyone, not even Gerry when he got into the chorus of *The Wiz*. Daphne was too happy to notice anything except her own delight at being there. With a quick hug back, she broke away to make a manic circuit of the studio. Humming, she touched her fingers lightly to the barre, the mirrors, the bench where people sat to take a break, the old record player, the rickety piano used when Bobby Lemon came to play for them live. She greeted every piece of the room, then leapt a joyful jeté above the center of the floor. Irene watched, her homely face lit by a beautiful smile.

"I'm going to change!" Daphne sang out, snatching the shopping bag. She disappeared into the changing room, still humming.

Irene turned her eye on Frankie and whatever had been holding Frankie up all this time dissolved. Her knees began to buckle. Her head felt wobbly atop her spine. Irene pulled her down on the bench and pressed her shoulders against the wall to steady her.

"What the hell is going on?"

"Margaret was arrested…"

"I read the papers. How did you get involved?" Irene sounded angry, but then Irene always sounded angry. It was only ever a question of degrees.

"She's a kid. I couldn't leave her there alone. She needs me."

"There isn't a maid or someone?"

"It was Casilda who called me. She said that Mar…She couldn't do it on her own. She needed help."

"I warned you, didn't I Frankie? That Margaret Rodney would take advantage…"

"No one took advantage. I want to help."

"What about the family. Where's the family on this?"

Frankie didn't answer.

"Oh, for Christ's sake! No one?" Irene scratched the top of her head, exasperated. "A lawyer at least? Someone? She made you responsible? You're a 20 year old girl…"

Frankie bristled. "21. I'm an adult."

"Great. 21. So you're more than ready to be the mother of a 12-year-old. Frankie, you know how fond I am of Daphne. It's bad enough she has to be caught up in this mess. I'm fond of you too. I don't want to see you become collateral damage."

"I'm fine, Irene. Anyway, it's only for a few weeks. Margaret'll be home soon. It'll all blow over…"

"Can I put on 'All At Once'?" Daphne was on the floor, hovering by the record player. "We've still got half an hour 'til class."

Irene nodded. Whatever she'd been about to say died on her lips, but the frown lines stayed between her eyes. She gave Frankie's hand such a quick squeeze that maybe it didn't happen.

Frankie pulled herself off the bench. "I'll put my on shoes."

Ellen had never expected her relationship with Franklin Li to last long. The only question was when and how it would end. Lately she'd been under pressure to decide. Valda and Dieter's proposition, which she'd initially assumed was a tease, was serious. She'd never had a three-way and the merest thought caused a spasm that was halfway to coming, but with the Oelrichs officially raising money for *A Thing or Three*, this was more than a little complicated. It was impossible for her to fuck them and Franklin, and stay in business with both. Could she risk giving up one for the other? The Oelrichs were full of promise, physical and financial, but would they deliver? Franklin, she knew, was dependable on both fronts. Ellen had heated arguments with herself: remember your priorities; nothing could be more important than producing *A Thing or Three*; what would be best for the show? The tension was becoming unbearable when deliverance came from an unexpected source.

The Li parents descended on New York without warning and in the best of spirits. They had found their golden child a suitable wife. Moreover, the young woman and her parents had also arrived in town and were also staying at the Plaza. An introduction was arranged, in the company of both sets of parents, in a private dining room. Smooth, confident Franklin Li came away strangely abashed. Not only were the bride-to-be's blood and credit lines impeccable, but her degree in Art History was from the Sorbonne. And she was gorgeous. Franklin didn't say as much, but Ellen could see it in his face when he ticked off Wei Wei's marriageability points. Fluency in five languages didn't cause the lazy eyes or the secret smile that twitched around his mouth. The man was utterly smitten, love—or at least lust—at first sight.

Franklin broke the news of his engagement with a stern benevolence that made Ellen wonder if someday he might not switch to a criminal practice and evolve into a judge. He and Ellen would still be friends, he assured her, and business partners, but their other relationship would have to end.

Ellen accepted graciously. So graciously that Franklin turned overtly sentimental and kept sending expensive gifts: the Mont Blanc pen; the bit of carved jade that felt wonderfully cool and intricate when you worried it with your fingers; the oversized pearl, on its long cord of black silk, which never suited her but which would become, in another sixteen months, a perfect gift for Jill. She wore the leather coat when the four of them went to the Four Seasons to celebrate and wish him a safe flight to Hong Kong for the wedding. After dinner, she shared a cab with the Oelrichs, a cab that stayed on the East Side. The leather coat, worn over nothing but the belly chain, was a huge success.

♫

Ahuva dressed as if she were going to her own funeral. *In mourning for my life*, she thought, without a trace of irony. She refused to wear jeans today. The occasion required an element of respect. It was probably pretentious to wear a black skirt and top, but it was the only skirt she had and, once she put it on, the top was a natural choice. She brushed her hair until it shone. She would have put it up in a messy knot, at which she was now adept, but she didn't want to block the view of someone who might be sitting behind her. Respect. For the same reason, she wore the little gold balls instead of long earrings that might jangle. She decided not to wear mascara.

Her heart was breaking. Ahuva knew what it was to cry into a pillow all night, but she'd never felt this bad before. Even when she'd landed here from Israel, half a world and a language away from everything she'd ever known, she'd found a tiny thread of comfort to hold on to. She'd known she'd see Israel and her family again, just as she'd known that Byron, while leaving her, would still be somewhere. She'd never before lost anything that had disappeared from the planet. When the curtain came down this evening, *Lake Song* would be as gone as yesterday's lunch.

She was miserable. Her stomach ached and her hands were clammy. She hated thinking about the next few hours, but how could she not attend the last performance? The last performance. No, final. "Last" could mean most recent, while "final" was...final. Fin. Finis. The same in almost every language.

What am I to write at the bottom of the page

Just before they put 'finis'? What am I supposed to say

To have the last word?

The perfect, gloomy song. Every time she thought about it, she remembered what Ric had said about the compelling darkness of the song it had replaced, the one Berenson originally wrote for Kostia's goodbye. Hard to believe a song could be sadder than "The Man Who Wished." She tried to push it out of her head, but what popped up to replace it wasn't much better. "Fireflies," the song Bronwen Davies sang on the Tribute album. Did Marshall Berenson have a window into her heart? Whatever she was feeling, he always seemed to have felt it first and put it into words as she never could have done.

The thing about illusion

Is it doesn't last forever

And it cannot come again.

Maybe, someday, she would see another production. At a summer theatre. Or years from now, maybe a teacher like Bert Gruen would put it on in school and her daughter would play Masha. Or someday, if there were any justice in the world, people would realize it was a classic and bring it back to Broadway, like *Anything Goes* or Gilbert and Sullivan. It didn't matter. It wouldn't be the same. They could do a hundred productions of *Lake Song*, but none of them would ever be The Show. That would be over after today, gone forever except for the cast album and her memories.

She met Ellen and Leonard outside the Regale. It had seemed obvious, when Ellen proposed it, for them to go together. Frankie should have been there too, but she still hadn't been heard from.

"Dark side of the moon," Leonard joked. The girls looked at him blankly. "Pink Floyd?"

"Pink Floyd?!" Ellen screeched. "Since when are you Mr. Rock and Roll?"

If this is what it was going to be like, Ahuva wished she weren't sitting next to them. She'd rather be alone with her misery. Then Leonard reached for her hand and gave it a squeeze. She squeezed back automatically, before looking up. There was sympathy plastered all over his face.

Leonard shrugged sheepishly. "Sorry. Trying to break the tension. Unlike this one, who's pretending it doesn't exist." He jabbed a thumb in Ellen's direction.

Ellen made a face and mashed out her cigarette. "Okay, I'm sad too. Are you happy, asshole? I'm sure as hell going to miss Joe Bigelow. Until he gets another show, he'll be exiled in New Jersey. Damn, this really is fucking sad."

"It really is," Leonard agreed. "So, get it over with?"

Ellen nodded. She put an arm around Ahuva. Leonard took her other side. They would march through the lobby as a unit. Ahuva was surprised by the sudden flood of warmth she felt for both of them. Solidarity. Love, like the Maharishi said; she only had to open herself up to find it.

"I'm going to an ashram this summer," she blurted out, apropos of nothing.

Ellen's eyebrows nearly hit her hairline. "India?! Holy fucking…"

"The Catskills," Ahuva corrected, wishing she hadn't opened her mouth. "This time. Maharishi Narang said I was still too young for India." It sounded better than not being ready. And she was too young to go to India alone; she would be, as long as she had to depend on her parents for airfare.

"Still pretty far out," Ellen said respectfully.

"Good for you," said Leonard, giving another squeeze.

The lights started flashing. Five minutes. Only five minutes.

But everything is possible only for a moment.
Wonder is too frail a thing to tether to a chain.
Anything too wonderful will only last a moment;
Holding it forever
Is something you will always wish in vain.

♫

Margaret Rodney wouldn't be coming home any time soon. There was a call from her lawyer. Bail had been refused. She'd be staying in an Arizona prison until her trial, after Labor Day. He hadn't wanted Daphne to hear this on the news.

Frankie was stunned by the news. She'd been certain that any day now everyone would see it was all a mistake and Margaret would come home. On the other hand, she was relieved to hear the voice of a responsible-sounding adult. Melina still hadn't been heard from. After Antigua, the Fannings had fled to Greece, where Melina's father had a small island. Some reporter had tracked them down, and gotten a famous black eye for his resourcefulness.

"What are we supposed to do next?" she asked Mr. Kerrigan. The housekeeping money was getting low, though Casilda thought she could stretch it another month. What they were more concerned about was the rent. Which wasn't rent, Casilda had explained, but some kind of fee that people who own apartments pay to the building board. Frankie, for whom this was a new concept, wasn't clear on the details, but she understood that Casilda was afraid that, even though Margaret owned the apartment, the building would seize on any excuse to throw them out. The reporters, lurking around every corner, trying to sneak in, were driving the other tenants crazy. And what about Daphne's school? There was still another month until summer vacation, but the principal had already asked Frankie whether Daphne would be coming back in September. She and Casilda were doing their best, but now it sounded like this was going to drag on for months and months.

Mr. Kerrigan let her babble on until she ran out of breath. He cleared his throat. "I don't know," he said.

"What do you mean you don't know?!" Frankie's voice zoomed up to a note Donny had never managed to coach her to reach.

Mr. Kerrigan explained that he was Margaret's criminal attorney. He knew nothing about her financial arrangements. He'd never met her until her mother had arranged for him to represent her in this case.

Another shocker. Frankie had completely forgotten that Rosamund Eschenbach was still alive. Unlike Melina, she was an entirely offstage presence in Frankie's dealings with the Rodneys. Except for her twice yearly visits to Arizona, Daphne communicated with her grandmother through the mail. The old lady was so deaf that she never made phone calls. Someone nearby to her must be handling things on her behalf.

Mr. Kerrigan seemed to guess Frankie's next thought before she could even say it. "Mrs. Eschenbach lives in Paradise Valley." There was a pregnant pause while Frankie digested this. Daphne's grandmother lived in the same town as Uncle Ned, as the victim. "I'm sure you can understand why she wouldn't want Daphne down here."

"But there's no one else." Frankie blurted it out. "You have to help us."

"I'll pass the message along to Mrs. Eschenbach," he said, sounding uncomfortable.

"You do that!!"

Afterwards, Frankie felt bad for snapping at Mr. Kerrigan. It wasn't his fault. At least he'd thought to call them at all, which was more than either Daphne's sister or grandmother had done.

He must have also been as good as his word. A few days later, Frankie got a call from Chase Manhattan Bank that an account had been opened in her name. Two thousand dollars had been wired from a bank in Paris, from Margaret's half-sister it turned out, Ned's sister Beatrix. And it was lawyers writing on behalf of Beatrix Murray who informed Frankie that the family trust would continue to cover all of Daphne's expenses—including the apartment, which they owned—until such time as permanent arrangements were made for the child.

♫

The Saturday following the final performance of *Lake Song*, the Regale was opened for a sale of the retired set dressings and wardrobe. The cast had already bought items to which they'd become sentimentally attached: Medviedenko's leather satchel, Masha's pince-nez. James Lord would have taken the seagull himself, except he learned that Becca and Chris wanted to hang it over their new mantel.

As was her custom, Ruth Mann had pulled out what she considered to be the most significant costumes she'd designed for the show. She would warehouse these in a climate controlled cubby she maintained in Sunnyside, along with the rest of what she called, straight-faced, the Ruth Mann Collection. The archive was destined for a museum, although Ruth kept changing her mind as to which one. When she felt that costume design was clothing design, she favored FIT. At other times, wanting to limit access to those who were following in her footsteps, she leaned towards the New York Public Library's collection at Lincoln Center. Recently, her dear friend Diana Vreeland had begun pressuring her to consider the historically referential aspect of costume design, as well as her own legacy as a designer, and donate the lot to Diana's Costume Institute at the Metropolitan Museum of Art. Wherever they eventually ended up, they weren't on sale now. Not Nina's fluttery storm-colored "seagull" tatters from her final entrance. Certainly not the blue beaded gown and the robe that created the dramatic reveal. One of Masha's layered black weeds was also missing, the one with the bitter green petticoat that flashed in and out during the "Schoolmaster" soft shoe.

Arkadina's dressing table, which Ellen especially coveted, was not on view. It turned out to have been owned, all along, by one of the producers, Sara Bradley, who'd only loaned it to the production and wanted it back. It was just as well. Looking at the price tags on the smaller items, the dressing table would have been an unjustifiable several months' rent. She did manage to score the hand mirror, however, which was less substantial than the rich silver it appeared to be from the audience. It was pricy for what my father, the antiques dealer, called "white metal" but Bronwen Davies had gazed at herself in it—or pretended to do so—eight times a week for 30 months, which gave it a different kind of value. Leonard insisted on buying it for her as a birthday present. He bought Trigorin's walking stick for himself. With the money she saved, Ellen splurged on one of the blankets that covered the dying Sorin at the end of Act II. It was useful, being pleasantly soft wool, in an attractive blue and green herringbone. And she'd always get a little kick out of thinking she was still sleeping with Joe Bigelow, who'd nabbed the other blanket for himself. She already missed him.

Ahuva, wanting something Lil had used, bought one of the large decks of cards used for "Bezique." She also picked up one of Masha's black-edged handkerchiefs.

Frankie selected a perfume bottle from the dressing table. Her arrival, with Daphne Rodney in tow, stunned everyone. She'd gotten all their messages, she explained. She'd meant to call back, but things were always so crazy now...They almost didn't recognize her, which made Frankie laugh. It was the contact lenses, she explained. With Margaret in prison, the worst of the feeding frenzy had moved to Arizona, but there were still reporters and photographers crawling all over. One had found out about Irene and followed her and Daphne to the studio. A man in their class was an ex-Marine and threw the guy out, practically kicked him down the hall. Frankie had gotten permission to spend some of their allowance on a disguise wardrobe and a few wigs for both of them, but each time they went out it was harder to dodge the press. It was Sean, the doorman, who'd pointed out that no matter how she was dressed all the photographers recognized her glasses. He suggested she get contacts, and the lawyers agreed. She'd always wanted contacts, so it was kind of a bonus. They weren't comfortable, she admitted, but she was optimistic about getting used to them and meanwhile it was much better than her very identifiable Volkswagen headlights. So far it seemed to be helping. She and Daphne had managed to come out today without anyone noticing.

No one had met the child before and they had to fight against their instinct to stare. She was amazingly ordinary; a little chunky, too, which surprised them, considering she was such a dancer. Frankie whispered that she'd been overdoing the pasta and chocolates and Frankie didn't have the heart to pressure her. There was comfort in carbs, at least for a while. When this was all over and Margaret was back home, she'd most likely be sentenced to a month of iceberg lettuce and boiled shrimp, but she'd be so happy that she wouldn't care.

Daphne was a sweet kid, the others agreed when they told me about it, as of course they could hardly wait to do, sprawled around my dorm room after the first performance of *The Buddy System*.

She was a little shy, they said.

Leonard was the only one who didn't find that surprising. "Of course she's shy." He did the eye-rolling-with-goofy-grin that was his usual way to show exasperation while trying not to get his head snapped off by his more assertive friends. "She was probably always shy. Anyway, having your mother accused of conspiracy to commit murder would be enough to turn anyone shy. We're strangers to her, remember? She doesn't know any of us. We don't know her either. We only think we know her because Frankie's been talking about her all year."

Kevin, who hadn't been at the *Lake Song* sale agreed with Leonard. "She's a kid whose mother basically disappeared. All alone in that enormous empty apartment with Frankie and the maid, her mother in jail halfway across the country, and no one is telling her anything."

"Frankie is," Ahuva objected.

Kevin shook his head. "From what I hear, Frankie's telling her that her mother'll be home any day now. I don't know, maybe Frankie even believes it. She's probably steering clear of the coverage, to protect Daphne, but Len and I have been reading it and it does not look good."

"It doesn't," Ellen agreed vigorously. "I asked Franklin. He was fascinated that I knew someone connected with the case."

"He's an entertainment lawyer," Ahuva said disdainfully. "I would think Frankie knows more about it than he does. Than any of us."

She had a point. Frankie actually knew Margaret Rodney. She would know better than, not just us, but all the people on the news. The rest of us were complete voyeurs, drooling over the drama, getting a thrill out of projecting the worst possible outcome. We might as well be stuffing ourselves from giant buckets of greasy popcorn. Meanwhile, that poor kid.

It was one thing everyone could agree on: whatever Margaret had or hadn't done, the child hadn't asked for any of it. Now that they'd all met her, Daphne was a real person and we were all a little guilty about the false sense of importance we'd assumed from knowing Frankie.

"Why did you drop the last chorus of 'My Better Half'?" Ahuva made it clear that she wanted to change the subject.

I was happy to oblige. Like any actor, I expected a little ego boost from my friends. Though they'd rented a car and driven all the way up to see *The Buddy System*, they'd hardly said a word about it. The entire conversation had been about the end of *Lake Song* and Margaret Rodney.

♫

Not long afterwards, I was home and looking for what would be the last summer job of my student career. Don't get me wrong: I fully expected to remain a student for another couple of years. I intended to get my MFA from Yale Drama. Once I got in, I'd be acting every summer, so this would be my last temporary grunt assignment. Perversely, as if to put me in my place, all the jobs went into deep hiding. Things were looking grim when I had a call from a fellow Drama major who had work lined up with a costume shop. It turned out her place needed a few more people for July.

It was a long hot July, hotter even than June, which had been unusually sticky. Ahuva missed out on it up in Hurleyville. It surprised me that the Geffners let her go to an ashram. I suppose in the balance, the influence of a mysterious Eastern religion was nothing compared to the benefits of their daughter being several hours away from the empty Regale theatre.

Frankie had her hands full, of course, taking care of Daphne. Ellen had her complicated life to juggle, and Leonard had Kevin and weekend escapes to the beach. As for me, well...During the Great Depression, my father's mother had sewed shirts in a sweatshop downtown. It kept the family going so that, someday, I could exist...and go to a posh private college...and earn my book money sewing in a sweatshop downtown.

POLINA

Bezique!

DORN

A friendly game would be a treat:

TRIGORIN

A soothing balm, my dear. [*to the others*] She hasn't slept in days.

ARKADINA

My nerves are all a-fray.

POLINA

We know how sensitive you are.

ARKADINA

The mattress in that sleeping car...!

DORN

Your deal.

KOSTIA

Now that they're here, it all seems real.
I cannot bear it, how they gossip and they play
While Sorin fades away.
[*he exits, followed by Masha*]

ARKADINA

Where are you going? Oh, he drives me mad!

DORN

He's overcome, forgive him.

ARKADINA

Not his manners; it's his beard—
How can he be this old?!

TRIGORIN

I have a dix!

ALL

Bezique!

DORN

Carte Blanche!

ARKADINA

Is Dorn developing a paunch?
I can't help noticing his waistcoat pulls a bit.

POLINA

His tailor botched the fit.

ARKADINA

I hope that he refused to pay.

POLINA

Trigorin's getting rather grey.

TRIGORIN

A brisque!

ARKADINA

Do you still find it worth the risk?
It's quite remarkable to last so many years.

POLINA

My love and your career—
There's something to be said for hanging on.
We have a common marriage...

ARKADINA

You have nothing of the sort!

POLINA

Not us, the cards we hold.
We call the trick.

POLINA and DORN

Bezique!

ARKADINA

Declare!

TRIGORIN

It was a trifling affair.

DORN

They always are with you. A different
    girl each night.
When do you ever write?

TRIGORIN

It's all a part of making art:
A chain of girls and broken hearts

POLINA

Revoke!

DORN

I sense you think that I misspoke
About poor Sorin's state...

TRIGORIN

It's clear as day to me.
Irina won't agree;
She's found that willful blindness
    serves her well.

ARKADINA

It's not the cards you're dealt; it's
How you play them when they come.

TRIGORIN

I've crossed the Rubicon.

POLINA

Another round?

ALL

Bezique?

[*They shuffle and deal; Masha returns*]

MASHA

There's nothing here for me to do
    now Kostia's door is barred.
I've done as much for Sorin as I'm
    able.
I can't just sit here watching other
    people playing cards.
If only we could make another table.

MEDVIEDENKO

I'd happily be "dummy."

SHAMREYEV

Never understood this game;
Sometimes I think that's why they all
    suggest it.

MEDVIEDENKO

The time! I must be setting out. I
    don't mean to complain...

MASHA

Then don't. Good night. You won t
    hear me protest it.

DORN

Four Jacks.

TRIGORIN

He's always thought I was a hack
And now that he has some
    success...you saw the sneer...

POLINA

Ridiculous, my dear.
It isn't that you're widely read,
But that you share his mother's bed.

DORN

A meld!

TRIGORIN

You win again! I've always held
One shouldn't bet against
A doctor...

POLINA

In the end
We're all gamblers, my friend

ARKADINA

Why do we even play this silly
   game?

DORN

We could play whist or belote...

MASHA

Rotate partners for piquet?

SHAMREYEV

A six-hand game of cribbage?

POLINA

I could fancy écarté.

ARKADINA

My head won't hold a sequence.

TRIGORIN

Someone pour another round.
My friends, it's been a charming
   evening.

ALL

Bezique!

The new, unlisted telephone was ringing off the hook with calls from Mr. Kerrigan, from a spokesman for the family trust and once, notably, from Beatrix Murray in Paris. Frankie had never spoken with someone overseas before. Everyone agreed that no one could have handled things better than Frankie and Casilda, but a longer term solution was called for. Hounded by the press, unable to attend school, Daphne was a prisoner in her own home, a home, moreover, riddled with sad memories. The atmosphere in New York wasn't healthy for the child. She needed to feel secure in her environment. Eventually, extensive enough communication was held with Rosamund Eschenbach that a decision could be reached. Rosamund's niece Doris lived in Ann Arbor, nicely distant from both New York and Arizona. Doris had two girls of her own, the older recently married and the younger about to leave for college. She missed having someone to take care of and, in Michigan, Daphne would have both the freedom of anonymity and sufficient healthy outdoor sports to fill her spare time. Doris's husband Jack agreed that they would take her. After the trial, when Margaret was released, she would join Daphne there. The apartment was going on the market; the address was too well known. Once the fuss died down, the family would buy them a new place, in another city, to make a fresh start.

Daphne was scheduled to leave for Ann Arbor two weeks before Labor Day. Anything she wanted to bring with her, including her furniture if she chose, would be shipped out ahead of time. As for the rest, she and Frankie and Casilda were to go through the house and decide what should be packed up for storage and what would be left behind.

It was a big job. Casilda, was staying on until August 31st to wrap things up. Frankie volunteered to stay with her and help. She told Mickey it was part of the job, so he wouldn't worry. Not that he would anyway. Overall, he'd been pretty blasé about all this, except that one time the reporters caught them and she'd ended up on the evening news. He'd been more excited about that than he'd been about *Mother Courage*. And Eunice...Eunice had practically grabbed the phone out of his hand, pouring out phony sympathy "for the dear little girl." Eunice had never shown any interest in the Rodneys before, only pleasure at Frankie spending the summer and Christmas anywhere other than Patchogue. All it took was a major scandal, plus the press referring to Margaret as a "socialite" and an "heiress." Now Eunice wouldn't stop angling for some inside gossip to share with her coffee klatch of over-the-hill Suffolk County bombshells, which was why Frankie got into the habit of calling Pop on Eunice's card nights.

Going back to Patchogue would be hard. It didn't matter that the trust wouldn't be paying her anymore after Daphne left. Frankie would take every day in the city that she could get. She was still amazed they'd paid her as much as they had $150 a week once the trust finally got involved, and they'd insisted on back pay for April. She'd saved almost all of it. She would be okay for the rest of the year at least. If she got a job pretty fast, maybe she wouldn't have to tap into it at all. She could maybe even move out. She'd made some calculations based on the "roommate wanted" cards on the boards. Starting with what the train from Patchogue cost her, another $250 a month, if she was careful, would handle all the necessities in a place where she could have her own room: rent, food, all the utilities, including her answering service. If she could put aside enough for a solid year, $3000…make it $3500, because she'd need to buy a futon and keep a reserve fund for emergencies…Yes, when she had $3500 in the bank, she'd do it, she'd move out. Maybe she should hold off and use some of what she had to get her teeth fixed, like the photographer and that agent guy had suggested. It would be expensive, but if a better smile would land her a commercial, she'd make back the money in a few months. If the commercial went national, she might even have enough to get a studio apartment all to herself; it wouldn't cost that much more than a roommate. Wouldn't it be amazing if the trust decided to give her a bonus of some kind and she could do both at once, her teeth and an apartment? Not that she expected such a thing—she wasn't getting laid off from a real job like Casilda was—but it was nice to fantasize.

They were giving Casilda a generous check, a combination of severance and a thank you bonus for staying on the way she had. She'd almost fainted, blurting out to Frankie that she'd have enough to go home to Ecuador and start a restaurant. Then she ran to church to light a candle for Margaret's soul because she felt uncomfortable that Daphne's misfortune had become her own good luck. It was Frankie's opinion that Daphne would be glad to see something good coming out of this. Frankie was right. Daphne was so excited when she heard that she broke out into a feverish set of triple time steps. Maybe it was just knowing that some kids, at least, would be reunited with their mom.

It was Daphne's idea for Frankie to ask the trust if Casilda could take a few useful things from the kitchen.

The secretary who took their call seemed surprised by the request. "Anything she wants. Take it all. Otherwise it's going out. It's not worth putting things in storage that can be replaced. The family only wants to store the better pieces: any antiques, the sterling. That sort of thing. And anything of sentimental value of course."

"And Margaret's clothes," Frankie added absently. In her head, she was starting to reconsider some of the items they'd already tagged with "keep" stickers. "Or does Mrs. Eschenbach want those shipped to her in Arizona?"

"I'd suggest giving them all away. Even if they fit, they'll be out of style, assuming…"

"Assuming?!" Frankie's voice rose to her upper register. This woman was assuming that Margaret was guilty, that she would be in jail for years!

The secretary coughed uncomfortably. "Storage," she said shortly. "But use some discretion."

The first way Frankie used her discretion was to not relay the subtext of that conversation to Daphne. All she said was that it made no sense to hold onto anything Margaret didn't like or was maybe tired of.

By that time, Frankie's answering service had relayed a message from Ahuva, who was back from her ashram and apparently had time on her hands. Frankie was grateful to take advantage. There were a ton of things to do before the movers came. Ahuva was great at organizing things, plus she really got into it. Indeed, she showed up with an actual clipboard and a lot of thoughts about relabeling everything with a system of codes that she'd devised on the subway. That, plus the fierce intensity in her shoulders and smile, made Daphne shrink into herself until the box of chocolate jelly rings from Ahuva's father's shop restored the sunshine.

Ahuva was gung-ho to see everything that they'd already done and "get the house in shape." She clearly thought focusing on Margaret's closets was a waste of her talents. It was, but Frankie didn't care. Emotionally, she needed Ahuva as a crutch to get her through this. When all that was involved were Italian table linens and Daphne's dance scrapbooks, it had been easy to make packing a kind of game. The thought of Margaret's clothes, however, made Frankie's stomach churn with memories of her own mother's death. Having a someone else around, someone kind but not personally involved, would add a precious element of detachment to the proceedings.

It was silly, she knew, but the closed door to Margaret's bedroom gave Frankie a haunted house feeling. Pausing on the threshold, she made a feeble attempt at humor. "Okay, ladies. Since Diana Vreeland couldn't be here today, Daphne, you're in charge."

Daphne grinned. "Yes, ma'am! Mamma is going to be so happy we're getting rid of The Mistakes for her." She'd developed some enthusiasm for the project, which she decided was the kind of massive wardrobe overhaul Margaret always meant but could never bring herself to do. She scooted past them, leading the way.

Like every room under Casilda's care, it was clean and tidy. There was a ghost of stale cigarette smoke and Joy. It could have been a hotel, except for the closet. Margaret's closet was a walkway between her bedroom and bath, each side fitted out from floor to ceiling with custom cabinetry: panels of honey-colored wood concealing a battery of racks and drawers and shelves. Like a movie, Frankie thought, grinning at Ahuva in gleeful surprise.

There was no answering smile. Ahuva's legs folded down to sit on the carpet. Setting aside her clipboard and pen, she shook her head in disbelief. Her own wardrobe, she stated, implying Margaret could benefit from her example, fit neatly into a small closet and four dresser drawers, and was more than sufficient for any contingency.

"Who needs this many white blouses?" she demanded, affronted by a rack of shirts.

Daphne assumed the martyred politeness of the meticulously schooled. "You wouldn't wear satin in the summer." She selected her words carefully, intuiting that this was a language that Frankie's friend didn't speak. "Or for daytime. Night and day are different, just like seasons. And of course days are different depending on what you're doing. You'd wear this for lunch at Mortimers." The shirt she held to her chin was soft and clingy, with ruffles at the wrist and throat. "Well, with the Chanel suit," she corrected herself. "If the jacket has a different collar, one of the others would be better. But not this one!" She pulled out another shirt and giggled. "Not for lunch in the city! You'd only wear this to the beach, or on someone's boat."

The white gauze tunic was a lot like the tops Ahuva had been living in since Kaye had introduced her to the Maharishi, enough so that it made Frankie suddenly realize that she wasn't wearing one today. That wasn't the only thing different about her appearance. Ahuva's plain blue T-shirt was tucked neatly into her jeans, there were small turquoise studs in her ears and her hair was pulled back in a ponytail. She almost looked preppie.

Ahuva held up her hand, crossing-guard style. "Forget I asked. You can do the shirts another time. There must be some other way I could be useful." She sighed balefully.

"Boots," Daphne said promptly. "And winter shoes. Check the bottoms. If Mama hasn't worn them by now, they were a Mistake."

It was shocking how many garments a rich woman would have that she really didn't like or need. From one drawer alone, Daphne pulled out ten scarves that made her wrinkle her nose and say "Christmas present" before tossing in the dump pile. Then there was the wildly printed Missoni muffler with the tangled silk fringe. Margaret loved that one. So much, Daphne giggled, that she'd accidentally bought it twice! Frankie found it mind-boggling that someone would shell out a hundred bucks for a scarf even once. At Daphne's urging, she took the spare; Ellen would appreciate it.

Some "Mistakes" had been optimistically bought a size too small, usually because they were signature pieces of their season, things one absolutely had to have, and Margaret's proper size was sold out. There was also a significant collection of casual items worn once or twice, purchased for vacations that had disappointed. Other Mistakes were hysterical, like the sheer jumpsuit that was even more outrageous than Barbra Streisand's Oscar outfit a few years ago; too outrageous for Margaret, considering it still had the tags on.

That was probably the strangest item, but a lot of the evening things were a mystery, especially to Ahuva. Every time she wrinkled her nose and said "Who would wear that?!" in a particularly disgusted tone of voice, Daphne could be counted on to light up like a Broadway marquee and say something like "Oh! Mama wore that to a party at Gloria Vanderbilt's. It was in *Town and Country*. We can't give that one away!"

Frankie held up a classic black cocktail dress. "Or this one. Just like Audrey Hepburn. Your mom must wear it all the time."

Daphne shook her head. "Never. She got it for the school concert. Last year she wore this," she pointed to a sparkly peach confection. "But every other mother was wearing black. Mama doesn't really like herself in black. And since I won't be going back there, she won't need it again."

She said it so casually. She was so used to not going that she probably wouldn't really absorb it until her first day of school in Michigan. This Doris had better be a good person.

Frankie ran her hand over the heavy silk. It seemed a pity to put it on the discard pile.

"Try it on," Daphne suggested. "I bet it would be pretty on you. "

Frankie held back. "It's too expensive." She assumed it was. Who knew what a dress like this must cost?

Ahuva shrugged. "Daphne says Margaret doesn't want it. It's you or the thrift shop." That's what they were going to do with the discards, give them to a good cause. Ahuva was making a list from the Yellow Pages to go over with Ellen, to find out which were the shops where people would actually buy clothes like these. Then she'd take care of delivering everything. She insisted she had plenty of time and was happy to help. Something was going on with her, but Frankie didn't feel she could open that conversation with Daphne around.

"Please!" Daphne urged, pushing Frankie, still holding the dress, to face the mirror. Standing behind her, she hooked her chin over Frankie's collarbone, pouted winsomely and pointed. "See how pretty? Come on, try it." She was in a lighter mood than Frankie had seen her in ages, except when they were at Irene's. It made all the difference, having another person here.

Frankie let Daphne convince her. Anyway, when would she ever have a chance to have a dress like this? She pulled off her shirt and jeans and stepped into it. As she pulled it up, the fabric caressed her bare legs. She had a real silk blouse at home, but it felt nothing like this. Now she understood what all the fuss was about.

Daphne zipped her up the back. The bodice was just-just across Frankie's boobs, but she thought a different bra could fix that. It would have to. There was no way she wasn't keeping this dress.

"You look like a movie star! Doesn't she, Ahuva? Oh! Now it's your turn. Pick something!" Tilting her head, Daphne gave Ahuva a thorough stare, then turned to frown at the tumble of discarded party clothes. She squealed and plucked out a dress. "This one! It's a Pucci, you know. Mama wore it to dinner and another woman in the restaurant was wearing it too, so now she won't wear it anymore. Too bad, because she really likes it. Come, on! Look, it matches your shirt."

The print had a lot of the same blue as Ahuva's T-shirt, the one she called her signature color. To Daphne's obvious delight, she surrendered.

The Pucci was too tight to sit in, which was too bad, but now that she was undressed, Daphne insisted she try on something else. Humming all the while, the girl flitted from one to the other, holding garments under their chins, zipping zippers and tying bows, treating them like living dolls. They were all about the same size, but Margaret's hips were a little slimmer than Ahuva's, her shoulders broader than Frankie's, and she was flatter-chested than either one of them. Still, with Daphne's determined assistance, they each found things to adopt, especially among the more casual Mistakes.

With the decisions made, they folded as many of the discards they could into shopping bags. They were going to need more. Ahuva said she'd also bring a couple of boxes from her parents' store, to use for things like bags and shoes.

They finished a few minutes before Casilda called to say dinner was ready. Ahuva agreed to stay. While they were eating, Daphne wheedled her into "a sleep over."

When Daphne finally went to bed, Frankie poured them each a glass of sherry and was finally able to ask Ahuva if everything was okay.

"Fine," Ahuva said.

Frankie didn't believe her. "How was the ashram? I don't even know what to ask about it."

"Interesting. Not what I expected. You know, Daphne is a great kid."

"Great," Frankie agreed. Ahuva's face had shut down. Whatever it was, she didn't want to talk about it. Frankie could change subjects, too. 'I called Connie the other day. She had a postcard from Bron, from London. She's in rehearsal for a new Alan Ayckbourn play. You know. The guy who wrote *Absurd Person Singular*."

"It's excellent that she's working again," Ahuva said emphatically. "Lil is doing *Importance of Being Earnest* at Lincoln Center in October. Abba read the *Arts and Leisure* section for me while I was away."

"Joe Bigelow is playing Max in *Sound of Music* in Boston over Christmas season, Ellen says."

"I miss them." Ahuva's eyes almost brimmed over. She sniffed back the tears and grimaced. "I miss all of it. Don't get me started. Who's on Johnny Carson tonight?"

"He's on vacation. It's John Davidson this week."

Ahuva rolled her eyes. "Maybe there's a movie."

♫

Ahuva didn't want to talk about the ashram.

What was there to say? Everything was about the Wheel, and the Wheel wasn't anything; it just was. Period.

The sun rose. There were no window coverings in the dormitories, so you automatically awoke along with it. Everyone chanted. There was yoga and yoghurt. There were chores, everyone working in the garden or the kitchen or the dairy, or helping to clean. Assignments changed every week. You would have thought they'd want people to stick with one thing and get good at it, but the goal here was pilgrimage, not expertise. To absorb each experience and move to the next, the way you stimulate all your chakras. The Wheel. There was lunch, some kind of rice with vegetables from the garden and lentils and Indian style bread that Ahuva couldn't stop thinking of as pita. The week she was on kitchen she tried to be original and make falafel, which the rest of the group informed her was an Indian food called "pakoras." They were the same thing as far as she could tell, except for being fried in ghee instead of oil. When she said as much, instead of being noted for originality, she was indulgently smiled over as yet another example of the Oneness of the Universe.

More chanting after lunch was followed by outdoor meditation, to feel One with Nature. This was followed by the day's lesson. The teachers were never as interesting as the Maharishi.

Afternoon chores ended half an hour before dinner, to give you time for private meditation. She found a tree behind the dairy that felt secluded, with enough background noise that no one would hear her guiltily singing show tunes under her breath. Her sloka, so powerful at home, was only one more chant among many here. She craved breaking out with something that was hers alone.

Dinner was the same as lunch. There was more chanting afterwards, less like prayer and more like a party. There was singing and dancing, and people played music. Some of them were very talented. They were so self-effacing that she felt embarrassed singling anyone out.

"We all have talents, Yayaati," said the sitar player when she tried to compliment him. "They are only gifts when we share our joy and release them, without judgment."

One final group chant closed the day. Everyone hugged. You padded off to your bed to sleep, swaddled by one-ness and tranquility, until the sun rose the next morning to do it all over again. And again. And again.

The ashram. Nothing to talk about.

They called her Yayaati there, the name Maharishi Narang had given her. Someone told her it meant traveler and said it was a compliment. Ahuva wasn't so sure. Maybe it was one of Guru's little jokes. Traveling meant you started from one place and ended up somewhere else. Ahuva was wandering around in circles.

It would have been special to go to India, but she had a hunch the ashram there would have been much the same. Even as meditation and chanting opened you to the beauty of the world and the oneness of its fabric, the routine was meant to free you from what the Maharishi called "misguided hunger" for acceptance and high regard. All moving through the same patterns, everyone was valued equally. Being One with the same Universe. On the same Wheel.

So how did Kaye Victor do it? Kaye wasn't like everyone else, not remotely. She was vibrantly individual as well as uniquely talented. And she never pretended that she wasn't. She used those gifts to rise to the top of a fiercely competitive profession. How do you do that and still be One with the Universe? If she didn't know Kaye, Ahuva would have assumed this was impossible. No, this puzzle was solvable; she must be missing a big piece. All these months with the Maharishi had brought only questions, no answers—and she had begun to doubt that her questions were the right ones. She felt dense, which she did not appreciate at all. If there was one thing she had always been confident of, it was her intelligence.

She didn't want to talk about it.

♫

It's spring that's supposed to feel like the beginning of a new year, with the return of the sun and all that sap rising, every cell in your body crying out to reproduce and your brain confusing that with references to moonbeams and roses and wine. But even if you're not a kid in school, it's autumn that really gets you going: that first cool breeze against your skin, that first ruddy stain hemming the leaves…warning sirens. Winter hibernation is on the way. You snap to high alert, your mind suddenly razor sharp and your internal clock kicking into high gear, anxious to cram everything in. It's time to reap, and if there's nothing lying around to reap, then you'd better come up with something soon and finish it off before the calendar goes dark.

God knew Ellen was busy enough. September and October openings were going full throttle, with Gloria handling a fat lot of them. But *A Thing or Three* had stalled and the waiting was driving her nuts. It turned out that summer was not when rich people want to bother with backers auditions. They're all too busy lolling around expensive sand and water. Which, the way Valda airily explained it, was followed by a fall…beg your pardon, "autumn" social calendar jammed with openings and then, as holiday season draws near, all those newspaper-worthy fund raising galas.

Valda thought the second week in January would be the time to start pushing again. In the meanwhile, she suggested they all take a break. She and Dieter planned to follow the snow. They'd missed last ski season because of her leg. Now, when the Oelrichs weren't buying every parka on Madison Avenue, they were training rigorously in order to be back in shape before Aspen in November: living on yoghurt and nuts, hiking Bear Mountain and doing endless pool laps at the 92nd Street Y. Valda joked they hardly even had time to fuck.

Ellen didn't mind that part. Once the initial excitement had passed, the threesome had become extremely ordinary. Dieter was athletic but perfunctory, and Valda seemed to enjoy the idea more than the act. Franklin Li had been a much better lover. Ellen would have enjoyed telling him so, but there was no appropriate moment for that kind of conversation. When they saw each other, hardly ever anymore, she found herself talking not to a friend or former lover but to the man she'd met her first day on temp duty: beautifully polite, but all business. With Joe stuck between Jersey and Boston, she was feeling a serious itch below the waist as well as frustration over the show.

Drumming abstractedly on the table that was her desk, she yearned for action. She felt enough at loose ends that when Felix Ayre called out of the blue, she didn't hesitate.

Enough time had passed that it was an undiluted pleasure to sink back on the tired old couch and listen to the familiar music of his voice. Since Canada, Felix been all over the world: in Yugoslavia, playing Vincent Price's brother in some cheesy horror film; on the West End, directing and starring in a production of *Present Laughter* with Penelope; even in LA, which he ostensibly hated, eating scenery for a few weeks as a debonair villain on some evening soap. He had stories galore to tell about all of these. And plans, of course. When did Felix not have plans? This time, instead of attempting an entire season, he was focusing on a single production.

"What I would really want, if I had my druthers, would be for me and Pen to do *Present Laughter* here, but we just made it under the wire with the London run. Bloody man practically kidnapped her. I blame Lionel of course. Who knew that scholarship was so sexy?"

Ellen didn't bother to disguise the fact that she hadn't a clue what he was talking about. Her days of needing to impress Felix were so long gone she could hardly remember them. "Meaning what?"

"Didn't you hear? Didn't they toll the bells or muffle the horses' hooves or some such? I know I wore a crape band for a week, until she finally noticed and tore it off my arm. Nearly ripped the silk on that dressing gown. Yes, Ellen, I have been in deepest mourning. My beloved Pen is gone. Finis..." Placing a hand over the glass coffin where her wax heart would be, he dropped his voice to its lowest register and slowly intoned "Married." Only, being Felix, he pronounced it as Hamlet would "marry-ed."

"Married?!" That was a surprise. Ellen had suspected Penelope of deliberately dating impossible men so that she could say she'd tried, and continue her peculiar relationship with Felix. The only one that had seemed at all serious had been... "Not the art historian?!"

"Indeed. One and the same. That sunburned Western type with a hut in the desert. Though as Lionel, damn him, introduced them, I must assume the professional credentials at least are impeccable. Still, New Mexico? Do they even have art in New Mexico?"

"Georgia O'Keefe," Ellen offered.

"Touché." Felix sighed loudly and flung himself backwards in his chair, the better to sprawl. He took a restorative sip of his whisky. "I suppose I will have to go and see for myself. Eventually. Not now. Pen married is strain enough but Pen in an interesting condition is beyond endurance. If she suddenly showed up here, I'd probably have to hide behind the arras. Though I don't expect she will until it's well over. At her age, they say it's best to stay close to home. I only wish for her sake that home were somewhere civilized."

"Wait, are you saying Penelope is pregnant?"

"What did you think I was saying? Yes, of course. Why else would she have married the man? Barefoot and pregnant, with Indians rampaging at her front door."

"I don't think there's rampaging," Ellen absently corrected. This was fascinating. She'd never been sure how old Penelope was but, fabulous as the woman looked, it had to be past 40. Could you still become pregnant at that age? Maybe it was Sydelle's endless carping about having "settled for" Harry at almost 30 that had led her to think otherwise. Ellen wasn't sure she felt comfortable staying on the pill that long. She'd have to ask Planned Parenthood for more information about IUDs. Damn, it was exhausting being a woman.

"She rather likes the desert," Felix was reflecting, mournfully. "She went to Reno to divorce me, you know. Said she found the open spaces extremely calming. I'd assumed she was covering for a fling with some brawny cowboy. Perhaps I ought to have believed her."

"Maybe she loves this...what did you say his name was?"

"Ben. Isen something. Stadt, stern, blatt...one of those. A member of the Tribe. Ah, that should have sounded a warning bell. My golden *shiksa* has always had a weakness for us Chosen types. So, back to the business at hand." Felix was always one to turn on a dime.

She should have assumed she hadn't been asked over merely to gossip. "Business, yes."

"As I was saying, I want to mount a single play. Something classic, naturally. A jewel of a production, enough to make people clamor for more."

"And offer to fund a season?"

He beamed. "From the very first, you've always understood me so perfectly. Yes, exactly. And I've decided on *The Man Who Came to Dinner*. I'll play Whiteside, of course."

"I can see you in it. I mean, I would like to."

He nodded. He'd expected her to say that. "Such fun to cast! There's a young woman I met up in Ontario who would be wonderful as Maggie, the secretary. Dana has exquisite comic timing, and she's been longing to give New York a try. And I would love to get Blythe Danner for Lorraine, if I could pin her down. What a marvelous voice she has. Don't you think?"

"Yes. You know who does great Kaufman and Hart? Joe Bigelow." She couldn't remember if Joe had ever done any Kaufman plays, but she had nothing to lose by making a pitch. The play had several parts he might work for.

"Ah, yes. Our friend Joe. Wouldn't that be fun?" Felix looked at her sharply. For once, she didn't blush, but he knew what she was thinking all the same. "I will certainly take that under consideration. Once I am one hundred percent certain of the funding, that is."

"Here I was thinking you must have most of it, to be thinking so seriously about casting."

"Oh yes. Nearly all. Only one teensy wrinkle." He smiled his most winning smile.

The warning flags went up. Finally, the real reason he'd invited her here. "And that is?"

"I was introduced to a marvelous new organization. American Heritage Theatre, they're calling themselves. Angels, and a few academics I think, with the mission of creating a vibrant national theatre."

"You mean like the National Theatre in London? It would be wonderful to preserve our theatre tradition like that."

"It would be wonderful if America realized it *had* a theatre tradition beyond *Oklahoma* and *Carousel*," Felix noted, with some asperity. "But I'll take what I can get. They've got the money and have been looking around for a way to get their feet wet. They want to eventually start a theatre so, as you can see, this might be a marriage made in Heaven."

"It sounds perfect, Felix." It did. Exciting enough that her instinct for self-preservation had to fight with her desire to volunteer to help. "What's the catch?"

He shrugged. "Nothing really. Only that, with all of one's energies engaged on mounting a production of this scale, one doesn't have the time to do it."

She noticed the shift to the impersonal pronoun and cooled her tone accordingly. "To do what?"

"Oh, just a little contest they're running. For new playwrights. They don't only want to preserve, they want to nurture young talent."

"Laudable."

"Yes. Yes of course it is. Only one doesn't have time to read 20 scripts."

"Only 20?" she said, before she realized what she was saying. "Is this a secret contest?"

He flicked away her comment. "They hardly expect one to read through a mountain. These are the semifinalists. I'm to read through and add my notes, which will be provided to the lucky writers. The board will then select a winner and two runners-up...I believe it was two. In any case, the runners-up get a cash award. The finalist receives an Equity Showcase."

"They're very generous, your American Heritage people."

"Too generous by far. They expect one to produce and direct the showcase."

"Aha."

He shuddered. "Indeed. You can see that this would be impossible."

"No, Felix, I don't. They're putting up the money for your show. If this is all they want, a couple of months of your time..."

"Where to begin, dear girl? Perhaps if someone I could depend on would read through the manuscripts and whittle them down to, oh, the most promising three? And assist with the producing efforts...the most arduous of which, as you wisely point out, is already done...Perhaps such a person would receive an Associate Producer's credit. Such a boost for a resume: Associate Producer of a Felix Ayre production!"

She hated to agree, but it would be. It might be exactly what she needed to ratchet up her credibility and help get funding for *A Thing or Three*. And she'd have a great foot in the door with a brand new theatre organization. Maybe she'd even get to work on *The Man Who Came to Dinner*. "I can't afford to quit Gloria," she mused aloud.

"No of course not," he eagerly agreed. "Bird in the hand."

"It would be a huge amount of time. I'd be working two full-time jobs. Three once January comes." She shook her head.

"I would insist that they pay you an honorarium," he declared. Felix was invariably generous, so long as it wasn't coming out of his pocket.

"And you'd introduce me to all of the American Heritage people. I mean, they'd all know who I was and that I was working with you. Not reading the scripts," she hastened to clarify. "I expect you wouldn't want them to think you'd farmed that out. But the producing bit."

"Absolutely." Felix stuck out his hand.

She took it and shook.

He topped off both their glasses. "To theatre!" Felix toasted.

"To theatre!" she echoed gladly.

♫

We all rallied around to support Frankie when the Rodney trial came on the docket in Arizona. They flew her out to testify as a character witness, probably the best character witness the defense could have wished for. The accusations never made sense to Frankie. The only Margaret she knew was a generous, if sometimes flakey, friend and a loving, devoted mother. She said as much on television to the celebrity reporter who later wrote a book about the case where she referred to Frankie as "Daphne's babysitter." When this reporter tried to wangle some exclusive details about her months with Daphne, Frankie steadfastly refused to say a word. It was the fellowship of orphans. For as long as I knew Frankie, she and Daphne continued to correspond and, every year on Frankie's birthday, there was a long-distance call from Michigan. Whatever else Margaret Rodney might or might not have done, she had chosen her child's guardian well.

The trip to Arizona and the interview were the final act of the Rodney case, although Frankie had to suffer through the airing of the television movie, based on the book, two years later.

For now, life went back to normal. Normal was no bargain. Frankie had fully expected to feel a little uncomfortable in Patchogue after so many months away, but it was worse. Eunice and Mickey made her feel like an intruder. When she came down to breakfast, they acted surprised to see her and stopped whatever conversation they were having, making cold polite comments about the weather or the news. She innocently mentioned they were out of Cheerios and was told by her father, more sharply than was necessary, "We only eat Raisin Bran." If she tried to help out, like empty the dishwasher, it would be met with a frown from Eunice and Pop mumbling how they didn't do it that way anymore.

As if that weren't bad enough, during Frankie's absence, Eunice had crept into every corner of the house that was still left to her, except for Frankie's bedroom. The bathroom—the guest bathroom, as Eunice pointedly referred to it—had been redecorated, with all of Frankie's things swept into shopping bags "to keep them out of the way" and left in her bedroom. With no similar excuse, her winter coat had been removed from the downstairs closet and dumped on her bed, with her snow boots and galoshes on the floor beside it. The last remnants of Martha had been expunged from downstairs. Even her cherished genuine Waterford crystal rose bowl was gone from the living room. Mickey had always said it reminded him of his mother, who'd been born in Waterford. You'd think that would have kept it safe. That, plus it was expensive; Eunice respected expensive. It broke, Pop explained when she asked. It got knocked over by the handle of the vacuum cleaner. Frankie tried to picture the angle at which a vacuum would have to be held for the handle to sweep across the coffee table. There was no point in pressing Mickey. He was already defensively red-faced, spinning a long story about how upset Eunice had been, how she'd moped around for days until he bought her that fancy Lucite cigarette box and table lighter, the latest thing from Fortunoff, to make her feel better.

Frankie watched him wait for her reaction. She shrugged. "I was just curious, Pop. Too bad. I know how much you liked it." And she changed the subject. She didn't cry, not even later, back in her room with the door closed. Maybe clearing out the Rodney home had made her tougher about things, about losing them.

She had to get out. The Rodney money was almost enough to make it possible, as long as she didn't tap into it for other things.

After so many months, it wasn't easy to get back into the swing of auditioning, but she made herself go to practically every open call she saw posted, anything she was even marginally right for. On Eunice's card night, she baked a double batch of Tollhouse cookies. She wrapped them in waxed paper with pretty ribbon, tucking one of her postcards under each bow. The next day, she made the rounds, handing them out at all the agencies that placed extras and to the assistants of every soap casting agent.

Meanwhile, she needed to earn money. Several times a week, she read through all the help wanted ads: the trades, the *Daily News*, the bulletin boards at Equity and the Drama Book Shop. She put up her own flyers on the bulletin boards, her service number on a fringe of tear-off slips, saying she was available for housesitting and pet sitting. "Fee negotiable" is what she wrote, but she'd probably do it for free if it meant few days away from Patchogue.

At least she was working at Alfie's again. The day she got back from Arizona, she took the train in and went straight to the restaurant. She said she'd take anything Alfie could give her—covering for sick days, Tuesday nights, anything. Timing was in her favor: one of his girls, an understudy for *Shenandoah,* was getting rotated into the chorus next month; another was dating Tony Roberts and kept calling in sick. He gave her three days, one of which was Friday.

The tips were good, but not enough. She would have to work harder if she was going to move out. Still, the happiest hours of her week were the hours she spent there.

These days, the restaurant was the closest she felt to having a home. One night a week, she stayed at Ellen's, which was really nice of Ellen. She wished she could do more in return besides comp her a drink at Alfie's...which was really nice of Alfie.

Craning her neck a little so she could see past the cloakroom counter, she could make him out, sitting at his usual post on the front bar stool, bent over his paper, that baby spot, bouncing off the mirror, reflected in his patent-leather hair. To think she'd been afraid of him once. Really he was one of the kindest people she knew.

She checked her watch. Ten o'clock. It would soon be time for the last wave of customers. Even with all the out-of-towners, who had a very limited idea of what things should cost, Frankie got her best tips each week from Friday night pre-theatre dinner guests. The customers she liked best, though, were the ones about to come in, the Tuesday night post-show drinks crowd. There weren't a lot of them, but they were all theatre people. They tipped well, because they'd all waited tables or checked coats in their time and never lost the feeling that someday they might need to once again. And they made a point of talking to her, even if it was only "How are you today?" or "Can you believe this weather?"

It was comforting. She'd expected some comfort at Irene's too, but everyone there was too conscious of Daphne's being gone. They treated her like an invalid. Still, she knew they meant well. People were mostly nice—

with one big exception she kept firmly blocked from her mind. Which wasn't too hard most of the time.

Frankie was getting better and better at managing what went through her head. She got through her vocal exercises without ever hearing Donny's voice or feeling his hands. Except when she was at Irene's, she spent whole days never thinking once about the Rodneys. Her rare thoughts about *Lake Song*, which the Rodneys had pushed into the distant past, were a pleasurable nostalgia and mostly happened when she got together with Ahuva, who couldn't let it go.

"Ollie! Hi!" So funny to be thinking about Ahuva just when Ollie Blanchard hands her his coat.

"Frankie!" He leaned over the counter and kissed her cheek. "Don't you look wonderful! Where have you been keeping yourself?"

"I was doing some private tutoring," she said. It was actually Leonard's idea that she should say this if anyone asked. Ellen, who had Barnum's attitude towards publicity, was all for her mentioning Margaret Rodney at every opportunity, but Frankie didn't want to be asked questions she had no intention of answering. "Are you in something now? I didn't know…"

He shook his blond curls and smiled. "Starting rehearsal in a couple of weeks for *The Pirates of Penzance* in Chicago. No, I was at *Chorus Line*. My friend Crissy went on tonight. Actually, I'd better get moving. I'm supposed to grab a table."

"Go," she said, making a shooing motion with her hand. "Sorry I can't get to Chicago to see you. It sounds like fun."

He stopped a few steps away and turned back. "You know," he confided. "I played the Pirate King in high school. It almost feels like cheating to get paid to do it now."

"I wouldn't mind that kind of cheating," she said wryly.

Laughing, Ollie gave her a thumbs up and walked away.

Frankie smiled happily to herself. She liked moments like this, moments that made her remember that she was not the same girl who'd been dumped from NYADA almost two and half years ago. That poor girl, always worried what people would think of her, trying so hard to pretend she wasn't afraid. Well, she knew her way around now. She'd acquired skills and confidence and a SAG card. It was even good that she'd loved and lost—every artist had to do that. And the responsibilities she'd taken on, first Bron and then Daphne…she would never have imagined herself doing any of that.

She knew people and people knew her. She hung Ollie's coat in the best spot on the rack and gave it a fond pat. No, she sure wasn't that girl anymore.

She was a woman, 21 years old and on her way to the life she'd always planned. Progress might have been slower than she'd hoped, but there had been progress. And the next step was getting the hell out of Patchogue.

♫

The world around us shifted and we scrambled to find our bearings. This is when my father had the heart attack.

I'd returned to campus at the end of summer, joyfully digging into the mountain of senior year efforts. Graduation beckoned. At the end of May, I would take my place in the adult world, a world in which my talents would, at long last, be appreciated. Until then, there was the show that was my Drama Department honors project, a History thesis paper, and the yearbook. Everything required 100% of my time and energy—and everything was due at once. I paused only to take the train down to the city for a dentist appointment. My mother and my sister were waiting at the gate at Grand Central. It didn't take a genius or even an almost-college-graduate to figure out that something was very wrong. The last time anyone had met my train was when our dog died.

My father hadn't died. It was merely an extreme new episode in the story of his heart, a saga that framed my sister and my college careers being prefaced, as it was, by his diagnosis of severe angina my freshman year and concluding with his death the year after her graduation.

This first official cardiac event was severe enough that it would require a long patch in the ICU before they would transfer him to a regular ward to complete his recovery. We were only allowed to visit him one at a time. My father was physically a large man and had the kind of personality that sucked most of the air out of an average room. It was odd to see him so diminished by the hospital gown, the bars of the hospital bed, and grim-looking hospital paraphernalia surrounding or attached to his unusually pale body. It was odder still to find him quiet.

I can't remember what we did when we left the hospital. Did we go out to the diner? Bring in pizza? Heat up some Weaver's frozen fried chicken? Surely one of those three. We were all exhausted; especially my mother, who'd lived a lifetime in the ten hours since she'd overcome her terror of driving to shove him into the passenger seat of our station wagon and race to the ER. We had a quiet weekend. I went to the dentist. We all went to the hospital both days. Sunday afternoon, guiltily feeling I was running away, I took the train back to school.

♫

Seventeen nights later, my show debuted at an open dress rehearsal, before an audience of visiting Alumnae. My friends sent telegrams, as if it were a real Opening Night; and on Saturday, Ahuva and Ellen and Leonard and Frankie rented a car and drove my mother up to Poughkeepsie.

I was only able to hang out with them for about an hour before I had to grab my sandwich and head for the theatre. There was so much talk about my father (who was out of the ICU but still in hospital), that what I mostly learned was how much catching up I had to do. I had been so absorbed in my own dramas that I'd missed out on everyone else's.

It wasn't clear to me what was going on with Ellen's show, but Felix was back in her life and she was helping him with some project. She was unusually reticent about her sex life, something I put down to my mother's presence. Ellen always had great respect for my mother, who was so different from her own. Leonard was applying to grad school, Kevin's anthropology friends having gotten him interested in Comparative Religion of all things. Frankie, as usual, had a funny story. This one was about being an extra in a movie shot on Jones Beach. It was a period piece. Her bathing suit looked like the one from her parent's honeymoon pictures and she'd worn a rubber bathing cap that made her ears ache. No one was allowed to talk between takes because the star of the movie was Method; if he heard any modern conversation, it would break his focus.

It was the first time I'd been with Frankie since Daphne left town. It was a relief to see her so happy, even though Ahuva and Ellen both whispered to me that there was a lot of shit going on with Eunice. During my Thanksgiving break, everyone promised, we'd have a giant sleep over at Ellen's and I would know everything.

"Though I'll probably be late," Ahuva said importantly. "Unless we do it Monday or Tuesday."

"I'm at Alfie's Tuesdays," Frankie added.

"So Monday then." Casting her eyes in her favorite raised-brow-lowered-lid expression, Ellen flicked an ash so emphatically that my roommate's kitten thought it was a game and leapt onto her wrist. It had claws like tiny needles. "Fuck!"

"Is your family going away for Thanksgiving?" my mother asked Ahuva.

She shook her head. "I have a job!"

I knew she meant something that wasn't her parents' store, where she'd been working again. "That's great!"

"Wonderful, dear," said my mother, politely. She'd already hinted, when Leonard mentioned grad school, that it wasn't too late for Ahuva and Ellen to go back to college.

Ahuva grinned. It was absolutely the happiest I'd seen her since the day she'd heard they'd posted the closing notice for *Lake Song*. "Only temporary, but I'll be House Manager at STC."

"How did you manage that one?! I mean, I know you'd be a great House Manager…" I knew she would. I'd spent two years in that role at the campus black box theatre and Ahuva was better than I was at the kind of work it required. "But when did you go back to STC?"

"I was in the Village last week and there was an STC poster in the window of one of the shoe stores. It was for *No Exit*. Remember? *Huis Clos?*"

I remembered. It was on Mr. Solganik's French 4 reading list. In our year, Heidi and I hadn't been able to make any sense of it either. I wrinkled my nose.

A burbling snort of happy laughter. "I know! But I wanted something to do that night. I miss the theatre. And STC is safe. It's downtown."

We knew what she meant. Ahuva was trying to avoid the theatre district these days. We'd all heard the story about the last time she walked past the Regale, and how her stomach cramped up so quickly she almost hadn't made it to the Milford Plaza. It was a story no one wanted to hear again.

"It was either *No Exit* or a foreign film at Bleecker Street that I'd never heard of. And this was STC. I thought I'd see if they could use some volunteers for the next show. I know I said I wasn't going to work for free anymore, but Queens is driving me crazy."

"And they do good work there," Ellen said generously.

Ahuva nodded. "The next show is *Trojan Women* and it's going to be stellar."

"Eileen Herlie's playing Hecuba, right?" Leonard contributed.

"How do you even know that?" Ahuva exclaimed. "I've never even heard of Eileen Herlie."

"Some Classics friend of Kevin's is involved. He did the literal translation for the playwright, who's a British feminist…maybe a Communist, too? Something political. She's very big over there."

"What's her name?" Having indulged my Anglophile tendencies with an airmail subscription to *Plays and Players*, I assumed I knew the names of all the up and coming British talent.

"I can't remember." He brightened. "They did it at the Royal Court last year."

"Herlie was Gertrude to Burton's Hamlet," Ellen said, simultaneously implying that everyone should have known this and that there was nothing further of important to know.

"Well she's playing Hecuba and Alison Fleming, who played Hedda is also in it…"

"Probably Andromache," Ellen and I said, in almost perfect chorus.

"You remember what happened with *Hedda*," Ahuva continued. "They had to extend the run an extra month. Betsy, the house manager, thinks this is going to be even bigger. And she'll be out for most of the run. She's pregnant. She'd been going crazy trying to figure out how they'd manage with only volunteers. When I said I had some time, you should have seen the hug she gave me. I thought it was probably hormones. I never got the impression she liked me that much, but apparently she was very impressed with my work. She said it was a relief to think someone reliable would be there a few days a week. So I told her, depending on the job I got, I'd try to be there as much as possible. Which was when it happened. She gave me this look and said "Aren't you working now?" And I told her I was looking and then she snapped her fingers." Ahuva acted it out, accompanying the gesture with Eureka-wide eyes. "And she said 'we could hire you to cover for me!'"

"It's only logical," Ellen said, doing the eye thing again. "How did they think they don't need a house manager?"

"They didn't think that," Ahuva said, with some asperity. "They have Betsy. They can't afford two people. They're not Lincoln Center, you know."

"I won't ask what they're paying you," Ellen said.

Leonard hit her in the arm. "Probably more than what Felix paid you that first year. Jesus, El."

"You're right. Sorry. At least they *are* paying you. And it'll look great on a resume."

"My first professional theatre job!" Ahuva wriggled her shoulders.

I gave her a hug. Then I hugged everyone else. I had to leave and they'd be piling into the car immediately after the show. "Enjoy the show. I hope." I made the self-deprecating face we make before we share our art with friends. "I can't wait to see you all next month. Thank you guys for coming up. Thank you so much."

There's a big part of me that would like to freeze them there. Ahuva, her face lit with excitement over the job at STC. Leonard, easier in his skin than he'd ever been before, thanks to love-returned and a path to the future. Ellen, reaching out to life with both hands, finding new possibilities around every corner. Frankie, danger averted, back on track to fulfill her promise. And me, the success of my show making me feel that all my dreams were justified and about to come true.

27 – HEAVEN HELP THE HOMELESS WAYFARER

NINA

I am the wind,
I am the seagull on the wind,
I am the feather on the seagull,
I am nothing, I am all:

I beat my wings against the winter,
Stretch my breast across the sky,
As I soar through endless
    cloudbanks
'Til my wings and heart are weary—
I am lonely, I am free.

And I yearn to lay my bones down,
But I sacrifice to wander
And there is no home for me:
There is a haven for the sailor,
But no haven for the bird who sails
    the breeze over the seas.

Heaven help the homeless wayfarer.
Heaven help the dreamer and the
    seeker.
Heaven help the blistered feet, the
    aching heart, the ravaged soul.
Heaven speed the constant search,
    and blunt the constant woe.
Heaven help the homeless wayfarer.
Heaven help the dreamer and the
    seeker.
Heaven bless and Heaven keep,
And Heaven grant a quiet corner
    now and then in which to sleep.

KOSTIA

I am the lake,
I am the willow on the lake,
I am the quiver in the willow,
I am nothing, I am all:

I bare my chest against the winter,
Stretch my fingers to the sky,
And I push through earth and gravel
'Til my roots are deep and weary—
I am timeless, I am new.

I am lonely in forever,
And I yearn to slake my thirst
With something sweeter than the
    dew:
There is a lover for the swallow,
But no lover for the willow in whose
    crest she builds a nest.

Heaven help the homeless wayfarer.
Heaven help the dreamer and the
    seeker.
Heaven help the throbbing head, the
    aching heart, the ravaged soul.
Heaven speed the constant search
    and blunt the constant woe.

KOSTIA & NINA

Heaven help the homeless wayfarer.
Heaven help the dreamer and the
    seeker.
Heaven bless and Heaven keep.
And Heaven grant a quiet corner
    now and then in which to sleep.

No, nothing dramatic happened after that hour in the living room of my campus apartment. They didn't all die on 9/11—two of them no longer even lived in New York by then. Nor did any of us perish in the AIDS plague that was about to hit the theatre world so hard, though we all knew people who did. Within a few years of that night, people we knew would die falling from mountains, be paralyzed in boating accidents, and be raped and murdered in a home invasion—but none of us would. Nor did any of us die tragically young in any of the more common ways: no drug overdoses; no vehicular homicides; only a minor cancer scare or two that was quickly addressed. We all made it past 60 with only the usual bumps and abrasions of life.

With only ordinary achievements and fleeting moments of happiness as well. Wasn't there supposed to have been more? In stories about a group of young people, all bursting with hope and promise and determination, doesn't something wonderful happen to at least one of them? Not necessarily. Not in real life.

No, nothing glorious happened to any of us, for all that we'd been so very certain something would, those few short years of *Lake Song* having been an endless chain of enterprises of great pith and moment.

It's impossible not to be sentimental about those years. We didn't understand how innocent we all were—yes, even Ellen. Or how very young. I know I felt old and battle-worn before I was 20. So much had happened; *a moment as long as a life*, to borrow a phrase. I remember feeling, when I hit 28, that I had to hurry, that I had already missed out on winning the race but, if I tried one last sprint, I might at least cross the finish line.

♬

My father recovered from that particular heart attack in time to drive me to New Haven for my grad school audition. In the interim, he'd embraced his new status as a chronically ill man, using his vulnerability to dodge the disagreeable and cut short any arguments he might be losing. My mother lost weight, my sister lost sympathy and I had my first encounter with acid reflux. Despite this, my directorial efforts on my honors project resulted in an A and a small award from the Alumni association, I submitted the first draft of my History thesis on time, and my co-editor and I shipped all our pages to the yearbook publishers. By that time Simon had again broken up with me, for good (until that final brief reconciliation after which I, once and for all, broke up with him). By early second semester, everything was tidied away. I could sit back and enjoy my final months of college. Or try to; it was hard to enjoy the present when I was so fixed on the future.

I had wanted to be an actress from the time I was seven years old. Of course, like most children who don't grow up in the business, I initially thought I wanted to be a Movie Star. At eight, I understudied Mrs. Duck in the 3rd grade play. Linda came down with chicken pox the night before Assembly and I discovered that what I yearned for wasn't fame and fortune, but the magic of making a story real for an audience. At 14, making an entrance to thunderous summer camper applause as Dolly Levi-born-Gallagher, I accidentally stumbled onto the actor's duality of being both marionette and puppeteer, a description that barely hints at the deliciousness of the sensation. To make a character live with such bone-deep conviction that you feel possessed by her truth, while simultaneously secretly enjoying the quite conscious satisfaction of pulling the strings, is a form of ecstasy; ecstasy in any form being, as you know, the closest we humans come to feeling like gods. It is necessarily fleeting and, once tasted, relentlessly sought to repeat; although, as Marshall Berenson tells us, *anything too wonderful will only last a moment. Holding it forever is something you will always wish in vain.*

My parents, both of whom had missed the experience themselves, were determined their children should have the advantage of a college education. Young and overly conscious of the risks inherent to adult life, it never occurred to me to do otherwise, but I knew in advance that I would major in Drama. Before I'd ever set toe on campus, the college that chose me had experienced a student they were confident would be The Great Actress of our generation (an epithet that all the instructors pronounced with implied capital letters). From the first minutes of Introduction to Theatre, we were constantly bombarded with the faculty's nostalgic sighing over this awkwardly named Meryl Streep. The Department scanned each incoming class, praying for her successor. Short bosomy Jewish girls didn't fit the prototype. As the Department firmly rejected any whiff of professional practice (including, I would later learn, effective guidance in seeking post-graduate training), this was the single aspect of my education that actually prepared me for an acting career; I would go on to experience 15 more years of being similarly "typed out" in the early rounds of the audition process.

The stage filled my heart. Through semester after semester of casting disappointments, I remained fiercely hopeful that my enormous talent would ultimately triumph. I heaped my schedule with student productions. Where I wasn't cast, I worked as crew. I was delighted—and determined—to grab as much as I could. Someday I would relish the Department's collective embarrassment when I won my Tonys. My first step towards that glorious future would be Yale Drama.

On the way up to New Haven, despite being nervous to the point of carsickness, I was buoyant with anticipation. My hair had been cut and blown the day before and I wore an expensive ensemble—treasure of a miraculous post-Christmas sale at Bonwit Teller—that was sure to emphasize my serious intent and set me apart from the ranks of silly girls who thought acting would be fun. Quaking but confident, I kissed my father goodbye and waved him off to the nearest diner.

Candidates were directed to a large waiting room rimmed with single chairs. We avoided one another's eyes; every person of your own sex was competition. Tensely balanced on the edges of our individual seats, we might as easily have been sitting in separate cells, staring blindly at the overhead lights, frantically mouthing the words to our monologues as if they were prayers.

A staff member came in to welcome us and say a few words about the program. I doubt anyone there registered anything other than white noise. Surely nothing caught my ear until the end.

"We're proud of the actors we produce," he concluded. "Every actor who completes our program has a thorough grounding in theatre and a well-trained instrument. There's a young woman who recently graduated who we believe will be the greatest actress of your generation."

The warmth fled from the room along with my confidence. Instantly cold with foreboding, I mouthed it along with him.

"Meryl Streep," confirmed the voice of doom.

If that was the benchmark, I already knew I would be weighed and found wanting. I'd lost before I even entered the audition room. I wore the same lovely skirt and sweater for the NYU audition that was my backup plan. Like poor Byron Weeks before me, I suffered the false hopes of being placed on a wait list. They were my only hopes. No one in the Department thought to mention the fairly new acting program at Julliard or a number of other good MFA options. I only knew about the program in Texas because it had taken someone from each of the two classes before mine; I couldn't see myself in Texas.

And so I wore the same sweater and skirt a month later when the Bloomingdale's recruiters came on campus. I was young and immature. I had neither calluses nor defenses, nor, with a college loan looming over me, money. My dreams died as quickly as Florida citrus in a freak snowstorm. If I couldn't go to graduate school, I couldn't afford to try and be an actor; in which case I didn't much care what I did. Not caring, when asked why they should offer me a spot in their Assistant Buyer's program, I told the Vice President of Accessories that I was smart as a whip and cute as a button. He offered me the job. I took it.

I detested it. I detested my life, cut off from anything that had any meaning to me. I imagined the iron bands around my chest must be what asthma felt like. The reflux, which had calmed down before graduation, returned. Every morning on the subway, I counted the hours until I would be home. At home every night, I only wanted to sleep.

So I quit, which is probably one of the five bravest things I ever did in my life. I was afraid of a vast empty future, but terrified that if I stayed, everything I was would disappear. I'd never quit anything before, and had no idea of what to do next.

Only my friends kept me from being paralyzed. Ellen immediately put me to work, "designing" costumes for the showcase she was producing for Felix. As the men in the play were meant to wear tuxedos, which would be rented, this meant whipping up a simple dress for the leading lady, who would accessorize it differently for each of the two acts.

Ahuva gave me the name of the photographer who did the publicity stills for STC, and I got my first headshots. Frankie took me to ModernAge to make copies and postcards, and then she explained what it was that I should do with them.

Frankie showed me the ropes. In the beginning, I couldn't go to union calls or hang out with her in the Equity lounge, but we could make the agency rounds together, dropping our headshots into the wire baskets outside the locked doors. She introduced me to the agency that did the promotions and we spent a day on opposite sides of 59th Street from one another, giving out free samples of a gum that squirted fruity gel when you bit into it. At some quiet hour, we'd meet up at Howard Johnson's or the Edison or the grubby place with the red leatherette seats, hunker down in a booth in the back, and practice our monologues to each other.

When Frankie was cast in the comic-murder-mystery showcase, I helped her run lines and volunteered to usher. I ushered for Felix's showcase, too; and for a couple of shows at STC, where Ahuva's temporary job had turned into a permanent part-time gig; and for a production of Ric's new play at the Puerto Rican Traveling Theatre. A few days a week, I sold clothes in an oddly provincial boutique on the Upper East Side, where one of my coworkers was a retired operetta soubrette and another roomed with a drag queen. Real life at last.

By the time *A Thing or Three* was in rehearsal, I was studying voice with a friend of Ritchie Edelstein and Soap Opera Acting at Weist-Barron, and had just been cast in a showcase of my own. I'd been out in the world for almost eight months and was chomping at the bit to take it by storm.

That was when we called in my one contact.

It's not unique to the Arts that it matters who you know, but it is more pronounced than in other fields. In any arena, if you can't deliver once you get there, the contacts won't have meant a thing; but without them, you often can't get through the door to try.

My parents had a connection from their dating days, a neighborhood friend who'd famously worked his way up from the mailroom at William Morris to become a top talent agent. It was Eddie's parents who had fixed up my parents in the first place and his sister who, on one famous occasion, talked my mother into giving my father a second chance. His cousin was my mother's best friend. At some point and in some way, Eddie heard I wanted to be an actress and offered to come see me if ever I was in anything that showed me off. It was the kind of thing people said to be polite. I don't think he expected we'd take him up on it. My mother had told him about *The Buddy System*, but the run was at the same time as the Cannes Film Festival...or so he said. When I got the showcase, my mother called again.

You could arguably say that was because of Eddie's family that I had been born. He apparently felt some responsibility, as he didn't exactly put her off. By now he was living almost full time on the West Coast. He arranged for me to meet his junior in New York, an ambitious young man I'll call John.

I hadn't been so excited since the day of my Yale audition. I was much wiser now. I knew that a serious thespian wouldn't be caught dead in chic coordinates. I wore jeans, my Frye boots (for height), and my one silk shirt. I wore small earrings that wouldn't swing distractingly should he want to put me on camera (the one useful takeaway from that Soap class). My hair had cooperated, my nails weren't chipped and my makeup was impeccable. I was ready...so very ready!

The William Morris offices were half a mile and a universe away from the kinds of places Frankie and I visited on our rounds. Everything was modern and, if not marble, then leather or aluminum or glass. In Reception, my name was taken by one of a trio of young women who were as polished as the desk they sat behind. The table by the sofas held the trades, *Architectural Digest* and, in a nod to Los Angeles, a bowl of fruit.

John kept me waiting only 20 minutes and greeted me with a polite air of getting-it-over-with.

I shook his hand warmly and gave him my brightest smile, the smile I thought of as Scarlett-at-the-barbecue because, to summon it, I would make Vivian Leigh's entrance in *Gone With the Wind* run through my head. I'd prepared to open strong, with an invitation to next month's showcase, but he forestalled me by asking how I knew Eddie.

"My parents," I explained. "It was so nice of him to speak with you about me. I really appreciate you taking the time..."

John had been leaning back in his chair. He suddenly popped upright, new interest sparkling in his eyes. It was as clear as a caption running across his chest: maybe Eddie wasn't wasting his time after all. "Oh, great! Your parents, isn't that nice! Would I know them?"

It was question that had a right answer and a wrong one. The right ones being numerous: Liz and Dick. Lucy and Desi. Jimmy and Roslyn. Even to a film man, Phyllis and Adolph would have sufficed.

My answer was the wrong one: "I don't think so. They grew up together. Actually, funny story, Eddie's sister introduced them."

John deflated to his original slouch. He gave me five more minutes: an unimpressed scan of my resume, a shrug when I said I hoped he'd be my guest at the showcase.

I should have lied and said Steve and Eydie. Eydie Gorme had gone to high school with my mother and Eddie's cousin. The singers were past their peak, but they still had enough of a name that maybe John would have felt an obligation to take me seriously.

He drummed his hand briefly on the desktop, jumped to his feet and came around to my side of the desk

"It's a tough business," he deigned to say. "Especially for your type. We've got too many ingénues on the agency rolls already."

"Well, I appreciate your seeing me," I repeated feebly, standing with as much poise as I could muster. "It was very nice to meet you."

I held out my hand again at the door, and made sure to flash one more bright smile.

His lank handshake was accompanied by a perfunctory, "Good luck."

Maybe he would have had second thoughts if he'd watched my performance on the way out. I beamed and nodded at the glossy reception trio as if to imply they should expect to see me again. I kept a smile plastered across my face in the elevator and a spritely bounce in my step as I walked across town to the subway farthest from the William Morris building.

I only stopped when I reached the luncheonette on Third Avenue, and snagged a stool at the counter. I let my face fall and my shoulders sag. I ordered a cup of coffee with a danish that I would never eat. I was in no rush to get home and answer my mother's eager questions. She hated when she couldn't give her children what they wanted or protect them from hurt. I needed an hour or so to simply feel bad, without having to handle her distress at not being able to make things better.

I feel some of that same distress now, thinking back on that naïve, thin-skinned young woman, wishing I could reach across time to help her, or at least comfort her. Poor serious little thing, she bruised like a banana.

My generation was raised to believe devoutly in the American Dream: that if you applied yourself and persevered, you could be Anything You Wanted. Those of us who were drawn to the arts understood there was an extra factor to consider: talent. I was serenely unconcerned. Like Frankie, like hundreds upon hundreds of us, I was convinced of my own talent. I had only to put in the work and, I believed implicitly, eventually talent would out. I have a lovely note from Joan Rivers, a response to a fan letter I wrote when I was maybe 13, assuring me that this was indeed so. Each rejection, therefore, was a rejection of that talent; I was working hard, so if I wasn't succeeding, I must be deluded about having it.

It took years for me to grasp the enormity of the challenge that I'd set myself. There are so few theatre roles for young women each season that there are better odds that a priest will become a bishop than that an actor will land one. One year, I amused myself at curtain calls by counting the women and men on stage. I saw between 40 and 50 plays that season, and for every seven male performers there was one female. I can't say the proportions were exactly swapped in the audition halls, but were you to eyeball the lines of men and women waiting to be seen on any given day, they would look very much like the average breakdown for public restrooms.

With hundreds of women trying out for each available female role (which might as easily be a grandmother as the girl next door), a director can afford to see only those who exactly match his vision of the character. I've tried to explain this to theatrical friends who live and work in smaller countries, where craft is emphasized and actors are expected to be versatile. Our country is so large and diverse that if the character is conceived as a one-legged six-foot tall redhead who speaks fluent Lithuanian, in New York alone there are bound to be five or six adequate actors who fit that bill exactly. The director needn't compromise on a shorter, albeit fiercely talented, woman who will dye her hair, practice her limp and be coached to a sufficient Lithuanian accent.

The real world, it turned out, was college on steroids. I was rejected as casually as I rejected a pair of shoes in a store window: not because of the quality, but simply because the look wasn't what they had in mind. It wasn't about my talent. I rarely got to the point where anyone bothered to investigate whether or not I had any. Once I accepted this, I got better at rejection. Eventually, I would be able to laugh at the talent agent who told me, at aged 27, that he couldn't send me out on commercial calls for "mother" roles because I was too short; at the casting agent who wouldn't let me read for the Wendy Wasserstein play because I was "not ethnic enough for the Jewish girl, but too ethnic looking for the WASP;" at the assistant director who admitted I was a dead ringer for the woman who'd played the part on Broadway but explained that, for the road company, they wanted to "distance themselves from the original."

I can see myself so vividly, waiting on lines: in my brown herringbone coat in the face-roughening cold; huddled under a busted umbrella in the pouring rain; sweat trickling down my back in the 90 degree sun. I can smell the scuffed floorboards of the studios where I took jazz and tap, the musty stairwells of the about-to-be-condemned building that housed my final acting class. I can see the painted cinderblocks and dingy linoleum of the audition rooms; and I can see myself, striding across those rooms to be judged or ignored, flashing my smile, making sure to call the casting intern by name as I handed over a copy of my headshot that, at the end of the day, would end up in the trash, another dollar down the drain, back when a dollar could get you a round trip subway ride.

I got better at rejection, but I never had enough success to make up for it. It became more and more difficult to explain my life to my sister, who asked sharply when I was going to get a real job, or to my friends who'd gone through graduate school, started families or had careers on Wall Street (which you could do then with a Liberal Arts degree). Eventually I got tired of banging my head against cinderblock walls. But that's another story. A story I could never have imagined when I was young and life was full of promise.

When all of us were.

So much *longer ago and farther away than it seems*.

Time, as Marshall Berenson, Albert Einstein or any *Doctor Who* fan could tell you, is a relative construct. It seems like all this happened yesterday. On the other hand, these days, I blink and a decade has passed. *A flick of an eyelash*. Everything disappears before I notice. Even the city I knew no longer exists, except in my memories.

And so, my story draws to close.

Not an end. We all live.

We all stayed in touch to some extent for a decade or so, Ellen and Ahuva and Frankie and I, only gradually drifting apart. I could tell you about those ten years in detail, except I've already gone on for far too long.

You probably think this book should have closed with a tidy wrap up. The Happily Ever After bit. Reader, she married him. Or, less happily but conclusively. And so we beat on. Frankly my dear, I don't give a damn.

Life is never so neat as the stories we tell of it.

And how long is Ever After anyway?

28 – FOR THOUSANDS OF YEARS (REPRISE)

NINA

Men and lions, partridges and arks,
Ev'ry worm that wriggles, ev'ry dog that barks;
Ant'lered stags, and hawks and bees and others;
Th'unforthcoming fish that dwelt beneath the waters:
All are gone, gone, gone.
Life is done, done, done.
On the empty Earth
Is a fearful dearth.
In the wake of death
All is cold, cold, cold, cold, cold.

Five months was plenty, though we didn't know this until much later. On the night when I finally saw *The Trojan Women*, Ahuva was in top form, all bustling importance and happy smiles. At STC, as in many small theatres, the job of house manager and box office manager combine and, since the success of *Hedda Gabler*, the volume of work had steadily increased. Despite longer runs, ticket demands could be heavy and, on prime nights, ticklish to fulfill. Ahuva initially found great satisfaction in formalizing guidelines for VIP tickets, straightening out the office, organizing neglected paperwork, setting up more logical systems for making deposits and managing the roster of volunteers. With typical Ahuva enthusiasm, she'd plowed through the mess, and with typical Ahuva efficiency, she got it sorted out. The co-op that ran STC, including her old teacher, Deb, was thrilled. They decided that the growing subscription audience was generating enough dependable income that they could afford to keep Ahuva on permanently, part time. She accepted the offer.

When she told us, she seemed delighted. Only when she quit the following year did she confess that the job had begun to pall even before Betsy came back with the baby slung against her chest. Being a house manager might have been a job in the theatre, but it wasn't *of* the theatre any more than working for Mr. Nudler had been. Everyone at STC went out of their way to learn her name and say "hi" if their paths crossed; those who had anything to do with front of house were loudly grateful; but she was never part of the backstage family and that was what her heart longed for. She forced herself to accept that there weren't any jobs that would make that dream come true. She couldn't perform or write or direct; she couldn't design anything. She couldn't be a producer, like Ellen, because she couldn't bring herself to ask people for money. It would be decades and multiple attempts at reinvention before she'd wonder why she'd never got around to trying stage management.

At this point in time, however, she made the hard decision to give up theatre and make a fresh start at a different life. A year after that night in my campus apartment, Ahuva applied to college. She didn't tell us until the acceptance letter had arrived.

She began NYU the year she was meant to have graduated from SUNY. It would be an entirely different experience from that sad semester upstate.

Ahuva was conscious now that it was when she was overwhelmed by choice that her palms were certain to start sweating, her heart to palpitating wildly and logical thought to flee from her mind. It was so easy to be crippled by endless possibilities, to be so afraid of missing something that you missed everything altogether and action became impossible. But *anything is possible, if only for a moment*. The trick was to have a specific goal. When she had one, Ahuva knew she was indomitable. She would throw herself into NYU with the same valiant doggedness that she'd employed to conquer the English language, with the same single-minded purpose with which she'd hacked a path from one side of the Regale stage door to the other.

The vastness and variety of the university would not be permitted to confound her, not this time. The new Ahuva Geffner was a confident woman (a word she had begun to ostentatiously employ when most of us were still saying "girl"). She had a second chance and she was determined not to waste it. She would accept that she could never comprehend, no less sample, everything on offer. She would narrow her vision; she would breathe and focus.

For her first semester, Ahuva scrupulously filtered the mountain of university offerings to those areas of study that appeared to have practical application. Ellen's experiences in the job market inspired her towards Introduction to Law and Society; there were lots of jobs in the legal field. She'd selected a first level accounting course for the same reason, but her advisor informed her that Stern students had first crack and it always closed out. He suggested that, if she liked math and logic, she try computer science as an alternative; computers were a coming thing. Considering her goal, it might have seemed odd to choose Behavioral Psychology, except that Ahuva knew she had a tendency to see things in black and white; whatever she ended up doing, she would need a better grasp of nuance. Because she loved languages, she allowed herself a linguistics course as a treat.

It was more of a treat than she'd expected. If someone could have designed a man for Ahuva, I think he would have come out very much like Vilem. Vilem wasn't the best looking man she ever dated. Not much taller than she was, he had a wiry runner's build. Beneath his static halo of ginger hair (apparently an exit strategy for excess energy), his face was elfin, with the crinkly eyes and crabapple cheeks of the Normal Rockwell Santa, and a close-shaven beard that implied a pointed chin. But he was a force of nature, utterly charming and, as anyone could tell within 15 minutes of meeting him, brilliant. He had the same accent as Jakub and a similar sense of humor. Both of her parents were crazy about him, which went far to soften the blow when, after they'd been dating less than a year, Vilem asked her to move in with him.

Wrapped up in Vilem and her studies, Ahuva was in a world far removed from the theatre district and the Maharishi's studio. When the old gang managed to get together for coffee, or the one or two times she was able to meet us to catch a show, she would expound at length on both of her new enthusiasms, eyes shining. I'm sure Wilde or Whistler must have coined some epigram about the aura of smug satisfaction that accompanies the honeymoon period of a serious relationship: it is that ubiquitous, and it's always irritating to those in the vicinity who are currently unattached. This was not only Ahuva's first requited love, but they had set up housekeeping. The honeymoon effect was magnified to the extent that I never expected to like Vilem as much as I did when I met him. But like him, I did. I can't think of anyone who met him who didn't. And they were great together.

Ahuva blossomed. That initial Law and Society course having been a revelation, she had declared herself as Pre-Law. The practice of law, with an order and logic that she described as "elegant," seemed tailor made for her. Vilem was delighted; his previous girlfriend had won a fellowship to Trinity, Dublin. He expected his women to be educated and successful, as well as smart. Not surprisingly, Ahuva minored in psycholinguistics. She did brilliantly in college this time, finishing her BA in three years, graduating with high honors and an acceptance to law school. It was an extremely competitive arena. Disappointingly, NYU, her first choice, had wait-listed her but Fordham was equally impressive. Jakub, though he would have preferred the lower ranked Cardoza for cultural reasons, was overjoyed.

Five years after *Lake Song* ended, you should have seen Jakub glittering with happiness and pride at her graduation. I was seated with the overflow on the Student Center rooftop during the ceremony, but I joined them afterwards for lunch and got to witness it firsthand.

He was gaunter than when I'd seen him last, his eyes sunken and shadowed, his face more thickly lined, and yet he was radiant. Malke, too, despite her smiles, seemed to have aged. We made happy conversation about Ahuva's academic honors, and her exciting future. Everything was now and would continue to be wonderful. She was leaving the next day for a well-deserved rest, to unwind for a few weeks with the family in Israel, and Malke kept reminding her about various gifts she'd promised to deliver.

It wasn't until lunch was over, and Ahuva and Vilem left us at the corner, that Jakub gave way. It had been a long, emotional day and he had a bad heart. There were plenty of seats on the off-hour E train. Jakub collapsed into one and began to deflate. I understood, suddenly, that it was only sheer will power that had kept him going. Jakub wasn't in pain now; he was simply, finished. His daughter was a college graduate, on her way to becoming a lawyer, and loved by a good man. Jakub had led her to the promised land; he could see it from the top of the mountain; he didn't need to enter it. Station after station, I watched the life force drain out of him. Getting off one stop before the Geffners. I kissed them both goodbye and noted the incredibly sweet sadness on Jakub's face. I'd never witnessed this before, but I somehow I knew that he was letting go. It was the last time I ever saw Jakub Geffner.

Less than a week later, an unusually subdued Malke Geffner called to tell me that he'd had a massive heart attack; that the EMTs had arrived quickly and worked over him for almost an hour, but there had been nothing they could do; that she'd called Ahuva in Israel. This was where Malke's voice broke, the point at which she related having to tell Ahuva that her adored father was gone. Ahuva had caught the first plane home. Vilem was camping in Canada and couldn't be reached. Hope was picking Ahuva up at the airport. Would I mind coming to the apartment and being there when they arrived?

"I can't be with her alone," Malke said, her voice shaking again. "She won't forgive me."

"What could you have done?" I asked. "You did everything."

"I'm here and he's gone," she replied.

Maybe if she hadn't been in mourning, if Vilem hadn't been so focused on finishing his dissertation; maybe then law school would have satisfied her. We hardly saw her, she was so busy with work. There were hundreds of cases to read, with hundreds of precedents she would someday be expected to cite. It was later, after she'd made the decision to leave, that she confessed how dry and meaningless she'd found it. Rote learning had none of the elegance that had initially attracted her to the study of Law.

She lost heart. She withdrew from law school after the first year. She lost Vilem...or Vilem lost her...We never knew the details and it doesn't matter, except to them; they lost each other.

She moved her belongings back to her old room and, resolutely pushing past the fateful memories of her last aborted visit there, spent much of the summer with her family in Israel.

On her way home, Ahuva stopped in London to find solace in what was most dependable, in Marshall Berenson.

Theatre lovers tend to forget that there was a period of several years when Marshall Berenson, official national treasure, couldn't get a new show on the boards, when the only Berenson work to be seen in the USA was on school or summer stages. It was the dawn of the blockbuster era. There was still sufficient Puritan residue in our culture that no one had yet proclaimed outright that "Greed is Good," but philosophy was already shifting: in every industry, a modest profit had begun to be considered as much a failure as no profit at all. By those standards, theatre was a non-starter. There hadn't been anything close to a theatrical goldmine since *A Chorus Line* (we were still a year away from *Cats*). Berenson's shows, expensive to mount, with odd subject matter and highbrow music, were particularly risky, and therefore peculiarly unattractive, except to those investors who suffer from Red Velvet Curtain Disease. If you're thinking of last year's Academy Award winning film adaptation, you must be shocked to learn that American investors once appraised *Wardenclyffe Tower*, in particular, as failure material. Remember: this was when the digital revolution was in its infancy; technology and science stories had only fringe appeal at best and the name of Tesla was on hardly anyone's lips.

In London, however, where the arts continued to be separate from industry, there was more risk tolerance, especially for an artist as esteemed as Marshall Berenson. That particular summer, while New York remained void of Berenson, London boasted, not only the original production of his newest musical, *Wardenclyffe Tower*, but the first full scale professional revival of *Playing the Palace*. Both were enormously popular.

Ahuva said that *Playing the Palace* was tremendous fun live. It was bawdier than it had seemed in either the cast album or the film version, or maybe that was just how English did comedy. The crowning moment for her was right after intermission. Before "Royal Progress," the ensemble number that the album notes had taught us opened Act II, the fire curtain lifted to reveal Fyodor and Wong Sing, at opposite sides of the stage, facing away from one another, silhouetted against a scrim that was lit to imply sunrise. The instrumental from the Entr'acte shifted gracefully into a faintly familiar musical phrase and the actor playing Fyodor opened his mouth to sing an unfamiliar verse. A shiver ran down her spine. The musical director had spliced together a number for Fyodor and Wong Sing, setting bits of the solos that had been cut from the original production. Ahuva *had* heard this melody before: when Marshall Berenson himself had sketched it out for her on his piano, on that magical afternoon when they'd shared a plate of cookies and a pitcher of lemonade. She felt herself smiling even while her eyes filled with tears. Lost in the memory, she missed half the jokes in "Royal Progress." She had to run to Keith Prowse the next day and buy the cast album, as well as the multiple copies of *Wardenclyffe Tower* she'd already budgeted, songs unheard, for everyone's Christmas present.

Ahuva was lucky to get into *Wardenclyffe*. From the expression on the ticket broker's face, he'd thought she'd won the lottery. The seat in the nosebleed section of the Lyceum reminded her of the night we first saw *Lake Song*. Staring down at the curtain, listening to the overture, she'd felt that same head-to-toe tingle of anticipation. Nothing would ever be as wonderful as The Show, but *Wardenclyffe* was stellar. Enough so that she came back to the theatre the next day at 3 PM to wait on the returns line—a London refinement we all agreed should be taken up by the New York theatres—and managed to see it a second time.

"Good theatre karma," Ahuva calls it; something that sticks with her to this very day, as if somewhere, the Universe is apologizing.

Back in New York, after registering with several temp agencies, Ahuva bought a copy of *What Color is Your Parachute* and began figuring out what to do next. She also began religiously haunting the TKTS booth, catching up on whatever shows she might have missed. Thanks to the London interlude, the theatre had returned to the forefront of Ahuva's life.

It was now that she became briefly involved with the St. Bart's Players, the venerable amateur theatre group working out of St. Bartholomew's Church on Madison Avenue. In one of the last copies of *Backstage* that I picked up before taking my first sabbatical from acting, I saw a casting notice for their upcoming production of *The Boy Jones*. It's an ambitious show, requiring an unusually large chorus, which is probably why the Players decided to reach beyond their membership. I told Ahuva about this, assuming she'd want to make herself a note to see the show in November. What she did was go to the chorus call.

This was how she met Phoebe, another alto. They were fated to become friends. A big fan of Isobel Talisker, Phoebe used to hang around Talisker's house, hoping to catch a glimpse of the great actress. Talisker shared an alley with Marshall Berenson. Phoebe confessed to having occasionally rummaged through the trash there. Once, she said, she'd found bits and pieces of what looked like a game, with a name was so funny that she never forgot: it was called Berensonopoly.

Though they stuck around for a handful of shows, St. Bart's wasn't satisfying to either of them. The Players included too many professional and quasi-professional performers. There were only two musicals done each year and, when a show had a small chorus, singers like Ahuva and Phoebe didn't make the cut . Phoebe didn't care about being in a show so much as having a community to sing with. Ahuva might have found satisfaction in helping run the company, if only there hadn't been so many other members already entrenched in all the significant positions.

Ten years after *Lake Song* closed, Ahuva was living uptown, in her second year working at Columbia. Her "parachute" had pointed her towards teaching (almost as though everything since high school had been a detour) and being a departmental secretary was a cost-effective way to pay for a Master's at Teacher's College. She found the Ansonia Show Choir on one of the bulletin boards and dragged Phoebe to one of their "open door" nights. They were a newish group, enthusiastic, musically sound and operationally ragged. Almost immediately, it became the center of both their lives. Someday it would even lead Phoebe to meet her husband—not in their choir but through it, the year they participated in the Choir Olympics in Salzberg.

But that was yet to come. At this point, half a lifetime ago, it was enough to be part of a community and, on Ahuva's part, to feel that her involvement was making a difference.

And after that? Ahuva might have been born for teaching, bringing order out of chaos, inspiring young people to look to their passions and try. Her professional decision worked out well. Love, not so well. While teaching math at a high school in Brooklyn, she met Rainer, a graphic artist and widowed father of one of her students. Rainer was very handsome and terribly French. European men always felt more familiar to her than the Americans she dated. She moved in with him when the son went off to college. The relationship was passionate; so was the ending, with Ahuva wanting to have children, and Rainer declaring that he was an artist and couldn't be expected to commit to one woman. There was already at least one other in his life, it turned out, living a few streets over.

Leaving the neighborhood wasn't enough. Ahuva wanted to get out of New York entirely. Someone told her about the American Schools Abroad program. She signed up and did several tours on an Army base in Germany, enjoying the opportunity to travel Europe to her heart's content. In those years, she only came back to the States once, for the Broadway run of *The Summer Lands*. We saw it with Ric and Jay, having both lost touch with Frankie and Ellen by then; this was fifteen years after *Lake Song* had closed.

Probably Berenson's most heartbreaking work, *The Summer Lands* starred our old Medviedenko, Peter Beckwith, as the man of science who is torn between his mission of debunking mediums and his yearning to contact his dead wife. Reviews were mixed. The four of us, however, adored it. Fortunately, so did someone at PBS, and the production was captured for Theatre in America. If you get the DVD and watch it on a large enough screen, you'll probably feel the same chills as we did at the Act I closing number, "Across the Veil." Ric and Jay didn't think to grab an intermission smoke until it was too late; that should tell you how shaken we were.

After the show, we went around to the stage door, something none of us did anymore. Ahuva didn't expect Peter Beckwith to recognize her. Except for his voice, I doubt we would have recognized *him* without a *Playbill*; who would have expected that scarecrow to grow so stolid and substantial in middle age? In any case, she'd only ever known him to say hello. No, it wasn't about being recognized, though it would have been natural to harbor a wish that maybe, *maybe* he would; Ahuva only wanted to recapture the feeling of standing at the Regale all those years before. In the final throes of my abortive acting career, I felt stunningly self-conscious, as if standing there waiting for other actors was an admission of my own failure; I kept to the back, far enough away from the door to disassociate myself from the cluster of fans. Under the lamppost, Ric and Jay finally got their smokes. We were all close enough to hear Ahuva's happy laugh at the crowd's little cheer, when Beckwith walked out. Ahuva's genuine laugh is distinctive, a full-bodied "Ha!" ending on a cheerful hiccup. We instinctively looked at her. So did Peter Beckwith, pausing over the *Playbill* he'd been signing and cocking his head as if trying to identify what had sounded so familiar. The moment passed and so did Peter Beckwith, but it was enough to give all of us a spark of delight.

We grabbed Ahuva and set off for Joe Allen's, Alfie's having shuttered several years before, four old friends in the mood to have a nightcap and share memories.

I'm trying to remember if was during this trip, the *Summer Lands* visit, that Ahuva had lunch with Vilem and met his wife. They were definitely back in contact. They corresponded while she was abroad—primitive as it was, we did have email by then—and gently turned themselves into friends. After that lunch, she befriended his wife, too. If it wasn't that week, then it was soon after her time in Germany, during the period she lived in the States again. I vacillated between admiring this and being appalled. None of my relationships ever had enough substance to leave that kind of residue. Even if they had, I couldn't imagine coping with my successor as Ahuva did, with grace and generosity.

Ahuva will insist that she has no talent and is lousy at relationships. I would argue with her on both of these; but yes, the kind of talent and the kind of relationship that she most yearned for continued to elude her. In a romantic novel, Vilem would have remained single until some perfect storm of timing and location would have thrown them back into one another's arms. Or Ahuva would have run across Byron Weeks somewhere in Europe. Or there would have been a mysterious stranger, someone as talented as Byron, as brilliant as Vilem, as handsome as Rainier, who would have stumbled across her path.

Life is not a romantic novel. She never found that good man. Nor did she find an outlet that would satisfy her by requiring her to apply her intelligence and efficiency towards something creative. This never extinguished her conviction that something wonderful was around the next corner. Always intrepid, always pushing herself to be positive, Ahuva kept searching: from house manager to law student; from student to teacher, on two continents; from teacher to business analyst for a technology company, and then, in what seemed like an inspired leap, to events planning for that same company. After a few years, each enthusiasm burned itself out and it was time again to seek. Maharishi Narang had named her well: Yayaati; Traveler.

Twenty-five years after Lake Song, as if Jakub and Vilem had been magnets pulling her there, she ended up in Prague. She lives there to this day, teaching English and sometimes math. She is exotic there, the American from New York who speaks perfect, unaccented Czech. Much less exhausting than fighting to be someone special in a city where everyone is constantly striving to be extraordinary.

Now and then, when they need her, Ahuva works with a small local theatre company that is making a name for itself with daring chamber productions of American musicals. It's not the grand arena she once imagined for herself, but they appreciate that she has something unique to contribute and it brings her joy. On my last visit, I got to see their original Czech production of *Riding a Bicycle*; I didn't understand a word, but it was tremendously exciting theatre.

We went out for beer and betons with Youri and Milos and the cast, and I told them at great drunken length how much I'd enjoyed the show. At moments like that, the years fall away. Ahuva blossoms again, and becomes the girl I remember hanging off the poles in a subway, singing in gleeful harmony. *A moment holds all of a life.*

29 – IF EVER YOU NEED MY LIFE (REPRISE)

NINA

If ever I dreamed of love, what did I know?
I thought it was a fairytale and I the princess. But I was the sacrifice. And now I hear your voice; I die again.

Whenever you needed salt, there were my tears.
And when you needed sustenance, you took my very blood. My body was
Your youth. My fantasies, my soul became your books.

When you needed a rocket to the moon, I carried you on my wings.
Born by the winds of innocence, I never imagined you'd wring
Me of every last heartbeat,
And then you would leave.
And still I am waiting—if ever you need.

Ellen Janow came very close to making her dreams come true on her very first try.

Thanks to Gloria's borrowed connections, the contest winner's showcase got more press than most and was counted a solid success. American Heritage Theatre was happy to give Felix a green light for *The Man Who Came to Dinner*, which opened just in time for his Whiteside to garner a Tony nomination (he lost to Al Pacino). More importantly, they agreed to give Ellen an Associate Producer credit. As Felix had anticipated, this burnished her reputation with the Angel community and, by that October, Threesome Productions had sufficient funds to project an April opening.

Casting began the first week in February, before Valda and Dieter returned from the slopes. Ellen plunged into managing the audition process. With Franklin mentoring Peter Korn, his new junior associate at Keppel & Grace, she was also doing the bulk of the paperwork and handling all the typical emergencies, like scrambling for a replacement when the lighting designer suddenly dropped out. She didn't mind. Even when she was terrified of fucking up, it was exhilarating.

It was during the callbacks that Ellen first noticed the leggy brunette whose intriguing deep blue eyes turned almost the color of Elizabeth Taylor's whenever she wore pink or purple. Jillian Woodlawn (certainly not the name she was born with) wore a lot of pink and purple. She was a smart cookie. The old fashioned description suited Jill, who seemed to have unpacked her personality from a trunk marked "round-heeled babe with a heart of gold." Jill wore lipstick redder even than mine, cat's-eye eyeliner and black fishnet hose with seams up the back. She didn't joke—she made wisecracks. She sang with a natural belt and, despite her coal country origins, a Brooklyn accent. Her strongest talent, though, was dancing. Frankie, by now considered something of an expert by our group, admired her tap skills. She could Fosse up a storm; and she could high-kick like a Rockette. In fact, that had been the dream that brought her to New York from West Virginia. It didn't pan out. Despite her stage presence and obvious ability, the Rockettes turned her down twice. A saucer-eyed ingénue at her last audition sweetly suggested that she didn't seem the type. This was true. The Rockettes were resolutely wholesome under their spangles. Jill was a little coarse, in an indescribable way that spurred Leonard to wonder if she'd ever done porn. When we later learned from a smitten Ellen that she'd been making most of her recent living as an exotic dancer, it seemed inevitable.

The timing of her arrival couldn't have been more perfect. Joe Bigelow was in LA, *The Man Who Came to Dinner* having inspired his agent to submit him for a bunch of television work, and Valda and Dieter had moved on to an Italian couple they'd met at Chamonix. Jill was talented. Jill was street-smart and cocky. Most of all, Jill was desirable. In quick succession, Ellen and Jill flirted, went out for a few drinks, and had sex for the first time.

The camaraderie Ellen had with Joe Bigelow was rare among her relationships. She preferred casual romps with people of whom she was less fond, relishing seeing herself reflected in her partner's eyes as someone free and powerful, or else playing La Belle Dame Sans Merci, deliciously controlling another person's pleasure. She'd reveled in the knowledge of Ruth Mann's deep need to restrain her. Half the allure of Ruth and the entire episode of her threesome with the Oelrichs had been how these antics fed the image of wild, daring Ellen Janow. So did sex with Jill.

"You know, all strippers are lesbians," Ellen informed us. "They get off watching the men go crazy for what they can't have. And what they're missing! You have no idea what it's like with a dancer." She skewed her eyes heavenward in rhapsody, and then winked. "It's a good thing I had that knee surgery."

Ellen couldn't get enough. "I wish she would just sit on my face all day," she sighed over coffee one afternoon, setting off a battery of spit takes in our booth. "That woman!"

Soon, Jill was at Ellen's nearly all the time. Her own futon, in the Hell's Kitchen living room of a couple of gypsies, was nice for empathy, but lousy for privacy and sleep. She didn't officially move in, but her wheat germ and yoghurt stocked the refrigerator, her leotards and fishnet hose dripped off the towel rails. On opening night, Threesome Productions gave each of the cast members a bottle of champagne; privately, Ellen also gave Jill Franklin Li's pearl pendant.

Smitten was the word. It wasn't only sex. Jill brought out feelings that she'd never acknowledged having. Ellen, who had always needed to feel in control of a relationship, surrendered to Jill. She allowed herself to be tender and vulnerable. And yet, she yearned to protect Jill, assuring each of us in turn that this tough little urchin was really as fragile as the famously pea-beleaguered Princess.

It was a glorious couple of months for Ellen. *A Thing or Three* was an obvious freshman effort for all the talent involved, but rough-edged comic cabarets were enjoying a brief flutter Off-Broadway. Reviews were decent.

The box office was steady enough. To top it off, she had Jill: feisty, seductive, agile and always provocative Jill.

If she hadn't been so wrapped up in Jill, would she have noticed before it was too late? Ellen would batter herself for years with that question. The answer was probably not. Franklin Li, hadn't seen it coming either.

Three years and six weeks after *Lake Song* ended, Jill's paycheck for *A Thing or Three* bounced. At the bank, Ellen was told the account had exactly one dollar in it. She called Franklin, who was as confused as she was. He checked the books at the end of every month; there had been almost $50 thousand.

No one answered the phone. When Ellen and Franklin finally went in person to Park Avenue, the doorman shook his head and wouldn't let them up. The Oelrich's had moved out, he informed them, and they'd left no forwarding address.

The details were never discovered. The Oelrichs disappeared into Europe, never to be heard of again. Franklin bitterly asserted that they were cons, that this had been their plan all along. It was his pride talking. It made no sense that they'd invested nearly three years in *A Thing or Three* for a bankroll that loomed large to Ellen, whose yearly salary from Gloria was closer to $22 thousand, but would merely be chump change to socialites who lived like Valda and Dieter.

Ellen immediately laid the blame on the Italian couple they'd met skiing; after all, there had been no hint of anything shady until they'd paired up. Frankie took umbrage at the implication that Italians were criminals by nature and was extremely cool to Ellen for a while.

The show closed. Ellen couldn't bear to face Gloria, who'd made a small investment as encouragement. She quit her job and started temping again. Jill went back to exotic dancing until she decided New York wasn't the place for her and she took off for the West Coast.

By then, Ellen was working for Felix.

Ellen was Felix's right hand at American Heritage Theatre for the entire two-year lifetime of that noble failure. Their company delivered solid, often inspired work, but Broadway audiences preferred their theatre new or starry. The New Phoenix Repertory Company a few years prior and Tony Rancall's National Actor's Theatre some years later met the same brick wall. America has never rallied behind a National Theatre, a state of affairs that many theatre lovers, including me, continue to mourn.

Towards the end of AHT, Jill returned briefly to Ellen's life. Los Angeles had not been a success for her and she was hoping the New York scene might have changed. She moved in. Ellen broke up with her latest boyfriend, owner of a small local chain of shoe stores. We all thought she was making a terrible mistake, but she was happy.

When AHT folded, Felix reprised his disappearing act but this time Ellen wasn't left holding the bag. She even collected unemployment, a luxury she'd never imagined.

It had been a productive couple of years. Ears and eyes open, she'd learned enough about making a theatre company run that she was able to talk her way into a summer at the Williamstown Theatre Festival. Jill locked in a revue on Cape Cod for July and August. Separation would be hard but they agreed in advance that stories about their extra-curricular activities would add spice to the fall.

It was a refreshing summer idyll but nothing more. Ellen had cherished some hopes that the pool of young talent might yield a new property to produce. Since Franklin had managed the legal issues around the Threesome failure, she was free to start again. Although she met a lot of people, none of her new contacts led either to a property or to a job. Fortunately, Gloria had more coming in than she and her current assistant could handle and she was happy to feed Ellen some freelance work. The AHT Foundation, whose new mission was nurturing young playwrights, paid her to write some grant applications.

Jill's career was similarly stalled. The only jobs she picked up after the summer were a couple of trade shows at the Coliseum. She didn't have Ellen's patience. She couldn't, she observed; dancers only have so much time. Early in the year, she took off for Vegas.

Ellen was bereft. She moped all winter, treating us to tipsy declarations of celibacy.

It was a relief to everyone when Williamstown cropped up again. This time they called her. They offered her a better job, a longer one that began while the season was still planning and included the paperwork after.

Several of the well-known actors who regularly performed at Williamstown had bought houses in the area and summered there with their families. One of them had an Irish nanny whose brother, a promising playwright, was invited to come and stay in August. Ciaran Kelligher made the most of his visit. Clever enough to understand the benefits of being a professional Irishman, he hung around the Festival, chatting people up with spontaneous warmth and disarming frankness. I think even Harry was charmed when they finally met. It was hard not to be. The man was a bloody leprechaun: not the compact pot-bellied variety, but slim and long-limbed, with a boxer's broken nose, and long fingers that Ellen assured us were as clever as they were elegant. His clothes were worn with such flair that no one could say if their invariable shabbiness was born of necessity or artistic affectation. But what made him memorable were his impish smile and acute, wicked wit.

Ciaran struck up Ellen's acquaintance at the bar one cabaret night. He later admitted that, earlier that day, he'd seen her talking with Nikos and Dick Cavett and assumed her to be more important than she was. They instantly hit it off. She was delighted to introduce him to everyone that she did know and, once she read the two plays that he'd confidently lugged across the Atlantic, determined to help him. Here was the talent she'd been hoping to find. The green-card marriage was a logical next step.

Harry and Sydelle were so elated by Ellen doing anything as conventional as marrying that they sprang for a small party at Sign of the Dove after the City Hall ceremony. The bride wore belted green silk, green, according to Ellen, being an appropriate color for marrying an Irishman, and Sydelle having wearily agreed to compromise on color as long as the dress had a decorous neckline. The groom was rakishly handsome in a fine wool suit jacket over a white dress shirt and his best jeans, a look not so common in those days. It was only when leaning in to kiss congratulations that you noticed the faint aroma of thrift-store cleaning fluid. After lunch and a champagne toast, the happy couple took a cab up to the Pierre, for a weekend honeymoon courtesy of Harry and Mo. They spent much of it planning how to forward Ciaran's career.

By the time Ellen began work on the next Williamstown season, Ciaran's had become a familiar face on the New York scene, enough that one of Nikos's more important assistants agreed to read the new play that Ellen casually provided. He liked it enough to promote it for a showcase on the small stage.

I drove up with Leonard and Kevin to see it. The play was darkly funny, in what I would later understand to be a typical modern Irish way. None of us entirely liked it, but we agreed that Ciaran could write and the production served him well. The artistic director of a Baltimore theatre company attended that same performance and loved it enough to take out an option.

Nine years after *Lake Song* closed, Ellen and Ciaran were living in Maryland. His play had been a great success there. When the theatre commissioned him to write another, he proposed to Ellen that they relocate. He had no desire to spend another three months going back and forth, as he had for the first production. Ellen had already been toying with the thought of trying a city with more resident companies where she could maybe get on staff. She had nothing other than sentiment keeping her in New York. She agreed. Away from New York City, her resume, and her recommendation letters from AHT and Williamstown, not to mention the one she wrote for herself on Felix's behalf, were loudly impressive. Initially hired as assistant to the managing director of an up-and-coming theatre, she would eventually take over when her boss moved to Chicago.

Baltimore is only a few hours away, but state-to-state phone calls were still charged as "long distance." In any case, we were all so busy, it was hard to schedule the time. We gradually lost touch.

When Harry died, I didn't hear about it until Ellen came to town several months after to handle some paperwork for Mo. This must be difficult for younger generations to grasp. Today, even if we live half a world away and haven't seen each other for years, we know the minute a friend's cat dies. Before social media and smart phones, it was common for distance to cause even good friends to lose touch unless they both enjoyed writing letters.

During that brief visit, I had coffee with Ellen and Frankie somewhere downtown. It was an odd, uncomfortable hour. Frankie already knew about Harry, but she hadn't told me. We were already drifting apart, though our final break had yet to come.

What I know going forward is patchy. Fourteen years after *Lake Song* closed, Ellen and Ciaran split up. I remember being sad when I heard. I knew it had begun as a green-card marriage, but they were genuinely fond of each other and I was still enough of a romantic to hope it had blossomed into more.

Ciaran went out to Costa Mesa for a production of one of his plays and had an affair with the leading lady. He and Ellen had each had their affairs over the years, but neither minded; their marriage was, after all, a business partnership. This time, however, he fell passionately in love. They divorced. He moved to Los Angeles and gravitated to television. I see his name on my screen all the time.

Around the same time, Sydelle moved to Boca. That was certainly a surprise—Florida wasn't exactly simpatico with Sydelle; but her sister and brother-in-law were making the move, and without Marlene, Sydelle would be all alone. Once she moved, Ellen had less reason to come to New York. When she did come in, it was usually to see some shows, and she often went straight to Leonard and Kevin's place.

I can't recall the last time we spoke.

Twenty-three years after *Lake Song* ended, Ellen was the only person I'd ever known who was apparently making a living in theatre.

Heidi was in from Israel on one of her biannual visits. The cuisine in Israel was still almost exclusively Mediterranean. Until the Russians started arriving in droves, you couldn't even get the smoked fish of our childhood, which I (such a New Yorker) thought of as quintessentially Jewish. Whenever Heidi came to town, her to-eat list was as long as her shopping list. That day, we'd gone to Second Avenue deli for egg creams and pastrami. As we were paying, we ran into someone else from high school.

"Man!" he said, after we'd all exclaimed and hugged several times. "This is such an effing small world! I was in Baltimore a few weeks ago and you'll never guess who I saw. Remember Ellen Janow? She was so surprised I recognized her. I dunno, she looks basically the same. More surprise she recognized me!" He ran a rueful hand over where his signature 'fro no longer grew. "Damn, she was so good in *Arsenic and Old Lace,*" he said, naming the class play that had been Ellen's single venture onto a stage. "I was sure she'd go pro. But she never went into acting, she said. Seems she runs this theatre in Belvedere. I can't remember the name. She said they do a lot of new plays."

That was the last I heard until recently. Thirty-six years after *Lake Song* ended, Leonard and I reconnected on Facebook. We did what's become the usual thing: exchanged a flurry of messages laying out the bare bones of how we've lived since the last time we were in one another's lives. I know he and Kevin are no longer together, that he's married to someone else and that he and Seth still run their family business. Leonard has always kept in touch with Ellen. From him, I learned that she still lives in Baltimore but has retired from theatre. These days she raises funds for a not-for-profit that helps young LBGT runaways. It's a good second act.

I can't rightly say I that I know her, but I'm proud that I once did.

30 – THE MAN WHO WISHED (REPRISE)

KOSTIA

The man who wished
Wished for too little and too much—
He wished for happiness

What am I to write at the bottom of the page
Just before they put 'finis?' What am I supposed to say
To have the last word?

Is it thought? Is it action? Or maybe conversation?
What would be the right—or should I say appropriate—sensation
To hold them, their attention;
Or release them, loose the tension?
What to give them as my very final moment?
The last word...

That's the story of my life.
That's the story of my art.

Do I think? Or do I act? Or will they talk about me?

Frankie Cecchi kept making the rounds, always certain that the break that would change everything was right around the corner. Soon after I left Bloomingdale's, she showed up for one of what was about to become our regular coffees, bouncing on the vinyl seat in her excitement. She'd just come from Equity and seen a call for *Cherry Orchard* auditions next week. It had been quiet lately, so any play with several good parts for young women would have been good news, even an unpaid showcase. Better still, this *Cherry Orchard* was a Soho Art Theatre production, directed by Wardell O'Hare.

Frankie hadn't had any contact with O'Hare since *Gooseberries*, almost three years before. He must have been putting on shows all this time—the man had his own theatre—but she hadn't noticed. Maybe they'd occurred during periods when she'd been taking care of Daphne or Bron, or maybe he'd cast everything entirely from within the company. After *Gooseberries*, she'd been a little insulted that he hadn't invited her to join that company. She'd certainly paid her dues, working her ass off for nothing but subway fare and disappointing results. The experience had resolved Frankie to narrow her focus to showcases that might attract more attention: new plays, preferably comedies, performed in venues more amenable to casting agents.

Cherry Orchard was a special case. There were two good parts for her: the serious Varya and the flighty Dunyasha. Either one would show her off and be sure to get her more work. Best of all, Dunyasha, the funny role, was a maid. Considering her previous success with comic Chekhovian maids under O'Hare's direction, we both figured she'd be a shoo-in. She probably wouldn't even need to do her comic monologue, but she polished it to perfection.

Frankie stayed at Ellen's the night before, to be well rested. She later told us her hair and makeup looked great (something that she never said, so they must have). Entering the theatre, familiar ground, she felt relaxed and confident. Unlike her previous experience here, this was a full-scale audition. There were others waiting in the lobby. She said it didn't even make her nervous. When her name was called, by a serious young man she didn't know, she laughed before correcting the pronunciation.

The theatre looked exactly as she remembered it, down to the ratty sofa. The serious young man led her down the aisle and held out her headshot to Wardell O'Hare, seated in the front row.

O'Hare also looked exactly the same. Same pointy beard, same odd eyes. It was probably even the same Irish sweater.

"Frankie Cecchi," the assistant announced, shocking her by repeating it correctly.

"Hi, Wardell," she said, holding out her hand. "It's so great to see you again!"

O'Hare looked at her blankly. "Yes?"

Letting her hand drop, she shifted slightly to get more light on her face and smiled again. "It's me, Frankie. From *Gooseberries*, remember?"

"*Gooseberries...*" he drawled, as if he'd never heard the word before.

"I was your ASM. And I played the maid." She gestured to her stomach, sticking it out.

His face didn't so much as flicker. "I meet so many people. Have you done a lot of Chekhov?"

"Only *Gooseberries*. But I love..."

"My company are all experienced Chekhovians..." He flipped over her headshot to read her resume.

"Yes, I know. I still remember the breathing exercises...Maestro..."

He wasn't listening.

She felt like she was in a bad movie. She took a deep breath. "I have a monologue prepared." She already knew it was a mistake but she was damned if she'd give up so easily.

He sighed and pointed two fingers at the stage area.

Frankie knew, down to her bones, every spot in that monologue that should get a laugh. As each one passed without reaction, her body tightened. She began to force the emphasis. Her voice grew shrill. She couldn't help herself. There is nothing as silent as a space that should have held laughter. An hour later, her two minutes were up. She delivered the final line with her arm lifted, held it for an extra second, and let it drop.

"Thank you," she mumbled.

"Yes," he said, waving a dismissive hand.

She trudged back up the aisle, retrieved her coat and left. "What the hell just happened?" she wondered.

She called me and told me the story. I said the same thing, except I said "What the fuck...?" I told her it only confirmed what we'd all suspected: Wardell was clearly certifiable, as well as an asshole.

Ellen stopped by Alfie's after work, heard the story and said exactly what I said, adding that he couldn't direct for shit and no one worth knowing would drag their asses downtown to see the garbage he put on.

472

As she did with most things that hurt, Frankie made the incident into one of her funny stories. It had a somewhat happy ending.

If she'd gotten *Cherry Orchard*, she wouldn't have been available to audition for the showcase that she *did* get. The new comic murder mystery, performed in a rehearsal hall on Eighth Avenue and 47th Street, attracted a lot of agents, a handful of whom approached her during the run. Her small but critical role showed her off to good advantage.

One agent, though he wouldn't sign her, set her up for a few LORT auditions before her lack of callbacks made him change his mind; another sent her on go-sees for some commercials until her teeth and skin were deemed to be deal-breakers. This is where the happy ending falls short.

She did get a job—ironically, from someone who hadn't come to the showcase. One of the dozens of agencies to which she'd sent flyers and postcards, an agency that handled extra work but hadn't used her in a long while, put her on their call list. Frankie showed up for a day of filming and was upgraded to be the stand-in for the minor star who was playing the girlfriend. It was five weeks of work. Surely it would be the start of something big.

It wasn't. Yet again, two steps forward, one step back. The stand-in job didn't lead to anything more. The money, the most she'd ever earned as an actress, was enough to keep her until something else turned up.

It seemed that something always did when she needed it most (although the timing could be a nail-biter). Everyone who ever met Frankie wanted to help her. All the years I knew her, her mother's friend Rhoda cut her hair for free. As many times as she had to leave Alfie's, he always took her back. One of Alfie's customers thought of her when his receptionist burst an appendix and ended up in the hospital for nearly a month. Tyler Moss called her out of nowhere, to be temporary nanny to the children of a visiting diva.

Once—but I'm jumping ahead a couple of years—she was having coffee with Connie dePaul, and Connie mentioned they needed another assistant dresser on *Sugar Babies*, where the chorus had a lot of quick changes. Older and wiser than the last time Connie had tendered such an offer, Frankie grabbed it. The work was enough to qualify for the union...and for the subsidized housing project that focused on low-income working members of the theatre community. Finally, Frankie could get away from Patchogue.

Another event, which started less than happily, ended well for Frankie. Two-and-a-half years after *Lake Song* closed, she slipped on some ice by Penn Station and chipped a front tooth. Her mouth, always her Achilles heel for film work, was worse than ever. To add insult to injury, she no longer matched her headshots, a magnitude of tragedy that only another broke actor will completely understand.

She couldn't afford to get caps, but she couldn't afford not to. She called everyone, hoping someone knew of a dentist who would work out a reasonable payment plan. Ahuva suggested she try the Dental School clinic at NYU. Luck was with Frankie. The students were about to start a unit on caps and crowns, and she could get the necessary work done for little more than the cost of lab fees. It was at the clinic that she met Dave-the-dentist, who she would date until he decided to return home to Omaha. A friend of Dave's was a freshly-minted orthodontist. As the weekend receptionist for the orthodontics practice, Frankie earned a tiny salary that was more than offset by a substantial professional courtesy discount. She got the braces she'd always needed and could count the months to a camera-ready smile.

Even before she broke her tooth, Frankie had begun taking voice lessons with Irene's cousin Bobby, who sometimes played piano for her tap classes.

We spent a lot of time puzzling over Bobby Lemon. Five-foot-nine in thick-soled construction boots, Bobby had a gruff alto voice and buzz-cut hair and always wore chinos with either plaid flannel (winter) or blue cotton (summer) button-down shirts. We ultimately decided that Bobby was a very butch lesbian. At the dawn of the 80s, what else would we assume? Glam rock had its androgynous stars, everyone was familiar with drag performance, and Ellen knew a straight man who was a weekend transvestite, but Bobby wasn't like any of these. Except for Renee Richards, whose story was on everyone's lips that year, most of us weren't aware of the transgendered among us, and if the phrases gender-fluid and genderqueer had taken shape, they certainly hadn't launched into the mainstream. Whatever Bobby was or wasn't, Bobby was a gifted voice teacher and thought the world of Frankie and her talent. Under Bobby's coaching, Frankie gradually expanded her range and, more critically, gained the confidence that her ability to put over a song was far more valuable than any notes she could or couldn't reach.

Every January, Bobby's students put on a "Post-Christmas Cabaret" at a club in the Village. It cost them each $100 but it was worth it. Since the performance always included surprise appearances by a few of the successful artists that Bobby had helped along the way, you never knew who might show up in the audience. The year of Frankie's debut, Leonard found himself watching the show through a veil of Bernadette Peters' curls. He nearly had a heart attack. Being Leonard, he demurred at saying hello but, at the end, waited in the aisle for her to pass. She smiled warmly and wiggled her fingers so he was familiar to her (whether or not she knew why). More important for Frankie and other performers, there was also a sprinkling of agents and the occasional song-writing team.

Frankie longed to do one of Masha's numbers from *Lake Song* but her upper register wasn't up to "Black" and Bobby felt "The Schoolmaster and His Wife" was too insubstantial. Instead, she and some guy named Kent did a hilarious rendition of "Carried Away" from *On The Town*. They brought down the house. Kent got a new agent and was almost immediately cast as Kenickie in a road company of *Grease*. Frankie, in her new braces, auditioned for Frenchie in the same production, but didn't get it. She didn't get an agent either. She did, however, get one to agree that, if she saw a job she wanted to go out for, as long as he wasn't already submitting someone on his books, he'd be willing to submit her. As always, Frankie took this small gain as a victory.

Buoyed by the audience response to "Carried Away," she told Bobby she wanted to build a club act. There were plenty of bars in the city that had small stages to lend out as a way of drumming up business on a quiet night. Your take would usually be half the cover charge and maybe a tiny percentage from drinks. Unless you accompanied yourself on the piano, it probably cost more to perform than you'd make back, but it was great experience and, if you kept at it and showed you could pull in an audience, someone might offer you a paying gig. Bobby helped her select songs that were vocally achievable and allow her to display a mix of moods. Frankie started writing down the stories she wanted to tell in between the numbers. It didn't take long for her to have a 75 minute set.

Frankie did her very first club date at one of the Irish bars across the street from the Coliseum. It had snowed a few days before, which meant that the streets were full of dirty slush, not the best weather for drawing a crowd. She'd sent flyers and follow-up postcards to every talent agent and casting agent in town; not one showed. Nonetheless, it was a full house. Frankie had a lot of friends; everyone came and most brought other friends.

From the moment Frankie stepped out, in her Judy-Garland-traditional black tights and white shirt, a magenta feather boa flung around her neck, she commanded that room like a pro. Even I, who'd been her audience for countless rehearsals, was surprised. It was the performance of her life. She poured her heart out from that tiny stage. Comic numbers that seemed made to order; Broadway standards she could let loose and belt; even an affecting torch song that was a little beyond her range: she sold them all with the panache of a seasoned cabaret performer. Her patter with Bobby Lemon (who played for her that one time) and her occasional ad libs to the audience were quick and funny. We laughed heartily at every joke and applauded hard after every number, understanding that we were a part of it too.

The owners of the venue were impressed. Before Frankie left that night, they invited her to come back soon.

It was spring when she returned, this time with a pianist our own age, another of Bobby's protégés. They had a nice energy together. Scott was more willing to go with the flow than Bobby had been, which worked out well as, the more club dates she played, the more Frankie departed from the script, stretching out her patter. Making people laugh had always been her favorite thing. Now she basked in it and, the more she got, the more she craved. She played with her set, focusing more on the comic material, cutting out some of the ballads she'd worked so hard on with Bobby, turning one wistful number into a gentle parody of itself. After a while, she started punching her laugh lines, making the anticipated response obvious to the audience.

We still laughed. With the gift of timing and a gravelly cartoon voice, Frankie was naturally funny. We anticipated our part in the choreography now, but we didn't mind because Frankie always had a puppyish appeal that put everyone in her cheering section. We laughed, we applauded, we assured her that, any minute now, her break would come. After all, the talent agents always said that you had to narrow your focus, pick your type and sell it hard, and Frankie had found hers. She did a club date every month or two, and in between, she brought new confidence to her auditions. And yet none of the casting agents or directors ever said "Yes! Here's what I'm looking for!"

They weren't saying it about me, either. In those years, I was probably closer to Frankie than to anyone. Ahuva was absorbed in Vilem and school. Ellen was producing, or working hard to stay afloat while trying. Frankie knew a lot of actors and dancers and singers, but she was the only one out there who I knew. I'd lost touch with the theatre crowd from college, except for Carol, who'd modeled overseas and was now doing commercials and workshop productions of gritty award-winning playwrights. I had a lot more in common with Frankie, both of us juggling a full-time search for acting work with part-time paying survival jobs. We were a pair of travelers supporting each other on a yellow brick road to the stars.

Then I became addicted to Shakespeare and managed to earn enough at my survival jobs to cover a summer acting program in England.

♫

It's impossible to think of Frankie at this time without bringing myself into the mix. It's trite but true to say that we'd been drawn together by what we had in common and were drawn apart by our differences. We shared the same unswerving vocation, the same pure-hearted dream. Frankie pursued it with unshakeable conviction in her path and talent and, despite all frustration and setbacks, content. For Frankie, the Way was the destination; as long as she was pursuing that path, she was an Actor. I was less pure in my vocation. If I ever had any kind of faith, in anything, I surely lost it before the age of nine. My path was as unavoidable as magnetic north is to a compass needle, but I found no "there" there. All those classes I took, all those audition monologues, had me in a perpetual state of wannabee. "So what do you do?" people would ask me at parties, on blind dates, at alumni association events. And my throat would seize up, until I would eventually mumble along the lines of "Well, I'm working in a boutique uptown, but I'm trying to act." I simply couldn't bring myself to say "I'm an Actor." For that, I needed work—even unpaid work—and I was hardly getting any.

Ten years after *Lake Song* closed, the year that I would turn 30, I heard about the summer program in England and saw it as my last chance. When they accepted me, I was wrapped in a fairytale. This would be it, you see. After a decade of trying, here is where my acting career would at last come to fruition. I would be appreciated over there. Someone would offer me an acting job. And maybe I would meet a wonderful Englishman and we would fall in love. Yes, I sold myself on the whole Cinderella story. I was wrong, of course. No fairytale for me. But I met some marvelous people. One of my instructors was a pretty wonderful English actor, with a lifetime of experience and stories to share. When he expressed astonishment that I wasn't "working all the time" back home, it was one of the most important moments in my pathetic career. His belief in my talent, and the regard of my peers whose work I admired, confirmed for me that I had not been wrong to try. I still wasn't working but, to eyes other than my own, I was an Actor after all.

I returned home with a renewed sense of purpose, and set to auditioning with energy and confidence. The work that summer, and the Shakespeare performance classes I'd taken the year before, had also rekindled a thirst to learn. If I wasn't getting work—or even showcases—I needed something more stimulating than the bathroom mirror. I'd been foolish to limit myself to singing and dancing lessons all those years when, compared with my competitors in the market, my gifts in these areas were meager. My strength was straight theatre, comedy and drama both, and most especially those dramatic comedies where it was critical to marry timing with line delivery; I was very good with words. I decided I would take an acting class—if I could find the right one. When I tried to encourage Frankie to do the same, she took it as an insult. After all, she was the one who'd had a professional theatrical engagement before she was even 18, and with Thierry Dupontel.

I was accepted into the workshop of a director as equally well-known as Thierry, a man with his own theatre festival and an international reputation, a man so consequential that even Ellen was impressed. She should have been—she'd spent a couple of summers working for him. Nikos also taught at Yale, but this was his professional workshop. I couldn't believe he was willing to take me. One of the women in this workshop was in the midst of co-producing and starring in an Off-Broadway show; another was in the chorus of *42nd Street* on Broadway; one of the men had been on a soap for a few months: working professionals.

For the first six months, nothing I did was right. Nikos raked me over the coals after every scene. I cried a lot—never in front of him—and gritted my teeth and forced myself to try again. I had to concede that whatever I'd been doing for the past decade wasn't working or I'd be getting jobs. If I really wanted to act, I had to start from scratch. This man, this great director, must have seen some potential, some glimmer of what my instructor in England had seen, or he wouldn't have accepted me. I vowed to work my ass off learning how to please him. I did work my ass off. The first time he gave me one of his non-compliment compliments, the adrenalin surge had me high for two days.

Frankie didn't get it, but I had other acting friends who did. That was the most tangible result of my summer in England, that Frankie wasn't my only friend pounding the pavement. We saw each other less often now. When I wasn't working at my latest survival job, I spent a lot of my time rehearsing scenes for class. Frankie spent more and more of hers in Irene's classes and at tap revival events. Our paths had started to diverge.

♫

Towards the end of my first year in the workshop, Frankie was cast in another showcase. Again, it was an original comedy. This time the stage was on Theatre Row. Frankie, now an experienced cabaret performer with an almost-beautiful smile, was certain that this production would be The One. I was excited for her. This was going to be the year that we were both finally going to make a dent in that brick wall.

It turned out, like so many showcases, to be a vanity production. The play was awkwardly written, the characters flat, the humor strained. It was obvious where we were supposed to laugh. I did, though it felt like a duty. Frankie's first entrance was a relief. As always, she brought a jolt of energy to the proceedings. Things perked up a bit during that scene, though not enough to save the show. Her next appearance was a letdown.

For all the years I'd known her, I'd been inspired by Frankie's courage. Each time that I gave up acting for a while and tried to adapt to what my sister pointedly called "a real job," I was awed by Frankie's ability to carry on. To my admiring eyes, she walked the highline without a net. Watching that night's performance, it occurred to me for the first time—or maybe this was simply the first time I allowed myself to think it—that the armor that made Frankie seem so free and brave in life was boxing her in on stage. If we could only see ourselves as clearly as we think we see someone else.

Frankie was naturally funny—her voice and her timing would always ensure she got laughs—but she could have been doing an audition monologue for all that she worked with the other actors in the scene. I hadn't noticed this in the murder mystery, where her role was significantly smaller, but I saw it here: she wasn't listening, an engagement that had been emphasized to me so many times since that first Shakespearean scene study class. Her performance, all punched laugh lines and winks at the audience, had no more dimension than the maid she'd created for *Gooseberries* a decade earlier.

Frankie should be so much more than this. Sad at heart, I laughed and applauded politely throughout the play and thought about what she could be if she did what I was doing. If she found a good teacher to work with, she would surely break out of that box and be as amazing as she was supposed to be.

If you've ever seen friends perform, or had friends show you their paintings or ask you to read their stories, you know the stress of having to say something afterward. If you genuinely liked and/or admired it, it's a happy challenge to find words that will make it clear that your reaction is genuine and not colored by the friendly desire to approve. If you didn't like it, the challenge is how much to not say. You can get yourself off the hook by smiling, saying "It's wonderful!" and nodding agreement at everything the radiant artist volunteers in support of that allegation. We do this all the time, friends cheering friends, artists cheering artists. Sometimes, however, you feel that maybe a good friend should give more than an empty pat on the head. Sometimes, wanting to help, you make the mistake of forgetting what people don't want to hear. I made that mistake that night.

I went backstage and hugged her.

"You were so funny," I said. "You always are. Even if the play's not great." I whispered the last part, thinking she'd giggle along with me.

She didn't. That should have been a red flag, but I didn't spot it. I kept barreling on.

"You have so much presence. Everybody woke up whenever you came on. I guess I just wished the director had given you more to work with. I've been learning so much this year, about how to open up...You're so talented..."

"Enough to get this showcase," she said, face and voice turned to ice. "A new play by a promising playwright."

"More than this showcase," I said, digging myself deeper into the hole. "You're such an amazing natural comedienne. You could learn to do so much more with your talent."

She began searching over my head for someone else to talk to.

"I didn't mean..." I lamely tried to shrug my way out of it. "I really do think you're amazing. I guess I meant that this show...doesn't show you off the way you deserve. Always the problem with showcases, I guess."

Someone else was coming around the corner. She waved at whoever it was.

"Well, thanks for coming," she said, brushing me away.

"Glad to," I said. "I'll call you during the week. We need to make a lunch date for your birthday."

We never met again.

I re-ran what I'd said. Had I sounded critical? Patronizing? Fuck, I hadn't meant to. I'd only wanted to help, to get her out of that box.

I left messages on her machine for almost two weeks. I even wrote her a letter. She never replied.

Eventually I took the birthday wrapping off the rare Blues album I'd found for her at Colony and put it on my own shelf.

Forty years after *Lake Song* closed, you ask: "What ever happened to Frankie Cecchi?" That's a good question. If anyone I knew was going to make it, surely it would have been Frankie. She was distinctive, with her funny voice and mobile face, and she carried herself with an air of destiny. So maybe she wasn't the next Carol Burnett or another Gilda Radner. Maybe we'd inflated her talents because she was the first person any of us knew with a resume and an Equity card, and because we cared for her. But she was certainly as good as any number of people who were out there making a living. And she stuck it out. That's what it takes, according to the ones who succeed—sticking it out.

I know she kept trying, years and years after I'd thrown in the towel. I always seem to know a few people who do extra work in the city, and every now and then one of them tells a story about an odd-voiced eccentric woman named Frankie who said or did such and such on the set of some film.

I never stopped keeping an eye and an ear out for her. There were so many times when I've opened a *Playbill* fully expecting to see her name. Or I'd watch commercials for new sitcoms, thinking she might be that year's belated overnight success.

Frankie did eventually show up on my television, in 2003 or 2005, for about thirteen weeks. It was a commercial for National Grid. She was one of a dozen carefully diverse customers giving a smiling "thumbs up" for clean energy. The first time I saw her face flash by, the size of a postage stamp, I jumped from my chair and squealed with excitement. That was almost thirty years after *Lake Song*. It seems to have been the peak of her career.

What happened? Frankie had charisma and timing and a natural gift for making people laugh. She had drive and unquenchable certainty. All of that together wasn't enough. it takes more than that. *It takes grit, determination and an awful lot of luck.*

Luck. That's what Frankie didn't have. Or me. Or any of half a hundred talented, intrepid people with whom I had the privilege and joy of sharing a scene study class.

What happened to Frankie?

I don't know.

What happens to any of us?

Fireflies in a garden
Making magic of everyday things,
Phosphorescence on gossamer
    wings
In the violet air, see them glisten.

Baby stars in the twilight,
Tiny lanterns for fairies at play;
Morning sunlight will burn them away;
If you blink while they're there, you
    will miss them.

And knowing that they have to
    disappear,
You try to capture glory in a jar,
For you yearn to hoard your
    pleasure;
Then you look upon your treasure
And you're holding but the cinder of
    a star.

Fairy rings in the forest;
Step inside them, the world disappears.
When the spell breaks, you tremble
    with tears,
And you yearn to return where it
    started.

But the splendor has vanished;
Spells once broken can never resume.
Might as well try to lasso the moon—
You are certain to end
    brokenhearted.

For everything you felt was but a
    dream
And dreams can never bear the light
    of day.
The thing about illusion
It is doesn't last forever
And it cannot come again.
Everything is possible if only for a
    moment.
Wonder is too frail a thing to tether to
    a chain.
Anything too wonderful will only last
    a moment;
Holding it forever
Is something you will have to wish in
    vain.

Fantasy has its moments,
Just like fireflies or flickering flames.
You imagine it's calling your name—
Such a dangerous trap! Just resist it.

When you wake to the sunlight
Mourning over the marvels you left,
Wisest course is to try to forget:
Let them fade into shadows and
    whispers.

There isn't any substance in the charm.
Pretend you never heard it call your
    name.
There's temptation to surrender
To a radiant delusion
When life is full of pain:
But everything is possible only for a
    moment.
Wonder is too frail a thing to tether to
    a chain.
Anything too wonderful will only last
    a moment;
Holding it forever
Is something you will always wish in
    vain.

What am I to write at the bottom of the page

  Just before I write 'finis?' What am I supposed to say

  To have the last word?

There's no cure for "red velvet curtain disease." It's a form of addiction.

There isn't any substance in the charm.

Pretend you never heard it call your name.

If your craving was of an audience nature, it's a functional addiction that is easily sated by regular tickets.

Those with more participatory yearnings end up on one of several tracks.

Some happy few do succeed in carving out careers and making a living. Not all have names you would know if you weren't a fellow sufferer but, like the happy audience members, theirs is a functional addiction.

Others succeed barely enough to justify carrying on. I've known a few of these: actors who manage to occasionally act, playwrights who get the occasional production, and so on. They mostly continue to rely on alternative sources of income (survival jobs, spouses, inheritance) to keep afloat. These artists get enough fellowship and professional acknowledgement to blunt their cravings, but are always itching for the next fix.

Then there are those who tried and, burnt out by either failure or a disproportion of pain to pleasure, walked away. Most can comfortably manage the cravings with teaching or community theatre, and with regular dosages of audience.

For a few of us, even being in a theatre is a painful reminder of what was lost or never was. I take my seat, half an hour before curtain, and take deep breaths to halt my suddenly skyrocketing pulse. The last whiffs of tobacco have long since been steam-cleaned or reupholstered out, hot lights are being replaced by LEDs, but there's still the aroma of anticipation. The audience trickles in, chatting and laughing. They marvel at the painted ceilings and chandeliers and moldings or, in the minimalist modern theatres, whatever feature seems unusual in the room. My eyes are also drinking in the sights, but to my eyes each theatre is populated with the ghosts of the productions that I've seen there before.

My past flashes before my eyes. I sat way up there, I remember, for that play with the wonderful monologue that sent me running to the Drama Book Shop so that I could memorize it for auditions. I recall sitting over on the side, burning with anger because the acting was so bad and I knew so many fiercely talented people who weren't getting cast. Or was it the play that was so bad, and I was furious because my friend's play on the same subject was a hundred times better and hadn't even been able to get a staged reading? I will never forget sitting three rows from the back, in the center but a few seats in from the left aisle, straining my neck around the defensive tackle in the seat in front of me so as not to miss a second of those magical performances that left me exhausted and shaking and with every cell in my body longing to do the same.

If the show that night is bad, I am angry for days afterwards. If the show is acceptable, I am wistful and sad. If the show is wonderful, my heart soars skyward for a few hours, then plummets down to earth aching and empty. Rage, sorrow, anguish. Sometimes I ache so much that I don't go to theatre at all for months at a time. But the addiction is too strong. Eventually I am always pulled back.

Ahuva and Youri will be here in a few weeks. Milos has decided to come, too. The four of us will go to the Al Hirschfeld Theatre, which used to be the Martin Beck, and see what Meryl and Kevin can do. Theatre karma has once again kicked in for Ahuva; it turns out Maria Dearborne is playing Polina.

What happened to me? I finally wrote this book. I have, at least, fulfilled that promise.

That's the story of my life.
That's the story of my art

APPENDIX

For those of you who can't imagine a love story without seeing a portrait of the beloved, I've included the content of some relevant pages from the *Playbill* that I kept from the first time I saw *Lake Song*. It's a bit crispy around the edges, but it still has my ticket stub stapled to the page opposite the credits; it's that habit I have of recording history.

What I haven't included, though it was fascinating to see them just now, were the ads from that *Playbill*. Saturday, March 24, 1973. There were refined ads for various brands of cigarette and Catherine Deneuve for Chanel No. 5. On the fashion pages, plaid was all the rage; though there were also predictions of a return to the "Gatsby" look, thanks to how cute Mia Farrow looked in the (new) movie. I'd forgotten how horrible the shoes were then; our feet looked as though they were strapped to bricks.

I get downright weepy looking at the ad for Hawaii Kai, a long-defunct restaurant where I attended a few glamorous birthday parties, wearing plastic leis and drinking fruit punch out of Tiki glasses. There are also all the restaurant chains that have disappeared. In 1973, midtown Manhattan supported six La Crêpes plus a Magic Pan, a couple of La Bonne Soupes, and five Steak and Brews, not to mention a few remaining Schraffts and the original Friday's.

For me, there are so many memories on all those pages. For you, I've only included the few that specifically have to do with *Lake Song*. You'll find the credits, the "Cast, in Order of Appearance," the listing of musical numbers (also in order of appearance), and the "Who's Who." As you've already noticed, the lyrics to all the songs have been included in this volume, heading each chapter. Mr. Berenson and his publishers were kind enough to give permission to reprint this material. I thank them enormously for that, and so should you.

REGALE THEATRE

James Lord
IN ASSOCIATION WITH Sara Bradley PRESENTS

LAKE SONG

A NEW MUSICAL
MUSIC AND LYRICS BY **MARSHALL BERENSON**
BOOK BY **IAN KRAFT**
SUGGESTED BY A PLAY BY ANTON CHEKHOV

STARRING

BRONWEN DAVIES	MAX BULLOCH	LILITH BRASSLOE

FEATURING

REBECCA LEWIS KAYE VICTOR CHRISTOPHER PRUITT
OLIVER BLANCHARD JOSEPH BIGELOW PETER BECKWITH
MARTIN KORN WAYNE ALAN CARNEY

MARIA DEARBORNE FREDI COURTLAND LINDA SCHILLER CAROL KELLY NANCY PARDOE
TYLER MOSS RALPH CERUTTI CHRIS MANHEIM ANDREW STOWE JEFFREY HALL

SCENIC DESIGN	COSTUMES DESIGN	LIGHTING DESIGN
IVAN SCHURMAN	RUTH MANN	ZORA MIKLOS

MUSICAL DIRECTION BY FRANK PIRELLI

CHOREOGRAPHY BY **CHRISTINE JOLLEY**

DIRECTED BY
JAMES LORD

CAST

(in order of appearance)

Semion Semionovich Medviedenko .... PETER BECKWITH

Maryia Ilyinichna Shamrayeva (<u>Masha</u>) .... KAYE VICTOR

Piotr Nikolayevich <u>Sorin</u> .... JOSEPH BIGELOW

Konstantin Gavrilovich Trepliov (<u>Kostia</u>) .... CHRISTOPHER PRUITT

<u>Yakov</u> .... WAYNE ALAN CARNEY

<u>Nina</u> Mihailovna Zaryechnaia .... REBECCA LEWIS

<u>Polina</u> Andryeevna Shamrayeva .... LILITH BRASSLOE

Yevgheniy Serghyeevich <u>Dorn</u> .... OLIVER BLANCHARD

Irina Nikolayevna Trepliova (<u>Arkadina</u>) .... BRONWEN DAVIES

Boris Aleksyeevich <u>Trigorin</u> .... MAX BULLOCH

Ilyia Afanasyevich <u>Shamrayev</u> .... MARTIN KORN

plus: Servants, Peasants, Friends: RALPH CERUTTI; FREDI COURTLAND; MARIA DEARBORNE; JEFFREY HALL; CAROL KELLY; CHRIS MANHEIM; TYLER MOSS; NANCY PARDOE; LINDA SCHILLER; ANDREW STOWE

TIME
Turn of the Century
PLACE
Russia

UNDERSTUDIES
Understudies never substitute for listed players unless a specific announcement is made at the time of the appearance

For Arkadina—NANCY PARDOE; for Polina—MARIA DEARBORNE; for Trigorin—JEFFREY HALL; for Nina—LINDA SCHILLER; for Kostia—WAYNE ALAN CARNEY; for Dorn—RALPH CERUTTI; for Masha—FREDI COURTLAND; for Sorin/Shamrayev—TYLER MOSS; for Medviedenko/Yakov—CHRIS MANHEIM; for Servants/Peasants/Friends—CAROL KELLY and ANDREW STOWE

MUSICAL NUMBERS

ACT I

"Two Years" .... Polina

"Lake Song" .... Company

"Black" .... Masha, Medviedenko

"Nothing" .... Kostia

"Something" .... Sorin

"Everything" .... Polina

"Anything" .... Dorn

"Moscow" .... Arkadina

"For Thousands of Years" .... Nina, Company

"Nothing" (reprise) .... Kostia

"Famous People" .... Nina, Kostia

"As I Am" .... Arkadina

"A Subject for a Short Story" .... Trigorin

"Moscow" (reprise) .... Company

"If Ever You Need My Life" .... Nina, Trigorin

"Bandaging the Wound" .... Kostia

"Kiss, Kiss" .... Arkadina, Trigorin

"The Horses Are Waiting/New Life" .... Company/Nina

ACT II

"Two Years" (reprise) .... Polina, Company

"The Schoolmaster and His Wife" .... Masha, Medviedenko

"A Woman Loves" .... Polina, Masha

"Four Miles" .... Medviedenko

"The Man Who Wished" .... Kostia

"Bezique" .... Arkadina, Trigorin, Polina, Dorn,
Kostia, Masha, Shamrayev

"Heaven Help the Homeless Wayfarers" .... Nina, Kostia

"For Thousands of Years" (reprise) .... Nina

"If Ever You Need My Life" (reprise) .... Nina

"The Man Who Wished" (reprise) .... Kostia

WHO's WHO IN THE CAST

BRONWEN DAVIES (Arkadina) a favorite of two generations of American film audiences, makes her Broadway debut in *Lake Song*! Orphaned in the London Blitz, Miss Davies and her brother came to LA to live with their aunt, a wardrobe mistress at MGM. It was there that she was discovered by director George B. Seitz, who needed a young English girl to play opposite Mickey Rooney in *Andy Hardy and the Princess*. America was charmed by the lovely Miss Davies, who went on to be featured in many MGM films including *Captain Marigold, Patsy, Clouds Unfold, Dombey & Son* and *Dear Brutus*, winning Academy Award nominations for the last two. At the pinnacle of her early career, David Selznik chose Miss Davies from among Hollywood's brightest starlets to play Mimi in *The Bohemians*, opposite British matinee idol James Lyttleton. The popular young acting couple returned to London after their marriage. Beginning with a triumphant production of *The Importance of Being Earnest*, the Lyttletons delighted British theatre-goers in such plays as *Romeo and Juliet, The Taming of the Shrew, Much Ado About Nothing, Private Lives, Cyrano de Bergerac* and a landmark production of *Three Sisters*, directed by Mr. Lyttleton in which the Lyttletons played Masha and Vershinin. Miss Davies's subsequent stage ventures include *Blithe Spirit, Candida, Not Mary, Quality Street, A Doll's House* and the first English language production of Beckett's *Stone Cold*.

She returned to film acting as snoopy American millionairess Debbie Webber in a trio of beloved comic mysteries, the popularity of which inspired her successful BBC comedy, *Our Bron*. When the British Invasion turned America's eyes firmly toward London, Hollywood rediscovered Bronwen Davies, who found herself playing Americans in Britain and English women in America in such "mod" comedies as *Good Will Ambassador, Goin' Goin' Go Go* and *Mrs. Babcock Goes to Parliament*. *Lake Song* reunites Miss Davies with Marshall Berenson, for whom she originated the role of Angelica in *Concerto for Flute and Heart* on the West End, and with Ian Kraft, who wrote *Princess of Oranges* especially to showcase her talents. Miss Davies is also very pleased to once again work with Lilith Brassloe, with whom she starred in Mr. Kraft's *Marriage à la Mod*. Miss Davies is proud of her artist-son Richard and her daughter Cressida who is currently studying acting at RADA.

LILITH BRASSLOE (*Polina*) literally exploded onto the London stage at the age of seven as a tiny human cannonball in her parents' music hall act, and has been thrilling and delighting audiences ever since. From childhood appearances as pixies, fairies and flowers, her grace and charm led to steady work in musical revues. The great Cole Porter plucked her from the chorus of the West End production of *Anything Goes* to understudy the role of Reno Sweeney,

489

the first in a string of roles that established Miss Brassloe as a major star. She has since sparkled in countless musicals, including *Happy End, Du Barry Was a Lady, Sail Away* and *Marx!*, just to name a few. For her performance in *Cold Comfort,* the London Theatre Critics voted her Actress of the Year. A radio broadcast of *Nicholas Nickleby*, in which she played both Mrs. Kenwig and Mrs. Crummles, showed directors that Miss Brassloe didn't have to sing to be funny. Thereafter, she was featured at the Old Vic, Stratford-upon-Avon and in London's West End, in plays as varied as *Lysistrata, Romeo and Juliet* (as the Nurse), *The Way of the World, Dinner At Eight, You Can't Take it With You* and *The Importance of Being Ernest.* Her considerable success in *Skin of Our Teeth* suggested her as Tallulah Bankhead's replacement in the West End production of *Night of the Iguana*, inaugurating a new phase of her career. Miss Brassloe went on to challenging roles in *The Balcony, The Madwoman of Chaillot, Mrs. Warren's Profession* and *Entertaining Mr. Sloane.* Ian Kraft wrote the parts of Agatha in *Lettuce Alone* and Prunella in *Marriage à la Mod* especially to showcase her singular talents. Americans first got to see what all the fuss was about when Miss Brassloe appeared in a post-war revival of Noel Coward's *Design for Living.* She has since enjoyed huge success in this country, creating such unforgettable Broadway roles as Mona in Marshall Berenson's *Riding a Bicycle.* As the lascivious Mrs. Wentwhistle in *Last Gas Before Highway*, Miss Brassloe won both the Drama Critics Circle and

Tony awards, and received an Academy Award nomination for recreating the role on film. Hollywood has enthusiastically employed her on both large and small screen. She has appeared in such films as *Casino Royale, Black Diamonds* and *The Pink Panther Prowls Again,* made guest appearances on *The Carol Burnett Show, The Judy Garland Show, The Lucy Show* and *Gilligan's Island* and was doused with water on *Laugh-In.* Miss Brassloe was a regular panelist on *Quiz-Cycle*, and been a favorite guest of American TV talk shows. She has toured the US, Great Britain and Europe with her one-woman cabaret act *Sweet and Brassloe*, which won an Emmy Award for Best Variety Special when it was televised in 1968.

MAX BULLOCH (*Trigorin*) was most recently seen on Broadway as Larry in *Slings and Arrows*, for which he received a Tony nomination. Moviegoers can look forward to seeing his performance in the film version, which is due for release later this year. The versatile Mr. Bulloch is equally well known for his musical and classical work. Last summer, to both critical and popular acclaim, he performed the unusual feat of playing Petruchio in both *The Taming of the Shrew* and *Kiss Me Kate* in repertory at the Stratford, Ontario Shakespeare Festival. Previously, he had appeared with the Festival in productions of *The Tempest, Heartbreak House, The Beggar's Opera* (Macheath), *Tartuffe* and *The Servant of Two Masters.* For many years, Mr. Bulloch has been associated with the Actors Theatre of Louisville, both as an actor and more recently, following the success of his production of *The Tempest* (a play with which he is particularly associated), as a director. Among the many Louisville productions in which he has played leading roles are *Arms and the Man, Murder in the Cathedral* (Beckett), *The Duchess of Malfi, The Tempest* (playing both Caliban and Prospero in various productions), *The Crucible* (Proctor), *Othello* (Iago) and *The Country Wife*. In addition, Mr. Bulloch has performed dramatic roles with professional companies in every state except for North Dakota. He made his Broadway debut as Michael in Marshall Berenson's *Concerto for Flute and Heart*. Other favorite musical roles include Mike in the National tour of the revival of *Rosebud*, Emil in *South Pacific*, Billy Bigelow in *Carousel* and Stuyvesant in the Lincoln Center production of *Knickerbocker Holiday*. Mr. Bulloch has appeared on television in episodes of *Bonanza, Ironside, Medical Center, Mission Impossible* and as a Klingon commander in *Star Trek*. Film work includes featured roles in *The Parallax View, Thunderball, The Godfather, The French Connection* and *Green Skies, Blue Hills*. He is the proud father of Stephanie and Michael.

REBECCA LEWIS (*Nina*) first stepped on a Broadway stage as Gretl in *The Sound of Music*. Subsequently she was featured in *Fiddler on the Roof, Here's Love, The Roar of the Greasepaint...*(Girl), *Carnival* (Lili) and as Ngana in James Lord's production of *South Pacific*. A graduate of the Neighborhood Playhouse, Miss Lewis's performance credits also include *Romeo and Juliet* (Juliet) and *The Wild Duck* (Hedwig). For her performance as Anya in *The Cherry Orchard* (with Anne Baxter), Miss Lewis was the winner of a Theatre World Award.

KAYE VICTOR (*Masha*) previously played Masha in a production of *The Seagull* in London, where she worked for several years following her studies at LAMDA. Miss Victor was a featured performer on the West End and at the Old Vic, where other roles included Lady Anne in *Richard III* and Jessica in *The Merchant of Venice*. For her performance in *Cold Comfort* (starring Lilith Brassloe), she was voted Most Promising Newcomer by the London Theatre Critics. Miss Victor debuted on Broadway in *The Prime of Miss Jean Brodie* and was most recently seen on this stage as Marie in *The Boy Jones*. NY work includes *The Rothschilds* (Hannah) and the Lincoln Center production of *The Crucible* (Mary Warren). Favorite roles run the gamut from Kattrin in *Mother Courage* to Jo in *A Taste of Honey*, both at the Guthrie Theatre, and include Isabella (*Measure for Measure*), Varia (*The Cherry Orchard*), Lucy (*The Beggar's Opera*) and the title character in *Trelawney of the Wells* (the last three at ACT). She would like to thank Miss Brassloe and J A Narang for inspiration.

CHRISTOPHER PRUITT (*Kostia*) was seen in New York last year as Norman in *Moonchildren*. Previously, he had performed Off-Broadway in *Godspell* and *The Fantasticks*. Following his graduation from North

Carolina's School of the Arts, Mr. Pruitt worked at Arena Stage in Washington, where he was featured in such plays as *Waiting for Lefty, The Skin of Our Teeth*, and the world premiere of David Marash's *A Heavy Reckoning*. In his spare time, Mr. Pruitt may be found at various jazz clubs in the city, singing with The Medium Band.

OLIVER BLANCHARD (*Dorn*) sang his first public notes in Salt Lake City, as a boy-soprano with the Mormon Tabernacle Choir. This led to an interest in light opera, and eventually to featured roles across the US in productions of *Iolanthe, The Pirates of Penzance* and *The Desert Song* as well as *Fiddler on the Roof* and *My Fair Lady*. He has since appeared in the National Companies of *1776, The Buddy System, Applause* and in the revival tour of *Rosebud*, playing opposite Alice Playten. *Lake Song* marks his Broadway debut. Mr. Blanchard studies acting with the wonderful Uta Hagen.

JOSEPH BIGELOW (*Sorin*) first beguiled Broadway audiences during the original run of *South Pacific* when he was promoted from the chorus to become the last sailor to don the coconut brassiere. Subsequent favorite credits include roles in *Kiss Me Kate, We Bombed in New Haven, The Beggar's Opera, Barefoot in the Park, Guys and Dolls, Finishing Touches* and Ian Kraft's *Marriage à la Mod*. Classical theatre aficionados have seen him in Central Park productions of *Twelfth Night, Henry IV, Part 1* and *The Cherry Orchard* as well as the Lincoln Center production of *The Crucible*. Mr. Bigelow's association with the music of Marshall Berenson includes creating the roles of Maestro Antonelli in *Concerto for Flute and Heart*, John of Stout in *Playing the Palace*, Arthur in *The Buddy System* and most recently Mr. Jones in *The Boy Jones*, for which he received a Tony nomination. Soap fans will recognize him as Dr. Von Kleinhaus on *One Life to Live*.

PETER BECKWITH (*Medviedenko*) is extremely proud to have made his Broadway debut in the chorus of *Riding a Bicycle*. Broadway audiences have more recently seen him when he understudied the role of Nathan in *The Rothschilds*. Other musicals include *Fiddler on the Roof* (Motel), *Dames at Sea* (Lucky) and *Grease* (Doody), the last two Off-Broadway. From his first professional engagement, acting as "Nana" in a production of *Peter Pan* in his hometown of Louisville, Kentucky, Mr. Beckwith has frequently played animals on stage, such as Snoopy in *You're a Good Man, Charlie Brown* and Bottom in *A Midsummer Night's Dream*. Favorite human roles include Trinculo in *The Tempest*, the 3rd Knight in *Murder in the Cathedral* and Guildenstern in *Rosencrantz & Guildenstern Are Dead*.

MARTIN KORN (*Shamrayev*) is a veteran of 23 Broadway shows. From his debut in the chorus of *High Button Shoes*, Mr. Korn includes among his credits such memorable productions as *Call Me Madam, Fiorello!, Wildcat, Little Me, How to Succeed in Business..., Riding a Bicycle, Coco* and, most recently, *The Boy Jones*. Before starting rehearsals for *Lake Song*, Mr. Korn fulfilled a lifelong dream by singing the role of the Major General in the Civic Light Opera production of *The Pirates of Penzance*.

WAYNE ALAN CARNEY (*Yakov*) graduated from Carnegie Mellon in 1969 and has been working professionally ever since. He began at the Pittsburgh Playhouse, where he was featured in *Hay Fever, Aladdin* and *Life With Father*. He has since appeared in Philadelphia in *The Fantasticks* and in New York productions of *The Roar of the Greasepaint...* and *The Mikado* (as Nanki Poo). Last year he made his Broadway debut in *The Boy Jones*. On television, he has been seen as Dirk on *Another World*.

RALPH CERUTTI has recently been seen on Broadway in *1776* and *Rosencrantz & Guildenstern Are Dead*. He debuted as understudy to Cornelius in *Hello, Dolly!*, a role he went on to play in the National Company. Favorite credits include roles in *George M!*, *Jacques Brel...*, *Damn Yankees, Private Lives*, and Don, in the National Company of *The Buddy System*. People with long memories may recall Mr. Cerutti's professional debut as a classmate of Mary's on *The Donna Reed Show*.

FREDI COURTLAND makes her Broadway debut in *Lake Song*. A native Californian, Fredi has worked extensively on television, where credits include guest spots on *The Monkees, Room 222* and *The Doris Day Show*. She has played a variety of roles Off-Broadway and in stock, including such

plays as *Dames At Sea* (Joan), *Cabaret* (Sally), *Funny Girl* (Fanny), *Oliver!* (Nancy), *You're a Good Man, Charlie Brown* (Lucy) and *Rosebud* (Joan). Fredi dedicates this performance to her mother, Dilys Watts, who sang and danced her way through dozens of MGM musicals.

MARIA DEARBORNE may best be known as the voice of "Pretty Kitty" in the cat food commercials. She began singing jingles to earn her tuition for a Master's degree in English Literature. On a dare from a fellow singer, she auditioned for the original production of *The Buddy System* and found herself understudying the role of Barbara, which she later played in the National Company. She has appeared in productions of *Hello Dolly!, Showboat, Oliver!, Kiss Me Kate* and as Joan in the Broadway revival of *Rosebud*. Most recently, New York audiences could see Miss Dearborne as Cousin Connie in the long-running hit *Gal From Kalamazoo*.

JEFFREY HALL's Broadway credits include the revival of *Rosebud*, in which he played the part of Mike opposite Maria Dearborne, *1776* and *Marriage à la Mod*. He has also been seen in productions of *Major Barbara, Ring Around the Moon* and *Orpheus Descending*. Films include *Mean Streets, Bonnie and Clyde, Little Big Man* and *The French Connection*. He considers his luckiest break being cast as El Guyo in a production of *The Fantasticks* featuring the beautiful Catharine Trewer, to whom he has now been married for six years.

CAROL KELLY makes her "legit" Broadway debut with *Lake Song*, though she danced in New York's largest musical show for two years—as a Rockette! Miss Kelly has played featured roles in *Fiddler on the Roof, Peter Pan* and *Rosebud* in her native Texas, and has toured with the National Company of *Playing the Palace*. She is a member of The Jolley Crew and studies voice with Ernie Adano.

CHRIS MANHEIM numbers among his credits such varied roles as the Scarecrow in *The Wizard of Oz*, Dick in *Rosebud* and Linus in *You're a Good Man, Charlie Brown*. A native of Chicago, Mr. Manheim entertained his home town for two years as a member of the Second City Players. He is excited to be making his Broadway debut in *Lake Song*.

TYLER MOSS was seen as Pickering in the recent Jones Beach production of *My Fair Lady* with Alfred Drake, and immediately before that on Broadway in *The Boy Jones*. Among his favorite Broadway credits are the classic musicals *The Pajama Game, Damn Yankees, Fiorello!* and *How to Succeed....* and Marshall Berenson's *Always Forever..., Playing the Palace*, and *The Buddy System*. He is proud to have supported such great leading ladies as Katharine Hepburn (*Coco*), Angela Lansbury (*Mame*) and Carol Channing (*Hello, Dolly!*). When not on stage, Mr. Moss may be found at Break A Leg, his NY store devoted to theatrical memorabilia.

NANCY PARDOE will immediately be recognized as "Marge" from TV's *Jill Williams Show*. On Broadway, she has been featured in *Riding a Bicycle* and *Marriage à la Mod*. Other stage work includes the National Tour of *The Buddy System, Dames at Sea* (Mona), *Oh, Coward!* and *The Odd Couple*. On film, she has appeared in *It's a Mad, Mad, Mad, Mad World*. Television work includes featured roles on *Adam 12, Medical Center* and the innovative weekly musical series *That's Life*.

LINDA SCHILLER makes her Broadway debut here, having graduated last spring from the New York Academy of Dramatic Arts where she was featured in productions of *The Trojan Women* and *Can You Hear Their Voices?* Miss Schiller hails from Boston, and owes much to her experiences on the Cape Cod summer circuit. She has particularly enjoyed performing in *Carousel* (Julie), *Rosebud* (Rosebud), *The Mikado* (Yum Yum), *Camelot* and *The Pirates of Penzance*.

ANDREW STOWE got his start as a young magician in Nebraska City. A local talent competition led to an appearance on the Mickey Mouse Club's "Talent Roundup." In addition to Broadway appearances in *Fiddler on the Roof* and *Applause*, Mr. Stowe's credits include national tours of *Rosebud* and *Mame* and two seasons with the Oregon Shakespeare Festival. As "Andre the Magnificent," he hosts a Sunday morning TV show for young people.

JAMES LORD (*Director-Producer*) is simultaneously represented on Broadway by *Lake Song* and the Tony

Award winning *Danny Boy* (now in it's third year). Mr. Lord has served in his present capacity for three previous Marshall Berenson hits: *The Buddy System, Always Forever Never Again* and *The Boy Jones*, as well as directing the Broadway production of *Concerto for Flute and Heart*. Other dual-credit productions include *South Pacific, The King & I* and *Dangerous Music*. Mr. Lord served as producer for *Baby Blue, My Love & I* (both with Kenneth Gillian), *Under Milkwood, Taxi Dance* (Tony winner), *Carolina* and *Mr. Edmund*. He has directed productions of *Aida* and *Mephistophle* for the Metropolitan Opera. His first film as director, *Pipe Dreams*, won him an honorable mention at the Cannes Film Festival. Mr. Lord is currently preparing to direct a film in Italy starring Michael Caine.

MARSHALL BERENSON (*Music and Lyrics*) won the Tony Award last season for his music and lyrics for *The Boy Jones*, and shared an award in 1960, with composer Bernie Melchik, for his lyrics for the now-classic *Rosebud*. Berenson's career began when his mentor, composer Henry Peet, selected him to complete the lyrics begun by the late Meyer Tong for *Cry Out Loud*, going on to fully collaborate with Peet on *Concerto For Flute and Heart*. His first solo venture, the innovative *Riding a Bicycle*, earned much admiration from critics during its brief Broadway run and recently enjoyed a successful production in Chicago. Mr. Berenson has provided both music and lyrics for *Playing the Palace, The Buddy System* and *Always Forever Never Again*, receiving three

Tony nominations in the process. A production of *Always Forever...* will be seen in London later this year. Mr. Berenson has provided the soundtrack for the films *Voyage of the Carpathia* and *Shoot From the Hip*, as well as James Lord's *Pipe Dreams*.

IAN KRAFT (*Author*) has been writing for the stage for more than thirty years. He is best known, on both sides of the Atlantic, for his award-winning comedies including *Marriage à la Mod, Off License, Lettuce Alone, Princess of Oranges, Olly Olly Oxen* and *Cold Comfort* (a recent London Theatre Critics Play of the Year). Currently, he is represented on the West End by *Ciggies and Gum*, starring Felicity Kendall and Eric Porter. His previous collaboration with Marshall Berenson, *The Boy Jones,* earned him a Tony award. Thanks to Public Television, American audiences will soon be able to enjoy Mr. Kraft's four-part BBC biography of the great Shakespearean actor Henry Irving, *The Manner of His Speech*. In addition, writing as "Jack Straw," Mr. Kraft is the author of the popular "Lucullus Fen" mystery novels.

RUTH MANN (*Costume Design*) is additionally represented on Broadway by her Tony Award-winning costumes for the current revival of *Once in a Lifetime*. Miss Mann previously worked with Mr. Lord to create costumes for his acclaimed production of *Aida* at the Metropolitan Opera and for his revival of *South Pacific*. In collaboration with Ivan Schurman, Miss Mann recently designed a space-age production of the *Ring Cycle* for the National Opera of Canada. Through her long and happy associations with the American Shakespeare Festival in Stratford, Connecticut and the Mark Taper Forum in Los Angeles, Miss Mann's designs have regularly delighted theatre audiences on both coasts. Her creations have graced many films and she has twice been nominated for an Academy Award (for *House of the Rising Sun* and *Paris Best of All*).

CHRISTINE JOLLEY (*Choreographer*) has shared each step of her theatrical career with Marshall Berenson and James Lord. Ballet-trained Miss Jolley found her true calling as one of the three Swans "loaned" by Dance Theatre to the original production of *Concerto for Flute and Heart*. She went on to dance for the greatest theatrical choreographers of this century, including De Mille, Robbins and Fosse. She was appointed dance captain in the original Broadway production of *Rosebud* and went on to choreograph the revival of *Rosebud*. She also assisted Danny Blinken with the award-winning choreography for *The Buddy System*. Last season, Miss Jolley won both Drama Desk and Tony awards for her choreography of *The Boy Jones*. Away from Berenson and Lord collaborations, her many successes include productions of *The Roar of the Greasepaint...*, *Can-Can*, *Oklahoma*, and *Flower Drum Song*, and projects as varied as the dance interludes for *The Tempest* at the Stratford Ontario Shakespeare Festival, musical staging for a recent Liza Minnelli concert tour, and half-time extravaganzas for two Super Bowls.

Television work includes *The Little Match Girl* (for which she also acted as assistant director) and the 42nd Annual Academy Awards. Her own company of actor/dancers, The Jolley Crew, tours the tri-state area, enchanting schoolchildren with contemporary interpretations of myths and folktales. Miss Jolley has just been appointed to a national creative team that will be responsible for the Bicentennial festivities planned for July 4, 1976.

ZORA MIKLOS (*Lighting Designer*) is an award winning designer (including a Tony award for *The Boy Jones*) and a photographer of considerable talent. She is currently represented on Broadway by *The Clock Struck One*, as well as by the long-running *Gal From Kalamazoo*, which has taken her designs around the world. Other Broadway credits include *Concerto for Flute and Heart*, *Hastings on Hudson*, *Johnny Blackheart*, *My Last Duchess*, *Dangerous Music*, *Mrs. Sprat*, the recent revival of *Angel Street* and *I Love You, Sandy Beach*. Since 1967 Miss Miklos has been the lighting designer for Ballet Ashkenazy. She also has designed light shows for the Hayden Planetarium, the National Air and Space Museum in Washington DC and The Reuben Fleet Space Theatre in San Diego. Her two volumes of photographs, *Nine Ladies Dancing* and *Limelighting* have both been published by Rizzoli.

IVAN SCHURMAN (*Set Designer*) has a career that reads like a history of 20th century set design. He began in his late teens, as an apprentice to Diaghelev's Ballet Russes. Early

496

experience with ballet and opera stood him in good stead when he emigrated to Los Angeles, where he designed for everyone at MGM from Busby Berkeley to Vincente Minnelli. During that period, Mr. Schurman continued his off-screen work, designing, amongst others, the ill-fated production of Brecht's *Tomorrow and Tomorrow*. Moving to New York and returning to his first love, dance, Mr. Schurman began a fruitful collaboration with George Balanchine, for whom he designed many important productions, including a setting of *Coppelia* that is used by New York City Ballet to this day. Mr. Schurman instituted the design training program at the Stratford, Ontario Shakespeare Festival, a program currently headed by his daughter Nathalie Duvall. His relationship with the festival has also produced sets for productions as varied as *The Tempest, Anything Goes, Heartbreak House* and *The Beggar's Opera*. For James Lord, Mr. Schurman designed sets for *Mr. Edmund, Concerto for Flute and Heart*, and, most recently, *The Boy Jones*. Other especially noteworthy designs include the Peter Brook production of *Peer Gynt* and the gravity-defying sets for the National Opera of Canada's *Ring Cycle*. Mr. Schurman has been married to dancer Nadia Zelinkova for forty happy years.

FRANK PIRELLI (*Musical Director*) is pleased to reprise his recent *The Boy Jones* collaboration with Berenson and Lord. His association with these artists goes back to the years he served as assistant to his mentor, the late Alvin Benton, on *Playing the Palace, Riding a Bicycle* and *Always Forever Never Again*. Mr. Pirelli also served as musical director for the recent revival of *Rosebud*. Other recent productions include *Carolina, Bye Bye Birdie* (Jones Beach), the New York Shakespeare Festival production of *The Twelfth Night*, and *Oh Lady! Lady!* at the Goodspeed Opera House. He designed incidental music for *Love's Labour's Lost* at the New York Shakespeare Festival, and Andre Serban's Boston production of *Blood Wedding*, Mr. Pirelli is a graduate of the Julliard School of Music. He is especially proud to conduct the Pirelli Quartet, which includes his wife Monica and their sons Robert and Charles.

SARA BRADLEY (*Associate Producer*) served in the same capacity for *The Boy Jones, Always Forever...* and *Playing the Palace*, as well as for *Danny Boy, Carolina* and *Mr. Edmund*. In conjunction with The Ridley Group, Miss Bradley has produced three international tours of the Martha Graham Dance Company, and was one of the team responsible for last year's Rudolf Nureyev tour. Descended from impresario Ezra Quinton, she and her brother, playwright Quinton Bradley, are proud to represent the fourth generation of an American theatrical family. Miss Bradley has produced several of her brother's plays, including *Last Tuesday Moon, Elastic Plastic Miracle* and the Broadway production of *Refracted Flight*.

AFTERWORD

In *The Music Man*, con man "Professor Harold Hill" informs River City that he is the creator of the revolutionary "think system:" in his band, the boys need only hold their instruments and think hard about the "Minuet in G" and, ultimately, they will be able to play it.

I can make a good case for having written this book via the "think system." The seeds for the story came to me before I'd turned twenty. Back then, I knew I was in no way ready to write it. I knew I needed experience: both the acquired writing skill to shape the story and the years of life that would put it into perspective. So I scrawled some character notes (my stories always begin with characters) and stuffed them into a manila folder for "someday."

Chasing Fireflies (it had that title from the start) always stayed in the back of my mind, calling out to me during dull patches in my various survival jobs, or while giving away free cigarettes in midtown Manhattan or waiting in the endless lines actors endure in hopes of getting seen for a shot at a job.

Five or maybe six years after I had the idea, it occurred to me that if I expected to be able to quote freely from the musical-within-the-novel, I'd have to write it myself. It would be easier to base it on some existing story than to start from scratch. With my imagined cast as a rep company, I considered various classical plots until I understood, in one of those happy lightbulb-overhead moments, that Chekhov's *The Seagull* was perfect for my purposes. We didn't have Google or Wiki then, but I was able to establish to my satisfaction that there hadn't yet been a musical version of sufficient magnitude to be confused with what I decided to call *Lake Song* (apologies here to anyone who's written one since). I broke down the play into a series of song opportunities, gave final names to my actors, and was off and running. In my own rambling, "think system" kind of way.

Whenever I needed something to play with, I worked on the songs. Here's where I apologize to the fictional Marshall Berenson for not providing lyrics that support his legendary status. With one particular burst of creative energy, I blitzed out a "Who's Who" section for the imaginary *Playbill*, providing backstory (I was on a small professional roll at the time and feeling rather playful). But each time I tried, after a few weeks of work, I'd put the work aside. I still wasn't ready.

Sometime in the late 1980s, following my first cycle of playwriting, I made my maiden attempt at writing an opening chapter. It was deadly. I returned *Fireflies* to the back burner and focused instead on converting an abandoned film script into prose. That effort became *Wisdom*, my first completed novel (aka "excellent practice").

Pushing 40 and having resigned myself to the fact that my acting career would end without my ever, beyond one memorable audition, setting a toe on a Broadway stage, and with my face and my voice having never ended up in the same film, I took another stab at kicking off *Fireflies*. It still refused to take off. I put it away again. Still always thinking.

Every couple of years, I'd try to raise the curtain on *Lake Song* and the three girls who loved it. The music of the story never sounded right, and every single time I would set it aside. Considering my innate pessimism, it's amazing that I never gave up. I was certain that if I let my subconscious mull it over long enough, someday I would find myself playing the opening bars of the "Minuet in G."

I wish I could remember how and when, so that I could tell you, but I can't. I can only say that I sat down one weekend and wrote the story of Frankie and Judy Garland. And I knew, with that visceral knowledge you have that something is right, that I'd found the key and the show would go on.

And yet I paused. Because I'd also just begun work on shaping (another) rejected film script into my novel *The Breast of Everything*, a story for which the time seemed perfect. Next, I decided it would be sensible to try my hand at genre fiction. While working on *The Upsilon Knot*, I had a strong sense that I'd fallen into an important progression: that those two books and one more (which became *Under the Bus*) were necessary groundwork for the skills I'd need to write *Fireflies* the way I wanted to. With decades of emotional weight behind it, *Chasing Fireflies* had evolved into a marathon that I had to train sufficiently to run.

Here I am crossing the finish line. After all these years of thinking—nearly 40, but who's counting?—the story has finally come out and it sounds very near to the tune I'd been humming in my head.

It should come as no surprise that I have had a lot of supporters and inspiration along the way.

Odella Schattin has supported this effort all the way back to the Big Bang with flags flying; and more recently, by spending precious hours attempting to clean up my more egregious errors (any slippage that remains is entirely of my own doing!). I cannot thank her enough and only hope she is pleased with the result.

Big big thanks to Bil Vargas, Dorit Sapir (thanks extra for that map!), Denis Hutchinson, Thandi Brewer, and usual suspects Alan Salant, Honey Seltzer, Tom Wilinsky and Örjan Blix, for endless cheerleading. Special thanks are due to Tavie Phillips, for convincing me (though she won't remember the conversation) that there might be an audience for this story and to Sue Dubrovich for gentle but emphatic reassurance.

I am grateful to every acting teacher I ever had, from Jack Farrell and his improv classes for tweens, to Irma Jurist and Harry Uher at the Neighborhood Playhouse, to Sondra Green and John Clingerman who love and respect the spoken word. Most especially, I am deeply and eternally grateful to the late and extraordinary Paul Daneman and Nikos Psacharapolous for the lessons they taught me and for validating my dream; thanks to them, I can remember my acting career as a noble failure rather than a willful mistake.

There is a special place in my heart for Fred Sidewater, who volunteered to help when others, asked, refused. For incredibly gracious fellowship to one who was a very small actor indeed, thank you to (chronologically): Timothy Hutton, Tovah Feldshuh, Jeff Bridges, Gene Wilder, Richard Pryor, Al Pacino, Barbet Schroeder and John Waters. A wry but not unappreciative nod to Sidney Lumet for publicly affirming that I "wasn't wooden." Warm gratitude to Sondra James for her kind guidance and my second act, to Paul A. Levin for bringing us together, and to Deborah Wallach, Harriet Fidlow and Kenton Jakub for their acceptance.

Much loving thanks to every acting or theatre-minded friend I've ever had, most especially to Karen and Jeanie C and Harvey, to Kathleen and Robin R and Bob B. Curtain call bouquets to Joy and Jeff T and Berc, and to FHHS SING! '71 & '72 and Look In Their Minds; to Roberta, Marie, Carol, Carolyn, Cyndi, Kim, Tony and Merle, and to the June 1975 VC production of Company. Applause for Louise, Adele A, Walker, Lizzie, Elizabeth, Bob R, Margie and BADA '85; for Serena and for Vicky, Robert, Amity, Susan W and Jeff B; and to all my classmates, scene partners, fellow extras and loopers, and everyone who waited on the line.

Finally, from the bottom of my theatre-loving heart, to those who made the magic, thanks for the memories:

Adolph and Betty; Bill; Cole; Cy; Ed; Frank; George and Ira; Irving; James; Jerome; Jerry H; Jule; John & Fred; Jonathan; Leonard; Meredith; Richard and Lorenz and Oscar; Richard and Robert; Sheldon and Jerry B; Stephen; Steven; Yip and Harold

Anton; Alan; Anthony and Peter; Arthur; AR; Beth; Brian; Caryl; David; Douglas; Eugene; GB; George and Edna and Moss; Howard; JM; John; Michael; Noel; Oscar; Tina; Tom; Tony; Wendy; Will

Both Alan As and Alan B; Anthony; Benedict; Brian; Charles; Chip; Christopher; Cyril; Derek and Ian and Edward; Frank; Gene; Geoffrey; George H and George S I; Hal; Harvey; Hugh and Hume; Jack; James Earl; Jason; Jerry O; Jim; Joel; John; Kenneth; Kevin K and Kevin S; Larry and Laurence; Len; Lewis; Liev; Mandy; Mickey; Nathan and Norbert; Ralph and John; Robert M and Robert B; Roger; Sherman; Tom and Tommy; both Tony Rs; Zero

Alexis; Angela; Ann M, Ann R and Annie G; Audra; Barbara and Barbra; Bea; Bernadette; Beth F and Beth H; Bette and "Betty" and Bonnie and Blythe; Carol and Carol; Cate and Kate; Chita; Cherry and Colleen; Cynthia and Cicely; Christine; Debbie and Debra; both Donna Ms; Dorothy; Elaine; Ethel M and Ethel S; Glenn and Glenda and Gwen; Glynis and Hermione; Helen; Jane; Jessica; Joanna; Julie A and Julie H; Judy and Liza; Judi and Maggie; Judith; Laura; Mary and Madeleine; Patti; Penny; Phyllis; Rosemary; Roz; Stockard; Yvonne; Zoe C and Zoe W

And all the rest, as many as there will always be lights on Broadway.

Lori Berhon, New York NY, May 1, 2017

ABOUT THE AUTHOR

A one-time actor and playwright, Lori Berhon continues to live in her home town of New York City where she occasionally attends the theatre and is furious (if it's bad) or heartbroken (if it's good) for a week afterward. A card-carrying member of the American acting unions for an embarrassing number of years, her only Broadway performances were auditions and she has never managed to get her face and her voice into the same film. Her playwriting career was even less perceptible. *Chasing Fireflies* is her valentine to the unrequited love of her life.